I0772834

ENSNARED BY THE PACK

THE COMPLETE SERIES

TESSA COLE

Gryphon's Gate Publishing

Ensnared by the Pack: The Complete Series

Copyright © 2024 Tessa Cole

All rights reserved. No part of this book may be reproduced in any form or by any means without written consent, excepting brief quotes used in reviews.

This is a work of fiction. Names, places, characters, and events are entirely the product of the author's imagination or are used fictitiously, and any resemblance to persons, living or dead, actual locals, events, or organizations is coincidental.

Gryphon's Gate Publishing

550 King St. N.

PO Box 42088 Conestoga

Waterloo, ON

N2L 6K5

Print ISBN: 978-1-990587-51-1

WOLF DECEIVED

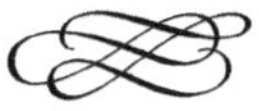

AUDREY

Tonight, my wolf would awaken. It would. Fifth time was the charm, right?

I glanced up, checking the time. The full moon was almost perfectly framed by the large hole in the thick canopy of branches and leaves surrounding the pack's sacred grove, indicating it was only a few minutes until midnight and then— Then! Then I'd become a real shifter.

I nervously ran my hands down the front of my simple white dress. I'd bought the dress on my eighteenth birthday, eager to become an adult in my pack, ready to meet the animal half of my soul even though I knew I'd have to wait ten months before the summer solstice to join the others who'd turned eighteen that year for our first shift.

Except that solstice had come and gone, and my wolf still hadn't woken.

A part of me wished our pack was like the other packs, born with our animal natures fully awake, shifting around six or seven years old whenever we wanted and not needing to wait until our eighteenth birthday. But then I would have had sixteen or seventeen years of being the laughingstock of my pack and not just five.

Instead, centuries ago, the then pack alpha paid a witch to halt our transformation until we were eighteen. It was a way to protect ourselves from being discovered by the humans and it had made us a significant pack in North America. We'd been able to build our own village out in the open instead of hiding away from the humans and gain influence and prosperity in a world that would have hunted us down if they'd known the truth.

Then a little over twenty-five years ago, Michael had tried to exterminate every human on the planet — as well as all of us hidden supernatural beings — and Gabriel made a deal with every super in hiding to join the fight.

The deal had turned the tide of the war, and the need to hide, to avoid children losing control and shifting in front of a human, no longer mattered. The world knew about shifters and vampires and demons and angels. We were the heroes that had helped save humanity, and now we were the pack that couldn't shift until we were adults.

And I was the girl who couldn't shift at all.

But this year would be different. I could feel it.

This was my year.

The full moon was a good sign. Those who awakened under the full moon were said to be stronger, more connected with their wolves.

This year my wolf would awaken and I'd become an adult and get the hell out of this town. Not that I technically wasn't an adult at twenty-two — at least according to the humans — but as far as pack law was concerned, I was still a child.

On top of that, once my wolf wakened, I wouldn't look like a target to every supernatural being I came across the moment I left pack land, since while my essence told every super who saw me that I was a shifter, it also told them I was so weak I was practically human.

Merrick, our pack's alpha, wouldn't be able to use any of that as an excuse to keep me here any longer. Although I had a bad feeling he'd find some other excuse. No money, no family, no something I'd never been able to have in the first place. I was free labor, and according to him I *owed* him for taking me in when my father killed himself thirteen years ago.

He always told me he could have let someone else take me, but no, my father had been a valued member of the pack even after he'd come back from the war broken and haunted by the things he'd experienced, and Merrick had been obligated to take care of *family*.

That, of course, had been a lie, but I'd been too young to realize the truth until it was too late. Not that I'd have been able to do anything about it.

No one defied the alpha, especially someone who was still considered a child.

Joan and Shea, with their perfectly coifed blond locks, stepped into the sacred clearing with their younger siblings who'd turned eighteen a few months ago, and a chill rushed through me as my pulse picked up.

I inched back toward the deeper shadows of the grove where the pale moonlight didn't reach and tried to make myself look smaller, even though I knew I wouldn't be able to hide from their enhanced night vision unless I was in complete shadow. But it was the best I could do. I had to be here for the ceremony so I couldn't just run away.

Hopefully they wouldn't notice me and everything would be fine. They were here for their siblings, not me. But their attention instantly jumped to me as if they'd been looking for me and it didn't matter if I made myself smaller or not.

Joan sneered, catching me trying to will myself invisible, and my pulse pounded faster. Sometimes it worked. Sometimes when I couldn't just flee, I managed to hide in the shadows and not be noticed, but I should have known they'd search me out. I was guaranteed to be here. I was tonight's amusement. And now I looked like prey. Prey that Joan had been toying with for years.

She'd had her eye on Sterling, Merrick's son and my sort of — definitely unwanted — brother since we were little. She'd been furious when I'd moved into his house, her tormenting reaching new heights that had often sent me to the nurse's office until she'd realized

I'd actually become Sterling's slave. Then they'd joined forces, honing their skills to make my *accidents* look more like accidents and learning that waiting for an attack elicited as big or bigger a reaction than actually being attacked.

God, I should have just run when I'd started fantasizing about it years ago.

I certainly should have done it after the first summer solstice when I didn't shift.

I should have stolen what I could have easily carried so I could pawn it in the next town over and taken the bus as far away from here as possible, like to Union City. That was on the other side of the country and had a whole vibrant supernatural quarter. Surely the wolf pack there would take me in. I'd become damn good at cooking and cleaning, so I at least had a few useful skills.

Except it didn't matter where I went, Merrick would find me. As soon as it came out that I was a shifter who couldn't shift he'd know where I was because there wasn't anyone else out there like me. And yeah, I'd spent the last five years back in my old high school's library at their one remaining clunky student computer, searching the internet for anything that might tell me why I couldn't shift.

"Every time you show up you just prove the rumors true," Shae snickered with a wicked gleam in her eyes that made my pulse race even faster because she knew I couldn't refuse the ritual until I actually shifted. "You're just a mutt. Not even shifter enough to have a wolf. Your mom fucked a human and your dad was too stupid to know the truth."

Except I had proof that wasn't the reason I couldn't shift. There wasn't such a thing as a half shifter. Children of human-shifter pairings were either shifters with the ability to shift and the essence of a shifter, or human with the essence of a human. There was no in between like me.

Joan barked a shrill laugh, and her younger sister and Shae's younger brother joined in.

"Stupid must run in the family," Joan cackled, her voice rising and drawing the attention of the two dozen others in the grove. Not that she needed to speak up. Shifters had excellent senses — smell, sight, and hearing — once their animal-soul had awakened. "You're never going to shift."

"I think we should change the ritual this year," Sterling purred as he slunk out of the shadows and drew up close behind me, making me jump. His ferocious power rolled over me, threatening to dominate me and force me to my knees in submission just by being near me, and I realized he'd fully suppressed his power to sneak up and surprise me. "I think we should make the mutt run when she doesn't shift."

AUDREY

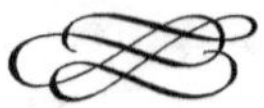

A SHUDDER SWEPT THROUGH ME AS I FOUGHT TO KEEP STANDING AND not kneel in front of Sterling like his power demanded. They'd made that threat before and followed through with an incident that had left me limping for weeks. I'd thought once they'd become adults the bullying would stop, that they'd get on with their lives, but I'd been wrong. I was too much fun and with their animal natures fully heightened, they used me to hone their new hunting abilities.

Sterling nicked a claw against the back of my neck with a sharp sting and sauntered over to Joan as I slapped my hand over the wound.

The warm blood oozing from the cut coated my palm. It wasn't deep, but it wasn't a papercut, either. Swell.

It would heal when I shifted… if I shifted—

No. I *would* shift tonight. But until then, I'd draw even more unwanted attention.

He cocked a pale eyebrow and smirked, the look doing nothing to diminish his striking appearance. He was a devil in an angel's skin, blond, beautiful, with a naturally sculpted physique, and a cruel speck of black nothingness for a heart. He knew full well that he'd made it so that if I didn't shift, the newly awakened wolves, with their predatory senses suddenly on overdrive from being repressed, might see me as prey and attack instead of going on the run with the alpha, and there was nothing I could do about it.

Joan sniffed sharply and sneered, her lips curling back revealing her extended canines. "She always smells like prey."

Shae inched closer to me, her eyes darkening as her wolf's nature rose closer to the surface, her hunger clear in her expression. Even her brother and Joan's sister, on the verge of awakening their wolf but not yet wolves, drew closer, their noses working, picking up the scent of my blood.

My pulse roared and I fought the urge to hug myself.

Don't look like prey. Don't. Or at least not any more than you already do. Stay. Calm.

But I wouldn't put it past them to double back after the shift took over the newest adults of the pack and that thought terrified me.

Merrick and our packs' beta would lead their first run, but those who'd already shifted didn't have to join in and didn't have to stay with the group like the newly made adults did. And if I didn't shift, I was a target just waiting to be attacked.

"If you kill her, who will clean your house?" Royce asked.

A hint of his power rolled over me as he stepped out of the shadows on the other side of the circle and sauntered toward the group, but then he pulled it back completely like he always did when he was around Sterling, like a good beta should. His eyes were just as dark as the others, his wolf close to taking over, but his expression remained flat, not hungry, and I was almost relieved to see him.

Almost, because he'd never attacked me or put me down. Of course, he'd also never publicly gone against Sterling to stop him. As far as everyone was concerned, he was on team Sterling. Like almost everyone else. He had, however, since that first year when I hadn't shifted, been making little comments to protect me and subtly distracting Sterling and Joan so I could slip away before things got out of hand. And while he'd been doing it for four years, I still had no idea what to make of it.

"Of course, when her wolf wakes tonight, you'll need to find a new housecleaner regardless. She'll be an adult and able to move out of your house. You know," Royce added with a pointed look at Sterling, "that thing kids do when they become adults."

"There's no point in moving out of my father's house. It'll be mine soon," Sterling huffed, jumping right to Royce's jab about still living at home. "And she'd still be an unmated female with ties to the alpha. Dad will want her to stay until he can find her a suitable match."

My thoughts lurched at that. "He what?"

Had Sterling just implied that Merrick was going to arrange who my mate was?

Everyone's attention snapped to me. The force of their ferocious natures pressed against my senses, and I froze.

Crap. One wrong move and their wolves would take over and they'd attack. Or rather they'd *let* their wolves take over.

"Your mate would have influence over the alpha. You *are* my sister," Sterling said even though he'd made a point over the years to remind me that I wasn't his sister. "Every male in the pack knows that."

But that was just another excuse. I didn't have any power and everyone in the pack knew it. The only way I could get power was if my mate was powerful. Of course, that was if I stayed. If I left... yeah, the odds of me having power in a different pack were slim, too, but that was better than being here.

"Dad probably won't even wait for your wolf," Sterling said. "You're old enough. You need a good match. One that looks good for our pack. Since by pack law you're still a child, it'll be up to him to find you a suitable mate."

He flashed me a wicked smile, wrapped an arm around Joan's waist, and led her, Shae, and their younger siblings away.

My heart slammed inside me, no doubt audible to everyone around me. Would Merrick let me leave even if my wolf woke this evening?

I'd be an adult. He'd have to.

Now my wolf had to show up. It wasn't the dark ages and our pack didn't have arranged matings, but I wouldn't put it past Merrick to use me as political leverage. He was pissed that his wife had left him for a human and pissed that our pack no longer had the same political influence over the other North American packs that it used to have.

And he was really pissed that he hadn't been asked to be the North American shifter representative in the Joined Parliament where supers governed pretty much the whole supernatural world. There was no way he'd sacrifice his precious heir with an arranged mating to improve his position among the other packs, which left me as the sacrificial offering to his political goals.

AUDREY

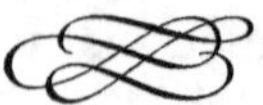

As if thinking about him made him appear, Merrick strode into the sacred grove. My attention, along with everyone else's, jumped to him. Even with his ferocious power only partially released, it still crackled against my senses and thickened the air. It didn't press against me, willing me to my knees like Sterling's had, but that was only because he wasn't trying to exert his will on us.

He reached the center of the grove and the group closed around him, ready to begin the ritual. Everyone about to meet the wolf-half of their soul was dressed in white, while everyone else was stripping out of their clothes since the nature of our magic that allowed us to shift completely destroyed whatever we wore.

For those of us about to be adults — *please, oh please let me become an adult tonight* — the destruction of our white clothing symbolized our transformation from child to adult. For everyone else, it was better on the bank account to strip first instead of constantly having to buy new clothing.

"It's an auspicious night," Merrick said, his voice a deep rumble as he turned his attention to the moon and I kept mine on him, determined not to see something I didn't want to see — like Sterling naked. "Wolves that wake under the full moon are leaders in our community. Much will be expected of you."

The eleven teens about to take their first transformation into adulthood drew closer, stepping into the circle of moonlight.

"You're so sure your wolf won't wake that you're not going to join them?" Royce asked, suddenly right beside me, his voice low.

"My wolf can wake just fine over here," I hissed back, fighting the urge to glance at him.

He'd played this game with me before. Two years ago, he'd come up beside me during the ritual and I'd gotten an eyeful of his honed physique and semi-hard cock. I was sure my eyes had bulged out of my head as my face had burned with embarrassment.

I knew it was stupid. Shifters were naked all the time.

Except our pack *wasn't* naked all the time. We were essentially humans with aggressive tendencies until we were eighteen and because I had yet to shift, I hadn't been involved in any of the hunts or games.

The only times I'd seen anyone naked was that one time I'd accidentally walked in on Sterling in the bathroom — and gotten my arm broken for my mistake — and the four other times I'd attended the transformation ceremony. But during the ceremony it had been night and hard to see much of anything unless someone had been standing right beside me, like Royce had... and now was.

"Audrey," he murmured, his voice strangely soft, surprising me and straining my control to keep my attention on Merrick in the center of the grove. "Tonight's your night. I can feel it."

I huffed a bitter laugh despite my hope that my wolf would wake tonight. "Yeah, because I'm supposed to be a leader in our community?"

"Why wouldn't you be?"

Because no one would listen to me. I was the girl who couldn't shift, the girl who scrubbed floors like Cinderella and was about to have a prearranged mating like a woman from the Dark Ages. And no, there was no Prince Charming or fairy godmother who was going to give me a happily ever after. Happily ever after didn't happen in real life.

Except the moment I thought that, I thought of Mila and her fated mate. She'd heard the power of a rare fated mating call with a shifter from another pack and had left town last year. We'd grown up together, her friendship never wavering even after Sterling, Joan, and their friends ramped up their bullying. She'd tried to resist the call, put off being with her mate, but it had made her miserable. I hadn't wanted her to leave, but I also didn't want to stand in the way of her happily ever after, so, after a lot of promising that I'd join her new pack the minute my wolf woke, she'd left.

She had a happily ever after. Maybe I had a fated mate as well. If I had one, Merrick couldn't arrange my mating and my mate might be able to protect me from Sterling, or better yet, he'd be from a different pack like Mila's mate.

Which was childish wishful thinking. A man wasn't going to solve my problems and really, what kind of pathetic woman would I be if I hoped a man would whisk me off my feet and rescue me?

A tired, scared woman with very few options, a tiny voice said inside me.

But a fated mate just wasn't in my cards. Just like my wolf awakening probably wasn't either. And if I was going to be free of Sterling and his fan club, I was going to have to take matters into my own hands.

I bit back a sigh and focused all my attention on Merrick and the others in the middle of the grove. Merrick pulled off his shirt, preparing to shift, and the group inched closer, drawn by his power.

I felt the tug as well, a tightening in my chest, but I stayed where I was. If I didn't shift, I didn't want a new, possibly out-of-control wolf to notice that I'd been bleeding and possibly still was.

He chanted the Ritual of Welcoming and Transformation and the pressure in my chest grew stronger. But this wasn't a precursor to my wolf waking, just the alpha evoking the magic that would allow the wolf half of our soul to wake.

The pressure had happened the previous four solstices. The first time I'd thought I was really going to shift. The second time I was hopeful. Now I knew something else needed to happen. I just had no idea what.

Then searing agony exploded in my chest, stealing my breath and dropping me to my knees.

This was it. I was going to shift. My wolf was going to wake and I could get the hell out of this town.

But the pain was blinding, unlike anything I'd experienced before, and my sudden joy that I was finally going to be a real shifter snapped to panic.

This wasn't how a shift was supposed to feel. Shifting was natural to our kind, our body turned to liquid and reformed in our animal form, as easy as breathing. It didn't hurt and it certainly didn't feel like I was being burned alive and ripped apart from the inside.

I clenched my jaw, fighting the agony, desperate to not draw attention to myself, especially in such a vulnerable position on my hands and knees. Sterling would use this weakness against me, probably use it as proof that I was never going to shift and Merrick needed to find me a mate before everyone in the other packs realized the truth. Although how he'd explain my complete lack of power to anyone looking at me and not mention that I couldn't shift was beyond me.

"What do you know, she is a shifter?" Joan snickered.

"She isn't if it hurts," Sterling replied, pushing away from his father and striding toward me.

He grabbed my ponytail and yanked my head back as another explosion ripped through me, this one with a deafening gong that reverberated through my whole body.

"Let her go," Royce snarled, grabbing Sterling's wrist and twisting, breaking his hold on me.

"Fuck off," Sterling shot back, his power flaring, crushing against me, demanding I bow down to him.

He reached for me again, but Royce shoved him before he could grab hold, and he stumbled back.

"Stay away from her," Royce growled, kneeling beside me.

My gaze leaped up to his, shocked that he'd defend me against his best friend in public. There was no going back from that. Sterling would be pissed, and Royce had just lost his chance at being pack beta when Sterling took over from his father.

But then our eyes met and all my thoughts vanished, burned away by the power roaring and clanging inside me, and I was falling falling falling into his dark eyes.

They were bottomless and consuming and filled with power. He wasn't as strong as Sterling, couldn't command the same number of shifters to the same degree, but he still had the potential to crush me with a howl. And yet I knew he wouldn't.

Because he was mine.

My mate.

His eyes widened and the fire swept back into my chest, leaving my limbs and face cold, but I was barely aware of it, of anything. We might not have known each other very well, but once we did, we'd be in love forever. That was how fated mating bonds worked. They were precious and rare, a strange side effect of the spell that had taken away our ability to shift until we were eighteen, and those with fated mate bonds were revered among the pack.

I did have a happily ever after.

And Royce had a high enough status in the pack that even if Sterling chose someone else to be his primary beta when he took over, I'd still be safe from their torments. Sterling would lose face if he continued to pick on me. I was no longer the girl who killed her mother just by being born, or whose father had killed himself, or who couldn't shift.

I was now the girl with a fated mate.

AUDREY

Sterling growled low and opened his mouth to say something, but his father barked his name.

"He's not your beta if he defies you. He never was," Merrick said.

Around him, the adults were shifting, their bodies transforming in a quick, fluid motion from one shape to another, starting on two legs and ending on four. Ripples rolled through a few of the teens, their forms shuddering, solidifying back to human, then shuddering again. The wolves beside them drew closer, offering support with physical contact while Merrick shifted, raised his head to the moon, and released a long, deafening howl.

Awaken and run.

Power rolled through the grove and those teens whose forms were already starting to change dropped to their hands and knees and shifted. The others started to lose their form and Merrick howled again.

His alpha's command, to take my true form, to wake and run, squeezed inside me. I had to obey. I wanted to obey. I was pack — and I sure as hell wasn't even close to being an alpha and able to resist his power.

But just like the last four years, no matter how much I wanted to obey, nothing inside me responded to his call, not a growl or huff or a sense that my body had the capability of being anything other than human.

My throat tightened with disappointment, but I pushed it aside. I wasn't done yet. My wolf could still wake. I could still shift. I just needed to try harder, concentrate more, something, anything.

Awaken, Merrick roared in my head, as if he knew I needed another stronger push to shift.

His golden gaze seized me from across the grove and the pressure crushed around my heart.

I fought to breathe, to will my body into transforming. Please. This was my year. I was going to shift. I had to shift. Even with a fated mate, I wanted to shift. I wanted to be what I'd been born to be. A wolf shifter, a supernatural being, a predator, not some helpless prey who wasn't shifter enough to be a super but not human enough to be human, either.

I squeezed my eyes shut and searched inside myself for even just a spark of ferociousness, a flicker of animalistic power, something, anything.

But there was only me. There had only ever been me. Weak, fragile, so close to human I should have just been born human.

Pathetic, Merrick huffed inside my head. He turned away from me and released another howl. The rest of the group responded and they took off into the woods, leaving me panting against the pressure that remained in my chest, my soul aching and empty.

Did I even have a wolf? How many times could I come to the grove on the summer solstice and not shift before I accepted the truth?

I was a shifter who couldn't shift.

I *was* pathetic.

I pressed my forehead to the forest floor, gasping in ragged breaths, the deep musty scent of dirt doing nothing to steady me and ground me within my body because I didn't want to be where I was. I didn't want to be aching and empty in our pack's sacred grove. I wanted to be running through the forest with the other wolves. I wanted to be recognized as an adult, hell, even just a person.

My eyes burned and my throat tightened with tears I didn't want to shed. Crying was weak. Except I *was* weak. Sterling was right. He'd always been right. I was prey and would always be prey.

And I needed to remember that and get home before Sterling, Joan, and Shae could double back and attack me and—

No. They wouldn't because Royce still knelt beside me. They might not have figured out yet that he'd protected me because of our fated mating call, but they knew something was up, and they'd figure it out soon enough. Then Royce would join me as the laughingstock of the pack. Mated to the shifter who couldn't shift.

I cracked my eyes open and glanced at him, my forehead still pressed against the cool uneven ground, too tired to bother raising my head. He hadn't touched me or said anything the whole time, but from his expression it looked more like he wasn't sure how to approach me instead of horrified that I was his fated mate.

"So much for this year being my year," I said.

"I don't know," he said with a shrug. "How many of us can say we've heard a fated mating call?"

He offered me a soft smile. It lit up his face and I was struck with how handsome he was. Compared to Sterling in his shining captain-of-the-football-team blond glory, Royce with his spikey brown hair and muddy brown eyes hadn't stood out as good looking. He'd been handsome, but nothing compared to his friend. But his smile, so real and comforting, turned him into an angel and it was breathtaking. I wasn't sure I'd ever seen him smile like that.

The thought sent whispering heat teasing down my spine. This was a smile just for me. His mate.

"Well of the current group available, I'd say a hundred percent of us can say we've heard a fated mating call," I replied with a soft laugh.

He rolled his eyes at me. "Your sample size is too small. Two isn't enough for anything. Well..." He coughed and glanced away. "It's enough for ah... something else."

"Like completing the mating bond?" I wasn't sure how I felt about that even knowing that was the next step for us.

Yes, Royce was my fated mate and I couldn't pretend I hadn't heard the call. I hadn't thought it would come with an explosive fire that would make me feel like I was being burned alive — Mila hadn't said anything about that — but we knew so little about the call that everyone's call could be different. Perhaps the magic needed for my and Royce's souls to recognize each other had to be stronger because I was a broken shifter.

On the other hand, completing the bond meant having sex with someone I barely knew. Not that knowing him would change anything. We'd still be fated mates. I'd just hoped I'd be a little less self-conscious about the whole sex thing before I actually had sex. Especially since I'd never actually *had* sex before. It had been hard enough to keep Mila as a friend and next to impossible to find a guy to have any kind of relationship with.

And while I knew I was going to have to admit that to Royce before we completed our bond and he probably wouldn't judge me, I wasn't prepared for the look he'd give me when he realized I was a virgin.

"How about coffee first?" I suggested as I pushed up to my feet and leaned against a tree to steady myself.

"I'd love to," he said, standing as well, his hands reaching for me as if to help me with my balance but stopping before making contact, still uncertain of himself. "But I don't think we can afford to wait. Not even for coffee." He glanced across the grove in the direction the pack had gone. "Sterling wasn't lying when he said Merrick was going to arrange a mating for you. I overheard the alpha on the phone the other day. He's going to send you to the Albuquerque pack."

"Albuquerque?" I was surprised he wasn't sending me to Union City or to a pack in Europe. Albuquerque wasn't close, but it wasn't exactly far away, either. Except getting rid of me wasn't the plan. Using me as currency to buy what he wanted was, and if that was the case— "Isn't the Albuquerque alpha the head of the North American Shifter Alliance?"

"And they just had a seat open up at the table," Royce said. "It's not the JP, but it's the next best thing."

"Does he honestly think the alpha will give him that seat once he learns he's been sent a defective shifter?" It didn't make sense, not for something like that. But then if he wasn't going to mate me to a shifter for his own political gain, why would he arrange a mating for me?

"It sounded like it didn't matter whether you could shift or not," Royce said.

My pulse picked up. I really didn't like the implications of that. The Albuquerque pack had a renowned supernatural research facility and if Merrick wasn't shipping me off to be someone's wife, he could be shipping me off to find out why I was a shifter who couldn't shift. And I didn't want to think about how they were going to gather their data.

"We can't risk Merrick denying our bond," Royce added, inching closer to me and reaching a tentative hand to cup my cheek.

My pulse fluttered at his touch and at the desperate look in his eyes. I leaned into his palm and warmth billowed in my chest and radiated over my cheek where our flesh met.

God, it felt so good to be touched. Since Mila had left, there hadn't been anyone to satisfy my shifter need for physical contact, and I hadn't realized just how much I missed it until now.

"He can't deny a fated mating call," I replied, my voice turning breathy and the heat in my chest sinking low within me, the need to seal our bond rising even though it had only just been awakened. "Even if we haven't said our vows and completed the bond, we're still fated mates."

His gaze dipped to my lips and the heat blossomed into an achy need. What would it feel like to kiss him? What would it be like to do more? Unlike me, I was sure he'd had practice, had kissed someone, probably a few someones, before. He'd probably *been* with a woman, too.

And now I was even more self-conscious of the fact that I'd never been intimate with someone.

"I don't want to bet on Merrick respecting a fated mating call," Royce murmured, inching even closer, his breath feathering across my lips. "I never thought I'd have a fated mate and I'm not going to lose you before I even know you."

The need and fear in his eyes matched mine. Merrick couldn't be trusted. He'd use me however he saw fit and the only way to guarantee that didn't happen was to seal my mating bond with Royce.

"Okay," I breathed. "Take me to your place."

"Sterling could still catch us before we get there." Royce brushed his lips against mine. Desire shivered all the way down my body, inflaming the aching need between my thighs. "Let's do it here in the sacred grove under the summer solstice's full moon."

AUDREY

"Okay," I said again, unable to come up with another word, unable to think past the knowledge that I was about to seal a mating bond with someone let alone my fated mate.

My heart pounded as Royce slipped his hand behind my back, tugged me close against his naked body, and captured my lips in a scorching kiss. It was strong and powerful and overwhelming.

I gasped at the ferocity of his passion and he slipped his tongue into my mouth, teasing me, adding to the fiery mating call within me that was about to explode once again into an inferno of desire.

I tangled my fingers in his hair, clinging to him, gasping for breath, dizzy against his onslaught. His cock, trapped between our bodies, hardened, proof of his desire for me, fueling my need and my certainty that this was right.

"God, Audrey," he growled against my lips. "Say your vow so I can say mine and we can be together."

"Blessed be the moon and her children," I said.

He nipped at my lips and reached under the skirt of my dress, sliding his hands up my thighs to cup my bare ass — since I hadn't wanted to destroy one of my few pairs of underwear shifting — and pressed his length against me.

"And blessed be this sacred vow," I continued, my voice getting breathier by the second.

He rolled his hips, rubbing himself against me through my dress and ratcheting up my need.

The fated mating call rang again, louder this time than before. It vibrated through me, a powerful, deep, resounding *gong* filled with certainty that drowned out everything else. Royce was my mate. We belong together. We would always be together. We—

"I answer the call—" Royce prompted, reminding me that I needed to finish the vow and awaken the binding magic that joined two shifters' souls together so Royce could say his vow and we could seal our bond.

"I answer the call and join my soul with you, my mate," I finished. "My *fated* mate," I corrected myself.

The call rang again, and the need and heat that had awakened with the fated mating call ignited every cell in my body. I was going to change a part of my essence, bind it to my mate in a way only two shifters could bind themselves together, and that meant calling on a primal magic that affected the very core of my being.

"Perfect," Royce purred, his tone suddenly cold and dark, making my thoughts trip.

That wasn't what he was supposed to say. He was supposed to—

He grabbed my ponytail and jerked my head back, holding it at a painful angle.

"Royce, that hurts." I squirmed in his grip, but he held tight and glared down at me, his face a mask of dark satisfaction and malice. The love and hope and fear that Merrick would deny our mating was completely gone. There was no indication that he'd heard the call, that he wanted to take the sacred vows with me and seal our bond. "Royce—"

"About time," Sterling said, jerking my attention from Royce's cold eyes to him. He sauntered naked from the shadows on the other side of the grove, directly in my line of sight as if he didn't want me to miss seeing him, his lips curled back in a wicked smile. "Did you have to play with her first?"

Royce spat on the ground by our feet and wiped his mouth with the back of his free hand. "She needed to believe the call was real so she'd say the vow."

"The call wasn't real?" How could a fated mating call not be real? It was fate, two perfectly aligned souls finding each other. It couldn't be faked.

"Of course it wasn't, mutt," Sterling said. "Pay a witch enough and you can get a spell to do anything."

But it had to be real. It *felt* real.

Royce had protected me from Sterling, publicly defied him. He wouldn't have done that if he wasn't my fated mate. I needed him. Everything in my soul said we belonged together. "You're lying. It's real. You feel it." I turned to Royce. "You have to feel it. We're fated mates. We—"

Royce jerked my head back farther, sending sharp pain slicing through my scalp. "You honestly think my fated mate would be a wolf who can't even shift?"

"But I felt it." I clawed at his hand, desperate to break his hold. His words cut into my soul and the power of the incomplete mating bond heaved inside me, urging me to seal it.

Be with him. He's our mate. It's real. Real!

I didn't know how I'd gone from one minute determined to leave the pack the second my wolf woke — or didn't wake this evening — to desperately needing Royce. It didn't make sense. But the desire to seal my bond with him was overwhelming. It consumed me, thrumming and burning, begging for completion. It had to be real.

"I heard the call," I gasped. "It was real."

"Fuck she's stupid, isn't she?" Sterling spat as he uncovered a vial with a red glowing liquid from his pile of clothes.

"And pathetic," Royce snarled, wrenching me up by my hair until my toes skimmed the ground, his greater shifter strength more than enough to lift my weight with one hand. "You're a shame to this pack and I can't believe Merrick let you live after your first solstice when you didn't shift. We'd never be mates."

I clung to his wrist, trying to hold myself up, my bare feet skittering over the moss, trying to find enough footing to support my weight. My thoughts whirled and stuttered, the compulsion from the newly formed bond tearing into me as horrible realization hit me. The incomplete vow was why I suddenly couldn't live without someone I barely knew, why I couldn't let him go when only minutes ago I'd been perfectly fine without him. I'd started the magic to seal our bond and it was now compelling me to finish.

I had to fight it, refute it now before it completely took over. Sure, if Royce didn't complete his half of the bond, it would eventually fade, but that could take months, possibly years, and I was *not* going to spend any time pining over someone who didn't love me.

"Why?" I gasped, straining to focus past the clawing need threatening to tear me apart.

I needed him.

No. I was strong enough without him.

But you can't shift. You're not a wolf. You're nothing but prey.

"You're sick," I forced out. *And I love you.*

No. I. Don't.

"How could you manipulate the calling like that?"

Come on. Concentrate. Refute it.

"Because I needed someone with an incomplete mating bond," Sterling said with a sneer before striding to the center of the grove. "I'm going to make our pack powerful again, but I needed a sacrifice." And from the look in his eyes, that *sacrifice* involved something horrible and he was more than happy to sacrifice me.

Oh no.

Oh no no no.

I heaved and clawed against Royce's grip. "Let me go."

"It's like you were made to be our pack's sacrifice," Sterling continued as Royce wrenched me toward the center of the grove, his steps even, unaffected by my flailing. "No one will miss you and you don't even have a wolf. You're not really a member of this pack."

"Mila will miss me," I said.

Come on. Refute the bond and break the magic. He'd said he needed an incomplete mating bond so if I severed the magic empowering it, he wouldn't be able to sacrifice me.

But I couldn't get my thoughts to focus to work up enough willpower to break the magic. I needed Royce. I didn't want to die. How the fuck had no one noticed Sterling was insane?

"Mila is too busy with her *fated* mate," Royce chuckled, his tone for *fated* mocking, twisting my need for him tighter which only deepened my disgust at myself. How could I have been so stupid? No one would be a fated mate to a shifter who couldn't shift. I should have known something wasn't right from the very beginning.

"It's a shame the guy we picked for her turned out to be half decent," Sterling replied, turning my aching desire and screaming frustration into a sudden, fearful cold.

They'd manipulated Mila just like they'd manipulated me? Her guy wasn't her fated mate? For all I knew she didn't have a fated mate, either. I had to warn her that her mate was manipulating her. Except he'd happily taken his vows with her and completed their bond, and I hadn't sensed that he didn't love her... of course I hadn't sensed that Royce was deceiving me, either.

"Yeah, well, we couldn't risk bringing someone else in on our plan," Royce said. "He had to be just as oblivious as the bitches."

They laughed as if it was the funniest thing in the world to mess with someone's emotions while Sterling poured the glowing red contents in his vial on the ground and hissed a few sharp words I didn't recognize.

Magic exploded around us. It slammed into me, stealing my breath, and roared into a wild black whirling mist that shot up from the ground and poured into the sky turning into thick black clouds that blotted out the moon.

"All right, god of power," Sterling yelled. "Accept our sacrifice and show yourself."

AUDREY

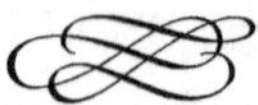

Lightning sliced through the clouds and black misty tendrils rushed around me, digging into my essence, seizing the pressure and heat in my chest from the incomplete mating bond and yanking on it, trying to pull it from my body.

Oh, shit.

I mentally scrambled to hold it in and break the magic. He couldn't complete the sacrifice if he didn't have an incomplete bond.

"I refute him!" I screamed into the vortex, heaving against Royce's grip. "I refute this asshole. I take it all back."

"Too late, mutt," Royce snarled. "The god has you bound and he's about to eat you alive."

"No." I tried to knee him in the groin, but he turned to the side and my knee skimmed his hip instead, so I rammed my heel down his shin, drawing a snarl of pain.

"Fucking bitch," he roared and backhanded me.

The impact broke my nose and shot agony through my face. Blood gushed down my chin and splattered on the ground. A brilliant flash of lightning streaked from the clouds and blasted into the center of the grove with a resounding *boom*.

"Come and take your sacrifice," Sterling called out.

More of my blood splattered on the ground followed by another blast of lightning and roar of thunder.

"I refute you. I refute you," I gasped. *Please, I refute you.*

The incomplete bond trembled and chilled. I was doing it. Just a little more and this would all be over. Sterling and Royce would be pissed, I'd have to fight for my life to escape, but the assholes wouldn't get whatever it was they wanted.

"I refute you!" I yelled

"And he doesn't care." Royce's fingers turned to claws and he tore through my dress and dug deep gouges in my chest.

Agony sliced through me, a mix of physical and magical pain, and I screamed. The incomplete mating bond ripped into my soul deeper and more painful than Royce's claws ripping into my flesh. The magic still thought he was my fated mate, and the pain of my mate's attack was overwhelming, stealing every thought but the desperate one to run. *Run now. Now!*

The lightning crackled and roared, illuminating the grove brighter than daylight and filling the air with the reek of ozone. Then the black mist burst apart, revealing an enormous column of rippling air, like heat rolling off asphalt on a summer's day, and radiating an enormous, crushing power.

Royce threw me to the ground at Sterling's feet, and a large red clawed hand reached out of the rippling air. It grabbed me, the claws piercing my back and chest, adding to the agony wracking my body, and the creature hoisted me up as it stepped fully out of the ripple.

It looked like a greater demon with large, leathery wings, fangs, and ram's horns protruding from his forehead. But it was bigger. A lot bigger. Which meant it was enormous since greater demons were already some of the largest supers in all the realms. It also didn't radiate any heat like a demon, let alone the enormous amount of heat that a greater demon was said to radiate with its essence fully released, and every inch of its skin — save for whatever lay under its loincloth — was red like a bad movie version of the devil where greater demons looked more-or-less human.

"She's weak, but she smells delicious," the monster snarled, revealing a mouth full of sharp teeth, "like sorrow and desperation." His tongue flicked out, swiping through the gashes Royce had carved into my breasts, lapping at my blood.

Oh God, oh God, oh God.

I wrenched in the monster's grip, driving its claws deeper into my body, my fear consuming all pain as well as all logic. I was pinned in its grasp, flailing wouldn't free me, but I had to do something. I was *not* going to be eaten by some monster. No way in hell.

Then a wave of power coming from somewhere behind me crashed over me with the command to kneel, crushing my insides because I couldn't move.

Sterling and Royce did drop to the ground and Merrick stormed into the grove.

"You broke into my safe and summoned it?" Merrick roared. "You idiot. He'll kill us all."

"He'll make us strong," Sterling shot back and he lunged at his father, somehow defying the alpha's power that was still squeezing my insides.

Merrick jerked out of the way, his eyes wide, likely with surprise that Sterling was strong enough to defy his power, but Sterling moved with him and rammed both sets of his claws into Merrick's chest. The alpha grunted in pain and slashed at Sterling's back, but Sterling ducked down, tearing his claws through Merrick's belly, and dancing out of the way.

Blood gushed onto the ground, and Merrick grabbed his stomach in a weak attempt to stop the bleeding. But the wound was too deep, eight long gashes that practically opened him up. Even with his heightened healing ability and the ability to heal by shifting, the injury was too great. Shifting now would just kill him. He needed to get to a hospital.

"Even better," the monster roared. "More power and more desperation." It tossed me aside like a discarded doll and dove on the wounded alpha.

I slammed into a tree, pitched forward, hit another tree with my head, and crashed in a heap on the ground, the world spinning around me.

Through my wavering vision, I watched the demon shove his hand into Merrick's gut, rip something out, and eat it.

Merrick screamed and my stomach heaved. That was going to be me—

That could still be me.

Merrick might be the main course now, but I could still be dessert. I had to get up and run.

I heaved up to my hands and knees. Darkness swam across my vision, but I forced myself to keep going, grabbed the tree beside me, and climbed to my feet, sending another wave of darkness that threatened my consciousness.

The monster howled in delight, catching my attention and giving me a perfect, horrific view of it drawing another strangled cry by tearing off Merrick's arm and chomping on it like a chicken wing.

My stomach heaved again and I staggered to the next tree, deeper into the forest and the shadows. I moved to the next and the next, the sounds of the monster eating Merrick ringing in my ears, propelling me forward.

That would be me. I would be next. *Run. Run run run.*

I forced myself to move faster, the trees and underbrush becoming shadowy blurs, my vision just as bad in the dark as a human's because I didn't have a wolf form yet. But I couldn't be more careful. I had to get as far away as possible before they noticed I was gone.

Just keep running. It doesn't matter where so long as it's away from that nightmare.

Branches caught on my dress and in my hair and whipped stinging slices against my bare arms and face. My toes caught on roots and bumps hidden in the darkness making me stumble, and rocks and branches sliced my bare feet. I bashed my shins against larger stones, rammed my hips and shoulders into tree trunks, but kept running.

I had to get farther, move faster. Go go go.

Sterling had let that thing eat his father alive.

My breath rushed in short, painful gasps.

Alive!

I jammed my foot on something, wrenched to the side to keep my balance, and slammed into a tree trunk. Pain shot through my face and the world spun and went black for a second.

Blindly, I staggered forward. I couldn't stop. Not for anything. But my foot hit empty air and I crashed forward, tumbling down a rocky incline and splashing into deep, freezing, rushing water.

The current wrenched me under and tossed me around and around. My body screamed for air, but I couldn't find the surface. My shoulder and the side of my head slammed into something hard, and sparks flashed across my vision before being consumed by writhing watery darkness.

I scraped against something else, broke the surface, somehow managed to gasp in a watery breath, but was shoved back under before I could even think to get my bearings and save myself.

I was moving too fast and my lungs screamed for air. I was going to drown and I was sure I hadn't gotten far enough away from that monster.

At least I wouldn't be alive when the thing ate me.

KNOX

I CRESTED THE RISE, MY FOUR LEGS CARRYING ME UP THE SLOPE FASTER than my brothers on their two legs, and scanned the horizon. A dark red smear stained the eastern edge of the sky while the wind gusted, stronger on the hilltop than the valley below, and I could smell the moisture in the air.

A storm was fast on its way. A real one. Not like whatever had lit up the night just after midnight, jerking us from our sleep. From the color of this morning's sky and the ache in my right haunch — not to mention we were a month into the summer storm season — the coming storm would be bad, and we'd need to find cover soon.

Except I was pretty sure the real storm was the least of our worries, which was why Cyrus hadn't told us to turn around and head to the closest patrol shed to take cover.

Whatever had summoned that lightning had been powerful. After the first blinding flash and bone-rattling boom, a giant wave of power, that I'm sure had been felt all the way to Stonehaven, had crashed into us.

The wave had disappeared, and the night returned to quiet, but we couldn't risk thinking that because it had stopped everything was fine. Lightning didn't just come out of nowhere once then disappear.

Not on a cloudless night. And it certainly didn't come with a wave of power.

The malicious god, Tzanagoth, was said to have fallen asleep in the heart of Anakar, the ruined temple complex in the center of the forest that lay before us, and while no gods had yet to wake from their magical slumber, we needed to confirm that this one hadn't finally broken the spell.

"Do you see anything?" Cyrus asked from halfway up the hill.

I raked my gaze over the thick forest beyond. The lightning had struck somewhere in the middle of those trees, but with them crowded close and the thick mist rolling and whirling between the trunks, I couldn't see anything in the predawn gray that might indicate what had happened, even with my excellent night vision. Which made me even more unsettled.

"I really hope it wasn't at the Anakar ruins," Bishop said, climbing to the top of the hill with Cyrus and stopping beside me. He reached down and brushed his fingers through my fur, trying to calm me with his touch even though I could sense his own worry through our twin bond.

I jerked away from him and loped down the hill.

I didn't need his touch to help calm me. I was fine. I wasn't even that upset.

So long as I was out in the open, preferably in my wolf form, I was fine, and I'd continue to be fine. I'd been fine for over a year.

But every time I got a little worried and it slipped through our bond, Bishop got concerned, like he was afraid my wolf was going to fully take over and I'd go feral again.

My wolf huffed at that. It hadn't really taken over, either. *So don't blame me.* Our fear had. That was the real beast inside me, the thing I battled with every day that I never admitted to anyone, not even my twin.

Very few in our pack had ever gone feral, and no one would have expected it from one of the alpha's sons. We were supposed to be the pack leaders, warriors at the front of the battle against the dangerous beasts roaming the land.

Of course, after Bishop had pulled me back to myself, everyone had *expected* I'd have a relapse. Even my brother. I was the strange one, the odd one, the one who didn't bother to smile for the sake of being polite. They said I liked the hunt too much, that I preferred my wolf form over my human one. I was already more wolf than man.

And they were right. My wolf didn't have to live up to expectations and didn't have to smile and be social when surrounded by too many people. I was free as a wolf in ways I'd never be free as a man, and I didn't give a fuck about my obligations as one of the alpha's sons. Just point me in the direction of a battle or hunt. That's all I wanted.

I found a break in the underbrush and a narrow game trail leading deeper into the trees and waited for Cyrus and Bishop to catch up. Mist curled over the ground, cold and thick, and the scent of forest decay and dirt sat heavy in the air, along with the teasing smell of a rabbit and some squirrels.

I ignored the urge to hunt down the rabbit and focused on smelling beyond the obvious forest scents for anything that might be dangerous.

We were almost done with our patrol of our borders and had already had to fight a small pack of grimalkins who thought one of our farmers and his livestock looked delicious. For all we knew, the rest of the grimalkins' pack had holed up here since the pack we'd fought had been smaller than usual and we didn't routinely patrol the Darkweald forest.

Not that they'd be smart enough to figure out that we ignored the forest since it was almost a day's march from the closest farmer and there were unwelcoming spirits in these mists. But without us patrolling the area, to their animal minds it might have seemed like a good place to call home.

I sniffed again. There was something just at the edge of my senses. A sweetness? A freshness? Something that didn't belong... or maybe it did. Maybe there were flowers in the heart of this murky forest. A god's power often influenced the area where he or she slept. Perhaps Tzanagoth's magic had made it possible for something to bloom in the forest's perpetual twilight. Although given that

Tzanagoth was a malicious god, I wouldn't have expected any flowers to bloom, especially ones that smelled sweet and fresh.

Smell anything? Cyrus asked in my head.

I pushed through the underbrush, stepping fully into the shadows and mist, and scented the air again. The sweet freshness grew a little stronger. It was definitely coming from somewhere to my left, but that didn't mean anything. I was supposed to be smelling for trouble while we headed straight to the ruins, and this didn't smell like trouble.

I'm scouting ahead.

Cyrus huffed his agreement, the communication more sensation than sound. He knew that if I didn't say there was trouble then there wasn't trouble.

I bounded down the trail a bit then slipped off the path into the underbrush, heading deeper into the forest to my right, away from the sweet scent. Cyrus and Bishop would stick to the path in their human forms while I'd search the surrounding area for signs of danger. Just because I couldn't smell something dangerous, didn't mean that something wasn't out there and hadn't left evidence behind.

The sweet fresh scent on my left continued to tease me despite purposely heading away from it, and my wolf started to double back toward it before I fully realized what we were doing.

I heaved myself back on track. Normally I'd just let him take over, especially since it was easier for him to be in control in our wolf form, but we couldn't lose ourselves in the hunt or even just curiosity right now. That lightning and power had announced the possibility of something seriously dangerous, and our brothers were depending on us to help keep them safe. As much as my wolf and I wanted to say fuck it to the world and all our obligations, we never wanted to endanger our brothers again.

This way, my wolf snarled, wrenching my head back toward the sweet scent. *Trouble.*

Something that smells good isn't trouble. Although I'd met more than a few females who'd smelled good and they'd certainly been trouble.

The wind gusted, swirling the mist and filling the air around with a hint of that sweet fresh scent and a big whiff of coppery tang. Blood. Lots of blood. Wolf shifter blood. And from the sweet freshness, female blood.

My wolf took off before I could come to the conclusion that it was necessary to check out what had happened.

A wolf shifter meant it was a pack member and everyone in the pack would want to know what had happened and who it was. Our pack wasn't small, but it wasn't too big that we didn't know or know of everyone in it, and someone had been seriously hurt.

KNOX

Pack has been hurt, my wolf growled to Cyrus and Bishop, racing faster as if he couldn't get to whoever it was quick enough. He must have recognized something about the scent that I hadn't, which was uncommon for everyone else but not for me. I spent days, sometimes months at a time in my wolf form, letting him control our body and wasn't completely aware of everything he did or everyone he encountered.

They could be dead, Cyrus replied grimly. He must have gotten a sniff of all that blood, too.

My wolf snarled at that and I crashed into a thorny bush, not caring that it scored my skin. The cuts weren't deep and even if I didn't shift, they'd heal soon enough.

I don't smell decay, Bishop replied quickly in an obvious attempt to calm my wolf.

Cyrus grunted at that. It could be too soon for decay to set in but he didn't want to say anything and risk setting me off. Now even he was walking on eggshells around me.

I shoved through the bush, my gaze instantly caught by a bit of white something, and jumped off the short steep edge of the river-bank into the mud.

The something white was a torn, filthy, bloody dress, on the broken body of a woman sprawled face down in the mud a few feet away. Scrapes and bruises covered her, and four deep wounds punctured her back as if she'd been stabbed with a wide, thick blade.

With the wind hissing through the trees and the rushing water, I couldn't hear from this distance if she was alive or not, but I couldn't see her breathing and I had a horrible feeling the injuries on her front would be worse.

I padded to her side, shifted, and gently rolled her over, my vision snapping to red, my anger roaring in my ears.

I was right. Her front was worse. Her face was one big bruise, her eyes swollen shut, her nose broken and still weeping blood, and the front of her dress had been ripped open, revealing four gashes, clearly claw marks, sliced across her chest.

Watery blood oozed from the wounds, pooling in the muddy puddle beneath her, and my anger blazed stronger. They hadn't just beaten her. They'd tortured her. Those slices weren't deep enough to kill right away and the sensitive flesh of both her breasts had been cut.

And the pack had thought *I* was a monster when I'd gone feral.

I'd never toyed with anyone like that, never tossed a person away in the river like they were garbage.

A growl bubbled in my throat. I didn't recognize her, not by her battered face or her matted, muddy blond hair, and neither I nor my wolf recognized her scent, but that didn't matter. I wasn't going to leave her here for the scavengers. She deserved to be taken back to pack land and given a proper burial.

And then I was going to hunt down whoever had done this to her and rip him to shreds.

My wolf heaved under my skin, determined to take over and start hunting now.

Just breathe, Knox, Bishop said, his voice in my head filled with worry. He wasn't even trying to hide his concern.

He and Cyrus pushed through the underbrush a few feet away from the thorny bush I'd gone through and staggered to a stop.

"We're going back to town," I snapped, picking up her limp, still slightly warm body, and cradling her against my chest. "We're going back now and burying—"

A gurgling gasp escaped her lips, followed by weak, ragged coughs, and water trickled from her mouth.

Fuck, she's alive? How the hell was she alive and I hadn't noticed? I was holding her in my arms. I should have heard her heartbeat.

But I was just so furious over what someone had done to her and — now that I was concentrating and up close — I heard that her pulse was slow and weak, barely there.

The eyelid on her least swollen eye fluttered and another gasping, weak cough, wracked her body.

"We have to get an elixir into her and get her back to town," Bishop said, hopping off the bank into the mud and reaching to take her from me as Cyrus opened his pack to get the precious ampul of healing elixir every patrol team carried in case of an emergency.

But before I could hand her over, another cough shook her, her eye cracked open, and her gaze locked on mine.

Heat and pressure erupted in my chest, roaring through me. My knees gave out and I dropped to the mud, clutching her, unable to look away.

Mine. She was mine. Every cell in my being knew she was mine—

No. I was hers. The power came from her. Somehow, without having said the vows and awakening the mating magic, she was binding our souls together.

The force tore into my essence, weaving through it and wrapping around it, growing tighter and tighter. She was trapping me. The cage of a soul bond was locking into place around my heart and if it solidified, I'd never be free.

No. Stop. I can't be trapped. I won't be trapped.

"Stop," I gasped.

She didn't respond, just kept staring at me... or staring through me. I wasn't sure which. I wasn't even sure she was actually conscious.

Her breath stuttered and she whimpered, but I couldn't tell if it was from the magic or her injuries.

"Stop it," I growled. *Don't do this. Don't trap me.*

But the force of the magic surged, burning and hardening, tightening around my heart and soul until I couldn't breathe. Darkness crowded around me, crushing down, threatening my consciousness. I had to get free, had to stop this. Fight. Kill. Tear it all to shreds.

My wolf heaved and snarled, sensing my panic. It would protect me, protect her, protect what was mine—

No. We couldn't be bound together and I wouldn't be able to refuse the bond if my wolf took over. As much as it didn't want to be trapped, it somehow didn't see this mating as a cage like I did. It thought she was his and needed to protect her. Binding our souls was the first step in ensuring she was safe.

"Refute it with me." I shook her, desperate to wake her up. We could break the spell if we both refuted it before it took hold. If she knew that she was bonding to a complete stranger, she'd stop. She had to stop.

"Knox!" Bishop wrenched the woman from my arms, his eyes wide.

The distance stretched the magic between us, tearing at my soul, heaving me toward her, and Cyrus grabbed me around the waist and pulled me back.

The woman whimpered again and her eyelid slid shut, but that didn't sever the connection between us. The magic had fully awakened, and now that she was unconscious, she wouldn't be able to refute me as her mate and end this. It was up to me and the force of my will alone.

"I refute you," I said, heaving against Cyrus's bear hug, my body still trying to get to her. "I refute you. I won't have you. You're not my mate!"

Ice exploded in my chest, tearing through the heat and pressure of the mating magic. It froze the magical cage around my heart and the chain binding me to this woman but didn't shatter it. I'd managed to cut off an active connection from my soul to hers, but I was still trapped, and even though we had yet to fully seal the bond, this stage was still permanent. I didn't know if there was any way to break it other than death.

CYRUS

WITH A FURIOUS ROAR, KNOX WRENCHED OUT OF MY GRIP AND SHIFTED, retreating into his wolf like he always did when his emotions were heightened.

"What just happened?" Bishop asked, as I cracked the wax seal on the ampul's stopper and dribbled the half ounce of elixir into her mouth. "Did she just mate bond with you?"

It sure looked like she had and from the look in Knox's eyes, he was pissed. I just wasn't sure if he was pissed that he'd been put in the position in the first place and forced to refute her or if he'd failed and was now stuck with a mate he didn't want.

Knox hopped onto the bank not acknowledging Bishop's remark and pushed through the bushes back to the trail.

"She was barely conscious," Bishop added, hurrying through the bushes after him. "I'm not even sure she knew who you were, and you didn't say your half of the vow. Do you even know her?"

Do you? You're familiar with a lot more females than I am, Knox said, his mental tone on *familiar* clear that he really meant fucked.

"No, I haven't slept with your mate before," Bishop shot back.

She's not my mate, Knox snarled.

Bishop glared at him. "I can feel the bond. You're blocking it, but it's there."

Guess he was pissed over not being able to break the mating magic before it took hold. Which was bad on so many levels.

Out of all of us, Knox was the worst one for the woman to have forced a bond on. He barely got along with others, shifters or otherwise, and he certainly wasn't interested in female attention. It was like Bishop, our youngest brother, had gotten all of the desire for social situations and flirting and had left Knox with nothing.

Except that wasn't really true. Knox hadn't been so closed off when we were children. At least not before the accident. He'd been a shy, somewhat reserved child, but he hadn't actively fled interacting with people, not like he did now, and I couldn't help but wonder if that distance he put between everyone except me and Bishop had been the reason for his fall into feral madness. There just weren't enough people he cared about to keep his primal nature at bay. One stress too many and without social support, our wolves took over to protect us.

And that was something I was going to have to keep an eye on. The stress of being forced into a mating he didn't want could be enough to tip him back into feralness.

So could losing that mate — whether he wanted her or not — and given the state of her injuries, I wasn't convinced that one ampul was going to be enough to save her.

"We need to get another ampul in her," I said. "We make for the patrol shed." Where we had one more dose of the healing elixir.

It was an hour out of our way if we wanted to go straight back to town, but I doubted she'd make it that far. I wasn't even sure she'd make it to the closest patrol shed. The healing elixirs worked wonders, but they weren't quick, and it took more than one — more than two actually — to bring someone back from the brink of death.

Except two was all we had access to. I could only hope it would be enough for her to hold on long enough to get back to town.

The wind gusted, swirling the mist and bringing with it the deep scent of rain. The storm that had been promised on the horizon had arrived and sooner than expected, making the shed an even better choice than heading straight to town.

I glanced back toward the heart of the forest. We still had no idea what had caused the lightning and power wave earlier this morning, and the longer we waited the greater the chance any clue as to what had happened would be washed away. But the woman was a priority. Even if she hadn't just soul bonded with Knox, saving her life was still a more immediate problem than investigating the lightning.

We hurried over the hill and into the valley on the other side. The clouds thickened, growing darker and darker and blotting out the sunrise. They released their promised downpour when we were only halfway to the shed. Stinging sheets of rain pelted us and wind gusts stole the breath from my lungs. But with no other obvious place to find shelter on the rolling grass and farmlands — and in need of that second ampul — all we could do was press forward as fast as we could.

We were drenched and shivering by the time we yanked open the shed door and hurried inside, Knox rushing in as well, surprising me.

He immediately shifted — thankfully resisting the urge to shake out his fur and spray everything in the tiny shed — and went to work starting the fire, leaving the woman to me and Bishop.

I grabbed the shed's only ampul of healing elixir from the hidden compartment by the door, cracked the seal, and dribbled it in her mouth. She looked even paler than when we'd first found her, and I was certain that wasn't just because the storm had washed away most of the mud and blood from her skin.

Blood still oozed from her deepest wounds and now her lips were blue. Even with the second ampul we still needed to warm her up and tend to her wounds, and I could only pray she hadn't lost too much blood and that two ampuls would be enough to save her.

I glanced at Knox, who was so focused on building the fire that it was painfully obvious he was trying not to look at the woman. I had no idea how to deal with this mess. If the bond had been set, they were going to have to seal it or there was a good chance they'd both go mad.

Except Knox was stubborn and would fight it. Probably to the point of irrevocable damage to both of them. How did I convince him to accept a mate he didn't want?

Hell, for all I knew she wouldn't want him, either.

Would they be able to break the magic if they both agreed? I'd never heard of anything like that happening once the bond had been formed, but then I'd never heard of anything like a bond forming without anyone saying the vows, either.

Knox had been adamant in refuting the bond. It should never have taken hold in the first place, and the magic remaining in the woman would have eventually faded. It wouldn't have been quick, usually months, but it would have gone away.

Except Bishop had said he'd felt Knox's mating bond, which meant it had progressed further than just one person starting the spell.

Did that mean this woman had intended to purposely trap Knox in a bond? We were the alpha's sons, and while it was expected my mate would join me in leading our pack there was precedent for the mate of a second or third son to become the female facet of the alpha unit. Of course, that was usually because that woman also took the first son as a mate as well, but there'd been that one rare female who hadn't mated both brothers.

Except I knew every eligible female in our pack and didn't recognize her. She didn't even smell like any of the other pack members. And if she'd really wanted to ensnare one of us with the goal of becoming a part of our pack's leadership, it would have been easier to trap Bishop. He wasn't wary of women like Knox was.

That and unless it had backfired on her, I doubted her plan was to be found almost dead in a river, hours away from our patrol route. She'd have had no way of guaranteeing that we'd even go into Darkweald... unless she was responsible for the lightning and the power.

Except given how weak her shifter essence was, indicating that she was almost powerless, it was even harder to believe she'd been responsible for last night's wave of power than her planning to trap Knox in a bond.

No. Whatever had happened to her and however she'd managed to mate with Knox, it hadn't been planned.

And that only meant I needed to stop trying to figure everything out right this second and focus on saving the woman.

CYRUS

I STRIPPED OUT OF MY WET CLOTHES AND TOOK HER FROM BISHOP.

"I'll get some fresh water," Bishop said, but Knox pushed past him, reaching for the bucket by the door before Bishop could grab it.

"I'll go," Knox growled not bothering to look at us, and he march back out into the storm.

"We're not going to be able to convince him to hold her to warm her up," Bishop said as he stripped out of his wet clothes as well and opened one of the many waterproof trunks at the back of the small room.

I laid the woman on the floor by the hearth as close to the fire Knox had started as was safe and sliced open the rest of her dress with a claw. "You honestly thought we might? I doubt we'd be able to convince him to do it even if we were in a room ten times this size."

"We both know he's not an asshole. I thought he'd be concerned enough to use their bond to help comfort her," Bishop replied, pulling on a dry pair of pants then grabbing another pair for me along with the pack with our non-magical healing supplies. "If she wakes, she'll be in pain and probably confused. The bond is new, but his presence will still help keep her calm."

The door flew open, and Knox stormed in with a bucket filled with water from the well. His gaze instantly locked on the woman, her battered body now fully exposed, the scrapes and bruises and bleeding gashes on her chest bright against her pale skin.

His eyes, which were almost perpetually dark with his wolf not the brown with green flecks he'd been born with, narrowed and the muscles in his jaw tightened. "I'll keep watch." He set the bucket beside me and stormed back outside.

Yeah, wishful thinking to hope he'd want to hold her. He wasn't purposely cruel, but this went so far beyond what he was comfortable with, I wouldn't be surprised if he stayed in his wolf form for days.

"Let's get her wounds cleaned and dressed. With luck the clothes in his pack aren't too wet and they'll dry before she wakes. We can at least give her his scent."

We used up all our clean gauze and linen packing the stab wounds and gashes on her front and the stab wounds on her back and then binding it down with strips wrapped around her chest. Bishop set down a blanket, laid down, and, mindful of her injuries, drew her close, his bare chest to her mostly bare back in the hopes that any flesh-to-flesh contact from him and not just her mate would help her. In the very least, his body — along with a second blanket that I set over both of them — would help warm her.

I pulled Knox's damp, but thankfully not drenched, shirt from the bottom of his travel pack and set it on the floor by the fire to dry then dug through the supply trunks for rations. We hadn't eaten breakfast, choosing to chase after whatever had brought the lightning, and if we were going to have to wait out the storm, we might as well eat something.

The trunks were maintained on a seasonal basis, kept fully stocked for those rare occasions, like now, when a patrol didn't have time to hunt and needed shelter. Something I was grateful for since there was no way of telling how long the storm would last. It could be a few hours or, if it had originated over the lands where a few of the storm gods slept, it could be days and we'd need the dried food supplies for our meals.

For the woman's sake, I hoped it blew over quickly. I could still barely hear her pulse even with two ampuls of elixir in her, and while it took time for the elixir to work, the fact that she hadn't responded yet wasn't good.

Giving her a third one would have better increased her chances of survival. Except we didn't have a third one. And if we did and it was already too late for her then I'd just be throwing away valuable elixir.

I found a bag of dried oats and set them simmering in a pot of water over the fire then sat by Bishop and the woman to mind our meal and monitor the dryness of Knox's shirt. I didn't know how Knox would react to Bishop holding his mate while she was naked and injured, and while flesh to flesh contact might be better for her, it would be safer for Bishop if she were dressed.

Being possessive wasn't common for our pack, not like some of the other shifter species and packs, but it wasn't completely unheard of, either. Even if Knox didn't have the possessive trait, it was still common for newly mated males to be overprotective of their females, and just looking at this woman made all my protective instincts rise up and howl. And I wasn't soul bonded to her.

"Where do you think she came from?" Bishop asked his voice low, barely carrying over the storm howling outside.

"I don't know." I brushed a dark blond strand of wet hair away from her swollen and purple cheek. Shining sisters, it hurt just looking at her. "Even if she didn't come from one of the other packs, I doubt she'd have come from the north. There isn't a town within a five day's journey from the north side of Darkweald, if there's a town out there at all."

And she certainly wouldn't have been alone. She'd have been with at least a dozen others regardless of where she'd come from. Even if she'd come by sea — the safest way to reach pack lands — and landed in Savaria, the port city four days west from our town, she still wouldn't have been traveling alone.

As much as we and the other sentient races had spent generations trying to tame these lands, the power seeping from the sleeping gods was too strong. The beast and spirit population never diminished, it could only be kept back, and that meant traveling between civilized lands was dangerous even for a group of armed warriors.

"Whatever her situation, it can't be good," I mused. "Spirits don't usually do this kind of damage and a beast would have finished her off and eaten her."

"Unless she managed to escape and got swept down river," Bishop suggested, but he didn't sound as if he believed that.

A lot of her scratches and bruises could be explained by her fleeing through the forest and being tossed down a rushing river, but the puncture marks in her back and front and the claw cuts across her breasts without any other mauling injuries suggested it hadn't been a beast. She would have had more claw and teeth marks on her arms. People almost always raised their arms to defend themselves and beasts always slashed and bit those easy targets.

"That still doesn't explain why she was in Darkweald in the first place," I said. "She has no power, she's barely a wolf, and I doubt she'll have much more when she recovers."

If she recovers, a worried little voice whispered to me.

And if that happened, there was a chance we'd lose Knox to his wolf again. Permanently this time.

BISHOP

Cyrus growled — I wasn't sure he was fully aware he was doing it — and leaned forward to stir our breakfast. I couldn't sense his emotions like I could Knox's, but I knew him well enough to know the growl wasn't anger but fear. It had barely been a year since Knox had come back to us, and this woman threatened to shatter what little hold he'd managed to regain of his humanity.

In the blink of an eye, she'd mate bonded with him, and I still had no idea how she'd done it or why.

Unlike the mythical angels, our mate bond was more symbolic than symbiotic. Yes, a bond was formed with magic from our soul and that could increase an emotional connection between mates — or in the case of me and Knox, between twins — but she couldn't draw strength or power from him like an angelic bond, so bonding with him couldn't have been a desperate attempt to live.

She whimpered, making my pulse trip. Waking up was a sign the elixir was working, but given her injuries that probably wasn't the best for her. She was going to be in pain and there wasn't anything we were able to do about it.

The patrol sheds weren't stocked with sleeping elixirs since those were even more precious than healing ones and there was always a chance a beast or a thief would come by the sheds and find the hidden compartment and steal it. And even though there'd been extensive studies, no one had found a non-magical sedative or painkiller that worked on shifters. Warriors on patrol we're expected to just tough it out if they were so badly injured that they needed both the team's and the shed's elixirs. No one thought we'd need to tend to a female barely clinging to life and that it would be better if she remained unconscious while she healed.

I brushed my hand over her damp hair, trying to calm her. We couldn't afford for her to fully wake and panic over being surrounded by strange men. She could hurt herself worse than she already was. But it would have been better if it was Knox holding her. Even if her human mind didn't recognize him, her wolf would, and that might be enough to help her.

Except even with his reinforced mental barrier hard and cold between us, I could still feel his emotions seeping through: rage, frustration, confusion, and on top of all that fear.

His fear was so strong it twisted in my chest, making *me* afraid. I didn't know if my fear was just because of his, or if I was also afraid he'd retreat fully into himself and let his wolf take over again, or worse, lock his wolf down and do the only thing that we knew would fully sever the mating bond before it got too strong: kill her.

I tightened my grip on the woman and curled more protectively around her, unable to help myself.

I couldn't believe she'd meant to bond with him. I wasn't even sure she'd been conscious, so there was no way for her to know who she was bonding with, if she'd even been aware that she was bonding with someone in the first place. This wasn't her fault and I wouldn't let Knox take his fear out on her. If her mate couldn't be trusted to protect her, I would.

And with the way things were, it was going to be up to me. Cyrus was obligated to protect the pack, and he wouldn't hesitate to imprison or kill her if he thought she was a threat.

Cyrus got up, grabbed a small pot of honey along with bowls and spoons for three from the trunks, then checked Knox's shirt.

"This is dry and the oatmeal is almost ready," he said, no indication in his voice that he thought the woman was dangerous. "Let's get her dressed so she's not completely naked when Knox comes in for breakfast."

Now it was my turn to huff at him for making a ridiculous statement. "You honestly think he'll come in and eat?" Sure, lying with her was a lot more involved than sitting in the same room with her, but he'd still made a point to sit outside when we all knew no one and nothing would be out in the storm and there was no point in keeping watch.

"I'll make him," Cyrus said, his wolf rising to the surface and darkening his eyes. "Now prop her up so we can get his shirt over her head."

She wasn't very big, so it was easy to support her head and sit up at the same time. She whimpered, her breath turning sharp with pain, but thankfully didn't wake, and with the two of us, we easily pulled on Knox's shirt, which was practically a dress on her — an extremely short dress, but still a dress — then settled her back on the floor.

I set the blanket back over her but didn't lie beside her so I could eat. With another soft whimper, she curled in on herself and pulled Knox's shirt up to her nose. Her breath evened out and frustration twisted in my chest.

Her reaction to his scent, even while unconscious, was proof she needed him and hard proof that she and Knox had indeed mate bonded. Knox should be here with her.

The muscles in Cyrus's jaw flexed at that, as if he'd needed proof and not just my word about the bond, then pulled his attention away and spooned out three helpings of oatmeal.

Breakfast is ready, he called out, speaking in both my mind and Knox's.

I'll catch something on the way home, Knox growled back, including me because Cyrus had.

We'll be hampered by the woman. I don't want you hunting, Cyrus insisted.

I'll make it home without eating then. If it hadn't been obvious before, it was clear now, Knox was avoiding the woman. He could usually handle an hour, let alone a quick meal, in the shed before he became too uncomfortable in the small space.

We don't know when the storm will end. We need to eat and we need to talk, Cyrus growled a hint of his power slipping through the link. *You can go back outside when we're done.*

We can talk just fine right now, Knox huffed.

No. Cyrus's eyes flashed to full black and his canines extended, his wolf threatening to take over. *You'll eat and you'll eat now!*

His power raced through the mental link, flooding both Knox and me — since the only way Cyrus could command someone as powerful as Knox was to not hold back — and I scooped a mouthful of bland, boiled oats into my mouth before I had a chance to sweeten it with the honey.

Knox whined on the other side of the door, being a stubborn asshole and fighting the command.

Now! Cyrus barked, sending another wave of his power crashing over us.

The woman cried out, Cyrus's power affecting her even while unconscious and not directly connected to our mental link, and the shed door flew open as if her pain and not Cyrus's command had been what had compelled him to come in.

BISHOP

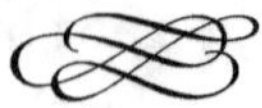

KNOX STOOD IN THE DOORWAY IN HIS HUMAN FORM, WATER DRIPPING from his hair and down his naked body into a puddle at his feet. His gaze locked on the woman and for a second his expression was ragged and filled with desperate heartbreak before vanishing behind a mask of anger.

"You're a fucking asshole," he snarled, his fear picking up and his eyes jumping over the walls of the small shed.

"And we need to eat and talk about what we're going to do with the woman." Cyrus gave a pointed look at the third bowl of oatmeal by his knee.

Knox trembled for a moment, still fighting Cyrus's command, then dropped to the floor beside me and picked up his breakfast.

"We're not going to do anything." Knox shoveled a large spoonful into his mouth and dutifully chewed and swallowed, glaring at Cyrus the whole time. "The second we get home, I'm going to ask Whil if she can break the bond."

"The bond is already set." I could feel it even through the mental shield he'd put up preventing me from fully connecting with him with our twin bond. He'd frozen the mating bond — not just blocked it like our bond — cutting himself off from the woman as fully as he could. But it didn't matter what he did, he couldn't sever it.

Cyrus frowned. "Do you think Whil can break it?"

"She's a sorcerer. She's figured out how to take the water leaking from Airmed's resting place and turn it into a healing elixir. If she can't break the bond outright, then some god has empowered water or sap or a flower or something that can." Knox's gaze flickered to the woman and he angrily ate another spoonful of bland oatmeal. "I don't care how long it takes. I won't be trapped in a bond."

It sounded like he'd spent more than just the short time he'd been outside thinking about this. Had he thought about asking Whil to break our twin bond?

My wolf snarled at that. Knox was ours. Just like our mate would be — and I wasn't going to think about the fact that we'd always thought Knox and I would share a mate because of that.

We shared a bond very few did, and my wolf and I would fight with everything we had to keep it. We were two halves of the same soul, more than just brothers. We wouldn't allow him to force the pain and emptiness of a broken bond onto us, and we didn't want him to force that on the woman, either. She was in enough pain already.

"Breaking the bond will hurt both of you," I pointed out, even though it didn't need pointing out. Everyone knew breaking a bond — which as far as we knew could only be done through death — was devastating for the surviving member. And that was why not everyone spoke the vows to awaken the magic for a mating bond. Not because they didn't love their mate, but because our world was dangerous and warriors often didn't want their mates to suffer if something happened to them.

"I won't be trapped," Knox insisted as if that explained everything. And perhaps it did. He'd been trapped in the dark in that cave-in for days when we were kids and he'd never been the same since. The hint of panic I felt through our muted bond was the same panic he felt surrounded by too many people, in a crowded room or, hell, even just spending too much time in a small room. To him they were the same as being trapped under all that rubble.

Still— "She should have a say in the matter, too." It wasn't just him who was going to suffer the effects of their broken bond.

"No," Cyrus said, shocking me. "Knox tried to refute her. He has every right to break the bond whether it hurts her or not. He shouldn't have to be stuck with a mate he doesn't want."

Well, when put that way...

"No one should be stuck in a loveless mating." Cyrus's gaze drifted to the woman and his wolf rose to the surface, but I couldn't tell if it was anger at the situation with Knox or his situation and the possibility that, as the oldest, he was going to have to mate with someone he didn't really love for the sake of the pack. "Besides, we don't know anything about this woman. She could be cruel and self-ish. She's weak, maybe she ended up almost dead in Darkweald because she was trying to become more powerful in an unnatural way."

"You think she had something to do with the lightning?" Knox asked, his attention locked on his meal, his fear starting to seep stronger through our connection even though he'd only been in the shed for a handful of minutes.

"I first thought no, but trying to get Tzanagoth's power would explain why she was in the forest." Cyrus sighed and pushed a damp lock of hair that had come loose from his braid out of his eyes. "We won't know until she wakes and we have no idea when that will be."

"Even then," Knox growled, finishing his meal and storming back to the door. "I don't care if she's a goddess of absolute goodness. I'm breaking our bond."

KNOX

I couldn't get home to Whil fast enough. It felt like forever before the storm passed when really it had blown through quickly and only took up the morning. But then we moved at an agonizingly slow pace, trying to balance speed with not aggravating the woman's injuries and worsening her condition.

The woman. My mate.

There just was so much wrong with those two words.

A mate meant someone living with me, around me, crowding me. Just the thought made my pulse race. It was difficult enough to be around my brothers and they understood me. This woman, like everyone else, wouldn't.

And it didn't matter that my soul and my wolf were certain that wouldn't be the case, that she, even if she wasn't as broken as I was, would still accept me. That was just the mating bond.

It was already hard to ignore her, to resist the need to gather her in my arms and comfort and protect her, and that desire to be near her, to do more with her and seal the bond, would only get stronger the longer the situation went on.

As it was, I'd only managed to hold myself back because Cyrus had commanded me to eat and the shed's fifteen by fifteen windowless space had made me feel — a lot more than usual — like I was suffocating.

It had been easier to ignore the frozen bond in my chest once I was outside, but not by much. There had only been a door and a few feet between us, and my wolf really wanted to shove Bishop aside and take his place beside her. It was certain with her in our arms, the small space wouldn't bother us so much.

I wasn't convinced. Nothing alleviated the anxiety of feeling trapped except getting outside. Outside was the only place I was truly safe.

Except now we were outside, the gloom of twilight heavy around us, and there was no door separating us. I tried to roam ahead, but even if Cyrus hadn't cared how far I went, I couldn't get very far. The chain around my heart that I was determined to keep frozen kept yanking me back, drawing all my senses to her.

I'd heard that the compulsion from the mating bond to be with your mate in every way, especially when it first formed, was powerful, but this went beyond powerful. It was consuming. She needed me, needed to be protected and held and loved. It didn't matter that I didn't even know her name. She was mine and there wasn't anything I wouldn't do for her.

Which wasn't true. It was gods damned not true.

I only felt that way because of the magic connecting us. It wasn't a real emotion. It couldn't be, so I concentrated on wrapping more mental ice into the cage around my heart and the chain linking us together.

She whimpered and my wolf snarled. Bishop needed to be more careful. She would be better off with me carrying her.

Fuck, no. I wrenched my attention back to the rolling grass-covered foothills and the shadow of the towering mountain in front of us and the faint glimmer of light at the mountain's base. Home.

Focus on home and getting to Whil and getting free. The woman was just fine with Bishop. Given her injuries, she would have been whimpering and moaning just lying in the shed. Besides, her pain, while regrettable, didn't matter.

I didn't care.

I couldn't care. Not if I wanted to get through severing our mating bond as unscathed as possible.

This ordeal would be over soon. I just had to hold on a little longer and keep the ice around my heart strong. I sure as hell couldn't give in and hold her. Holding her would lead to other things. Nothing serious because she was too badly injured, but some gentle kisses wouldn't be a prob—

Stop it! No holding. No kissing. No nothing with this stranger.

Why couldn't I remember she was a complete stranger?

For all I knew Cyrus was right and she'd been trying to strengthen her pathetically weak essence by waking Tzanagoth.

It was full dark by the time we reached Stonehaven, the pack's town that sprawled down the mountain's sloping base. The original buildings at the top — Old Town — were almost a thousand years old, although thankfully they'd been modernized over the years. They were big and blocky, and with the exception of the alpha's residence, which was surrounded by gardens, were crowded together with a mix of shops and residences interspersed with a warren of gardens and small parks all surrounded by the original town wall.

Over the years, though, the pack had grown beyond the couple hundred that Old Town could hold and with the area surrounding our land becoming safer, houses and shops had been built beyond the wall, the architecture growing more modern the closer you got to the edge of town.

Much to my surprise, Lucius, Zavier, and Whil waited on the outskirts of town with two travel packs resting on the ground by their feet.

Lucius, our first beta and primary advisor since he'd retired from being huntmaster — and was really better suited to administration than battling beasts — along with Zavier, his nephew and newly made warrior who showed great promise, were dressed to travel.

"What's wrong?" Cyrus asked the second we were in earshot. We'd arrived later than scheduled, but given the strange lightning, a late arrival would have been expected. Zavier might have been sent to greet us to find out if we needed anything immediately, but Lucius and Whil would have stayed in the Residence. And no one would have brought travel packs with them or worn the protective leathers necessary to travel the mountain pass to Savaria and the lands beyond.

"Jundar called an emergency meeting of the Mountain and Sea Alliance to discuss the increase in beast activity in the area," Lucius said, his attention on my mate.

My wolf curled his lips back, but I managed to swallow his growl before we released it.

She was *not* my mate. She was just a woman. I didn't want her. Anyone could look at her and it didn't matter, and while I wouldn't be able to stop Cyrus from telling everyone I was mate bonded to her, I'd hoped he'd spare me the attention and keep it between us and Whil.

And if I really wanted that, I couldn't afford to get all protective and reveal the situation on my own.

Except no matter what I did, my focus always returned to her. I'd yank it away, be determined not to pay any attention to her, and be unable to resist seconds later.

"We need to head out," the older man said, "but we wanted to wait until you got back before we left. I'm assuming you investigated that lightning and power wave?"

"We didn't get a chance," Cyrus said, his expression dark.

Yeah, strange lightning and power, and now the towns on the other side of the mountain were experiencing the same increase in beast activity we were. Not good.

"We found her in Darkweald barely alive," Bishop added. "Two ampuls of healing elixir this morning and she's still unconscious."

"What happened to her?" Zavier asked, drawing closer to get a better look and making my pulse pick up. He was young but of an age where he was courting potential mates—

I shook my head, trying to clear it.

He wasn't going to flirt with my mate. She was unconscious and she wasn't my gods dammed mate!

Bishop tightened his hold on her, drawing her closer to his chest as if he, too, instinctually wanted to protect her, and even that made my wolf heave within me.

We should be holding her, protecting her.

Jeez. How many times was I going to have to tell myself we wanted nothing to do with her? We didn't even know her.

"We don't know what happened," Bishop replied.

"We'll send a hunt team out in the morning to restock shed twelve and see if there's anything in Darkweald to indicate what happened," Cyrus said. "Unless you know what happened," he added, turning his attention to Whil.

The willowy fae with her ever-so-slightly glowing skin pulled her bright green gaze up from the woman.

Damn it! Was everyone going to stare at her? Did Whil know about the mating bond?

I mentally rolled my eyes at myself. Of course she knew. She could sense bonds and magic and all manner of things shifters couldn't. She'd have known I was chained to the woman before Lucius and Zavier had even spotted us on the road.

"I have a few theories," she replied, thankfully not mentioning my unexpected mating bond with a stranger. "But nothing concrete."

"Anything we need to deal with immediately?" Bishop asked, his worry over the situation seeping into me even though I was actively trying to keep him out.

"Probably, but until we know more, there's nothing we can do." She frowned, and her gaze drifted to the rolling hills beyond the town that were cloaked in darkness and thankfully not back to the woman.

"And with that, I should get going." Lucius nodded at Zavier who started to race back into town.

"Wait," Cyrus said, and a shiver of his power rushed over us even though I knew he wasn't purposely trying to command us. "You better be taking at least half a squad."

"I might be retired, but I'm not an idiot," Lucius huffed, and Cyrus jerked his chin at Zavier, giving him permission to continue on his errand. "If Jundar is concerned, then the pass isn't safe even in the daytime."

Which meant our situation was worse than we'd first thought. Beasts in the pass meant they were getting closer and closer to our town, and if they were also encroaching on the borders of Ciliaran and the other towns, states, and kingdoms in the Alliance then that meant for some reason there'd been an increase in their population and that would endanger the lives of all our farmers as well as trade among our communities.

I had a bad feeling that something dangerous was on its way, and I could tell from everyone's expression that they feared the same thing as well.

And if something dangerous — or rather something more dangerous than usual — was coming our way, I couldn't afford to be distracted by this bond. It was getting harder and harder to focus on the conversation between Cyrus and Lucius. It'd be even harder in the middle of a battle.

Lucius's attention flickered back to the woman. "I hope rescuing one life doesn't endanger everyone else's."

The asshole! My wolf seized control of our body, sent a wave of our power over all the shifters in the group, demanding submission, and snapped at Lucius, not caring that we were raising suspicions. Lucius dropped to one knee, his eyes wide at the sudden use of force, while both Cyrus and Bishop staggered.

KNOX

"Enough," Cyrus barked, his own power tearing mine apart and forcing me to bow my head in submission to him. "We weren't going to leave her for dead. I'm going to assume Jundar will ask for more warriors. Tell him we want more healing water for Whil to refine in exchange."

"Yes, alpha," Lucius said, still kneeling.

"Good. Now—" Cyrus turned to Whil who, because she wasn't a shifter, hadn't been affected by my or Cyrus's power. "Walk with us. We need to talk."

Without waiting for her response, he strode down the main street toward the center of New Town.

She quirked a sculpted golden eyebrow, her attention sliding to me then the woman — Oh yeah, she knew the truth — then rushed to fall into step beside him.

Bishop hurried to walk on Cyrus's other side, and I pushed ahead, trying to get them to hurry up. The sooner we dealt with the bond, the sooner I'd be free. But the urge to stay by the woman's side, to shift, to take her from my brother churned inside me, and I kept slowing, drawn to her whether I wanted to be or not.

"You should probably be talking with Nova instead of me. She's the party planner," Whil snickered once we were out of earshot from Lucius. "It can be a surprise party for the rest of the pack." She burst out laughing. "I don't think anyone bet that you'd be the first of the alpha's sons to mate."

This isn't funny, I snarled as we reached the main square in New Town and took the lead, bounding up a narrow side street with shallow steps leading up to the Old Town wall. The last thing I wanted was to march past the dozen pubs and restaurants lining Main Street while having this conversation. Even if only my brothers and Whil could hear my side of the conversation, people could figure out the truth from Whil's responses. *I don't want a party. I want it broken.*

"You what?" Whil missed the first step and stumbled up the next three.

Cyrus grabbed her arm before she fell, helping her right herself. "Is that something you can do?"

"Why would you make the bond if you don't want it?" she asked.

Because I didn't make it. I rushed up the stairs and around the corner, but my wolf jerked me to a stop and the frozen chain in my chest strained to draw me back to her. We couldn't see her anymore, we needed to go back.

No. We could wait. Bishop would catch up soon enough.

But damn it. We didn't want to wait on anything. She was ours and we needed to seal the bond and properly claim her.

For the love of—!

There was no way in hell we were claiming her. Even if we wanted to, she was in no condition to have sex.

Which, jeez, wasn't the point.

Bishop, with his precious, unwanted cargo, rounded the corner and the pressure in my chest eased.

"We don't know what happened," he said. "We found her near death and when Knox picked her up, she initiated the mating bond. I don't even think she was conscious."

"I didn't think it was possible to initiate that kind of bond while unconscious." Whil laid a hand on the woman's forehead. "At least certainly not for shifters."

"But it is for other races?" Cyrus asked.

"Angels have no control over their mating bonds. No words, no conscious thought. It could be with a complete stranger they've never met, and they could be barely alive, and the bond would still form," Whil explained as we rounded another corner and reached the road that followed the Old Town wall around the original town. "But she's clearly not an angel."

"Are we sure?" Cyrus asked. "Her essence says she's one of us, but it's weak. Could she be a half-breed?"

"Not with an angel," Whil said. "Even if the portals to this realm were unlocked and the beings from the Realm of Celestial Light decided to pay us a visit, angels can only procreate with other angels. There are no half-breeds. And even if one of her parents was something else, you're either born a shifter or you're not. There's no in between."

I don't care what she is, I snapped as we reached the main gate to Old Town and hurried up the road to our home. *I only care that this fucking bond is broken.*

"Watch your tone," Cyrus growled in warning, his power rolling off him. Whil was a revered member of our community and had been so for almost a thousand years — despite the fact that she still looked about thirty. With her ability to weave raw magical energy into spells, she could have easily taken over the pack at any time, but instead, chose to just be a councilor, offering her wisdom and abilities when asked.

My wolf whined at Cyrus's power and the woman whimpered, sending more churning desperate need twisting inside me.

Bishop's worry increased as well, and for a second all the emotions and need were too much. The road was too narrow, the walls of the buildings on either side of me too high. I needed space. I had to get out of there, but the bond wouldn't let me leave her side. I was going to suffocate from the pressure.

"We have to do something," Bishop said.

We reached the courtyard in front of our residence, the grand, three-story fortress only visible against the shadow of the mountain because of the lights at the main doors and in a dozen of the windows. Home. Except the thought of going inside made my chest tight. I had to stay out here, regain my mental equilibrium. And somehow, my wolf actually agreed with me.

Except if Whil could break the bond right away—

"I don't know if it's possible to break the bond. I need to do some reading," Whil mused, shattering what little hope I had that this mess would be fixed immediately. "I also need to talk to her..." She drew the word out as if expecting one of us to give her a name. When we didn't supply her with one, she shrugged. "She might have a clue about what happened. If she wasn't conscious during the bonding, then maybe there was something else going on and it isn't a true bond. It might not be as permanent as it looks."

"You mean there might be a way to break it?" Bishop asked.

"If it's a false mating bond, maybe," Whil said, "but I'll need more information."

"I want to talk to her first," Cyrus said, pulling open the front door and holding it for Whil. "We don't know if she's dangerous. For all we know she's connected to that wave of power."

Whil's expression turned grim. "That's something else I need to think about."

Figure out how to break the bond first, I said, managing to stay outside despite the pressure closing in around me.

I didn't care how important that lightning and power were, I was losing my mind. There was too much pressure from too many things, and I was going to lose control over one of them. I didn't want to risk that one thing being my need to resist the compulsion to seal the bond. Sealing it gave it strength and then all possibility of breaking it would be lost whether it was a fake bond or not.

AUDREY

I TOSSED THIS WAY AND THAT ON A DARK OCEAN OF AGONY, MY WHOLE body on fire. Sharp pain sliced through my face and chest while throbbing pain radiated through the rest of me. I tried to open my eyes, but couldn't, wasn't even sure if I could turn thought into action, and was dragged deeper into the painful darkness.

A moment later — or was that an eternity? — I bobbed back up to the surface. Voices murmured around me and the agony in my body burned stronger. I strained again to open my eyes. I couldn't just lie there. That monster was after me. It might have eaten Merrick, but that didn't mean I was off the menu. But the painful darkness dragged me back under again.

Another eternal moment and a wave of power threatened to crush me. I hadn't even clawed my way back to the surface. Sterling had to be furious to radiate everything he had and pound into my subconscious like that, which meant I was in danger. I *had* to wake up.

Wake up. Open your eyes. Run.

But the more I struggled, the deeper the darkness dragged me down. The pain and fear and knowledge that I'd been so stupid was too much. Better to curl into the darkness and hide from everything.

At least in the darkness I wasn't weak, wasn't so pathetic that my life was considered worthless by my pack.

A trickle of cold seeped into the darkness.

I was so pathetic my fated mate didn't even want me.

The cold grew, pushing the pain to the edge of my senses. But instead of something flooding into the hole carved inside me, the cold just kept pushing, making the hole bigger and bigger, leaving me frozen and achingly hollow.

Of course my fated mate wouldn't want me. I was a shifter who couldn't shift. I was so weak my wolf nature refused to wake or even acknowledge me. Who wanted to be stuck with someone like that for the rest of his life? No one. I wasn't good for anything. Sterling had been telling me I was useless from the moment I moved into his house, and Royce had said the same when he'd refuted our fated mate bond.

Except the fated mating call hadn't been real. Royce and Sterling had used magic to manipulate me.

But that thought only made my insides twist with shame. I should have known fate would never bond me with someone as powerful as Royce, and I certainly should have known that even if by some miracle the fated mating call had been real, Royce would never have accepted me.

And now I had who-knew-how-many months suffering this painful, hollow ache of the incomplete bond until it went away.

Except a part of me feared it wouldn't go away.

It felt too powerful. A frozen emptiness that threatened to completely hollow me out into a lifeless shell. It felt locked within my cells, imprinted in my soul, a permanent reminder of how foolish I'd been.

To think I could be loved, be free, be anything other than myself.

I was weak *and* stupid and the only reason I was alive was because I'd gotten lucky and Merrick had stumbled across Sterling's ritual before that monster could eat me.

Oh, God. That monster!

I woke with a start, my pulse pounding along with my head... and my face... my whole body, really. I was one enormous aching bruise. But strangely not much more than that when, given the injuries I'd had when I'd raced blindly into the forest, I should have been in agony.

The icy hollowness, however, was stronger than before, threatening to overwhelm me, so perhaps I was just too numb and heartbroken to notice how much pain I was in.

The rich scent of wood smoke and something else, something deeply masculine, hung in the air, wrapping around my senses, and while I had a strange feeling it should be comforting me, it couldn't penetrate the icy emptiness consuming me.

I dragged my senses away from the scent and opened my eyes. I lay on my side, covered with a soft blanket, facing a plain white wall and a simple, large window. Outside I could see sunlight streaming through a large leafy tree branch and beyond that brilliant blue sky.

None of which gave me any clue as to where I was. I wasn't in my room or anywhere in Merrick's house — or rather Sterling's house now that he'd murdered his father — since the window frame didn't match any I was familiar with.

Something creaked behind me and my pulse leaped into a rapid beat again. I wasn't alone. Wherever I was, someone was watching me.

Please don't let it be Royce or Sterling... or that monster. I didn't know why they'd have kept me alive and in a bed, when they'd tried to serve me up to that thing last night. I would have expected them to lock me in a damp basement to await whatever they planned. But being comfortable in a bed could easily be another way to torture me before putting me back on the menu.

I glanced over my shoulder. A large, intimidating, beautiful man sat in a chair between me and the door, watching me with moss green eyes. His expression was hard but that only seemed to accentuate his rugged, masculine beauty.

His shoulders were easily twice as broad as mine and his biceps probably the size of my thighs. Without a doubt he was a foot to a foot and a half taller than me, and I was about average height for a woman. His brown hair had been shaved at the sides but left long on top and twisted into a thick braid that reached the nape of his neck, making him look like a Medieval warrior. Add to that at least a day's worth of scruff on his square jaw along with the enormous feral energy radiating from him, and it was obvious he was a powerful, dangerous wolf shifter.

Relief flickered through me, but the feeling barely burst to life before being consumed with fear. Just because I didn't know this man, didn't mean I wasn't still at Sterling and Royce's mercy. This man could be a mercenary hired to keep the pack in line now that Merrick was dead, or worse, to keep *me* in line until it was time to sacrifice me.

AUDREY

"I'M NOT GOING TO HURT YOU," THE MAN SAID, HIS VOICE SOFT BUT still gruff as if he wasn't quite sure how to deal with me, which didn't fit with him being Sterling's hired muscle. "What's your name?"

That really didn't fit with being hired muscle. Even if Sterling hadn't bothered to mention my name, the kind of guy he'd hire to watch me wouldn't care. That and why hire someone when there were more than enough members of the pack who'd happily guard me then hand me over to a monster?

I should have thought of that from the start. If Sterling was now the alpha, his father's betas would need to prove themselves to keep their position in the pack, and while I'd thought most of them were okay men, I didn't really know them well and wasn't sure how far they'd go to keep their position in the pack.

But if that was the case, did that mean I'd managed to escape? Was I actually free?

The icy hollowness swelled, overwhelming me for a second. Even if sacrificing Merrick to the monster had gotten Sterling whatever he wanted, if I ever showed my face anywhere near pack lands, Sterling would go after me. He'd probably have someone keeping an eye on Mila in her new pack just to see if I'd go to her.

If I had, in fact, managed to escape my old life, I had to make a clean cut. I couldn't reach out to Mila in any way, and I had to figure out how to get as far away from pack lands as possible — and I doubted that wherever I was, was far enough.

I needed to figure out how to get out of the country— hell, go to Europe or Asia if I could find the money. It didn't matter that my wolf hadn't woken and I still looked like an easy target for any super looking to cause trouble. I would fight with everything I had to keep the freedom I'd somehow managed to achieve.

"Your injuries have healed enough that you can shift out the rest," he said, carefully standing as if afraid moving too quickly would spook me... which it probably would. Just sitting he'd been intimidating and now, towering over me, he was terrifying.

"There's a bathroom across the hall. Why don't you get cleaned up and I'll find you some clothes." My stomach growled, making his lips quirk. "And some food," he added as he opened the door revealing a glimpse of another white wall and the edge of a doorframe. "I'm Cyrus."

"Audrey," I murmured and he left before I could thank him.

I didn't know why he was helping me or if I could actually trust him. Just because he wasn't connected to Sterling didn't mean I was safe with him. Of course, if he'd wanted to hurt me, he'd had plenty of opportunity while I was unconscious.

I sat up and pushed back the covers, my body throbbing in protest, the pain strong enough to cut through the cold emptiness. Someone had changed me out of my transformation dress, wrapped bandages around most of my torso, and put me in an oversized, loose shirt. Probably Cyrus.

I wasn't sure how I felt about that. I'd never been naked in public before. Hell, I'd never been naked in private with another person. But he was a shifter and not from my pack, so he probably didn't have the human hang-ups I did about nudity. Royce had already ripped open the front of my dress so I'd probably been flashing it all when he'd found me.

My throat tightened at the thought of my dress. That dress had held all my hopes for the last five years. It was gone and so was the life I knew.

I couldn't go back, even if for some ridiculous reason I wanted to. I could only go forward and to do that I needed to figure out where I was and how to get farther away from Sterling. I could only pray that as a wolfless shifter I'd be able to go unnoticed or that he wouldn't bother searching for me. Although I had a horrible feeling that if he knew I was still alive, nothing would stop him from coming after me.

And again, there was nothing I could do about that right now.

I climbed out of bed and headed to the bathroom — which was right across the hall like Cyrus said. The room was luxurious with white marble floors, counters, and tiles, and shiny chrome fixtures. An enormous mirror sat over the vanity, and I cringed at my reflection.

My not-blond-but-not-brown hair hung half loose in a tangled mess while the rest was still captured at an odd angle in the hair elastic I'd used for my ponytail. I also had two black eyes and was covered in bruises and scratches, although they weren't nearly as fresh as they should have been, which meant I had to have been unconscious for more than a day.

A large tub sat at the back in a bay window that looked out onto a small garden, and while I really wanted to just soak and relax, Cyrus had promised food and I was hungry.

I started the water in the stand-up shower, which was more than big enough for a man Cyrus's size, and grabbed the hem of the shirt. It was enormous on me, hanging past my butt, and would have been loose on Cyrus, but that only meant it would be quick to take off.

Was that a clue about the type of man Cyrus was? He anticipated he'd need to shift at a moment's notice and wore clothes that were easy to take off since our shifting magic destroyed whatever we wore?

I pulled the shirt up over my head and was instantly enveloped in that rich, smoky scent again. God, it smelled so good. Like home... even though I hadn't thought I associated home with wood smoke.

The icy hollowness inside me shuddered and the warm comfort of the scent turned into longing and need. I ached to be surrounded by that scent forever, to be fully embraced by it, have it fuel my need into a burning desire, and set me fully ablaze. I didn't want to discard the shirt on the floor, step into the shower, and wash the scent from my skin. My soul ached for it to accept me, welcome me home, caress me, touch me, love me.

A part of me knew I felt the way I did because of the incomplete mating bond, but another, smaller part, a part I'd been ignoring and denying because I'd had to survive, knew deep down the incomplete bond only shone a light on what I'd desperately craved from the moment I found my father in a pool of his own blood in the bathtub.

Tears burned my eyes and I tossed the shirt to the farthest corner of the bathroom.

Fuck you, Royce, for making me feel this way. Fuck you for reminding me that I was broken and no one wanted me.

Those horrible feelings had been dragged into the stark light of reality and even when the icy emptiness of the incomplete mating bond faded, I'd never be able to forget about how I longed for something I couldn't have. So clearly pointing out what I ached for was the cruelest thing he'd ever done to me.

Fuck you and Sterling. Fuck all of them.

My throat tightened.

And fuck me for being stupid enough to believe them.

A tear rolled down my cheek and I furiously brushed it away. I didn't want to cry. I didn't want to be emotionally pathetic as well.

But the tears kept leaking from my eyes, my soul and body weeping despite my mind's determination to be strong.

Damn it. I'd had a plan. I'd finally worked up the nerve to leave whether my wolf woke or not. I'd been cautious to leave the pack because, weak as I was, I thought I'd be in more danger out there than staying where I was, but I'd never just given up.

I couldn't have been more wrong about being safe with Sterling and Royce the psychopaths.

Cautious had nearly gotten me killed.

Shame burned my cheeks and anger flickered, a miniscule flame, in the icy hollowness in my chest.

God, I wanted to rip off Royce's and Sterling's cocks and feed them to that monster. But they were stronger than me in every way. Ridiculously so.

The most I'd be able to accomplish would be yelling at them and then they'd probably kill me.

Resigned with the burning knowledge that life really wasn't fair, I unwrapped the bandage around my chest.

Wads of bloody gauze plopped on the floor, a testament to how injured I'd been. Royce's claw marks were ugly red gashes down the front of my chest, and without the ability to shift, they'd scar. I'd have a permanent reminder of his betrayal not just hidden in my soul but sliced into my skin for any future lover to see. Hell, even a low-cut neckline would show them off to everyone.

My throat tightened again with emotions I really didn't want, and I stepped into the shower and leaned my forehead against the tiles, just letting the warm water stream down my back. If I was smart, I'd hurry up and clean myself. The more I stood still, the more the icy hollowness would affect me, and a part of me was afraid it would be too much and I'd give up, just like my father had.

He and my mother hadn't been fated mates and they hadn't created a magical mating bond, but I'd gotten the impression from him and everyone around me that they'd loved each other deeply. Her love and support had been what had held him together and kept the nightmares at bay when he'd returned to the pack after the war.

Logically I knew he'd held on for as long as he could after her death before the nightmares had become too much and he'd killed himself. But there was still a little girl inside me who felt abandoned, felt she hadn't been enough for him, and was afraid she had the same emotional weakness he'd had.

My shifter essence was weak. Why not the rest of me?

I shoved those thoughts as deep down inside me as possible. I hadn't lost my love and hadn't survived years of brutal war. I'd had the shit scared out of me for a few hours and been tricked by an asshole. Killing myself would just be letting him win, and I was *not* going to let him win. I'd survive just to spite him and Sterling and everyone.

AUDREY

Determined to ignore the icy hollowness until it went away —
because it was *going* to go away — I grabbed the bar of soap on the
small ledge at the back of the shower and worked it into a lather. I
washed the grime from my hair and picked out the tangles as best I
could without conditioner, then turned my attention to my body.

Just reaching up to my head pulled at the gashes in my torso. The
wounds on my front had healed enough that they wouldn't open up if
I scrubbed too hard — and I suspected the wounds on my back were
the same — but that didn't mean they weren't tender.

I ran my soapy hands over my chest, carefully washing away the
dried blood without hurting myself. If I closed my eyes, I could
almost pretend I was having a shower like normal.

Except the moment I did, I became hyperaware of the hollowness
inside me. It was icy and aching and thrumming with longing that
grew with every slide of my hands.

The edge of my palm brushed my nipple and the longing swelled,
oozing heat into the cold, making me ache for a touch that was never
coming.

It was just another thing that was cruel about tricking me into
starting the mating vows and then leaving me hanging. A mating

bond heightened sexual desire and I had no one to be sexual with... well there was Cyrus.

Even if he was intimidating, he was handsome. Maybe he'd be interested in a little something. I knew in my heart it wouldn't be the same as having sex with my mate, but since I didn't have a mate—

Oh, my God! What was I thinking?

Even if he was interested, I didn't know him. Did I really want to have sex with a stranger just to relieve the pressure? Worse yet, did I want to have sex *for the first time* with a stranger just to relieve the pressure? How did I even go about asking for that?

You're cute and I'm a horny virgin, you wanna...?

Jeez. The situation wasn't that bad. I could barely feel anything. Really... even if I was getting hornier by the second.

No. I was *not* going to ask Cyrus to have sex with me.

If things got too bad, I'd just take care of myself by myself. I'd done that before. It would be enough to get me through the worst of it while the incomplete bond faded away.

And now I was also determined to ignore the aching longing. A few more things to ignore and I'd have to change my middle name to Denial.

I scrubbed down as quickly as possible, not caring that I aggravated my injuries — pain was better than the aching longing — and hurried out of the shower. I'd just finished drying myself off and was trying to figure out what to do about clothing since the only thing I had to wear was the towel or the shirt that I didn't — and did — want to put back on when someone knocked on the door.

"Clothing," Cyrus said, and he opened the door a crack and set a pile of silky blue fabric on the floor along with a pair of strappy tan sandals.

I picked up the fabric and it unfurled into a backless dress that was secured at the nape of the neck and the small of the back with ties. It hung to my ankles and covered everything it was supposed to cover, but I still felt naked wearing it. The soft fabric clung to every curve and without a bra, I couldn't hide my peaked nipples. I could only hope Cyrus thought I was cold and not turned on like I really was.

Why in God's name would he give me a dress like that? Had I been wrong about his intentions?

And damn if it didn't make it even harder to pretend the only thing I was feeling from the mating bond was cold emptiness.

I stepped out of the bathroom and Cyrus's eyes narrowed, making me cross my arms over my chest, even more uncomfortable in the flimsy dress than before.

"You won't get pity walking around like that," he said, his voice still gruff and now edged with a hint of frustration. "You might as well shift out the rest of your injuries."

"I'm not looking for pity." But I also didn't want to tell him that I couldn't shift. He might have saved my life but that didn't mean I could trust him, especially if he learned how weak I really was. "I appreciate you saving me."

"Want to tell me what you were doing in Darkweald to begin with?" he asked, striding down the hall, forcing me to scramble to catch up.

"Darkweald?" I didn't recognize the name. How far had the stream washed me away? I thought I was familiar with the names of everything on and around pack lands.

Of course, I didn't remember a stream anywhere near the sacred grove... and I wasn't sure what to think about that.

The hall opened into a grand front entrance with an enormous glittering chandelier, massive front doors, and a thick, red rug. We stood on the second level at the edge of an equally grand staircase that started split in two on the ground level, curving up and around a wide entrance, met again halfway up creating a broad landing, and split again to the hall where Cyrus and I stood and to another hall across from us, suggesting the building had two wings.

Every surface was clean and well kept, just like the bathroom and the room I'd woken in. This wasn't some abandoned mansion Cyrus had found and was squatting in while he passed by, and it didn't seem

like a bed and breakfast or short-term rental, either. It was too...
grand for something like that.

Except that didn't make any sense.

There wasn't a mansion like this anywhere near pack lands. Even
if I'd never gone beyond the area owned by the pack, I would have
heard from the others about a house like this, occupied or otherwise.

Of course, if I'd been unconscious for a few days, we could have
easily driven across the state. Which meant I could be one step closer
to getting as far away from Sterling, Royce, and that monster as
possible.

"Yes, Darkweald," Cyrus pressed, leading me down the stairs.

The entrance that was framed by the split stairs opened into a
large empty room lit by indirect sunlight coming through dozens of
windows. They were smaller than expected, looking like they
belonged to a much older building. But I didn't get a chance to get a
good look before Cyrus headed away from the grand entrance down a
wide hall and took me to a kitchen big enough for a medium-sized
restaurant.

There were dozens more of the smallish windows along the far
wall, but these faced a different direction and full sunlight streamed
through. A door at the back stood open, letting in more sunlight
along with a warm, fresh breeze fragrant with the scent of flowers and
herbs, and beyond lay a garden, a tall stone wall, and a towering
mountain.

I was still in the mountains so he hadn't taken me two days east. I
might not be as far away from Sterling as I'd hoped, which meant I
needed to figure out how to get moving.

With literally nothing, possibly not even the scraps of dress I'd
been wearing for the transformation ceremony, I was going to have to
walk across the country and rely on the kindness of strangers to
survive. That, or find work to earn enough for a bus ticket to get me to
Union City.

"Well?" A hint of his power rolled into me with that word.

I opened my mouth to answer him but managed to snap it shut
before the truth poured out. Even if I lied about my age and said I was

performing my pack's transformation ceremony, he'd still know exactly who my pack was, and I couldn't risk him trying to take me back.

Could I even mention being betrayed and almost sacrificed to a monster?

My cheeks burned with shame.

For all I knew, this guy might think he'd get a reward for returning me.

"You're not strong enough to resist me," he said, opening a tall cupboard and revealing a strange looking fridge inside.

Swell. Of course, he'd just force me to talk. That was what powerful supers did to weaker ones, which only reminded me that I hadn't stood a chance in my pack, and I wouldn't in the real world, either.

AUDREY

MY throat tightened and the icy emptiness inside me swelled. "I'm not strong enough for anything," I replied, moving toward the light pouring through the open back door, hoping that the warm air would ease the frozen ache.

"So?" Cyrus asked, but he didn't add more power to his word, giving me the chance to respond of my own free will, surprising me.

"I trusted someone I shouldn't have." I stepped into the sunlight and turned my face to the sky to stare up at two moons.

My thoughts stuttered. Two.

I squeezed my eyes shut, but when I opened them again, the moons were still there.

What the hell?

"Don't make me force you," Cyrus said

A hint of power returned to his words, and I was about to open my mouth again when a man, more handsome than Cyrus and almost as tall and muscular rounded a large bush in the garden.

His warm brown eyes widened with surprise when he saw me, and he flashed a smile that would have stopped my heart if it hadn't already been stopped with shock over the two moons.

"You're awake." His gaze swept over my face and his smile

faltered, making me cringe. From the essence radiating off him he was as powerful — or awfully darn close to being as powerful — as Cyrus. And while he didn't look as intimidating, that didn't mean he wasn't going to use his power to force me to talk.

"Why didn't you shift?" he asked, his tone filled with concern and not reproach like Cyrus. "Your injuries have healed enough. It's safe."

"I'm not so sure about that." I pointed at the moons. "I'm seeing double."

Except the moons were clearly two distinct objects, one white and normal looking, the other slightly pink and smaller. Not to mention nothing else was doubled.

"I'm still unconscious. That's what this is— Or dead." No, if I was dead, I wouldn't have the icy emptiness threatening to consume me or the constant, throbbing whisper of need beneath that cold.

"You look conscious to me," the new guy said. He glanced up, looking for what I was looking at, but from his lack of reaction, he clearly didn't see anything wrong.

"If you don't see it then this has to be a dream."

"See what?" Cyrus growled.

I pointed up. "Two moons."

The new guy glanced behind me, his now weak smile melting into concern. "What about the moons?"

What about the moons! "There are *two* of them."

"And?" Cyrus huffed.

"Proving this is a dream and I'm unconscious somewhere bleeding to death."

"I don't understand how the Sisters prove you're dreaming," the new guy said.

"They even have a name." Of course they did. Because dreams were like that.

Except I had no idea where I'd come up with the two-moon thing. I didn't read or watch a whole lot of science fiction or fantasy so I doubted my subconscious would gravitate towards something like that, and nothing else about this felt like a dream...

Was I in another realm?

There were a number of portals all over the planet. Some led to a specific realm like the one in Rome which only went to the Realm of Celestial Light, but there were others that could go to any number of realms if you had enough power and the right spell or the right kind of super with you.

I turned to Cyrus. "Where did you take me?"

There wasn't a portal anywhere near pack lands, but there was at least one within a two-day drive.

And if I was in another realm, did that mean I was safe? It was farther than I thought I could ever get from Sterling, but I didn't know much about the other realms and had no idea how dangerous this one might be.

"You're in Stonehaven," Cyrus said, filling a glass with water at the sink.

"No, what realm?"

The new guy frowned. "Are you saying you're from another realm?" He pulled out a chair at a nearby table and gestured for me to sit.

I frowned back at him. If he didn't know I was from the mortal realm then— "You didn't bring me here?"

"We found you in Darkweald forest." Cyrus set a plate with a sandwich along with the glass of water in front of me then sat in the chair opposite me. His dark green eyes locked on me and power rolled off him, making my insides tremble, but he didn't push — not yet at least — and force me to talk.

"You were badly hurt," the new guy murmured, taking the seat beside me.

Then realization hit me. If I was in a different realm, I must have gone through the portal Sterling had made to summon that monster. That monster was from this realm.

My pulse leaped, suddenly racing. Was I safe here from that thing?

Oh, my God! Were there more of them?

If there were more of them maybe these guys knew how to defend against them. They were certainly strong shifters. Stronger than Sterling and Royce. Maybe a monster like that was nothing to them.

The new guy brushed his fingers across the back of my hand, jerking my attention— hell, my whole essence to him. He was so close I could see the green flecks in his warm brown eyes.

"You're safe," he said, his voice soft and soothing, easing some of the panic.

But that only made me aware of his fingers on my skin, the heat radiating from his body, easily seeping through my thin dress, and the aching longing thrumming in my soul.

I struggled to focus beyond my growing need. "You know how to kill those monsters?"

A hint of concern flickered in the new guy's eyes.

"What monsters?" Cyrus asked.

"It looked like a greater demon in his natural form but all red like a movie monster." And it had started eating Merrick while he was still alive.

I shuddered and my gaze dipped to the sandwich Cyrus had made me as my stomach churned.

"None of what you just said made any sense," Cyrus said.

"I've read about greater demons," the new guy replied. "Whil has a book that mentions them. But I don't know what this movie monster is."

"It's—" How did I explain? Did they even have photography here or would it be easier to compare it to a painting or a play?

Except that wasn't the point. Confirming that these men knew about the monster and were capable of dealing with it was.

"It was big and red with horns and claws and ate people," I said.

The muscles in Cyrus's jaw flexed but he didn't react as if he knew what I was talking about, and the new guy's eyes grew bigger.

"Do you think—?" the new guy started, but Cyrus shot him a hard look, stopping him mid sentence.

"We need to talk to Whil," Cyrus said.

AUDREY

CYRUS STOOD AND HEADED TO THE BACK DOOR, STILL OPEN AND STILL letting the sunlight pour into the kitchen.

"So you don't know how to kill it?" I asked. Which meant there weren't dozens of those monstrous things wandering around this realm.

The new guy stood and motioned for me to follow Cyrus. Practicality made me grab my sandwich even though I was no longer hungry. I still had no idea what I was doing or where I was going, but I couldn't afford to do anything on an empty stomach, especially if I hadn't eaten in a couple of days.

Outside, I turned my face to the sun, hoping it would warm more than just my skin, but the warmth couldn't penetrate the frozen emptiness inside me, and I feared nothing ever would.

The other guy — whose name I still had to learn — drew up close behind me, too close for my comfort even though I was a shifter and as a species we had a smaller personal space than most. But I couldn't tell if he was close because his personal space with strangers was practically non-existent or for some other reason.

From the outside, the mansion looked more like a Medieval castle, made from large stone blocks. It stood three stories — four or five stories at the six turrets — and was surrounded by gardens and a high wall.

Beyond the wall, I could see a few more buildings tucked against the rise of the mountain and suspected there were more on the other side of the mansion. These buildings were plainer, more practical than the castle, but still made from large stone blocks, and past them stood an even taller wall.

Then we rounded a corner and stepped into a shaded grove. It wasn't very big, not like my pack's— my *old* pack's sacred grove in the middle of the forest, but with the trees clustered in a circle and pruned so their branches in the center framed the sky, it was clearly a grove.

Cyrus led us around the grove and down a slope to a strange building that was half English cottage and half greenhouse tucked against the large protective wall. Bushes and trees and vines crowded around the building and everything was in bloom regardless of their season, spring irises and tulips blooming beside fragrant roses and black-eyed Susans.

Something flickered at the edge of my vision... or was that the edge of my senses. It tugged at me, pulling my attention from the impossible cottage to the shadows in the grove above.

The icy emptiness shuddered and the aching need swelled.

I was suddenly hyperaware of the new guy, his muscular body close behind me. It was as if I could feel his body heat, which was impossible since he wasn't *that* close. But he was even more handsome than Cyrus and with that smile of his and his kinder attitude, he'd be an even better choice to alleviate the need caused by my incomplete mating bond.

"Whil," Cyrus called out, stopping at the cottage's open door and surprising me. He struck me as the kind of man who'd just barge in and make demands. He was more than powerful enough to be the alpha of a pack, and in my experience wolves that powerful didn't ask, they took.

"In the library," a feminine voice called back.

"Our guest is awake," he said, not going into the house as

expected, but heading around to the greenhouse part and stepping through an open door from one garden bursting with life to another one.

Interspersed among the vines and branches and leaves and blooms were shelves crammed with books and jars and scrolls. The floor — wide flagstones when there was floor and not moss or grass or other groundcover — was set in wide steps, except they didn't go in one direction. There were a few going up on the right to a tall bookcase and a few going down to a bench while another two steps were raised in the center of a small pool.

The room was larger than I expected, and we wandered to the back where there were more bookcases, fewer windows — although the ceiling was still glass — and a mismatched seating arrangement that consisted of a short, old-fashioned couch with only one arm, a more modern looking chair with thick cushions, two more simpler chairs, and a stool.

On the floor, surrounded by uneven piles of books, sat the most beautiful woman I'd ever seen. She was so stunning she seemed to glow, caught in a perpetual stream of sunlight that haloed her entire body, made her long golden hair shimmer, and accentuated the delicate tips of her pointed ears.

My breath caught. She wasn't just a woman, she was a fae woman. And from how pointed her ears were, she had to be full fae.

"Am I in Faerie?" I asked, my voice breathy with awe.

The fae had sent a few sorcerers to help with the war, but they'd kept to themselves and very few people had actually seen one. The only evidence that they had even helped were the few faekin — men and women who were half-fae — wandering around the mortal realm. There were only a few pictures of a few faekin on the internet, never any fae, and only one faekin sat in the Joined Parliament.

The woman raised a sculpted eyebrow and glanced at Cyrus as he sat on the couch. The movement exuded power and danger, and I doubted he was purposely trying to intimidate me. This was his natural state. A predator.

"She thinks she's from a different realm," Cyrus replied.

I shot him a dark look. "I don't think. I know. My realm doesn't have two moons."

Cyrus matched my dark look and let a hint of power roll over me. "You could be lying."

"Why would I be lying?"

"Come here." The woman — what had Cyrus called her? Whil? — pushed the books in front of her aside to make room for me on the floor. "You're not in Faerie, but I am fae. I'm Whiltierna. Everyone calls me Whil."

"Audrey," I said, stepping over a small pile of books to get to her.

Whil held out her hand, palm up. "The boys found you in Darkweald."

"That's what Cyrus keeps saying," I replied, sitting in front of her and placing my hand in hers.

Golden light radiated from her skin and a warm caress of power curled over my hand and up my arm.

"A malicious god sleeps in Darkweald. You could have gone there with evil intentions," she said.

I huffed, and the power seeped over my shoulder and into my chest. It oozed around my heart, soft and sensual, but couldn't get past the ice to fill the emptiness inside me.

Nothing would fill it. I was going to be broken and empty forever.

I tried to push that thought aside.

It will fade. It has to fade.

"Oh child," the woman breathed. "That's a nasty curse."

Both of the men leaned forward.

"Did she get it from Tzanagoth?" Cyrus asked.

"No, this is old. Handed down from generation to generation." The woman raised a gaze filled with sadness and captured me with eyes the color of new leaves.

My cheeks heated with embarrassment. One quick look and she knew I couldn't shift.

"Did you go to Darkweald to use Tzanagoth's power to break your curse?" Cyrus pressed.

"No," I said.

His power rolled over me, stronger than before.

"I'm from the mortal realm," I insisted, my body bending forward of its own volition to submit to him. "I don't know what Darkweald is or anything about this Tzanagoth."

Whil shot Cyrus a look and his power vanished. "How do you know about the realms?" she asked.

"Supers—"

She frowned at me.

"Supernatural beings," I corrected. Guess she wasn't familiar with the short form. "We came out of hiding about twenty-five years ago when the archangel Michael decided to cleanse the earth of the *human infestation*. The entire planet learned in one horrible attack that angels and the Realm of Celestial Light were real and so was almost everything else."

The new guy pulled the stool closer to me and sat. "Everything?"

"They didn't go into a whole lot of detail in school, but yeah. There are hundreds of realms, maybe thousands—"

"And you can learn about them later, Bishop," Cyrus said, cutting me off. "We need to know what happened, and we need—" Cyrus snapped his mouth shut, cutting himself off.

Clearly, I wasn't supposed to know whatever that second bit was.

The other guy — Bishop — sighed. "So, what did happen?"

I was stupid enough to think Royce was my fated mate and had trusted him too easily. And I still had no idea what Cyrus's intentions were.

"Two guys from my pack summoned a monster and tried to sacrifice me to it," I said, not wanting to get into all the embarrassing details but knowing I needed to say enough so they'd think I'd told them everything. "The alpha interrupted them and it tossed me aside to eat him. I wasn't thinking clearly. I was bleeding and hit my head so I'm not quite sure what happened, but I think I ran through the portal the thing came out of to get to the mortal realm."

There. Straight to the point. Everything they need to know without all the embarrassing details.

My gaze dipped to the sandwich still in my free hand and

Merrick's screams shuddered through me, making my stomach heave.

"It ate him," I murmured, the words slipping out.

"Who?" Whil asked.

"The alpha. It started ripping him apart and eating him while he was still alive."

More of Whil's power seeped into me, pressing against the icy barrier but unable to break through. "How did they open the portal to summon it?" she asked.

"I don't know. They poured a potion on the ground and there was black mist and lightning."

"Just a potion?" Whil's grip on my hand tightened. "There had to be something else."

Yeah, an incomplete mating bond.

Whil's gaze flickered up to Cyrus and his power surged over me.

"There's more," he growled. "Tell her."

I bent over, my forehead pressed against the flagstones in forced submission. "The alpha mentioned something from his safe," I gasped.

"What was it?" Whil asked.

"I don't know."

"You're hiding something," she insisted. "I've cast an intention spell and I know there's something you're not telling us."

AUDREY

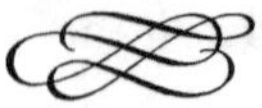

The pressure from Cyrus's power grew, crushing inside my frozen chest. "I won't let you endanger my pack," he said, his voice low. "If someone from your world woke and summoned Tzanagoth, someone here could figure it out, too. What are you hiding?"

"It's not important." *Please.* I didn't want to say it. I didn't want to confess I was so weak and desperate that I'd believed someone powerful like Royce was destined for me.

But Cyrus's power kept growing and it didn't matter how hard I clenched my jaw, the words still poured out. "An incomplete mating bond. They needed an incomplete mating bond."

The pressure vanished and the icy emptiness roared back in. "The only way for that to happen—" Cyrus said not needing to finish his sentence.

He was a shifter. If he knew about mating bonds, then he knew I was stupid enough to initiate one and was then rejected.

"Yeah." My throat tightened with emotions I really didn't want, and I collapsed forward, sobbing, the shame and frustration and aching cold too much to hold back.

It will pass. It will pass. Please, God, make it pass.

It's not going to pass, a voice filled with burning anger snarled in my head.

It will. It has to. If it didn't, I had no idea how I was going to hold out. I already teetered dangerously close to the edge of complete surrender. I didn't know how much longer I could hold out before the incomplete mating bond made me think the only way out was death.

I hadn't thought the grief would be so strong. It was just incomplete, a connection between my soul and Royce's hadn't been made so I shouldn't have felt as if a piece of myself had been ripped out.

It won't. It isn't incomplete, the voice growled.

What? How?

But the second he said it, I knew it was true. I could feel the bond around my heart, partially woven into my soul, and I could sense it was linked—

Oh, God.

It was linked to whoever was speaking in my head. I didn't even know who he was. He didn't sound like Cyrus or Bishop. But I recognized his scent, the dark rich aroma of wood smoke, and every cell in my being knew he was mine. Forever. My mate.

I felt cold and empty not because the bond was incomplete, but because he'd frozen our connection. He didn't want me and was fighting the bond with everything he had.

My gaze jerked across the greenhouse to a large, black wolf stalking across the uneven floor toward me.

"Why?" I gasped. It didn't make sense. If he didn't want the bond, why accept it? *Why say the other half of the vow and finish it?*

I didn't. He curled his lips back, baring his long canines, and growled at me. *I refuted you and you forced it on me anyway.*

"I what?" How could I have done that? Even if I'd been aware of what I was doing, I wouldn't have been able to force the bond on him. He had to say the vow and accept it.

You forced it on me. He captured my gaze with his strange black eyes, and I knew, through the bond he didn't want, that he meant every word he said. *I don't want it and I don't want you.*

His words shot ice into my heart with an agony more painful than anything I'd experienced before.

I was nothing, weak, unwanted. Not even my mate wanted me. He didn't want me with every fiber of his being.

His hate and anger tore into my soul deeper than his claws could have. It would have been less painful if he'd attacked me.

"Not true," I gasped. "It's not true."

It is, my mate snarled.

No. It couldn't be. *I am worthy. I deserve to be loved. I'm stronger than this.*

But the icy hollowness crushed inside me. I couldn't catch my breath. I kept gasping, kept trying to draw in air, but it wasn't enough. Nothing was going to be enough.

I scrambled to my feet. I needed space, air. *God, please. Why can't I breathe?*

The pressure from Cyrus's power crashed over me. He said something, but I couldn't understand his words, could barely hear anything beyond the rushing in my head and the anguish in my heart.

My mate didn't want me.

No one wanted me.

I didn't want to feel that way. I shouldn't. I was strong enough to survive living with Sterling and strong enough to survive almost being sacrificed to a monster. I could survive this. I just needed to get away from them, away from *him*, from everything, and breathe.

I staggered, fell to one knee, pushed back up, and kept going toward the door.

I had to escape this madness, even though I knew there was no escape. No, that wasn't true. There were two ways to escape. His death or mine, and given his strength and the strength of the others around me, it was going to be mine.

I should just give up, stop fighting, and face the inevitable. I might have escaped that monster, but I couldn't escape this. My only way out was death. I couldn't even run away. Even if I could somehow evade my mate, the emptiness and anguish would always be with me.

And yet my body kept trying to escape, trying to find enough space within me to breathe, because a small, desperate voice inside me was certain that if I could just breathe, I'd be able to fight the overwhelming emotions. *Please, I need to breathe.*

"Stop," Cyrus roared, his voice cutting through the rushing in my head.

His power surged and dropped me to both knees, but my body kept fighting, crawling even as the pressure pushed me down. I needed to escape.

God, why had I been so stupid?

BISHOP

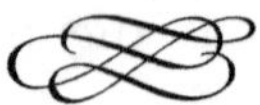

The woman, Audrey, heaved against Cyrus's control even as I tried to get him to stop. Tears streamed down her cheeks, her expression filled with the terror and anguish of a panic attack, making my heart break for her. Then a glittering stream of golden magic caressed the back of her head and she passed out, put to sleep by Whil's spell.

"What's wrong with you?" I demanded, glaring at Cyrus and giving him one last mental shove with my power, drawing an *oomph* but doing little else. "You didn't have to force her to tell us about the incomplete bond and you certainly didn't have to force her to stay. I could have caught up to her outside, and I could have gotten her to tell us everything without terrorizing her."

"And I needed to know she wasn't a threat." Cyrus snarled back.

"Well, she's not." And it had been obvious the moment I'd looked at her, broken and bleeding, in the river. She hadn't deserved what had happened to her. No one had.

"And you," I said, shooting my glare at Knox before picking her up and cradling her in my arms. "She just confessed she had an incomplete mating bond as part of what happened to her, which means those men who tried to kill her either murdered her mate before they could finish saying their vows or one of them made her fall in love with him then betrayed her." And I wasn't sure which made me angrier. Both were horrible.

I jerked my chin at Cyrus, telling him to get off the couch, so I could set Audrey on it.

I was trying to break the bond, Knox growled, a hint of regret whispering through our bond before he clamped down on it. *Get her to refute it with me.*

"Without telling her what you were doing?" I asked as Cyrus got out of my way. "She's just had her heart broken and you told her you didn't want her."

I don't.

"But you didn't prepare her. All you did was flood her with rejection without warning while the bond is telling her you're supposed to love her." I laid her on the couch but didn't want to let her go and couldn't pull my attention away from her to keep glaring at my brothers... not that a hard look would change their minds. I was the flighty brother, the one who jumped from idea to idea, the flirt, the one who'd rather make a joke than an enemy and they both saw that as a weakness.

That only proves how weak she is. She didn't even try to fight back, Knox snarled.

"We don't know what her story is," I insisted, more pieces of my heart breaking. "Someone tried to kill her and she just lost her mate." And got an asshole in his place.

On top of that, her essence was weak. Depending on if her weakness was something she'd been born with or had for a long time — and with Whil's comment about a curse that might be true — fighting back might have never been an option for her, so it might not be a first instinct for her.

"After that little demonstration of *affection*," I said to Knox, "I have no doubt she'll be more than willing to try to break the mating bond with you."

Cyrus turned to Whil. "Did anything she say explain how she bonded with him without either of them saying anything?"

"No, and this bond can't be broken with just intention," Whil said, sitting on the edge of the couch and laying a hand on Audrey's forehead. "As much as I hoped it wasn't, now that I've gotten a better look at it, I know it's a real mating bond, not something else masquerading as one as I'd hoped. You might not have sealed it yet, but it already runs deep between you."

I don't care how strong it is. Find a way to break it. Knox's lips curled back and he growled at Audrey. *She's not my mate. She never was and never will be. I won't accept her. Ever.*

He stormed from the cottage, a flicker of furious emotions rushing through me before he clamped down on our bond as well.

"So that's it, then?" I asked. She was going to be stuck with my brother for the rest of her life when she'd thought she was going to spend it with the man she loved.

"Not necessarily," Whil replied. "It didn't form in the natural way so there's still a chance there was something about what happened to her that might be a key to breaking it. But the odds aren't good."

"I don't want to lose him because of some woman," Cyrus said. "And I don't want him stuck with someone we can't trust."

"She told the truth about what happened to her," Whil said, brushing a lock of hair away from Audrey's eyes. "And my intention spell confirmed that she told us everything she knew about how that monster, which I assume was Tzanagoth, was summoned." She frowned. "Although I'm not entirely sure he was actually summoned."

"Still," Cyrus said, a small wave of power rolling off him like it did when he was worried and not paying attention to controlling himself. "She didn't shift out her injuries. She's clearly trying to manipulate us."

Whil sighed and moved her hand from Audrey's head to over her heart. "She didn't shift out her injuries because she can't. That's the curse."

Cyrus stared at Whil as if he couldn't believe what she'd just said then groaned and rubbed his face, suddenly looking exhausted and a little guilty. "Of course she can't. This just keeps getting better and better. Knox would rather stay in wolf form and now has a mate who doesn't even have a wolf form. They don't even have that in common."

"Can you break the curse?" I sat on the floor beside the couch near Audrey's head. How much suffering could one woman take? The person she loved was gone, her home was gone, and she couldn't shift. I couldn't imagine not having a connection with the wolf half of my soul and not being able to shift.

"There's a way to unlock it, but the release mechanism is damaged... maybe blocked? I'm not sure." Whil closed her eyes and raised her chin, a sign that she was using her magical senses to get a better look at the curse. "It's woven into every cell in her body. Even if I were in Faerie, I wouldn't have enough power to break it. A master sorcerer might, but I'm not a master sorcerer."

"And not what we should be worrying about," Cyrus said, squaring his shoulders and putting on his "alpha of the pack" expression, the same one Mom used to wear when she needed to ignore her emotions for the good of the pack. "We need to break the mating bond without killing either of them and figure out if we're in danger from Tzanagoth. I'm not willing to bet the safety of the pack thinking that the malicious god is now in Audrey's realm."

"I wouldn't bet that, either," Whil said. "The portals to the other realms were locked by powerful magic. Two shifters wouldn't have enough power to break that lock, not even harnessing the magic within a mating bond, which is what sounds like happened."

"So then what?" Cyrus asked. "The monster was her imagination and she really didn't come from this other realm?"

"No. The spell could have opened a temporary crack or a rip between the realms. I'm not entirely sure how, but theoretically, with enough power and maybe the right spell, it's possible. But something as powerful as a god probably wouldn't have been able to pass through it. What attacked her alpha probably was a temporary manifestation of Tzanagoth." Whil picked her way through the piles of books to a shelf partially hidden by a flowering vine. "What I don't know is if summoning that temporary manifestation broke the sleeping spell on him or not."

"If he's still in our realm and now awake, wouldn't we have felt his presence?" I asked. Everything I'd read about the gods said they radiated a powerful essence when conscious and if he was awake, I doubted he'd have stayed within Anakar's ruins.

"We'll know more when the hunting party returns," Cyrus said. His gaze slid to Audrey and the muscles in his jaw flexed, and I could practically hear the wheels in his head turning as he tried to decide what to do with her and if it was worth the time to save our brother when our entire pack could be in danger.

And while I wanted to argue and tell him we couldn't lose Knox, I also understood that the pack came first. Even before family.

"I won't know what to look for regarding Tzanagoth until we hear from the hunting party," Whil said before Cyrus could make the difficult decision to let Knox and Audrey suffer.

"You have until then," he replied then turned his attention to me. "Take care of her. Everything will be easier if she's not having a meltdown."

"You should have thought of that before you made her submit," I said.

"Don't start," he said, sending a wave of power washing over me. "You know I had to get the truth. We can't be divided on this. Not if we're going to keep Knox."

And as much as I hated it, he was right. It didn't matter what I thought of Audrey. She wasn't family and she wasn't at risk of going feral. Although from that panic attack it looked like there might be a chance she'd completely melt down and kill herself, a thought that had my wolf rising to the surface with the need to take over and protect her.

"If it comes down to it and we have to pick one or the other, we pick Knox." Cyrus's expression softened. "I don't like it, but if we lose Knox, I could lose you, too. Your twin bond is almost as strong as a mating bond even though it shouldn't be, and you were a mess the last time he went feral."

I hated that those were our choices, but I couldn't fight Cyrus on this. "Fine."

"Bring her to dinner." His gaze dropped to her and his expression softened even more. "We can introduce her to our betas and I can show her that I can be pleasant."

He left and I turned my attention back to Audrey. She looked at peace, but her cheeks were still damp from her tears and her face was still bruised from her ordeal. She'd already gone through so much. I didn't want to accept that our choices were her or Knox. There had to be a way to save both of them that didn't involve forcing them to accept their bond.

The only way we knew how to break a bond was if one half of the bond died but what about transferring it? It was often easier to redirect something than stopping it completely.

"Can a bond be transferred?" I asked.

Whil froze her hand hovering over a book about to take it off the shelf. "What are you thinking?"

"That it might be easier to redirect a spell than break it."

"And if it's possible, who would you suggest we redirect the mating bond to?" she asked. "It would need to happen soon. She and Knox aren't going to be able to resist the compulsion to seal the bond for long. There wouldn't be a lot of time for her and her new mate to get to know each other."

Yeah, and while I could ask someone to take the bond, that idea didn't sit well with me. It made my chest tighten with a confusing mix of emotions. She was Knox's mate and I could feel their connection. The desire from their bond seeped through our twin bond and while it was only a fraction of what Knox was fighting, it added to my wolf's desire to protect her, hold her, love her—

"I already have a connection with Knox. I can feel their bond," I said. "It would probably be easier to move the mating bond to me."

Whil looked at me and raised a sculpted eyebrow.

Yeah, I was coming up with another one of my ridiculous ideas.

Except it wasn't ridiculous. The situation wasn't Audrey's fault or Knox's and neither of them deserved to suffer. Knox didn't have the social skills — and didn't want them — to nurture an unexpected relationship, but I did, and from what I'd seen so far, Audrey seemed like a kind, genuine person who'd just gone through the worst day of her life. And my wolf wholeheartedly agreed with that assessment.

If she was willing, we could make it work, if, of course, it was possible to redirect Knox's half of the mating bond.

AUDREY

I woke to the bright scent of fresh-cut grass, flowers, and the rich aroma of damp dirt then realized I was still in Whil's strange greenhouse library. Above, through the leaves and branches and the glass ceiling, the sky was starting to darken, the precursor to night when it had been the middle of the day when I'd had that panic attack and passed out.

Bishop sat cross-legged on the floor beside me with his back against the couch and an enormous book in his lap. His head was tipped forward, but a few small braids at his temples kept his jaw-length hair out of his eyes. It was long enough that he could have tied it back with an elastic, but just like with the over-sized shirt I'd woken up in, the braids indicated he was prepared to shift at a moment's notice.

He raised his gaze to meet mine and for a second, I was drowning in his warm brown eyes. Mesmerizing green flecks caught the lamp-light, pulling me in deeper and deeper, like just how I'd fallen into Royce's gaze when I'd heard the fated mating call.

"How do you feel?" he asked, his voice soft, sending a shiver of need rushing through me even though I doubted he intended his tone to be sensual.

Turned on, cold, ashamed and—

And a whole bunch of things I didn't want to think about.

"Awful. Cyrus didn't have to force me to bring up the mating bond," I said, focusing on the one thing that didn't have to do with me being weak or foolish or anything else. Anger I could do. Anger was safe.

He offered me a soft, sad smile. "Would you have said something otherwise?"

No. The sooner I forgot about that mistake the better, except— "I would have when I found out I was bonded with a complete stranger."

"I know this must be difficult for you, but if you can think of anything else that happened to you that might help."

"Help how? My mate bond bound me to a man I've never met before who despises me." The ice inside me swelled along with the memory of how much he didn't want me. "I don't think hashing out the details will help him understand."

He'd hate me even more once he knew the truth. It was bad enough he was stuck with a weak stranger for the rest of his life, it would be worse once he knew I was naive and stupid, too.

"Your bond with Knox didn't form the normal way so maybe there's a way to break it," Bishop said.

My chest tightened at my mate's name, but I couldn't tell if it was with desire or grief.

"His name is Knox? Do you know him? Does he—?" The pressure tightened. Not desire or grief. Fear. I was feeling fear. He was so angry with me, his fury ice in my veins, would he take out that rage on me? "Does he have a temper?"

Bishop's eyes darkened and his power shuddered around him, threatening to release before he regained control. "He'd never lay a finger on you," he said, jumping to the conclusion — and likely seeing the fear in my eyes — that I was worried my unwanted mate would be abusive. "My brother is angry and he usually goes off by himself when he's upset, but he can't get as far away as he wants with the mating bond newly formed and still unsealed."

The word *unsealed* turned some of the cold back into aching desire. The bond didn't care if he hated me or that it had been a mistake to bond with him. It needed to be sealed and that meant having sex... and if we didn't do something about it, eventually the bond would compel us to have sex whether we wanted to or not.

"He's your brother?" I asked, trying not to think about the inevitable sex or, if we somehow managed to resist the bond long enough, the insanity.

"And Cyrus," Bishop said.

And they'd taken me to an enormous building that had to be the alpha's residence. They'd also looked right at home in the kitchen, which meant one of them was this pack's alpha.

It had to be Cyrus. His power was enormous, and while I could sense the others were strong as well even though they were holding back, Bishop was too nice and Knox was too angry.

"So I've accidentally forced a mating bond on the alpha's brother." Just great. The weakest wolf in existence had forced herself into an alpha's family.

"It wasn't your fault. The bond was meant for someone else." Sadness filled Bishop's eyes, and for a second, I couldn't understand why. Then I realized he didn't know I'd been tricked. He thought my intended mate had been killed before he could finish our mating vows. "With luck we'll be able to find a way to break the bond and you can mourn properly."

I contemplated going with the lie. It would mean no one in this realm would know I'd been so foolish, but I was a horrible liar and I'd feel uncomfortable getting sympathy from everyone for a lover I hadn't lost.

"I wish it was like that," I said, my cheeks heating with shame. "I wish there'd been someone who'd wanted to mate with someone like me."

Bishop's sadness turned to knowing, but without any disgust like I'd feared. "I think being tricked into falling in love with someone might be worse."

"Yeah, the asshole is probably still alive and laughing at me," I said bitterly. And if I was stronger...

"How long did he play you along?" Whil asked, stepping out from behind a flowering shrub carrying a tray with a teapot and cups.

"Thankfully, not long. Somehow they found a witch who could make a spell or potion or something that imitated a fated mating call."

"A fated mating call?" Bishop asked as Whil set the tray on a nearby table.

Right. He didn't know what that was. That was something only my pack experienced. "It's a side-effect of the spell that—" My throat tightened. *Come on. Just say it. Whil has already sensed the truth.*

"A side-effect of the curse that prevents you from shifting," Whil finished for me, pouring tea into a cup and offering it to me.

I took the cup and stared into the pale green liquid. "A long time ago the alpha of the pack made a deal with a powerful witch to enspell us, or rather my ancestors. The wolf half of our soul is kept asleep until the summer solstice after our eighteenth birthday."

"Why would someone do that?" Bishop asked, horrified.

"Humans hadn't taken well to supers in our realm and it was a safety precaution. Unlike the other packs, we didn't have to worry about a child shifting where a human could see," I replied. "Because of that, we were able to have stronger connections with human communities, and my pack— *that* pack became one of the most powerful packs on the planet."

"And when your wolf finally wakes all the senses that had been repressed that you should have had a lifetime to acclimatize to, burst into existence," Whil said.

"Sometimes those senses lock onto a similar soul, a perfect mate," I said. "It's like— it *was* like fire and pressure and a vibration in my soul that shook my essence. I don't know if that's what it's supposed to feel like or not since it wasn't real." There were only a couple of fated mates in the pack, but I hadn't talked to them about the fated mating call, and all I had to go on were rumors about what it felt like.

"Sounds like an angelic mating brand," Whil said, leaving her cup of tea only half poured and heading to a bookshelf hidden behind a small tree with bright autumn leaves.

"I looked at Royce and I just *knew* he was my mate." I blew at the steam curling from my cup, my hands starting to tremble. "I didn't know him very well. I didn't have a lot of status in the pack before my eighteenth birthday, and when my wolf didn't wake, I lost even more status. Royce said—" I huffed a bitter laugh. Royce had said a lot of things that hadn't been true. "He said he was afraid the alpha would deny our mating. He was friends with the alpha's son and next in line to be the first beta."

"So you rushed to say your vows," Bishop said, some of the sadness returning to his expression with a huge helping of pity.

Swell. Although I should probably be happy it was pity and not disgust like how my pack looked at me. I'd tried every day to be better, stronger, enough, but that hadn't made my wolf wake or my pack treat me any differently.

"Then they cast the spell and summoned the monster and you know the rest." I tried to raise my cup to my lips to take a sip but my hands were shaking too much.

"Here." Bishop took my cup from me and set it back on the tray.

Why was I shaking? I couldn't figure out my reaction. Of course, all I could really feel was icy hollowness and aching yearning.

He captured my hands between his, his palms warm against my skin, and held my gaze with his warm brown eyes.

"How long have you been afraid?" he murmured.

"For as long as I can remember," I whispered. Even when my father had been alive, I'd been afraid. He'd yell in his sleep, lose his temper, break things. It was his bad memories and it hadn't been his fault, but my existence had always been precarious.

"Whether we break the bond or not, you're safe here." He brushed his thumb against my cheek and I realized I was crying. My body was finally reacting to the shock of what had happened, but I was too twisted up inside by the mating bond— or rather Knox *rejecting* the mating bond to feel it.

"I'm a shifter who can't shift. I don't have any value."

"Whoever told you that is dead wrong," Whil said from behind the tree. "We all have something to offer. I'm a sorcerer, but my ability to channel raw magical power from the Realm of Faerie is so small it's almost laughable to call me a sorcerer. But here in this realm, I'm a counselor and archivist and researcher. You just haven't figured out where you fit yet and it sounds like your previous pack didn't give you a chance to find out."

It sounded so easy when she said it like that and I desperately wanted it to be true, but I knew it wasn't so simple to be seen as something more than the girl who couldn't shift.

"Now let me do my work here. You have a dinner to go to," Whil said.

"Dinner?" I asked.

Bishop offered me a soft smile. "Cyrus wants to prove he isn't a complete asshole and has asked that you join us and our betas for dinner."

"I don't think that's a good idea." I really didn't want a repeat of being forced to submit, especially with a larger audience, and I didn't trust that Cyrus wouldn't do it. That and I still looked like I'd been beaten up, which would make people stare at me and ask questions I didn't want to answer. "I should stay and help Whil. Two heads are better than one, right?"

"Can you read Sennari, Common Fae, Latin, or Ofuin?" Whil asked.

"No." And I hadn't even heard of half those languages. Well so much for that. "I still think going to this dinner is a bad idea." I gestured to my face as if Bishop — who'd already figured out so much without me having to say anything — wouldn't have realized why I didn't want to meet other people.

"You can't avoid meeting our betas until you're fully healed. You'll be living in our house for a while, and they need to meet you right away so they don't think you're a threat." Bishop hooked his finger under my chin and brought my gaze back to his, making the aching need inside me swell. "And no, you're not living someplace else," he added before I could suggest the idea. "Even if you're only Knox's mate for a little while, you're still family right now."

"And if we can break the bond and I'm no longer Knox's mate?" I asked, holding his gaze.

"We'll help find a place for you, whether it's here at the Residence or in town."

The intensity in his eyes grew, fueling my need, and I broke eye contact, dropping my attention to my hands in my lap.

It sounded too good to be true. And maybe it was, but I didn't have any choice. I couldn't leave because the bond would compel me back to Knox so we could seal it whether we wanted to or not and it was already pretty insistent.

Even if the situation was half as good or a quarter as good as Bishop made it out to be that was still better than where I'd come from. I could live with that... if my bond with Knox didn't drive me insane first.

AUDREY

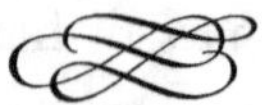

WE WENT STRAIGHT FROM WHIL'S COTTAGE TO A DINING ROOM LARGE enough to host fifty people, although the long table was only set for eight at the one end. The room wasn't the enormous one I'd seen from the front hall, that room had been the size of a ballroom— it probably *was* a ballroom. This was a "more intimate" dining room.

The thought made a hysterical laugh bubble in my throat and I tried to swallow it back. Merrick's house had been big, but it hadn't been a castle. It had one dining room for about ten people, and if he wanted to meet with more, he hosted them in the ballroom in the town's main hotel. Somehow, I'd gone from Cinderella trapped by a big fish in a tiny pond to Cinderella at the end of the story in a castle. The only thing I didn't have was a prince.

I glanced at Bishop as he led me to a chair two seats down from the head of the table and pulled it out for me.

Maybe I did have a prince. Although being nice to me didn't mean he was interested and I was also mated to his brother.

So yeah, no prince for me.

Cyrus already sat at the table along with another man who only radiated a fraction of the power of the alpha. I didn't know if he was holding it back out of respect for Cyrus or if he just wasn't very powerful... which didn't make any sense. He had to be holding it back.

This was a dinner with the pack's betas and an alpha didn't pick weak betas.

The man had a similar build to Cyrus, big, bulky, and intimidating with a shaved head and piercing blue eyes, which only added to the theory that he was holding his power back. He couldn't look like an equal in power if he was also an equal physically. No alpha would allow that.

Beside him sat a beautiful woman radiating more power than the guy, and somehow, I could tell she was actually holding her power back. She wore a dress in the same style as mine, sleeveless, backless, and with fabric light and silky enough to show off every sleek curve and ripple of muscle. Hers was a deep green which brought out the gold in her eyes and the red accents in her light brown hair. It showed off her long neck and sculpted arms, and I'd bet if she stood, she'd have a six-pack and a great ass.

I was more or less fit — housecleaning could be hard work — but I didn't look nearly as good in the dress as she did and my nipples were still "at attention" with my constant, ever-so-slightly turned-on state. I would have been embarrassed about it if both of them hadn't looked at my face and forgotten to check out the rest of me.

Swell. Yep. I can't shift. Make your jokes now. Give me your disgusted looks. Bring it on.

Bishop cleared his throat and they jerked their attention away from me, but two more men and another woman strode into the room and took their seats. Now *they* stared at me.

Wonderful. I sat in the chair Bishop had pulled out for me, but that only made the man across from me raise his eyebrows in surprise.

"Knox's seat?" he asked, his attention jumping to Cyrus.

"Easier than adding an extra place setting," Bishop said, sitting in the chair beside me.

"Because bringing out silverware and an extra glass is a hardship," the new woman said. She wore a red version of my dress made from a material that was thicker than mine — thick enough that it might have better disguised my nipples — and had her dark hair piled on her head in an intricate updo.

With her attention on Bishop and only Bishop, she gracefully sat on the chair beside Green Dress. Her power wasn't particularly strong, and this time I clearly felt like she wasn't holding back, which shocked me. Maybe she wasn't a beta but a mate of one of the men.

Or maybe Cyrus wasn't like all the alphas I'd heard about and everything I knew about alphas and how to *be pack* was wrong.

"It's a waste to leave the spot empty every night," the leaner of the men Red Dress had entered with said. He sat beside her, his power similar in strength and also not suppressed, and offered me a warm, if confused smile, his attention on my face — most likely my black eyes.

"To answer the question you're all dying to ask," Cyrus said, drawing everyone's attention. "And I know it isn't 'will Knox be joining us for dinner' because you know he never does. This is Audrey. She'll be staying with us for a while," he said. "And yes, the rumors are true, she's the one we found injured in Darkweald."

"Rumors?" the other new man said with mock innocence as he took his place beside Lean Guy. He was older than the others with a hint of gray at his temples and deep laugh lines around his eyes.

He'd shown up in a black, lighter-material version of a kilt, his broad muscular chest and arms on full display. He wasn't as big as Cyrus or the man sitting across from me, but there was a sharpness to his features, a strong sense of feralness churning just under his skin that made him seem even more dangerous than Cyrus. A constant trickle of power radiated from him as if he was almost as strong as Cyrus or Bishop, was trying to fully contain it, but didn't have the same kind of control at suppressing it as the brothers did.

Cyrus rolled his eyes at him as if the man made comments like that all the time, the sense of humor a strange juxtaposition to the sense of wildness radiating off him. "We all know Zavier said something before he and Lucius headed out."

"That boy just can't keep his mouth shut," the guy across from me said.

"Give the boy a break," Green Dress said with a laugh. "When was the last time the alpha's sons went out on patrol and came back with a woman?"

"Are we talking about all of them or just Bishop?" the older guy chuckled, making Red Dress shoot him a dirty look.

"And really, Cyrus," Green Dress continued, "if you wanted to keep things quiet, you shouldn't have asked to borrow a dress while I was in the middle of meeting with half of my staff."

Bishop threw his head back and laughed. "You went to Nova for a dress? Audrey was out for hours. There was plenty of time to send someone to get something."

Cyrus shot Bishop a dark look. "It is what it is. She didn't need clothes until she woke and we had no idea when that would be."

"You fell asleep in that chair after I checked on her," Green Dress said. "Didn't you?"

Cyrus huffed and Bishop turned to me, his eyes bright with amusement. "We'll get you some clothes tomorrow when I show you around town."

"You don't have to do that," I said. I was already in their debt and still didn't believe that they wouldn't demand something in return.

"Better me than him," he said with a laugh, jerking his thumb at Cyrus. "He wouldn't know what looked good on a woman if it slapped him in the face."

The others at the table burst into laughter and the tension evaporated. Clearly that was an inside joke.

"I don't care if I look good. Just... more... covered," I murmured, my cheeks heating. "I'm not used to wearing something so..."

"Convenient to take off?" Green Dress said, making my thoughts jump to my achy need to seal the bond— hell, to just have sex with someone, anyone, my body didn't care who.

Everyone at the table stiffened ever-so-slightly and adjusted in their seats, suddenly uncomfortable, and I realized they'd just gotten a huge nose-full of my desire.

My cheeks burned hotter. Just great. You couldn't hide anything from a shifter. And while I'd known that, I hadn't really experienced it. Aside from school where only our teachers were shifters — and were probably used to smelling all kinds of things — Merrick had kept me more or less isolated from the rest of the pack. I'd been too busy for extra-curricular activities and only Mila had wanted to be my friend, and after I'd turned eighteen and my wolf hadn't woken, I'd been even more of an outcast.

Bishop cleared his throat and Cyrus's glower darkened while the older guy burst out laughing. The lean guy shot the older guy an exasperated look and pinched the bridge of his nose, while Red Dress's gaze fluttered up to Bishop with a heated look in her eyes then quickly looked away.

"That wasn't where I was going with that," Green Dress chuckled. "I meant given that you haven't shifted out the rest of your injuries, you probably aren't accustomed to shifting all the time."

"Is it really cold where you come from?" the exasperated man asked.

My embarrassment burned hotter, racing over my whole face and down my neck. "No. It's... complicated."

"And you're clearly not used to proper etiquette," Red Dressed huffed, her dark brown gaze flickering to Bishop again as if she couldn't keep her eyes off of him. And really, I couldn't blame her. Bishop was hot. Gorgeous and funny and kind. Who wouldn't want to be with him? "You don't release pheromones like that at the dinner table and if there's a risk of that happening you don't attend dinner."

"Lighten up, Velora," the older guy said. "She's young, she could be nearing her first heat and just hasn't figured out what the signs are or how to control it yet."

Oh. My. God! Did he really say that? Now my face was hotter than the sun. Yes, we shifters experienced periods where our sexual needs were stronger, usually in our late teens and early twenties, but it wasn't like a true heat like actual wolves.

"If that's the case then she shouldn't have come to dinner," Red Dress, Velora, said.

"She's our guest," Cyrus growled, letting a wave of power ripple over the table. Everyone's eyes jumped to him. "I told her to come. I wanted you to meet her so you don't accost her in the halls. Her reproductive cycle isn't your business—"

Green Dress raised an eyebrow at that, making Cyrus roll his eyes at her.

"Fine. Yes. If it's a problem, then it's yours, Nova, but only yours." He slid his glare over the others. "No, she's not accustomed to our ways. From the little she's told us, her pack is very different."

The guy who was exasperated with the older guy sat forward. "How different? Where do you come from? Are there actually any communities up north?"

I opened my mouth but I had no idea how to respond to that. Would they even believe me? Cyrus hadn't and had only accepted what I said as truth because of Whil.

"Very different," Bishop answered for me, "it's hard to explain, and she doesn't know."

His hand dipped under the table and settled on my knee, sending a ripple of calm through me as if he were my mate or a close friend and not someone I'd just met.

But that only reminded me of how shifters needed physical contact to help steady the animal aspect of their soul — even for those whose wolves were still asleep — and how I'd been without that kind of comfort since Mila had left. My reaction to Bishop's touch said I'd been without for so long anyone was good enough to steady my soul, even a stranger... albeit a kind stranger, but still a stranger.

Of course, the achy throbbing from the unsealed mating bond also didn't care he was a stranger or even my mate, and I gave the room another, mortifying, blast of my desire.

AUDREY

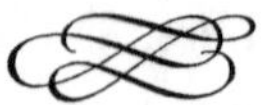

THE MUSCLES IN CYRUS'S JAW FLEXED AND HIS EYES GREW EVEN DARKER, his wolf rising to the surface. Red Dress shot me a look of pure murder, while the older guy looked like he might cry from the effort of holding in his laughter.

"She'll be here for a while," Cyrus said, his voice clipped, "There'll be time to ask her questions later." His hard gaze slid to me. "But only if she wants to talk."

Oh, so now I have a choice?

"She's not a threat and may have to make Stonehaven her home," Cyrus continued.

"So, what you're really saying is let's pretend we're not assholes so we don't scare her away?" the older guy asked with a chuckle.

"Too late for that," the guy across from me said.

Cyrus glared at them, but the edges of his lips were quirked as if this was just the way dinners went with this group: light, fun, slightly dysfunctional like a good family, nothing at all like I'd seen with Merrick and his betas.

The thought made my chest squeeze, but I shoved the sensation back before it overwhelmed me. I had enough on my plate without being jealous of the *family* in front of me having dinner together

"So, the assholes around the table who we apparently trust with our lives are Finn—" Cyrus pointed to the guy sitting across from me. "He's the watch commander in Stonehaven, and Nova, the town's head physician." She was the woman in green who thought my reproductive cycle might actually be her business. "Beside her is Velora, who deals with all things administrative, Thane our chief of finance, and Deacon, our huntmaster in charge of the hunt teams." He was the older, mostly-naked guy, and he flashed me a warm, friendly smile. "Lucius, our primary advisor, is away on a diplomatic mission so you won't be able to meet him for a while."

After the introductions, the conversation thankfully turned away from me and who I was and where I was with my reproductive cycle and moved to lighter conversations about what was going on in town.

Two women brought out dinner as if we were in a restaurant, and I studied both of them, looking for signs of stress or fear, any indication that they were being treated badly, but it looked like they were content serving the alpha, his brother, and their betas.

I'd have to keep my eyes and ears open, but given how Bishop and Whil had treated me and how Cyrus's betas were even comfortable enough to tease him, I suspected what I saw was the truth. The people here were happy and Cyrus forcing me to tell him about the most embarrassing and shameful moment in my life was him being a protective alpha... like a good alpha was supposed to be.

Although could I really believe what I saw? I knew I wasn't a perfect judge of character, but I hadn't thought I was terrible. Except I hadn't seen being manipulated into starting the mating vows and almost sacrificed to a monster coming... although would anyone?

Regardless, I couldn't believe what I felt because I'd fallen for the fake fated mating call and I sure as hell hadn't thought that Royce would try to murder me.

The food was good and looked like food from home. I didn't know if that meant this realm was more or less the same as the mortal realm or not, but I was grateful I wouldn't have to adjust to blue goo or yellow sludge or something else unappealing.

Bishop's hand returned to my knee over and over again as the meal went on, a reassuring anchor as if he just knew his touch, even though we barely knew each other, would keep me calm. Not that I was going to run screaming from the room — where could I possibly go? — but my mind kept stuttering.

One moment I was fine, the next I remembered I was in another realm, I was mated to a man who didn't want me, I—

Bishop squeezed my knee and I refocused back on what Nova was saying.

"—early morning shift." She pushed her chair back, stood, and gave Cyrus a warm smile. There was a familiarity in it that spoke of a deep friendship and perhaps a little more. It made the hollowness in my chest swell, reminding me that I had a mate who hated me. "If you want to keep the rumors under wraps, I recommend not barging into my next meeting. Twice in as many days and people might start to think you've finally got your eyes on a mate."

Bishop choked on his wine and started coughing, his face turning red, making Nova quirk an eyebrow in curiosity. Velora shot me another withering look while Thane looked concerned, Finn angry, and Deacon like he'd just heard the best joke ever and was, for whatever ridiculous reason, trying not to laugh.

"Stop stirring trouble, Nova," Cyrus said. "It's been a stressful couple of days."

"So I can tease you tomorrow once you've recovered?" She batted her eyelashes at him in exaggerated innocence.

"Nova," he growled and she winked at me, her smile getting bigger.

"And you," she said to me, "should probably go to bed."

Her words spiked my desire again, and I became hyperaware of Bishop's hand on my thigh, the power radiating from his body, soft for now but I knew it could be hard and powerful in a second... and yeah, I was fully aware of the double meaning of that thought.

Finn groaned, and Velora huffed and left, while Thane pinched the bridge of his nose again, and Deacon roared with laughter, unable to hold it back any longer.

Embarrassment burned my face and neck, hell, my whole body,

and if I'd thought Cyrus would have let me leave, I would have fled like Velora.

Cyrus released a sudden burst of power and I trembled with the need to kneel. Everyone's attention snapped to serious as if they hadn't expected that reaction.

"That was mean, Nova," Cyrus said.

"You're right. I'm sorry," she replied, her expression turning thoughtful as if Cyrus's reaction had made her reevaluate what she thought about me... or maybe him? Or had she purposely made that comment to figure out what Cyrus thought of me?

The idea was laughable. Even if I hadn't been mate bonded with his brother, he'd never be interested in me. It had to be obvious to everyone in the room I wasn't suppressing my power so they all knew I was weak, and Cyrus knew I couldn't shift. I wasn't mate material for an alpha or even the alpha's brother.

"What I mean," Nova said, all mischief gone from her expression, "is that you should shift out the rest of your injuries first *then* go to bed. And don't think shifting is enough. It just *looks* like enough. Even after you've gotten rid of what's left, your body is still processing the trauma you experienced. Needing two ampuls of elixir means a substantial amount of trauma. It's best to sleep it off." She shot Cyrus another strange look. "I'd have preferred her to have spent all day in bed like I prescribed." Then she turned back to me, her expression softening. "If you feel tired tomorrow, don't push through. Don't be a stubborn idiot like everyone else here at the table. Take a break."

"Right." I stood, taking that as my cue to leave. And even if it wasn't, I didn't want to stick around and risk any more comments that would embarrass me.

Bishop stood with me, and we left the dining room as Nova said something — too quietly for me to hear with my still-human hearing — and Cyrus growled in response.

"Nova certainly is something," I said once we were far enough away that they wouldn't hear me.

"Yes, she is," Bishop said with a brilliant heart-stopping grin, and

I couldn't figure out if he was just impressed with her or attracted to her.

A sliver of jealousy oozed through me. I wanted to make Bishop smile like that, *and* I wanted to be as brave and bold as Nova. She teased her alpha, knowing it would piss him off and didn't care.

Of course, that also spoke to the type of man Cyrus was. He might not like Nova's ribbing but he still let her have her fun and be herself. He let all of his betas be themselves.

"She and Cyrus would have actually made a decent mating if she hadn't grown up with us like a sister."

"Her and Cyrus?" I burst out laughing. Surely that was a joke to lighten my mood. "I barely know either of them but I know he'd strangle her before they even got to the mating ceremony."

Bishop led me into the large front hall and we started up the grand staircase. "What you saw isn't exactly what it's like between them. He's worried about a lot of things right now, which worries Nova. He gets... well, like the way you saw him tonight and in Whil's cottage, and Nova digs in deeper with the teasing."

And one of those things he was worried about was me. "I really didn't mean to mate bond with Knox."

"I know you didn't." We stopped in front of my bedroom door, and Bishop hooked his finger under my chin, urging me to look up at him. His touch shivered through me and my desire burned stronger.

I resisted him, unable to look him in the eyes, knowing he could smell my arousal. God, why couldn't I keep it under control? But I knew why. He was kind and gorgeous, and feeling desire for him, hell even for the mate who didn't want me, was better than the icy hollowness threatening to consume me.

Except I was never going to let myself cross that line because I didn't know Bishop or any of these men and I was mated to his brother. If we couldn't break the bond, we'd either have to figure out another way to deal with it or accept it, and if it came down to accepting it, it would be less awkward if Bishop and I had never been intimate.

"I'm sorry about the—" My embarrassment burned hotter.

"It's not your fault." The pressure under my chin increased and I gave in and looked up, falling into his stunning brown eyes and mesmerized by the brilliant flecks of green scattered through his irises.

He was so close I was fully wrapped in his bright, fresh-cut grass scent and could feel the heat from his body through the thin fabric of my dress. My mostly-hard nipples tightened all the way, and my desire heated, warming a little more of the icy hollowness... particularly the area between my thighs.

Now there was no doubt — if there'd been any before — that I wanted to have sex with Bishop.

"The mating bond wants to be sealed so it's increased your sexual desire," he said, his voice husky, teasing a shiver down my spine.

I knew that. Except my desire was supposed to be for my mate, not every hot guy around me.

His wolf's darkness flickered in his eyes but he kept his animal side buried. "The fact that you're so sensitive and the bond is only a few days old suggests it's strong."

"Or not normal," I replied, my voice breathy, my body aching. "That might make it easier to break." And that had to be the case because strong meant no hope, it meant always feeling Knox's hate for me and this aching need to be complete, and I didn't want to live feeling like this for the rest of my life.

Bishop glanced down, and I realized I'd placed my hand on his chest and was leaning in to him. The darkness in his eyes flickered again, and a hint of it stayed, turning the brown almost black and making the green flecks brighter. The soft power emanating from him grew stronger and his attention moved to my lips.

My pulse picked up. *Please kiss me.*

It wasn't as if I was in love with Knox.

Of course, I wasn't in love with Bishop, either.

He inhaled deeply, taking in my scent, and released a low rumble. *Yes, just lean forward. Kiss me.*

Royce had stolen my first kiss but I ached to give Bishop my second... and third and fourth and—

With a soft, barely audible groan he squeezed his eyes shut and took a step back.

The icy hollowness swelled and my throat tightened.

He didn't want me. No one wanted me. I was weak and useless and—

No. I'm mated to his brother.

God, why was that so hard to remember?

But that was because Knox's rejection of our bond, even though it hadn't been intentional, magnified the hurt from all rejections.

"You should rest," Bishop said, his tone a little too bright. "Especially since you can't shift out the rest of your injuries. Come down for breakfast whenever you're ready and I'll show you around town."

"You really don't have to do that," I said, my voice still breathy even as the cold grew stronger.

If I hadn't been mated to his brother, he would have kissed me.

If I hadn't been mated to his brother, I wouldn't have wanted to throw myself at a complete stranger.

"You should probably keep helping Whil find a way to break this bond," I said, my chest tightening. My soul didn't want to break the bond even though it was the right thing to do. I didn't know Knox and it wasn't as if we were fated mates or anything. He was just the first person to touch me after I managed to escape that monster.

Remember that. Just keep remembering that.

"She has an apprentice who'll help her," Bishop said. "Tomorrow, I'm all yours."

Oh, how I wish you were.

He strode back to the grand staircase and I hurried into my room, my face on fire.

Mated to his brother. Mated to his brother. God damned mated to his brother.

AUDREY

THE RICH SCENT OF WOOD SMOKE WRAPPED AROUND ME AND MY EYES fluttered open. I lay on a soft bed of... I wasn't quite sure what. It looked like moss but felt more like bedding. Above me, two moons, one white and one slightly smaller and pink, were framed by tree branches heavy with leaves, and I realized I was in the small sacred grove outside the castle.

Except I had no idea how I'd gotten there.

Last thing I remembered, I'd gone to bed after that awkward dinner with Bishop, Cyrus, and their betas.

Now I was in their sacred grove... wearing my simple, white transformation dress.

This had to be a dream.

Something moved at the edge of my vision and I sat up, my pulse racing. Given what had happened the other night, I wouldn't have been surprised if that monster haunted my nightmares for the rest of my life.

But instead of the red-skinned monster, it was Bishop who stepped out of the shadows and into the circle of moonlight.

Except he didn't look right. He looked angry and hard, not the warm, gentle man who'd talked to me in Whil's greenhouse library. His hair partially hid his face, hanging forward and not braided back at the sides, and his eyes were dark and edged with a dangerous wildness.

He wore the practical pants that looked a little like cargo pants that he'd been wearing when I'd been awake, although these were black, not brown, but wasn't wearing his shirt, giving me an eye-full of his honed, muscular torso... or at least how I imagined his torso to look since this was a dream.

The breeze shifted, bringing with it more of the wood smoke scent and not Bishop's clean, fresh-cut grass scent, and the yearning within me swelled, overwhelming the icy hollowness.

This wasn't Bishop. This was my mate. His brother. And because I hadn't seen him in human form, my psyche had turned him into a more dangerous version of Bishop.

"I don't want you," he said, his voice low, his power rolling through me as he took a step toward me, his body belying his words.

But instead of making me bow in submission like it should have, it heated my insides, filling me with a tremendous, aching yearning. "I didn't mean to bond with you."

"Did you mean to bond with the man you said the vows to?" he growled, suddenly sounding angry that I'd wanted to bond with someone else.

"I thought he was my fated mate." My throat tightened and my cheeks burned, even as my desire grew stronger. "I thought we were destined for each other."

The words sounded ridiculous. How could I have possibly thought Royce was my destined mate when my real mate was standing right in front of me.

Except that wasn't true, either. Knox wasn't my real mate. He was just the man unfortunate enough to be caught up in the magic of my mating vows.

"No." The wild danger radiating from him grew stronger. "He's not your mate. I am."

"You're just saying that because this is a dream. You don't want me." He'd just said so, and he'd also made that perfectly clear in

Whil's greenhouse library — if the constant aching cold of our rejected bond wasn't enough proof.

"No," he snarled. His canines extended and the look in his eyes turned ferocious, and even though he was still in his human form, I knew I wasn't talking to Knox the man anymore, but his wolf. "You're mine."

He closed the distance between us before I realized what was happening, grabbed a fistful of my hair, jerked my head back, and crashed his lips against mine in a savage, ravenous kiss.

The icy hollowness inside me shattered, and desperate overwhelming need roared into every cell in my body and heaved at something powerful and wild deep within me. I needed him close, closer, needed him in me, needed to feel the bond between us empowered and alive. The bond just needed a spark, an electric magical jolt to bring it fully to life.

I tangled my fingers in his hair, digging my nails into his scalp, and kissed him back, that wildness hidden deep within me taking over and answering his hunger with its own.

With a snarl, he shoved me back, pinning me against a tree with his large powerful body.

"You. Are. Mine," he growled into my mouth, the words ringing within me like the gong of the fake mating call. "Mine forever."

"Yes," the wild something within me moaned.

I clung to him as he tore open the front of my transformation dress and roughly palmed my breast, still kissing me as if he were drowning and I was the only source of air. I wasn't going to think about how this was all a dream and how the gong of the fated mating call was merely an echo of what I'd experienced for real.

I ached to be desired, loved, accepted, and in this dream, the man who I'd accidentally forced a mating bond on was willing to give me all those things.

He roughly plucked and pinched my nipples, the pain building a need that was already threatening to consume me. Aching heat flooded my core, and moisture oozed down the inside of my thighs.

"Mine." He released my breast, palmed my mound, and shoved two fingers up inside me without warning.

I gasped at the sudden invasion, but my inner muscles fluttered with the promise of a release and my next breath came out on a low, desperate moan. My hips rolled, my body knowing what it wanted, but he yanked his fingers out instead of satisfying me and brought them to his lips.

A low growl rumbled in his chest, and he inhaled deeply, taking in my scent. My breath hitched at the sexual hunger in his eyes, and it stalled altogether as he sucked one finger clean then the other.

"Who is your mate?" he demanded.

"You are," I breathed.

"Say my name." He shoved his fingers back inside me and pressed his thumb against my clit but held it there, not rubbing the sensitive nub like I needed.

I rolled my hips again, but he pushed back, pinning my rear to the tree, holding me captive his hand in my hair controlling my head and his fingers inside me controlling my pelvis.

"Say. My. Name," he snarled.

"Knox." He jerked his fingers out and back in, the force jolting the breath from my lungs.

My inner muscles rippled again and my body trembled. I had no idea where in my subconscious this was coming from for me to dream this. Maybe it was because I knew how to make myself come with my fingers combined with how angry he was. Maybe I'd just spent too long fantasizing about what sex would actually be like.

He jerked his fingers out again and shoved them back in, snapping my attention back to him.

"Who am I?" he demanded.

"Knox," I moaned. "My mate."

"That's right." His fingers moved out and in faster and faster, his thrusts powerful, violent.

I clung to him. It was the only thing I could do captured between his hands and trapped against the tree, but I didn't feel helpless or in danger, not like I would if I'd been cornered by Sterling. No, I felt powerful. The icy hollowness was gone and a sun blazed within me, its heat and light reaching into every crack, every extremity, every cell of my body. My soul was alive with power and desire and that wildness that had been hidden within me until Knox had brought it out with his kiss and touch.

He pounded into me until I was wound so tight, burning with so much need, that it exploded out of me in a shattering, screaming rush. My inner muscles clamped down on his fingers with an orgasm more powerful than any I'd experienced before, stars flashed through my vision, and his expression turned smug and satisfied.

"You belong to me, and I will make him submit and claim you," he— no *his wolf* said as the stars faded and darkness consumed the grove.

AUDREY

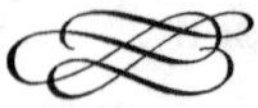

I woke thrumming with a need more powerful than what I'd experienced so far, but still drowning in the ice of my frozen mating bond and confused as hell until I remembered it had all just been a dream.

Knox hadn't ripped an explosive orgasm from my body and hadn't claimed me as his. And I certainly hadn't heard the fated mating call ring in my soul. I didn't even know if that was what Knox really looked like. Hell, I didn't even want the bond with someone who didn't want me.

I shoved the covers aside, the fabric brushing against my hyper-sensitive skin, put my dress on — because that was all I had to wear, and I wasn't going to tempt fate by trying to race across the hall naked — and hurried to the bathroom to warm up and relieve the pressure in my core with my own fingers. If I scrubbed really well afterward, no one would be able to scent my arousal and as long as I didn't think about the dream — or anything else for that matter — I wouldn't end up embarrassing myself today.

Who was I kidding? I'd already embarrassed myself in front of everyone last night. Most of the pack's betas knew I was desperate for sex even if they didn't know it was because of a mating bond. Why not just share that with the rest of the town? Hell, the betas hadn't been sworn to secrecy about me, so the town probably knew already.

Maybe I could convince Bishop to skip the town tour and just stay in. We could go back to Whil's, and I could keep them supplied in tea or something while they searched for a way to break the mating bond.

Except the odds of breaking the bond were slim, and if Knox and I didn't seal it — which with him despising me was the likely scenario — I was going to be horny for the rest of my life.

Which was something I was just going to have to figure out how to deal with.

Maybe instead of going to Whil's we could just stay in my room and alleviate the sexual compulsion from the bond. It had been a bad idea last night and it still was this morning, but I was going to scream if I didn't have an orgasm and the one in my dream clearly hadn't been enough.

Besides, Knox didn't want me, so he shouldn't have a problem with me sleeping with his brother.

Except the thought of Knox going to some other woman to deal with the desire from the mating bond made me want to storm out of the bathroom, find him, and yell at him... even before he'd done anything.

And really, my reasons for not sleeping with Bishop hadn't changed.

Jeez. Dealing with my situation by myself was the only safe option.

Steam from the shower misted the mirror, indicating it was warm enough, and I hopped inside.

The water hit my sensitive skin and my core trembled in anticipation of coming even before I'd done anything. The memory of Knox kissing me like his life depended on it, all his ferocious power focused on me, not to make me submit but to turn me on, flooded me.

He could have made me kneel before him but he hadn't. Of course, that was because it was just a dream. From the ferocity and anger that had roared through the bond when he'd told me I wasn't his mate, I knew if anything happened between us, he'd demand my complete submission. He'd probably even claim me with his teeth.

The trembling in my core grew at the thought and I let myself fall into the fantasy. He'd want my submission, but he wouldn't hurt me. I'd be able to trust him because he was my mate.

If he was here in the shower, he'd turn me to face the spray and take me from behind. He'd push his cock into me while he arched me back, a hand on my neck to hold me in place and show me he was in control and the other between my thighs rubbing my clit.

I turned to face the spray just like in my fantasy, letting the water beat against my neck and chest. The water splattered against my thrumming body, tightening already taut nipples. In my fantasy, with my chest pushed out, they'd grow even more sensitive. Tingles would rush through me every time I drew a breath that would push them deeper into the spray, and my breath would get faster and faster.

Knox would pound his length into me over and over again just like he'd pounded his fingers into me in my dream, twisting me tight until stars flashed behind my lids again.

I pushed a finger inside me and rubbed my thumb against my clit. His breath would rush over the back of my neck and cheek and as he came inside me, his wolf would take over, extend his canines, and bite into the muscle between my neck and shoulder.

My inner muscles spasmed at the thought and tossed me over the edge. The orgasm wasn't as mind-blowing as the one in my dream, but it still left me trembling and breathless and satisfied — which had been the whole point of the exercise.

The throbbing need receded, once more overwhelmed by the icy hollowness, and I finished washing with a mix of bittersweet emotions. Sure, I wasn't going to lose my mind if I didn't have sex, but the emptiness wasn't much better than the need, just less embarrassing, and a part of me feared sex would never live up to the fantasy, even with someone as handsome — and likely experienced — as Bishop.

I pushed that thought aside. Thinking about Bishop and sex was a bad idea, especially since the Knox of my fantasies had had Bishop's face.

I dressed, finger-combed my hair so it wasn't a complete disaster, and went to the kitchen.

Bishop was waiting for me just like he'd promised. He sat at the kitchen table reading a book with two other books open in front of him. When he saw me, he flashed a heart-stopping smile and thankfully didn't sniff or make a face or say anything about my perpetual state of heightened arousal.

A selection of meat and fruit and pastries sat on the counter, the platters half empty as if a few someones had already taken their breakfast and left, and I filled up a plate and sat in the chair across from him.

The door leading to the garden was still open, and I could see the morning sunlight in the greenery beyond and smell the mix of fragrant herbs and flowers on the breeze.

"You ready for the grand tour?" he asked.

"Absolutely." I didn't know what was going to happen with the mating bond. If we couldn't sever it, I didn't know if I wanted to stay in the same town as Knox. Of course, I also didn't know if the bond would let me leave Knox. But if we could sever the bond and I did survive, perhaps this could be my new pack.

Bishop was kind and friendly, and Cyrus, while not entirely friendly, didn't strike me as cruel — although I hadn't thought Royce was cruel, either. Their betas seemed to like and respect them, and I'd gotten a sense of genuine friendship among everyone at dinner last night. I was weak, and I might never be able to shift, but maybe they'd accept me like Bishop had said they would in Whil's cottage yesterday. Maybe there was a place where I belonged.

AUDREY

ONCE I'D FINISHED BREAKFAST, BISHOP LED ME BACK TO THE GRAND staircase and out the front doors into a wide, open courtyard. An intricate bricked driveway — that may not have been an actual driveway in this world since I had no idea if they had cars here — led from the gate at the far end to the main steps of the house. It curled around a fountain with two enormous wolves on either side of a woman pouring water from a large urn and was edged with well-maintained gardens. Beyond stood the tall stone wall I'd seen yesterday and the stone buildings clustered together.

"This is the alpha's residence," Bishop said, turning and gesturing to the castle.

I turned with him, taking in the impressive structure with its grand front entrance and two distinct wings. Somewhere behind the large building was the kitchen's back door, the herb garden, private grove, and Whil's cottage. And looming above it all, stood a snow-topped mountain range as impressive as the mountains in Oregon.

Then Bishop led me beyond the wall protecting the alpha's residence into Old Town which was a collection of old stone buildings crowded close together creating a warren of alleys and nooks and small hidden gardens clustered within another stone wall that was thicker and higher than the wall around the alpha's residence.

It would have been gloomy and claustrophobic if it wasn't for the myriad flower boxes on window ledges and balconies blooming with a cacophony of colors.

Beyond Old Town lay New Town and as we walked down the main street leading away from Old Town's gate it was like traveling forward through time. The farther we walked, the wider the road grew and the newer the buildings looked. The side streets also grew wider, more like the streets I was used to, and while stone was still the predominant construction material, the blocks grew smaller and more precise in size like bricks. The brickwork also grew more fanciful with decorative ornamentations and there was more variety in the architectural styles.

There were more people in the newer part of town going about their business like it was a normal town, and if I didn't pay too much attention to the fact that there weren't any cars but hand-drawn carts and bicycles instead, I could pretend I was in any town in my realm. They had indoor plumbing and lights that seemed to work like in my realm, but with the town on the edge of the mountain with various slopes and stairs and winding paths, motorized vehicles weren't practical so the fact that I didn't see any cars didn't mean there weren't any in this realm.

Just like Nova and Velora, many of the women on the street wore the same backless dress I did and some of the men wore wraps like Deacon, suggesting that whatever their job was, they shifted frequently. But there were also people, both men and women, wearing clothes like Cyrus and Bishop did: pants and loose shirt which was a good sign that I'd be able to find something that covered more of me.

We wandered down to a large market on the edge of town, which I could hear from a few blocks away before we'd even rounded the corner of what looked to be a low, long warehouse. The market was filled with people talking and laughing and shopping. They were predominantly wolf shifters but there were humans and other shifters — who I could tell were shifters from their essence but not what kind — along with a few people with lizard-like features with human-like essences.

The space was packed with permanent and temporary stalls, tents, and horse-drawn carts, creating maze-like pathways almost as narrow as the "streets" in Old Town, and my nose was assaulted by a dizzying array of scents from various foods and wood smoke to people and animals.

"You're lucky you showed up in the summer," Bishop said. "The market isn't nearly as fun in the winter."

"This is incredible." I stopped at a permanent vendor's stall. It was a good-sized shed with a garage-style door that was opened all the way, revealing bins and shelves packed with books.

"A woman after my own heart," Bishop said, flashing me another one of those smiles that made my pulse skip. "Do you like to read?"

"A little." I hadn't had a lot of time to read. Merrick and Sterling had kept me busy cooking and cleaning for them, and I hadn't had a lot of money, since my cooking and cleaning were considered payment for living with them and my father had died with very little money and no property.

I ran my fingers over the spines in the closest bin but was unable to read any of the titles. "But it doesn't look like I'm going to be reading anything here," I added.

"I could borrow some primers from the school and teach you," he offered.

"That's still going to take a while, and I'm pretty sure you have better things to do with your time." Of course, if this realm was going to be my new home — and given that Cyrus hadn't initially believed I was from a different realm, indicating it didn't look good that Whil would be able to open a portal and send me home — I was going to need to learn things and being literate could help me find a job in this pack that didn't involve housecleaning. Except—

"If the books aren't in English, how are you speaking English?" I asked. There hadn't even been a moment with Cyrus where he spoke a different language then realized I didn't understand and switched.

"We're not," Bishop replied. "Well, you probably are. I asked Whil about that yesterday since you seemed to understand us right away."

"Let me guess. It has something to do with magic," I replied.

"Pretty much," Bishop said. "According to Whil all portals to our realm, permanent and temporary ones like the one you came through, have a sort of communication magic on them that enspells whoever passes through so they understand the language of whatever realm they're entering. But it's only for speech, which is why you can't read anything."

"Well, that's convenient." I picked up a colorful child's picture book and admired the art but still couldn't guess what was written beside the pictures.

"Your realm, along with a few others, and our realm used to be closely connected. The greater beings in our realm used to be worshiped as gods in the other realms."

"Used to be?" I put the picture book back and searched for a book for even younger children, one that might be like the reading primer Bishop had mentioned just to see if I could figure anything out.

"They might still be," he said. "But they haven't left our realm in a thousand years. A sleeping curse infected all of them, and the leaders of the other realms sealed off all the portals afraid that the curse would travel and infect the other realms."

"But if the portals were sealed, how did I get here?" I put the book back and looked at Bishop. "And if this realm has a sleeping curse on it, why is everyone still awake?"

"We're not entirely sure how you got here, although Whil has a theory," Bishop replied as we wandered away from the book vendor and headed to the next vendor over, a large red tent with a swirling gold pattern on it. "And only the greater beings were affected by the curse. But the leaders in the other realms didn't know that at the time and now Whil has no way of telling them that it's safe to reopen the portals."

"So Whil has been unable to return to Faerie for a thousand years?" And given that I hadn't seen any other fae it was probably a good guess that there weren't other fae here, or fae she was close to.

Was she homesick? Would I become homesick even though I had no one to return to?

I didn't think so. Sure, I'd miss Mila, but she had a mate and was happy, and being here was a lot better than being there.

I drew in a deep breath, savoring all the competing scents. I still wasn't certain about Bishop and Cyrus, and I certainly wasn't certain about my unwanted mate, but I still felt freer than I ever had before.

With a skip in my step, I hurried to the red tent and reached to pull back the flap.

"Ah, Audrey," Bishop said, "You might want—"

I stepped through the flap and froze. It was filled with lingerie of all shapes and sizes and colors in silky fabrics and see-through fabric and—

Desire surged through me, making the young woman minding the tent sniff and give me a knowing smile.

"Not this one," I said, turning and trying to push Bishop back before he could enter, my face on fire.

"You sure?" he said, his eyes bright with mischief. "Every woman needs a few nice things to make her feel sexy."

"Feeling sexy isn't my problem." Or at least, feeling like I needed sex wasn't. "Besides, what would I do with them? I'm trying to get rid of a mate, not win one," I whispered, praying I was only loud enough for Bishop to hear.

"But not forever," he whispered back.

AUDREY

"You're safe here and you're allowed to make plans for the future," Bishop added, his voice soft and filled with a gentleness that made me want to burrow against him and never leave the comfort of his touch.

Instead, I pressed my palms against his chest to urge him to step back onto the street, but my thoughts stalled at the feel of all that powerful muscle hidden underneath his shirt then jumped to last night's dream and how I'd imagined what all that muscle had looked like and felt like and—

Bishop's wolf darkened his eyes and his nostrils flared, taking in my scent.

"I can't make plans. Not really," I forced out, my voice breathy. "There's almost no chance Whil will be able to break the mating bond and I'm certain lingerie won't change—" I glanced back at the shop attendant who was eagerly watching us. "It won't change *his* mind about me."

"So don't buy it for him." His gaze flickered to my lips as if he was thinking of kissing me and my need flared stronger. "Buy it for yourself. Let yourself feel beautiful."

I slid my hands up his chest, raised up on my toes, and tilted my head up in invitation. *Please kiss me.* Making myself come in the shower hadn't been nearly enough. Of course, having sex with Bishop wouldn't satisfy my need, either. The only one who could was Knox and he didn't want me.

The icy hollowness enveloped some of my desire, and my throat tightened with the grief of rejection that I didn't want but couldn't stop feeling because of the damned mating bond.

The desire in Bishop's eyes shifted to worry, as he clearly saw my change of thoughts. "However this works out, it will be okay. I'll keep you safe. I promise."

Except he couldn't promise that and there wasn't anything he or I or anyone could do about it.

So move on. Move forward. It's the only thing I can do.

I forced a smile and stepped back. "I'm pretty sure I asked for clothes that involved more material, not less."

His worry blossomed into a heart-stopping smile. "You're right. As my lady wishes."

We left the lingerie store and slowly wandered around the market, Bishop letting me explore everything at my own pace, not just the clothing stores. People smiled, waved, and chatted with him while I shopped, but I never felt like he was ignoring me. It was clear the pack loved him, just like it had been clear last night that the betas loved him and Cyrus, and a part of me was grateful he was drawing their attention away from me and my bruised face... after, of course, they all stared at me.

By late morning, Bishop carried two bags full of clothes and another with a practical pair of hiking boots.

It was too much. I could have gotten by with a shirt, a pair of pants, and the boots, but Bishop kept adding things when we went to pay. He even added a pink version of the dress I was wearing when he thought I wasn't looking even though I'd stressed practical clothes only.

A part of me heated at the idea that he wanted to see me in a dress again even though I'd already nixed the idea of lingerie. But just because I'd said no, didn't mean I could stop my mind from imagining the fantasy of him releasing the two simple ties and letting the silky fabric slide off my body.

Now I sat in a small park with benches, picnic tables, and a playground for the children while Bishop got us lunch.

Children ran around laughing and yelling one third fully clothed, another third completely naked, and the final third as wolf pups.

Their joy was infectious and I couldn't help smiling, but it was a bittersweet smile. If our pack hadn't paid that witch all those years ago to prevent us from shifting until we were eighteen this was what our playgrounds would have looked like. Shifters being themselves, free from the moment they were born. They wouldn't have been able to shift until at least five or six years old but they'd still have been connected with the wolf half of their soul from the moment they were born.

Two of the pups started wrestling and a woman at a picnic table called out to them, but they ignored her. Another woman nearby laughed and said something, and the first woman chuckled with her. Then the first woman stood, slipped out of her dress, shifted, and bounded over to them.

It was so natural it took me a moment to realize I hadn't been shocked at her being naked. She was a mom with her kids and was stopping a fight before it got serious. She'd just so happened to strip and shift to do it.

I turned away before my bittersweet joy at watching the kids play turned completely sour.

My childhood had been what it had been and I was what I was. I couldn't change it or me no matter what I wanted, and I wasn't going to let Knox's rejection of our mating bond make me feel sorry for myself about that.

I'd decided I was done with that in the lingerie tent, and I was going to stick with that decision.

Still, I wasn't sure I could keep watching the family and life I hadn't had so I let my gaze wander over the rest of the area instead of the playground.

The park sat at the edge of town on the far side of the market. A dozen large old trees delineated two of its sides from the rest of the market, but the third and fourth sides were wide open. The grass had been cut to the edge of the park but not beyond and was the only thing indicating where the park stopped and the rolling grassy foothills began.

Beyond stretched a breathtaking vista, and if I didn't look up at the ghosts of the two moons, I could almost pretend I was close to home in the mortal realm. Green and yellow grass speckled with flowers waved in a gentle breeze, white clouds scuttled across a brilliant blue sky, and the yellow sun warmed my skin.

One of the larger clouds drifted over the sun, and the wind gusted, making the grass ripple and undulate like water. The bigger movement accentuated a break in the ripple as if the grass were parting around something.

Probably a rock. We were in the foothills after all.

But the cloud scuttled away with another gust and the bright sunlight seemed to shine a spotlight on something black within the grass that wasn't a rock. Probably a shifter. Whoever it was wasn't big enough to be a full-sized wolf but could have been a kid or teen. He or she was probably honing their stalking skills, and while it seemed strange to me to see a youth hunting, just like the pups playing on the playground, it was probably common here.

A dozen feet away I caught glimpses of two more black shapes slinking through the grass together. They drew closer to the edge of the long stalks and I couldn't tell if they were practicing hunting as a pack or if the two of them were hunting the single wolf.

Then the solo wolf lifted his head and howled, revealing that he wasn't a wolf but a dog with a wide, square head and short black fur.

Dozens of howls responded and the two wolves— no dogs, the dogs that had been at the edge of the grass, raced into the park. They attacked a woman, wrenching her to the ground and killing her before I had time to call out.

The park erupted into chaos, people screaming and running, grabbing children and leaving their shopping and lunches.

More dogs barreled out from between the stalls and tents onto the street. Even though they looked like dogs, they attacked like big cats, pouncing and clawing as well as biting and tearing into people who weren't fast enough to defend themselves or flee. Men and women shifted, not bothering to undress, sacrificing their clothes to the magic that made them shifters, while others stayed human but grew claws.

A wolf lunged at another dog-creature coming out of the tall grass. It tried to get on top and bite the dog's neck or claw open its belly. But the wolf could barely catch it and when it did, it couldn't sink its teeth or claws into the dog's hide.

I scrambled from the picnic table, abandoning my new clothes, and raced into the market's maze-like streets away from the chaos.

The crowd jostled me, too many people trying to squeeze through the narrow space at the same time. Ahead of me, a man with a wailing toddler bumped a small girl, knocking her down, but didn't even glance at her. He probably didn't even know he'd run into her.

I grabbed her arm and hauled her to her feet. She gasped a thank you and we turned to keep going, but a desperate scream, somewhere ahead of us, stopped us in our tracks. The crowd heaved, people pushing and scrambling to change directions.

"This way," the girl said, yanking me back a few steps to a narrow space between two permanent sheds.

With her small stature, she easily slipped inside and quickly headed toward the band of sunlight on the other side. I hesitated for a second. I was bigger than her and it was going to be a tight fit. I didn't want to risk getting stuck... except if it was a tight fit for me, it would be an impossible fit for the dogs.

Oh, this is a bad idea.

I shoved myself inside, needing to exhale and take little gasping breaths to fit. The girl had already vanished out the other end and all that lay ahead of me was the narrow strip of sunlight.

Behind me, I heard the crowd race past, then the dogs. Someone screamed, the sound desperate and filled with agony, and the breeze gusted past me filled with the metallic tang of blood and something dark and foul that could only have been from the dogs.

I shoved my way forward, the rough wooden walls pinning me in, catching on my dress and scratching my bare skin. My heart pounded and fear twisted my gut into a frozen knot. I couldn't turn my head to look behind me and had no way of knowing if any of the dogs had noticed me.

Then wild, ferocious barking roared behind me followed by heavy violent banging that shook the sheds.

My heart jerked into overdrive. At least one of the dogs had noticed me and was trying to break through the sheds.

I strained to shuffle faster, desperate to get to the ever-growing band of light at the end.

The dog howled and snarled and the sheds shuddered again. Wood cracked and crunched, the sound shooting ice through me and the foul scent swept around me as hot breath hit my bare arm.

Oh, God. It was right behind me and I couldn't even turn to face it... and I had no idea if not being able to see my death coming was the better option or not.

The end of the sheds drew closer as it snarled and crashed into the sheds again. More wood crunched and something wet grazed my elbow.

Shit shit shit.

I heaved myself sideways in a desperate, awkward dive for safety and toppled out the other side, crashing onto the cobbled street. The dog smashed through the rest of the sheds and bounded toward me, and I scrambled to my feet, but there was no way I'd be able to outrun the thing.

Then two gray wolves leaped on it, clawing and biting and trying to pin it to the ground.

Run, a male voice barked. It sounded a lot like Finn and was backed with a wave of power that had me racing away from them and the heart of the market before I fully knew what I was doing.

The foul smell from the dogs and the cloying reek of blood choked me. All around me people screamed, children wailed, dogs barked, and wolves howled. A part of me howled at the fact that running was the only thing I could do. I couldn't shift and even if I could, I didn't know how to fight. I didn't even know if it was possible for a wolf to take down one of the dog-monsters.

I raced around a corner into a small, recessed area and stumbled to a halt. A dog had cornered a group of children and — from the two medium-sized bodies laying a few feet away from the trembling group — had already killed two of them.

A scrawny boy, probably about twelve, held a wailing toddler, while two little girls cowered behind him, one sobbing, the other deathly pale and silent. A slightly larger boy who looked to be about the same age as the other one stood in front of them, snarling at the dog with his canines and claws extended.

There were only two ways out of the area, the narrow path I'd run out of and a wider path big enough for the shattered vegetable cart lying a few feet away. But neither was an option. The dog had the kids backed into a corner between two shallow vendor stalls — also filled with produce and nothing that could be used as an effective weapon — and the stalls stood in front of a tall wall that didn't have any windows.

The only way the kids were going to get away was if something distracted the dog, and with no one else around, that something had to be me. No way was I going to leave these children to their fate, no matter how stupid it was to draw the dog's attention.

AUDREY

"Hey!" I yelled at the dog, keeping close to the path behind me so I could make a run for it and have as much of a head start as possible.

The dog swung its large, blocky head at me and snarled, and the sobbing girl leaped away from the group in the direction of the larger opening. But the dog jerked his head back to them and lunged at the girl.

The boy defending them grabbed her arm and shoved her behind him as he dove to meet the dog's attack. My pulse stalled. It was a suicidal move, and I didn't need my imagination to know the boy was going to be ripped to shreds like the two other kids already on the ground.

I grabbed a piece of the broken cart roughly the size of a baseball bat and barreled at the dog, screaming.

The creature batted the boy aside, its claws tearing into his back, and leaped at me.

Oh fuck oh fuck oh fuck.

I heaved to the side, somehow avoiding its claws, and bashed the dog over the head. The strike didn't even make it hesitate. With a roar, it lunged at me and I ran, praying it would follow.

It did but caught up quickly and rammed its blocky head into me, shoving me forward. I hit the ground, losing my makeshift club, caught a glimpse of darkness out of the corner of my eye, and threw myself to the side.

The dog's claws tore through my dress and into the cobblestones, and I rolled away, narrowly avoiding another swipe.

My elbow hit my club and I grabbed it and swung with all my might. It broke over the dog's head, stunning it long enough for me to scramble to my feet and yell at the kids.

"Run!" I screamed at them. A pressure of something thud-thudded in my chest and all of the kids bolted.

The dog turned to go after them, and I threw myself at it, ramming my shoulder against its side and only managing to redirect its attention.

Yep, I was going to die.

At least I was going to do it saving a bunch of kids and not being eaten by a monster to give the assholes Sterling and Royce more power.

The dog snapped at me, its teeth grazing my arm, and I stumbled back, lost my balance, and fell.

Thankfully the kids ran. The pale-faced girl tripped and the bigger of the two boys picked her up and slung her over his shoulder with his supernatural strength. His dark gaze met mine for a second, his expression filled with fear, but he knew what he had to do, and that wasn't to save me. It was to save the younger kids.

The dog snapped and swiped at me and I rolled out of the way again. A flicker of pain grazed across my back and I tried to scramble to my feet, but the dog rammed me with its head and knocked me back down right into the corner the kids had been in.

Shit.

With a snarl, the dog dove in to bite me, but a huge black wolf bounded out of nowhere and tackled it.

They rolled across the blood-slicked cobblestone, biting and clawing and snarling, their bodies twisting and heaving in a violent struggle.

I staggered to my feet, knowing I needed to get the hell out of there. If the wolf didn't win, I was as good as dead.

But before I could run, the wolf snapped its teeth on the dog's throat and tore open its flesh.

The dog collapsed, its blood gushing around it and the wolf, and I clutched the edge of the stall beside me, my pulse still pounding and my body trembling.

"Thank God," I gasped. *Oh, thank God.*

The wolf raised his head, capturing me with piercing, black eyes flecked with green, and everything within me froze.

Knox.

I didn't know his wolf form well enough to recognize him, but I knew in my soul the wolf in front of me was Knox.

Knox had saved me.

My whole being strained toward him, my soul aching with the bond he refused to accept.

Blood dripped from his snout as he stared at me, no growling, no angry words, nothing. It was like everything, all thought and sound, even the air, had been sucked from around us and we were suspended in this moment.

Him and me.

Bound together with a bond neither of us wanted. Forever. Trapped by our circumstances.

The icy hollowness inside me remained cold, his rejection still strong, but it didn't grow, didn't threaten to bring me to my knees with emotions I didn't want and couldn't control.

"What the fuck!" Cyrus roared from down the wider road, shattering the moment.

The world rushed back to life around me, people yelling, but not screaming, the foul reek of the dogs and the metallic bite of blood, but also the seductive wood smoke scent that my soul insisted belonged to me.

Knox raced away, neither brother acknowledging the other — although they could have communicated telepathically and just not included me in the conversation — and Cyrus stormed toward me.

He was breathtaking and terrifying and completely naked, revealing every powerful, dangerous inch of his body. His eyes were black with his wolf, his canines and claws extended, and blood streaked across his chest indicating that while he'd fought in wolf form — since he was naked — he'd also just been fighting in his human form, too.

Unable to stop myself, my gaze followed the streak of blood on his chest down to his partially erect cock, and my breath stalled. He was bigger than I expected, certainly bigger than the glimpse I'd gotten of Sterling all those years ago.

The throbbing need inside me surged, and all I could think about was how would it feel to have all that dangerous power holding me, pushing into me, driving me crazy.

"Don't you ever pick a fight with a grimalkin again." His power rolled off him in a great wave with his fury.

I jerked my attention up and met his glare while clinging to the edge of the vegetable stall to keep standing. I would *not* submit to him. Not when I knew what I'd done was right.

"I don't care how noble the cause or how many children you think you can save. You'll never do that again."

"You're not my alpha," I snarled back, even though the smart thing would be to submit and keep my mouth shut. But I'd just run for my life again and had been helpless *again.* I was furious to the point of tears that I was useless, that the only thing I was good for was being a sacrifice, even if this time it had been my choice. There was more to me than that. There had to be.

"You're mated to my brother," he growled. "That makes me your alpha and I'm giving you a direct order. Do I need to make you submit to acknowledge it?"

More power rolled off him and I clutched the stall, refusing to give in. "I wasn't going to let that— that whatever it was kill them." And now that I thought about it, that dog, or rather, grimalkin, could have easily killed them. It had played with them first, picking them off one at a time and building up their fear, and would have continued to do so if I hadn't stepped in.

"It almost killed you," he said as he stepped close, using his size to intimidate me — and with all his muscle and towering above me, he sure as hell was intimidating. He trembled, a low, dangerous growl rumbling in his chest, and anger blazed in his eyes along with— was that fear? "Your death hurts my brother."

It was fear. Just not fear for me.

"My death will solve his problem." I strained my neck to maintain eye contact in a direct challenge. I didn't care if he punished me over this. I'd been punished for everything else. This at least was worth it. "I will *never* abandon a child."

If I could help it, no child would ever suffer like I had. Those kids had needed someone to protect them and I was there. It was that simple. It didn't matter if I could have won the fight or not. Someone had needed to do something.

Something plopped on the ground by my foot, the sound wet and heavy, and Cyrus stepped back and looked down, breaking eye contact first and drawing my attention down as well.

I stood in a small puddle of blood. Of course I was. I was probably covered in blood with all the rolling around I'd done fighting the grimalkin. Hell, who was I kidding? I'd been running for my life there hadn't been any fighting involved.

But there was something else important about the pool at my feet...

Except with the adrenaline rushing from my body, I couldn't make my mind focus enough to figure it out.

There was blood all over the area, pools by the bodies of the two dead kids and by the dead grimalkin, but here...?

"Fuck," Cyrus snarled and he jerked forward as my legs gave out and the world went black.

CYRUS

I caught Audrey as she passed out, hefted her into my arms, and marched down the street to where Nova had set up her medical team.

Damn this woman.

I'd seen the kids run past and Audrey fighting the grimalkin and knew exactly what had happened since I already knew she knew how to run away. She'd chosen to stay and sacrifice herself to distract the grimalkin so the kids could escape.

And if it hadn't been the stupidest thing she could have possibly done, I would have been thrilled to learn that Knox's unwanted mate was willing to risk her life to save children.

But she'd known she hadn't stood a chance and knew that breaking the bond by dying could break Knox's spirit, and she'd made the choice anyway. And while she had no idea that Knox could go feral if their bond suddenly shattered, it still made me furious that she'd choose suicide by grimalkin to solve her problems... even if it was to save children.

Fuck.

Knox would have made the same choice without giving it a second thought.

So would I or Bishop.

And as much as I really didn't want to admit it, the glimpse I'd gotten from her before Knox had leaped in and killed the grimalkin, had been breathtaking. Even with her dress torn and her face bruised and body scratched, she'd been stunning.

She'd radiated a determination and ferociousness that told me exactly how she'd survived the attack that had left her almost dead in Darkweald.

I had no doubt that there was a wolf inside her. I just didn't know how to break her curse and let it out. Even if that wolf wasn't powerful, she was going to be magnificent. She'd be a fierce mother and when she found her confidence, like I'd seen tiny glimpses of at dinner last night, she'd be a dazzling mate.

Knox was a fucking moron for not giving her a chance.

And now she was in my arms with her blood oozing down my bare chest while my partial hard-on from just holding her was getting harder by the second, despite my worry about how much blood she was losing.

I was never going to hear the end of it.

There was no way Nova wouldn't notice I was turned on and she'd jump to the correct conclusion that Audrey was the cause.

Nova's team was in the large square at the edge of the market by the main road, a wide open space with a fountain that allowed for easy access to the hospital for the most seriously injured, as well as a place to treat those not as injured or who couldn't be moved without first aid first.

Doctors, nurses, and medics rushed to save lives, and civilians helped out by cleaning minor scrapes and applying pressure to more serious injuries until someone could help. Nova stood at the front of the chaos doing triage and directing people to various sides of the square.

It always shocked me a little to see her so serious, even though we'd grown up together in the alpha's residence, and I knew she was an exceptional doctor and leader. To me, she'd always be the bratty little almost-sister who used to leave frogs in my bed or get up in the middle of the night and change my alarm clock so I'd be late for school.

She turned and saw me holding a bleeding Audrey and sporting a raging hard-on and rushed down the street to meet us.

"How bad?" she asked all business, but I knew the second Audrey was safe and Nova had time to catch her breath she was going to bring up the whole mate conversation that she'd brought up at dinner.

"I didn't get a chance to get a good look, but we have to treat it like it's serious."

Her lips twitched.

Here it came.

Except her attention dipped to Audrey's face and her still obvious bruises and serious-Nova returned. "Why didn't she shift before bed like I told her to?"

"Because she can't," I said. It wasn't my place to share that particular detail, but Nova needed to know to treat her properly. "I don't know if she even heals like a shifter. You have to treat her like she's human."

"Are you sure?" she asked, hurrying us to the righthand side of the square where there were more people and supplies, not to mention more people scrambling to save lives.

"Whil has already confirmed it."

"Well, shit. Practically no essence and can't even shift." She caught the attention of a nearby medic and indicated he needed to take over triage then grabbed a blanket from a cart of blankets and set it on the ground near a packed medic's bag and a lineup of supplies ready to be used.

I laid Audrey facedown, her cheek on the blanket, and knelt beside her, concern finally weakening my hard-on. Blood smeared her back, oozing from four gashes, and trickled down her ribs. She was going to have more scars to add to the still bright red scars from all the wounds she had when we found her.

"I hate to say it, because she was really sweet at dinner last night," Nova said, pulling on a pair of gloves and laying two thick pieces of gauze on half of Audrey's wound, "but you can't take her as your mate. No one will accept her as an alpha."

She directed my hands to the gauze and I applied pressure. "I'm not interested in mating her."

Nova shot my cock a quick look, quirked an eyebrow then grabbed a bottle of saline and went to work. "I've never seen you react this way to a woman."

Which was true and scared the shit out of me. If it had been any other woman, I would have already handed her over to someone else and sought out Bishop, Finn, and Deacon to deal with this attack, but I hadn't. I'd personally carried her to Nova. And while I could lie and say I'd needed to be there in person to tell Nova that Audrey couldn't shift, I could have easily passed that information on to whoever I'd handed her off to and Nova knew that.

I could lie to myself and say I was protecting Knox, but that wasn't entirely true. There was something about Audrey, something that made me angry and protective and on-edge in a way I'd never been before.

Except there was still a chance we couldn't trust her and Knox was potentially stuck with her for the rest of his life and without a doubt, Bishop was sweet on her.

For the sake of the pack, I had to keep my head on straight.

But seeing her fight that grimalkin along with feeling her resist my power while refusing to break eye contact and submit to tell me she'd always sacrifice herself to protect children had made my wolf sit up and take notice in a way he'd never noticed another female before and—

Head on straight, for fuck's sake.

"She's been through hell and she's alone here, Nova," I ground out, as Nova put two new pieces of gauze on the wounds she just cleaned and redirected my hands.

And Audrey's hell had been worse than I'd imagined. After dinner, Bishop had joined me in my office and filled me in on what he'd learned about Audrey while they were at Whil's. She'd been told her whole life she was worthless because her essence was so weak and she'd been afraid for a long time, which Bishop assumed meant she'd been abused when she was younger.

The fact that she'd fought that grimalkin to save those kids and then yelled at me about never abandoning a child just added to Bishop's assumption about how she'd grown up.

"She needs people on her side," I finished. "That's it."

Now it was Nova's turn to roll her eyes at me. "Sure it is."

"There are more important things to worry about right now."

"Yes, and you being attracted to her is a problem," Nova said.

Fuck, I need to get out of this conversation without making Nova even more suspicious.

"I'm attracted to a lot of women," I huffed, trying to sound indifferent.

But my words only made Nova narrow her eyes at me, reminding me that I was a fucking idiot if I was going to get anything past her.

It was like I was eight again thinking I could lie to her and she'd buy it. She'd never bought it and I never learned because a part of me wanted her to call me out on it, needed her to. She, like Bishop and Knox, kept me honest with myself.

"Bishop is attracted to anything with a uterus. You're not," she said, cracking the seal on an ampule of healing elixir and dribbling the liquid into Audrey's mouth. "It sucks in a lot of ways. But you have to do what's right for the pack."

"I'm not the alpha's only son," I growled. I hated that Nova was right, hated that whether I wanted Audrey to be my mate or not, I didn't have a choice.

"Knox will never accept leading the pack and Bishop would need one hell of a woman to make the hard decisions and demand submission when necessary. That or share the alpha mating with another man or woman," she said, motioning to Harris, her second-in-command, to come over. "And we both know the only people he'd share a mate with is you and Knox."

Harris handed a bag of supplies to someone else and hurried to Nova's side.

"Stitch her up," she ordered as she stood and peeled off her gloves. "It's not as bad as it looks but with her essence so weak, I don't want to take any chances."

"Not bad? She's unconscious." And I was painted in too much blood, not to mention the gauze beneath my hands was red and wet.

"She passed out because she overexerted herself and is still recovering from her previous injuries." Nova's expression softened.

Yeah, she could see right through me. I'd spent a dinner with Audrey, that was it, and I was already more attracted to her than any other woman in the pack. What a fucking mess.

Another medic came up beside me and took over applying pressure to her wounds, and I forced myself to move away from her.

She wasn't mine. She was Knox's or maybe Bishop's if the bond could be broken, and she was going to be fine. I had more important things to worry about, like figuring out how those grimalkins got so close to town and why there were so many of them.

AUDREY

Once again, I was enveloped in the rich, comforting scent of wood smoke and my eyes fluttered open to see Knox, or rather dream-Knox, storm toward me from the shadows and into the moonlight bathing the sacred grove beside the alpha's castle.

Power rolled off him, igniting my desire instead of demanding submission just like the last time I'd had this dream, and my core clenched in anticipation. It didn't matter that he looked furious, ready to tear me apart. I burned for him, for all that ferocity pounding into me... even if this was just a dream.

"You fought that grimalkin," he snarled.

Swell. Dream-Knox was going to yell at me like Cyrus had.

I started to rise. No way was I going to face him sitting on the ground, but he pounced on me, capturing my face between his large hands and kissing me with the same wild passion as before.

He pushed me back to my knees, grabbed my hair, and deepened the kiss. His tongue invaded my mouth, possessing me, stealing my breath, and making the need from our mating bond turn to molten desire between my thighs.

"You fought that grimalkin," he growled into my mouth. "I knew you were a fighter." He pulled back just enough for his dark wolf's eyes to capture me, his gaze boring into me as if he could see my soul—

No, my wolf. It was as if he could see my wolf.

"I knew the second your soul reached into mine you were my mate. Determined, ferocious, powerful."

A flicker of ice from human-Knox's rejection sliced into my need, reminding me that this wasn't real. "I'm not powerful. I'm—"

"You're a fucking goddess," he said. "You just need to wake up."

But if I woke, this dream would end and I didn't want it to end.

"I *will* make him see the truth," Knox's wolf said. "You're mine. You've always been mine and you'll always be mine."

The gong of a fated mating call reverberated through me, just like in the dream last night, and I tangled my fingers in his hair and smashed my lips against his. I wanted to believe that mate bonding with him hadn't been a mistake, that it had been fate, and he was as much mine as I was his.

And for this dream, he was.

The wild thing inside me, my dream-wolf waiting to be woken, flooded my veins, igniting the cells in my body. Power rolled off me, crashing against Knox's, shooting sparks around us. It *thu-thudded* in my heart, and another resounding gong boomed, ringing in my ears, my body, my soul.

"Mine." His grip in my hair tightened and he slipped his hand beneath my skirt and shoved two fingers into my soaking wet core.

I gasped and he pushed his tongue deeper into my mouth, wild, hungry, unable to get enough. His need sang through our bond as aching and desperate as mine, connecting us in a way that should have terrified me, but didn't because this was a dream.

Except there was also a painful edge to his need, a tremendous fear from human-Knox that wolf-Knox was determined to conquer.

He pounded his fingers into me while his lips on my mouth and his hand in my hair held me captive unable to do anything but submit to the pleasure. The impacts jolted the breath from my lungs and shot snaps of hot-white need through me that added to my desire slicking his fingers.

"Who do you belong to?" he snarled.

"You," I gasped.

"Who?" He ground his thumb against my clit and the snaps turned into a blazing, twisting inferno.

"You, Knox," I moaned as the gong sounded again. It boomed through every cell of my body and erupted in my core. My muscles clenched tight around his fingers, but he kept pounding, drawing the orgasm out into ragged, shuddering pleasure.

Stars flashed across my vision again and my breath came in short sharp gasps. I sagged in his arms, but he didn't give me time to recover. He flipped me over, grabbed my hips, and pushed his thick cock into my entrance.

A long, ragged groan escaped my lips, the sensation of him filling me, stretching me, overloading my senses.

In the back of my mind, I knew it would feel different when I did this for real... although maybe not. I was so wet, so boneless from my first orgasm, that I might be able to take him without pain.

"You," he said, his voice low and dangerous, making my core flutter as if I hadn't just come. "You are my goddess."

He withdrew and pushed back in, again and again, pulling my hips back to meet his thrusts, our skin slapping together, our breaths bursting from our bodies with each ferocious, delicious impact.

Pleasure spun me tighter and tighter and I couldn't catch my breath or get my bearings. There was only Knox and his cock hitting an amazing spot inside me and our bond blazing with heat and light and power around my heart.

With a snarl, he grabbed my throat and urged me to sit up, capturing me against his powerful, muscular chest while his other hand went to my clit, his fingers hitting the sensitive nub and shooting another small orgasm through me.

"Oh, God," I said, my body shuddering at his savage, mind-blowing assault.

"More," he growled, his fingers furiously rubbing my clit, taking that small orgasm and exploding it into spinning, screaming, shattering release.

More stars— no, fireworks tore through me as Knox clamped his canines in my shoulder and came. His cock swelled and his hot cum surged inside me.

He clung to me, buried to the hilt, his tense body wrapped around me and his teeth in my flesh.

Aftershocks rippled through me, over and over again, and I sagged into his embrace, boneless and overflowing with the most amazing sensation.

His canines slowly shrank back to human-size, but he kept his lips pressed against my shoulder.

"I need you, Audrey," he murmured, his lips brushing my skin and sending a teasing whisper of an aftershock rushing through me. "*He* needs you."

I tried to open my mouth to ask what he meant, but my eyes slid shut and when I reopened them, I was lying face down in my bed in the alpha's residence.

My body throbbed with unsatisfied need because I hadn't just had the most amazing sex of my life, I'd only dreamed it. That, and my back hurt a bit.

Right. Cyrus had yelled at me, there'd been blood, my blood, and then I—

I guess I passed out. Mid-yelling.

Swell.

I turned my head to see if he was sitting in the chair glaring at me again, the movement ratcheting up my need, making me hyper-aware of the fact that I was naked, and that heat and moisture pooled slick between my thighs. It would just be my luck that he'd want to continue his reprimand the second I regained consciousness, and that would probably just turn me on more.

The image of him completely naked, his large, powerful body on full display as he stormed toward me, flooded my mind's eye.

My inner muscles clenched and a low, needy moan, escaped my lips.

I squeezed my eyes shut fighting to regain some control over my body. *Please don't be in the chair. Don't be in the chair.*

I wasn't going to survive if he was. I'd beg him to have sex with me, but he'd probably just glare at me, which would turn me on even more because I was an idiot like that.

Fuck. I needed to get a hold of myself.

I cracked my eyes open, but thankfully the chair was piled with the clothes Bishop had bought me and not Cyrus, saving me the embarrassment of throwing myself at him and ripping his clothes off.

Now to just spend the rest of my day... my life like this. Because my state of near-constant arousal wasn't natural.

Maybe I should have sex with Bishop. Just to take the edge off. He was still the best choice between him and Cyrus, but all the reasons for not sleeping with him were still there.

Which left me to deal with my desires myself, like always.

I turned to push the blanket aside to get up and go to the shower, but just that little movement sent another, more powerful tremor rushing through me. Another low needy moan fell from my lips and I collapsed back on the bed, already panting with need.

Embarrassment burned my cheeks, and I pushed my face into my pillow, trying to stifle the sound. The bathroom was just across the hall, but if anyone was waiting for me outside my door, they were going to know right away that I needed an orgasm, and they wouldn't even have to smell my arousal to know that.

If it was anyone other than Bishop or Cyrus they'd all think I was at the height of my first heat. And if it *was* Bishop or Cyrus... I didn't know if I'd be able to control myself.

The only way around this was to try and take the edge off my need so I could get into the bathroom and finish myself off properly.

I rolled onto my back, but not even the sting of lying on my injuries cut through my sex-induced haze. With a groan, I dipped a finger through my soaking wet folds and slid it over my clit. Just a quick one. That was all I needed. But the instant I touched myself, I melted into my touch and my fantasy turned into my dream... and to a very naked Cyrus.

BISHOP

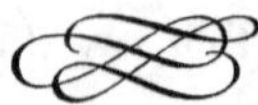

I pressed my back to the hall wall beside the door to Audrey's bedroom and squeezed my eyes shut, my cock so hard it hurt. Her arousal flooded my senses, and it took everything within me to stay on this side of her door.

Whil had discovered something about the mating bond, and I'd come to check to see if Audrey was finally awake so we could find out what. Except when I'd reached to open her door, she'd cried out in pleasure.

The sound had shot straight to my balls and turned me instantly hard, and I'd heaved myself against the wall to stop from rushing in to see what was going on, who she was having sex with.

But as I stood there, sucking in breath after breath that did nothing to ease the need thrumming through me because the air was rich with her scent, I realized no one was in the room. There were no other scents and the only sounds inside were her breaths and soft little mewls.

What was she doing—?

My cock strained against my fly.

Fuck me. I knew *exactly* what she was doing. She was getting herself off.

Relieving the pressure from the mating bond, more like it.

I knew it was strong. I could feel the bond in Knox even though he'd mostly blocked our twin bond. It urged him to claim her, but I hadn't realized it was so strong that Audrey had become desperate. She and Knox had only been mated for a few days, and while yeah, she could just be giving herself a little something because she wanted to, the mewls coming through the door were too desperate and her breath was too fast for something casual.

You could help her with that, my wolf rumbled inside me as he reached for the doorknob.

No. I jerked my hand away. Knox and I had shared a few women before and while matings with more than two people were uncommon in our pack, it wasn't frowned upon like in other packs or cultures, but I had no idea how the mating bond would affect him. Especially with him so determined to fight it.

If we couldn't break it, he and Audrey were going to end up crashing together, and I feared anyone caught in the middle, even me, was going to get torn apart.

Afterward... yeah, they might consider adding another mate to their bond, but not before.

And while I knew I didn't need to put my cock in her to make her come, I didn't know if I'd be able to resist the temptation.

My wolf growled, heaving inside me trying to take over.

He certainly wouldn't be able to resist.

And not just because her arousal had been driving both of us crazy for two days now, but because we liked her. She resonated with something inside us. I wasn't sure what. Watching her cry in Whil's library, her body trembling with the fear that she'd been living with her whole life, had made my protective urges go into overdrive, and then I'd been unable to stop touching her during dinner. I *needed* to comfort her soul almost as much as I needed to comfort Knox's.

But Knox was avoiding everyone and pushing the issue with him that he needed physical contact to steady his soul would only make him retreat more, so I'd tried to steady Audrey's soul — and in turn my own.

Except I hadn't gotten steadier. I'd dreamed of her the last two nights... well, her and Knox. I'd watched them crash together, their passion wild and unstoppable. My wolf had rumbled his desire but strangely had been content to watch. Somehow, despite it being a dream and my fantasy, the dream-wolf-me knew Knox needed Audrey more than I did and that my time would come.

Last night's dream had been so hot I was surprised I hadn't come while I was sleeping. Knox had claimed her, dominating her with his lips and hands and cock, making her scream with pleasure until she was trembling and sated and the bond between them radiated brilliant golden light.

I'd wanted so badly to join them, to claim her as well, but my wolf held me back, saying over and over again that it wasn't time.

My subconscious didn't seem to care that I didn't know her. It had already decided it had seen enough and wanted her. And Knox bonding to her only made it better.

She released a loud shuddering moan, the sound shooting straight to my cock, and the scent of her arousal grew thicker. She'd come and from the sound of it hard, and all I could think about were my dreams and how my dream-wolf knew my turn to push into her hot wet sheath would come soon.

The pressure inside me exploded, shattering my control, and my cock swelled.

Fuck. I was going to make a mess in my pants then have to do the walk of shame through the house back to my room to change if I didn't do something quick.

I leaped into the bathroom, undid my pants, and jerked out my cock. My cum erupted from me before I'd fully closed the door, spurting onto the bathroom floor, the force of my release bringing me to my knees.

Oh, fuck.

My wolf snarled, his essence surging, and I struggled to control him.

Now is the time, he said as if he were my dream-wolf.

But reality and dreams were two different things and as much as I wanted to add Audrey to my bond with Knox, for the three of us to mate in all the ways possible, that didn't mean that was what Knox or Audrey wanted. And *they* were the ones trapped in the mating bond.

But my wolf didn't give a fuck about respecting Knox's bond or how complicated the situation actually was. He wanted to storm across the hall, make her come again and again until she was drunk with pleasure and I was once again ready to drive my cock into her warmth.

Maybe Whil's news was that she'd found a way to transfer the bond to me like I'd suggested.

More cum spurted onto the floor.

Fuck, this was the orgasm that just wouldn't end and it pissed my wolf off to no end that I was wasting it on the floor and not inside Audrey.

Which was a whole other level of fucked up. He'd never wanted pups before, never, until this moment, cared who we slept with. We'd enjoyed the chase, the flirting, the fucking, but that was it.

It had to be the mating bond with Knox influencing my wolf and our most primal instincts despite him trying to block our connection. The feelings were too sudden. They had to be his— or rather his wolf's feelings for Audrey. His wolf had wanted to accept the mating bond when it had first formed and Knox had fought him and won... but how long would that last?

If my dreams were prophetic in any way — which they weren't — he wouldn't last long.

I stared at the puddle of cum on the floor in front of me, my cock still semi-hard in my hand even though I'd just blown my load and then some.

I really hoped Whil had good news about the bond, either breaking it or transferring it to me. Because if it was anything else, I wasn't sure how long *I'd* be able to resist her. I didn't want to have sex with her if my feelings weren't real. It didn't matter that I'd had casual relationships and one night stands before, my wolf had decided that Audrey was different.

AUDREY

AFTER THREE POWERFUL ORGASMS, THE ICY HOLLOWNESS OF KNOX'S rejection was finally stronger than the thrumming compulsion from the mating bond and I felt almost normal getting out of bed and putting on one of the slip-off dresses so I could go to the bathroom and take a shower.

Bishop stood in the hall, leaning against the wall beside the bathroom door. His expression was hungry and his wolf-darkened eyes captured my attention the second I opened the door. He took a deep sniff, making my pulse trip with renewed desire and my cheeks heat with embarrassment.

"I can't help it," I murmured, wrenching my gaze to the floor between our feet. "Maybe I am going into heat."

God, wouldn't that just be my luck? But that would explain why it wasn't just Knox I wanted.

"Have you had a heat before?" Bishop asked, his voice soft, low, caressing my senses like silk across my hyper-sensitive skin. "Do you know what it feels like?"

"Women in my pack don't have one until they have a wolf form." I clung to the doorknob, frozen in the doorway, my mind desperate to hide in the bathroom or back in my room, but my soul aching to grab Bishop by the shirt and drag him in with me.

"The bond might have set it off. Whil might be able to tell you." He took a large step away from me and the bathroom door. "She also has news about the bond."

My gaze jerked back up to his. "Can she break it?"

"I don't know." He swallowed hard and his eyes returned to their honey-brown color, his wolf retreating back inside him. "She can wait until you've had a shower and we've gotten you something to eat."

"Right." I hurried the few steps across the hall to the bathroom before I gave in to my desire to grab Bishop. But the second I opened the door, his fresh-cut grass scent swept around me, along with something deeper, richer, that made me instantly think of sex, and my desire overwhelmed the icy hollowness again.

"Oh shit," he hissed, freezing me in place in the doorway and making my pulse leap. "Your bandages. I should help you with them."

He cleared his throat and drew up close, his body heat and power rolling over me. I clung to the doorframe, determined to not move or look at him or anything other than stand there and let him help me.

He quickly tugged off whatever had been taped to my back then retreated down the hall, and I hurried into the bathroom and closed the door, escaping from him.

Except I hadn't escaped from his intoxicating scent and now I was trapped in the bathroom with it, aching as if I hadn't just come — three times!

Oh, God.

I really hoped Whil had figured out how to break the mating bond or had a potion or spell or something that could deal with this insatiable need for sex.

I powered through a cold shower, not even bothering to turn the hot water on and not caring how my back stung, toweled myself off, then had to retreat past Bishop back to my room for a change of clothes.

When I stepped back into the hall fully dressed, Bishop's wolf was hidden deep within him and he looked like the friendly guy I'd first met. We went to the kitchen, grabbed some pastries and apples, and walked to the back of the alpha's grounds to Whil's cottage.

We entered through the greenhouse library door and headed to the seating area at the back where we found her, Cyrus, and a big, black wolf.

Knox.

Our eyes met and my breath left my lungs— hell, all the air vanished from the greenhouse, sucked out by the tension and yearning and aching need ignited in the space between us.

A churning, tearing mix of icy hollowness and blazing desire swirled inside me and my body trembled, trapped between the need to throw myself at him — even in his wolf form — and the need to run away.

"Sit," Cyrus commanded, his power wrenching my attention up from Knox, who sat on the floor in front of the couch, to Cyrus sitting on the couch. He pointed to one of the plain wooden chairs, and I plopped down on it before I could stop myself or even think of picking a different one.

Bishop shot Cyrus a dark look but didn't argue with him as he sank onto the cushioned chair between me and Whil. The fae woman sat on the floor among her piles of books where she'd been the first time I'd met her, making me wonder if the piles were just "part of the furniture." Except a few of the books were distinctly different from the ones the other day, indicating that this was how she organized herself while she worked.

A large tome sat on her lap, opened to a spot near the back, and I stared at it, hoping that if I focused on it, I wouldn't look at Knox... or think about him... or about last night's dream.

The book's pages were yellowed with age and the edges rough as if they had been made by hand and the text looked handwritten in a dark, red-brown ink.

Was that blood?

Nah, who wrote a book in blood?

"What are you doing with the grimoire found in one of the death gods' temples?" Bishop asked.

Shit, maybe it *was* written in blood.

She smoothed her hands across the pages and looked at me. "I found this book in a market in Savaria three hundred years ago and bought it to keep it out of the wrong hands. I never thought I'd use anything within its pages."

I didn't like the sound of that. I'd been going on the impression that they weren't going to kill me. Cyrus had been furious that I'd fought that grimalkin because my death could have killed Knox or driven him crazy.

But what if they were just looking for a way to save Knox from the horrible side effects of a broken bond? If I died too soon, it would hurt Knox, but now that Whil had found a solution, they were free to kill me and end this madness.

"I ah..." I glanced back the way we'd come even though I couldn't see the door to the outside, my pulse suddenly racing. "I..."

"Stay," Cyrus snarled, his power locking me in my seat before I could think to run. "Let's hear what it is before panicking."

Bishop set a hand on my knee, his touch easing some of the fear but not all.

"No one is killing anyone." He turned his attention to Whil. "Right?"

"Sort of," she said. "You're not going to kill someone, but some*thing*. You're going to kill your bond." She opened her mouth, paused as if she was listening to something, then looked at Knox. "I'd say the most dangerous part is getting there. I can't say for certain how dangerous the spell is, but there's evidence in this tome that says it shouldn't kill either of you."

"Who?" Cyrus asked as if he knew what she was talking about.

I glanced at Bishop. He didn't look confused at all.

Swell.

Knox had said something with his telepathy and hadn't included me in the conversation.

"Knox and Audrey have to go," Whil replied. "They both need to be there for the spell to work. But they need to walk into the heart of one of the death god's lands, so a dozen hunters at least would probably be best."

Cyrus frowned. "The closest death god is north of Darkweald, but that's still at least a nine day hike. We can't spare a dozen hunters. We need to figure out how the grimalkins got so close to town and if there are more of them. We'll need all the bodies we've got protecting Stonehaven."

"I'll go," Bishop said then shot Knox a hard look. "Better one of the strongest fighters than a dozen weaker ones."

"Two," Cyrus said, rubbing his face, looking exhausted. Had he stayed up all night dealing with the grimalkin attack? "Two of the strongest fighters. I'm not letting my younger brothers walk into a death god's lands by themselves."

Right. Because I didn't count. I wanted to be upset about that, but I couldn't deny reality. If those grimalkins were an indication of how dangerous this world was, I wasn't going to be helpful on this trip. The best I could hope for was to not get in the way and not fuck up when it came time to do the spell to break our bond.

And really, I should be ecstatic. Whil had found a way to break our unwanted mating bond without killing either of us— or at least it *shouldn't* kill either of us. If it worked, I'd no longer be in a constant state of arousal, and the frozen emptiness inside me that threatened to shatter my soul would be gone.

I'd finally be able to live whatever kind of life I wanted.

I just had to walk into the lands of a death god and murder my bond. How hard could that be?

WOLF DENIED

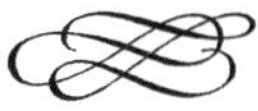

ENSNARED BY THE PACK: BOOK 2

AUDREY

The plan was simple. Walk into a land where a death god slept, go to his altar, and cast a spell to kill my unwanted mating bond with Knox.

Except from everyone's expressions, I doubted it was as simple as it sounded.

There were probably monsters between here and there, like those grimalkins that had attacked the town or worse. But since I'd only been in this realm a few days, I had no idea what to expect or what to fear.

A part of me believed that I should just fear everything. That would be safest. I didn't know anything about where I was or even who I was with... especially the three brothers leading this pack.

Cyrus was enormous and while gorgeous, was gorgeous in a hardened-warrior-dangerous-bad-boy kind of way. If our shifter abilities didn't heal us when we shifted — and if we were in my realm, the mortal realm — he'd probably be covered in tattoos, wearing a leather jacket, and riding a big, chunky, loud motorcycle. He'd probably throw me to those grimalkins without a hint of remorse if he thought it would protect his pack and wouldn't hurt Knox.

Bishop on the other hand was dangerous in the completely opposite way. Also gorgeous, he had a warm, disarming smile, and was kind, gentle, and supportive, and while I didn't think he'd purposely hurt me, he could easily break my heart. He'd probably left a trail of broken hearts all over town and didn't even know it.

While Knox... Knox hated me. Even if binding my soul to his had been an accident — and I wasn't sure he completely believed that — I'd still trapped him in a mating bond, and I could feel his hatred for the bond and me with frozen certainty in the core of my being.

And just thinking about it made the cold hollowness surge, swirling in and around the aching, desperate need to seal our mating bond with sex.

But the desire to have sex with him — or hell, one of his brothers — wasn't the real emotion in all of that. It was his rejection of me and I couldn't blame him. My power was so low I wasn't worthy to be anyone's mate let alone the mate of someone powerful enough he could be the alpha of his own pack... if he had any desire to lead.

On top of that, I couldn't even shift. My wolf was still asleep. It hadn't woken on the summer solstice of my eighteenth birthday like it should have nor after four more awakening ceremonies, and I feared the wolf half of my soul would never wake. I feared I never had a wolf form in the first place and everyone was mistaken about me being a shifter.

Sure, my essence said I was a shifter, but how could I call myself one when I couldn't shift?

And who would want to mate with someone like that?

"All right," Cyrus said, his intense, moss green gaze jumping from Knox, still in his enormous black wolf form, to Bishop who sat beside me, his hand resting on my knee in an attempt to steady my soul even though we weren't mates or even close friends. "Deacon, Nova, and Finn can handle leadership and security for the town while we're away. Lucius can take over when he gets back."

Bishop nodded his agreement, but Whil, the stunning fae with an ever-so-slightly perpetual golden glow, frowned and opened her mouth to say something.

"I know it isn't wise for the three of us to walk into a death god's realm," Cyrus said before she could argue with him. "But until I'm dead, I'm still the alpha of this pack. It's my decision."

Whil's bright green eyes narrowed. "You'll have to inform Nova that if things go badly, she and Deacon will need to take over."

"Velora is going to love that," Bishop groaned.

The muscles in Cyrus's jaw flexed. "Nova is more powerful and Deacon works better with her."

"You mean Velora is strung so tight Deacon will spend his time riling her up and nothing will get done," Whil huffed, tucking a strand of shimmering golden hair behind her delicately pointed ear. Then she turned her attention back to the book that hopefully had the answer to freeing me and Knox from our bond without either of us dying.

"Bishop," Cyrus said as he stood. "Find out everything we need to know about the spell. I'll organize our betas. We'll head out first thing tomorrow morning."

"Tomorrow morning?" I asked, the words jumping out before I could stop myself. "It's morning right now."

I wasn't really a part of this conversation and shouldn't have said anything. Sure, I had to go in order to break my mating bond with Knox, but they hadn't asked my opinion and even if they had, I wouldn't have had one. Hell, I hadn't even heard a quarter of the conversation about breaking the bond because Knox hadn't included me in his telepathic communication with the others.

But waiting until tomorrow meant I had to suffer a whole extra day with the nerve-wracking frozen hollowness of Knox rejecting our bond and the achy longing to have sex to seal it. A longing that was growing stronger and stronger and wasn't focused solely on Knox. My body didn't seem to care who I had sex with as long as I had sex.

And Bishop was just so kind and gorgeous and it was a struggle just sitting in Whil's greenhouse library with him beside me, the heat of his hand burning my flesh through my pant leg.

"It'll take half a day to pack our supplies and organize every-thing," Bishop said, squeezing my knee, his tightening grip ratcheting up my need and not calming me like he probably hoped.

"And it will take most of a day to get to the closest patrol shed," Cyrus added. "There might be more grimalkins in the area and if we have access to shelter, we shouldn't ignore it. Whil, have you got a map of the area?"

"Somewhere. Give me a minute to find it," she replied.

"You've got until tomorrow morning." Cyrus turned and headed toward the door of Whil's strange greenhouse-English cottage-library as Deacon pushed through the foliage and flowers and hurried into sight.

"The hunt team has returned from Darkweald," he said as he picked his way across the uneven floor to get to us in the mismatched seating area at the back. He wore the same black kilt-like-piece of clothing he had at dinner the other night and nothing else, exposing his broad muscular chest and making my desire spike because hey, he was a good-looking guy and my body wanted sex sex sex. He still also radiated the same sense of feralness, but it didn't seem quite as dangerous after watching him roar with laughter at Cyrus's — and my — embarrassment.

His golden-brown gaze jumped over the group of us, hesitating on Knox, and finally stopping on me, and he raised an eyebrow, his lips quirking as if he'd thought of a joke he didn't want to share.

"No sign of the malicious god," he reported, not commenting on what he obviously wanted to comment on — which was me being a part of some conversation between Whil and the three brothers. "But there's magic present in the ruins. Whil should check it out."

Cyrus's expression darkened. "Just great. Okay, change of plans."

AUDREY

"The ruins are on our way," Cyrus said. "We'll go with Whil and Deacon and a small hunt team to check out this magic then head north. Deacon and the team should be enough to protect Whil on the way home."

Deacon frowned. "North of Darkweald? Why are you going there?" His attention jumped to me, his expression strange. Everyone thought because I'd been found in Darkweald Forest, that I'd come from the north somewhere. "Are you going home?"

"I don't think I can go home." And if I could, I wasn't sure I wanted to.

Back home I was the weak, pathetic shifter who couldn't shift and had no status in my pack. The alpha's son — who was now the pack alpha since he'd murdered his father — and his best friend had tried to sacrifice me to a monster for power because they thought that was all I was good for.

I'd only spent a few days here, but I fit in more and was accepted more in this strange realm than I ever did at home. Although I supposed these people could turn on me since I'd already proven I was a terrible judge of character. For all I knew, the moment my bond with Knox was severed Cyrus and Bishop would decide I was worthless, and I'd be back to being an alpha's slave.

"You don't know you can't return home," Bishop said, his tone soft, sending a shiver of need rushing through me.

Deacon's eyes widened and his nostrils flared, while Cyrus's glower deepened, and Knox started to growl.

Swell. I'd just given everyone a big nose-full of my desire because shifters could smell every damn thing and I had no control over my body right now.

"If you're smart, you should wait until her heat is done," Deacon said, his lips quirking again as if he was trying not to laugh. "Or help her get it out of her system."

Yes, please! With Knox... or Bishop... Cyrus would do...

No damn it. Just no.

My cheeks burned with embarrassment even as heat pooled between my thighs.

Jeez. I only thought having sex with them was a good idea because of the mating bond. Knox would never have sex with me, Cyrus was barely being nice to me, and I didn't know if Bishop was only being nice because of his brother.

Did I really want to have sex for the first time with someone who didn't love me? Hell, who didn't even like me?

Fuck off, Deacon, Knox snarled, his power rolling off him in waves that made me want to slip off the chair and kneel before him in submission. *We leave at dawn.*

With a low, dangerous growl at Deacon that made the man raise his hands in defense and take a big step back, Knox stalked out of the greenhouse.

"You should probably assemble an all-female hunt team," Cyrus added, his voice gruff, and he, too, strode out of the greenhouse with Deacon at his side.

"Please tell me there's a way to control this," I groaned, turning to Whil. Maybe magic would help me get through the next nine or so days it took to get to the death god's altar.

"I wish there was," she replied, "but nothing can affect a mating bond... although I'm surprised at how strong the need to seal your bond is. It's only a few days old. You should have been able to go at least a week or two before your need to seal the bond is too strong to resist."

"Is she also in heat?" Bishop asked. "Would that affect her?"

"Possibly. A mating bond can set off a heat. Nova would probably be able to check your hormones to confirm, but there isn't much she can do about that, either," Whil said, focusing on me. "From what I know about wolf heats, you just have to get through it. Ideally with a partner, or a couple of partners, with decent stamina."

Swell. I bet Bishop had decent stamina. Cyrus too. And Knox... well, he *was* their brother. Stamina probably ran in the family.

Oh. My. God! Stop thinking about sex!

Except— "Heats aren't this powerful in my realm. They increase a woman's sexual desire, but not to the point of driving her crazy."

I'd never heard of a shifter being desperate to have sex with anyone and everyone. Not even one from my pack where our wolf nature and all its instincts burst fully to life when we were eighteen and sometimes overwhelmed us. Not to mention, I still didn't have a wolf form.

"How am I even in heat? I can't shift?" I groaned, frustrated and angry that even though I'd escaped Sterling and Royce and my pack, I was still a slave. Only this time I was a slave to my body's needs.

"Interesting," Whil said as she stood and headed to a bookcase. "There must be something about this realm that affects a female's hormones compared to your realm because heats in this realm are quite strong."

"So more magic?" Just like the magic that let me understand what everyone was saying even though no one spoke English. Except this magic was far more inconvenient.

"I'm sorry," Bishop said, rubbing circles on my knee and turning me on more. "I wish we could wait for your heat to be over, but the longer we wait, the harder it will be to resist the mating bond."

I fought a churning mix of desire and fear. I wanted to break the bond as soon as possible, but I was about to spend nine days —

longer if things didn't go well — with two incredibly hot men, and a man my soul said was my mate. I didn't know if I'd be able to hold out against the growing pressure.

"Once this is over you'll be able to choose who you want to spend your future heats with without fear of completing a mating bond," Bishop added.

Yes, with you.

No, damn it.

I stood and jerked away from him, praying a little distance between us would help me. "I'm not ready for this."

"It's okay," Bishop said, his voice soft. "I'll help you."

"With *everything*?" I asked, heat flooding my core and embarrassment burning my cheeks.

"Yes, even with sex, if that's what you want. No expectations."

Oh God, yes.

Except a small part of me, the part that wasn't desperate and needy or grieving from Knox's rejection said having sex with Bishop was a terrible idea.

"I don't know. I'm not— I haven't—"

I'd only ever had sex in my dreams and only recently at that. Not to mention, I knew the real thing would be nothing like what I'd fantasized about. Hell, I hadn't even really kissed a man since my first kiss with Royce didn't count.

Sex also meant complications. If we couldn't break the mating bond, Knox and I were going to have to figure out our relationship and my original reasons for not having sex with Bishop were still the same. I didn't want Knox angry because I'd slept with his brother. That would be bad for me, but also bad for Bishop and his relationship with his brother.

Wolves were notorious for being possessive and it wouldn't matter if I'd had sex with Bishop while Knox and I were trying to break the bond. He could still end up furious.

Except not everything in this realm was the same as my realm. Maybe wolves here weren't possessive. Maybe Knox wouldn't care.

My need tightened into a desperate ache and my breath picked up. Bishop was kind and gorgeous. Maybe it wouldn't be so terrible for him to be my first even if neither of us wanted a relationship. Women had casual sex all the time.

Except any kind of sex came with the risk of pregnancy and I wasn't on birth control. Merrick, my pack alpha — my *old pack* alpha — and the man who'd raised me after my father had died, wouldn't have ever bothered with the expense and there'd been no one in the pack I'd wanted to have sex with so it hadn't been worth the humiliation to ask for it.

I'd just have to hold myself together.

And if I couldn't?

Fuck. I didn't know if I could.

"Please tell me you have birth control in this realm," I groaned.

"Nova can set you up," Bishop said, standing and gesturing to the door. "Her main office and clinic are in the north wing."

"I think she's still at the hospital helping with the injured from the grimalkin attack," Whil said absentmindedly, pulling a book from her shelf.

"I'll come back to learn about this spell and help you look for that map." He turned his warm brown gaze to me and my pulse stuttered. "Remember," he said his voice soft and low. "You don't have to be afraid and you don't have to deal with this alone."

Except if I didn't want to break down and jump him or Cyrus, being alone would probably be best.

AUDREY

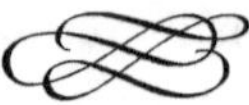

BISHOP LED ME OUT OF WHIL'S STRANGE ENGLISH COTTAGE greenhouse and my gaze instantly jumped to the majestic mountains towering close behind it. They were so much like the mountains in Oregon where I'd grown up and yet—

My gaze lifted to the two moons hanging in the sky. One was white and looked like "the moon," the other was a smaller pinker version. I was definitely not in Oregon anymore, or even in my own realm, and I couldn't even pretend I was.

We headed around the side of the alpha's residence which looked like an enormous Mediaeval castle complete with multiple wings and turrets and into Old Town. Unlike yesterday, Bishop took the direct path down the twisted, sloping main street and avoided the warren of narrow streets and hidden gardens. We quickly passed through the main gate in the large stone wall surrounding Stonehaven's original buildings and headed into New Town.

The hospital turned out to be a large, square building just off the main street. Its stone blocks were smaller than the blocks that made up the alpha's residence, but bigger than the buildings closer to the outskirts of town, suggesting the building wasn't hundreds of years old like Old Town, but still not new. There were also two new additions — one much newer than the other if the brick size was anything to go by — indicating that the community kept adding to its facilities as the pack's population grew.

We avoided the large courtyard with the wide doors at the front of the building that looked a lot like the entrance to the emergency area and instead entered through a modest foyer with a dozen comfortable-looking chairs and a wide reception desk.

Two young women sat behind the desk and they brightened when they saw Bishop. Then their attention slid to me. The younger of the two, a blond with short curly hair, kept her smile, while the other woman, also blond but with long hair, glowered for a split second before plastering on a smile so bright it hurt to look at her.

Yeah, Bishop had definitely left a trail of broken hearts — or hopeful hearts — behind him.

"Nova will be checking on the more serious patients," he said, nodding at the women and walking past them toward a staircase.

They both frowned as if they'd hoped he'd stop and talk— or rather flirt. I suspected if I hadn't been with him, he would have, and I had a bad feeling I was making enemies in my possibly-new pack just by being with him.

"If we can't find her at the nurses' station," he continued, "we can wait for her in the breakroom."

We went up to the second floor and down a long hall with plain white walls and a polished stone floor. It didn't have the institutional feel that hospitals in my realm had, but it was clearly designed to be practical and easily cleaned.

Wooden doors with windows lined the hall. Some stood open, some were closed, but almost all of them were for single-bed patient rooms. I didn't get a good look inside — or Bishop would have left me behind — but the equipment looked basic, suggesting this society wasn't as advanced as mine. Save for the lights, which turned on and off with a switch, nothing else indicated that they had electricity... which meant the lights were probably magical.

Men and women, mostly in loose, pale blue shirts and pants that looked a lot like scrubs, moved up and down the hall, coming and going from rooms.

We were just about to reach a T-intersection at the end of the hall when we passed a room with an enormous man in the doorway. He turned and I realized it was Finn, the pack's head of security.

His piercing blue eyes widened at seeing us then narrowed and he stepped into the hall. "Just the man I needed to talk to," he said to Bishop.

Bishop glanced toward the T-intersection and sighed. "The nurses' station is just around the corner. I'll catch up in a minute."

"Sure." I didn't want to stand around listening to Bishop talk business with his beta, but I was still uncertain about being around strangers by myself. Hell, even being around people I knew used to be dangerous, which was why unless I'd been meeting my best friend, Mila, I'd stayed at home.

"What's she doing here?" Finn asked once I'd rounded the corner.

His voice was low and I had to strain to hear it, but the edge in his tone made me stop on the other side of the corner to listen.

I didn't know what kind of man Finn was. Sure, he might have been one of the wolves who'd saved me during the grimalkin attack, but that didn't mean he liked me, and from the sound of it, he didn't.

I also didn't know if it was worse that he'd more or less been pleasant to me during dinner the other night and hadn't shown me how he really felt or not. At least with my old pack, I knew no one liked me and they made no attempt to hide it. I couldn't risk assuming that because people here were polite to me, I was safe.

"I thought Nova was taking care of her at the Residence," Finn added.

"I thought I'd show her our medical facilities," Bishop replied, his tone neutral and thankfully not announcing to the other man that we thought I might be in heat and was going to talk to Nova about birth control. Because Nova had been right. My reproductive cycle wasn't anyone's business but mine and hers and whoever I picked to get me through it.

"So now you're showing her the facilities?" Finn's tone turned exasperated. "Does Cyrus really have his sights set on her for his mate? You know the pack will never accept someone so weak."

His words stung. They shouldn't have. I hadn't been accepted before so it was foolish to think I'd be accepted now. And really! Cyrus wasn't interested in me as a mate and I wasn't interested in him… at least not for a permanent relationship.

I was smart enough to know someone like him never mated with someone like me, especially when any other woman in this pack would make a better choice.

I couldn't even fantasize about someone powerful coming along who wanted to mate with me and protect me. Not that I'd fantasized about that a lot, but Royce had made it perfectly clear when he'd faked our fated mating call and then tried to sacrifice me to a monster that no one with any kind of power would ever be interested in me.

My weakness was why Knox had rejected me right from the beginning and why he hated me so much. The weakest wolf in existence had forced a mating bond with him. I'd hate me too if I were him.

Which was logical and true and made my chest and throat tighten.

No one wanted me, and I couldn't convince myself the thought came from Knox rejecting our unwanted bond. His rejection only made the truth perfectly clear.

"Cyrus is strong enough to hold the alpha's position by himself," Bishop said, surprising me by not agreeing with Finn as well as not denying that Cyrus was interested in me becoming his mate. "He doesn't need a strong mate to help."

"But he'll lose all respect if he picks someone so weak and he'll be challenged for leadership," Finn replied, his tone shifting from anger to worry. "I'm sure once she stops looking like she's been beaten up she's cute and all, but we know nothing about her. She hasn't even shifted out her injuries, which means she's either vying for sympathy or doesn't have the strength to do a proper shift when she's hurt. Neither is good for an alpha's mate. Their pups could be powerless too and then there'd be a question of succession."

"She might be practically human," a new, masculine voice said. "But I heard she faced off with a grimalkin to protect a bunch of kids. That says something about the type of woman she is."

"Doesn't mean she'd make a good alpha's mate," Finn shot back. "Doesn't mean she'd make anyone a good mate. Would you want her to be the mother of your pups?"

"Well, I—" the new voice began.

"Of course not. No one would," Finn answered for him.

The icy hollowness inside me surged, crushing my chest. I fought to breathe as tears burned my eyes. No one wanted me. No one had ever wanted me.

The emotions are just Knox rejecting the bond. It's just Knox.

But I couldn't convince myself of that. The cold kept growing, devouring me from the inside. I was useless and weak.

Bishop and Whil had said there was a place for me here, but they were the only ones who believed that. My life in this pack wouldn't be any different than with my old pack and once my bond with Knox was broken, Cyrus and Bishop would kick me to the curb or turn me into their personal slave like Merrick had.

Except that was only if my bond with Knox could be broken and if I survived breaking it.

Maybe it would be better for everyone if I didn't survive. If I ended things now, the guys wouldn't have to risk their lives going to the death god's altar.

Maybe my father hadn't been weak when he'd taken his life. Maybe he'd just realized the truth: that everyone would be better off without him.

Except I hadn't been better off. Merrick had taken advantage of my ten-year-old naivety and used me. His son, Sterling, had used me, too. No one had been around to protect me and no one ever would.

Damn it.

Tears rolled down my cheeks and I furiously swiped them away.

I was stronger than this. I'd survived for years as the lowest of the low in my pack.

And what I felt was just the God damned bond.

I shoved away from the wall and Finn's hurtful words, not bothering to listen to the rest of the conversation. Being weak didn't mean I was helpless. I'd proven that facing off against that grimalkin — even if that grimalkin would have killed me if Knox hadn't saved me. Knox and I would break our bond, and if this pack couldn't accept me as a person then I'd find some place that would.

I'd survived almost being sacrificed to a monster. I could sure as hell survive this.

AUDREY

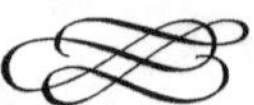

WITH MY SHOULDERS SQUARED AND MY DETERMINATION PUSHING DOWN the grief caused by Knox rejecting the bond, I marched to the nurses' station.

An exhausted-looking nurse stood at the chest-high desk with an open folder and a pen in her hand, the pen hovering above the page as if she couldn't figure out what to write or as if she'd zoned out and forgotten what she was doing.

"I'm looking for Nova," I said. I wanted to get this conversation over with and get away from any more gossip about me before my fragile hold on my determination shattered... or before my desire returned and everyone in the building knew I needed to have sex.

The woman glanced up and opened her mouth to say something, but her expression flashed from exhausted to concerned and I gritted my teeth.

"Nova," I pressed. I hadn't looked in a mirror, but from her reaction, it had to be obvious that I'd been crying. Past experience told me my eyes were red and my face splotchy, and I could only hope because I hadn't been crying for long, I'd look closer to normal by the time Bishop was finished talking with Finn.

That asshole who I should have told off instead of running away... and maybe if I see him again I will.

The thought shocked me and yet didn't shock me. Talking back had always ended in punishment, but so had everything else, and I guess I'd finally reached the end of my rope. I was sure I was going to cry and be a horny basket case again — and again and again — before all of this was said and done, but I also had a strange new wildness inside me. It was as if the sensation from my dreams with Knox, that I actually had a wolf buried deep in my soul, was affecting me while I was awake.

And if it got me out of this building without looking like a complete and utter mess, I didn't care if that was just my imagination or not.

"Audrey," Nova said from down the hall as she stepped out of a patient room. She wore the blue *scrubs* that everyone else was wearing even though she was the town's head physician and one of Cyrus's betas. Her light brown hair was pulled back in a ponytail and while she didn't look as exhausted as the nurse, she did look as if she'd been working with little rest since the grimalkin attack yesterday.

"Why are you out of bed?" she asked, striding to the nurses' station and setting a pile of folders on the desk. The exhausted nurse gave her a quick nod then headed down the hall and stepped into one of the rooms.

I was supposed to stay in bed? No one had mentioned that or even tried to mention it. But of course, they were distracted with breaking my bond with Knox because Knox was their priority, not me.

"No one mentioned it," I replied. And really, I felt fine, or as fine as I could get given the circumstances.

She threw her hands up and huffed in frustration. "Why do I even bother giving them instructions? The grimalkins are a distraction, but Cyrus was clear about your... condition. He should have at least told Bishop to not let you walk all over town as if you're perfectly fine."

"My condition—?" Oh. Right. The *condition* that meant I couldn't shift and I healed more like a human than a shifter. And as much as I hadn't wanted that particular detail getting out, Nova had needed to know how to properly take care of me.

"Like I said the other night," she added. "You might look and feel fine right now, but you'll still get tired faster because your body is still processing the trauma. It's best you rest." Her attention flickered over my face but she didn't react to my red eyes or splotchy skin.

"I'll make sure she stays in bed after this," Bishop said behind me, his words instantly making me think of him naked and in bed with me.

Hot need shot straight to my core and flaming embarrassment heated my cheeks, overwhelming the last of the Finn-induced-Knox-rejecting-our-bond grief which wasn't the solution I wanted for either my emotional problems or my splotchy skin problem. Just great.

"Will that be before or after you make her march back up to the Residence?" she asked, her voice dripping with sarcasm.

"If she gets tired, I'll carry her," he replied.

My thoughts lurched to being in Bishop's arms and more heat flooded me. Both Bishop and Nova sniffed, unable to keep pretending that I wasn't flooding the hall with the scent of my arousal.

Unbelievable. Now I couldn't even get through a conversation without embarrassing myself.

"But this is important. Audrey needs to discuss her... *options*," Bishop said, his tone making options sound like a dirty word. "The sooner the better."

And now I was thinking about last night's dream and my core was trembling in anticipation. Humiliation burned my whole face, seeping into my hairline and down my neck.

"Can you please stop talking about it?" I croaked. "I'm sure Nova's already figured it out."

"Come on," Nova said, her tone softening. "We can talk in here."

She led me to the end of the hall to an empty patient room, ushered me in, and gave Bishop a "no way in hell" look when he tried to come in as well.

"Wait by the nurses' station. If Audrey wants to talk to you about it, she will." She pointed back down the hall, then shut the door in his face. "Is this your first heat? Has anyone in your family talked to you about it?"

She motioned for me to sit on the bed as she sagged onto the chair beside it.

"It's ah... It's complicated," I said.

I had no idea if I should tell her the truth, or if she'd even believe that I'd come from a different realm and heats were different there. Cyrus and Bishop hadn't believed me until Whil had confirmed it and neither of the guys had mentioned it to their betas at dinner the other night. That, and bringing it up might distract Nova from the real problem — me about to jump on any passably good-looking guy I came across — and the sooner I figured out what my options were the better. And I hoped to God they had some form of birth control here.

"Where I'm from women don't experience heats this powerful, so I'm not sure how different this will be." Not that anyone in my pack had talked about heats or that heats were an issue for any shifters in my realm. "I'm guessing it's like what I know, that I'll have a heightened sex drive for about a week, except it'll be ten times stronger." Of course, that was if what I felt was an indication of what to expect, and also assuming I actually was in heat and not just being compelled by the mating bond.

"Heats can be powerful, and from your reaction, it looks like yours is going to be pretty strong," she said. "Knowing you can't shift makes this quite unusual. The weaker shifters tend to have weaker heats so I would have thought you'd have little to no reaction. I'd like to draw some blood and run some tests."

"Will that help you figure out how I can deal with this?"

Her expression softened even more and I wondered if she thought I was younger than I really was. How old were women in this realm when they got their first heat? In my realm, it was late teens or early twenties for shifters who hadn't had their ability to shift suppressed until they were eighteen, and with my pack it was shortly after their first shift. But no matter how similar this realm was to mine, I couldn't assume anything.

"With Whil's help we've discovered lots of amazing medications, but nothing to ease the symptoms of going into heat. Because you're unmated and with the amount of pheromones you're releasing, I suggest you avoid public places until you've gotten through it, get physical contact, and—"

Need shivered down my spine and, from Nova's subtle sniff, I released another nose-full of desire.

"The contact doesn't have to be sex," she said with a soft chuckle. "Although given the strength of your symptoms already, it would probably be best. But even just increasing the amount of touching and cuddling with someone close to you will help if sex isn't the direction you want to go."

Except the only people I knew in this realm were Bishop and Cyrus and it would be a challenge to stop at just cuddling since every time Nova said the word sex I thought of them. Of course, that was if either of them were even willing to cuddle with me.

Logically, because I was a shifter, I knew my soul needed physical contact even though my wolf hadn't woken. I'd been reeling since I'd come to this realm and my body had been seriously injured twice now. Bishop placing his hand on my arm or thigh wasn't nearly enough to keep me steady. I needed more. A lot more.

Nova frowned. Guess she'd just listened to what she'd said and realized I was alone and didn't have someone to cuddle with. "When was the last time someone held you?"

Too long.

I swallowed a bitter huff. Mila had joined her mate's pack just over a year ago and before that maybe once every couple of months because Mila, once she'd become an adult, had gotten more responsibilities with her family and the pack. We hadn't really cuddled since high school which had been about five years ago.

But I'd gotten by with minimal cuddling all this time and I'd get by without significant contact now as well. I just had to wait until my soul naturally steadied... and pray nothing else happened before then to shake it.

Nova's frown deepened and a hint of her power that she'd kept tightly controlled until now rolled over me. But I didn't get the impression she was trying to make me submit. No, it felt more like she was upset and her control had slipped.

"Sorry." She pulled her power back. "From the look on your face, I'd say it's been a while and not by your choosing."

"I didn't have much value in my previous pack and I have no family," I said, trying to keep my tone even. "So there weren't many options for cuddling."

It was just the way things were for someone so weak and there was no point in keeping it a secret. Even if I hadn't already told Cyrus and Bishop, everyone would figure it out. Hell, despite what Bishop and Whil had said, some of them, like Finn, had already decided I belonged at the bottom of the pack.

Nova's expression darkened and her power slipped her control again, sending a wave of pressure sweeping over me before she yanked it back. "Okay, since you're touch starved, I'd recommend you spend your heat at the heat clinic. Wilder and his men will be able to help you through it."

"And by helping me through it you mean...?" Was she suggesting that they have sex with me?

"I mean with you being touch starved, the best way you can get through a heat this strong is with sex. Physical contact will still help you better manage your symptoms, but in your situation, I'd say sex is the ideal."

Holy shit, she was!

She was prescribing I go have sex with a bunch of strangers.

Except if heats were a lot stronger in this realm than in mine and always had been, it made sense that their culture would develop differently and have ways of helping single women deal with it.

"The men regularly take the inhibitor extract, but just to be safe we'll get you a dose. It'll be good for four months." She stood and headed to the door. "If you don't mind Bishop coming along, we can go to the dispensary right now. If not, I can send it to your room in the Residence."

"He already knows what's happening." I huffed and hopped off the bed. "I'm sure everyone within a twenty-foot radius knows what's going on with me."

"Oh, thirty feet at least," Nova said with a chuckle and a mischievous smile, the same smile she'd had when she'd been teasing Cyrus at dinner. "It's a miracle you didn't have a trail of men following you down the street by the time you reached the hospital."

"They know they couldn't handle me," I quipped back. "I'm crazy enough to face down a grimalkin by myself."

And they didn't want to accidentally knock me up and get stuck with a pup who was just as powerless as I was.

But that was a sour, aching thought that I wasn't going to acknowledge. I'd managed to ignore the grief of Knox rejecting my bond during my conversation with Nova and if I went down the "no one wanted me" rabbit hole, I'd start crying again.

"Well, worry not. Wilder will definitely know how to handle you," she said, sending a wave of need shooting hot and heavy to my core. "I want to wait until you've had another day of healing, but I can get you set up in the clinic tomorrow and after your first session you'll be in much better control of your needs."

Except I was leaving tomorrow morning to head north to break my bond with Knox. Wilder definitely wouldn't be *handling* me.

She opened the door, wafting my scent into the hall. Bishop, who was leaning against the wall across from the door, straightened and cleared his throat. His warm brown gaze locked with mine and my pulse stuttered, my whole body aching for him.

As much as I wanted to believe I could hold myself together, my hope was quickly slipping away. Knox and I were going to have to have a conversation, and I could only hope that we could break the bond and he wouldn't try to kill one of his brothers for sleeping with me.

KNOX

AUDREY STOOD IN THE CENTER OF THE SACRED GROVE, HER WHITE DRESS luminous in the moonlight, and I knew I was dreaming. Again.

It was the same dream I'd had every night since she'd bonded her soul with mine. She always looked stunned to be there, always so fragile even though I knew she had the willpower of any alpha if not the power, and my wolf always took over and made me rush to her side.

We crashed together like we had all the other nights, and I tangled my hand in her hair and possessed her mouth with a hunger I couldn't deny, her sweet, fresh scent mixing with her rich arousal and driving me crazy.

It was hard enough holding my wolf back and not giving in to the bond when I was awake, especially when it was obvious she was in a near-perpetual state of arousal, and it was impossible in my dreams.

"You're not going north," my wolf snarled at her as he tore open the front of her white dress with his claws and roughly palmed her breast. "I won't let you."

"You have to," she gasped against my lips— *his* lips.

He captured her face between our hands and pulled back, glaring at her. Her brown, golden-flecked eyes locked with mine and it was as if I could see into her soul.

She ached with longing and fear just like I did and that made my wolf furious. She didn't believe him when he'd told her she belonged to us. She believed the ice I'd wrapped around our bond to keep her out was proof I didn't want her.

And I didn't. Just thinking about the bond made my pulse pick up with fear and anger. She'd trapped us. She'd fucking trapped us and going north was the only way to escape, no matter how dangerous it was for her.

"No," my wolf growled. "You're mine. He *will* submit."

The hell I will, I thought at my wolf as I tried to wrench myself away from her.

But my wolf crashed my mouth back onto Audrey's and that power hidden in the depths of her soul — that my wolf wanted to be there because this was just a dream — rolled from her body. It washed over me and my power rose to meet it.

Sparks burst around us and the need to take her, claim her, possess every part of her, surged inside me.

She tangled her fingers into my hair, her blunt human nails digging into my scalp, her body arching toward me. Her arousal clouded the air around us, heady and sweet, and my wolf plunged his fingers into her wet pussy, drawing a moan of pleasure. He didn't want foreplay, he wanted to fuck. He wanted to fuck her until she screamed his name and submitted to our bond like she'd done for the last two nights.

It was like this every dream. She had a power that surged up within her and heaved against ours, fighting me, taunting me, seducing me in a wild, primal dance of dominance. She didn't even know she was doing it even as her body submitted to us, her need driven by our unwanted mating bond—

Not the bond. She'd want us without it, my wolf said, trying to shove me further inside myself, determined to make me shut the fuck up while he fucked her. *She's ours. Always has been—*

Always will be. Yeah yeah yeah, I snarled back. *In your dreams. Which this fucking is.*

My wolf roared, inside me and out loud, and Audrey froze, her power vanishing between one rapid beat of my heart and the next, her body trembling like prey. A horrible feeling that could have only come from her through our bond swamped me, souring my desire.

She'd been in this position before. She'd been in the arms of a man, kissing him. She'd thought he loved her and he'd betrayed her. That was how she'd gotten the four ugly red scars slicing across her chest that showed up even in my dreams. That was why we'd found her in the river barely alive.

And now both my wolf and I were pissed off.

"You're mine," my wolf said, slowly inching his fingers out of her pussy, trying to reignite her primal desire. He needed to bury our cock inside her and sink our teeth into her flesh, claiming her again and again and again. He needed to show her with our body that he would never forsake or betray her. "My mate. Mine. I won't let you sever our bond."

"You're only saying that—" Her breath hitched as my wolf brushed the pad of our thumb over her clit. "You're saying that because that's what I want you to say." A shiver rippled down her body and her long dark lashes fluttered shut. "He doesn't want me." *No one wants me.* "I'm only powerful here in this fantasy. I didn't give him a choice and I won't burden him with a mate he didn't pick himself who can't even shift."

"I chose," my wolf replied, pushing our fingers back inside her and rubbing down on her clit, our body vibrating with a need that had to be released. "I accepted the bond. I knew the truth the moment I caught your scent."

Her eyes rolled back and she arched into me, her body begging for me even if her power had yet to reignite.

"You. Are. Mine." He tightened our grip in her hair and tugged her head back.

Another shiver of anticipation swept through her and her power flickered back to life. Her eyes darkened, her pupils dilating with desire along with a hint of the wolf we could sense buried inside her, and her lips parted in invitation. But my wolf glared down at her, holding her still with our grip in her long blond hair and our fingers in her pussy, waiting.

"Knox," she breathed.

"Who do you belong to?" he demanded, our lips a breath away from hers but not touching and our fingers buried inside her, not moving, making it clear he wouldn't satisfy her until she submitted to his truth: that she was our mate.

"Please, Knox—"

"Who?" he growled, wrenching her head back farther, exposing her neck.

Her breath came in short sharp gasps, heaving her small breasts toward us, taunting us to lick and suck her, to build her up. Her hips tried to move and the scent of her arousal thickened, her need desperate. But he kept our fingers locked within her and our thumb frozen on her clit, not giving her any relief.

For fuck's sake. Give her what she needs, I snapped at him, trying to take over. She didn't deserve to be tortured like this even in my dreams. She wanted to be fucked, needed it. She needed it in real life, too, but if I wanted to break our bond, I couldn't give in to that... no matter how hard I was or how much my balls ached.

"You." Her power rolled up from the depths of her being, fighting her submission to us, and slammed into me more powerful than the previous dreams.

A deep gong sounded, reverberating through me, making the ice I'd woven around my heart and the magical chain binding our souls together tremble.

My pants vanished — because this was a dream — and my cock sprung free.

"You, Knox. I belong to you."

I needed to be buried inside her. I needed to hear her scream my name.

Fuck my wolf and fuck this dream.

"Always," my wolf replied as *I* — not my wolf — captured her lips in a wild, possessive kiss.

I claimed her mouth, desperate and hungry for something I'd never had before and never wanted until now: acceptance.

I didn't know if the real Audrey would ever be able to accept someone like me, someone who would rather be a wolf, who didn't like crowds or, hell, even people, and someone who couldn't stand to be in my own bedroom in the Residence because the room was too small. But it didn't matter. This was a dream. She'd submitted to my claim which meant for this brief moment she accepted me. And from the way she kissed me back and held on to my head, keeping me close, she craved me as well.

I pushed my fingers in and out of her, building her up. Her channel was slick and hot, and her hips rocked into my hands, her body perfectly matching this wild primal dance between us. It was driving me crazy imagining what it was going to feel like to push into her, but even in my dreams she was tight, and I didn't want to hurt her. I wanted her boneless and soaking wet when I took her. I wanted every nerve ignited so she felt every inch of me.

"Knox," she moaned, a shiver rolling from her head to her pussy, her inner muscles fluttering around my fingers. "Mate."

The word shot like lightning straight to my cock. I ground my thumb down on her clit and pushed her over the edge. Her muscles clamped around my fingers, but I kept sliding them in and out of her, drawing out the tremors.

"Oh, fuck," she gasped, her body twitching, her hips riding my hand, greedy for every last drop of pleasure, and this time, unlike last night — because I was in charge and not my wolf— I waited until she was done before impaling her on my cock.

"Oh, fuck," she groaned again, as I pressed her back against the soft, mossy ground, and pushed inside her.

Her muscles still fluttered around me, her hot slickness easing just enough of the pressure and friction so I could smoothly bury myself to the hilt in one powerful stroke. Fuck, she felt so good, so perfect. So mine.

I sucked in breaths heavy with her arousal and her sweet scent, my balls aching, pausing to savor the feel of her. Her power crackled against mine, bright golden sparks flickering at the edge of my vision and teasing along my spine. Her brown eyes were slightly glazed with pleasure, her expression was pure bliss. A soft golden glow radiated from her skin and once again she looked like the goddess I'd glimpsed when she been fighting that grimalkin. Except now, instead of a warrior goddess, she was a goddess of desire.

"Mine," my wolf said and her face lit up with a brilliant smile.

Until we set her free, I whispered to myself then I gave myself over to my wolf and my primal need.

We pumped in and out of her, picking up speed, stealing her gasps and mewls with our kisses, and turning them into moans of pleasure. Her body and power crashed against ours, driving us wild, but somehow we managed to hold ourselves together until her whole body tensed with another orgasm and she screamed my name. Then we lost it, hammering into her, chasing our own release, until we exploded inside her.

Her pussy milked us, greedily contracting around our cock, drawing out both of our orgasms, and my wolf preened with satisfaction.

Our mate was happy and satisfied and our mating bond was even stronger.

My pulse stuttered.

Oh, fuck. The ice around the chain binding us together had cracks in it and the chain itself was bigger and thicker.

I told her you'd accept her, my wolf said, his smug satisfaction souring the afterglow of coming.

I haven't accepted her, I snarled back. This was just a dream, a fantasy, a way to relieve the pressure of the mating bond. I didn't want a mate. I couldn't be trapped like that.

You did accept her. You fucked her this time, not me.

I stared down where my cock was buried inside her.

Fuck me. My damned wolf was right. I hadn't just been a passenger like I'd been the previous two nights. Tonight I'd taken control and claimed her... and I had a horrible feeling that even though this was a dream, I'd just made our real bond that much harder to break and that much harder to resist.

CYRUS

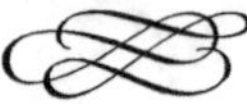

I stood in the courtyard outside the Residence with Deacon and his all-female hunt team, glaring at the brightening eastern horizon and trying to keep my power under control.

Yesterday, Bishop had told me he'd overheard Nova tell Audrey to spend her heat with Wilder, and my wolf had lost his shit. It had been a struggle to get through the rest of the day without flattening everyone around me with my power and even more of a struggle last night to keep my wolf under control and not march us to Audrey's bedroom and give her what she needed.

My wolf snarled at me, still pissed that I hadn't given in to *that* desire.

Nova had told Audrey to go to Wilder. Wilder of all people!

It didn't matter that he was experienced and sensitive and the best man for the job. My wolf refused to accept that Audrey had to go to some other man to satisfy her blatantly obvious needs and was furious that I wouldn't give him a chance to take care of her.

Fuck! It was ridiculous.

My wolf had never cared what the women in our lives did, even the handful of women we'd had somewhat serious relationships with. We weren't jealous. So long as everyone talked about it and agreed, multiple partners weren't a problem. My brothers and I had grown up with two dads and there were a number of multi-partner matings in town so it wasn't unheard of.

It also wasn't like Wilder was going to mate with her. He or one of his guys — or all of them if she so desired — we're going to help her get through the overwhelming need of her heat. He'd treated tons of women before and he'd continue to treat them until he decided to retire. Audrey would just be another patient.

But I couldn't convince my wolf of that, and I couldn't even convince myself that my reaction was because it was obvious Bishop was falling for her or that she might have to become Knox's mate if we couldn't break the mating bond.

She was suffering and *I* needed to take care of her.

I gritted my teeth and mentally clenched harder at my power. I had to stay in control and not let myself be distracted by a woman I couldn't have, even if I actually wanted her... which I didn't, damn it.

As much as I didn't want Nova to be right about who I could take as a mate, she was. I'd already heard whispers about how weak Audrey was while making my rounds and informing our betas that the three of us were leaving to take Audrey north. I'd also gotten a number of concerned looks and outright objections, particularly from Velora and Finn.

It seemed the rumor mill was determined to believe I wanted Audrey even though I *knew* mating with her would cause problems.

Which was ridiculous. Hadn't they seen how Bishop couldn't stop staring at her at dinner or that she'd been shopping with Bishop the other day, not me? How had they jumped to the conclusion I wanted her as my mate and not Bishop?

But the bigger problem was that my wolf didn't give a fuck that they thought she wouldn't make a good mate. She'd been willing to risk everything to save pups. It didn't matter if she had power or not, that made her perfect.

Except that didn't necessarily make an ideal alpha, and if I took Audrey as my mate, she'd become the pack alpha with me, and without power, it would be a constant battle to have people respect her and not challenge us for leadership.

Whil hurried around the side of the Residence, her small travel pack hanging at her hip, the strap slung across her chest. "I'm sorry. I couldn't decide which book I might need more."

"We're still waiting on Bishop and Audrey," I replied.

Whil's gaze swept over the group. "Knox?"

"He's waiting just outside the Residence's walls." Before Audrey, he would have been in the courtyard, close to the hunt team, although still not a part of the group. But now, he couldn't even be near that many people, even if half of the people were wolves.

Bishop had mentioned yesterday that Knox was becoming more withdrawn and he was worried. His twin had a stranglehold on their twin bond and the most Bishop was getting from Knox was his desire for Audrey. He wasn't even getting anger or fear anymore and those were usually the emotions Knox couldn't hide from Bishop.

Do you want me to send Lyra to get them, Deacon asked in my head.

But the front door opened before I could respond, and Bishop and Audrey hurried out dressed to travel and carrying their packs.

"My fault," Audrey murmured, her cheeks flushing and her gaze dropping to her feet making it obvious her heat had been what had delayed her. "I'm trying to get it under control."

I glanced at Bishop. His expression was pinched and he gave a slight shake of his head in response to my silent question. She hadn't turned to him for help. She was still trying to deal with it alone.

My wolf heaved under my skin at that thought and a whisper of my power slip my mental grasp.

"I'll control it," she insisted, mistaking my released power as anger at her inability to control a bodily function that could be hard to control at the best of times.

And is impossible right now because she's touch starved, my wolf snarled at me.

Which was information Nova had snapped at me when I'd gone to her for extra elixirs and medical supplies and told her we were taking Audrey north.

But it wasn't something I could wait out or do anything about. We had to get to the death god's altar before Knox and Audrey lost their minds or had sex and sealed a bond neither of them wanted. The best we could do would be to try to find time to hold her without succumbing to her scent... because I had a horrible feeling once my wolf got a taste of her, he was never letting her go.

The image of my face buried between her thighs jumped into my mind.

Fuck me.

"Stay downwind," I said, clamping down on those thoughts.

With a snarl, I swung my travel pack onto my shoulder. It was stuffed with my supplies and Knox's — since he'd probably spend most of this trip in his wolf form — and wasn't heavy enough to weigh me down, but that meant it wasn't a distraction from my wolf's thoughts about what it wanted me to do with Audrey.

"Eyes open for grimalkins," I barked, striding toward the front gate. "Deacon, you and your team lead the way."

Deacon, a large gray wolf, bounded in front of me, and the rest of his team, four sleek brown wolves, followed. Ahead of them, a large black shadow slipped down the road, keeping to the shadows and as far away from Audrey as his unwanted bond would let him.

Thankfully we were up early enough that there weren't a lot of people around to see our group marching down the sloping twisted streets and heading out on the main road toward the last patrol shed. Unfortunately, I knew we hadn't left unnoticed and the rumors that Bishop and I had left with Whil, a hunt team, and Audrey, would spread through town before sunset.

I hadn't thought taking care of Audrey in our residence and introducing her to our betas would be enough to start rumors, but it had been, and I could only imagine what the rumors were going to be by the time we got back.

Which really, was so low on my list of things to worry about it was ridiculous that I was even thinking about them now.

But there were only two things I could do on the long walk to patrol shed twelve: keep my eyes open from trouble, something

Deacon's team was already doing, and think. And because the walk was slower than I wanted — because Whil and Audrey didn't have the stamina of a wolf — we needed to watch our pace. And that gave me far too much time to think.

Really, I should be thinking about the grimalkins and how they'd slipped past our hunt teams and territory patrol teams as well as the town's watch or why Jundar had called an emergency meeting of the Mountain and Sea Alliance because of increased beast activity in neighboring areas. Except my thoughts kept jumping back to Audrey.

Audrey who needed someone to protect her and nurture her confidence. She'd faced off against a grimalkin, she'd survived the horrible ordeal that had brought her to our realm, she had the soul of a fighter, but it was buried deep within her, just like her wolf... just like my wolf wanted to be.

And now I was thinking about sex again. Wonderful.

AUDREY

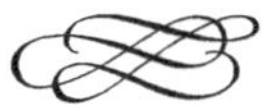

WE walked all morning, took a quick break at lunch for water and a handful of rations — since wolf shifters with an awakened wolf could live on one meal a day if they needed to — and walked for the rest of the afternoon.

After we'd left town, Deacon and his hunt team had spread out into the tall grass, searching the area for trouble and letting Cyrus and Whil take the lead, while Knox remained out of sight.

I'd hung back — and downwind from Cyrus — with Bishop. By his sniff and the darkening of his eyes the moment I'd opened my door this morning, he'd known I'd done some serious masturbating in an attempt to ease the aching desire of my heat, or my mating bond, or whatever the hell it was that was driving me crazy.

Thankfully, he hadn't commented on it then and didn't bring it up during our walk. Instead, he talked about safe stuff like the pack's territory and trade with a seaport on the other side of the mountain.

My feet had been sore when we'd stopped for lunch and they, along with my legs, were killing me by the time we stopped at a wooden shed forty feet off the road. Hell, all of me was sore. My pack that hadn't been heavy at the beginning of the day now weighed a ton and I was hungry and exhausted, and we'd only been walking for one day!

I had no idea how I was going to make it the nine days it was going to take to get to the death god's altar.

Except I was just going to have to. Cyrus was already pissed at me. It would be better to prove I wasn't completely pathetic and figure out how to pull my own weight on this journey. I wouldn't be able to help in a fight, but I could still—

God, I had no idea what I could offer. I'd never camped before, had no idea how to start a fire without a lighter or a match, and didn't know the flora well enough to scavenge for food to help make our rations last.

It looked like the only thing I could do right now was keep up, follow any orders Cyrus gave me, and not complain.

"Drop your pack in the shed, grab the bucket just inside the door, and draw water from the well for the hunt team," Cyrus said to me.

"Right." I trudged to the wooden structure and opened the door.

The shed was... a shed. One door and no windows. It was a fifteen-by-fifteen wooden structure that was smaller on the inside because of trunks and shelves and a tall rack filled with firewood along the back wall and left-hand corner. The ground was hardpacked dirt, which wasn't comfortable but safer than a wooden floor, and there was a small hearth and fieldstone chimney against the righthand wall.

I found the bucket, grabbed it, and set my pack where it had been, then headed to the well a few feet away.

Cyrus still stood on the road with Whil beside him, scanning the sea of grass and wildflowers all around us. He said something to her, too quiet for me to hear, and she nodded, her attention locked on something far off in the distance.

Their expressions were grim, but I didn't know if it was because of what we were planning on doing, the grimalkins that had attacked the town the other day, or the strange magic the hunt team had found.

And really, it didn't matter. I doubted they'd tell me, and even if they did, I wouldn't be able to help. The most I could do was follow Cyrus's instructions and draw water for the hunt team... whatever that meant.

I went to the old-fashioned well, complete with a rope-bucket pully system, and drew up a bucketful of water then dumped it into the bucket I'd taken from the shed. I wasn't sure what else I was supposed to do with the water and was on the verge of asking Bishop — who was building a fire in a firepit halfway between the shed and the road — when one of the sleek brown hunt team members came out of the grass, dropped a dead rabbit at Cyrus's feet, and went straight to my bucket. She murmured a *thanks* in my head and drank deeply then headed back into the grass.

Bishop got the fire going, Cyrus took the rabbit and thankfully headed away from the shed into the waist-high grass to skin and gut it where I couldn't see, while the other hunt members visited my bucket and drank.

I wasn't sure what else to do so I made sure the "drinking" bucket was always full. But it was a hurry up and wait kind of job and the exhaustion from walking all day sank into my body and mind, dragging me into a heavy numbness.

Around me, the breeze, starting to cool as the sun set, ruffled my hair and made the tall grasses *shush*.

Stillness.

Shush.

Stillness.

Shush.

The icy hollowness dimmed and so, too, did my achy need as if I was softly separating from my body.

A flurry of birds that looked a little like sparrows but not quite took off from the grass stalks, tugging me back to myself, strengthening all my unwanted emotions. They chattered with each other and scolded whatever had disturbed them then flew away, leaving a heavy, peaceful near silence in their wake.

I'd only experienced the near-silence a few times before since the only place I'd been able to find it had been in the heart of my old pack's forest and it usually hadn't been safe to be there.

There was an energy in the silence, a gentle vibration that filled the air and called to me.

It said I belonged, that I was home.

There was too much noise everywhere else, too much energy from others. But in the silence, I could feel my primal connection with nature and could imagine that connection came from the wolf asleep inside me.

I let my mind and body drift again and the gentle vibration changed, my senses zeroing in on a ferocious feral power. It was just a whisper, his power was fully contained, yet somehow I could still sense it.

Of course, my soul would always sense it, would always be drawn to it, and would always recognize it.

Because he was my mate and every fiber of my being believed he always would be.

Knox.

I hadn't even caught a glimpse of him all day and I knew if I turned around to look, he'd stay hidden in the grass.

The icy hollowness and the grief of rejection fluttered in my chest along with my achy need to seal our bond, but the sensations didn't overwhelm me, and I'd never been so happy in my life to be too exhausted to feel anything.

"Audrey," Cyrus barked.

I jerked, my eyes flying open. I hadn't even realized I'd closed them.

"Fill up the bucket and bring it." He strode past me and headed into the grass away from our makeshift campground.

The bucket was already full, so I picked it up and followed him.

He turned so the breeze was at his back — reminding me that he didn't want to catch the scent of my uncontrolled desire — squatted and held out his bloody hands.

"I didn't get a chance to talk to you before we left," he said his voice gruff as I hefted the bucket and poured a stuttering stream of water onto his hands so he could wash them.

My heart did a strange flipflop that I attributed to my perpetual state of semi-arousal. Maybe he wasn't as angry at me as I thought. Gruff did seem to be his natural state. Even during the dinner with his betas where he'd lightened up a bit — mostly because Nova kept teasing him — he was still kind of surly. Maybe I could actually trust him not to turn on me the second my bond with Knox was broken and that there was a place for me among his pack that didn't involve me being a slave.

"You can't fight and you can't shift, so I doubt you can hunt," he said, crushing the flicker of hope I'd had that he thought I was actually worth something. "How different is our realm from yours? Would you be able to tell what plant is and isn't poisonous?"

I wouldn't have been able to tell what plant was poisonous back home. "Probably not, but I—"

"I'm guessing the stars are different, too," he said, cutting me off before I could say I could learn. "If they were the same, would you know how to find your way back to town?"

"No."

His eyes narrowed and a hint of his power rolled over me. "How basic do I need to go? If you don't have a starter, can you start a fire?"

That was basic? I was pretty sure most people didn't know how to start a fire without a lighter or match. Sure, they'd probably seen the stick thing on TV before, but I doubt they'd tried it and I had a feeling it was a lot harder than the movies made it out to be. But that was my realm. Maybe every child here learned how to start a fire without a starter in preschool.

His gaze bore into me, his wolf rising to the surface and darkening his eyes, reminding me that in this situation, I was prey and he was the predator. Hell, in every situation I was prey.

"What *can* you do?" he growled, the pressure from his power growing, demanding I answer him.

But as he so aptly pointed out, I couldn't fight and I couldn't hunt. In this situation, there wasn't anything I could do. I didn't know anything about surviving in the wild. I hadn't even watched any of those survival TV shows. If we were back in the town though—

I thought about what I could and couldn't do that didn't involve creating a spreadsheet for a computer they didn't have or writing an essay on a history that didn't exist in this realm. My possible list of skills was far too short. All I could really do was clean and cook, and I wasn't sure my cooking skill would be helpful in this situation since I'd never cooked over a campfire before. Hell, I couldn't even read and write anymore since I didn't know this world's language and the magic that let me understand them and be understood only worked with verbal communication.

The thought made me sad and frustrated. What had I been doing with my life? Nothing. Not a damn thing.

No.

I shoved those feelings as deep down as I could before they fully woke the grief from Knox rejecting our bond.

I wasn't lazy or stupid. I hadn't been *allowed* to do anything.

"Anything?" he pressed, his power compelling me to answer.

"No." My throat tightened and my grief gained strength despite my determination to ignore it.

Damn it. There had to be something I could do. I couldn't be completely useless.

Except, right here and now, I was.

"There's nothing," I forced out.

Cyrus grunted and straightened, glowering down at me as if he'd suspected what my answer would be and still didn't like it.

"The first few rabbits should be ready soon," he said and took the mostly empty bucket from me and strode back to the well. He refilled it then headed to the campfire and sat.

I stared at his broad, straight back, fighting to regain control of my emotions before following him. But I was exhausted and the best I could manage was to hold back my tears. Because damn it, I was *not* going to cry just because Cyrus, like everyone else in my life, had pointed out I was useless.

I should have been used to it by now. Sterling and his friends had reminded me almost every day that I was worthless. But no one knew me here and a part of me had hoped even though I was next to powerless and couldn't shift that the shifters here would see me in a different light.

With a sigh, I waded out of the tall grass to the hardpacked earth and stone area where Bishop, Cyrus, Whil, and two wolves — one of them Deacon — sat around the campfire. Two rabbits had been skewered on a long metal stick which was propped up by metal stands on either side, creating a rotisserie, and the smell of roasting meat wafted over me.

"Here," Whil said as I approached, and she dipped a metal cup into the water bucket and held it out to me.

"Thanks." I took the cup and scanned the area for a place to sit, preferably away — and hopefully downwind — from Cyrus.

"Come," Bishop said, patting the ground beside him. "Sit with me."

AUDREY

I took the cup, trudged the remaining few feet to Bishop, and sagged to the ground, finally off my feet. But before I could settle, he grabbed me around the waist and hauled me into his lap.

"What are you doing?" I asked, my voice suddenly breathy as soft, sensual need swept through me.

"Before we left, Nova reminded me that I'm an idiot," he replied, his breath feathering across my skin.

A shiver of desire swept through me, but thankfully I was too exhausted, and it wasn't strong enough to compel me to beg him to have sex with me. Except that didn't stop my mind from jumping to the dreams I'd been having where Knox — looking like a moodier version of Bishop — made me come with screaming satisfaction, or remembering the look in Bishop's eyes the other day when I'd stepped out of my bedroom. He'd looked almost as hungry as dream-Knox with his wolf-darkened eyes.

My attention flickered across the fire to Cyrus, my fantasy sliding to him. I'd actually seen him naked and knew just how perfect and powerful his body was. His gaze caught mine, but his expression didn't change, as if he didn't have any feelings about his brother holding me... or was hiding them. There wasn't even a hint of power and I didn't know if that meant he approved or if he didn't want to start a fight.

"You've suffered two traumatic events in the last few days and you don't have anyone here to help steady your soul." He pressed on my shoulders, urging me to lie back against his chest even though I was sure he could smell my increased arousal.

His length hardened against my butt.

Oh yeah, he could smell it.

"You'll be better able to manage your heat if your soul is steady."

I moved to look him in the eyes, shifting my rear against him and making his breath hitch. "I'm not sure this is a good idea."

Need made his eyes even darker, but his expression was tight as if he was determined to control himself. "I'm not going to take advantage of you," he murmured. "I'll keep you safe. I promise."

His words swirled more heated desire into my chest, but on top of that— No it was *stronger than* that, there was something else, something softer but just as enveloping. It was like the energy I'd felt earlier by the well while embracing the near silence whispering in my heart: connected, safe, home.

I'd never experienced anything like it before. The sensation wasn't strong, but it was there, a ghost in my cells, a vibration that called to the wolf nature I feared I didn't really have, a foundation that would support me.

"What is this?" I breathed, pressing my hand over my heart.

"Our shifter connection," Bishop replied.

But that was impossible. Cuddling with Mila had never felt like this, and while those closer to each other, like mates and siblings, had stronger connections, close friends could have just as strong a connection.

Except perhaps a stronger shifter connection was just another magical thing that was different in this realm.

"Come," he murmured, urging me to relax and fully accept his embrace. "It'll help. I promise."

With a sigh, I gave in and leaned back. Distracting, achy need aside, it felt good to have his arms around me, and I was just too tired to fight him or do much of anything about our mutual attraction.

I turned my attention to the fire, watching it flicker and sway in the soft breeze, and let myself drift on the warmth of my shifter connection with Bishop. My eyelids fluttered closed and the exhaustion of the day sank deeper into my bones.

"Hey," Bishop said, taking my water cup — that I was about to dump in my lap — and setting it on the ground. "You need to stay awake until you eat something. Talk to me, tell me something about yourself."

"You already know the gist of it." I didn't want to talk about myself. As Cyrus had proven, my life had been simple and secluded, and the only other thing of note he and Bishop didn't know was how I was the one who found my father in the bathtub after he killed himself. And I really didn't have the emotional strength to bring that up. "There isn't much else."

"I'm sure there are lots, like ... have you ever seen an angel?"

Cyrus grunted, took the rabbits off the spit, and speared two more. I wasn't sure what the grunt meant. Bishop had been curious about angels — about my whole realm actually — and Cyrus had shut his questions down because they'd had more important things to worry about at the time.

"I haven't seen one in person," I told Bishop, "but I've seen them on TV."

"TV? What's that?" Whil asked, gingerly picking apart the rabbits and distributing the pieces among four metal bowls.

"It's—" How could I explain it? I didn't think they had electricity and I had no idea what level of technology they did have, not to mention if any of my realm's technology had a magical replacement in this realm.

"Do you have photography?" I asked. Bishop frowned. Maybe the realm's magic couldn't translate the word like it hadn't with TV. "It's a way of capturing an image on a specially treated—" Hmm, I couldn't say film. If they didn't know the word photography, they probably wouldn't understand *film* in that context. "—a specially treated piece of paper?"

"No," he replied, as Whil handed us our bowls of roasted rabbit.

Okay, so... I guess it would be best to just really simplify it. I picked up a piece of meat and blew on it to cool it off while trying to figure out the best way to explain it, but it was a struggle to focus and keep my eyes open.

"Well... we have... devices that let us capture images. Still ones, like a picture, and moving ones like a play."

"How is this related to this TV?" Cyrus asked, his voice jolting me as if I'd been on the verge of falling asleep. His gaze met mine, dipped to my hands then rose again. "Eat."

Right. Food. I really *was* hungry, but eating just seemed like too much work, and Bishop's embrace was so warm and relaxing and—

"Eat," Cyrus insisted, and a soft wave of his power jolted me awake again and made me pop a piece of meat into my mouth before I fully realized what I was doing.

"You don't have to force me," I said.

"Kind of looks like I do," Cyrus replied. "I'm going to keep waking you up until you've finished what you've been given."

Another soft wave of power made me eat more of my dinner and I glowered at him.

Cyrus met my glare, his expression smug and cocky, which did nothing to diminish his attractiveness. In fact, that cocky confidence and smirk that said he knew he didn't even need to use a fraction of his power to make me submit only made him more attractive.

"Now tell Bishop about this TV before he dies from curiosity," he said.

"What, no power? Not going to force me to tell him?" I huffed and popped more meat in my mouth before he made me do it.

"Do I need to?" he growled, sending a shiver of need rushing through me.

Oh, yes—

No! No no no. My body might have thought Cyrus making me

submit was exactly what I wanted, but it wasn't. What I really wanted was to feel his power like I felt Knox's power in my dreams, not controlling me, but awakening that wild and primal something within me.

He quirked an eyebrow, a whisper of his power teasing over me.

"The TV?" Bishop prompted.

I wrenched my attention away from Cyrus before my desire overwhelmed me. I liked being in Bishop's arms, liked the warmth and comfort and sense of *home,* and I didn't want to ruin it by trying to rip his clothes off and have him take me while everyone around the campfire watched.

"We watch the images we've captured on the TV." I finished off my meat, but Bishop took my bowl and replaced it with his which was still full.

"That's not fair."

"I can eat later," he murmured. "But you're not going to last for the next two rabbits to finish cooking."

"Fine," I grumbled, shoving more meat into my mouth before Cyrus could command me. "I've seen the angels in the Joined Parliament and I've also seen footage from the war of angels fighting Michael's nephilim."

The fire snapped and I realized I was starting to drift off again.

"Do you miss it?" Bishop asked.

I finished my mouthful but the idea of moving my hand to pluck more meat out of the bowl and eat suddenly seemed exhausting.

"I really miss cars," I sighed. How was I going to handle another day of straight walking, let alone eight more days after that?

BISHOP

AUDREY'S EYES SLID SHUT AND SHE WENT LIMP IN MY ARMS, FAST asleep. My bowl started to slide from her fingers, and I caught it and set it on the ground before she spilled it.

Aaaaand she's out, Deacon said in my head with a chuckle. *I'm actually surprised you didn't have to force her to stay awake to eat, too.*

Cyrus grunted at that, probably pissed that he'd been forced to make her eat in the first place. He didn't like to use his power like that, but she'd been falling asleep before the rabbits had even finished cooking and, like me, he probably doubted she'd stay awake long enough to start dinner let alone finish it.

How much did she manage to eat? he asked, his tone clear that if he didn't think she'd eaten enough, he'd wake her again.

Not enough considering we walked all day and are going to walk most of the day tomorrow. She sighed and shifted against my rock-hard cock, snuggling closer.

I gritted my teeth and fought to keep my promise to her. Just because I said I wasn't going to do anything didn't mean I didn't want to. And with her delicious, seductive scent filling the air around me, it was getting harder by the minute — my cock as well as the effort to resist.

We can put the leftover rabbit in some oatmeal in the morning, I said, trying to keep my mental voice calm and not give away how much she was affecting me. I was sure it was obvious to everyone that I was attracted to her, but I didn't want Cyrus to worry about me being distracted. He had enough to worry about already.

Deacon, still in his wolf form because he and his hunt team would remain as wolves for the entire hunt unless necessary, stared at me.

You sure you want to take her north? From her scent, she's only days away from a full heat. His golden gaze dipped to her and I instinctively tightened my grip. My wolf and I *needed* to protect her even if Deacon wasn't a threat.

It was obvious she was struggling with the journey already even though she hadn't complained. After lunch, her pace kept getting slower and slower and her gait had become uneven. Without a doubt, if she wasn't in pain now, she would be in the morning.

With the strength of her heat already, I doubt just holding her is going to be enough to get her through, Deacon added.

It might be more effective than you think, Cyrus replied.

Deacon snorted. *That sounds like wishful thinking. You best make your situation clear to her so she doesn't get the wrong idea.*

She won't be getting the wrong idea, Cyrus growled. *I'm not sleeping with her.* He turned to me and frowned. *Did you see her reaction to your soul steadying hers? It's like she's never been held before.* A ripple of power slipped his control, revealing his frustration, and he yanked the last two rabbits from the spit. *We deal with that and she'll be fine.*

I doubt that, Deacon huffed. *If no one has held her before, she'd be insane— well, more insane than whatever that fantasy tale was that she was telling Bishop, so someone has obviously held her. Jeez, Cyrus, this isn't like you.*

Would everyone stop telling me what I think or feel, he snarled back. *I haven't suddenly forgotten my duty to the pack.*

Then why the hell do the three of you have to be the ones to personally see her home? Deacon demanded.

Cyrus growled and I clenched my jaw. Knox had been adamant

about not telling anyone other than Whil what had happened, but given that we were going north into dangerous lands, Deacon wasn't going to be happy with a "just because" explanation.

He'd probably also been hounded by Nova to get the truth before we parted ways tomorrow afternoon. And while those two were the most laid-back betas on our team, they were the least likely to accept "just because."

Fuck, Knox snarled in my head. He wasn't as involved in the day-to-day running of the pack, but he still knew our betas and knew Deacon wasn't going to give up. *We're not taking her home. Somehow she mate bonded with me without either of us saying the vows and Whil thinks there's a way in the northern death god's realm to break it without killing either of us.*

Deacon's gaze jumped to mine then across the fire to Cyrus. *You're shitting me.*

Cyrus met his stare.

The fire crackled and popped then popped again.

Holy fuck! He burst out laughing, his wolf chuffing while his mental voice roared through our heads. *That's god-level fucked up. If she was going to manipulate any of you with a love potion, she should have targeted you,* he said, looking at me. *Out of all the guys she could have picked. Fuck! She picked Knox?*

She didn't pick me, Knox snarled back. *It just happened.*

"Likely a nasty side-effect of the magic that brought her to this realm," Whil whispered, loud enough for us to hear but soft enough to not wake Audrey since she didn't have telepathy like we did.

This realm? She's from a different one? Well, that explains the weird conversation you had, he said excepting Whil's explanation without hesitation. *Oh, Great Sisters, that poor girl. Mated to Knox.* Deacon's laughter abruptly stopped. *Shit. No wonder her heat is driving her crazy. You haven't sealed the bond.*

"That's part," Whil replied. "But given that she's said heats in her realm aren't powerful, I suspect there's something about this realm affecting her. It could be the same with soul-steadying touch. Which means she might not need as much touch because of where she's from, or she'll need more because this realm is changing her and she's already at a deficit."

Sisters! She just couldn't catch a break. Abused, betrayed, thrown into an unfamiliar realm, and mate bonded with someone who didn't want her, and now that bond and this realm were changing her body in unexpected ways.

She's going to need help adapting, I said only to Cyrus and Knox. *If holding her isn't enough, I can take care of her. You don't have to worry about her getting the wrong idea. Knox—?* I shouldn't have needed to ask his permission, and he was smart enough to figure out I was going to have sex with Audrey if she needed it, but I needed to know he'd be able to control himself if or when that happened.

Do whatever the fuck you want, he snarled. *I don't care.*

A sliver of anger seeped past the block he'd put on our twin bond, but it was too slight for me to figure out if he was pissed at the idea of me having sex with her or pissed at himself.

Don't get attached, Cyrus added. *We can't forget that this might not end well. If it comes down to her or Knox, I'm picking Knox.*

You don't have to remind me. I know our priorities. Except telling him that made my wolf heave inside me.

We loved Knox. He was our other half, and even though he was actively trying to keep me out right now, we were and always would be connected.

But even though there was a risk his wolf would take over and go feral, he was still stronger than Audrey. And keeping Audrey safe, even if it meant having to convince Knox to accept their mating bond, was the best way to keep Knox safe.

And she's going to need more than just help, Cyrus added, more of his power slipping, his worry about the situation growing. *She can't fight or hunt or start a fire.*

Audrey groaned but didn't wake, and I glared at Cyrus. *Control yourself, she needs her sleep.*

She needs a fucking miracle, Cyrus shot back. *She can't do anything.*

My wolf, already dangerously close to the surface because I was holding Audrey, wrenched free and took over.

Don't you dare say that where she can hear it, my wolf snarled at him. *Her sense of self-worth is fragile and Knox rejecting their bond isn't helping. If she's never been held and she now needs it to the same degree we do, her emotional state is even more precarious.*

I know, Cyrus growled back, his power flickering then vanishing before it could affect her again. *She's going to be exhausted, but we need to teach her everything we can. If she gets separated from us, she won't survive.*

She won't get separated, my wolf snarled back.

You can't guarantee that, Cyrus said, his wolf taking over as well and glaring back at me. *We protect her by making her stronger.*

Agreed, I replied.

Agreed, Knox's wolf whispered through our twin bond so softly I wasn't sure Knox was aware his wolf had spoken.

AUDREY

I woke alone in the windowless shed. Someone, probably Bishop, had brought me inside and covered me with a blanket, and from the light leaking around the door, it looked like I'd slept all night and into the morning.

With a groan, I sat up. My legs and feet throbbed from walking all day yesterday while the rest of me throbbed from yet another sexy dream.

Like before, Knox had pounced on me like I was his favorite meal, and I'd gone from those initial first moments of confusion to wet and ready in a heartbeat — thank you dreams!

This time, he'd lifted me up, pinned my back against a tree trunk, and brought me down onto his cock in one fast powerful stroke. As usual, all I could do was hold on for the ride and submit to the pleasure, so I'd wrapped my legs around his waist and let him pound into me until stars burst across my vision and his cum exploded into me.

The memory sent a miniature climax shuddering through me and a sensual moan escaped my lips.

I pulled the blanket over my head and groaned. I'd hoped I was too tired for another sexy dream or that somehow leaving the town would help, but nope. Exhaustion or change of location didn't matter, and, like all the times before, I woke only partially satisfied and aching to give myself a little more.

Except I should probably practice a little self-restrained. After today, I wouldn't have privacy. I'd be out in the open, camping under the stars with the guys and I couldn't just give myself an orgasm with them watching.

The thought of Bishop and Cyrus with hungry, wolf-darkened eyes and hard cocks watching Knox push into me sent another miniature climax rushing through me.

Oh, fuck.

I *liked* that idea.

What was wrong with me?

The mating bond was urging me to have sex with Knox and I was in heat. I had to be. *That* was what was wrong with me.

There was no point in hiding it or feeling ashamed. As soon as one of them opened the shed door, or as soon as I stepped out, they were going to smell that I was just as achy and desperate this morning as I was yesterday morning and the morning before that. And if I was going to get through this journey without begging Bishop or Cyrus to sleep with me or giving in and sealing my bond with Knox, I was going to have to relieve the pressure.

I pushed my hand down the front of my pants and ran my finger through my folds. I was so wet I had to have come in my sleep, and I was still strung so tight, I came almost the second I rubbed my slickened finger over my clit.

Jeez, we couldn't get to this death god's altar soon enough.

I gave myself two orgasms, hoping it would be enough to take the edge off, then squared my shoulders, my cheeks hot with embarrassment despite my determination to not be ashamed, and stepped out of the shed.

All the men instantly turned to look at me, even Deacon, still in his wolf form, who stood forty feet away on the road. Swell.

My embarrassment burned hotter, searing over my whole face and sweeping down my neck. But I made myself march to the fire, checked the direction of the smoke, and sat downwind from Cyrus.

"It's going to take half the day to reach Anakar," Cyrus said, not addressing my obvious arousal, his attention locked on the pot hanging from the rotisserie over the fire. "We'll make sure Whil and the hunt team are set, then carry on."

I nodded as Whil scooped what looked like oatmeal out of the pot into a bowl, added a spoon, and handed it to me.

"I want to get as far away from Darkweald as possible before we stop for the night," he continued, still not looking at me.

"I understand," I said even though I wasn't a hundred percent sure he was talking to me.

"Good." He stood and dumped the bucket of water on the fire. "You've got ten minutes."

"Good morning to you, too," I mumbled to his back as he strode away. His shoulders stiffened, obviously hearing my words with his better-than-human hearing, but he didn't turn back and scold me.

"He has a lot on his mind," Bishop said as he gracefully sank to the ground beside me, slid his hand under the back of my shirt, and pressed his palm against my skin.

His touch reignited the fire in my core that I'd tried to get down to a manageable level with my morning orgasms.

"Not going to pull me into your lap," I breathed.

"If we want to leave in ten minutes, probably not a good idea," Bishop said, his voice strained. "But you still need as much contact as we can give you."

"You mean, *you*," I said around a mouthful of oatmeal flavored with chunks of last night's rabbit. "As much contact as *you* can give me."

"Cyrus will help if you need him." Bishop's attention jumped to his brother and his expression grew sad. "But he's got obligations to the pack and he's worried—"

"It's okay," I said, cutting him off, knowing he was going to bring up the fact that I was a powerless shifter and not worthy to be Cyrus's mate whether I wanted to be his mate or not. Right now, I was turned on and achy, not icy and hollow, and I wanted to keep it that way. "I understand."

I finished my breakfast and washed my bowl and the oatmeal pot while Bishop took the telescopic metal pieces making up the rotisserie, shrunk them down, and secured them in his pack.

Everyone grabbed their packs and we headed off again, this time leaving the road to wade through the thigh-high grass. My feet and legs started complaining right away but there wasn't anything I could do about it, so I tried to distract myself by looking at the stunning scenery of endless rolling foothills and, when we reached the top of a hill, the forests in the distance.

By mid-morning we crested the top of a tall hill and looked down at a thick, dark forest. Mist seeped from between the trunks and melted the second it reached the sunlight, and the weight of something dark and ominous whispered against my senses.

It felt like the power I sensed from the shifters around me, particularly Deacon and Cyrus who had so much power they struggled to contain it, except somehow I knew it wasn't coming from a shifter.

"Stay on the trail and stay by Bishop," Cyrus said, his attention locked on the forest. "There are beasts and spirits in Darkweald. Some more dangerous than grimalkins."

He didn't wait for me to answer before striding down the hill toward a marginally wider opening among the trunks. Four brown wolves rushed down the hill ahead of him and slipped into the misty darkness. Deacon stayed with me, Bishop, and Whil, while Knox was already in the forest.

I hadn't seen him since the meeting in Whil's greenhouse cottage, but I could always sense him, and my attention kept jumping to wherever I felt he was even though I couldn't see him and didn't want to look for him.

The marginally wider opening among the trees was a narrow trail that forced us to walk in single file, leaving me feeling exposed on either side the second we crossed the threshold into the forest and were cloaked in shadows and mist and silence. There was no bird song or even the sound of leaves rustling in the wind.

The only sounds were our footsteps crunching on dead leaves and twigs, and the heavy ominous power seemed to muffle even that.

It thankfully didn't grow in strength, but it was like it had substance and had plugged up my ears and nose.

"Do you have spirits in your realm?" Bishop whispered as if he didn't want to disturb the hush among the trees or perhaps grab the attention of whatever possessed the ominous dark power.

"I don't know. I've never seen or heard of one, but that doesn't mean they don't exist in my realm," I replied, although for all I knew his realms spirits were supers I already knew about and were called something else.

"They're manifestations of a god's power," he said. "The closer you get to a god or goddess's resting place, the more likely you are to encounter one."

"How powerful are these manifestations?" I asked, peering into the thick, misty shadows around us. The guys had said there was a malicious god sleeping in this forest, which meant these spirits wouldn't be friendly.

"They get more powerful the closer you get to the god."

"And how close are we getting?" Although I had a bad feeling I already knew the answer.

Too close, Deacon said in my head. *To the heart of Anakar. But most of the area is out in the open, so we should be fine if we leave the forest before sundown.*

Which would explain why Cyrus didn't want to spend the night here... not that I'd want to spend the night even with just the pressure from the ominous power.

AUDREY

WE CONTINUED IN SILENCE, EVERYONE TENSE, INCLUDING CYRUS, searching the shadows for danger. Power rolled off him as well as Bishop and Deacon, crackling against my senses, but thankfully not compelling me to do anything... well, maybe it was. I couldn't stop peering into the shadows as well, twitching every time I thought I heard or saw something. And oftentimes, that something was the rusty fur of one of the hunt team members who followed on either side of us, weaving between the trees and bushes.

I wasn't sure how long we walked before we reached a break in the trees. According to my feet and legs and back, it was all day, but it couldn't have been since Cyrus had said we'd reach Anakar by noon. Beyond, bathed in brilliant sunlight, was a large stone arch carved with images of people in agony, welcoming us to the partial ruins of a large town... or was it a temple complex?

The trail widened, becoming the remains of an old road paved with wide, flat stones, although at least half of the stones were missing or covered in layers of dirt and debris. Two dozen wide, shallow steps led up to a courtyard-type area with the crumbling remains of what once had been a large fountain with an enormous statue — now worn beyond recognition by the elements. It sat in the courtyard's center, surrounded by crumbling one- and two-story buildings, some no more than just a partial wall and the outline of where the other walls had stood.

Beyond that, towering above the remains of the buildings, was the temple, an intricate structure with dozens of spires and gaping black windows.

Deacon took the lead, taking us past the courtyard into a maze of narrow streets littered with rubble and forest debris. Mist curled among the stones where the sunlight couldn't reach and the dark power pressing against my senses grew stronger.

Then the maze opened up into a grander, bigger courtyard with a fountain and statue right in front of the temple. Unlike the statue in the previous fountain, this one was in good condition, clearly showing the monster that Sterling had summoned.

My pulse lurched as I looked up at the thing that had tried to eat me and *had* eaten Merrick while he was still alive.

Its leathery wings were spread wide, and his head, with its ram horns curling from his forehead, was tipped back, his mouth open. He had a person in each hand, their expressions filled with horror, and one hand was raised up to his mouth to devour the unfortunate soul.

That had almost been me.

And from what Sterling and Royce had said, they'd known that was going to be my fate. They really were psychopaths and I hoped to God that thing had eaten them as well. It would have served them right.

Four pillars, carved showing more people in pain, stood around the fountain marking a large square in the center of the courtyard, and between the two on my left, hanging in the air, was a tall shimmering thread.

"That's definitely magic," Whil said, heading toward the shimmering thread. Cyrus and Deacon followed her, stopping a good distance from whatever it was to examine it.

"Do you know what it is?" Cyrus asked.

"It's a rip in our realm," Whil replied, keeping her distance as well and slowly circling the *rip.*

Beyond the rip, the forest had taken over the buildings, crowding close to this one side of the courtyard.

I walked to the trees' edge and peered into the shadows. I couldn't see more than a few feet into the gloom, but when I closed my eyes and concentrated, I could hear the rushing of fast-moving water.

"It's the rip I came out of," I said, a confusing mix of hope and fear and frustration churning inside me.

"Does this mean Audrey can go home?" Bishop asked.

Did I want to go home?

No. I was happier here than I'd ever been back home.

But once the mating bond was broken and I was back to just being a powerless shifter would Bishop and Cyrus treat me like Sterling and Royce had? Would I want to return home then?

The rip's shimmering brightened and instead of just rippling air that distorted the statue beyond it — like the air over hot asphalt on a summer's day — a forest grove appeared, one that looked a lot like my old pack's sacred grove.

Now that I could get a good look at it, I could see that the window was tall, stretching taller than the statue but only a foot wide, and as I watched, a sparrow, chased by a crow, darted through the rip. The crow swooped after it, but one of its wings clipped the milky, shimmering edge of the rip and burst into flames, burning so hot and fast the bird was complete ash before it could hit the ground.

My churning emotions shifted to fear and, much to my surprise, disappointment. Maybe I did want to go home.

No, it wasn't going home that I wanted, but to show Bishop my realm. He'd been so interested in hearing about TV and I knew he'd be amazed to actually see it.

"She's not going home through that," Cyrus said, his voice gruff.

"Then how did she make it through?" Bishop asked.

"It was probably wider when it was first made," Whil replied. "But there's nothing maintaining it so the magic that created it is fading, and the rip is shrinking. Eventually, it'll disappear."

Cyrus gave Whil a nod and grunted then shielded his eyes and looked up. "We have a little time before we have to move out. Audrey, eat something. Bishop, you're with me and the hunt team. I want to search the area for trouble. Deacon, you're with Whil."

He jerked his chin and two of the wolves from the hunt team followed him across the courtyard and around the edge of the temple.

Bishop drew up close to me and slipped his hand under my shirt, pressing his palm against the small of my back.

My churning emotions eased and a flicker of that warmth and calm I'd felt last night replaced them.

"You okay?" he asked, his eyes soft and sad. "I know you weren't happy in your pack, but it's still home."

"There are things I wish I could show you, but I'd much rather be here than there." I shrugged and gave him my warmest smile. His eyes darkened and my body heated.

With a groan, he yanked his attention away and cleared his throat.

"You should eat and I should patrol," he said, then he marched away before I could respond.

I sat in the shade on a chunk of stone at the edge of a crumbled building, pulled out my bag of dried fruit and meat, and stared at the strip of green in the rip.

Whil walked around the rip a couple more times then, with Deacon at her side, headed to the temple. I wasn't sure what she was looking for, but I had to remember that her trip here wasn't about finding me a way home. It was about determining if the magic that had brought me here had awakened the malicious god and taken him to my realm.

From the dark, ominous power pressing against my senses, I suspected the god was still here, and from the fact that we hadn't been attacked or heard of attacks in the last few days since I'd come here, he was still asleep. But that didn't mean he wasn't close to waking up.

Fear shivered down my spine. Merrick, my old pack's alpha,

hadn't stood a chance against that monster, and while Cyrus, Bishop, and Knox were all more powerful than Merrick, I had no idea if they'd be able to kill it.

Could someone even kill a god? Not to mention even if they did win, no one would get out of that kind of fight without injury, most likely life-changing injury.

AUDREY

I CHEWED ON A TOUGH PIECE OF DRIED MEAT AND WATCHED THE LEAVES in the trees through the rip flutter in a breeze I couldn't feel. From the sunlight filtering through the branches, it looked to be about the same time of day there as it was here, and I could almost imagine I wasn't in a different realm.

Rustling sounded somewhere beyond where I could see, then Royce stepped into sight.

Instinct seized me and I froze as my pulse lurched into a desperate, rapid beat. He'd gleefully tried to sacrifice me to a monster. I had his claw marks scarring my chest, marks I'd never be able to get rid of even if my wolf did eventually awaken because they'd already healed. They were forever a part of my body, a reminder that he and Sterling were psychopaths.

And a part of my soul still wept at his rejection, still believed he was my destined mate, even though it had all been a manipulation and my soul had picked someone else.

Well, fuck that.

I tried to shove aside the unwanted grief as well as my fear and feed my anger.

What I felt was an after-effect of the spell he'd used to fake the fated mating call, nothing more, and that disgusting spell was why my soul thought Knox was my mate and why I'd forced a soul bond on him.

I wasn't in love with Royce and never would be. Just like I wasn't in love with Knox. And while Knox could still hurt me, and was hurting me by rejecting our unwanted bond, Royce couldn't touch me anymore. He couldn't get through the rip to get to me— Hell, he might not even be able to see through it like I could.

As if he could hear my thoughts, he glanced at the rip and looked straight at me. His eyes flashed wide for a second, revealing his surprise, then his lips curled back in a wicked smile.

"Well, look who's still alive," he sneered.

I stood and glared back. He couldn't get to me, but I refused to stay sitting and look up at him, even from a distance. Sitting was a weaker position and I wanted to make sure he knew he hadn't broken me and never would.

"How's your incomplete mating bond, *mate*?" he asked.

"It'll fade," I lied. I didn't want to bring Knox into this. For all I knew, he'd side with Royce about how useless I was and I wouldn't be able to fight the grief from our rejected bond. "Soon you'll be nothing more than a bad memory."

"You keep thinking that." His smile darkened with dangerous glee. "We got that witch to put extra juice into her spell. That feeling of emptiness, of utter rejection?" he said. "That feeling will never go away. It's just going to keep on growing until you lose your mind and kill yourself."

My breath stalled and I fought to keep the fear that was now rushing through me from my expression.

It was never going to go away?

But it had to. I couldn't spend the rest of my life feeling like this.

"That's a lie," I said, forcing myself to hide my fear and keep my voice strong.

"You're going to kill yourself just like Daddy." He jerked forward a step, and I flinched even though I *knew* he couldn't get to me.

He threw his head back and roared with laughter. "He ate a bullet in the bathtub."

And there'd been so much blood sprayed across the dated yellow tiles.

"How will you do it? Got a gun? Got pills?"

The grief and icy hollowness that I'd been trying so hard to ignore surged, consuming my anger, and my eyes started to burn with tears I did *not* want to cry in front of Royce.

No one wanted me—

Damn it. It isn't a real emotion.

Except it was and the rejected bond was just shining a spotlight on how I'd felt after finding my dad. I hadn't been enough for him to fight his PTSD from the war. I wasn't enough for anyone.

"Looks like you're going to have to find something sharp and slit your wrists." Something rustled out of my line of sight and he glanced over at whatever it was. "Look who's still kicking," he laughed.

Sterling stepped up beside him, his expression darker, although he still seemed pleased — in that same psychopathic sick way that Royce did — that I was still alive.

"Well, well, well," Sterling purred. "Are you broken yet?"

"Never," I spat back, blinking away my tears. I might be hurting, I might get beaten down and be a complete mess, but I refused to let Sterling and Royce break me. "And you can't get to me anymore."

His expression snapped to sudden, violent rage, and a ferocious wave of his power slammed into me.

"Come," he snarled.

My body jerked forward a step.

Oh, shit. He can control me through the rip.

I fought to step back, but all I managed to do was to stop myself from moving forward.

"I'm alpha and you're pack. You belong to me. Come," he growled.

No. No way in hell. Never.

"I'll always be able to get to you," he sneered.

His compulsion squeezed my chest and I stumbled forward a few more steps. I clenched every muscle in my body and glared at him. His power wasn't as strong as Cyrus's, and I'd managed to resist him... at least until I'd passed out. I wouldn't give in to Sterling. I wouldn't.

"I. Said. Come."

"Fuck you," I spat back even as his compulsion heaved me forward another step.

The wind on their side gusted, blowing a flurry of dead leaves at the rip, half of them flying through and half bursting into flames.

Sterling's eyes lit up with wicked glee. Forty more feet and that would be me.

No. Fuck no!

Something small and quiet *thu-thudded* around my heart, and I staggered back a step, shocking myself and — from the look on their faces — shocking Royce and Sterling as well.

Holy shit, I'd defied his command.

But his rage returned, wilder and darker than before, and his face turned red with the strength of his emotion. The ghostly image of ram's horns flickered around his head, curling from his forehead, and the dark, ominous power I'd been sensing since we'd entered the forest slammed into me and seized my muscles.

I staggered forward a step and then another and another, running full out toward the rip.

Oh shit. Oh shit oh shit oh shit.

I mentally clawed inside myself trying to find whatever power I had that had let me take a step back, but there was nothing inside me, no hint of a wolf or wisp of shifter power. I tried to fall, to let my body go limp, but Sterling's command was too strong, and my body wouldn't obey me.

Please. There had to be something I could do. I'd survived that monster — barely, but I'd survived — I couldn't go out like this.

Kneel! Knox yelled inside my head, and a massive wave of power crashed into me, seizing all my muscles and stealing my breath.

I dropped to my knees, gasping for air, the warring pressure from Sterling's power and Knox's making it difficult to breathe. Royce and Sterling dropped to the ground as well and Knox bounded out of the shadows of a crumbling house. He stopped beside me, growling and baring his teeth at the psychopaths.

"Found yourself a new alpha," Sterling snarled, defying Knox's power and heaving up to one knee. "He's not stronger than me."

He raised his hands and black things — shadows, demons, I had no idea what they were — exploded out of the ground in a stinging shower of stone and dirt.

They whirled around us, too many to count, their bodies twisting and expanding into flying snakes. They were all black, black scales, black leathery wings, and black teeth, so many black shark-like teeth. The only things not black were their glowing red eyes.

Sterling howled with laughter but abruptly stopped when the shimmering around the edge of the rip flickered brighter.

"Kill them," he snarled. "When the window reappears, I want to see their bodies torn to pieces."

The rip shimmered again, and Sterling, Royce, and my old pack's sacred grove vanished, the rip, once again, turning into a rippling thread of distorted air.

Then the snakes attacked in a writhing, hissing mass. One swooped at my head, I swatted it aside, and dropped to my knees, praying if I was on the ground, I'd be a smaller target.

Snarling, Knox caught a snake in midair with his teeth and, with a sickening crunch, bit it in half, then swiped his claws through two more. Another one sank its fangs into his back and I ripped it off, but that left me open, and two more bit my arm and back.

Screaming, I tried to wrench them off, but more snakes latched on and another wrapped around my throat.

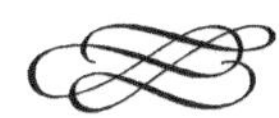

AUDREY

I wrench ed the snake from around my neck before it could strangle me, panic making me slam it against the ground again and again until its strange, glowing red blood had splattered me, Knox, and the ground.

My breath sawed in my chest from exertion and fear, and I had no idea how we were going to survive this or even just escape.

"What the fuck?" Cyrus roared, suddenly right beside me.

He yanked the snakes off me then swiped his claws through three more, splattering me with more blood.

I wrenched another snake off Knox and bashed it against a snake on the ground, killing both of them. My back, arms, and legs stung where they'd bitten me, and while the snakes weren't enormous, they weren't small either, and my arms were starting to get tired from all the swatting and yanking and swinging.

"How many are there?" Bishop asked, rushing up to us and boxing me in between the three of them.

"No, fucking clue," Cyrus growled. "I've killed at least a dozen but it doesn't look like I've made a dent."

Someone howled, and I glanced through the writhing swarm. Three of the four hunt team members were halfway between us and the temple, biting and clawing at snakes, while the fourth lay on the ground. Blood — our colored blood, not the snakes — rushed around her, and I jerked to my feet.

I couldn't really fight, but maybe I could do something to save her.

"Stay," Cyrus barked, his command slamming into me before I could go.

"She'll die."

"You'll die and my brother will be fucked," he snarled back as a snake on the ground shot out and dug its fangs into his calf.

I stomped on the snake with a stomach-churning crunch. "Your brother will be free."

"You don't know that," he said, tearing through two more.

Across the courtyard, Deacon and Whil bolted out of the temple followed by more snakes. She shot a golf ball-sized blast of golden light at a snake, and it fell to the ground, but two more took its place.

There are too many, Cyrus said in my head. *Deacon, you and your team get Whil out of the forest.*

"I haven't finished my investigation," she yelled back as she and Deacon reached the three remaining hunt team members, and they all fought their way closer to us.

Send a hunt team in to investigate before you come back and don't return without at least two teams.

"And when the window is open, don't let anyone from my realm see you," I said, stomping on another snake.

Cyrus shot me a dark look that said once we were safe he was getting answers whether he had to compel them out of me or not.

Deacon, you, Nova, and Finn decide if the town can spare two teams, Cyrus added, slashing a snake out of the air just before it bit me. *If not, don't come back. Knox, get Audrey out of here.*

Get on my back, Knox said, surprising me that he'd allow me to touch him let alone ride him. He was big, bigger than all the wolves in my old pack, almost the size of a pony, but still—

"I'm too heavy. I'll slow you down," I said. "I can run."

Get. On. My. Back. His command seized me and I scrambled onto his back before I could stop myself.

"Stop commanding me." His power made me lean over him and grab fistfuls of fur, enveloping me in his rich smoky scent.

Then do what I say when I say it. He leaped forward, his muscles bunching underneath me, his movement smooth and powerful as if he wasn't carrying me.

He barreled through the snake swarm, past the crumbling buildings, and into the forest. The snakes flew after us, hissing and snapping. One bit my thigh, but Knox bashed us against a tree, knocking the thing off and sending throbbing pain through my leg.

He leaped and wove his way through the trees and underbrush. Leaves and branches sliced at my cheeks, and I buried my face against his neck to protect it, fully wrapping myself in his scent.

Home. He was where I belonged. We were meant to be together. Always.

I struggled to concentrate beyond the warmth in my soul at our physical contact and the heat between my thighs at the knowledge that I was straddling him. It didn't matter that he was in his wolf form at the moment. He could shift into a man and be completely naked and ready in an instant.

Behind us, Cyrus and Bishop crashed through the underbrush, racing after us in their human forms, but they weren't fast enough to keep up and Knox quickly outpaced them, awakening a gnawing worry within me.

There were just the two of them and there were so many snakes, and I didn't know if they'd be able to outrun them. Of course, they could sacrifice their clothes and shift, but that thought didn't make the worry disappear.

"We have to go back for them," I said, tightening my grip in his fur as if that would alert him to how much we had to go back. "We can't leave them behind."

They can take care of themselves, he said, not slowing. *You can't.*

"Knox, please."

No.

"Knox—" Damn it. I hated that he was right. I could jump off and run back to Cyrus and Bishop, but I wouldn't be any help, and that was only if I could find them. And only if Knox didn't command me back onto him.

"They're your brothers."

He didn't reply, just kept running. The hiss and rush of air from the swarming snakes died off, but he didn't slow or hesitate until we crashed out of the underbrush onto a trail similar to the one we'd taken into the forest.

My emotions churned, a complicated hot mess that I just couldn't seem to control. My body screamed at me to have sex with Knox, now now now, but I also felt warm and safe and comfortable just like I had when Bishop had held me, while my stomach was heavy and aching with worry for Bishop and Cyrus along with the fear that Sterling and Royce would be able to reach me even now.

And on top of all of that, I was angry.

Angry that I couldn't escape those psychopaths, that I'd been wrong about being safe on this side of the rip, and that I'd been useless in that fight.

Knox rounded a curve in the trail and slowed down to a fast walk. Up ahead lay the way out, a brilliant opening, framed by the forest's dense, dark branches and mist.

What the hell were you thinking talking to them? Knox demanded, finally deciding to speak to me again as we crossed the threshold into the too-bright light of late afternoon.

I'd been thinking that I wanted to prove to Sterling that even if I didn't have any power, I was strong and a survivor. I'd never fought back before. I'd always kept out of sight as best I could and taken what he'd given when he found me. I'd thought for once I was safe and I could tell him how I really felt.

Boy, had I been wrong.

And jeez, I can't believe you thought that asshole was your mate, Knox added, his mental voice thick with disgust, as if everything was my fault because I was too stupid to know the truth.

"Don't you dare!" I shoved off his back, stumbled, my sore legs unsteady, then found my balance and glared at him.

His dark eyes captured mine and my soul wept that we'd lost

physical contact while my body flip-flopped between empty and cold, achy and hot, and angry.

"They're the ones who manipulated me. They enspelled me. I'm sorry the magic they used on me forced us into a mating bond, but don't you dare blame me for what happened." I wasn't stupid. I'd just been hopeful. So God damned, foolishly hopeful.

Royce had made me believe that there was someone out there who could love me, made me think I was worth loving. That, more than anything, was the cruelest thing he and Sterling had done to me. I hadn't realized how much I'd suppressed my hope, or how much hope I'd still had.

Shame and anger burned over my cheeks and forehead. In a matter of minutes, he'd given me everything I hadn't even known I'd been praying for.

It had happened too fast for me to fully process what was going on. I'd only known that a spark I'd kept hidden had suddenly burst into a flame and I wanted what the fated mating call promised.

Then he'd ripped it all away.

I'm not blaming you, Knox said, his voice still harsh and angry. *It's just obvious he isn't your type.*

"Oh, and you know my type?" I shot back. Not that I'd been given a choice. No one had been interested in me and the magic they'd used had convinced me we'd been fated for each other. "You've barely spoken to me, you want nothing to do with me, but you know my type?" Understanding hit me like a punch to the gut. "Right. He's powerful. Someone like me could never be with someone powerful like him."

Actually, I hadn't thought you were into assholes. He turned away, looking across the rugged, rocky landscape ahead of us clearly ending our conversation.

I glared at him as if I could will him into feeling all the frustration and turmoil and heartache I felt. I wanted to scream, fight, bash more snakes on the ground, something, anything to relieve the pressure building inside me. My insides twisted and everything felt too tight and too hot and too much.

I jerked a few steps toward the forest, needing to take action, even if it was just moving.

You're waiting here, Knox snarled.

"I know that," I snapped back, heaving myself around and marching away from him.

And you're not going far. A hint of his power fluttered over me and I ground my teeth, refusing to submit.

I stomped back toward the forest, getting a few steps farther before he growled at me, then marched away again.

Do something. Do something, my mind hissed at me over and over again. *Be useful.*

I raked my gaze around me, searching for something to prove my usefulness. Great chunks of rock jutted from a sloping, jagged landscape covered with moss and dense bushes, and in the distance were more forests. It looked more like we were higher up the mountains than lower and the only explanation for that was that Cyrus's pack's town wasn't in the foothills but a valley.

Except I hadn't seen any mountains on the horizon, which only reminded me that my realm's logic didn't necessarily apply here. And while I would guess that the river cutting through Darkweald Forest flowed through these rocks, I couldn't assume it was. Not to mention all this rock could have made it turn away from its north-south direction before we'd even left Darkweald.

Fine. I couldn't fill our canteens. Not that I'd be able to know if the water was safe. And while I could gather twigs from the nearby bushes, they wouldn't be nearly enough for a fire — and I doubted Knox would even let me go to the forest's edge to gather wood. I also couldn't tell if there were any good spots around for us to camp. Again, not that we'd stay this close to the forest and those snakes.

I turned back to Knox. A small pool of blood lay on the ground by his back paw and even though his fur was black, I could still see the sticky gloss of blood on his upper back thigh, shoulder, and snout.

Damn it. I'd forgotten my pack back at the ruins and I didn't even have supplies for first aid. Of course, given that he wasn't seriously bleeding, he could easily shift and heal himself which meant even if I had our supplies, I'd still be useless... and he'd be naked.

Oh, God.

I wrenched away from him again, making him growl.

For the love of— Stop. Pacing. His command jerked me to a stop. *I'm trying to listen for them.*

I sagged to the ground and closed my eyes. If I couldn't do anything and wasn't permitted to pace, I might as well listen, too. Not that my hearing was as good as Knox's, but it gave me something to focus on.

AUDREY

A moment later Knox huffed and the tension in his body eased, relaxing some of the churning worry inside me. I hadn't heard Cyrus or Bishop, but somehow I knew Knox had. It still didn't mean they were okay, but if he was relaxing, it meant both of them were still moving and that was a good sign.

A few minutes later, I heard their footsteps on the hardpacked earth of the trail and opened my eyes to watch them jog out of the gloomy forest into the afternoon sunlight.

Their shirts and pants were bloodstained and ripped, and Bishop's cheek was bleeding, the blood running down his neck and into his shirt, but neither of them were limping or holding themselves as if they were seriously injured.

I rushed to meet Bishop and tried to pull his pack from his shoulders. "You need to shift."

"He can wait until we're farther away," Cyrus said. His expression was hard, and he looked fiercer than normal with a wide streak of blood painted across his right cheek. "Can you wait on first aid as well?"

"Yes." From the bloodstain on my still-throbbing thigh — that was definitely bruised from being bashed against a tree — and on my ripped shirt, I knew I was bleeding, but I wasn't bleeding a lot. I also wasn't lightheaded, confirming that even though they stung, they weren't bad, which surprised me. I had no idea how I'd managed to get through that fight more or less unscathed.

"Good." He shoved my pack at me and glared. "Forget it again and it's gone. I won't pick it up a second time."

"Understood," I said, unable to stop myself from shrinking a step away from him.

Cyrus huffed and turned his glare to the sky. "We've got at least five hours until sunset. Knox, find fresh water so Audrey can quickly clean up and we can check her injuries before carrying on."

Bishop shot Cyrus a look.

"No." Cyrus strode away, their argument over before it had even begun, and followed the only path available that might or might not have been a continuation of the trail from the forest. "Want to tell me what happened back in the ruins?" he asked me.

Not really.

But there was no point in refusing to talk or lying. Cyrus would just force me to tell him everything or Knox would fill him in — because I had no doubt Knox had seen and heard everything.

"The men who tried to sacrifice me appeared on the other side of the rip. Apparently, alpha powers work through it and he wasn't happy I was still alive."

The memory of Sterling's power and the ghostly image of the malicious god's horns sprouting from his forehead shuddered through me.

"I hope Whil and the others are careful or the rip closes soon," I added. "I think Sterling got the power he wanted. When Knox stopped him from making me walk into the rip, he summoned those flying snakes."

"You think he'd attack the others even if you're not around?" Bishop asked.

"I think he's a psychopath who just got more powerful," I replied.

Bishop brushed his hand against my lower back and offered me a soft smile that I was sure was supposed to be reassuring and supportive but actually reminded me that I ached to have sex with him.

I tried to smile back without looking like I wanted to tear his clothes off and jump him then hurried after Cyrus.

Ahead, the path led down a steep slope and I couldn't tell if steps had been cut into it or not. There were enough places to step that I wouldn't skid all the way to the bottom on my ass, but that was only if I was careful since some of the *steps* were barely larger than my foot.

Below and beyond a thicket of scraggly shrubs lay the river, its water sparkling in the sunshine, and as much as I had said I was fine to carry on, I was grateful that I wouldn't have to go far before washing the snake blood off my face, hands, and arms. That, and I was starting to feel my aching legs and feet, along with every stinging bite from the snakes.

Maybe I wasn't so fine after all, and I'd only thought I was because of adrenaline.

Knox sat just before the thicket waiting for us. He was still in his wolf form, but his fur was no longer glossy and matted with blood, indicating that he'd shifted out his injuries while he'd waited for us to join him, which meant he'd been in his human form and naked.

That thought turned the sexual ache from Bishop's smile into a need as strong as the need I'd felt after I had one of my sexy dreams. It didn't matter that I hurt and was bleeding and filthy. My need to seal the bond, to have sex, to ease the pressure building between my thighs was suddenly overwhelming.

Damn it. I didn't want that. I wanted to break our mate bond. But if Bishop and Cyrus were going to shift out their injuries, they'd need to be naked too, and that—

My breath picked up and I tried to clamp down on that thought. Except I couldn't stop thinking about the one time I'd seen Cyrus naked. He'd been streaked with blood from fighting the grimalkins, and that had only made him look more ferocious and dangerous and incredibly sexy. He was all powerful muscle, honed from years of training and fighting, and his cock—

I was pretty sure I'd only seen it at half mast, but it had still been impressive. More impressive than Sterling at full mast when I'd accidentally walked in on him in the bathroom, something I wished I could bleach from my memory.

"Bishop." Cyrus jerked his chin toward the river, the muscles in his jaw tightening as if he knew what I was thinking — and while he didn't know the details, I had no doubt he could smell my arousal and knew I was thinking about sex. "Help Audrey."

My pulse picked up at the double meaning of his words.

"Come on." Bishop hopped down a three-foot ledge and held out his hand to help me.

I stared at it, afraid of what would happen if I touched him, afraid of how I wanted to throw myself into his arms and beg him to release the pressure.

He'd said he'd have sex with me if I needed it.

Did I need it?

Or did I just want it?

Did it matter?

Embarrassment burned my cheeks. Sex with Bishop complicated things, and having sex with him didn't mean he'd give me the thing I really wanted: someone to care about me. I didn't know if I'd be able to have casual sex with him and not have my heartbroken. And did I really want my first time to be out in the middle of nowhere, with his brothers listening while I was sore and tired and covered in sticky snake blood?

AUDREY

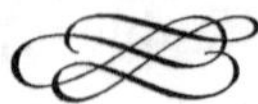

Bishop grabbed my hand, sending a shock of need snapping up my arm and shooting straight to my core.

My breath hitched and I dropped my gaze to my feet, afraid to look him in the eyes, as he tugged me forward, forcing me to hop down closer to him. Heat radiated from him, caressing my senses, urging me to lean into him, take comfort in his touch and in his body.

"I don't want to do something stupid," I murmured as he led me around the thicket and down to the river's rocky shallows.

"But you think you're going to?" he asked, his voice just as soft, although I was sure Cyrus and Knox could still hear us with their better-than-human hearing.

"I think I'm going to lose my mind and we've only just started this journey." I set my pack on the bank, sagged at the water's edge, and started scrubbing the snake blood off my hands. "I'm in no condition for anything and yet it's all I can think about. Hell, we just got attacked by flying snake things. I should be freaking out or something. And if we can't break the bond with Knox, then losing control now could make a bad situation worse." And now I was just babbling.

"Knox will understand," he said, kneeling on the ground beside me and washing his hands as well. He was close, but not as close as I wanted, and yet not far enough away.

"You say that but—" I splashed water on my face, cleaning away the blood.

"No buts," he said when I came up for air, and he hook his finger under my chin, drawing my gaze up to his.

I fell into his warm brown eyes, every part of me, body, heart, and soul, mesmerized by the bright green flecks in his irises. He was so beautiful and kind, and the warmth I'd felt when he'd held me last night had to mean we had some kind of a connection. Only a mate, family member, or very close friend could affect a shifter's soul like that, and he was neither a family member nor a close friend.

"Strong heats can require more than one partner to get through," he said, drawing my attention to his lips and making me wonder how they would feel against mine. "Even if you were happily mated, he'd understand if you needed extra help."

"But you didn't kiss me before," I breathed, leaning toward him, unable to help myself. We'd almost kissed twice now and every time he'd backed away. He had to have a reason for not kissing me and I doubted those reasons had changed.

"You weren't in heat." Now it was his turn for his gaze to flicker to my lips, and his wolf darkened his eyes with an intense desire that stole my breath. "Or at least, we didn't know you were in heat."

Right. My heat. And once it was over, his reasons would return. He'd told me yesterday he'd have sex with me with no expectations. I'd thought he'd meant it to reassure me that he wouldn't want a commitment if I didn't want one, but now I was sure it had been to warn me. We could have sex, but I shouldn't expect it to mean anything.

Sure, the look in his eyes right now said he wanted me, but I was releasing pheromones like crazy. Once my heat was over, I'd no longer be influencing him and he'd no longer desire me.

And right now, my body didn't care.

Hell, none of me cared. I *needed* relief. I was going to lose my mind and he was looking at me like I was desirable even though my clothes were ripped and bloody.

I closed the distance between us before I could second guess myself and pressed my lips against his. He stiffened and the fear that I'd misread the situation twisted in my gut.

Then he groaned softly and cupped the back of my head, gently holding me in place. This kiss was the complete opposite to my dreams where Knox had ferociously dominated me, pulling my hair and devouring my mouth as if he were starving. Bishop's kiss was tender, reverent.

His tongue teased the seam between my lips, asking permission, and his grip remained soft as if he were waiting for me to come to my senses and pull away. But my senses had vanished the second I'd thought of all three of them shifting into their naked human form, and now the heat in my core was lava.

I opened my lips to him, slipping my tongue into his mouth first, urging him for more.

A rumble rolled out of his throat and he kissed me harder, raking his tongue against mine and devouring my gasp of pleasure as his free hand pushed under my shirt and stroked a searing path up my ribs to my breasts.

My nipples were already tight, my breasts aching, and I arched into his touch no longer upset that this realm didn't seem to have bras... although now I was regretting not wearing that easy-to-slip-off dress. I could have been naked in an instant and wouldn't have had to worry about the awkwardness of trying to get my pants off.

The thought sent a flurry of nerves fluttering in my stomach. I was really going to have sex. Here. Now. I—

"Bishop," I gasped into his mouth. "I want—" He sucked on my bottom lip and his hand on my breasts dipped to the waistband of my pants. "But I've never—"

He stilled and my nerves froze into fear. Would he stop because I was a virgin?

Shit. I shouldn't have said anything.

"It's nothing. I—" I tried to press my lips back to his, but his hand that had been at my waist, slipped back up to my chest and gently held me back.

"No, it's something," he said, his voice husky. "Audrey, have you never had sex?"

The word sex shuddered through me. "I still need it."

He cupped my cheek with his large palm, his hunger softening a little.

"Please, don't make me beg," I implored, knowing how desperate I already sounded.

"I won't. I promise." His fingers dipped back down to my pants. "But I want you to enjoy it, so we need to go slow." He flicked the button on my fly. "And we don't have the time for slow right now, so—"

I opened my mouth to argue with him even though I knew Cyrus wasn't going to let us stay here long, but he pushed his hand down the front of my pants, and everything I'd just been thinking vanished.

"I'll relieve the pressure for now and we'll revisit this when we have time," he purred as his fingers teased through my curls and into my arousal.

I nodded, unable to form coherent words, and my hips rocked forward, my body knowing what it wanted even though all my experience had been in my dreams and with my own hands.

"Fuck, you're so wet," he groaned.

He swept his fingers across my entrance to my clit, and my inner muscles trembled. I'd been on the edge since I'd woken up this morning— Hell, I'd been on the edge for days and it wasn't going to take Bishop much to make me come.

Embarrassment heated my cheeks. I didn't want to come the second he touched me, but, God damn it, I was already so close.

He captured my lips again and teased his finger over my clit, twisting the achy, searing need inside me tighter and tighter. My breath turned ragged and my body trembled. I clung to him, my fingers digging into his shoulders, my forehead pressed against his, and then every muscle in my body contracted and stars flashed behind my lids.

A strangled sob escaped my lips, filled with relief and embarrassment and grief. It had happened so fast and wasn't as powerful as the one from my dreams. I wanted more. I wanted the fantasy. But this was reality and, if I was being honest with myself, the orgasm had still been a lot better than if I'd done it myself, even if it hadn't completely satisfied my body's craving.

Still shuddering, I collapsed against him. The warmth of our physical contact swelled around my heart, melting some of my embarrassment and grief.

He wrapped his arms around me and I nuzzled my face into the hollow of his neck, breathing in his fresh green scent. This was where I belonged, where I was safest. I was home.

Except I wasn't home.

Once this was over, all of this would be gone.

And I had to keep thinking like that. I couldn't afford to hope. I wouldn't survive my hope being shattered again. Not by Bishop. Because it was far too easy to fall in love with him.

BISHOP

I clung to Audrey, my wolf heaving inside me, fighting to break free. She needed more than a quick release, and my throbbing cock was more than ready to give it to her. But I refused to let him take over. We didn't have the time to do it right, and I sure as hell was going to do it right.

Calm the fuck down. She's a virgin, I snarled at my wolf.

But he didn't understand what that meant. He was a primal force, and the scent of her arousal was working him into a frenzy that I wasn't sure I'd be able to control for much longer.

We needed to protect her and that included relieving the pressure from her heat. He didn't understand that we couldn't just push our cock into her and make her scream with pleasure. He didn't understand that she needed to be wet and relaxed and feeling safe so her first time wouldn't hurt. And while her heat would help a lot in the wet department, I didn't want to risk it not being enough. My wolf didn't understand any of that. He wanted her now now now because she needed us now now now.

"Bishop," Cyrus said, his voice low, making Audrey tense against me, probably not realizing that wasn't his angry voice but his stressed-out voice... or suddenly realizing that Cyrus and Knox had heard all her strained gasps and her confusing sob when she'd come. "We need to get farther away from Darkweald."

"I ah—" She sucked in a ragged breath. "I think I should clean myself up... alone."

"You won't be able to patch yourself up by yourself," I replied, letting her push away from me. Her cheeks were red with embarrassment even though her expression was still hungry with desire.

"If you touch me—" Her gaze slid down my body to where I tented my pants, and her expression grew pained. "Cyrus should do it."

Do it? My thoughts instantly jumped to sex and my wolf snarled. I was here. I could take care of her. She didn't need my brother.

Except that wasn't what she was saying. She didn't think she'd be able to hold it together while I helped her, and we both knew we needed to keep moving. Even if those flying snakes didn't come out of the forest and we were safe from the malicious god's spirits, we still had to get to the death god's temple as soon as possible. And stopping for sex right now wouldn't help us. That, and I suspected from her sob that she had a lot of conflicting and confusing emotions around the whole situation.

"Okay." I forced myself to stand and climb back onto the bank. Cyrus had made it clear that he had no intention of sleeping with her and she probably sensed that in how he'd been keeping his distance from her.

I rounded the thicket where Cyrus and Knox waited. Cyrus's clothes were still ripped and bloody, but the streak of blood on his face was gone which meant he'd shifted out his injuries while he'd listened to me make her come.

I'm not sleeping with her, he said in my head.

Pretty sure that's why she asked for you.

He huffed and pushed past me, hopping off the bank onto the stream's rocky shallows.

"Get your clothes off and let me see," he growled, a hint of his power rolling off him.

Audrey stiffened and glared at him, the desire in her eyes shifting to frustration — which was probably Cyrus's intent.

"You don't have to make me," she snapped back, grabbing the bottom of her shirt and pulling it up over her head.

I turned away, sucking in deep breaths scented with her arousal that did nothing to ease my wolf or my raging hard-on.

Fuck. I needed to take care of that before I shifted out my injuries. If I couldn't get myself back under control, my wolf really would take over when I shifted and take us right back to her.

"Call me when they're done," I said to Knox, and marched farther away, trying to escape her scent. But it was on me, on my fingers, and clinging to my clothes, and I was going to have to figure out how to keep myself together while holding her this evening when we stopped for the night. Because as much as she probably needed a little sex, she still needed a lot of holding.

I yanked off my ruined shirt and shucked my pants. My cock jutted from my body, throbbing and hard and already leaking pre-cum, and with a groan, I gripped it tight in my fist.

I'd wanted so desperately to do more than just finger her. But I'd promised I wouldn't take advantage of her and a quick fuck when she'd never had sex before wasn't taking care of her. She deserved to be spread out on a soft bed, caressed, and gently teased until she was so wet and relaxed it wouldn't hurt at all.

I closed my eyes and the image of her on my bed in the Residence jumped into my mind. Her blond hair was splayed on the pillow behind her and her head was tipped back in pleasure offering me perfect access to her neck and the top of her shoulder.

My breath picked up and my canines extended in anticipation of claiming her even though this was a fantasy. I slid my hand to my tip, rubbing my palm over my pre-cum for lubrication, then pumped it back down.

I'd take my time with her, worship her, caressing and kissing my way down her body, and make her come before I even reached her sex. Her heat and inexperience made her hypersensitive, and I was going to take full advantage of that.

At the river, I'd barely gotten started with my fingers when she'd gasped and shuddered against me. I'd use that to bring her the most incredible pleasure over and over again with fingers, lips, and tongue, and then, once she was gasping and boneless and glowing, I'd slowly sink inside her.

I tightened my grip, working my hand faster up and down my length. She'd make those incredible sounds I'd overheard the other day when I'd been outside her bedroom, soft mewls and throaty groans and sharp gasps.

My balls tightened at the thought. Then she'd make that long shuddering moan— or better yet, she'd cry out my name like she cried out Knox's name in my dreams. Her body would light up with pleasure, our bond would light up with certainty, and—

Fuck.

My cock swelled and I shot cum onto the rocky ground in front of me. I clenched my jaw, fighting to swallow my own shuddering moan, and sagged back against the rock behind me to stay standing.

Fuck fuck fuck.

We didn't have a bond and I shouldn't be thinking like that until things were figured out between her and Knox. She had more than enough to worry about, and my wolf wanting to mate with her even though we barely knew each other could scare her away.

Hell, it was kind of scaring me away. Did I really want her as a mate or was that Knox's bond influencing me through our twin bond? And I wouldn't know the truth until they broke their bond or sealed it.

CYRUS

Bishop groaned, the sound just at the edge of my hearing, and my balls tightened in sympathy. Audrey's gasps and moans still rang in my ears, and the scent of her release hung heavy in the air around us. It was torture coming closer to her, forcing her to strip, and I could only imagine how much harder it was for Bishop actually having touched her.

Fuck me. I am not *sleeping with her. Not here. Not now. Not ever.*

And I sure as hell wasn't going to have a one-night stand with her. She deserved better than that.

She deserved the promise of forever.

But even if Bishop joined our mate bond, the pack still wouldn't accept her as an alpha, and I wasn't going to put her through that. No matter how much my wolf wanted her. She deserved to be worshiped and adored, valued for who she was not for how much power she possessed. Putting her in the public eye would only point out her weakness, and I feared she'd emotionally crumble and never recover from that.

She was already on the precipice. She might have glared at me for using my powers to make her strip, but even as she pulled off her boots and stepped out of her pants, she was shrinking in on herself. It was like watching a flower wilt before my eyes.

Now she crouched on the riverbank, her shoulders hunched, as she clutched her bloody shirt to her body, covering her breasts and groin as if she were ashamed.

Which made my wolf furious. Being naked was a natural part of being a shifter. If we didn't want to constantly be buying new clothes, we had to strip if we wanted to shift, and she had no reason to hide herself. It wasn't natural.

But that was just a reminder that *she* wasn't natural. Her pack had cursed themselves, preventing them from shifting until they were adults. She hadn't grown up with the casual nudity I had, and without a wolf form, she'd never needed to take her clothes off in front of anyone.

"Drop the shirt," I said, trying to keep my voice even and not reveal how much I was fighting to keep my wolf from wrapping our arms around her and comforting her. "It's only going to get in the way. I've seen it all already anyway," I added, hoping to relax her.

But she stiffened and turned red instead.

"That doesn't make me feel better," she murmured, dropping the shirt and thankfully not forcing me to make her. "Just hurry this up. I'm cold and—" A shiver rolled down her body from her head to her perfectly curved ass and her desire thickened around her. "And I'm pretty sure I'm not downwind from you."

No. No, you're not.

I bit back a rumble of desire and wrenched my gaze away from her to pull my first-aid kit from my pack. "You have a cloth in your pack. Wipe yourself down and let's see what we've got."

I heard her rummage in her pack and then the splash of water and turned to watch her slide the damp fabric over her shoulder and down her arm.

My wolf's focus snapped to her movement and the beads of water gathering on her skin. From this angle, I could see the swell of her breast, but her arm hid her nipple—

And now I was imagining the water beading on that dusky bud and my tongue licking it away.

Fuck me.

She had a couple of bites on her arm, as well as on her back, and I focused on those, reminding my wolf that while we wanted to claim her — which we sure as hell couldn't — she was still hurt and our first priority was to take care of her. We needed to assess her injuries, decide if she needed an elixir, and patch her up.

Surprisingly, she wasn't that hurt. She had a couple of nasty bites that Nova probably would have stitched up to be on the safe side since she healed like a human, a lot of cuts and scratches, and an enormous bruise blossoming over her right thigh, but nothing that seemed serious enough to warrant giving her one of our precious elixirs.

I patched her up as quickly as I could, trying to keep my touch professional and my expression distant, but by the time I'd taped on the last piece of gauze, her breath had picked up, her eyes dilated with desire, and her arousal thickened the air.

"We'll stop early tonight so Bishop can help you," I said, wrenching away from her to shove my first-aid kit back into my pouch.

Fuck, my cock hurt. I was hard from hearing her come and had only gotten harder as I'd patched her up. Touching and smelling her and knowing I was the one arousing her was pure torture. It didn't matter that her desire for me came from her heat and her incomplete mating bond and not from a genuine interest. My body and my wolf didn't care.

I needed to put some distance between us and she needed a good long fuck.

"I ah…" I heard her rummage through her pack again but refused to look at her. "Don't stop early."

I clenched my teeth, determined to not watch her get dressed. "You pretty much passed out the minute we stopped yesterday and today you're going to be even more tired."

"Good."

"Not good." My willpower cracked, and I glanced at her, grateful that she'd managed to put on the clean pair of pants that had been in her pack and was pulling down her shirt, hiding her breasts. "If your heat is affecting you this much, you're going to have to have sex. Cuddling with Bishop won't be enough. The sooner you deal with it, the sooner you'll be thinking straight."

"Cyrus, please." She pressed her hands against her chest, the motion she'd done last night when she'd felt Bishop's soul steadying hers. "I need this bond broken. My emotions are a mess, and if Bishop and I... It'll just get worse." Her cheeks flushed and she dropped her gaze to her feet. "What happened was a mistake. I can't — I'll—" She sucked in a deep breath, squared her shoulders, and met my gaze head-on again. Determination filled her expression even though her pupils were still blown out with desire. "No stopping early or starting late and no unnecessary breaks. I can push through. I *will* push through. I have to."

She was holding herself together on sheer will alone. I hadn't fully understood what she was going through with Knox rejecting their bond, hadn't thought she'd been experiencing the full effects so soon, but I could see the truth now. She'd been worn down to fragile glass in a matter of days and anything — like fearing Bishop would reject her once her heat was over — would shatter her. It wouldn't matter if I told her my brother was smitten with her. She didn't believe she had any value and couldn't imagine that someone would want to be with her.

And even if she could get past that, having sex with Bishop and knowing she'd never have it with her bonded mate — even if she didn't want that mate — could shatter her as well.

Fuck.

She was in a precarious position until the bond was broken. She probably didn't even know which emotions were really hers, which were the incomplete bond, and which were her heat.

"Fine," I forced out, my wolf angry that letting her suffer was the best solution to the problem.

I grabbed my pack and hopped up the bank, listening as she

scrambled to follow. My cock throbbed and my wolf heaved inside me. Fuck I hated this. I hated that my wolf had finally become interested in someone and I couldn't have her, and I hated that I was going to make her suffer even if it was at her own damned request.

Bishop, I snarled. *Did you hear any of that?*

Yeah, he replied, his mental voice solemn. *I'll carry her if she starts to slow down.*

You both know she won't want that, Knox replied as he bounded up the rocks. *She needs to prove how strong she is. To you and to herself.*

"And here I thought he wasn't paying any attention," Bishop muttered as he climbed up after him.

I can still hear you, asshole, he huffed. *Anyone who spends two seconds with her can figure her out. One look at her face and you know exactly what she's feeling.*

That just makes you *the asshole,* Bishop replied. *You're breaking her soul and endangering her life on the slim chance that we'll be able to break the mating bond at the death god's temple.*

Pretty sure being stuck with me for life is worse, Knox shot back as he raced out of sight.

Did he just...? Bishop asked me.

The effects of a mating bond goes both ways, I replied and while that comment meant Knox was softening up to his unwanted mate, it also meant he was determined to not keep her. Just like Audrey, Knox struggled with seeing himself for who he truly was.

AUDREY

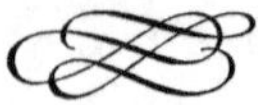

We hiked until I was sure I couldn't hike anymore and then hiked even farther. The sun sat low on the horizon when Cyrus finally stopped us for the night. My feet, legs, and back— hell, my whole body ached. The bruise on my thigh throbbed with every step, and the bite on my back stung, my backpack rubbing against it with each uneven step.

We'd stopped in an alcove, partially covered with a rocky overhang and sheltered from the wind on three sides. Our campsite sat at the edge of the woods that I'd seen far off in the distance and about sixty feet — and down a rocky incline — to the river.

Cyrus dropped his pack and tossed his and Knox's canteens to Bishop. "Fill those and set up camp. I'll get firewood."

"What can I do?" I asked, letting my pack fall to the ground. I was exhausted, just like I'd asked for, but if I didn't sit, I could probably help with something before I collapsed.

"Stay awake until dinner is done," Cyrus commanded and he marched toward the forest.

"It'll be easier with a job," I sighed, and Bishop offered me a sympathetic smile.

"Come on." He jerked his chin and I followed him down to the river. "Now take your boots off and soak your feet. According to the map, we've still got seven days until we reach the death god's territory and if we keep up this pace you're only going to feel worse."

"I'll feel worse if the bond forces me and Knox to seal it," I replied, sitting downstream from Bishop and pulling off my boots. "I think I can last seven days. Surely my heat will end soon. But I'm not sure if I can last longer."

"I've already promised that I won't let you do something you don't want to," Bishop reassured me.

I sank my feet into the cool water as he submerged the first canteen. "It's not just me fighting it. Wolves in my realm can be aggressive when it comes to their mate and the magic of this bond is..."

I shuddered, fighting my arousal, determined to stay in control. Except it was so much harder now that I knew what Bishop's lips felt like against mine, his hands caressing—

I clamped down on those thoughts and cleared my throat.

"The bond's magic is powerful. If it overwhelms Knox, he could hurt anyone who gets in his way," I finished.

Bishop closed the cap on the first canteen and started filling the second one. "Both of you are stubborn enough to resist it."

"I'd rather not press our luck any longer than we have to." My gaze flickered to Bishop's, but I managed to pull it away before I could fall into his warm, brown eyes.

"I understand," he replied, his voice husky. "You won't have to."

He filled the last canteen and then returned to camp, letting me soak my feet while he started to set things up. It probably wasn't entirely safe to leave me alone given that I didn't know how to defend myself and I was exhausted, but the water felt so good that I didn't want to say anything.

A little while later, Cyrus returned and I pulled my feet out of the water, letting them dry a bit, then shoved them back into my boots. I staggered up to camp to find Cyrus turning meat on the spit over a fire and Bishop sitting under the overhang, leaning against the rock wall. Knox was nowhere to be seen, but given how fast Cyrus had returned, Knox had to have hunted our dinner while Cyrus gathered the wood.

"Come here, beautiful," Bishop said, opening up his arms in invitation.

I huffed at the compliment. Even if I might be beautiful normally — which I wasn't — I certainly wasn't beautiful right now, not bruised and scratched up and exhausted. Still, I sank into his embrace, letting the warmth of being physically connected with him wash through me. The achy need from my heat and the mating bond swelled, but, as I'd hoped, my exhaustion was stronger than my desire, and all I really wanted was to lie against Bishop's chest, wrapped in his arms.

This was perfect. This was the way it was supposed to be. Well, not the complete and utter exhaustion or the constant ache from my body, but the sense of peace and belonging and home that seeped through my cells and into my soul.

The guys talked about how much longer it was going to take to get to the death god's altar and what they might expect, but I didn't join in. There wasn't much I could say because I didn't know anything about this world, and while I probably should have listened and learned everything I could about what I might encounter, I was just too tired and comfortable with Bishop holding me.

Their voices lulled me into a sleepy state where I hung, suspended between being awake and asleep until Bishop set a bowl of food in my hand and told me to eat.

I roused myself enough to eat without Cyrus forcing me with his power then lost the fight and let sleep take me while still in Bishop's arms.

The next morning, Bishop woke me at dawn after dream-Knox had brought me to climax with his lips but before my second orgasm with him inside me. I woke achy and needy and thankfully sore. Every muscle in my body hurt and it was easy to focus on my pain and not the thrumming need for a release or the icy hollowness of my rejected mate bond.

I hadn't expected my plan of being too tired for sex to affect my mornings as well, but a quick release in the bushes before I emptied my bladder took away enough of the pressure for the other sensations battling inside me to overwhelm my desire. And while it was the only practical way to deal with the situation, I couldn't stop my face from burning once I washed my hands and returned to camp.

Without comment, Bishop handed me a small bowl of oatmeal with last night's leftover meat while Cyrus dumped his canteen on our dying fire and packed up.

We walked all day and the next, and long before we reached the evening of the third day of my terrible plan, I was seriously regretting telling Cyrus to push our pace. I'd hoped I'd get used to all the walking, but it'd been a fantasy to hope I could get past the exhaustion and aches without resting for a day or ten. And while Bishop had gotten me good quality hiking boots, my feet just weren't used to it and I now had blisters.

But the pressure from the bond and my heat and the achy icy hollowness kept getting stronger, and I was certain the only reason I hadn't jumped Bishop again was because I was so tired.

I'd promised Cyrus I could push through and I would. The sooner we got to the death god's altar the better and not just because I was on the verge of snapping. Cyrus had said leaving town was dangerous, and while I hadn't seen any grimalkins or more flying snakes, I knew they were out there. I could feel them watching us, waiting to pounce, and like a lion hunting gazelle, I was fully aware that I was the weakest member of the group and the easiest target.

Now the sun sat on the western horizon just starting to turn the sky pink with the beginning of the sunset. If today was like the last couple of days, I still had at least an hour before we stopped, and I wasn't sure if my feet would make it.

Ahead of me, Cyrus crested a rise and paused, staring at the sunset. His eyes narrowed and he unclipped his canteen from his pack.

"Bishop, fill up our canteens," he ordered. "Knox says there's a cave up ahead so we're stopping for the night."

"But we have another hour," I said, despite my complaining feet.

An hour more of walking meant I was an hour closer to where I needed to be.

"And this is shelter," Cyrus replied, his attention flickering back to the sunset before shooting Bishop a stern look.

"Give me your canteen." Bishop held out his hand, and I unhooked it and handed it over.

He headed toward the river, while Cyrus led me around a jagged outcropping of rock and down a long, uneven slope with enough levelish rocky protrusions for footholds, so I didn't have to slide all the way down.

Another jagged pillar of rock and a scraggly pine tree that looked half alive partially hid the cave entrance and shaded it from the late-afternoon sun, illuminating only a few feet beyond the cave's wide mouth. Without my wolf form, I didn't have the night vision ability other shifters had, but from the sound of Cyrus's footsteps as he march into the gloom a few feet ahead of me, I could guess the cave was big.

"Sit over there and stay out of the way," Cyrus said, pointing into the darkness where there could be anything I could trip over or bang my head against.

"How about I wait here until there's a fire," I offered instead, making him frown. Then realization flashed across his face and his expression grew even darker.

Yeah, yet another reminder of how weak I really was.

I bit back a sigh and leaned against the mouth of the cave, too tired to be upset about it anymore. Right now, just like everything else, it was what it was and there wasn't anything I could do about it.

Bishop returned with our canteens and a handful of branches to start a fire but not enough to keep it going, and Cyrus left while Knox remained out of sight. I'd caught glimpses of Knox during the last couple of days, and last night I'd partially woken when Bishop moved me out of his arms onto my blanket and saw Knox sitting beside Cyrus near the fire.

I'd known Knox was avoiding me, knew it was for the best, but seeing him there, clearly having joined our camp after he knew I was asleep, had made the icy hollowness of his rejection surge inside me and even my sexy dream of him didn't push the sensation back to what it had been before.

Bishop got a small fire going, which didn't illuminate much more of the cave, and, like the previous nights, opened his arms to me. I sagged into his embrace, but while I was exhausted, I couldn't let myself relax enough to fall asleep.

The sense of something out there, something watching us, had grown stronger the longer I'd stood in the cave's entrance waiting for Bishop to set up the fire, and it hadn't gone away even with the warmth of his arms around me relaxing my body and soul.

Dinner was dried rations from our packs, adding to the feeling that I wasn't the only one on edge. If Knox wasn't able to hunt down anything for us to eat, it either meant there were other things in the area scaring off the smaller game or he didn't want to be distracted from protecting us.

But Cyrus and Bishop didn't say anything about it, and by the time I'd finished eating, I could barely keep my eyes open and didn't have the energy to ask. And really, would they even tell me? There wasn't anything I could do to help. Hell, given the condition of my feet, I wouldn't even be able to run very fast for very long.

AUDREY

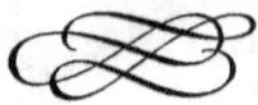

SNARLS AND YIPS OF PAIN AND CYRUS CURSING JERKED ME INTO SUDDEN awareness. My pulse leaped into a quick, frightened beat, and my attention jumped to the darkness beyond the illumination of our small campfire toward the cave's entrance where the sounds were coming from. But I couldn't see anything and had no idea what was actually going on.

"It'll be all right," Bishop said, sliding me out of his lap. "Stay here."

I nodded, still dazed from sleep, as he hurried to the mouth of the cave, claws extending from his fingers. But he didn't rush out to help the others. He stopped at the edge of the firelight, slightly crouched, ready for an attack. He was guarding me. Except from the sounds of Knox's low-pitched snarls and barks and Cyrus's grunts of exertion and pain, they needed his help.

I grabbed a piece of firewood and stood, putting the fire between me and whatever was out there.

"Bishop," I hissed, grabbing his attention. His eyes widened at me holding my makeshift club then he jerked his gaze back to the darkness but didn't move from his position at the entrance. "Go help."

"They're fine," he said, not sounding like he believed himself. "I won't leave you defenseless."

A wolf howled in pain and Bishop's back tensed. Fear swept cold and hard into my gut and everything within me said I had to go, help, save my mate. But I knew I'd only get in the way if I ran out there, which meant it was up to Bishop.

"Go. I'm not defenseless," I insisted, even though I pretty much was, especially if it were grimalkins out there. Back in Stonehaven, my club hadn't even made the grimalkin pause let alone stop it, and I doubted this piece of wood would do much better even though it was a little thicker. Still, the things yipping in the darkness didn't sound like the grimalkins I'd heard before. The cries that clearly weren't from a wolf were too high pitched, which meant it could be something smaller. And that meant my club might actually be useful.

The wolf howled again and Cyrus roared. My pulse tripped and my soul screamed at me. My mates were dying. They needed help. I *had* to help them. I had to do something... and that something was to convince Bishop I was safe enough without him.

"For fuck's sake, go," I snapped. "I'll scream if something gets past you."

His body trembled, his expression torn, which didn't make sense. Sure, he might feel an obligation to protect me even though I was a stranger, but his brothers were out there, and they needed him.

Unless he felt something more than an obligation toward me.

His soul steadied mine like no one else's. That meant we had a connection, something deeper than just friends who'd met a few days ago. Maybe he really did care. And maybe that was just what I wanted to believe.

And none of it mattered if Knox died because the mate bond would kill me or drive me insane.

"Bishop, please." Fear and desperation pounded through me, *thu-thudding* with my racing heart. "Help them!"

Bishop stiffened, his eyes widening for a second, then he leaped into the darkness.

The yips and snarls increased along with the grunts and growls from the guys. Someone, probably Cyrus, roared an inarticulate battle cry and something heavy landed with a wet *thud* near the mouth of the cave.

I tightened my grip on my club, my palms sweaty with fear, my eyes locked in the direction of the entrance. Standing behind the fire made me an obvious target and made it harder for me to see into the darkness, but it was also a small line of defense against anything rushing inside.

The wolf howled again, the sound sharp with pain, and my pulse lurched.

Oh, God.

Knox might hate me for accidentally trapping him in a mating bond and could have handled our situation better — although if he'd been kinder to me it would have been harder to resist the bond's compulsion to have sex — but I didn't want to see him hurt or dead. I didn't want to see any of them hurt or dead. I needed them so I could survive in this realm, at least until I got my bearings.

Except it was more than that. There was something about these men that drew me to them, called to me. I thought it was because the bond and my heat were making me horny and they were handsome, or because Bishop was kind to me, but there was something else, something more—

Something that was just my imagination. I was afraid to be left alone in the wilderness. If the guys couldn't survive out here, I didn't stand a chance. That was all. I already knew my emotions were a mess. I was mistaking my dependence on them for something deeper, something that didn't exist.

It was just the bond messing with my emotions. Just the bond. Once it was broken or sealed I'd feel the way I was supposed to feel toward them: grateful that they'd helped me and hopeful that maybe Bishop and I could be friends.

Cyrus roared again and the yips grew softer and softer as if whatever had attacked us was running away. Then the guys' footsteps drew closer and I blew out a relieved breath. Except they stopped before stepping into the light, making me tense all over again. Was the fight not over?

"You're *not* fine and no you're not just sleeping it off," Cyrus said, followed by a pause where I didn't hear a response, which meant he had to be talking with Knox who could only speak telepathically in his wolf form. "I *know* you're hurt worse than that. Now get in here and shift so we can tell if you need an elixir or not." Cyrus growled, the sound low and dangerous. "You know exactly how big the cave is and I don't fucking care," he snapped, his tone exasperated. "I *said* get in here and shift!"

A massive wave of Cyrus's power pounded over me, bringing me to my knees, stronger than anything I'd felt from him or the others before.

It crushed around my heart demanding obedience. I *needed* to shift. I had to.

Maybe my wolf hadn't woken because Merrick hadn't been my true alpha.

But the pressure of Cyrus's power kept building, stealing my breath until black spots danced across my vision and nothing else happened.

Through my darkening vision, I saw Bishop help Knox stagger into the cave, his body starting as his massive wolf, blood dark and shiny in his fur, before melting into his human form. He was still bleeding from a collection of claw marks over his thigh and back even though shifting helped a shifter's body heal, which told me just how bad that fight had been.

The pressure from Cyrus's power vanished and, still gasping for breath, I crawled the few feet to my pack and grabbed my first aid kit.

"Here," I called out, holding up the kit, ready to throw it to them, as Knox sagged to the ground near the fire and lay on his stomach.

Cyrus's eyes narrowed. "Do you know first aid?"

"The basics," I replied.

"Okay, good." He gave a tight nod, his response surprising me. I'd expected him to huff at that. I couldn't do anything else. Why would I be able to do basic first aid?

But come on. Clean the wounds, which they already were because the magic that let shifters shift destroyed everything — clothes, jewelry, and grime — check to see if any of the cuts needed stitches, which they probably wouldn't because his shift had already partially healed them, then apply bandages to keep the bleeding to a minimum until he had the strength to shift again. It wasn't brain surgery.

"Bishop, determine if he needs an elixir then guard the entrance," Cyrus continued. "Audrey, patch up the worst cuts. And you—" He turned his glare to Knox. "You're still bleeding so it's bad enough. Don't you dare shift until morning or you'll be useless all day tomorrow."

I'll be useless all night if I don't shift back, Knox growled. Now it was his turn to surprise me for including me in his telepathic communication with Cyrus.

"Better tonight while we're in one place than tomorrow when we need to move."

I can handle it. She doesn't need to bother.

Ah. He'd included me because he didn't want me touching him. My chest tightened at that, even as my core heated with desire.

Yeah, it stung that he didn't want my help, but if he was feeling half of what I was feeling, it might be difficult to ignore the compulsion from our bond even if he was injured and I was sore and exhausted. That was why he'd been keeping out of sight and joining his brothers at the campfire after I'd fallen asleep.

"No." Another wave of Cyrus's power hit me and I collapsed to the ground beside Knox.

"Would you *please* stop," I gasped.

The power vanished and I drew in as many deep breaths as I could as fast as I could, afraid Cyrus would unleash his power again.

"I'm going out to make sure they haven't double backed, which leaves Bishop to make sure you're protected, and Audrey to patch you up to slow the bleeding." Cyrus glared at Knox his expression clear that if Knox didn't obey, he wouldn't hesitate to use his power again and make him fully submit even if it flattened me. "I don't want your shift in the morning to take any more energy than necessary. There could be more jackals in the area, so suck it up."

With a snarl, Cyrus yanked off his clothes and marched away, his body melting into a massive black wolf, just like Knox, before he disappeared into the darkness.

"Fuck you," Knox snarled at Cyrus's retreating form.

"Well, you're clearly not in dire straits so you don't need an elixir." Bishop turned his warm gaze to me, the firelight flickering in his eyes mesmerizing me and tugging at that something inside me that I only felt because I'd been afraid they were going to die and I was going to be left alone, not because there was actually something between us. "If he takes a serious turn for the worse, call me."

He returned to the mouth of the cave and I moved to Knox's side, my gaze sliding over his body. He, like Bishop, wasn't as broad as Cyrus and his muscles weren't as bulky, but even bleeding, his back and ass were beautiful. He was all sculpted, sleek muscles, just like the Knox in my dreams. Even his hair was similar to my dreams. It was the same color and length as Bishop's except without the braids at his temples to keep it out of his face.

"Can we just get this over with?" he grumbled, turning his head to face the fire.

I wrenched my attention up, heat burning my cheeks from being caught staring at his ass but froze when I got a good look at him.

"Your face—" He looked exactly like my dream-Knox, a darker, more intense version of Bishop. It wasn't just that there were similarities because they were brothers, they were identical. Twins. They had to be.

"There's nothing wrong with my face."

"No, I mean. I didn't realize you and Bishop were twins," I said like an idiot, because of course I hadn't known they were twins. I hadn't seen Knox in his human form before.

I opened my first aid kit stunned that my dream-Knox was lying before me. I hadn't known what Knox had looked like and my subconscious had created an angrier version of Bishop. It was just ironic that what I'd imagined had been so close to reality.

Except it was closer than reality. It was as if I was looking at the man from my dreams down to the nuance of his expression and the intensity in his eyes. How could I have possibly imagined him in such perfect detail?

"Let me guess," he said, rolling his eyes at me. "In your realm twins are evil or something."

"What? No." I pulled out a clean cloth and wiped away the blood that had been seeping from the deepest wound on his thigh.

"Then why the hell are you looking at me like that?" he demanded, a whisper of his enormous power rolling off him and his wolf darkening his eyes, a precursor to violence. "I can tell by your arousal that you're attracted to Bishop, so it's not because you think I'm hideous."

"Well it's... I, ah..."

Come on, think of something normal. Not embarrassing.

Except now all I could think about was how my dream-Knox possessed me and drove me to an incredible high again and again.

My cheeks burned and I locked my gaze on my cloth. Except his beautiful ass was in my line of sight.

"Well?" More of his power rolled over me, threatening to make me tell him whether I wanted to or not.

"I've been dreaming of you," I blurted before he could force me.

KNOX

"You've been dreaming of me?" Just like I'd been dreaming about her?

That was not what I thought she'd say. I expected something like I was an asshole and it didn't matter that I looked like my brother.

"Yes, I have, I ah..." Her hands trembled as she taped a piece of gauze over the gash in my thigh. The scent of her arousal grew stronger and my cock hardened at the thought that maybe she actually did desire me.

Or maybe it was just the bond and her heat affecting her. But what her arousal really told me was what kind of dreams she'd been having. The same kind of dreams I'd been having of her—

Ah, shit.

We hadn't been dreaming separate dreams but shared ones. Bishop and I sometimes shared dreams, but that was because we had an unusually strong twin bond.

Which meant our mate bond was even stronger than I feared even though we hadn't sealed it. And it explained why the ice I'd swept around the chain in an attempt to reject it had weakened the night before we'd left. *I'd* claimed her that night in our dreams, not my wolf.

Fuck. I couldn't risk weakening my resolve and strengthening the bond even more, even in my dreams. The odds were already slim that the spell Whil had found would break our bond, and the stronger it was, the harder it would be to break.

I couldn't jeopardize our one chance to be safely free of each other. No matter how hard it was to control my wolf in my dreams, I had to stop him. It would be best if I didn't even talk with her— Hell, I shouldn't even see her. That would be the easiest way to stay in control.

I should warn her, tell her if she saw me again in her dreams she should avoid me... except that meant telling her that her erotic dreams were also my erotic dreams— or rather my wolf's erotic dreams, and so far, while she was awake, everything about sex embarrassed her.

Without a doubt, she'd be mortified to learn I knew about these dreams.

My brothers might have thought I was an asshole for wanting to break this mating bond, and I'd certainly been an asshole when we'd first met and I'd tried to make her hate me so she'd refute our bond and hopefully break it, but I wasn't *that* much of an asshole. I wouldn't humiliate her, wouldn't shatter the burgeoning confidence that I felt when we crashed together in our dreams. That would only push her wolf deeper inside her.

And she *did* have a wolf. If we shared the dreams, then the power I felt within her that rose up and sparked against mine was real. I didn't know how to awaken that wolf, but I knew driving her deeper into herself and embarrassing her — even if she had no reason to be embarrassed — wouldn't help her.

No, she could keep her dreams, they'd just change. She'd be alone in the grove, but because she thought it was a dream, it wouldn't be a big deal.

Yeah, that was the safest and kindest choice. For both of us.

"They're just dreams," she mumbled as she slid the cloth over my hip and across the top of my ass, the rasp of fabric making my cock go from "yeah, I could have sex," to "sex sex sex, now now now."

I growled and fought to stay on my stomach. If I rolled over, I wouldn't be able to control myself.

"Sorry," she said, mistaking my growl for anger at her. "I'm trying not to hurt you."

I opened my mouth to reassure her that I wasn't angry, at least not at her, then snapped it shut. If I told her I wanted her, right now in this filthy cave while I was still bleeding, the bond and her heat would crumble any resistance or common sense she had. She'd been on edge since we'd left Stonehaven and fingering herself in the mornings and that one time with Bishop hadn't been enough to satiate her needs.

She should have agreed to Cyrus two days ago and stopped early so Bishop could fuck her senseless. But from the glimpse I'd gotten of her in our dreams — now that I knew she was really herself — she wouldn't have had the confidence to just have sex with him. And even if she did, that wasn't what she wanted. It was obvious she yearned for a connection, yearned for someone to see her for who she was and accept her, broken bits and everything.

Just like I did.

We belong together, my wolf whispered.

No, she belongs with Bishop. I couldn't be anyone's mate. I was too broken. My chest was already tightening even though I'd seen the cave in the daylight and knew it was big, bigger than the ballroom in the Residence.

No one wanted a mate who couldn't spend more than half an hour indoors, who wouldn't be able to attend his own mate bond ceremony because there'd be too many people.

I'd thought I was furious that she'd trapped me in a mate bond, but I was really furious that I was trapping her. She might have been shy and painfully insecure about her abilities and her worth, but she had grit. She'd demanded Bishop tell her about our realm and how to survive while we walked instead of talking about other things that wouldn't be as useful. I didn't know how much she'd remember given that she was distracted and exhausted, but she was determined and that spoke to her true nature, the one hidden behind years of abuse.

She'd also faced off against a grimalkin when she knew she hadn't stood a chance and kept pushing day after day to get to the death god's altar as fast as possible to break our bond. She'd even tried to stand up against those assholes who'd tried to sacrifice her to a monster.

I'd given her grief about talking with them because it had ended in disaster and that had pissed me off. But the more I thought about it, the more I realized she'd been trying to stand up for herself.

She'd failed miserably, but that hadn't been the point. She'd tried.

I still couldn't believe she'd thought that guy was her mate. He'd made my hackles rise the second I saw him, and then listening to him taunt her, thinking she suffered from an incomplete bond and trying to get her to kill herself, disgusted me. She deserved better.

She deserves us.

Stop being an asshole. We won't be good for her. She deserves Bishop. But she wouldn't trust that Bishop had feelings for her until our mate bond was broken. And even if she somehow did realize the truth before then, it wouldn't be because of me. If I said anything, she'd just think I was trying to pawn her off on him instead of telling her the truth.

Audrey finished patching me up, grabbed the closest blanket to cover me then retreated to the other side of the fire. I sucked in a deep breath, trying to get my cock to calm the fuck down, and was flooded with her fresh, sweet scent.

Fuck. If I thought spending time at a dinner for dignitaries from other territories was bad, this was pure torture.

I tried to focus on those dinners. From the moment we could sit still, Mom had required the three of us to attend, and I suspected if she and our fathers were still alive, she'd still demand I show up in human form.

She'd probably been hoping I'd grow out of my aversion to people and crowded rooms and take my place with Cyrus and Bishop as leaders of our pack, but the sensation of being trapped and crushed, all the air sucked out of the room, never went away. It didn't matter how much time I spent with Bishop steadying my soul, I was irrevocably broken.

If my own twin couldn't fix me, nothing could. The only time I felt right was when I was outside in my wolf form. It was as if my human form was my secondary form and not the other way around.

Cyrus returned and took Bishop's place at the cave's mouth, and Bishop pulled Audrey into his lap and wrapped his blanket around both of them.

How are you feeling? he asked me as Audrey leaned into him, burying her face against his neck and breathing in his scent.

Like I should be a wolf, I replied, pissed that I was pissed because she was taking comfort in his scent and body even though I'd just told myself they belonged together.

If you can last the night, we can get in a full day's walk tomorrow, he replied.

Because the sooner we break this bond, the sooner you can convince her that you want to do more than help her with her heat?

The sooner I'll know if what I feel is real or the compulsion from your bond seeping through our bond. He sighed and brushed a lock of hair away from Audrey's cheek, relaxing her even more.

Had she fallen asleep already? She'd been pushing herself hard for days now and usually had to fight to stay awake during dinner. It wouldn't surprise me if she crashed the moment she felt safe and all the adrenaline had left her body.

If the bond can't be broken, I've asked Whil to see if she can transfer it to me. But if we can't do that either, you won't have to be alone in your relationship, he said, not surprising me at all. *I'll join your mate bond.*

Sounds like you've already figured out if your feelings for her are real. And I had no idea how I felt about that. I was jealous that she wasn't taking comfort in me, but not jealous at the idea that we'd share a mate. It would be best for Audrey and I wouldn't die or go insane. I could carry on as I had before while Audrey got the mate she deserved. It seemed like a win-win for everyone.

I always thought we'd end up sharing a mate, Bishop said as he pressed his lips against the top of her head and inhaled her scent. *I'm not at all upset that it's Audrey. There's something about her…*

There is, I conceded.

Bishop let my admission hang between us, not ribbing or encouraging me, knowing — because he knew me better than anyone — that I needed to come to terms with it.

I closed my eyes. Now Audrey's scent wasn't torture, but a comfort, as if admitting the truth had changed something inside me.

But it didn't change what needed to be done. The best possible outcome was to break the mate bond and set her free, then she wouldn't be able to doubt Bishop's intentions for wanting to mate with her and she wouldn't be stuck with me.

Now all I had to do was keep my wolf from jumping her in our dreams for the next four days and pray the spell Whil had found actually worked.

AUDREY

I woke the next day still wrapped in Bishop's arms, his bright, fresh-cut grass scent enveloping me. Knox was already gone, my blanket folded neatly beside my pack, and Cyrus was dousing the fire.

For once I was just regularly turned on and not frustrated from a night of dream sex, and my aches were more than enough to overwhelm the sensation.

It had to be because Knox hadn't shown up in my dreams. I'd opened my eyes to the grove and waited for him to pounce, but nothing had happened, and my real-life exhaustion had swept in. Too tired to stand and explore my dream world, I'd lain on the soft mossy ground, closed my eyes, and opened them again in the morning to the cave.

I had no idea why my dreams had changed, but I was grateful. Maybe it was because I'd been in physical contact with Bishop all night. Maybe that had been enough to steady my soul and control some of the symptoms of my heat.

"You should spend time with Nova when we get back. Build on your first aid knowledge," Cyrus said as he handed me and Bishop the equivalent of a granola bar. "There wasn't a lot of blood last night, but you didn't hesitate to pull out the first aid kit and you didn't care about getting it on your hands."

"Ah... sure." I didn't know how to respond. I hadn't imagined working in health care. Although I hadn't imagined any occupation. I'd just been dreaming of the day when my wolf would wake and it was safe to leave my pack.

"See," Bishop whispered in my ear. "There are things you can do."

"Not sure how well I'll handle something more serious," I replied.

"Hey." He hooked his thumb under my chin and urged me to look at him. "Don't diminish this. Not everyone would have thought to grab the first aid kit or been able to patch Knox up. Even if your place in the pack isn't with Nova's medical team that's still a skill not everyone has."

"You're right," I murmured, not wanting to argue with him. But just agreeing with him made my insides squirm.

I didn't know why it made me so uncomfortable to agree with him. But pulling out the first aid kit and patching Knox up didn't seem that extraordinary. It certainly wasn't that important, not in the big scheme of things like surviving in the wild and defending myself and others from monsters.

We ate a quick breakfast and left. According to the map, we only had four days left to go, but I feared those four days were going to be excruciating. My body hurt even before I'd started walking and two days later, on the morning of the eighth day, I had to keep reminding myself that I'd asked for this.

I'd asked Cyrus to keep going no matter what. I just hadn't realized he'd take me past the point of pain into a nightmare numbness where I knew I was hurting myself, but my mind had retreated into a narrow focus of putting one foot in front of the other so I could keep going.

Except there wasn't any other choice. I couldn't seal my bond with Knox and make it permanent and I'd only last for so long.

Only two more days, I chanted to myself. *Today and tomorrow. Two more days.*

I tried to focus on the morning sunlight streaming through the branches overhead and the sound of rushing water from the river out of sight but nearby. If I could find the semi trance-like state I'd been ending up in by the end of the day, I'd be able to ignore this morning's pain and push through until at least lunch. Except I'd never been able to reach that state first thing in the morning before and couldn't seem to find it now.

After almost two and a half days straight of rocky landscape, we entered another forest, and the forest's stillness surrounded us. Thankfully, the sense that we were being watched hadn't reappeared since the jackal attack two nights ago and the stillness wasn't the dark ominous stillness from Darkweald but the deep calm that made me feel as if my soul might actually be half wolf.

Ahead of me, Cyrus hiked up yet another a rise then half hopped half skidded down the incline on the other side, disappearing out of sight.

I bit back a groan and trudged after him. Yesterday morning, we'd gone over a rise and I'd lost my balance, nearly falling face first down the other side. After that, the guys wouldn't let me go down even the gentlest slope by myself without one of them standing at the bottom to catch me, and I ended up with their hands on me or their arms around me and my desire flaring hot and needy despite being sore and exhausted.

Bishop and I reached the top of the rise and I stared down at Cyrus and Knox standing in the middle of... was that a road?

I blinked, but the road didn't disappear. It wasn't a mirage from my exhausted mind. Below was an actual road running northwest, possibly following the river like we were, and east. It wasn't paved, but the ground had clearly been cut away and smoothed. Without a doubt, it was a road.

Bishop skidded down the incline then reached out to catch me and I followed, pushing out of his arms the second my feet were firmly on the road before my desire could burn out of control and I ended up groping him like I had the last time he'd caught me.

"Are we sticking to our original route?" Bishop asked. "This isn't on the map so I don't know if it'll lead to the death god's temple."

"Do we know when that map was made?" Cyrus asked, then he turned to Knox, paused as if he were listening to something, and nodded. "Agreed. If it turns fully north up ahead, it'll make traveling easier."

"If it does go north, we might run into trouble," Bishop replied as Knox bounded up the road. "The map is eighty years old, but unless this road is well maintained, it looks a lot newer than that. Either way, if it heads north that might mean the death god has new and active followers."

Cyrus took a long drink from his canteen, his eyes scanning the area although I wasn't sure what he was looking for. I couldn't sense trouble. With the birds chirping, the sunlight streaming through the leaves and branches, and the steady *rush* of the river nearby, the forest felt peaceful.

"Let me see the map," he said, turning to Bishop. But his attention caught on me and he sighed. "While we figured this out, why don't you fill our canteens."

"Sure." I took his and Bishop's canteens, left my pack with them — since there was no point in hauling it to the river and back — and headed up the road after Knox. The rise shrunk to half its height about fifty feet away and that would be easier to climb up than what we'd just skidded down.

The river wasn't that much farther, and I quickly reached its rocky banks and fast-moving water. Ahead I could hear the rush of a waterfall, it had to be close, but couldn't see it because the river turned slightly, and the trees blocked my view.

Carefully, I picked my way across the boulders and rocks to the water's edge and was about to dip the first canteen into the water when a young voice, from the direction of the waterfall, whooped and something splashed. More young voices and splashes followed then came a feminine voice calling out to slow down and stop running.

First a road, now a... pool party?

Bishop had said no one lived in this part of the realm, but clearly he'd been wrong. What I didn't know was if they were an opportunity for a night in an actual bed — *and* yes I could admit I was exhausted and willing to delay reaching the death god's temple by half a day for a real bed — or if they were dangerous.

Except they didn't sound dangerous. They sounded like a woman with kids playing in the river, but I had no idea how they'd react to me.

From what Bishop had told me, his pack had relationships with other packs and communities near theirs. There were also other territories and countries farther away, but not everyone welcomed strangers.

That, and the guys had just talked about the road indicating that the death god might have new worshipers. I didn't know what a typical death god worship session looked like, but best guess was that it involved death, and unwelcome visitors probably made the best sacrifices.

But I couldn't contain my curiosity and eased toward the sound, pushing through the underbrush and sticking close to trees and tall rocks for cover until a tingle of energy passed over me.

My pulse lurched and I froze. Had I set off a trap? Did they know I was hiding in the forest?

Someone moved up ahead, but no one came looking for me, and after a moment of waiting for yelling or magic freezing me in place or something, I dropped to my stomach and inched along the ground until I could see what was going on.

It was definitely a pool party and the pools looked man-made like the road.

A small stream from the waterfall had been diverted to pour down into a large pool. The water closest to the waterfall was dark and deep, but the ground sloped up along the pool's edges to create a shallow end and large patio area.

Half a dozen kids splashed in the deeper water, while two more raced up stone steps to get to a platform about six feet above the water. Three other teenagers, two girls and a boy, played with ten smaller children in a shallow waders' section close to me. The smaller children were a mix of babies and toddlers, most of whom were completely naked, while close to two dozen women hung out on the patio under umbrellas, sitting on lounge chairs, chatting, and watching the children play.

With the exception that their bathing suits were more like halter tops and shorts and the material didn't look like spandex, the scene looked like something out of a movie or TV show.

My pack had a community pool, but I'd never been stupid enough to risk going, so I'd never experienced a pool party in real life. But this was what I imagined it would look like. Lounging in the sun, chatting with friends while children laughed and called out to each other and had a great time.

No one looked like they worshiped a death god, although I wasn't sure what a death god worshiper looked like. I assumed they'd be dower and angry and not sunbathing and playing in the water with their kids. And none of them radiated any kind of supernatural essence. They were all human.

Still, Cyrus would be pissed if I just walked down there and ask if their town was nearby and if they had an inn or spare room I could use for the night.

I was about to sneak away when movement in the bushes near the far side of the wader pool caught my attention.

My heart dropped into my stomach, and I raked my gaze over the area where I'd thought I'd seen something. The last time I'd caught a hint of movement of something mostly hidden, the grimalkins had attacked the market and, people, including children, had died. I'd foolishly assumed it had been a young wolf practicing his stalking skills and I'd be damned if I'd make the same mistake twice.

It didn't matter that I had no idea who these people were or if they were even good people. If children were in danger, I had to try to protect them.

A gentle wind teased the leaves making up about a third of the canopy above. The sunlight and shadows danced over the underbrush and the rocky ground, making it difficult to tell if the things hidden in the bushes were rocks or monsters.

Please let me be wrong.

But there, at the edge of the brush, blending in with the shadows, was one of the large, bulky grimalkins that had attacked Stonehaven.

AUDREY

SHIT, WHY COULDN'T IT HAVE BEEN ONE OF THOSE JACKALS? I'D SEEN their corpses when we'd left the cave and they'd been half the size of the grimalkins. I was sure my club from the other night would have taken one of them down. The only reason Knox had had so much trouble was because there'd been so many of them.

The grimalkin was focused on the wading pool and not the slightly closer lounge area, and my fear turned into a hard, cold rock in my stomach.

None of the women looked like fighters and I couldn't see any weapons. Even if they were fighters and armed, they wouldn't reach the wading pool in time. I was closer, and while I didn't stand a chance against a grimalkin, I might be able to buy time for Cyrus and Bishop to arrive. I could only pray that with their better-than-human hearing, I was still within yelling distance.

The grimalkin tensed, readying to pounce, and I glanced around, looking for a weapon. Rocks or branches. Swell.

I grabbed the rock at my foot that was about the size of a tennis ball along with the closest fallen branch. The branch was almost too thick for me to wrap my fingers around, but it was longer than my last two "clubs" so hopefully that would mean I wouldn't be within claw's reach as often.

Then the large grimalkin leaped out of the bushes and so did I.

Oh, fuck oh fuck oh fuck.

"Cyrus! Bishop!" I screamed as I raced over the rocky ground, splashed into the wading pool, and barreled past the suddenly wailing babies and stunned teenagers.

One of the girls yelled and jerked toward me as if to fight me and defend the kids, but I ran right past her and threw my rock at the grimalkin.

I missed.

By a mile.

The stone landed in the water with a *plop* so far away from the creature it was embarrassing.

The grimalkin didn't even flinch but I didn't stop rushing toward it.

With a snarl, the beast leaped at me and I heaved out of the way, somehow managing to not get clawed or bitten and remembering to swing my stick as well.

My aim was too high, and the creature ducked and rammed its large blocky head into my stomach. But I'd faced that kind of attack before, and I managed to stumble back and avoid falling on my ass.

Ha! One point for me.

I smashed the stick against the grimalkin's nose, breaking the end off my impromptu weapon and making the beast howl in pain.

Two points.

Maybe I could actually do this.

But the grimalkin surged forward, swiping and snapping at me in a relentless attack, and all thoughts of fighting back vanished.

Just survive, I told myself as I scrambled to avoid being clawed. *Just survive until they get here.*

People and children screamed. I didn't know if all the babies and toddlers were out of the wading pool, and I didn't have time to check. All I could do was keep the grimalkin focused on me and stay alive long enough for my guys to show up.

The grimalkin's foul stench wafted over me, making me choke, and it swiped again. I jerked to the side, its claws narrowly missing me, but it leaped in, not giving me a chance to catch my balance, and rammed its head into my chest again.

My ass hit the hard ground, the ankle-deep water not enough to cushion my fall, and pain ricocheted up my spine. Water soaked into my pants, instantly weighing me down.

With a snarl, the grimalkin leaped and I scooted back on my butt. I didn't want to chance rolling away and getting caught face down in the water. It wasn't deep, but it was still deep enough to drown.

But I wasn't fast enough and the grimalkin's claws sliced into my calf, pain burning through my leg and my blood billowing out into the water.

I swung my stick at it one-handed, using my other hand to help me get out of the way and praying for a second where I could get back on my feet. I had crappy agility while standing and even crappier agility while on my ass.

Where the hell were Cyrus and Bishop?

Then my back hit something hard.

The edge of the pool.

Shit.

The grimalkin surged forward, its maw open to bite, saliva dripping from its sharp teeth, and its foul breath making my eyes water.

I jabbed forward with my stick, hoping to hit its eyes or nose, anything soft that would get it to back up so I could get over the pool's two-foot edge.

But my stick plunged into the monster's mouth, hit something then *popped* through. The weight of the grimalkin slammed into me, wrenched my stick from my hand, and crushed me against the pool's edge. Blood rushed out of its mouth onto my chest and neck but it didn't move. I'd killed it.

Somehow, I'd killed it.

Then Cyrus splashed past me and I realized there were two other grimalkins. Knox was already in the shallow water near the patio, keeping both of them away from the humans, snarling and biting, fighting to block off one grimalkin and pin the other. But it was a losing fight and even though the women and children were running from the pool area, Knox and the grimalkins kept getting closer and closer to them.

Bishop hurried to my side and hauled the grimalkin off me as Knox buried his teeth into one of the grimalkins' throats and tore it open.

A second later, Cyrus tackled the other grimalkin before it could rush past Knox. The grimalkin dug its back claws into Cyrus's stomach, but Cyrus held on, and with a roar — and a strength I hadn't thought possible — Cyrus snapped the beast's thick neck.

"Are you hurt?" Bishop asked, his gaze sweeping down my body as if he didn't trust me to tell him the truth and sending a shiver of desire rushing through me.

The muscles in his jaw tightened when he reached the gashes in my calf. With a low growl, he lifted me into his arms, not bothering to ask if I could walk and not caring that I was soaked in water and blood, then clamped a large hand around my calf to slow the bleeding.

"Two days. Two fucking days. That was all you needed to wait and then you could have done whatever the hell you wanted," Cyrus yelled, storming toward me as if he hadn't noticed he was bleeding. God, even when he was bleeding he was gorgeous.

Water soaked his clothes, clinging to his powerful body, leaving nothing to the imagination, including how well-endowed he was. Not that I needed help imagining his naked body. I'd seen everything and it was burned into my brain.

"I'd ask what's wrong with you," he huffed, "but I already know."

A woman with streaks of gray in her hair and wearing a loose beach dress splashed through the water toward us. Her face was pale and her eyes too wide with shock, but her expression was serious and determined. She was holding herself together to stay in control, and she was coming toward us instead of running away which made me think she was in charge.

"Is anyone hurt?" Bishop asked her.

She eyed Cyrus then looked at me, and I realized the entire front of my shirt was soaked with watery blood and giving everyone a show of my perpetually turned-on nipples. Thank God she couldn't smell my arousal like the guys could. Still, I crossed my arms and prayed someone would offer me a change of clothes while I waited for mine to dry... because the other option was waiting naked and that wasn't going to help the desire constantly raging through me.

"A few scrapes and bruises," the woman replied. "We should get you two to our doctor."

"Just Audrey," Cyrus replied. "A quick shift and I'll be fine. I'm just waiting until the pool clears out. Most humans I know don't appreciate public nudity."

The woman's gaze trailed appreciatively over his body and something inside me twisted. "I'm sure no one here would mind if you stripped."

"Mom!" a younger woman exclaimed as she hurried toward us. "You're a married woman."

"Doesn't mean I can't look," the older woman said with a sly smile.

"Oh, goddess save me." The younger woman rolled her eyes at her mother. "I'm so sorry. Thank you for saving us. I'm Hallie and this is my mother, Neera. Let's get you some dry clothes and have Ida check you out."

Bishop glanced at Cyrus and raised an eyebrow, and Cyrus gave an ever-so-slight nod.

"Is your village nearby?" Bishop asked.

"Not far. Will you be able to walk?" Neera asked Cyrus, her tone turning seductive. "Or should we wait for you to change forms?"

"Please forgive her," Hallie groaned. "There hasn't been a new handsome man in town since—"

"Since you snatched up the last one," her mother chuckled. "And now two more have shown up and saved your wedding day."

Cyrus grabbed our packs from the bushes where he and Bishop had left them and our canteens where I'd left them, and then Hallie and Neera led us out of the pool area.

"Are all three of you shifters?" Hallie asked as we stepped onto a wide, well-maintained path lined with what looked like patio stones.

The path led up a gentle slope until we were level with the river again and, from my glimpse through the trees, toward a collection of sturdy stone buildings. Much to my surprise, Knox fell into step beside Cyrus instead of returning to the shadows, but his posture was tense, and I hoped the villagers wouldn't mistake his worry as aggression.

"All four of us," Bishop corrected. "I'm Bishop, this is Audrey, Cyrus, and Knox."

Hallie leaned closer to us and dropped her voice. "Is he not shifting because he doesn't want my mother ogling him? I wouldn't blame him."

"Yeah, he's the best looking of the three of us," Bishop said with a chuckle. "Doesn't want to cause a commotion and all that."

"Better looking...?" Hallie's attention turn to Cyrus who walked ahead of us with her mother, and her gaze dropped to his perfectly outlined butt.

The something inside me twisted tighter and turned sour. No, not something. Jealousy. I was jealous this woman was checking out Cyrus even though he'd made it clear he wasn't interested in me. Not that I wanted him to be interested. I was just horny as hell from the mating bond and my heat.

Besides, if I was too weak to be his mate, a human would be even worse. And I was not going to think about how much it would hurt if he rejected me but accepted this human.

AUDREY

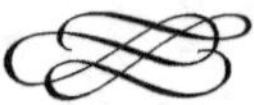

THE PATH TURNED AWAY FROM THE RIVER, AND THE TREES PARTED revealing a village huddled at the edge of a large meadow complete with grass and flowers, something I hadn't seen since entering Dark-weald. There were still areas where the ground was uneven and rocks jutted from the earth, but this wasn't the same rugged landscape we'd been traveling through.

The meadow had been divided into two areas, the first and larger area was a farm with a vegetable garden, a small orchard, a pasture for cows and sheep, and a flock of chickens. The second area looked like a park. The ground was more level and the grass had been cut. A large red canopy had been erected on one side decorated with ribbons and flowers, and in the center, wood had been piled high to make a bonfire, reminding me that Neera had said that Hallie's wedding was today.

Relief eased my sour jealousy but was quickly replaced with worry about having such a ridiculous response to some woman checking out the guys in the first place.

God, I couldn't wait for the bond to be broken and my heat to be over. Surely it would be over soon since it had been going for a week.

Cyrus wasn't mine. Neither were Bishop or Knox. I had to figure out how to survive on my own because once this was over, there was a good chance that's where I'd be. Alone.

Three men carrying swords and strange looking old-fashioned rifles rushed up the path toward us.

"Everyone is gathering in the square," one of the men said. "Are you the men who saved the women and children?"

"And woman," Hallie added, making the three men look at me, soaked, disheveled, bleeding, and in Bishop's arms. "She killed one of the grimalkins herself, and we should get her to Ida."

"Right," the youngest looking of the three said. "Of course." He blushed and palmed the back of his neck, looking embarrassed, but I wasn't sure why. I had my arms firmly crossed, hiding my nipples, so he couldn't see anything inappropriate.

"Come on," the first man said, grabbing the young guy's arm and pulling him away.

We continued into town, reaching a square that was filled with worried people. Knox's posture grew even more tense and the fur on the back of his neck started to rise. Thankfully, he didn't start growling or baring his teeth and drawing the attention of the villagers who were already afraid of being attacked by beasts.

At the far end of the square, a man stood on the steps of a larger, fancier building telling people to stay calm, that the protection stones were being checked, and yes, they were sending out a hunting party to ensure the wedding was safe.

Neera broke off from us and hurried into the crowd, while Hallie led us to a two-story building that backed onto the meadow. Women and children wrapped in towels gathered around the open front door and an older woman sat on a stool cleaning a nasty scrape on a little boy's elbow.

The crowd took one look at me and Cyrus and parted, letting the woman hurry all of us inside except for Knox — who slipped down the path along the side of the house, heading away from the crowd.

"So, this is the great warrior maiden all the kids are talking about," the woman said, walking us into a hall with long wooden benches on both sides and into the closest of four doors.

The room was a basic version of a patient room in a doctor's office with white walls and cabinets, a small sink, white marble counter, and a hard exam bed.

"Yep," Hallie said as Bishop set me on the bed. "All four of them are shifters and you should have seen it, Ida. Cyrus here—" she gestured to Cyrus "—killed one of the grimalkins by snapping its neck."

Ida's gaze jumped from my bleeding calf to Cyrus who was holding both packs and not bothering to apply pressure to the gashes in his chest — gashes that weren't bleeding as much as before since even without shifting, shifters healed faster than humans.

"If you're all shifters then you don't need me," Ida replied. "I'll just step out and find you some dry clothes while you shift out your injuries." She frowned. "In fact, why haven't you done that already?"

"Humans have a thing with nudity," Cyrus said, "and Audrey—" He glanced at me and I could see him trying to decide if he was going to share my not-so-secret secret. And while I respected that he was taking my feelings into consideration, I was still bleeding.

"I heal like a human," I said, saving him from making the decision.

Ida's eyebrows shot up. "Really? That's unusual. I took a specialized class in shifter medicine at the Royal Medical Academy, and I've never heard of that."

"It's a condition we're hoping to rectify by visiting the death god's temple," Bishop said, sort of lying, but not... except if the spell could break something as powerful as a mating bond, maybe it could break the curse my ancestors had put on our pack preventing us from shifting until the summer solstice after our eighteenth birthday.

"The death god's temple?" Hallie asked.

"Our wise woman found a spell that we think will help," Bishop replied as Ida cut open my pant leg and drew the fabric away from the gashes.

Three of the grimalkin's claws had caught my calf, the cuts slicing from the middle of my shin, down to my ankle. Even the top of my boot — which came to just above my ankle — was nicked.

"Let's get your boot off for a better look," the old woman said.

Bishop unlaced my boot and slipped it off, revealing the makeshift bandages I'd wrapped around my foot to help cushion the blisters on my blisters. Except the wrappings hadn't been doing the best job of protecting my feet since it wasn't even lunch and I'd already bled through them.

"Jeez, is that your other shirt?" Cyrus growled, his voice low, dangerous, making fear flutter through my chest.

Crap. I hadn't thought anyone would be upset since the shirt had already been torn in various places by the flying snakes. But Bishop had bought all my clothes and ripping up the shirt meant I'd wasted their money. I probably looked ungrateful for them helping and feeding and clothing me.

"I'm sorry," I murmured. "I didn't want to use up our medical supplies."

Ida carefully unwrapped my foot, exposing my many broken and bleeding blisters. Bishop hissed, his expression darkening, and Cyrus growled low in his throat as a wave of his power swept over me.

"I needed to do something," I insisted. Surely they could see that.

"You needed to tell me your feet were hurting you," Cyrus snarled then turned to Hallie who'd gone pale at the sight of my abused foot. "We need to stay the night. Do you have a room we could use? We can pay."

"You're not paying for anything," she replied. "But I'll have to ask around. Our inn isn't very big and my family from out of town and my fiancé's family have filled it up."

"Cyrus, we shouldn't slow down." If the inn was full, I was going to end up sleeping on someone's floor, which was somewhat better than the ground out in the open, but not by much. If a bed wasn't available and I was going to have another uncomfortable sleep, I might as well be closer to the death god's altar. "We—"

Cyrus glared at me and his power snapped my mouth shut, reminding me in no uncertain terms that he was the alpha and I was the weakest shifter in existence. And while he hadn't used a lot of power, he was more than capable of flattening me if I pressed the matter.

"We're fine with the floor," he said. "We just need shelter and assured safety for a night."

"Put them in old Mac's house," Ida suggested. "It's empty until the new village hunt master arrives and they'd probably appreciate the privacy."

"That's a great idea," Hallie said. "It's on the other side of town from the bonfire so my wedding celebration won't disturb you. I'll get some of the girls to help clean it up and air out the mattresses. We'll have everything ready for after supper and you're not paying for that, either. You're our honored guests. Attend my wedding and enjoy the food and celebration." A whisper of darkness shifted through her expression. "Without you, there might not have been a wedding."

"All right. Knox and I will join that hunting party to help ensure there aren't any more grimalkins hanging around." Cyrus shot me another glare. "Bishop, keep Audrey from doing anything stupid and that includes walking." He grabbed his pack and turned to Ida. "Is there a spare room I can shift in?"

"The room on the other side of the hall is also a patient room. You can use that," Ida replied, pouring something that smelled like rubbing alcohol onto a piece of gauze and dabbing it over the first gash.

Pain burned through my calf and I sucked in a sharp breath. Definitely rubbing alcohol.

"Do you need a change of clothes?" Hallie asked Cyrus.

"No, but Audrey apparently does since she ripped up her spare shirt." He marched across the hall into the other patient room, closed the door, and my thoughts instantly jumped to him stripping off his clothes.

Unbelievable. He was clearly pissed at me and I still wanted to have sex with him. I was insane. It was the only explanation. If I was going to have sex with anyone, it would be Bishop.

Except if the bond couldn't be broken, it was going to be Knox whether we liked it or not.

Swell.

BISHOP

Audrey jerked her gaze from the door across the hall where Cyrus had gone and groaned. The scent of her desire curled around her, and I fought my own arousal so I wouldn't embarrass her even more in front of Ida and Hallie, even as my wolf strained to take over and satisfy her.

Exhausting herself and walking until her feet bled hadn't been enough to control her heat, and after we rested in the village it was going to be even harder.

A part of me had wanted to argue with Cyrus about staying. We only had a day and a half until we reached the death god's temple, and she'd been suffering from her heat for seven days already. If she stayed in her current painful state, she might be able to hold out until we broke the bond, or her heat broke... which surely would be soon.

Except the rest of me hurt just looking at her feet. Hell, I had no idea how she'd managed to get as far as she had without asking for help. She needed to rest and she needed an elixir if she was going to carry on. Even if I carried her the rest of the way, she still needed medical attention and rest.

The only question remaining was how she was going to deal with the pressure of her heat. I wanted to respect her wishes, help her hold out until she knew for certain she was no longer mated to Knox, but given that she was craving Cyrus even in her current condition, that wasn't a reasonable expectation.

Besides, if she was going to give in and tend to her natural bodily needs, this was the place to do it. She'd have privacy, a bed by the sound of it, and time for me to do it right.

I was just going to have to approach her carefully and keep hold of my heart. I was certain Knox's bond with Audrey was affecting me, but I was now also certain that even without Knox's influence, I'd want Audrey.

Because of my bond with Knox, I'd been fighting what I felt, fighting what my wolf knew with absolute certainty and had been quietly waiting for me to realize.

Audrey was our mate.

She'd always been our mate and always would be. Fate had decided.

It didn't matter that she was powerless and couldn't shift — although I could feel a power inside her, had felt a ripple of it when she'd told me to help Cyrus and Knox during the jackal attack.

But it didn't matter if she ended up powerless and wolfless her whole life. My wolf and soul needed her, craved her, wouldn't be complete without her.

Except just because my wolf and I understood the truth, didn't mean she did. And even if she did accept the fact that we were fated for each other, it might not happen quickly. She'd been tricked by the promise of a fated mate and would be wary of it no matter what her heart told her.

That and she needed time to adjust to her new realm and new pack, to figure out who she was and what she wanted. She'd never been given an opportunity to become who she was supposed to be, and her bond with Knox, a bond I knew that was fated as well, only complicated the matter.

If only she'd bonded with me first. She wouldn't have had to deal with being rejected, something that had made her self-confidence fragile. And while I knew she was a fighter and determined, one blow too many or too strong could shatter her.

"I'll find you something to wear and get the girls started on Mac's house," Hallie said to Audrey then hurried out of the doctor's office.

The patient room opened and Cyrus stormed out with his and Audrey's packs slung over his shoulder and dressed in his clean clothes — washed and mended from our fight with Tzanagoth's spirits.

Audrey's arousal thickened, and my wolf heaved under my skin.

She needed us. Now. She'd needed us before, too. It had almost been a week and my wolf was still pissed that we hadn't eased her heat's symptoms on the rocky riverbank just outside Darkweald.

And it was furious that we'd only held her for the last seven days. We'd been so close and yet not nearly close enough. It wouldn't be satisfied until our cock and teeth were in her and a mating bond fully formed and sealed.

I swallowed back a growl and somehow managed to not pace as Ida stitched up the gashes in Audrey's calf.

"Now," Ida said, snipping the thread. "Let's get you upstairs and cleaned up so I can wrap these stitches and your feet."

Audrey moved to hop off the table, but I picked her up before her feet could touch the floor. "Cyrus said no walking," I murmured, my wolf making my voice husky.

Her eyelids fluttered and she shivered at my tone.

"Are you going to help me bathe, too?" she breathed, her desire making her bold even as her cheeks flushed with embarrassment.

"There's nothing wrong with your arms," Ida said with a chuckle, "and I'd appreciate it if you saved it for Mac's house. My tub isn't big enough for the both of you."

Audrey's flush swept down her neck and disappeared under the collar of her shirt — a shirt that was still wet, clung to her every curve, and was currently taunting me with her pert nipples since she'd dropped her arms to get off the table.

I followed Ida up the stairs at the back to a small apartment and set Audrey on the edge of a tub that, as Ida said, wasn't big enough for both of us, let alone just me.

"I should probably do this myself," Audrey said to me as the older woman gathered a handful of towels from a closet. "I don't think I can —" Her cheeks burned brighter and she crossed her arms over her chest, hiding her nipples again. "Especially if I'm naked."

"Right." I forced myself to step away from her and not wrap her in my arms like I wanted. Now wasn't the time. Not in Ida's house with the woman watching and probably not while she was confused by her bond with Knox. "I'll be in the hall if you need me."

With my wolf snarling at me in frustration, I stepped out of the bathroom and closed the door. My heart lurched, a painful twisting in my chest, and I gritted my teeth before my wolf compelled me back inside. With the exception of relieving herself and filling our canteens, she hadn't left my sight since we'd left Stonehaven and every protective instinct I had suddenly surged, riding a wave of furious anger from my wolf that I'd allowed her to leave our sight... even if we were only separated by a door.

I paced down the short hall into Ida's small living room and my wolf wrenched me back to the bathroom door.

Damn it.

I could wait however many minutes it took for Audrey to bathe. It wasn't like she was going to sit in the tub and relax like she deserved. She was just cleaning up.

Below, the building's front door opened followed by soft footsteps. It was someone light, probably a woman, and a few seconds later, Hallie came up the stairs carrying neatly folded clothing dyed in various shades of blue and a pair of soft tan slippers.

Her eyes widened when she saw me, and she froze in the middle of the living room, gripping the clothes to her chest, recognizing the predator in front of her.

Shit. I strained to get my wolf under control even though I knew it wouldn't work until Audrey was in sight again, or better yet, in my arms.

"They're in the bathroom," I growled, moving into the living room as far away from Hallie and the hall to the bathroom as I could get.

Hallie bobbed her head and hurried inside, and I could only pray she wouldn't change her mind about offering us a place to stay for the night.

Jeez. My instincts were going insane. Even standing on the other side of the living room with the bathroom door closed, I could still smell Audrey's fresh sweet scent and the heady aroma of her arousal that was growing by the second.

My wolf didn't care about what she wanted. She needed relief. She needed us.

The bathroom door opened and Audrey hobbled into the hall with one hand on Hallie to keep her balance and the other on her chest as if she were afraid to show off any cleavage.

Which was ridiculous. The dress wasn't cut that low and she looked incredible in it. Yes, she looked exhausted and her complexion was too pale, but she was still the most beautiful woman I'd ever seen.

Hallie's multi-blue clothing turned out to be a summer dress with thin straps. It skimmed the swell of Audrey's breasts, hips, and ass and hung mid-thigh, exposing most of her sculpted legs along with the ugly black stitches along her calf. Her blond hair was wet and hung loose, framing her face and drawing my attention back to her soft brown eyes, flecked with gold and filled with exhaustion and desire.

The pressure in my chest suddenly released, my wolf receding now that she was in sight again, and I swept her into my arms.

We returned to the patient room where Ida wrapped Audrey's calf in linen, then slathered ointment over her feet and wrapped them as well.

"I'd say stay off your feet for at least a few days, but I have a feeling you're going to continue your journey tomorrow," Ida said as Hallie helped Audrey put on the slippers.

"It's best if we get to the temple as soon as possible," Audrey said, dropping her hand from her cleavage revealing the tops of the ugly red scars marring her chest and shifting to the edge of the table as if she were going to jump off again.

"No, walking," I growled, a hint of my power slipping free, both me and my wolf furious at the reminder of the men who'd hurt her.

She was already self-conscious about standing out by having almost no power. Now she stood out even more since very few shifters had scars.

More of my power rolled over her before I managed to yank it back.

Her eyes narrowed and the muscles in her jaw flexed. "You don't need to force me," she said.

"I wasn't. And I'm not so sure about that. You keep trying to jump off that table and walk," I said, offering her my wickedest smile to distract her.

A shiver rolled through her and the scent of her arousal increased.

I slung my pack over my shoulders, then swept her into my arms.

She instantly relaxed against me, and the warmth of our connection swelled around my heart, steadying my soul as I was steadying hers. My wolf huffed in soft satisfaction. Even if she didn't realize it, her body and soul knew we were mates.

AUDREY

I DREW IN A LONG BREATH FILLED WITH BISHOP'S FRESH-CUT GRASS scent and relaxed into the soft power vibrating in my cells that had been awakened by his embrace.

I was tired — so damn tired — and it felt good to just be held, so I fought my rising desire at being in his arms. I didn't want to ruin it by giving in to cravings that were only going to make a complicated situation more complicated, and I really didn't have the mental power to figure anything out... if anything could be figured out in this situation.

Hallie handed me a basket with food and we took it to the meadow we'd passed coming into town. People were back in the field setting up tables, although the mood was still somber and stressed. I guess the hunt team hadn't returned yet to confirm that the village was no longer in danger.

Bishop picked a surprisingly soft spot in the grass and wildflowers on a gentle slope at the edge of the activity, and sat, placing me between his legs and letting me use his chest as a backrest. The position made me all too aware of his hard cock pressing into the small of my back and my desire flared stronger despite my exhaustion.

"What's in the basket?" he asked as he rummaged through his pack and pulled out his first aid kit.

I raised an eyebrow at him.

"Pretty sure Ida took care of everything," I said, grateful he wasn't going to bring up my heat since I had no doubt I was releasing pheromones like crazy. How could I not? I was in the arms of a gorgeous man who was kind and warm and a perfect gentleman.

He could have easily started something over the last couple of days while he'd been holding me and steadying my soul, and I wouldn't have had the willpower to stop him.

But he hadn't and that was making it even harder to remember that the spell to break my bond with Knox might not work and a relationship between me and Bishop would be impossible.

"Ida didn't take care of everything," he replied, "not if you plan on putting your boots back on and walking tomorrow."

He pulled out a small vial of healing elixir, cracked the wax seal on the stopper, and handed it over before I could argue that taking one of their precious elixirs for sore feet was a waste. Not to mention it would make it that much harder to ignore my heat. Being sore and exhausted was the only thing that had kept it in check.

"You know this is only going to make it harder to control myself," I murmured and I downed the bitter liquid.

I didn't want to feel better until this mess with Knox was over. That had been the plan. And while I was grateful for Cyrus deciding to spend the night in the village where I could sleep in a bed, being rested *and* healed was going to make the next couple of days very difficult.

"I know," Bishop replied, his tone strange. I couldn't tell if he was sorry for making my life more difficult or something else.

He pushed aside the cloth covering our food in the basket and handed me a sandwich then took one for himself.

The sandwich consisted of dark brown bread, pale meat, and green leaves that looked a little like spinach. I took a bite and watched the villagers work on setting everything up for the wedding.

This was supposed to be a joyous day for Hallie and her fiancé, and I hoped the hunt team returned with good news. She deserved to be happy. She'd found someone she wanted to spend the rest of her life with and that deserved a carefree celebration.

The thought made the sandwich turn to dust in my mouth. Would I get a wedding? I hadn't thought about having a mating ceremony and celebration, hadn't dreamed that anyone would want to mate with me. I'd only been thinking of staying safe and escaping when my wolf woke.

And then Royce had awakened desires I hadn't known I had and crushed them all at the same time.

I tried to eat another mouthful of sandwich but it didn't taste any better than the last bite.

I'd only get a mating ceremony if Whil's spell worked and if anyone decided they could mate with a wolf as weak as me. If it didn't, I doubted Knox would suddenly decide he wanted to celebrate our mating.

Only his brothers and Whil knew we'd bonded and it would probably stay that way. I was the unwanted mate, the embarrassment he wouldn't want to acknowledge. Ever. I'd be trapped worse than before because this time I'd have no chance of escape, not even a small hope.

God. How could I carry on? Knox and I would have sex, the bond would make us do it sooner or later, but our hearts wouldn't be in it.

Except I had a horrible feeling my heart would be in it. My soul wept for him, and clearly, his didn't weep for me, or he wouldn't have been filling our bond with icy disgust and rejection.

"What do I do if this doesn't work?" I stared at the half-eaten sandwich in my hand unable to bring myself to take another tasteless bite, the warmth from Bishop's body and soul no longer strong enough to steady me.

"We go to plan B," Bishop replied without hesitation. He set his own sandwich aside, wrapped his arms around me, and drew me back against his chest, enveloping me in his warmth. "We get back to Stonehaven and see if Whil can transfer Knox's half of your bond to me."

What the—? He'd ask Whil to transfer the bond to him?

I pushed up to stare at him. It didn't sound as if he was joking, and given how kind he'd been, I doubted he'd joke about something like this, but—

"Why would you do that?" I asked. "Why would you take Knox's half of the bond? Then *you'll* be stuck with me."

I knew he loved his brother, but I hadn't thought he loved him so much he was willing to sacrifice his own happiness to save him.

"Audrey." He cupped my cheeks between both palms, his expression determined as if he was trying to will me into believing his words. "I'll never be *stuck* with you. I'd be happy to be mated with you even if we weren't trying to break the bond with Knox."

That didn't make any sense. "You're powerful. You're a pack alpha and I'm—"

"Determined and beautiful and kind?"

"Weak," I corrected him. I didn't want him lying to me to make me feel better, because I knew none of it was true. "I'm weak. I can't shift and any pups I have could be just like me. No one wants a mate like that."

I'd overheard Finn say as much before we'd left Stonehaven, and I couldn't blame him or anyone else who thought that. As much as I didn't want it to be true, it was.

Bishop's eyes darkened, his wolf rising to the surface. "Anyone who can't see past that doesn't deserve you. I don't care if you can't shift. When we're back in Stonehaven, I intend to court you properly. I will earn your heart and be your mate."

My heart lurched, hope and fear swirling in my stomach. He sounded so certain, so determined, as if I was a prize he needed to win.

The hope fluttered stronger along with a lick of desire. He'd offered to help me with my heat with no expectations of anything else and I'd assumed it meant he was warning me off. Was he actually saying I shouldn't feel guilty or pressured if I didn't reciprocate his feelings? Did he actually have feelings for me? Except—

"If the spell doesn't work or if Whil can't give you Knox's half of the bond, I'll be Knox's mate for the rest of my life." I couldn't let Bishop's feelings for me grow, not until I knew I was free from the bond with Knox.

Bishop frowned as if he didn't understand what I was saying then realization flashed across his expression. "You think only two wolves can share a mate bond." He groaned with understanding. "That's why you've been trying to get through your heat without sex. You don't want to complicate your emotions and risk hurting yourself or Knox."

"I don't want Knox pissed at you if all this fails and we're still mates." Which was also a part of protecting my heart. I'd feel awful if I broke their relationship. I didn't know about Knox, but Bishop had already proven he'd do just about anything to protect his brother.

He wrapped his arms around me and pulled me tighter against his chest again. "Even if Whil can't transfer it, I'll join your mate bond," he said. "If you'll have me. Neither of you have to go through this alone. Multi-person bondings aren't common in our pack, but it isn't taboo like I'm guessing it is in yours."

My thoughts stuttered at that, my exhaustion making it hard to think. "So, you're saying I'd have two mates?" Had he really said that?

"Why not?" he replied. "Our mother had two."

I had no idea what to say about that. I'd never even had a boyfriend and now I was looking at the possibility of having two mates. Not that Knox would be interested in me.

Except I couldn't help thinking about what would happen if he finally embraced our bond. What would all that intensity from my dream feel like multiplied by two? And while my mind was certain being mated to both of them at the same time was a bad idea, my body thought it was great.

"So, I'd be mated to both Knox and you? At the same time?"

Bishop hummed low in his throat, probably getting high from all the pheromones I was releasing. "Only if you want." Then he released a soft huff. "Although not until Knox gets his head out of his ass."

My thoughts jump to my dreams where Knox had impaled me on his cock and pinned me against a tree. Except the tree turned into Bishop's hard, muscular chest, his hands teasing and tormenting my breasts, as Knox pounded into me. The impact would grind me against Bishop's cock and his growls of pleasure would sweep hot against my neck.

Need shivered down my spine and my cheeks heated at the idea of being caught between them... and liking it.

Except Knox would never go for that. He'd never want to have sex with me in real life even if we couldn't break the bond, so the fantasy of the three of us together was just that, a fantasy.

However, being with Bishop and having an emotional connection with him like I really wanted wasn't a fantasy. He'd just said so, and he'd always done what he said he'd do and hadn't manipulated, forced, or tricked me.

I had no reason to doubt his desire to have me as his mate or fear he'd reject me.

I yawned, my exhaustion a heavy blanket on the verge of dragging me under, and leaned back, savoring the feel of his body against mine.

Maybe I should stop fighting myself and take him up on his offer.

CYRUS

It was midafternoon by the time the hunting party finished searching the area around the village. Knox hadn't scented more than the original three grimalkins, and one of the village trackers had come to the same conclusion. That tracker had been the young guy who'd blushed the second he'd laid eyes on Audrey and had proven himself to be quite skilled, which pissed my wolf off even more.

Not only had he looked at her with desire, but he was competent and decent looking, too. He might have been a human, but that didn't mean Audrey wouldn't be interested. She saw herself as practically human. She might think a human would be a good match.

Or, if the spell to break her bond with Knox worked, she might think mating with a human was the only match available to her.

I bit back a growl as Knox and I passed through the magical barrier protecting the village from ill intent that had been fixed while we were hunting and mentally reached out to Bishop to find out where he and Audrey were.

We'd been too far away to communicate telepathically, and it had been driving me crazy not knowing what was going on with her. Was she being stubborn? Was Bishop giving in and letting her be stubborn?

He wasn't a pushover, but he was so in love with her that it wouldn't surprise me if he let her do something stupid in an attempt to nurture her fragile confidence.

Where are you? I asked him, another growl bubbling in my throat making my mental words harsher than I intended.

In the field where they're setting up for the wedding. Is there trouble?

Only with me and my wolf wanting someone we couldn't have and being jealous over a human. We were leaving tomorrow and Bishop wasn't going to let her out of his sight. Knox wouldn't, either, but he'd lurk in the shadows and watch, not hold onto her all night like Bishop would. I had no reason to be jealous of some random human.

I had no reason to be jealous at all.

She wasn't mine.

The image of her ramming her broken stick into the grimalkin's mouth and killing it flashed through me. She'd risked her life to protect children again, and my wolf was losing his shit, both because she'd been in danger and because she'd proven herself to be a fierce protector.

He didn't care that she was already mate bonded with Knox and, if Bishop had his way, be bonded with him before the year was out. It didn't matter to him that being with her could throw the pack's leadership into turmoil and put her in the spotlight to be criticized, something that wouldn't help her confidence. He was determined to have her, too.

We reached the edge of the field and Bishop glared at me.

Pull your power back before you get any closer, he snarled. *She's asleep and I'd like to keep it that way until the wedding gets started.*

Fuck, I snarled somehow managing to keep that thought to myself. I needed to pull myself together. I didn't want her. It was just her heat affecting me and as soon as it was over, my wolf would calm the fuck down.

I wrenched my power back under my control and marched to the grassy rise where Bishop lay. He was half propped up against the slope with Audrey cuddled against his chest, her nose buried in his neck, one hand tangled in his hair and the other pressed against his heart.

She wore a pale blue dress covered in flowers in various shades of blue. The skirt reached midthigh and Bishop had wrapped a hand under her ass to keep the fabric down so she wouldn't accidentally flash anyone walking by.

For any other shifter that would have been ridiculous. But Audrey was so shy, especially of her body, that the action spoke to just how much Bishop cared for her and how aware he was of her needs.

My gaze dipped from the sensual curve of her ass to the bandage wrapped around her calf and the soft slippers on her feet, and a hint of my power slipped through my control before I could stop it.

Audrey murmured, her brow pinching in discomfort, and snuggled closer to Bishop who glared at me.

I know, I huffed at him, pulling it back. *I'm just so pissed she didn't tell us about her feet.*

You're pissed that you didn't think of it before it got so bad, Knox replied, his ears swiveling and his gaze sweeping over the field, searching for danger even though Rafe, the town's magistrate and Neera's husband, had been assured that the stones creating the magical protective barrier around the village had been repositioned.

Unbeknownst to the villagers, the torrential downpour two weeks ago had shifted a few of them, weakening the barrier, which was how the grimalkins had gotten through.

When this is done, we should send Lucius to the capital of the Birialis Kingdom to negotiate. Their closest god is Alexiares, a god of protection, and they've figured out that the rocks near his resting place can create a protective barrier.

You think we can use them instead of building another wall around Stonehaven? Bishop asked.

If Birialis's king is willing to trade, it would mean we wouldn't have to restrict the town's limits again like our ancestors did with Old Town, I replied, because even if we did build another wall, Stonehaven could continue to grow and we'd overflow our boundaries again. *If we can't get the beast activity in the area to go down again, there will be more attacks and we can't fit the town's population within Old Town's walls anymore, not for any extended period of time.*

I sat in the grass beside Bishop and pushed aside the cloth covering the basket between us as Knox sat beside me, using me as a shield between him and Audrey.

He was still tense from being around the villagers, but he'd agreed that it wasn't safe for the villagers or for him to be on his own, not with everyone jumping at shadows looking for beasts. Someone could overreact and attack without thinking and then he'd be forced to defend himself, which would only turn a bad situation worse.

I was actually impressed with how well he'd held it together. There'd been a lot of people in the square crowding close to us, and he'd managed to stay at my side, something he hadn't been able to do even a month ago... although he hadn't had much choice today. Last month at our mother's and fathers' five-year memorial, Bishop had convinced Knox to try to join us, but before we'd even gotten thirty people in the square, he'd slipped back into an alley to watch from the shadows.

Has she eaten any of this? I asked. The basket was packed with sandwiches and fruit and it looked like only a few things had been removed.

She got through a quarter of a sandwich before she passed out, Bishop replied. *But I'll make her eat when I wake her for the wedding and then we'll make her eat again at dinner.*

Knox huffed. *Why bother waking her for the wedding?*

Because she'll also get rest tonight and I think she'll like it, Bishop said. *That and the villagers want to thank her. They've been pretty respectful since it's obvious she's asleep, but they keep looking at us and a mom has had to hold her kid back so he wouldn't wake her.* Bishop pressed his lips to the top of her head and inhaled her sweet fresh scent. *She'll be embarrassed, but hearing the villagers thank her will be good for her.*

I pulled out a sandwich and took a large bite. Not as much meat as I usually liked, but it was fresh and not fire-roasted game or travel rations so I wasn't going to complain, especially since after this we'd be back to whatever Knox could catch, what we could forage, and our rations.

I asked Neera if we could stay for a bit once we returned from the death god's temple, Bishop said. *We have to come back this way and if this spell works we won't need to rush home. All of us could use the extra rest.*

If it works, I warned. I didn't want him to get his hopes up. Yes, he and Knox could share a mate bond with Audrey, but she didn't seem interested in that idea. *If it doesn't work, she and Knox will be mates and have to figure things out. She hasn't shown any indication that she'd be open to a multi-person mate bond so that might not be an option for you.*

She hasn't shown any interest in multi-person mate bonds because she didn't know it was possible, Bishop replied.

My wolf jerked to attention at that and heaved within me. Did that mean he'd told her? Was she open to the idea?

I shoved my wolf back, fighting to stay in control. Even if she was open to taking another mate, she'd pick Bishop or someone else. I still couldn't be in the running. I had responsibilities to my pack.

So, like a coward, I changed the topic instead of finding out what she wanted. I filled Bishop in on the other things I'd learned about the village while struggling to keep my attention on the villagers and not on Audrey.

Kelna, the village, sat on the Birialis' border — a border that had been pushed out to settle Kelna sixty-three years ago. A rare moss grew in the caves near the village that absorbed the death god's powers that the villagers refined into a powerful, highly effective, and safe sedative.

I also learned that the death god asleep in the north was Makaria, a goddess of peaceful eternal rest. Her spirits wouldn't attack us like Tzanagoth's since she wasn't an evil or malicious goddess, but they could try to lure us into a slumber we'd never wake from, so it was best to avoid the death god's lands during nighttime.

More people started to gather in the field, dressed in finer clothes than I'd seen before, and Knox shifted beside me. We were a good seventy feet away, but he was still starting to become uncomfortable with the crowd.

Come on, I said as I stood. *The wedding is going to start soon and Bishop needs to wake her.*

I didn't want to leave her side, but I couldn't let Knox be by himself, not if he wasn't going to take his human form, and he needed to get farther away from the crowd.

We headed away from the wedding area but stayed within sight of Bishop and Audrey. He stroked her hair and murmured something to her. If he'd spoken normally, I would have heard him, but he didn't want to shock her, something my wolf appreciated even if he thought he should be the one holding her.

She lifted her head, her gaze rising to his, and her face lit up with a soft, drowsy smile. Everything within me froze — my thoughts, my heart, and my soul — mesmerized by her. It was like time stood still and I was captured in the warm comfort of that smile even though it was directed at my brother.

Fuck.

I heaved my attention away and managed to not look at her until Hallie, escorted by her parents, crossed the field toward the large red canopy where her fiancé, his family, and the priestess waited. Then I couldn't help myself. I wanted to see if Bishop was right, if she enjoyed the wedding... if she'd want a mating ceremony of her own.

She sat comfortably in Bishop's embrace, eating — thank the sisters — her attention on the ceremony. Her soft smile had returned, but it grew softer and sadder as the ceremony went on. She wanted a ceremony and didn't think she'd have one.

A low growl bubbled in my throat. I wanted to kill those assholes who'd raised her, who'd made her think she was worthless because she was powerless. It made me furious that she didn't even think love was possible.

Of course, Knox wasn't helping by rejecting their bond, but Knox was almost as broken as Audrey was and thought being bonded to him would be bad for her.

The ceremony finished and the celebration began. Platters of food were laid out on long tables and the bonfire was lit. Hallie brought her new husband to Audrey and they thanked her for saving their wedding, making Audrey dip her head, her cheeks turning pink with a soft blush.

More and more people approached Audrey and Bishop, bringing them food and drink, talking and making Audrey dip her head and offer shy smiles.

I grabbed a plate of food and rejoined Knox, who'd moved closer to them — although I wasn't sure if was aware he'd moved closer or not — as half a dozen small children rushed to Audrey's side. Two mothers quickly followed with apologetic smiles, but Audrey opened her arms to the smallest of the girls and let her climb into her lap while two of the boys regaled her with a retelling of her heroics at the pool.

More children gathered, and Audrey smiled and laughed and listened with rapt attention. She was radiant, a shy goddess completely unaware of the power she possessed, and my wolf fell even more in love with her.

She was going to be the mother of our pups.

He'd made up his mind no matter how impossible it was.

AUDREY

I sat in the V between Bishop's legs with a little girl who could barely walk sitting between mine and listened to a boy — this one probably nine or ten — telling an adventure story about his uncle.

I wasn't sure how much of the story was true or exaggerated, but I didn't care. His face was bright with excitement and so were the faces of the other children and adults around us, and he was thankfully drawing attention away from me and the summer dress I wore that was cut low enough to reveal the tops of the ugly red scars across my chest.

A little while ago the sun had sunk below the tree line, the sky turning to black velvet dotted with stars and lit by this realm's two moons, and I'd been hopeful that I wouldn't have to keep hiding behind the little girl.

But the villagers had brought out hundreds of lanterns to light the festivities and surrounded me and Bishop with a dozen of them, lighting us almost as well as the tables with the food and drink as if we were another "station" the villagers needed to stop at.

It had been non-stop since the ceremony ended. Everyone was polite, but I'd never had anyone pay this much attention to me before, and I certainly hadn't had so many people thank me.

It made my insides churn. I didn't know how to respond. That, and even as I sat there hiding behind a child and surrounded by others, I couldn't stop thinking about how I was pressed against Bishop's crotch and how after my nap and taking the elixir, I was no longer exhausted and sore.

The heat building in my core had quickly overwhelmed any ice and emptiness from Knox even before the wedding ceremony was done, and now I strained to concentrate on the people around us and tried, for the umpteenth time that evening, to make myself move so Bishop and I were sitting side by side.

But neither my thoughts nor my body obeyed me.

It felt too good to be this close to him. The warmth in my chest as his soul steadied mine infused into my cells. I was home. I was where I belonged. I was safe.

And I was horny as hell.

My heat was still going strong, stronger than I would have thought possible lasting longer than a week, and I had no idea when it would let up. Maybe I just needed to have sex and get it out of my system.

Bishop accepted another plate of sweets, the movement shifting his body against mine, his hard cock digging against my rear, and my desire spiked, hot and needy, momentarily stealing my breath.

I glanced back at him, but he smiled at the man who'd offered the food and answered his questions about being a shifter as if he wasn't affected by the pheromones pouring from me even though he was as hard as steel.

He'd said he wouldn't let me do something I didn't want to do. If I wanted to wait and see what happened between me and Knox, I had no doubt he'd wait even though he'd said he wanted to be my mate. But if the spell couldn't break our bond then Knox and I would have to have sex.

A chill whispered through my desire. Knox would want to get it over and done with. It would be a transaction, nothing more, and I had no idea how careful he'd be with me. Sure, in my dreams, I liked being overwhelmed by all his ferocious power, but I knew my body wasn't ready for something like that in real life.

Bishop, on the other hand, had been nothing but kind and gentle with me, and he'd already said he wanted to take his time, so I'd enjoy it.

The mother of the little girl in my lap returned after dancing around the bonfire with her husband for a couple of songs and crouched beside me. "Thank you for being so patient with her."

They'd tried to convince her to not bother me by sitting on my lap, but I didn't mind, and I assured them again that sitting with her was fine. She was adorable with soft brown curls and plump rosy cheeks and had been content to sit with me without fussing since before the sun had set. And then the other kids and a couple of their babysitters — two of the teens I recognized from the wader section of the pool — joined us, and the adults had felt safe to enjoy the party. They checked in on us periodically but the kids were great, and it felt... nice.

There was a small bitter pang at seeing the kids laugh and smile and talk with their siblings and parents, but also a sense of home. This was what a pack was supposed to look like, people coming together to celebrate and care for each other. This was what a family was supposed to feel like.

I hadn't thought about whether I wanted kids or not. I'd have needed a mate for that — or hell, even a one-night stand — and no one wanted to be with a shifter who was so weak. But for this one night, I felt like it might be possible, that I might be able to have those baby giggles and the excited storytelling and the sweet simple questions asked in such a serious way.

"It's bedtime," the woman said, lifting her daughter from my lap and turning to one of the younger boys in the group.

"Yes," one of the teens said while a man who'd been quietly sitting a few feet from us monitoring his children nodded his agreement.

"Say goodnight to Miss Audrey," another woman said.

The kids rushed to my side, a few crashing into me to hug me, and wished me goodnight before being led away... and leaving me alone with Bishop.

I raised my hands to cover my neckline even though Bishop had already seen my scars. Hell, he might have seen everything just like Cyrus had.

Heat surged through my veins at the thought of Bishop seeing me naked and my breath picked up. Now everywhere Bishop touched me burned with need and more moisture pooled between my thighs.

"I think I should go to bed, too." I met his gaze, his eyes dark, his wolf just under the surface, but he didn't move, just kept watching me, and I realized what I'd said might not have sounded like the invitation I'd intended. "I mean— I— I think you should take me to bed."

Jeez, that wasn't clear, either. He'd been carrying me around all afternoon and what I'd said could just mean I'd accepted that he'd carry me to bed not that I wanted to have sex with him.

"With you," I blurted out, trying to clarify, my cheeks burning. "I want to have sex with you."

Bishop chuckled, a soft, low rumble that made my insides flip with anticipation, then he picked me up, cradling me against his chest.

"Figured it out the second time," he said as he dipped down and brushed his lips against the top of my head. The touch was quick, barely a whisper that disappeared before I fully realized he was kissing my hair and ended far too quickly. "Thank you for trusting me."

"Well... ah..." My cheeks heated with embarrassment and I squeezed my eyes shut. I had no reason to be embarrassed. He'd offered and I'd asked. It was as simple as that. It wasn't like I was a nervous teenager.

Yeah, just a nervous twenty-two-year-old who'd never been able to ask for what she wanted before.

"I... ah..." God. I had no idea what to say now. I leaned into his embrace and drew in a deep breath of his fresh-cut grass scent, hoping it would help. Except all I could think about was how I was finally going to relieve the pressure of my heat with the most gorgeous man I'd ever seen. Not even the warmth and comfort of his soul steadying mine could ease the nerves skittering down my spine.

"It's okay," he murmured as he carried me away from the meadow and into town. "You don't have to say anything."

He carried me across the town's square and down a narrow street that quickly turned into a dark narrow path that wound through the forest. The path twisted around a large outcropping and climbed a dozen shallow steps that I could barely see in the dim light then opened up to a small glade on a rise overlooking the village.

Moonlight poured into the glade, illuminating a small one-story cabin at the far edge and a path cut through a swath of grass and wildflowers. The cabin had a wide porch that wrapped around three sides of the structure, and small lights had been light in the two front windows and the single attic window as if to welcome us home.

"Cyrus promised he wouldn't show up until we're done, so you don't have to worry about that," Bishop said.

The thought of Cyrus showing up early sent more nervous energy skittering through me. Except I wasn't just afraid of being seen naked and having sex. I wasn't even sure if my reaction had anything to do with that. My body *liked* the idea of Cyrus showing up, wanted him to watch... to participate.

My pulse picked up, and my cheeks and forehead burned. I was only thinking that because Bishop had said he'd joined my mate bond with Knox, that I could have more than one mate, and I'd been attracted to Cyrus from the moment I'd met him. Not to mention, I'd seen him naked and couldn't help wondering what all that powerful muscle would feel like when it was pressed against me.

Jeez. What was I thinking? I was in Bishop's arms and we were about to have sex. Why was I thinking about Cyrus?

Because I was aching and desperate and had put off dealing with my heat for far too long.

Bishop drew in a long breath and groaned. "Keep thinking whatever you're thinking about and I'm not sure I'll be able to make it to the bedroom."

"I—" Now my whole face, neck, and the top of my chest radiated heat. I couldn't tell him I was fantasizing about his brother.

"Oh, beautiful," he murmured, his voice sensual and gentle as he carried me up the three steps to the porch. "Sexy thoughts are nothing to be ashamed of. I promise. I'm going to make you feel good. So good. Just like you deserve."

He opened the front door and stepped into an open concept kitchen-living room with a large fieldstone fireplace on one side, a bathroom and bedroom on the other, and a narrow staircase leading up to a loft. Everything was wood or stone, the surfaces worn from use, and the furniture mismatched. But it was all clean and a hint of citrus hung in the air. It wasn't too overpowering but enough to tell me the place had been recently cleaned.

It reminded me of the cabin I'd gone to with Mila's family the summer before my dad killed himself. But that thought brought up a swirling mix of emotions that I didn't want to deal with, and I pushed them aside, letting the growing need of my heat consume them.

We headed straight into the bedroom, and Bishop sat me on the bed, sank to his knees before me, and looked up at me. Even in the dim candlelight, I could see his eyes were dark. His wolf was close to the surface and his expression was edged with a hunger that made my skin tingle with anticipation.

I was really going to do this.

My pulse picked up and I dropped my gaze to his chest, unable to keep looking him in the eyes.

Oh God, I was *really* going to do this.

"I know you're nervous, but you have nothing to be nervous about." He cupped the side of my face and teased his thumb over my cheek. "If at any time you want to stop, just say so."

I nodded, not trusting my voice, my mouth suddenly dry with nerves. Then he dipped in and kissed me. The kiss was soft, a tease and a promise, but it sent my pulse roaring into a wild, ferocious beat with a spinning mix of excitement and fear.

Jeez. What was wrong with me? It wasn't as if I hadn't kissed Bishop before. Hell, I'd even begged him to have sex with me.

But there was a huge difference between being swept up by my desire like I had at the riverbank outside of Darkweald and purposely deciding to have sex.

"Relax, Audrey," he murmured against my lips. "Give in to your desire. I'm not going to hurt you or laugh at you or abandon you once we're done. I said I was going to court you when we got back, and I have every intention of becoming your mate." He brought his other hand up, fully capturing my face and urging me to meet his gaze.

I fell into those dark depths, the green flecks bright as if they held impossible sparks of magic.

"Let me take care of you," he purred. "The way you deserve."

AUDREY

BISHOP DIPPED CLOSE AGAIN AND THIS TIME HIS KISS WAS FILLED WITH the hunger I'd seen in his expression. But unlike my dream-Knox where we crashed together and he kissed me with a ferocity that stole my breath, Bishop's passion was warm, encompassing, and empowering. He was holding himself back, determined not to overwhelm me. I could feel it in the tension in his arms, the flex of delicious muscle beneath my palms. This was my night, and if all I wanted to do was kiss, he'd leave it at that.

But I wanted more than just kisses. Nervous as I was, I still wanted it all.

I tangled my fingers in his hair and kissed him back with all my pent-up, aching need. I hungered for a release I'd been putting off for days and Bishop matched my intensity. He raked his tongue against mine and nipped at my bottom lip, fueling the throbbing inferno that had been growing inside me from the moment I'd woken in his arms that afternoon.

Then he shifted one hand to the back of my head to better control our kiss, while his other skimmed down my throat and across my shoulder. His fingers plucked at the strap of my dress and another icy flash of nerves rushed through me. He was going to see everything.

My hand jumped to my neckline in a useless attempt to hide my scars despite the dim candlelight and the fact he'd probably already seen them.

"Hey. None of that." He dipped down and kissed the back of my hand, right over top of my heart. "You don't have to hide from me or anyone else. You're beautiful and these scars are just a testament to your strength."

I huffed at that. "I'm not strong. I can't even shift."

"You're strong in other ways. More important ways." He nudged my hand away and pressed a gentle kiss just above the neckline of my dress where my scars peeked out. "You'd do anything to protect a child and you're willing to walk until your feet bleed to free Knox from your bond." His breath feathered across my skin, sending a shiver rushing through me from the top of my head all the way to my core. My desire turned to a molten heat, not wild like my dreams, but heavy and insistent. "That kind of determination and self-sacrifice is stronger than any alpha's power."

His fingers found the straps of my dress again and teased them off my shoulders. This time I didn't freeze, although I still couldn't silence the niggling doubt that Bishop would be repulsed by what he saw. It was rare for a shifter to have scars and I had far too many.

But he didn't hesitate as he slowly drew the fabric lower until just my nipples were covered. Then he teased the tops of my breasts until those tight buds were aching and my breasts felt heavy, yearning for more of his touch.

My breath had already picked up and I was soaking wet between my thighs. And all he'd done was kiss me. I squeezed my legs together, desperate to relieve the ache and not wanting to leave a wet spot on my dress, but then he swiped his thumb across my nipple and all thoughts vanished.

Need shot straight to my core and I gasped. My hands flew to his head and tangled in his hair, and I arched my back, urging him to put his mouth there as if this was one of my dreams.

Maybe it was. It sure felt like it. My body hummed with anticipation, every nerve zinging at the slightest touch or kiss or breath.

Bishop didn't resist my silent plea and pushed my dress beneath my breasts. With a low moan, he drew his tongue over my nipple in a long, heavy lick, that shivered up my body, stealing my breath.

Oh, God. I'd only dreamed that being kissed like that would feel so good.

He sucked on the aching bud and rubbed his thumb against the other, building my need until my breath was ragged and I was rocking toward him.

I clutched at his head, never wanting to let go until his hands slipped over my knees and up the insides of my thighs and Bishop said, "I want to feel you come on my tongue."

"Yes." *Oh yes. Oh my God, yes!* Sex was already so much better than I imagined and if Bishop wanted to go down on me I wasn't going to say no.

His lips curled in a sexy, wicked grin, as he grabbed the bottom of my dress and drew it up over my head, leaving me completely naked.

"You're so beautiful," he groaned, his eyes raking down my body, drinking me in, instantly melting the little tremble of nerves that came with being naked in front of him. "And your scent—"

He slid his palms up my thighs again, urging me wider to make room for him, and dipped in to press his nose against my mound and breathe in my scent.

"You smell like home."

His words swept heat around my heart, filling me with that warmth and calm and surety that I always felt when he held me as if our souls recognized each other... as if we were meant for each other.

Then he inched his nose lower and teased his tongue against me and all the warmth and calm roared into hot aching desperate need.

"Fuck, you taste good," he groaned then swiped his tongue over me again.

This time, the tip of his tongue flicked over my clit, and a jolt of liquid heat swept through me. My inner muscles fluttered and Bishop hummed a satisfied rumble that sounded more wolf than man.

He licked and sucked, turning that heat into a raging inferno. I didn't know what to do with my hands, so I clutched the blanket beneath me. My breath heaved, ragged and desperate from the pleasure and my hips started rocking into him, eager for more, eager for that final push that would send me careening over the edge.

And then he slid a finger inside me, found that magic spot, and sucked on my clit.

Every muscle in my body contracted and glorious sensation rushed through me as strong as my dreams. I'd been so wrong. I'd thought the fantasy was just that, a fantasy, and reality would disappoint me, but God— Why had I fought this?

Oh, right. Mated to his brother.

But that was no longer a problem. Even if the bond couldn't be broken, I could still be with Bishop. Monogamy wasn't my only option in this realm and I could only hope Knox would understand.

Gasping, I glanced down at Bishop who was still between my thighs slowly lapping at my sex and sending soft ripples of pleasure through me. His eyes were fully dark and they held a wicked gleam that sent more ripples rushing through me.

"Oh, yes," I breathed, reaching for him in invitation to move up my body and take me like his look implied.

"Not yet." He flicked his tongue over my clit, stealing my breath with a jolt of sensation. "I want to taste one more."

"One more?"

"Yeah." He raked his tongue over me and my eyes rolled back.

Oh. My. God.

A long moan escaped my lips, and he worked me up again with lips and tongue and fingers. This time, he teased me, bringing me to the edge, backing off, and bringing me to the edge again and again until I was panting and moaning and begging for release.

One more thrust of his fingers, and I was crashing over the edge, lights flashing behind my lids, a strangled cry caught in my throat. I spun around and around, riding a wave of incredible bliss that was stronger than even the ones in my fantasy.

When I finally managed to catch my breath and open my eyes, Bishop was standing and looking down at me.

"That's what I love to see," he purred.

I squirmed under his gaze, more ripples sweeping from my head down my body as if I was still on the edge, still ready for more. And yet I was also boneless and satiated and so incredibly relaxed.

His smile deepened and he pulled off his shirt, revealing his stunning, sculpted chest and abs. But before my gaze could drop any lower, he captured my lips in a searing, breathtaking kiss. Fabric rustled and I was sure he'd stepped out of his pants, but I couldn't focus beyond his lips.

He tasted like he had when I'd kissed him before, but also like something else that could have only been my release.

With a rumble, he grabbed my hips and urged me to move up on the bed. We shifted, never breaking our kiss, and ended up with me on my back and Bishop braced over me.

The kiss reignited the dying embers of my desire, and I clutched at his powerful, muscular shoulders, my hips rocking up, pressing against his hardened length, greedy for more, for all of it.

Bishop growled and his canines extended, grazing my bottom lip as he slid his length against me, grinding against my clit. Sparks flared inside me from the friction, drawing gasping moans that he devoured.

"Do you want this?" he asked, his voice rough, his body trembling with his control. "You can still say no."

"Bishop, please." I ground my hips against him, trying to get him where I needed him. "I said yes and I still say yes."

"Thank the Sisters," he gasped and shifted to press the head of his cock at my entrance.

I froze, my nerves returning, but he captured my lips again. He kissed me breathless, stealing all thought, adding to the fire once again rushing through my body, and slowly pushed inside me.

It was the most incredible feeling, pressure and heat and a building of that achy need that screamed to be released.

When he was buried all the way in, he paused, letting my body adjust to him, and broke off the kiss to look me in the eyes again. "Are you okay?"

"Yeah," I breathed unable to think straight, a tremor fluttering in my core. I was so incredibly full, and in a way I hadn't realized I needed to be filled, and every hypersensitive nerve was on overload, shivering and heating and singing at how amazing I felt.

"Just okay? I'm clearly not doing my job right." Slowly, he drew his hips back, sliding out before pushing back in.

A ripple of pleasure shuddered through me and I released a soft, breathy moan.

"That sounds better than just okay."

"It is. I just—"

He withdrew and pushed back in.

"I can't— I can't think— Oh, Bishop."

My eyes rolled back and I gave myself over to the sensations, to his comforting fresh-cut grass scent wrapped around me, the heat and home in my heart from our contact, and the pleasure building once again in my core.

Bishop slowly picked up his pace, his long, drawn-out strokes coming faster and faster. Waves of his power washed over me with every push, as if by giving in to his passion, he was losing control of his power. And just like in my dream, it caressed me, raised me higher. It didn't demand my submission but built my desire and whispered to that something within me that I prayed was my wolf even if it didn't rise to the surface like it did in my dreams.

Bishop plunged into me again and again, and I spun faster and tighter, until I couldn't breathe, couldn't think. I could only feel. And the feelings were overwhelming, heat and need and glorious bliss.

I reached the summit again, and Bishop swiped rough circles over my clit, tossing me screaming over the edge.

Fireworks exploded behind my lids and sensation engulfed me. Bishop continued rubbing my clit and thrusting into me, drawing out my orgasm until it was almost too much. Then he lost his rhythm, thrust hard, and released a heavy groan. I could feel him pulsing inside me, sending fluttery aftershocks through me, and I sighed, thoroughly satisfied.

I was ruined for other men and I didn't care. My first time was just as incredible as my dreams and I couldn't thank Bishop enough for that.

KNOX

I PACED THE GLADE OUTSIDE THE CABIN, THE GRASS AND WEEDS catching in my fur as I moved, my wolf heaving inside me and threatening to completely take over. He wanted to go in there, shove Bishop aside, and claim our mate. And I wanted to get the hell away from them.

But the fucking mating bond wouldn't let me leave, the chain binding our hearts together yanking on my soul every time I got too far away, and that made it even harder to ignore my wolf... and what was going on in the cabin.

Every time I got too close, I could hear them — and too close was the middle of the glade. Some idiot had left a window open and with my wolf's sensitive hearing, I caught every moan and gasp.

Fuck. I *needed* to be in there.

It wasn't right that Bishop was relieving the pressure from her heat. It should be me. Me!

I wrenched myself away from the cabin before I climbed the steps and broke down the door. But getting out of earshot didn't alleviate the pressure. Instead, I became more aware of Bishop's feelings, of his need for her, for her pleasure and his, and his growing certainty that she was his mate which only made my wolf heave and snarl more, determined to break free.

Stop, I snapped at him.

You stop, he growled back. *She's ours, our mate.*

And she deserves more than we can give her. Why couldn't he understand that? The bond wasn't real. It had been an accident, and if Audrey had been given a choice, she never would have chosen me.

Yes, she would have, my wolf insisted. *She's ours. She always has been.*

He jerked me back toward the cabin and I dug in my heels. A swell of lust poured through my bond with Bishop, and I was so hard my cock hurt, my wolf not caring that I wasn't in a compatible form to be with Audrey.

Then she cried out, her voice strangled with the force of her pleasure, and I was at the door, in human form, and reaching for the latch before I realized what I was doing.

"Don't," Cyrus commanded from his seat on the porch swing. His power snapped through me, not as strong as it could have been, but still forceful enough to make my wolf wrench toward him.

"She's mine," my wolf snarled.

"And you think you can control yourself enough to not make her terrified of sex?"

My wolf leaped at him and seized the front of his shirt, but Cyrus grabbed my wrists, broke my grasp with his incredible strength, and forced me to my knees with his strength and a burst of power.

"If you want the bond that badly," he said to my wolf, "control yourself. Then you can go to her. She's not an alpha. She's not even a wolf."

"She is," my wolf insisted. If our shared dreams were true, she was a wolf and she was powerful, possibly even an alpha. She just needed to wake up.

"She isn't right now. She's a scared woman whose world has been turned upside down. She has no survival skills, knows nothing about this world, and is being crushed by your human half rejecting her."

"Not for long," my wolf said. "He *will* submit. She's ours. She belongs with us."

Cyrus grabbed my throat, capturing it in one large hand, and yanked me close. His canines extended and his eyes darkened as his wolf rose to the surface. "She belongs with whoever she wants to belong with. And right now, that's Bishop. Have I made myself clear?"

My wolf growled a warning for him to let go and my power rolled over my body, threatening to attack even as I fought to contain it. "You want her, too."

"I want her to enjoy her first time and I want her to stop being so fucking scared all the time." He huffed. "And I want her to be terrified when she should be fucking terrified, like going up against a grimalkin."

"She's not your mate." My power grew stronger and Cyrus's rose to meet it.

Get your shit under control before you hurt Audrey, Bishop snapped in my head, his mental voice strained. The telepathic communication strengthened our connection and for a second I was inside Bishop, burying himself in her tight warmth.

Get your cock out of her, my wolf howled. *She's mine. Mine.*

Every protective, jealous instinct I had swamped me. I was the only one who could take care of her and I had to keep her safe. I was furious that I let myself take her on this dangerous journey and even more furious that my brothers had agreed to it. They didn't have her best interests in mind. If they did, they wouldn't have put her in danger.

Cyrus shifted his grip, capturing my throat in the crook of his elbow, jumped off the edge of the porch, and hauled me away from the cabin.

I heaved against his hold, fighting to get my feet under me to get better leverage, and my power slammed against his. The force crackled through the air around us. There was no way I'd be able to make him submit. Between the three of us, he was the strongest brother, the true alpha of our pack.

No. He wasn't going to take us away from her. He wouldn't. I had to protect her, claim her. She was mine.

With a snarl, I rammed my fist into his gut with everything I had.

He staggered, his grip loosening, and I wrenched free and lunged at him with my claws extended and my canines bared. There was no point in running past him. He'd just grab me. I had to eliminate the threat before I could get to her.

He sidestepped my attack and seized my arm, but I twisted with his grip, expecting his counter to my lunge, and sunk my claws into his gut.

"Fuck," he snarled and his free hand clamped around my throat.

With a roar, he lifted me up and slammed me onto the ground, his power aiding his strength and crushing inside my chest.

The impact knocked the breath from my lungs and before I could jump up and attack again, he rammed his fist into the side of my head.

The world lurched and darkened, the force of the blow again aided by his power, crashing inside my skull. He'd never augmented a punch with his power before, and it was more powerful than anything I'd ever felt from him.

Holy fuck. I'd known he was stronger than me, but I hadn't thought it was by that much, and I'd never have thought to augment my blow with the power that let me force other shifters to submit to me.

Then I blinked and we were in the woods, the cabin barely visible through the trees, and my mating bond was stretched painfully thin. He'd knocked me out?

He'd knocked me out and taken me away from her!

Roaring, I leaped at him, my wolf furious, my skin aching on the verge of shifting back into my wolf form.

"Sit," he commanded, crushing me with the full force of his power. I stumbled to a halt before reaching him and strained to resist, strained to show him I was strong enough to be her mate, and strained to get back to her, claim her, and protect her.

No, my wolf did. It wasn't me. I didn't want her—

Well, a small part of my human soul did, and I wasn't sure if that was just Bishop's influence or not. But that didn't matter. I couldn't be the mate she deserved. I had to keep remembering that. I couldn't let my wolf take over and fuck up her life. I had to set her free.

No, my wolf screamed. *I have to protect her. Mine.*

"I. Said. Sit." Cyrus's power surged, wrenching me to the ground. "You *will* let them have this and you *will* get your wolf under control." A hint of fear filled Cyrus's gaze before vanishing behind his hard, in-control alpha mask.

Shit. I hadn't seen Cyrus afraid like that since Bishop had brought me back from being feral.

Was I that close? I hadn't thought I was. But then, I hadn't realized I was losing control the last time.

Fuck. This was why I had to break the mating bond. I was ready to kill my brothers just to be with her. It didn't make sense. Bishop was making her happy which should make me happy. That was how it had worked with our fathers and mother.

But no. My wolf was furious and I didn't know if I'd be able to stay in control for two more days.

"You have to collar him," I forced out, even as my wolf tried to clamp my mouth shut and control me.

Cyrus's eyes widened in surprise. Collaring the wolf half of a shifter's soul was painful. It wasn't the sharp, agonizing pain of being hurt, but the crushing emptiness of being cut off from a primal part of yourself. It took an extremely powerful alpha to do it and wasn't permanent so it couldn't be used as a reliable punishment, but it could help in short term, desperate situations.

He hadn't been able to collar me when I'd turned feral because once my wolf had taken over it had been too late. That, and I doubted he could collar me without my help even with the amount of power he'd just shown. But I couldn't afford to lose it right now. We were in the middle of nowhere at least eight days from home and whether my wolf wanted it or not, we needed our brothers to get Audrey back to Stonehaven in one piece.

"Do it," I snarled.

"You're almost as strong as me," Cyrus replied. "I won't be able to collar you."

"I'll help."

The muscles in Cyrus's jaw flexed and he glared down at me. I'd gone feral once before, and there was a risk that once the collar was released and my wolf was free, it would consume me and I'd go feral again. And there was no guarantee that Bishop would be able to bring me back a second time.

"It has to be done," I insisted. There was no other choice. I wasn't going to be able to control my wolf for much longer. I could already feel him straining against my control. The only thing keeping me strong enough to hold him back was Cyrus's command to sit. "I'm not going to make it to the temple and then Audrey will be fucked."

Cyrus groaned. "Fuck. Fine. Okay."

He dropped to his knees in front of me and captured my head between his hands, forcing me to look him in the eyes. His power rolled over me, a crushing, suffocating weight, threatening to consume me, and my own power rose up to meet it.

I strained to hold onto it, not let it clash against Cyrus's but melt into it, empowering it even more.

No, my wolf screamed, straining to take over my body. *We have to protect her.*

"You have to weave your power into mine," Cyrus said, his voice tight with the strain of drawing on so much power and not releasing it right away. "I can't make you do it."

"I know." It was taking everything I had just to keep my wolf from possessing me.

My wolf howled and heaved and clawed, digging agonizing rents into my soul, fighting to make me submit to his will and claim Audrey.

Cyrus's crushing pressure grew, squeezing my chest and forcing me to suck in shallow gasping breaths. I tried to close my eyes to focus, but Cyrus had already seized control of that part of my body because he needed to see into my eyes to capture my wolf and collar it.

"Give me your power," he snarled. "Submit."

No. I won't let you. You can't have her. She's mine. Mine mine mine.

And she deserves better than us.

I mentally shoved my power into Cyrus's and it, along with his, slammed back into me. It tore into my soul, seized my wolf, and ripped it free from my human half.

Fiery agony sliced through me in a sudden, blinding flash, followed by complete desolation.

I tried to swallow my scream but couldn't. I had no control over my body. I'd given it to Cyrus and he was focused on locking my wolf away.

Then the power vanished, and he sagged back on his heels and released my face. I collapsed forward, a gaping emptiness numbing my limbs and filling my chest. It wasn't the same crushing pressure of our combined power, but it was still damn hard to breathe.

Cyrus stood with a groan. "I'll get you your clothes."

My clothes?

Right. My wolf was collared. I wasn't going to be able to shift until he was released, and I was going to have to figure out how to live in my human form, a form that made my insides twist and my skin crawl with discomfort.

AUDREY

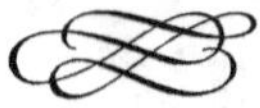

I woke with my cheek pressed against Bishop's chest and his arms wrapped around me, holding me close. An ache, not painful but certainly present, radiated from my core, reminding me of what we'd done last night, and a silly smile curled my lips.

I'd had sex.

And with a gorgeous, powerful shifter who'd *wanted* to have sex with me. I was no longer a virgin and it had been more amazing than I'd imagined.

A flutter of desire tightened my stomach. It wasn't nearly as strong as the desire I'd been fighting since I'd woken in this realm, more just a memory of what had happened and how I wanted to do it again.

In fact, the more I concentrated on it, the more it felt softer and sweeter, not wild and aching and desperate.

I released a relieved breath. My heat was finally over. It had to be. Having sex with Bishop had been exactly what I'd needed. I even felt steady enough that the icy hollowness from Knox rejecting our bond wasn't as strong, as if finding my emotional balance with my heat had helped steady all of me.

Bishop hummed, the sound rumbling in his chest beneath my ear, and rubbed gentle circles on my back with his fingers.

"Did I wake you?" I asked, glancing up at him. He looked absolutely delicious with his jaw-length brown hair mussed from sleep and an affectionate warmth in his eyes.

"I was already awake," he said. "I didn't want to move and disturb you. That, and you make the cutest noises when you sleep."

Heat swept across my cheeks and I ducked my head, burying my face against his chest again to hide my blush and breathing in his comforting fresh-cut grass scent.

He chuckled softly and shifted his hand from my back to my head and stroked my hair. "How do you feel?"

His question made my thoughts jump back to last night and I squirmed, sliding my body against his and savoring the feel of our flesh rubbing together.

"Good." *So so good.* "Thank you."

I glanced back up at him and his lips curled into a brilliant, breathtaking smile. "You are so beautiful."

My blush returned with a vengeance. "Stop saying things like that."

"Why? It's true." A hint of playfulness flashed in his eyes. "I think I'll say it every day from now on."

"Bishop—"

"Come here and kiss me, you gorgeous woman," he interrupted, his hands shifting to my hips to help me scoot up the bed to kiss him.

His lips were soft, the kiss tender. It wasn't filled with the passion from last night, but a reverence, a promise of more to come, a lifetime of warmth and love. He'd said he was going to be my mate no matter what and this kiss was a reassurance of that promise.

When he finally pulled back, I was breathless and well on my way to getting turned on. And from the hardness digging into my thigh, so was he.

"We should probably go have breakfast," he said, his voice deliciously gruff with desire. "Cyrus won't wait all morning and I suspect you don't want him walking in on us."

The image of Cyrus opening the door and watching us make love flashed through my mind's eyes. Except he was naked like he'd been after the grimalkin attack on Stonehaven and his eyes held the same hunger my dream-Knox had had.

A shiver of need rushed through me. Boy, my mind was really running away with the multiple mates idea.

But jeez. My heat was over and I was mated to Knox and practically mated to Bishop. I shouldn't be fantasizing about Cyrus. Especially since he'd made it clear he wanted nothing to do with me.

"Yeah," I mumbled, ducking my head and rolling away from Bishop to get off the bed. "That would be bad."

Yes. Bad. Bad bad bad... not sexy as hell.

I climbed out of bed, my feet still protected by the linen bandages and Hallie's soft slippers, placed them on the floor, and gingerly stood up. As I'd hoped, because I'd taken one of the guys' precious healing elixirs, they didn't hurt. And while the gashes in my calf still ached, it was nothing compared to yesterday.

"Your feet okay?" Bishop asked, grabbing his pants and pulling them on.

"I think so. I'll keep them wrapped up until I find my boots, but I shouldn't have any problem reaching the death god's altar."

"Good," he replied as he leveled a hard look at me. "And on our way home, you're going to tell us to stop when they start to bother you, so you don't permanently hurt yourself."

"I promise." If, of course, the bond was broken and we didn't need to hurry back to Whil to see if she could transfer it to Bishop.

Bishop's eyes narrowed.

"Promise," I insisted, grabbing the dress Hallie had given me — since I didn't know where my clothes were or if they'd even been cleaned.

Bishop huffed as I pulled on the dress.

"You're a terrible liar," he said. "But I get it. Neither you nor Knox asked to be bonded together."

And I'd promised myself I would do everything in my power to free him. I still wasn't sure if he blamed me or not. Sure, he'd said he didn't, but he'd been cold and distant and angry with me since the beginning — so very very angry — and the sense I got from him through the bond hadn't changed.

"Come on," Bishop said, pulling me from my thoughts, and we stepped out of the bedroom into the kitchen-living room.

Cyrus sat at the worn wooden kitchen table, eating a muffin with an apple core with a hank of grapes on the plate in front of him.

"They didn't know when we'd be up," he said, pointing to a basket at the center of the table. "So, they brought fruits and breads. Nothing that needed to be kept warm."

"No meat?" Bishop asked.

"They're not shifters. It probably didn't occur to them that we need extra protein." He shrugged and nudged the basket in our direction. "I'm just grateful for a bed and fresh food."

"Not complaining," Bishop said, pulling out the chair beside Cyrus and gesturing for me to sit. "Just commenting."

I sat and grabbed the first muffin I saw from the basket, not caring what kind it was. Cyrus was too close, but I couldn't have refused the seat without drawing more attention to myself. As it was, I felt like I had a neon sign on my forehead flashing "I had sex," and I couldn't stop myself from blushing.

My reaction was ridiculous and embarrassing. I was an adult. I could have sex with whoever I wanted, whenever I wanted, and it didn't matter if Cyrus had heard us... or if I'd fantasized about him joining us this morning.

My blush grew hotter and swept down my throat and across my chest.

Oh. My. God.

"I talked to Rafe while you two were entertaining the villagers at the wedding and he says there are the remains of a village just outside Makaria's circle of influence," Cyrus said. "It's three-quarters of a full day's hike, but just like Anakar, it's half a day to the temple."

"So, we make camp in the remains of this village, avoid running into any spirits after dark, and get to the altar tomorrow afternoon," Bishop said before taking a big bite of an apple.

A day and a half and then Knox and I would be free. God, I couldn't wait. And then Bishop and I could figure out our relationship—

Although now that I had a clearer head, maybe I should figure out myself before anything else. I really had no idea what I was doing or where my life was going. Once I was free, who was I? I didn't want to be the same Audrey who'd been betrayed by my pack, but I had no idea where I fit in this new one.

Bishop had said he didn't care that I was weak, but from the conversation I'd overheard in the hospital, not everyone felt that way. Did I care? If I was Bishop's mate, it might not matter.

Except others would look down on him for willingly mating with a shifter who couldn't even shift, and I didn't want to just be "Bishop's-mate-Audrey." I wanted to be more. I wanted to be "Audrey" without anyone else attached to my identity.

But before I could figure any of that out, I needed to walk up to that death god's altar and murder my mating bond.

AUDREY

Cyrus and Bishop talked about their supplies and the path they were going to take to get to the abandoned village, and I ate my breakfast without saying a word. Just like all the times before, I didn't have anything to offer to the conversation, so I just stayed out of their way.

When I was done, I gathered up their plates, washed, and dried them, then set them on the counter beside the sink while they talked about returning to Kelna for another night in a bed and resupplying.

Someone had returned my clothes, cleaned of the blood and grime from hiking for seven days and from fighting a grimalkin. They sat in a neat pile on the edge of the couch, right in front of my cleaned boots, and I gathered them, hurried into the bedroom, and changed then turned my attention to my injuries.

I wasn't sure if the gashes in my calf were fully healed so I didn't bother unwrapping the bandage to check. The linen was clean without any sign of blood and my pant leg covered it, so I decided not to touch it and to wait until we returned to Kelna just in case. I didn't want to risk an infection and use up another elixir when it could be easily prevented.

For my feet, I carefully unwrapped them and confirmed that my blisters were healed. They hadn't been as deep as the gashes, even if they'd been as painful, and I was relieved I was going to be able to walk, and not limp, the rest of the way to the death god's altar.

I was just finishing rewrapping them and carefully pushing them into my boots when someone knocked on the door.

"You ready to go?" Bishop asked.

"Yep," I replied, hurrying back into the living room. "And before you ask, yes my feet are healed."

"What about your calf?" He headed to the front door where our packs waited for us.

"Still a little sore, but a lot better than yesterday," I said, following him. "I didn't want to risk unwrapping it, finding there was a chance they could open up, and then doing a crappy job of wrapping it back up again."

He huffed, picked up my pack, and handed it to me. "I'm sure you wouldn't have had a problem rewrapping it. You patched Knox up after the jackal fight."

"Taping gauze over wounds that are going to heal in a few hours is different than securing a bandage that needs to withstand walking for a day or more."

"It is," he said picking up his own pack and stepping outside. "And I'm confident you would have been able to do it. You're more capable than you think you are."

"You're just saying that because—" I stopped dead in my tracks.

Knox stood at the bottom of the stairs in his human form. The resemblance to Bishop was uncanny. They had the same brown eyes flecked with green, beautiful sculpted features, identical builds, and even the same haircut. The only difference was Bishop kept his hair braided back from his face and Knox didn't. Oh, and Knox glowered like he wanted to rip something — probably me — apart.

Except his eyes weren't dark. His wolf wasn't fighting to take control. And that, along with the fact that he was actually fully clothed as if he was planning on staying in his human form, shocked me the most.

"You're human," I gasped, the idiotic, obvious words jumping out of my mouth before I could stop them.

I'd only seen him in his human form once — my dreams not included — and that had been a few days ago. Hell, I'd barely seen him at all since I'd accidentally mate bonded with him. He'd been avoiding me even while we'd been traveling together.

"I'm not a human. I'm a shifter," he snarled as he snatched my pack and walked away with it.

What the—

Why was he carrying my pack? It wasn't as if he'd suddenly changed his mind about me and wanted to be nice. The icy hollowness from our frozen bond was as strong as ever. He didn't want me. And I didn't want him or his help.

"I can carry my own pack," I called after him, but he just huffed and stormed into the forest.

"Come on." Cyrus jerked his chin, indicating that we should follow Knox, and not addressing the fact that he'd just walked off with my pack. "It's already well after dawn and it would be nice to get to this abandoned village before nightfall."

We walked until late afternoon only stopping for a quick lunch of dried meat and fruit before heading out again. Knox stayed in human form for the entire time, but he didn't join us for lunch and was always thirty or more feet ahead of us.

He also didn't return my pack and the only thing I could think of that would explain his behavior was that he didn't want to risk me slowing him down. He wanted to get to the death god's altar by noon tomorrow and be free of me, and I was too weak and pathetic to keep up. Which meant he had to carry my pack and as a result had to stay in human form.

And that was fine by me. Really. At least as far as my mind was concerned. I hadn't asked for the help, so I was still staying out of Cyrus's way and keeping up without complaint. My heart and soul, however, wept at the icy hollowness of his rejection and the thought that soon our connection would be shattered.

But I knew that grief wasn't my real emotion. I'd never wanted to be with someone who didn't want me. Even if it made my life better or easier, I'd never want that.

Besides, I had someone who *did* want me, and I couldn't wait to be free so I could be with him. That thought made it impossible to stop thinking about last night or to stop stealing glances at Bishop.

Shivers of remembered pleasure and waves of heated embarrassment rushed from my head to my toes every time our eyes met, and it took everything I had to concentrate on hiking over the uneven terrain and not falling on my face.

After lunch, the forest gave way to a barren, rocky wasteland that stretched as far as I could see. Only a few scraggly shrubs and weeds managed to grow, and I wasn't sure if *growing* was the right word since they were brown and brittle like it was winter and not the beginning of summer.

By late afternoon, we reached the long-abandoned village which turned out to be the barely standing remains of a dozen structures. All of them had been small, one-story buildings, and had long-ago lost their roofs. More than half had walls left standing, but those walls only reached waist or shoulder high and the rest had fallen over.

Cyrus picked the sturdiest looking house, a one-room building that hadn't been more than a thirty-by-thirty-foot box. One of the walls had been taken out by a neighboring house — if the rubble taking up half the floor space was any indication. But unlike the other house that didn't have as much debris, this one's two walls offered shelter from the wind. And while the wind wasn't strong at the moment — just enough to make me wish I had a light jacket — that could easily change once the sun had set.

"Bishop," Cyrus said, dropping his pack and pulling off his shirt. "You and Audrey gather firewood. Knox, see if you can find a well with safe water. I'll get us dinner."

He dropped his pants, giving me a front row show to his powerful, stunning body, and a rush of remembered pleasure shuddered through me, momentarily stealing my breath.

I turned away from him as he shifted, my cheeks heating, and listened as he ran away from our shelter on four legs. Beside me, Knox snorted, dropped my pack, grabbed the canteens, and left as well.

"I still can't believe you blush every time someone gets naked," Bishop chuckled.

"Yeah, well, you like it when I blush when *you* get naked." It wasn't much of a comeback, but it was the best I could think of while my brain was still short-circuiting on Cyrus's naked body and what it would feel like to have all that powerful muscle wrapped around me.

"That I do." He flashed me a heart-stopping smile.

I jerked away, my face suddenly on fire, caught my toe in the rubble, and careened forward.

But Bishop seized my wrist and yanked me tight against him, his arm wrapped protectively around me before I hit the ground.

Need shivered down my spine and my pulse stalled as his scent flooded my nostrils. One night with Bishop hadn't been nearly enough, and I couldn't wait to get back to Kelna and some privacy to go again. This time without the pressure of my heat egging me on.

"So, no flirting while you're trying to walk," he laughed. "I'll have to remember that."

"I can walk just fine. Even if you flirt with me." I rolled my eyes at myself. I'd just tripped because he'd smiled at me. "Okay, so maybe I'm a little distracted."

"Just a little?"

I huffed. "Fine. A lot distracted." I hadn't been able to stop thinking about last night and I wasn't sure I wanted to. Something good and amazing had finally happened to me and I never wanted to forget it.

"Is it your heat?" he asked as he tightened his embrace and pressed his lips against the top of my head.

I melted against him, letting the warm calm of being held seep into my soul.

Sure, I was a little turned on and yearned for another hot night in bed, but the feeling wasn't nearly as strong as it had been before, it felt more like a desire to be with Bishop again, not jump the first hot guy I came across.

Which had to mean my heat had broken. Finally. It had gone on for at least seven days and was finally done.

"I don't think it's my heat. I don't feel desperate or needy at all anymore. I just—" Another shiver of pleasure teased through me. "I keep remembering last night."

"So, you enjoyed it?"

"Do you really have to ask? I'm pretty sure I've spent all day with a stupid grin on my face while making moon eyes at you."

He laughed, the sound rich and welcoming. "Yeah, you have been. I just wanted to check." Then he released me and stepped back, his hand finding mine and gently squeezing. "Hopefully that was all you needed to tip you over the edge and break your heat."

"Yeah." Icy fear flickered through me. Was this where he told me it didn't mean anything? That he was just helping me out because my heat was driving me crazy?

I tried to push that thought aside. He'd said he was going to court me. He'd promised.

But Royce had made promises as well, and all my life, no one had wanted me.

"Don't you dare go there," Bishop said, hooking his finger under my chin and forcing me to meet his gaze.

"I know it's stupid and it isn't true." But I just couldn't help it. I might have felt steadier since having sex, but the icy hollowness and the soul-deep grief of having my mate bond rejected were still there. I was still afraid that Bishop was going to rip the rug right out from under me, just like Royce had.

"It isn't stupid," he said, his voice soft and his expression sad. "You were betrayed in the worst way and nothing has been easy for you. It's going to take time for you to believe that I'm not going anywhere and that you deserve so much more than what you'd been given."

"Yeah," I repeated, uncertain what to say to that.

"I'll wait for however long it takes, and I *will* show you every day that you are more than what everyone says you are and that you deserve to be happy."

Tears burned my eyes and my throat tightened. I wanted so desperately to believe him, wanted to believe that I could be worthy of being loved, but I couldn't make the tiny voice in the back of my head shut the fuck up.

"I'll wait for you, Audrey." He brushed his lips against my forehead and wrapped me in his embrace again. "I'll always wait for you."

AUDREY

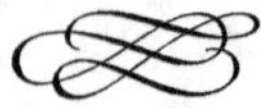

I clung to Bishop, silent tears trickling down my cheeks and soaking into his shirt. Hope was such a dangerous, fragile thing, and I couldn't withstand the terror of having it shattered again.

Bishop murmured soothing nonsense to me as he stroked my hair, and his soul warmed and steadied mine. I wasn't sure how long we stood like that before I eased out of his embrace, but thankfully it was before Knox and Cyrus returned.

I didn't want to deal with anything they might say or even the looks they'd give me. They thought I was weak, and crying over being told I wasn't alone and that someone cared for me, was probably pathetic in their eyes.

"Let's see if we can find enough wood for a fire," I said, wiping my face on my sleeve.

"Yeah." Bishop swept his gaze at the desolation around us and sighed. "Although I don't have a lot of hope for that. I think the best we hope for is enough to cook whatever Cyrus catches... if there's anything out there to catch."

We picked our way through the rubble, searching for anything that was more than a handful of stringy grass, and attacked every scraggly bush we came across. I was pretty sure the branches were too thin to be anything more than kindling, but unless we came across a wooden beam or piece of furniture or something it was all we had — and I suspected, given the condition of the buildings, that anything wooden had rotted away a long time ago.

"Ah, here's a big one," Bishop exclaimed as he peeked through the window of one of the best-preserved walls in the village.

I followed as he made his way around, revealing that half the house was more or less untouched, standing a good two feet taller than Bishop, while the other half had completely crumbled.

The "big one" was a shrub almost as tall as me with a trunk thick enough to make thin logs, and we got to work ripping the branches off until the remaining branches were too thick for me to break apart. Then Bishop took over, and I went to work breaking the thinner branches into campfire appropriate lengths.

As I worked, I let my attention drift to the wasteland beyond the crumbling walls. The sun was close to setting, the few clouds in the sky turning pink with a warm sunset that I couldn't feel, and far off in the distance, I could see a thick fog rolling over the rugged terrain getting closer.

A shiver slipped down my spine, this one from fear and not from my sexy memories, and I hugged myself against the chill.

"I heard that the fog shows up every night over the death god's domain," Bishop said. "But it doesn't reach the village, and it disperses in the morning,"

Which was when we'd march straight to the altar, cast the spell Whil found, and pray that it worked.

Tomorrow.

I sucked in a steadying breath. Whil had said the spell could kill anything magical within us and that included our bond. Would it also kill my curse?

I sat up straighter. Bishop had lied and told Ida and Hallie we were going to cast the spell to break the curse that prevented my wolf from waking. But what if that didn't have to be a lie? What if I could be completely free of everything?

I could be strong. People wouldn't look at me with disgust or pity. I could be the person I was supposed to be.

"Bishop," I said, my gaze locked on the undulating fog and the hope that lay within it. "Do you think the spell that can break my bond with Knox will be able to break my curse?"

He released a heavy sigh and my hope trembled inside me. That didn't sound good.

"I was hoping you'd forget I said that. I felt like we needed an explanation as to why we're heading to the death god's temple and breaking your curse was easier to explain than breaking a mating bond," he said, ripping off the last two branches to get to the trunk.

"That means the answer is no." What little hope I had twisted into heavy resignation.

Of course the spell wouldn't break my curse. My wolf was never going to wake and that was just the way it was.

"I'm sorry," he said crouching beside me and pulling me into a hug. "I asked Whil the same question and she said the curse that prevents you from shifting is woven into your essence. Given how the death spell works, she has no doubt casting it to break your curse would kill you."

"Swell."

"Hey, don't give up hope," he said. "After your bond with Knox is broken, we can move on to breaking that curse."

I nodded my agreement, my throat tight, and we finished tearing down the bush and headed back to our shelter.

Knox and Cyrus returned a few minutes later. Both had been successful which meant we wouldn't need to ration our water for the next two days and we didn't have to eat trail mix for supper.

After tossing us the canteens and saying the water was safe, Knox turned around and left. With a sigh, Bishop started the fire, and Cyrus set up the spit to cook the... raccoon? Gutted and skinned, I wasn't entirely sure what animal it had been and wasn't going to look at it too closely. It was food, and I was grateful.

I sat out of their way while they worked, wanting to help but afraid they'd refuse if I offered. It had been days since Bishop had tried to teach me wilderness survival stuff, but I had thought he'd stopped because I'd been exhausted, not because I was a bad student. Now I wasn't so sure, since this was a perfect opportunity for a lesson and it was obvious I was now fine.

I smiled and bit back a breathy sigh before they noticed. I was better than fine and by tomorrow afternoon, once the bond was broken, I'd be great.

I was still disappointed that the spell also couldn't break my curse, but I was trying hard not to focus on that. Knox and I would be free and I'd finally be able to feel exactly what I was feeling, not the heartbreaking, icy hollowness of his rejection.

"What are you smiling about?" Bishop asked as he lit the fire and sat beside me.

"That after tomorrow, my life will finally be my own." Unless Bishop and Cyrus turned on me the second Knox was safe.

I shoved that thought aside. It wasn't from me. It was my insecurities magnified by the rejected bond.

With a grin, Bishop drew me into his lap and wrapped his arms around me, sending warmth and calm radiating around my heart. Cyrus cocked an eyebrow as if he wanted to say something but huffed instead and stared at our dinner cooking over the fire.

"Any thoughts on what you want your life to look like?" Bishop asked.

"I don't know," I confessed leaning into him. "I haven't really thought about it. I hadn't been able to think about it in my old pack." I was the alpha's slave, and if Merrick hadn't been planning to use me as currency to buy a seat at the North American Shifter Alliance's table, I probably would have stayed his slave — even if my wolf did manage to wake. "And I haven't been able to think about it here because of everything going on."

But now my heat had been broken and the mess with the accidental mating bond would soon be over. Maybe it was time to think about the future. Except—

"The only thing I can do is clean," I sighed.

"Is that what you want to do?" Cyrus asked.

"I don't enjoy it. But everyone in a pack needs to be useful." Even my father had told me that. It hadn't just been Merrick and Sterling and the pack betas saying that to control me, and I believed it. I wanted to contribute. I wanted to matter. Even if it was just a little bit.

"I'm sure we can find something you like," Bishop said.

"My options are limited," I told him. "I'm not an artist, so I can't add to the pack's enjoyment and culture, and I can't read or write your language. Technically I can't even speak it."

"Whatever you decide on, it doesn't have to happen the moment you get back," Bishop replied.

I shivered, the night getting chilly now that the sun had set, and Bishop rubbed his large warm palms up my arms to warm me.

"If you want to be literate," he added, "you can learn without pressure. Our pack has always tried to encourage our members to follow their strengths."

That sounded so beautiful and yet— "I have no idea if I have any strengths. I'm not even sure where to start."

Cyrus growled and a flicker of his power washed over me before vanishing a second later.

Swell. I didn't know what I'd said to piss him off, but a release of power like that meant a strong emotional reaction. He was probably tired of holding my hand — not that he'd actually done a lot of hand-holding — and wanted me to stop sucking up all his time. I'd bonded with Knox and by the time we got back, he'll have lost two thirds of a month trying to fix it. He probably had a ton of work waiting for him when he got home. Bishop, too.

"House cleaning is probably a good place to start, though," I said, trying to sound positive and not worried. "I'll be able to pay for room and board while I figure myself out."

"You're not paying for room and board," Bishop said. "You're staying at the Residence."

"If she doesn't want to stay at the Residence, she doesn't have to," Cyrus growled.

Except I couldn't tell if he meant that to respect my desire for independence or if he was really hoping I'd leave his house and get out of his way.

"Of course, she doesn't," Bishop replied. "But I don't want her to feel like she isn't welcome once her bond with Knox is broken."

"And I don't want her to feel obligated because we're the pack alphas," he shot back and his hard gaze captured mine. "If I told you to stay in the Residence, would you say no?"

I narrowed my eyes. I wanted to say that I would say no, that I'd refuse him if he made it an order, but I probably wouldn't. It was safer to just go along with it until I could get away.

And I'd learned my lesson. I wouldn't hesitate the next time because I was afraid. I'd run at the first chance I got and never look back. I really liked Bishop, but I still didn't know him very well and I couldn't count on him protecting me from his brother.

"Thought so," Cyrus huffed and he turned back to our dinner.

In one breath he offered me independence and in the next, he reminded me of just how weak I was.

AUDREY

I woke at dawn the next day covered in a blanket and wrapped in Bishop's arms. The sense of warmth and calm of being in his embrace filled me with a heavy, relaxing warmth, although my muscles did ache a bit from having walked most of the day yesterday — guess I wasn't quite as healed as I'd thought I was.

Across from me lay Cyrus and Knox, both covered in their blankets and asleep. It shocked me that Knox still hadn't shifted back to his wolf, the form Bishop had told me he preferred. It, however, didn't shock me, that he'd waited until I'd passed out before joining us at the campfire.

His lids cracked open and his gaze jumped to mine as if drawn to me, unable to look anywhere else first. For a second the icy hollowness wasn't as overwhelming and hope that he didn't despise me for accidentally trapping him flickered inside me.

Even if we weren't permanently bound together, I didn't want him to hate me. If Bishop and I were going to be in a relationship, everything would be easier and less awkward — or as less awkward as things could get given the circumstances — if Knox didn't hate me.

Then his eyes narrowed, bursting my hope, and with a grunt, he got up. He shoved the blanket into my pack and marched around to the other side of the wall, taking my pack and that hope with him.

Only half a day to go, I told myself. *Half a day and it will be over.*

Knox might never forgive me, but by noon today he'd at least be free, and I wouldn't be able to sense that hate.

We ate a quick breakfast of dried rations, tidied up our campsite — since we were going to be returning to it tonight — and headed out.

The sunrise had burned away most of last night's mist, but there were still a few curls of it undulating in crevasses and shaded areas where the light had yet to reach, and a chill still hung in the air. As we walked, the land grew more even and more barren without a shrub or weed in sight, leveling out to look more like a cracked, water-starved desert than the rocky mountainous lands we'd been hiking, and it still hadn't warmed up.

It was hard to believe that all my hope lay in the middle of complete emptiness, and by midmorning, a part of me started to fear that the desolation around us was all there was. There wasn't an altar to a death god and there was no hope that the bond would ever be broken.

But Knox, who walked a good hundred feet ahead of us, kept going north. I didn't know if it was because he sensed something or if he just couldn't stop, couldn't give up on the hope that he'd be free.

I focused on the possibility that he sensed something. I'd come this far, walked until my feet bled. It couldn't all be for nothing. There was an altar and the spell would work. I would get my life back.

No, I'd get a better life. I was still a weak shifter who couldn't shift, but that didn't mean I was helpless. Humans did just fine without any shifting or magic, and I could find a place for myself in this realm. If it wasn't in Cyrus's pack, then a human community.

It wouldn't be easy, especially since I was illiterate, but for once in my life, I could make my own decisions, choose my own path.

And in a few hours, once we found this altar, I could get started.

Another hour later and I realized the ground ahead of us wasn't so flat. It was hard to see, just a bump on the horizon, but it kept getting bigger and bigger the closer we got to it.

That was the temple. I just knew it.

My pulse leaped in anticipation and I picked up my pace. Bishop and Cyrus didn't say anything, but they easily matched me, and we hurried toward the—

Lump.

It was a giant, three-story mound of earth in the middle of nowhere. It didn't look anything like Tzanagoth's detailed, multi-spired temple in Anakar, and I wasn't even sure it was anything. There were no windows and no doors — at least from this side. For all I knew, it wasn't even hollow.

Perhaps we had to climb to the top... except I couldn't see any stairs or hand and footholds, and the surface was smooth enough that climbing would be difficult. Or at least difficult for me. The guys could probably climb that thing no problem.

"Is this the temple?" Bishop asked, staring at it, his brow furrowed.

Cyrus glanced at the sun. It sat high in the sky indicating it was close to noon. The villagers had said if we left at sunrise and headed straight north, we'd reach the temple by noon.

Maybe we hadn't walked north. It was highly unlikely with Knox leading the way, but maybe.

There's an entrance on the far side, Knox said in my head, and presumably in Bishop's and Cyrus's as well since we all hurried around it to find Knox standing a good ten feet back from a dark, narrow entranceway. His posture was stiff and he glared at the entrance as if he were furious with it.

"I'll check it out," Bishop said and he headed inside.

The passage was barely wider than his shoulders and only a foot taller than him, and within a dozen feet, he disappeared into darkness.

With a growl, Knox paced a good fifty feet away from the mound then stomped back. Then his head jerked toward Cyrus and his growl deepened.

"I'll be fine," Knox snarled, a hint of darkness in his eyes. "This needs to be done."

"Then get ahold of yourself," Cyrus snarled back, his power crashing over me and dropping me to my knees before I realized what was going on.

I fought to breathe against the crushing force, my body bending forward and pressing my forehead to the ground in complete submission.

Knox groaned, dropped to one knee, and bowed his head.

"Better," Cyrus said and the pressure released me.

Fuck. I sucked in ragged breaths, my forehead still pressed to the ground, and trembled at the reminder of just how powerful Cyrus was. Sterling had been able to bring me to my knees as quickly, but never with as much force.

God, was that his full strength completely unleashed? I'd known he was strong, but that was so much more than I could have possibly imagined.

The tunnel is about a hundred feet and it opens into one enormous chamber, Bishop said, thankfully distracting me from just how terrifying Cyrus really was. *A bit of the ceiling has fallen in so light isn't a problem.*

Good, Knox replied. He squared his shoulders, his expression pinched as if the idea of walking inside made him angry, but he marched ahead anyway, a man on a mission.

And I suppose he was. He wanted the bond broken even more than I did.

"Come on," Cyrus said, holding out his hand in an offer to help me up.

I narrowed my eyes at it, wanting to snap at him for crushing me while trying to control Knox for whatever reason. But snapping wouldn't change anything. Flattening me was collateral damage and I wasn't important enough to be considered. Better to not pick a fight with a man who could crush me with a look and put me back into a lifetime of servitude. Even if he had agreed with Bishop about finding me a place in his pack where I was happy, he was still an alpha. He could easily change his mind.

I followed Knox down the passage with one hand dragging on the wall and the other held in front of me, slowing to a crawl once I was in complete darkness. The air was even cooler inside than outside the mound and damp even though the surrounding land looked like it was starving for water.

Cyrus drew up close behind me, a whisper of his body heat radiating against my back, but thankfully didn't complain about my pace. He just remained a hulking, intimidating presence at my back. One that, even though he'd just terrified me with his show of power, still sent a teasing shiver of need rushing through me.

I quickly tamped down on that. It was just more residual good feelings from having sex with Bishop. Cyrus was gorgeous in that sexy bad boy kind of way and now I knew how amazing sex could be. That was all.

After what felt like forever but was probably only about ten minutes, I could make out the end of the passage and a hint of light beyond. The light didn't get much brighter when I reached the end, but it was enough to tell I'd reached an empty cavernous room.

The edges of the room were draped in darkness and I couldn't tell if there were any other passages, while most of the floor was smooth flat ground. The exception was where the rubble had fallen from the ceiling and the coffin-sized slab of stone in the center.

The death god's altar.

Bishop and Knox stood by the altar, and Bishop had already pulled out the piece of paper with the instructions along with the vial of shimmering golden liquid Whil had given him to power the spell — since shifters couldn't summon magical power like a fae sorcerer or even a human witch.

"Let's get this over with," Cyrus said, nudging me forward and making me realize I still stood at the mouth of the passage.

"Right." My pulse picked up with hope and anticipation, and I hurried across the perfectly smooth floor, my footsteps echoing around me.

This was it. This would break our bond and I'd be free. For the first time in my life, I'd be free.

"You need to stand across from each other," Bishop directed, and Knox moved to the other side of the altar as I stepped up beside Bishop.

The altar was the only thing that hadn't been left plain. Unlike the outside of the temple/mound and the floor, it was carved in an intricated, mesmerizing swirling pattern so fine it must have taken hundreds of hours to complete.

"Now you need to prick your finger and smear blood on the death god's seal." Bishop frowned and ran his hands over the altar, sweeping away a thick layer of dust, revealing just how precise the swirling pattern was. "Here," he said, pointing to an intricate circular symbol in the center of all the intricate swirls. "Smear your blood here."

"Which finger?" Cyrus asked me, stepping up beside me, his claws extending from his fingers.

"How much blood do you need?" I asked Bishop, who was back to reading the piece of paper.

"It doesn't say. A good smear if you can manage it," he said with a shrug.

Which meant the wound was going to be deeper than a papercut, might need a bandage, and be a pain for a few days, but thankfully no worse than that.

"This one," I told Cyrus, holding out my left ring finger. It was a finger that I hopefully wouldn't use as much as my other ones for the next few days.

Cyrus nicked my fingertip, his claws so sharp I didn't feel it at first. Then my blood welled over my skin and I felt the sting. I smeared a large red streak across the symbol, squeezed my fingertip to draw out even more blood, and added another streak just to be sure while Cyrus nicked Knox's finger and he did the same.

"Place your palm on the seal and keep it there until the spell is done," Bishop commanded. "Whil's instructions say, don't worry if you touch the blood or each other. Knox, when I say go, I want you to pour Whil's potion over both of your hands and the blood." He uncorked the vial of golden liquid and handed it to Knox. "Then both of you repeat what I say. Got it?"

I placed my hand on the symbol and nodded that I understood, while Knox did the same, his fingers on top of mine, his hand almost big enough to cover the seal by himself.

A hint of desire shivered down my spine and pooled between my thighs, a reminder of the mating bond we were trying to break. Knox's eyes narrowed, and he sucked in a sharp breath as if he, too, could feel the urging from the bond.

Then the muscles in his jaw flexed, his eyes narrowed, and the icy hollowness of his rejection swelled, devouring the need and leaving me shivering not just from the cold in the chamber.

"Okay," Bishop said as he and Cyrus took a large step back.

Knox raised his gaze, finally meeting mine. His eyes were still a normal brown with no hint of his wolf, and for a second, I was falling inside their hard depths. They were so unlike Bishop's warm eyes and yet so very much the same, and I ached for him, for us, for what never should have been.

For just a second, hope and desperation flickered in those brown flecked with green depths, then he blinked, releasing me, and the hard mask he'd been wearing since I'd seen him in his human form returned.

"Ready?" he asked, his voice gruff, his body so tense a vein in his temple had started throbbing.

"Ready," I told him and he poured the potion out of the vial, trailing it over our hands and onto the seal and making sure some of it landed on the blood. A sudden jolt of power snapped through me and heat swept from my hand and up my arm, almost too hot in contrast to how cold I was.

"Oh, gree-ate god-ESS," Bishop said, his pronunciation strange as if he no longer knew exactly how to speak his own language.

"Oh, great goddess," I repeated.

"Oh, pow-erful ru-EL-er over the EEE-ternal slu-umber and the EEE-nd of all things," he continued. "I sta-and before you with hope-

E, DEE-sire, and HU-mility. Heear my plea and gr-ANT your greeatest mercies and might that I, your most HU-umble sea-er-vant, might sever and EE-x-cute the magic that Buh-hinds me. Oh, most REE-vered, awesome, and May-ges-tic ru-EL-er of death."

Knox and I repeated it all and waited...

And waited...

Time dragged forward with only the initial heat from Whil's magical liquid warming my hand and forearm.

My pulse pounded in my ears, and I held my breath, hoping and praying that it would work.

Knox deserved to be free. I hadn't meant to bond with him, hell, we didn't even know each other, he shouldn't have to be stuck with me for the rest of his life.

Please. If there was a death god asleep under my feet, please let her hear my prayer and free him. *Please.*

Sudden, ferocious light exploded from the shimmering golden liquid and the heat from the power turned into an inferno. It raced past my shoulder, into my chest, and flooded around my heart, stealing my breath, and painfully tearing into me, threatening to consume me. Every muscle in my body locked, the force of the power the only thing holding me up, and it jerked me upright, my head thrown back on a scream I couldn't release.

The pressure and agony was more powerful than anything I'd ever felt before. Even Cyrus's crushing power outside the temple that had brought me to my knees in an instant was nothing compared to the force ripping into my very essence.

But a mating bond was a powerful form of magic that no one had ever broken before. The magic needed to destroy something so strong had to be a force unlike any other, and I feared that force was going to tear me apart with the bond.

WOLF DESIRED

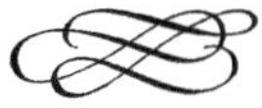

ENSNARED BY THE PACK: BOOK 3

AUDREY

BLAZING AGONY TORE AT MY BODY, RIPPING INTO MY CELLS, DIGGING into my essence, and igniting my soul. Everything was on fire and every muscle had contracted. I was frozen in place with one hand gripping the side of the death god's altar, the other pressed on top of the altar — my fingers brushing Knox's — and my head thrown back with a scream I couldn't release.

I tried to breathe but couldn't. Tried to move, to think, to do anything to relieve the pressure and the inferno consuming me, but I was stuck.

Panic squeezed even tighter around my chest, an all-consuming terror that I'd made a horrible mistake. Not because I shouldn't have been trying to break my accidental mating bond with Knox, but because the spell we'd hoped would break the unbreakable was going to burn me up and leave nothing behind. Even if somehow my body survived, I'd be a shell, my soul completely devoured.

The fire tightened around my heart, ripping at the magic binding me to Knox. It heaved the bond from my chest, wrenching me forward, stretching, tearing, straining.

Tears streamed down my cheeks, and I squeezed my eyes shut, praying for it to be over, to finally be free.

Then the fire exploded, and the force yanked my soul out of my body determined to tear it apart before slamming it back into my chest. The impact knocked me over, suddenly releasing all my muscles, and I collapsed on the smooth floor of the death god's temple.

Bishop rushed to my side and gathered me in his arms, cradling me against his chest and wiping the tears from my cheeks.

"It's okay," he murmured. "I've got you. I've got you."

On the other side of the altar, Knox groaned. He hadn't been thrown back and had collapsed on top of the coffin-sized stone slab. The weak light filtering through the hole in the domed ceiling caught in the green flecks in his eyes.

They were so much like Bishop's and yet so different. They mesmerized me, drawing me in, stealing my breath, and connecting with that messed up something inside me that said he was mine.

"Fuck," he snarled, and the icy hollowness of his rejection crashed over me, consuming the painful, fiery remnants of the spell.

Oh, God. The frozen emptiness was even stronger than before, and I didn't know if that meant our mating bond was stronger or just his determination to get rid of me.

"Shit," Cyrus hissed, laying a hand on Knox's shoulder. "It didn't work, did it?"

"No." Knox batted Cyrus's hand away, shoved past him, and stormed out of the temple.

My throat tightened and a tear I didn't want to cry rolled down my cheek.

It hadn't worked.

We were stuck together.

Forever.

Or at least until one of us died, and I had a horrible feeling Knox would rather take his chances on going insane when I died than spend the rest of his life with me.

A sob tightened my throat and I buried my face against Bishop's shoulder, fighting to keep it in.

I could do this. I could live with this.

Knox and I would have to seal our bond before it drove both of us crazy, but then I could convince him that I didn't expect him to behave like my mate. I could find a room to rent in Stonehaven and spend a quiet life cleaning houses or something.

It wouldn't be so bad.

Except my soul wept at the thought. It didn't want to be without Knox. He was my mate. We belonged together.

And he doesn't want me. Never did. Never will.

That was the cold hard truth I was going to have to live with.

"It's okay," Bishop murmured, stroking my hair and holding me tight. "We'll get back to Stonehaven and see if Whil can transfer the bond to me."

Right. Plan B. All wasn't lost. We just needed to withstand the compulsion of the bond to seal it for another nine days.

A roar echoed down the narrow passage, the only way into the enormous chamber, and a shock of ferocious fury swept through the icy hollowness.

Oh, shit. He wasn't going to wait for plan B. He was going to kill me. Now.

My gaze slid to the altar.

Would he think he'd be able to avoid the side-effects of losing his mate if he sacrificed me to the death god? Would Cyrus and Bishop let him?

A shiver swept through me. I'd already had one supposed mate try to sacrifice me and I'd barely escaped with my life. I doubted I'd be so lucky a second time. Especially since Knox was more powerful than Royce and Sterling.

I shifted my attention to Bishop, looking up at him through my lashes. He was so beautiful, his features sculpted, a dusting of dark stubble along his jaw, and warm brown eyes that could capture my soul.

He'd been kind to me from the start, had vowed to court me and make me his mate even if I was also mated to Knox. He wouldn't let him sacrifice me.

But would he be strong enough to protect me from his brother? From both his brothers?

Without a doubt, if Cyrus had to pick a side, he'd pick Knox's. He'd already made his priorities clear. His pack and family were first. Always first. And I was neither.

Bishop leaned back and met my gaze, his expression filled with so much concern it made my heart break and another tear rolled down my cheek.

No one had ever looked at me like that, like I mattered and I wasn't a burden even though I was. I'd yearned for someone to care for me like that all my life, and now it seemed I'd found someone just when everything was completely fucked up.

"Can you walk?" he asked, his voice soft as if he were afraid speaking too loudly would scare me.

I nodded even though I wasn't sure if my legs could hold me and reluctantly eased away from his embrace.

Knox roared again and a hint of alpha power squeezed around my chest. Bishop's attention jerked toward the passage, his body tensing, and an icy fear shivered down my spine.

Was Knox coming back? Was Bishop going to be forced to pick between me and his brother?

My throat tightened and more tears burned my eyes.

There was no contest. Knox was his twin, the other half of his human soul. It didn't matter how Bishop looked at me. A look was just a look. It didn't mean anything.

Cyrus marched back into the chamber and grabbed all three of our packs. "We need to go. I don't want to be on the death god's land when night falls. Carry her if she can't walk."

Then he marched back out. He hadn't even glanced my way and that only made the sinking feeling in my stomach grow. Some of Merrick's betas hadn't been able to look at me, either. They'd pretended I hadn't existed and that somehow absolved them of any responsibility for the child they knew their alpha was treating like a slave and abusing.

I sucked in a ragged breath, trying to steady my nerves. If we were leaving, Knox wasn't planning to sacrifice me. Which meant I might be the person no one wanted, but my life wasn't in immediate danger.

It was sad that that was my best situation... and that I'd have to be on guard for Knox or Cyrus to change their minds.

I sucked in another, steadier breath, and gathered the tattered remains of my determination. Bishop had a plan B and my heat was over. I could resist having sex with Knox for another nine days. It might only be eight if I could convince the guys to push our pace.

I could do this.

I'd already made it this far. I'd survived a man-eating monster. This unwanted mating bond was nothing.

And maybe if I kept telling myself that, I'd believe it.

"So," Bishop asked. "Am I carrying you?" A soft smile tugged at his lips as if he already knew my answer.

"No." I shoved up to my feet. My body was achy on a bone-deep level, but I couldn't have expected to go through that spell without some aftereffects.

I just needed to walk it off, perhaps get a night's sleep, and I'd be back to the way I was before. The way I'd felt yesterday morning when I'd woken boneless and satiated in bed with Bishop.

The memory of having sex with him shivered through me and I clung to the sensation. Feeling a little turned on was better than the icy hollowness any day. And now the sensation wasn't out of control. It was a low, sensual ache, burning at the edge of my senses. A memory that I could draw on to make myself feel better.

"Let's go," I told him.

So, plan A hadn't worked, plan B was a long shot, and I had no idea what plan C was... if there even was a plan C. But I hadn't given up during the years of suffering with Merrick and Sterling, and I wouldn't give up now.

AUDREY

I STRODE OUT OF THE TEMPLE, AN ENORMOUS, SHAPELESS, WINDOWLESS mound in the middle of flat, barren nothingness as far as the eye could see.

Knox paced about fifty feet away, his movement jerky, anger radiating off him. It shocked me that he was still in human form. I would have thought he'd have shifted before even getting out of the temple's dark passageway given that he preferred his wolf form over his human one.

Without a word, Cyrus handed one of the packs to Bishop and started marching south. Knox took that as permission to leave — I wasn't sure why he'd even stuck around — and, with a jerk of Cyrus's chin, Bishop hurried to catch up with his twin.

Swell. Just what I needed. Left with the brother who thought I couldn't do anything and that I was going to be a burden to his family and pack for the rest of my life.

I'd been trying to prove this whole walk here that I wouldn't hold him or anyone back. I might not know anything, but I'd been, and still was, determined to not complain and keep up.

I'd thought from our conversation last night where he seemed to have respected my desire to live independently that he was softening up to me. But now, from the tension in his shoulders and back, I guess I'd been wrong.

"I can carry my own pack," I said, even as the ache in my body grew, complaining about our current pace.

His gaze slid to mine, his moss green eyes edged with his wolf's darkness, his expression hard and unreadable even as it sent a shiver of desire teasing down my spine. Was he furious like Knox?

I huffed at myself. Of course he was.

He'd been angry at me since we'd left Stonehaven and now all hope of getting rid of the weakling was gone. Even plan B meant I was still part of the family... of course, if Bishop intended to court me regardless of the spell's outcome, I'd still end up part of the family.

My toe caught on an uneven crack in the almost completely flat ground, and I staggered two steps before catching my balance.

Cyrus raised one eyebrow as if he couldn't believe I'd actually found something to trip on.

"Walk for an hour without tripping. Then you can get your pack back." He jerked his attention back to Knox and Bishop, who were now at least a hundred feet ahead of us.

Fine. I could do that.

"We all knew the spell was a long shot," he said a few minutes later, his gaze still straight ahead. "Bishop's plan B has even worse odds."

"It might be possible," I insisted even though I knew Cyrus was right.

Still, the fae sorcerers that had helped the Angelic Defense defeat Michael had been incredibly powerful. Whil had said she wasn't magically strong, but that didn't mean she wouldn't be able to do it. I had no idea what was considered a "weak" sorcerer. She probably had more power in her baby finger than I did in my entire body.

"Anything is possible." Cyrus glanced at me, his expression soft and sad.

God, he was just as beautiful as his brothers except in a more rugged, edgy way, and seeing him look at me like that, like he actually cared, made my pulse stutter.

Had I been wrong about him? I'd assumed everything I did pissed him off, but maybe that wasn't true and he just wasn't great at showing his feelings.

Then his expression hardened, his walls returning, and he faced forward again. "But you're smart enough to know moving a mating bond isn't probable," he added.

"I don't have any other option. Knox doesn't want me." The icy hollowness in my chest surged and I fought to push it back.

"Both of you are going to have to accept the reality of your situation," he said, the angry edge returning to his voice. "The sooner you do, the better for Knox."

And there it was. The reminder that Knox was, and always would be, Cyrus's first priority.

"So, I just have to accept that I'm going to spend the rest of my life in a loveless mating because that's what's best for Knox, for the pack? You're just as bad as my old pack."

My toe caught on another crack and I stumbled again.

This time I couldn't catch my balance and careened forward, but Cyrus caught me before I could smash my knees on the hard ground and yanked me against his body.

My hands slid across his broad, sculpted chest, and his powerful arms surrounded me. His deep earthy scent wrapped around me like a blanket, comforting and warm until the warmth began to grow.

The last time I'd been this close to Cyrus, we'd been in Stonehaven and he'd been yelling at me for risking my life. And he'd been naked.

My breath hitched. I knew what all that bulky muscle looked like, and now I was getting a moment to know what it felt like to be wrapped in it.

The heat dropped to my core and turned the soft, achy memory of having sex with Bishop into something deeper and stronger.

"Are you saying you're not open to multiple mates?" he asked, his voice gruff. "Will you refuse Bishop? If Whil can't transfer the bond, you and Knox are stuck together, but that doesn't mean that has to be everything in your life."

I tipped my head to look up at him, and his gaze flickered to my lips before jumping back to my eyes.

"And you'd accept that?" I breathed, my lips tingling with the need for him to kiss me. "The weakest shifter in existence mated to both of your brothers?"

He cupped my cheek with his large palm. "I think we've already established that you're not the weakest. You've killed a grimalkin—"

"By accident," I reminded him.

"You've stood your ground against them twice, and you've walked until your feet bled on the chance you could set my brother free. Those are not the actions of a weak shifter." He huffed a soft laugh. "A foolish one, maybe, but not weak."

I dropped my gaze, unable to keep looking him in the eyes. I didn't know what to do with words like that. I'd never been good enough or strong enough or anything enough, and just hearing that maybe I was, that maybe Cyrus saw me as something more than a weakling, made my insides squirm.

"I can't shift," I murmured. "My children might have the same curse I have." And they might have the same problem. Unlike the rest of my pack whose wolf had awoken on the summer solstice after their eighteenth birthday, mine was still asleep and probably always would be... if I even had a wolf half to my soul.

"Bishop doesn't care." Cyrus brushed a stray lock of my dirty blond hair away from my eyes then hooked his thumb under my chin, forcing me to meet his gaze again. "He's never courted a woman before—"

"I find that hard to believe." From everything I'd seen, Bishop had left a trail of broken hearts behind him.

"Oh, he's dated and flirted, but his wolf was never interested. Not until you." His eyes dipped back to my mouth, and my pulse picked up, my body yearning for his lips on mine.

I leaned into him and breathed in his scent, my pulse pounding in my ears. Cyrus had never shown any interest in me before, and while a tiny voice in the back of my mind was screaming that this was wrong, this was how my body responded when I was in heat, the rest of me didn't care. He was stunning and powerful, and he'd never be mine, but oh how my body wanted a taste of what it would be like.

Then the muscles in his jaw flexed, and he slid both hands to my shoulders and took a large step back.

The sudden separation sent chills rushing over me, and not just because I'd lost his body heat. He was rejecting me. He'd had a moment of weakness, a moment my now throbbing core desperately wanted, and realized it was a mistake.

"You're not without options, Audrey," he said, his voice gruff. "Just remember that when Whil can't free you from Knox." He turned back toward Knox and Bishop, who were even farther ahead of us. "Come on. We're falling behind."

"Right." I fought to swallow my disappointment, confused about why I'd reacted so strongly to him, and hurried to catch up.

He set an even faster pace than before and I struggled to keep up. I was already achy — sore *and* turned on — and the longer I walked, the achier I became. I wasn't walking off the side effects of the spell, and now I couldn't stop staring at Cyrus's ass or his broad, powerful shoulders easily carrying the packs... one of which I should have been carrying.

On top of that, the chill in the air that had deepened the closer we'd gotten to the temple didn't warm up the farther we went away. Even with the sun still sitting high in the sky and blazing down on us, I shivered, which didn't help with the achy muscles.

The path grew rockier and scraggly weeds and bushes started to dot the landscape. Cyrus was hot enough that I could see sweat darkening the back of his shirt every time one of the packs shifted, which made me think of my hands sliding over his slick skin, those bulky muscles flexing as he drove into me.

Fuck. I squeezed my eyes shut. What was wrong with me? Why was I thinking about sex with Cyrus when I could be remembering sex with Bishop?

My thoughts lurched to the previous night and how Bishop's sleeker body had looked as he pushed oh-so-carefully inside me—

I stumbled over the uneven ground, the ache in my body sinking deep into my hips and back, making each step harder and harder.

A whisper of a breeze swept over us, rattling the dead stalks of grass, catching in strands that had fallen out of Cyrus's braid, and making my teeth chatter.

Hugging myself, I fought to control my trembling, but that upset my balance and I stumbled again, bashing my knee against a rocky outcropping.

Shit.

I swallowed back my curse, not wanting to alert Cyrus that I still couldn't walk a straight line without a pack, and limped forward. The injury wasn't bad, but the impact had jarred up my entire body, pointing out every achy muscle and joint.

Rocky landscape meant we were getting closer to the abandoned village where we were going to spend the night.

I just needed to push a little farther, and then I could take a break because I wholeheartedly agreed with Cyrus. I didn't want to be caught on the death god's lands after dark.

The guys had warned me about this realm's spirits that were manifestations of a god or goddess's power, and I didn't want to encounter any that belonged to a death god.

But as I raised my gaze to see where we were — and how far ahead Cyrus was — the world lurched to the side, and I bumped my hip against another outcropping.

Staggering, I clutched at the rib-high protrusion to catch my balance. The rock beneath my hand swam in and out of focus, darkening and lightening as if clouds were rapidly passing overhead even though there hadn't been a cloud in the sky.

The world lurched again despite not even looking up, and my knees trembled, threatening to drop me to the ground.

Something wasn't right and I wasn't going to be able to tough it out until we made camp. And even if I could tough it out, Cyrus had been pissed because I hadn't told him that my feet had been sore, bleeding messes for days. He hadn't yelled at me during our conversation about accepting my bond and I really wanted to keep it that way.

I looked up, gritting my teeth against my lurching, darkening vision. He was even farther away than before, but I didn't know if he really was or if that was tunnel vision.

"Cyrus," I gasped, my voice ringing in my ears. "I—"

My core clenched hard and a wave of clawing, desperate need stole my breath along with my vision. I sagged to the ground, my legs unable to hold me, the world so dim it felt like the dead of night. Shivers wracked my body. The trembling exacerbated my feverish aching and the painful throbbing in my core.

I needed sex.

I needed I needed I needed.

I couldn't think of anything else and my need was going to consume me if I didn't satisfy it.

CYRUS

My wolf heaved against my control and I fought to hold him back as I marched after Knox and Bishop.

What the fuck was wrong with me? I'd had Audrey in my arms and all I could think about was kissing her. She was hurt and scared, the spell she'd put her faith in had failed — and it looked like it had been painful — and I was thinking about what her lips would feel like and taste like.

I'd been trying to do the right thing and convince her to accept Knox as her mate, and then she'd tripped and I'd lost my fucking mind.

Of course, it wasn't really Audrey who needed to accept the mating bond, but she was the one who was going to get hurt the most. She needed to be prepared and understand that it wasn't the end of her world. Because the thought of her continuing to suffer made my wolf howl and threaten to take over.

I didn't want Knox to suffer, either, but no one, not even Bishop, was going to be able to convince him to accept his fate.

Unfortunately, the stubborn asshole's inner battle was tearing a rift between him and his animal half, and I feared when I released the collar containing his wolf, the beast would take over and we'd lose him again. This time permanently.

It had taken everything I had to keep the collar intact when the spell had failed and the pressure of being inside the temple had become too much for my brother.

Next time, I might not get so lucky.

And without a doubt, there'd be a next time before we decided it was safe to let his wolf loose.

Which was why I'd sent Bishop to walk with him. Bishop could help calm him down as well as add another layer of compulsion to the collar which would hopefully keep Knox contained until we got back to Stonehaven and attempted Bishop's next-to-impossible plan B.

But that had left me with shivering, too-pale, wide-eyed Audrey and the need to say something.

I wasn't good at placating or telling sweet lies to make someone feel better. That was Bishop's job. I was the practical brother. I saw problems and addressed them, and Audrey refusing to accept the inevitable was a problem that could shatter her burgeoning confidence.

If she embraced it, she could plan for it. The emotional blow wouldn't be so hard, and she wouldn't have to figure out her next steps while caught in an emotional whirlwind. Steps like where she lived and what she wanted to do with her life.

Just because she and Knox were mated didn't mean they had to live together, at least not until they grew more comfortable in the bond and it compelled them closer.

But I had a feeling she wouldn't think of that. Certainly not while she believed her life had been permanently turned upside down. I could even see her thinking that she belonged to Knox since power and strength had played a strong role in her old life. I'd gotten the impression that for her, the powerful owned the weak, and the weak had no say.

And then she'd tripped and every protective instinct I'd had surged along with my wolf's determination that she was mine.

For fuck's sake. I couldn't be her mate. No matter what my wolf wanted.

She couldn't ever be mine. I had responsibilities to my pack and they wouldn't see Audrey the way I did, wouldn't see the determined, resilient beautiful woman I'd caught glimpses of on our journey here. They'd constantly question and challenge her, and she'd retreat back into her shell.

No. I wouldn't do that to her.

If she could accept the idea of multiple mates, Bishop would love and support her in ways neither Knox nor I could. Knowing he cared for her and was more than capable of protecting her would have to be enough.

I swallowed back a growl and rolled my shoulders, trying to loosen the tension in my body. I needed my wolf to calm the fuck down. He'd been going insane since the spell had ripped through her body, her expression locked in agony, and he hadn't been able to do anything.

Nothing was going to happen with Audrey. Not now. Not ever.

Audrey gasped my name, her voice barely audible and strained, and the sound jerked me from my whirling thoughts.

I wrenched around to look at her and my pulse froze.

She was farther back than I expected, on her knees, and leaning against a rocky outcropping as if it were the only thing keeping her from completely collapsing to the ground. Her eyes were closed and even from this distance, I could see her breathing was short and shallow.

Shit. I should have paid closer attention to her.

I knew the spell had affected her. She hadn't been able to stop shaking since we'd left the temple, and her complexion had been pale and hadn't warmed up from the exertion of walking.

I rushed back to her and before I could even reach her, I was hit with the scent of her arousal.

Oh, fuck.

I was instantly hard, my balls aching and my wolf straining to break free. She was mine and she needed me.

My fear for her surged and I shoved it, along with the over-whelming desire to fuck her senseless, as far back as I could.

This couldn't be happening. Not in the middle of nowhere.

"Audrey," I murmured, kneeling in front of her and cupping her cheeks between my palms, urging her to look at me.

Her scent wrapped around me, sweet and heavy, and my wolf heaved, straining to take control. Sweat slicked her too-hot skin, pasting loose strands of hair to her forehead and cheeks, and she shook as if she were freezing. Her eyelids fluttered, cracking partially open, and I could see her pupils were fully blown and she couldn't focus on me. She probably couldn't focus on anything.

All of that were signs of a strong heat fever.

Damn it. I should have refused to try the spell and kept her in Stonehaven, should have insisted she spend her heat with Wilder at the heat clinic. He would have been able to manage her heat and not let it get so bad that she succumbed to the fever.

The urge to claim her, relieve the pressure that I'd been told was tearing her up inside, squeezed my chest. It didn't matter to my wolf that we didn't have shelter or any other comfort — like a bed — his instincts said she was ours and she needed us. Now.

Bishop. Knox. Get back here, I mentally called to them as a snap of power escaped my control and rushed through our connection.

What happened? Bishop asked, his mental voice sharp with worry, knowing if my control on my power was slipping that it was serious.

Her heat. I dropped both packs and gathered her into my arms, heat radiating from her body and her scent suffocatingly strong. *She's got heat fever.*

You said her heat was done, Knox snarled as he bolted toward me with Bishop close behind.

She said it was over, Bishop insisted.

But she's never had a heat before. Realization hit me. If she'd never had a heat before and heats weren't as strong in her realm, then she didn't know that they ebbed and flowed. Sex helped to relieve the pressure, sometimes for a few hours, sometimes for a few days. Of course, her heat had been going since we'd left town ten days ago, so it would have made sense for her to assume no symptoms meant it was over.

Shit, Bishop hissed as if he, too, had figured out what had happened.

I turned and raced south, passing my brothers, knowing they'd grab the packs and catch up.

Heat fever was serious and only the strongest female shifters experienced it if they didn't properly take care of their heat.

I didn't know if this meant Audrey was actually strong and her powers were imprisoned by the curse or if this was a result of our realm changing her body. It could also be the lure of the mating bond or the spell we'd just tried setting it off.

Hell, it could have been none of the above or any combination thereof.

What I did know was that I had to get her safe and comfortable because a heat fever could last a few days and be rigorous even with two or three partners.

And given that she couldn't have sex with Knox and hadn't given me permission to help, it was going to be up to Bishop to see her through this.

How could you let this happen, Bishop? Knox demanded. *You walked with her all morning. Even if you wanted to get the spell done, you didn't say anything after.*

I didn't know, my brother replied as he and Knox caught up to me with our packs, and I picked up the pace.

"She was shaking," I told them, "but I didn't think it was a fever. I thought it was a reaction to the spell."

"There's no point in laying blame—" Bishoped started but Knox cut him off.

"Yes, there is. If you'd been paying attention, we wouldn't have left Kelna and she wouldn't be faced with suffering in the middle of nowhere."

He shoved Bishop into a boulder, drawing a grunt of pain, and bared his thankfully still-human teeth.

"Control yourself." I released a sharp snap of power, making Knox huff and Audrey whimper. "You can't afford to break the collar. Not while she's got the fever. You could barely control your wolf when she just had regular symptoms."

"Fuck," he hissed.

I glanced at him, trying to determine if he was angry that he had to stay in control or not. "If you want to try Bishop's plan B then you need to keep your cock to yourself."

Audrey moaned, her fingers clenching my shirt, and she buried her nose in my shoulder, instinctually seeking my scent.

Knox roared and rammed his fist into the rock beside him, making Audrey whimper again and curl in on herself.

"We might not be able to get the fever under control at our camp in the abandoned village," Bishop said.

"We need to get to Kelna," I replied. The village that had graciously given us a cabin the other night was the best place for her. We'd have privacy and access to food, water, and shelter. We wouldn't have any of that at the abandoned village where we'd camped last night and there would be limited ways to bring her fever down at the camp as well.

The question was if Audrey would last the day it would take to run to Kelna.

BISHOP

WE RAN THE REST OF THE DAY, ALL THROUGH THE NIGHT, AND REACHED the small one-story cabin on the outskirts of Kelna by midmorning. The village leader had said we could have the cabin again tonight as a rest stop on our way home, and I could only pray he'd let us stay until Audrey's heat was over.

I'd heard about heat fever. It was part of our basic education all pack children had to take, although I'd never seen it firsthand. That was Nova's area of expertise, as well as Wilder's and anyone Wilder employed. But I hadn't thought it would be so bad.

Audrey huddled in Cyrus's embrace, shivering and sweating and whimpering and panting. Her eyes had cracked open periodically during our mad dash back here, but they were always glassy and unfocused, and I wasn't sure if she was even conscious.

Cyrus marched up the wooden steps leading to the wide porch and the cabin's door, and I hurried ahead of him and opened the door so he wouldn't have to adjust his hold on her.

He'd refused to hand her off, and while she wasn't much heavier than two of our packs combined, she'd soaked her shirt with sweat, along with the front of his shirt, and had blanketed him in her scent. A scent that had me partially hard despite trying to keep my distance and staying downwind. It had been difficult enough for me to concentrate on getting back here as fast as possible and not letting my wolf succumb to her arousal. I couldn't imagine how hard it must have been for Cyrus.

With a nod of thanks, he carried her straight into the bathroom, and I dropped my pack and Audrey's just inside the door then glanced back at Knox.

He'd stayed a good fifty feet away from her the entire run and now stood at the bottom of the steps, glaring at the inside of the small cabin as if he were furious with it... or actually thinking about entering.

His frustration and anger seethed through our twin bond along with a stomach-churning fear, and I was shocked Cyrus's collar on his wolf still held.

Even bolstered with my power, Knox's wolf was a force of nature and one whose mate right now was in trouble. It was a miracle his human half was still lucid.

His hands clenched into fists, but I couldn't tell if that was just his anger or him working up the nerve to follow Cyrus inside.

The cabin wasn't very big, but the main room was open and had good-sized windows that let in a lot of light. He could probably last a few hours, maybe even a little more before his claustrophobia forced him back outside.

But that would have been on a good day, and today wasn't a good day.

With a snarl, he dropped Cyrus's pack on the deck and retreated deeper into the glade surrounding the cabin.

Bishop, Cyrus called, jerking my attention back to the immediate problem. *We need to bring down her temperature enough for you to explain what's happening.*

I hurried into the bathroom to find her sitting on the floor propped up against the wall. Water poured from the tap into the stone tub that was big enough for her but not for me or my brothers, and Cyrus had already pulled off her soaked shirt.

Her breathing had turned short and shallow and her fingers

clenched the front of his shirt. With a soft moan, she strained her neck forward, her lips seeking his.

"Help me get her pants off," he said, his voice gruff and his expression pained.

I hurried to help and undid the tie keeping her pants on as he grabbed her around the waist and lifted. The movement made her whimper, and she leaned into him, her mouth brushing along his collarbone just above his shirt.

A growl rumbled in Cyrus's chest, low, barely audible, and we both pretended it hadn't happened. Quickly, I pulled her pants below her ass and Cyrus set her back down then retreated out of reach before I'd even gotten her pants down her legs to her boots.

"I need to let Rafe know we're back early and that we'll be staying a few days." His gaze swept down her body and the muscles in his jaw flexed. "Let me know what you need."

"She's going to need fluids and something easy to eat. At least until I can get the fever under control," I told him as I unlaced her boots and pulled them off.

Audrey tipped her head back and groaned, her hands sliding to her breasts to play with her nipples.

My half-hard cock stood up to full attention despite my worry for her, and Cyrus grunted and left. The next few days were going to be difficult for all of us and I didn't begrudge Cyrus retreating.

He might not think of Audrey as a potential mate, but I knew he was concerned about her — and not just because she and Knox were bound to each other. He'd been furious to learn she'd hidden her blistered feet from us because that meant he hadn't known she'd been in pain, and he'd been protectively watching her from a distance since he'd learned she had absolutely no survival skills.

I quickly unwrapped the bandage around her calf and checked the three scars and dozens of stitches that marked where the grimalkin had slashed her. The elixir had done its job and she'd been healed in record time. We were going to have to pull the stitches out soon, but after I'd gotten her lucid enough to understand what needed to happen and to relieve some of the pressure of her heat building in her body.

I unwrapped her feet — also healed — and set her in the tub. Audrey cried out when the cool water touched her too-hot flesh and clutched at my arms. Her shivering turned violent, and her breath short and sharp between her chattering teeth.

"It's okay," I cooed, wrapping an arm around her to keep her head out of the water. "It's going to be okay."

I didn't want to tell her that her body was going crazy, and she was going to beg for sex, never being fully satisfied until her heat was over.

She'd been a virgin three days ago and had blushed when she knew we'd been able to scent her arousal. Sure, she hadn't been a naive teenager, but she was still shy and inexperienced.

Her reaction to an uncontrolled heat could go two ways. She'd accept what was going to happen or be mortified by it.

She shivered and moaned, and I brushed her hair back from her face.

"I need you to open your eyes, Audrey." I didn't want to start relieving the pressure without her knowing what was going on.

But her breath picked up and her hips started rocking. A whimper escaped her lips and she fondled her breasts again, searching for a release that would be much easier to get with a partner.

Fuck. I wanted her consent. I didn't want to assume because we'd had sex the other night that this was okay. But there weren't any other options. I needed to break her fever long enough for her to be lucid and to do that, she needed an orgasm.

In truth, unless she wanted to seal her mating bond with Knox, Cyrus and I were her only options to get her through this. And from Cyrus's reaction, it looked like he was going to leave it all to me.

I suppose she could ask for one of the villagers. Maybe it would be better if she went through this with someone she'd never see again.

The thought made my wolf heave inside me. *We* were the ones who were supposed to help her. She was ours. Ours to protect and love. And right now, she needed both protection and love.

I pushed my free hand into the water and teased my fingers over her stomach and into her curls. Her breath hitched and her back arched, pushing her breasts up in invitation.

A low rumble rattled in my chest, my wolf rising to the surface but thankfully not taking control, and with a groan, I dipped forward. I sucked on her closest nipple and slid a finger between her folds, drawing a loud moan that was half pleasure and half relief.

Arousal still slickened her channel despite the water, and I slowly pumped my finger in and out of her. Her hips rocked up to meet me every time I plunged inside her and her fingers tangled in my hair, holding me against her breast.

Her moans grew louder and her rocking sped up, urging me to go faster. I added a second finger, pressed my thumb against her clit, and picked up my pace.

The cool water sloshed in the tub, slapping me in the face, spilling over the edge, and soaking the front of my shirt and pants. I abandoned her breast, earning a whimper of displeasure, even as she bucked faster, but moved to her mouth and was rewarded with a sharp gasp.

I plunged my tongue between her parted lips, matching my pace with my fingers. My cock throbbed, so hard it was painful, but I resisted the urge to pull her from the tub and impale her on it. If she agreed to more, I'd have plenty of opportunities to be inside her, to feel her slick heat clenching around me like it had the other night.

Then her channel started to flutter, indicating she was close, and I ground down on her clit. A second later she cried out her release, her back arching away from the tub and her muscles clenching around my fingers.

I pumped through it, trying to draw it out for as long as possible, as she panted into my mouth. Then she collapsed back against the tub, her body limp, and her eyelids fluttered open.

Thank the Sisters!

"Audrey," I said and her gaze drifted to me, her eyes still a little glassy, her pupils blown wide with desire, but she did manage to focus on me.

"Bishop?" A shiver rushed through her, drawing a moan, and her hips started rocking again, trying to draw out more pleasure from my fingers still buried inside her. "What's wrong with me?"

"You have heat fever," I said, letting her fuck herself on my hand. "It's the worst case scenario for a heat."

"But I thought it was over." Another shiver rolled down her body and her lips parted on a soft moan. "I wasn't going crazy with need after we—" A hint of a blush colored her pale cheeks even as she continued to use my fingers, and she squeezed her eyes shut. "What does this mean?"

"It means to keep the fever from overwhelming you and endangering your life, you need to have sex." I offered her a gentle smile. "Will you let me help you?"

AUDREY

I squeezed my eyes shut, trying to concentrate on Bishop's words, but that only made me more aware of his fingers buried inside me and the ache in my core that I couldn't relieve.

A shiver of a climax teased me, and I bucked faster against his hand, chasing it, desperate to make it bloom into a full orgasm.

"Audrey," Bishop said, cupping my cheek and tilting my head up, the precursor to a kiss.

I pried my eyes open, but he hadn't dipped close to kiss me and still watched me with pained concern.

"My fingers and mouth will help, but not as much as direct intercourse."

The promised climax I'd been chasing slipped away as if proving his point, and I whimpered in frustration.

"This could last for a few days and you might be delirious for most of it," he continued.

"But you'll take care of me?" I asked, my voice trembling with cold and need. God, I was losing my mind. I *needed* sex like I needed to breathe.

"I'll always take care of you," he said. "I just want you to understand what's going on." He brushed his lips against mine, finally giving me the kiss I desired.

It was just a whisper of contact, but it stole my breath and shot searing need straight to my core as if it had been more.

The bathroom — how'd we get back to the cabin in Kelna? — darkened and lurched, and I dropped my fingers to my clit, trying to get the heat to break and bring me relief.

"I've got you," Bishop murmured and he curled his fingers inside me, hitting a spot that made my muscles clench and sent light flashing behind my eyelids.

But the relief only lasted a few seconds before the ache returned and I was panting and rocking my hips again.

I tried to figure out what had happened, how I'd been stupid enough to think my heat was over, but I couldn't think past the need consuming me. It burned me up from the inside, overwhelming any attempt to focus.

"Come on," he said, pulling his fingers from me.

I whimpered at the sudden emptiness, my core thrumming, needing, desperate to be filled.

"Just hold on for a minute." He yanked off his shirt, revealing his stunning, sculpted physique then stood and dropped his pants.

His cock sprang free, standing at full attention and making my pulse stall and my mouth dry in anticipation. He was thick and long and bigger than I expected. I couldn't believe I'd had *that* in me the other night. No wonder he hadn't let me see or touch it. I would have gotten even more nervous for my first time and it wouldn't have been nearly as enjoyable.

And now all I could think about was wrapping my fingers around him and licking the glistening drop of precum from his tip.

I reached for him, eager for that taste, but he picked me up before I could grasp him. Water rushed from my body and poured over his hips and thighs, but he didn't seem to care. He carried me out of the bathroom, through the open-style kitchen-living room, and into the bedroom.

The room was furnished like the rest of the cabin with well-used, worn furniture, and the blanket, the linens, and the curtain on the window were mismatched, giving it a homey, lived-in feel. Someone had set out towels for us at the foot of the bed along with a pitcher of water and two glasses on the nightstand.

Shivers wracked my body, but I didn't know if they were from the fever burning me up or the anticipation of having Bishop inside me again.

"I promise I'll always take care of you," Bishop murmured, capturing me with one strong arm behind my waist to steady me on my feet and drying my back with a soft towel.

His hard length dug into my belly and the ache in my core burned hotter.

Moaning, I leaned into him, savoring his scent of fresh-cut grass and comfort, and slid my hands over his wet skin. My fingertips traced over his rippling ads before I dipped them lower, following the V at his hips down to his cock, and wrapped my fingers around him just like I wanted.

A deep, masculine groan escaped his lips, ratcheting up my need, and I teased my fingers up his length and slid them through the precum leaking from his tip.

"Fuck, Audrey," he gasped through clenched teeth. "I can't lose control. I don't want to hurt you."

"I don't care," I begged.

"I know you don't, beautiful. But still—" He palmed my mound and his fingers slid through my folds and slick arousal.

My body bucked into him, eager, needing, desperate, and I tightened my grip on his cock. "I need you. Please, Bishop."

With a groan, he captured my lips in a searing kiss and pushed me back onto the bed. I gasped into his mouth, my breath ragged, and his slickened fingers found my clit. More shuddering need and desperation roared through me, and I clawed at his head and shoulders. More. I needed more. So much more.

"Bish—" My core clenched, relief flooding me as I spun on sensation and light.

But just like the orgasm in the tub, the feeling didn't last. I couldn't reach the top, couldn't fall into satisfied bliss. I was consumed with a hunger that just couldn't be satiated.

Tears pricked my eyes. I didn't want this.

Please. How do I reach the finish line?

How long was it going to last? And was every heat in this realm going to be like this? I'd go insane.

Bishop pulled his hand away, the sudden absence of his touch making me sob. He hadn't even been inside me, but his retreat felt like a rejection. God, it was so much worse than Knox. Bishop had promised to protect me, take care of me, and now—

His cock pressed into my entrance and my spiraling thoughts lurched.

Oh, yes. Please, yes.

A mini climax shuddered through me, growing stronger with every inch he slowly pushed into me. It crashed into a full-blown release when our pelvises pressed together.

"Fuck," Bishop groaned, his body trembling.

He squeezed his eyes shut and sucked in long breaths, trying to get himself under control. But he was staying perfectly still to do it, and I just couldn't stay still, not long enough for him to get a hold of himself, not even for a second.

I needed more, stronger, faster. I had to move, had to feel his incredible cock sliding along the walls of my channel, building my desire higher and higher.

My hips rocked, moving the fraction they could with him pinning me down.

God, please. I need him to fuck me into oblivion.

I clawed at his powerful shoulders, digging my nails into his flesh, and strained to satisfy myself. But I couldn't get enough movement or friction.

Then Bishop growled low in his throat and opened his eyes. Darkness had flooded his irises, making the green flecks stand out in sharp contrast. His wolf was at the surface of his consciousness, if it hadn't already taken over.

"Fuck me," I begged, not caring if I was talking to the man or the beast. *Just please, fuck me.*

With a snarl, he withdrew and plunged back inside me. Hard. The impact shuddered up my body in a delicious wave that pulled a moan from my throat.

That seemed to be the permission he needed because he grabbed my hips, withdrew, and thrust back in again.

I bucked up to meet him, the impact reminding me of the wild sex with my dream Knox.

In the back of my mind, I was pretty sure my body wasn't ready for even a fraction of the aggressive sex I'd had in my dreams, but I didn't care. Nothing could stop the need screaming through me.

Bishop's fingers dug into my flesh hard enough to leave bruises, but that pain felt so good and there wasn't any other, not like I'd expect for having sex for the second time in my life. Only pleasure.

He pounded into me, spinning me tighter and tighter. I panted and moaned and begged for more. More more more.

The wave building inside me was stronger than even the ones I'd fantasized about in my dreams, and I clung to it as it took me higher and higher.

It broke with an eruption of bliss that crashed through me. Every muscle in my body clenched tight and stars exploded behind my eyes. It spun me around and around, darkness and light snapped through my vision, shot through every hyper-sensitive nerve, and rang in my soul.

A golden nimbus filled me and I was weightless, floating in bliss, warm and safe. I was home. Exactly where I was supposed to be.

Because Bishop was mine.

CYRUS

AUDREY SCREAMED HER RELEASE, AND I SQUEEZED THE HANDLE OF THE
cold cupboard and gritted my teeth, my cock still painfully hard. I
was going to have to take care of myself before I did something stupid
like run into the bedroom when she started begging for round two —
something my wolf really wanted to do.

A moment later, Bishop groaned his own release, and I'd never in
my life been more jealous of my younger brother.

If Knox and I— Hell, who was I kidding? If *I* took care of everything else — since Knox wouldn't talk to the townspeople to get
supplies and needed to stay as far away from Audrey as possible —
Bishop would be able to focus entirely on Audrey, and she wouldn't
need my help to survive a heat that had reached a fevered level.

And really, it was better that I kept my distance.

I didn't have her consent, and even if I did, having sex with her
would muddy the line between us. The line I'd been working hard to
make absolutely clear.

She couldn't be my mate and given how she'd been about sex
before the fever hit, I knew sex meant something important to her.
She wouldn't have sex just to have sex and that meant having sex with
her could give her the wrong impression about my intentions.

I heaved my attention back to the cold cupboard, taking stock of the handful of fruits and vegetables, the block of cheese, and the pitcher of dark green juice inside. It wasn't much, barely enough for the evening meal the villagers thought we'd need when we were supposed to return later today.

They were probably going to bring something over around dinner time like they had at breakfast the other day.

I should have looked for Rafe the second I'd left the bathroom like I'd told Bishop I would, but I hadn't been able to get very far before my worry about her condition forced me back. I needed to know she and Bishop were going to be all right first. Then I could look for the magistrate and his wife so I could beg for more of their kindness to let us stay the few days it was going to take for Audrey to get through a heat that shouldn't have been so bad.

Although maybe it had been inevitable.

Audrey wasn't from this realm and she'd already gone into her heat touch-starved —seriously touch-starved for someone from this realm. The fact that she'd said heats in her realm were almost non-events and how her body had already been on the verge of a normal heat before we'd even left Stonehaven should have been a clue that our realm was changing her.

I should have known even though she was an almost powerless shifter that she'd have the mother of all heats. And for all I knew, her incomplete mating bond with Knox could be making it worse.

Bishop stepped out of the bedroom with a set of long dark pink scratches trailing over his biceps. She must have drawn blood for them to be that dark. If she hadn't, his natural healing would have healed the marks before he'd even left the bedroom. He carried one of the towels I'd set on the bed, dropped it in a heap by the bathroom door then sagged onto one of the sturdy wooden chairs at the worn kitchen table.

"She asleep?" I asked, unable to keep my wolf's growl from my voice. I kept my back to Bishop, fighting to get my cock to calm the fuck down, and pulled an apple and a hank of grapes from the cold cupboard.

"And her fever is down a bit," he said. "I also managed to get her lucid enough to explain what was going on."

"Good." I sucked in a slow breath, determined to get myself under control, but that only filled my nose with a mixture of her fresh sweet scent and thick heady arousal.

Fuck it.

I was a guy and Audrey had been giving off pheromones like crazy since her fever hit. It'd be a miracle if I *wasn't* hard right now.

There was no way I was going to get through one day with the cabin smelling like her and sex, let alone three or four days without a hard-on. I was just going to have to accept that and move on — preferably to the bathroom where I could jerk off and relieve the pressure.

I turned to face Bishop and set the fruit on the table. His gaze dipped to the massive tent in my pants, and he cocked an eyebrow but thankfully didn't comment. Then he turned his attention to the food.

"We're going to need more than fruit," he said.

"I was just taking stock before finding Rafe and telling him what's going on," I replied as I filled a glass with water and slid it to him. "I'll go hunting after that. Hopefully, I'll catch something big enough to last the duration since you and Audrey are going to need meat to keep your strength up."

"I left a mess in the bathroom," Bishop said, downing the glass of water and standing. He was at half-mast again, Audrey's pheromones affecting him just as much as they were affecting me.

Except he can do something about it.

You can, too, my wolf told me. *You should. She needs you.*

I shoved that thought aside. Bishop was going to be her mate. I was just going to be her brother-in-law. I shouldn't help her. Not the way I wanted to.

I turned to the cupboards and pulled out a large blue ceramic bowl so Bishop could bring some of the fruit into the bedroom and wouldn't have to make a trip back into the kitchen.

"I'll clean up the bathroom. You go rest. We've been up for over a day and we have no idea how aggressive her fever is going to get." I put the rest of the grapes, two more apples, and a couple handfuls of blueberries in it and handed it to him. They still needed an actual meal with meat, but it was a start. "Next time she wakes, get her to eat something."

Bishop nodded, his expression tight with concern, and returned to the bedroom.

I sucked in another breath filled with the scent of Audrey and sex and went to clean up the bathroom. Depending on how her heat went, she might need more time in the bath or want to clean up in the shower.

Bishop had left his wet clothes and a puddle on the floor and hadn't drained the tub.

The memory of Audrey in my arms, clinging to me and breathing in my scent, her nose nuzzling my neck, her hot body pressed against mine as I carried her shot a burst of white-hot need straight to my cock.

She'd been in distress, her beautiful eyes squeezed tight, and strands of dark blond hair stuck to her sweaty forehead, and my wolf was going crazy, every protective instinct I had howling inside me.

She needed someone to fuck her.

And that someone was Bishop. Only Bishop.

But even though I knew that, I couldn't convince my wolf — or myself for that matter — that helping Audrey through her heat wasn't my job.

She's perfect, my wolf said. *A protector. A mother. Ours. She'll feel so good.*

The thought of pushing into her tight warmth made my balls ache.

We'd make her feel good, give her what she needs. A heat fever this strong is dangerous. We need to protect her. We need to mate with her.

I forced myself to my knees before my wolf could walk us into the bedroom and claim Audrey and shoved my pants down.

My cock sprang free, red and angry, precum leaking from my tip. I squeezed the base, fighting to get myself under control, but the only control I could muster was not going to her.

Fuck me. Why did she have to have the fever? I should have told her and Bishop to fuck every night since she'd started to fall apart on the second day of this stupid journey. All of this could have been avoided.

But she'd been a virgin and shy, and I'd thought if we dealt with her being touch-starved, everything would be fine. She wasn't a strong shifter. Her heat should have never reached a fevered level.

I roughly jerked my hand up and down my length, my grasp so tight it edged on painful.

Now we were stuck here for the next three or four days when we really needed to get back to Stonehaven. The longer we stayed, the greater the chance Knox would succumb to the lure of their mating bond and seal it, destroying any hope of Bishop's slim-to-none plan B.

That, and I couldn't put off my pack responsibilities for much longer. We still had an increase in beast activity in the area along with the strange rip to Audrey's realm in Anakar that could be dangerous.

And while I knew Nova and Deacon could handle most of the day-to-day operations of the pack, I also needed to get home to put some distance between me and Audrey.

My hips jerked forward, fucking into my hand with fast, aggressive thrusts as my wolf thought about how Audrey would pant and moan and then scream her release like she had for Bishop.

My balls tightened and tingles shot up my spine. I came hard, thick ropes of cum spurting into the water on the floor and a strangled cry caught in my throat.

Fuck me. I wasn't sure I was going to be able to wait until we got to Stonehaven to put distance between us.

CYRUS

After I cleaned the bathroom, I got out of the cabin as fast as I could, before Audrey's scent could make me uncomfortably hard again, and found Knox pacing a trench in the ground in front of the porch.

His posture was so tight, I was afraid he'd pull something, and when he wrenched around to march my way, I could see his eyes were wild — but thankfully not dark with his wolf.

By some miracle, the collar was holding. The question was, for how long?

"I should have known," he snarled at me. "Everything else about her is fucked up. Of course her heat would be the worst-case scenario."

"Bishop's got it handled." And just Bishop. No matter what my wolf wanted.

"Like he handled her heat before?" He clenched and unclenched his hands and his lips curled back in a snarl in an obvious challenge.

"We should have known, but we didn't," I told him, my wolf heaving to take control and put Knox in his place for daring to challenge us. He might be *an* alpha, but I was *the* alpha, and I had the strength to prove it.

But that wouldn't help him calm down and I needed him calm to keep the collar intact. Because when it broke, his wolf would take over and not care if Knox wanted to be mated to Audrey or not.

"I'm going to find Rafe and let him know we're here and that we need to stay. Then I'm going hunting. Come with me." Maybe putting some distance between him and Audrey would help.

"I can't hunt as a human." His gaze jerked to the cabin door and the muscles in his jaw flexed. "And I can't leave her."

"You can't fuck her, either," I warned. "She won't be lucid enough to say yes or no, and she has her hope set on Whil being able to transfer the bond."

"I'm not going to ruin any chance she has of getting rid of me." But he didn't look away from the cabin.

How much of his feelings were because of the bond and how much because he actually cared for her? He didn't like being around people, but that didn't mean he didn't have feelings. While he'd kept his distance from her and refused to talk to her, he'd spent the entire trip watching her.

Did he see what I saw? Did he see a shy, uncertain woman who'd been beaten down her entire life? And did he see how hard she was trying to keep up and be brave and face a realm filled with things she'd never experienced before?

Probably. He wasn't dumb. He just couldn't stand crowds or closed off spaces.

"Just hunt with me. Even if you stay in human form it'll help control your wolf from breaking the collar."

He turned his wild-eyed gaze back to me, his expression stricken. "The bond won't let me leave her. Not when she's like this."

"Are you going to be able to stay away from her?" I didn't want to force him to go with me, but we needed meat. I had to go hunting and I needed to know he wasn't going to cause problems for Bishop.

"Yeah." He huffed a bitter laugh and glance back at the cabin, his expression strained. "Never thought my *condition* would actually be good for something."

He stormed to the far end of the porch, jerked around, and came back, resuming his pacing. It set my nerves on edge, but I knew it was the only thing burning off the angry energy building inside him.

"I won't be gone long."

He grunted his acknowledgment but didn't look at me, and I headed down the path into Kelna.

The town was small, maybe five or six dozen houses, but the buildings were bigger than the average "village" house I'd seen in my travels on diplomatic missions with my parents and were well-maintained.

I found Rafe, his wife, Neera, and their daughter and her new husband, along with most of the villagers in the meadow behind the town. The wedding had been two nights ago, but it looked like the festivities were still going.

Both Rafe, the town magistrate, and his wife assured me we could stay as long as we needed and offered to send someone with food right away. I told her I'd collect everything after I'd gone hunting and take it to the cabin since I was positive Audrey didn't want the townspeople hearing her having sex.

The next five days consisted of hunting and picking up baskets of fruit, vegetables, bread, and baked casseroles, and doing my damnedest to stay out of the cabin and the overwhelming scent of Audrey's arousal.

As it was, I still had to jerk off multiple times in the day just to be able to focus. And I *needed* to focus because Knox was hanging on by a thread, Bishop was fully consumed with Audrey, and Audrey was getting worse. Not better.

A heat fever usually peaked at the end of the second day or the beginning of the third, then the need to mate slowly diminished over the next couple of days from every couple of hours to eventually a few times a day, and then the woman's temperature returned to normal.

But Audrey's temperature remained high — thankfully not dangerously high like it had been when it first started but still high — and the duration between matings was getting shorter and shorter.

It was mid-afternoon on the seventh day when I strode down the narrow path back to the cabin with a bundle of clean sheets and towels.

I was tired, having only managed sporadic sleep since we'd returned to Kelna, and the tension in my body made the headache I started two days ago pound behind my eyes. But I couldn't give in and stop. I had to keep taking care of her, and we'd been at the cabin long enough for Audrey and Bishop to have gone through all the clean bedding and towels in the cabin.

It didn't matter that Bishop said she was barely lucid with the biological drive to mate fully consuming her. She could have a moment of clarity at any time and I wanted her to know we were taking care of her.

It made my wolf furious that all we were doing was cooking and cleaning and keeping our gods damned distance so we didn't do something stupid.

I rounded the rocky outcropping and climbed the half dozen shallow steps carved into the stone ground up to the glade and followed the narrow path through the thigh-high grass and wild-flowers to the cabin.

Knox lay on the porch swing, his eyes closed, and his breathing slow and steady.

Thank the Sisters!

He'd finally passed out. He'd been pacing and snarling so much in the last few days, I was afraid that even if he didn't manage to break the collar containing his wolf, I was going to have to chain him up. He'd even begged me to do it just before dawn this morning when Audrey was whining and begging and desperate.

When this mess had started, I'd been jealous of Bishop — and a very small part of me still was — but now I was worried for him. I was pretty sure I dozed at least a little last night but every time I jerked awake, he and Audrey had been going at it. Without a doubt, he was getting even less sleep than I was.

I tiptoed onto the porch and cracked open the cabin door. Audrey's sweet fresh scent — a scent that made my wolf sit up, wag his tail, and yip with joy — wafted over me. Then the heady, rich scent of her arousal followed and my cock jerked to attention.

Fuck. Her scent was killing me. Every instinct I had screamed to satisfy her. By satisfying her, I'd be protecting her. And by protecting her, my wolf and I would prove to her that we were a worthy mate.

Because he *had* to have her. She'd do anything for pups who weren't even her own. We wanted a mate like that, a mate who wanted— no *needed* to protect those too small to protect themselves.

Inside, everything was quiet and I prayed that meant Audrey and Bishop had managed to fall asleep.

But I'd only gotten a few steps inside when the bathroom door opened and Bishop stepped out. He looked tired and worried, and even with the air thick with her sweet scent and heady arousal, he was only at half-mast — which meant he was as exhausted as he looked.

"Tell me you have more of that broth," he whispered.

"Did she drink it all?" Well, that was a miracle.

He hadn't been able to get her to eat anything and she was barely drinking water. And while the heat put her body in a state of conservation, that was only supposed to be for a few days and even a normal shifter with a normal fever came out weak and dehydrated. Which was why the pack tried to avoid letting a heat get to the fever stage and why Wilder and Nova had set up the heat clinic.

"Unless there's a pot in the cold cupboard I can't see, she's had it all." Bishop's expression darkened and he glanced at the partially open bedroom door. "But even if you make another batch, she's not going to be able to last much longer."

"Maybe that means the fever is almost over."

He shot me a hard look. Yeah, I didn't really believe that, either, but I couldn't let Bishop lose hope. He was the one who had to hold it together. Without him, Audrey's heat would never break.

He shuffled to the couch and sagged onto the worn seat cushion. "I have no idea how Wilder does it. I think I've gotten two hours of decent sleep in the last three days, and now it takes half a dozen orgasms to ease the fever long enough to give her ten minutes of peace."

"Wilder doesn't do it alone," I reminded him even as my wolf strained against my control. Bishop wasn't enough. Audrey needed us, too. "And this should have been over at least two days ago."

"I know." He raked his fingers through his hair, pushing it away from his face. "Whatever we're doing? It's not working."

I'd been thinking the same thing all day but couldn't figure out what we were doing wrong. The only thing I could think of that might possibly influence a heat and made Audrey's different from any other heat I'd heard about was her incomplete mating bond.

"It has to be the bond," I said and Bishop nodded his agreement.

"That's what I'm thinking and why the fever isn't breaking." He swiped his hand through his hair again. "What are we going to do? Knox refuses to accept her."

"He's still adamant that she shouldn't be stuck with him." I dropped the towels and sheets on the couch beside Bishop and headed to the kitchen to pull out what I needed to make another batch of bone broth. Because I *had* to do something.

"You know, sometimes she cries for him when the fever is riding her hard."

I knew. I heard her through the open windows. Knox knew it, too, and he usually retreated to the far side of the glade.

But as much as Audrey begged for Knox, that was the fever talking. She'd walked until her feet bled just to try a slim-chance spell to break their bond.

"I'll talk with the village healer about the sedative this town makes."

"Right," he said. "The moss in the nearby cave that absorbs the death god's power that they harvest and turn into a sedative. You said it even works on shifters."

Which was a miracle in and of itself. So far none of our doctors or researchers had been able to find a sedative that worked with our physiology. Not even Whil had found anything.

Bishop frowned at me. "Sedating her will help me get some rest, but I don't know if it'll break her fever."

"I'm not betting on that. I want to sedate her so we can take her home. If anyone knows what to do with her, it'll be Nova." As much as Nova had always been like a bratty little sister to me, she was a brilliant physician. Between her and Wilder's experience with hundreds of heats, surely they'd be able to figure out something that didn't involve her sealing her bond with Knox.

"Do you think sedating her will be enough?" he asked as a soft gasp and pained mewling came from the bedroom. His expression tighten, the worry in his eyes deepening, and he shoved up to his feet. "I don't know how many days she has left. She's already so weak."

"Neither of them wants the bond," I insisted even though we all knew the odds of Whil being able to transfer the bond to Bishop were just as slim as the spell that had failed. We had to try. That was what she wanted. "Sealing it has to be our last resort."

"If we can catch her in a moment of lucidity, I can ask her to bond with me," Bishop said. "Maybe that—"

"There's no guarantee she'd have the strength to form a mating bond and no guarantee that a new bond would break her fever," I said stopping him before he finished, knowing exactly where his train of thought was taking him... because I'd thought the same thing half a dozen times already.

But if a shifter was too close to death, it didn't matter if he or she said the words, the magic for a bond would never spark to life.

The only reason Audrey had been able to bond with Knox, even while she'd been on death's door, was because the mating magic had already been awakened and had been looking for someone to latch on to.

"We'll see how tonight goes and if she doesn't improve, we leave in the morning," I told him. I didn't want to sedate Audrey for seven or eight days, but I would if that was the only way to get her the help she needed.

The mewls turned to whimpering and my chest tightened with worry.

With a groan, Bishop hurried to the bedroom and I caught a glimpse of Audrey writhing on the bed. Her eyes were glassy, staring off into space, her hair was plastered to her forehead and neck, and she panted, short, shallow gasps as if she couldn't catch her breath.

In her consuming need, she'd pushed the sheet down to her hips, and her slight frame looked thinner, frailer. She'd lost some weight with all the physical exertion to walk to the death god's temple and it looked like she'd lost even more. She might not make it to Stonehaven. Not even if we sedated her.

CYRUS

Cyrus!

I woke with a start, my gaze darting over the moonlit glade, searching for what had woken me.

The Sisters were near full, their soft ever-so-slightly pink illumination bathing the long grass and wildflowers and, on the far side of the open space, lay a huddled form whose power felt like Knox's. No one else was around and there was nothing to indicate why I was suddenly awake.

Inside the cabin, Audrey whimpered and moaned, the sound hoarse and strained. She cried out with a strangled sob then almost immediately went back to whimpering, her orgasm giving her no reprieve just like she'd been all afternoon.

I squeezed my eyes shut, trying to will myself to go back to sleep. If we were heading out in the morning, I needed as much rest as possible.

I wasn't sure how I'd managed to fall asleep on the porch swing the first time with the sounds of the exhausted sex marathon going on or Audrey's scent taunting me every time the wind shifted, but I had, and I needed to figure it out again. It was the only thing I could do.

Fuck. Cyrus! Bishop gasped in my head, his mental voice filled with panic.

I jerked upright, my heart racing. *What's wrong?*

Get the sedative.

Audrey's whimpering grew louder and her moans more pained than pleasured.

Get the sedative now. Please, Cyrus. He groaned and mental whispers of soft, soothing words ghosted through me as he tried to soothe Audrey without breaking our connection. *I can't bring her fever down. I've tried cooling her in the tub. Even put in ice. Nothing is working. She isn't even giving me time to recover.* And I knew without him saying anything that he'd made her come as many times as he could before losing control and coming himself.

I scrambled off the swing as quietly as I could. I didn't want to alert Knox that anything was wrong. His wolf would break his collar and he'd seal the bond without a second thought.

Which would solve our current problem, my wolf snarled at me, pissed that we weren't doing everything in our power to help her.

It's a last resort, I snarled back. If the sedative didn't work then I'd talk to Knox and deal with the consequences — one of which could be Audrey hating me for forcing her to bond with a mate she didn't want.

I hurried inside and grabbed the bottle of sedative and dropper from my pack, grateful I'd visited the town healer right after my conversation with Bishop.

Hurry, he gasped. "It'll be okay. I promise," he cooed, his voice half in my head and half out loud.

Please let him be right, I prayed and raced into the bedroom.

Audrey lay on her side, her arms wrapped around her stomach and her knees pulled up. Desperate, heartbreaking sobs wracked her body and tears streamed over her cheeks onto the pillow.

Bishop lay tucked up against her, stroking her hair and murmuring to her while his other hand was buried between her thighs.

She whimpered and rocked into him, but from the sheen of sweat on her skin and how fast she was panting between her gut-wrenching sobs, I knew the fever was too strong to be satisfied with just his fingers.

Her body tensed and shuddered with a release, but her sobs didn't stop, and Bishop shot me a gutted look, his eyes begging me for help.

Get her on her back, head raised, I commanded and set the bottle of sedative on the dresser, as far away from the bed as possible without leaving the room. I didn't want to risk her fighting me like she had every time we'd tried to feed her.

The sedative had been a gift for saving the villagers from the grimalkins — just like the use of the cabin — but I suspected it was worth a lot and I didn't want to have to ask for more.

With a steadiness I didn't feel, I unscrewed the bottle, dipped the dropper in the pungent, glowing green liquid, and sucked up the dose for a human female.

When I turned around, Bishop had her partially rolled over, her head in his lap. She was still curled in a ball, hugging herself as if her insides hurt — which they probably did — but at least her head was raised mostly facing up. Hopefully that would mean she'd swallow the sedative and not let it dribble out of her mouth.

I climbed onto the bed, realizing that even in my panic I was fully erect, my cock straining against the confines of my pants... and that Bishop wasn't. Heat radiated from Audrey's frail body like an oven and her eyes stared off into nothing.

"Please," she sobbed. "Please. Why don't you want me? Please. I need—" Her sobs turned to agonized wails and she writhed on Bishop's lap.

I emptied the dropper into her mouth and Bishop followed the sedative with a sip of broth that thankfully encouraged her to swallow.

"Ida said it could take ten to fifteen minutes before it works and only if we've gotten the dose right."

"That long?" Bishop shot me a panicked look.

"Just keep her comfortable," I said, but her breathing turned ragged and her body jerked, her muscles starting to convulse.

Bishop shoved his hand between her thighs again. "We don't have ten minutes."

And Bishop was just too exhausted. Shifters had increased healing and stamina, but even we had limits, especially when we were sleep deprived.

Fuck. The fever had to be brought down long enough for the sedative to work, and I was the one who was going to have to do it.

For a split second, I thought about capturing her attention and getting her consent, but she was too far gone. I wouldn't be able to get her lucid in time to save her... if I could even get her lucid.

Fuck.

Fuck fuck fuck.

I jerked off the bed and yanked off my clothes. My wolf leaped to the front of my consciousness, thrilled we were finally going to do what we should have done days ago, but he didn't take over. He was happy to let me stay in control since he was getting exactly what he wanted.

Bishop watched with a grim expression but didn't say anything. He knew what had to be done, although he didn't know entirely how I felt about it. And he never would.

No good could come from telling my brother I wanted his mate when I shouldn't have her, and without a doubt, Bishop was going to woo her into being his.

I shoved those thoughts aside and tugged on her knees, urging her to open for me.

Her body jerked with another convulsion, and I took the split-second afterward, when her muscles relaxed, to pry her legs open and shove my hips between them. Bishop had two fingers pumping inside her and they glistened with her multiple releases and her body's need for more.

I watched them slide in and out of her, unable to tear my gaze away. Her breath turned into short, sharp gasps and her hips bucked violently. With a growl, he picked up his pace and ground his thumb on her clit, tearing another orgasm from her exhausted body.

Then he pulled his fingers free and I pushed inside her tight, hot sheath.

Audrey and I both groaned. Audrey with the relief of being properly filled, and me with the relief of finally being buried inside her. I'd been aching for her since before we'd even left Stonehaven, fighting my wolf to stay in control because I couldn't claim her like he wanted.

This was going to be the closest we'd ever get to having her and the circumstances made my soul weep.

A soft orgasm rippled through her, her walls fluttering around my cock, and she weakly rocked her hips, chasing it but unable to make it bloom in full. I slid my thumb over her swollen clit, helping it grow, and was rewarded with a breathy moan and her inner muscles squeezing me tight.

Fuck. I sucked in a breath, fighting the ache in my cock and balls and the need to pound into her and fully claim her. Even if she was mine, she physically wouldn't be able to handle that right now, and I needed to hold out until it looked like the sedative was taking over.

Audrey panted and trembled, her eyes glassy and unfocused. I couldn't stand to see her like that. I wanted her to rise up, embrace the strength within her that I saw every time she squared off against a grimalkin. And I never wanted her to fight one of those beasts again. I was the alpha. It was my job to protect her.

The urge the hold her, comfort her, protect her overwhelmed me, and I pulled her to my chest, my arms around her body supporting her. I hated how light she was, how weak. I hated that she had to walk all the way here, and I hated how the spell failed. Not because I didn't want to share her with Knox or that I thought Knox shouldn't be her mate, but because it had hurt her and had torn a gash in her far-too fragile hope.

I held her still and rolled my hips, sliding in and out in long, slow strokes. She'd already worked herself to exhaustion. I could take over now and do the work, give her what she needed.

Her desperate, sharp pants evened out into deeper breaths that turned into soft moans, and her hands tangled in my hair while she buried her face in the crook of my neck and breathed in my scent.

Another orgasm rolled through her and then another. Her moans grew louder, filled with pleasure, the sound of her satisfaction and her muscles clenching around me, straining my control. A warmth radiated around my heart, our shifter souls connecting and calming. It was as strong as the warmth I felt when my brothers' souls steadied mine... the same strength I'd felt as a child embraced by my mother or fathers.

It was the feeling of home.

And I only felt it because the stress of the situation heightened my emotions, not because it actually meant something.

Audrey came with a weak cry, and I continued to thrust into her, my pace building, my own release threatening to break free.

Another release shook her, strong enough to make her frail body tense against mine, but her cry of pleasure was weaker, softer.

"I think she's about to pass out," Bishop said. He leaned against the headboard, his expression exhausted. He looked like he was about to pass out as well.

His words shattered what little control I had, and I thrust faster and harder, determined to give her one more orgasm before I lost control.

She tried to rock into me, matching my speed, and pulled on my hair. Her lips captured mine in a weak, needy kiss, and my wolf seized control and kissed her back.

He knew I didn't want to cross that line of intimacy and wasn't going to let this opportunity pass him by. Having sex to relieve the fever was one thing, but kissing made it personal, deepened the connection between our souls, and sent searing desire straight to my cock.

She came with a sharp inhalation, her body tensing, her inner muscles seizing my cock and yanking me over the edge.

I came hard, my seed spilling into her satisfying my wolf even though he knew she was on birth suppressant and this wouldn't give us the pups he wanted.

Then she went limp, the sedative taking over, and I laid her on the bed beside Bishop. He watched me with wolf-darkened eyes, but I didn't see aggression in them from having been with his soon-to-be mate. No, they were filled with understanding.

Yeah. I was so fucked.

KNOX

Cyrus bounded out of the cabin in his wolf form and slipped into the dark forest surrounding the glade.

My pulse lurched. Something had happened. But I had no idea what.

The last time I'd seen him, he'd been sleeping on the porch swing while I'd been trying to sleep on the far side of the glade, as far away from the cabin as the mating bond would let me.

I hurried to the cabin before I realized what I was doing, grabbed the door that Cyrus had left open, and stared inside into the dark living room.

I didn't hear screaming or sex and Bishop wasn't calling me. Audrey had to be okay.

Except she wasn't... and if I didn't want her to be stuck with me with my fucked-up head, I had to let my brothers take care of her.

They had a plan, and I just had to keep my wolf collared and wait until we were in Stonehaven and Whil had transferred the bond before releasing him.

I shut the door and turned to head back to the far side of the glade but couldn't make myself step off the porch.

The pull of the mating bond mixed with my worries was just too strong. It squeezed my chest, making it hard to breathe and move and hell, just think about anything else.

Fuck, this was my worst nightmare. I hadn't even known that *this* was what I feared the most. But the terror howling and clawing and unable to break free from inside me was stronger than even the squeezing, suffocating panic that seized me if I was inside for too long or surrounded by too many people.

Everything in my soul screamed that I needed to protect her, and my wolf was losing his shit, furious that I'd let Cyrus and Bishop lock him away.

Her heat had been going on for too long and even if I hadn't overheard Cyrus and Bishop's conversation about it not stopping — and the theory that it wasn't going to stop until our mating bond was sealed — I'd be terrified for her.

I curled up on the porch swing, forcing more ice into the mating bond, praying that would help stop me from completely fucking up her life.

I couldn't take care of her the way a mate was supposed to.

I couldn't even cover the basics for a mate.

I couldn't spend more than a few hours inside, and I couldn't ask her to live like I did, sleeping in the tall grass outside Stonehaven or in the sacred grove outside the alpha's residence. Even if she could shift, she'd still need shelter for winter and the storm season.

But she couldn't shift and she'd want more than just "living inside." She'd want a life and she deserved to have one. She deserved everything her old pack had denied her: friends, family. Hope.

No. I couldn't be her mate. I couldn't be anyone's mate. I was too fucked up.

I squeezed my eyes shut and fought to still my racing thoughts. If the bond wouldn't let me leave the porch, then I needed to embrace the oblivion of sleep. In the morning we'd start the journey back to Stonehaven and then everything would be fine.

Hell, maybe whatever had made Cyrus race out of the cabin as a wolf had been whatever she needed and the fever would be broken by morning... and I wasn't going to think too deeply about what that might have been. A heat fever was dangerous and whatever he'd done would have been to protect Audrey.

I sucked in a slow breath then another and listened to the crickets. I could do this. Audrey could do it. Everything was going to be okay.

A soft thump jerked me awake and I sat up with a start. Inside the cabin, slow footsteps shuffled across the wood floor in an unsteady rhythm, drawing closer. Then a door squeaked and clicked shut, and a moment later, the shower started.

I strained to hear more. It hadn't sounded like Bishop. He was tired, but his steps would have been heavier and surer. Which meant Audrey was in the shower. By herself. Did that mean her heat had broken? Even if it had, she had to be weak. The fever had ridden her hard and she'd barely eaten or slept. Why was he letting her use the shower by herself?

What the hell was wrong with him?

I mentally nudged him and received a sleepy groan in response. Exhaustion and worry surged through our twin bond and I clamped down on it before it could affect me. I hadn't realized just how tired he was.

My wolf wrenched against the collar. If Audrey's fever was that bad, then we needed to go to her, not just to protect her, but to protect the other half of our human soul as well.

I gritted my teeth and squeezed my eyes shut. Bishop wasn't alone. Cyrus might have needed to go for a run, but he'd be back, and Audrey had both of them. They'd be fine.

But my wolf didn't believe that and a growing part of the human me didn't believe it, either.

Something inside *thumped* and all my senses snapped to high alert. Bishop remained asleep and the shower *shushed* in a steady, undisturbed stream of water. Audrey wasn't moving around, that would change the sound of the falling water.

Because she's fallen, my wolf snapped, his voice muted as if he were far away.

A surge of panic shot me to my feet. I wasn't sure if it was mine, my wolf's, or a combination of both. I couldn't assume the thump had been Audrey falling.

And yet given how weak she had to be, I couldn't assume otherwise.

I mentally reached for Bishop to wake him and make him check on her when a soft sob cut through the *shushing* water.

My wolf wrenched me to the door and flung it open before I realized what I was doing.

Panic seized my chest and I gripped the doorframe, stopping my wolf from forcing me inside.

She needs us, he snarled, his voice getting louder, his fear straining the magical collar containing him.

We can't. I tightened my hold on the door, fighting to stay where I was. The wood groaned, threatening to crack beneath my grip, and the walls of the cabin crowded closer together, proving exactly why we couldn't be her mate.

Another sob cut through the sound of the falling water and my wolf wrenched my unwilling body to the bathroom despite the pressure of the collar.

Audrey sat huddled in the corner of the shower just outside of the spray, hugging her knees to her chest. Her hair was wet and limp around her face and shoulders, her body too pale and too thin, and her eyes were squeezed tight in desperate agony.

The pressure in my chest that had been squeezing me since her fever had started crushed tighter, and I sucked in a sharp breath filled with her sweet scent and the scent of her arousal.

All fear of being closed in and suffocated by the small room vanished and my focus narrowed to just her, everything within me screaming to help her.

I turned off the water, crouched before her, and cupped her cheeks in my palms, urging her to look at me.

Her lids fluttered open and she locked gazes with me. Her eyes were surprisingly clear, the fever having eased enough for her to be lucid.

"Knox?" she gasped as tears rolled down her cheeks, the agony in her expression breaking my heart.

It should never have come to this. Bishop should have been taking care of her from the moment we'd left Stonehaven. Except if Bishop and Cyrus's theory was correct, that wouldn't have made a difference.

Only sealing the bond would have prevented this.

Her body tensed and her face scrunched in agony. A strangled moan escaped her clenched jaw and her breathing grew shorter and sharper.

My pulse lurched and I picked her up, not caring that she was getting my clothes wet. Sisters, she was lighter than when I'd carried her on my back to escape Darkweald. And that had already been too light for my liking. It spoke of neglect and too many days going to bed hungry. And now she was wasting away to nothing.

I had to get her to Bishop.

No. I had to end this.

Fuck.

I didn't want to seal the bond, didn't want to trap either of us. But there wasn't any other choice.

I set her on the counter and brushed her damp hair from her face. She stared up at me with her soulful brown eyes, the gold rings around her pupils shining bright, mesmerizing me and reminding me that I'd never been close enough to look her properly in the eyes to notice that subtle, beautiful detail.

The bond had already ensnared my soul, it was only a matter of time before this brave, determined woman fully ensnared my heart.

Before I realized what I was doing, I palmed the back of her head to keep her steady and captured her lips with mine.

Her breath hitched then turned into heavy pants, and she kissed me like she was starving. Her fingers clung to my shirt and her hips rocked up, pressing her slick heat against my painfully hard cock.

My wolf howled and heaved inside me, straining against the collar, determined to break free and claim her. She was ours and we'd neglected our responsibility to protect her for too long. We shouldn't have even left Stonehaven. We should have accepted the truth from the very beginning. She was our mate. She'd always been our mate and we'd just been waiting for fate to bring us together.

I bit back a growl, undid the tie keeping my pants up, and shoved them down my legs. My cock sprang free, jutting between us, and Audrey wrapped her small hand around it.

More tears rolled down her cheeks and she sobbed into my mouth.

"It's the only way," I said, my voice gruff and my throat tight with guilt.

"But you don't want me," she said even as she weakly stroked me and pressed me against her slick, swollen folds.

"I don't want anyone." I captured her lips again, my need for her tearing through the last of my resistance.

I needed her as much as she needed me, needed to fill her and complete myself, needed the bond that would only make us miserable.

I pushed into her, unable to hold back any longer. She moaned, the sound loud and satisfied, just like the sounds she'd made for my brother.

See, I could please her just as well as they did.

I would please her better because she was mine.

I tangled my fingers in her wet hair and tugged her head back, deepening our kiss, as I plunged into her again and again.

"Please, Knox," she begged against my lips. "Harder. Please, please, please."

I picked up my pace, pounding into her as she wept and begged for more, for me.

"Yes," she cried. "I need you, Knox. I need you."

"You're mine," I growled, my wolf straining to break the collar.

A shudder swept through her and her walls clamped around me as her eyes rolled back in pleasure, but I kept pounding into her. I wanted her to scream, wanted to brand my soul onto hers and shatter the fever consuming her. If we were going to make this sacrifice, I was going to save her.

Another orgasm tore through her and her moans grew louder. But the fever wasn't letting go. I could feel it rising again, feel the heat radiating from her skin.

My balls and cock ached, the need to fill her with my seed tightening every muscle in my body. But I needed to hold out, needed to make her come again and again. I needed her screaming my name.

"Who's your mate?" I snarled.

"You," she gasped, another weak climax rippling through her.

She was losing strength, which meant I was losing her.

"Who?" I yanked her hair, determined to get her attention and keep her from succumbing to the fever. Her eyes flew open and her gaze, filled with a wild heat, locked on mine.

"Say my name," I demanded as I pounded into her, my hand behind her butt jerking her toward me with each thrust. "Say. My. Name. Who's your mate?"

"You," she cried, her body trembling, her expression wild with pleasure. "You, Knox."

Every muscle in her body contracted, the force wrenching my own release from me. Heat shot down my spine into my balls, my canines grew despite my wolf being collared, and I sunk my teeth into Audrey's shoulder, claiming her.

She screamed my name again, her voice reverberating into my soul, ringing with a great, powerful gong. Every cell within me vibrated at the sound, aligned, and a brilliant golden light exploded behind my lids.

Mine.

She was mine. Forever.

Gods help me.

KNOX

AUDREY SAGGED AGAINST ME, HER BODY GOING COMPLETELY LIMP AND her breathing turning deep and steady with unconsciousness. The heat from her skin cooled, faster than I would have expected, but then her fever hadn't been a hundred percent natural. It had been spurred on by the magic of our mating bond.

Our now complete mating bond.

Warmth, unlike anything I'd ever experienced before, swelled around my heart, and a sense of calm, of being home, stronger than what I felt when my twin was steadying my soul, surged into the very essence of my being.

How could I have been so stupid to think sealing the bond with Audrey was a bad thing?

It was the most right thing I'd ever done in my life. Even my wolf, while still pissed that he was collared and yearning to claim Audrey again with him in control of our body, was satisfied.

But that still didn't address any of the reasons I couldn't be her mate. How could we possibly have a life together when I lived most of my time as a wolf and she couldn't even shift? I couldn't even spend more than a few hours inside.

That thought made me suddenly aware of the walls surrounding me. The bathroom wasn't the smallest I'd seen, but it was still an enclosed space with one too-small window.

Holding Audrey steady on her perch on the counter, I kicked off my boots, stepped out of my wet pants, and yanked off my soaked shirt. Then I carried her out to the porch, snagging the blanket on the back of the couch in the living room as I walked by.

I should have taken her back to the bedroom and left her with Bishop, but I wasn't ready to let her go. Just holding her was steadying my soul and I needed to stay calm. I had too many thoughts whirling in my head and no answers.

A low growl rumbled in my chest as I wrapped the blanket around us and settled on the porch swing with Audrey cradled in my arms.

She sighed in her sleep and nuzzled her nose into the crook of my neck, taking in deep, slow breaths of my scent while her sweet scent and musky arousal clung to me, fueling the sense of rightness.

Mine. All mine.

Except she wasn't just mine. She and Bishop had feelings for each other, and as much as I wanted to hold her and never let her go, I knew Bishop would be good for her. Better than me.

In fact, I should push him to claim her as soon as possible. Maybe his claim would distract her from our bond and she wouldn't be compelled to be with me.

She could have a normal life.

With my brother.

My wolf heaved against the collar, snarling and snapping his mental teeth at me. Giving her to Bishop and then trying to step away from her life was unacceptable. She was ours. We'd never leave her.

Even if it's best for her?

We're what's best for her, he growled, the collar making him sound far away and muffled.

But we weren't best. Hell, I didn't even know what to say to her when she woke. Even if she hadn't actually been fully lucid and the heat fever prevented her from remembering having sex in the bathroom, she'd know right away the mating bond was sealed. There was no mistaking the sense of completeness, of rightness... of permanence.

It felt so different from the heavy aching cage around my heart and the chain binding us together that had first formed and I'd filled with ice to keep us apart.

Ice and distance that I'd known had hurt her.

And now I really had no idea what to say to her.

Sorry wasn't enough. And neither was an explanation. Now that we were bonded, my reasons felt stupid and yet still so significant.

Fuck. I had no idea what to do. I'd never been in a relationship before. I'd had a few flings, most of them with Bishop at my side, before my wolf had taken over and I'd gone feral. They'd been pity or curiosity fucks, girls wanting to say they'd had the wild brother, the dangerous one. But none of them had been serious.

Hell, none of them had even been casual. How could they have been? I wasn't normal. I was fucked up. I didn't want to meet friends or family. I didn't want to be social and go to parties or dinners or events. I wanted to be left the fuck alone.

Until now.

But alone was the best option for Audrey.

She had a life to build, a fresh start waiting for her in Stonehaven, and my fucked-up head would only stand in her way.

Panic flooded my twin bond and I gritted my teeth, determined to not let it affect me. Bishop was awake and had just realized Audrey wasn't in bed.

I've got her, I told him. *We're on the porch swing.*

The panic shattered, followed by confusion then a stomach-churning mix of emotions flashing so fast they were nearly impossible to recognize as he realized I'd sealed the mating bond.

Yeah. That was how I felt about the whole situation as well.

Why? he asked, his footsteps hurrying across the living room floor and drawing closer to the door.

You know why. Her fever wasn't going to break unless the bond was sealed and now her fever has broken.

The door creaked open and Bishop stood in the doorway looking exhausted. His gaze slid over Audrey curled against me, her expression relaxed and peaceful, and he released a heavy breath.

Thank the Sisters, he said, sagging against the doorframe as the energy from his fear evaporated.

As soon as she's strong enough, you need to mate with her, I told him, even as a part of me roared at the words. She was mine. I was supposed to be able to protect her and fulfill her needs. But I couldn't and I never would.

You still need to develop a relationship with her, Bishop said as if he already knew that I planned to keep my distance after he bonded with her — probably because that's what I did with all the things I couldn't handle. It was always easier to say, 'to hell with it,' and move on. And it would be better for Audrey if I did.

Cyrus, still in his massive black wolf form, bounded out of the underbrush on the far side of the glade and raced toward us, stopping at the foot of the porch steps. His tongue lolled from his mouth and his sides heaved with heavy breaths as if he'd spent the entire time away from the cabin running.

Knox sealed the bond and broke her heat, Bishop said.

Good, Cyrus stepped forward, his form turning liquid for the blink of an eye before solidifying into his human form, and he marched up the steps to the door. *We still leave in the morning.*

Shouldn't we give her a day to recover? Bishop asked.

Cyrus glared at him and Bishop moved to the side to let him pass.

She can recover on the way. The fever might have done more than exhaust and starve her, and we can't chance Kelna's human healer not recognizing if there's a problem.

And while the healing elixir Whil made healed a lot of things, it didn't help with exhaustion, starvation, or rifts between our human and wolf souls. Given how Audrey's connection to her wolf was so buried she couldn't even shift, it wouldn't surprise me if the heat fever had created more problems.

The thought made me tighten my grip on her.

If I hadn't been stubborn, none of this would have happened, and the only way I could think of to make it up to her was to convince

Bishop to mate with her as soon as possible and stay the hell out of her life. Our bond was sealed and the overwhelming compulsion to be together was gone.

Audrey bonding with Bishop would overpower any other desires to be with me. It had to.

AUDREY

THE RICH SCENT OF WOOD SMOKE WRAPPED AROUND ME LIKE A comforting blanket and a reassuring calm heat filled my chest. I was safe. I was loved. I was home. The achy, icy hollowness from Knox rejecting our bond was gone and it was never coming back because we'd sealed our mating bond.

Oh, God!

My pulse lurched, grief and horror consuming all my warm feelings.

Knox and I had sealed our bond.

I was now permanently bonded to a man who didn't want me and was furious at me for accidentally bonding with him in the first place.

Tears welled in my eyes and I buried my face into the shirt of whoever held me.

It had all been for nothing. I'd walked until my feet bled and then walked some more, and it had been pointless.

Why couldn't we have held out longer? We'd just needed to get back to Stonehaven and Whil could have transferred the bond to Bishop.

But that had been a long shot. Just like the spell in the death god's temple.

Cyrus had warned me that I was going to have to face the fact that Knox and I were going to be mates, and I hadn't wanted to believe him. We'd been walking away from the temple and I—

My thoughts stuttered. I'd been exhausted and too cold. I—

Images of being with Bishop, of begging him to satisfy me as an agonizing, desperate need clawed at my insides flooded through me. I'd pleaded with him to fuck me again and again. I'd needed more more more, and he'd been all over me and in me, hands, mouth, cock. I could still feel the glorious pressure of him pushing inside me, of how he hit an amazing spot when he pushed in from behind. I'd needed him more than anything and had been relentless in seeking my pleasure.

More tears leaked from my eyes and I clung tighter to the shirt, pressing my face against a hard, sculpted chest.

I'd been an animal, consumed by my need, not caring about anything but having him fill me.

Heat burned my cheeks. I'd lost complete control.

Then Cyrus's face flashed through me and my body burned with the memory of him thrusting into me.

I'd had sex with Cyrus? That didn't make any sense. Cyrus didn't like me and he certainly didn't want to have sex with me.

Another set of strong hands wrapped around me, and I was pulled into someone else's embrace and enveloped in the scent of fresh-cut grass.

I tried to open my eyes, tried to drag myself to full consciousness and see what was going on, but I couldn't. Exhaustion pulled at me but wouldn't drag me back under and release me from the horror of my memories, and my sobs grew stronger.

A soothing hand stroked my head and a low voice murmured words my whirling mind couldn't register.

All I could think about was how I'd been out of control, how I'd demanded sex again and again from a man I'd wanted to be my mate, how my fantasy of having sex with Cyrus felt so real, and how I was now trapped in a bond with Knox.

Trapped. Forever.

My life in this new realm was over before it had begun, and the thought of being imprisoned in a loveless mating came out in desperate, strangled sobs.

I didn't know what to do.

There was nothing I *could* do.

Finally, my exhaustion dragged me back into darkness, and I drifted into a churning, black sea, bobbing up to catch blurry glimpses of rugged, rocky scenery passing by, small crackling fires, and soothing hands urging me to eat and drink a cloying bitter liquid.

I had no idea how long the darkness held me captive, all I knew was that every time I broke through, I remember how I'd been, how I'd begged Bishop and Cyrus and Knox to use me in every way possible... or had that been a dream? A nightmare?

What was even true anymore?

Maybe I was dead.

Maybe that monster had eaten me and this was hell. It was just as likely as me actually escaping Sterling and Royce and the pack, falling through a rip between realms, and landing in a place where they couldn't reach me. Even if I had my full shifter powers— Hell, even if I was strong enough to be an alpha, I'd never have the ability to open a rip or gate or anything else between realms.

A dark, menacing laugh rumbled, striking sudden, icy fear within me, and I froze, afraid to move, afraid to look like the prey that I was.

"You're desperate," a voice hissed in my ear, but when I wrenched around to face whoever it was, I found myself alone in my old pack's sacred grove. "Whore."

"It was my heat," I insisted. But that didn't release the shame that sat heavy and hot within me.

"Greedy cunt," the voice hissed in my other ear. "Greedy, desperate cunt. You begged for it. You'll always beg for it. You're begging for it now."

"No." I hugged myself. I wasn't like that. And yet mixed with the shame was desire to be with Bishop again like our first time before my fever, or to be with Knox just like how I'd dreamed, or to have Cyrus hold me with such tenderness as he thrust inside me.

"You're going to beg your mate and he's going to fuck you and still hate you because you're weak."

The words sliced into my soul, bleeding in more shame, while my voice, crying for Knox to give me more, begging him to fuck me, echoed around the grove.

"That," the evil voice said with a dark chuckle, "was a pity fuck. He had to seal the bond to save his life. Not because he loves you."

"The bond will help," I insisted. The bond was supposed to deepen the love between two people, but if there wasn't any love to begin with...?

"You're going to be his convenient cunt. You'll never say no to him and he's going to fuck all his hate into you."

"He won't." He wouldn't. "Bishop would never let—"

The menacing laugh roared around me. "Bishop is his brother. He's family, not some weak pathetic whore. He wants to fuck you with his brother because they're sick fucks and you're the sickest of them all. Do you honestly think two guys would want to share you?"

Was it all a trick? Was Bishop trying to manipulate me just like Royce had when he tricked me into thinking we were fated mates?

My throat tightened and tears burned my eyes. It couldn't be a trick. I believed Bishop. He cared for me. I know he cared for me.

"You're a convenient cunt who won't talk back. You'll take whatever they give you, you'll beg for it, and they'll laugh at how they've turned you into their toy."

"That's not true." Sure, Bishop had talked about sharing me with Knox, but it was to help me... wasn't it?

"You don't want to be used like that," the voice taunted, back to whispering right behind me. "Do you?"

I wrenched around, still alone in the grove where Sterling had tried to sacrifice me.

"You're only good to be a fuck toy or a sacrifice," he mocked.

"No."

"You know it's true," he said. "You can feel it in your soul... along with the bond keeping you prisoner."

"It's not true." Except I was so weak. No one had ever wanted me.

Not even my own father. Everything Sterling had told me over all those years had chipped away at me, breaking me down into something fragile that would inevitably shatter.

"You know you only have one option."

I had no options. I was trapped in the mating bond.

"You know what it is." The voice deepened, his tone cajoling. "It's in your DNA."

The image of my father's blood splattered over the yellow bathroom tiles flashed through me.

"No."

"Yes. Unless..." the voice turned wicked. "Unless you do want to be a begging cunt."

"No," I insisted, but I didn't know if it was to killing myself or being Knox's whore. I had more self-respect than that... didn't I?

"You do," the voice whispered. "He hurt you. He hates you. He fucked you without you saying yes. He and his brother are going to continue to use you. Do it."

"No," I whimpered. I didn't want to give up like that, didn't want to accept that happily ever after was a ridiculous fantasy for someone like me.

"Do. It," the voice screamed.

Something deep within me jolted and I screamed back, "No!" The wildness I'd felt when I'd dreamed of Knox surged. "Hell no."

I wasn't like my father. I was stronger than him, not as a shifter but where it mattered, where it *had* to matter. I might be afraid and ashamed, and I might make myself smaller to avoid being noticed by the predators around me, but I didn't give up.

I never gave up.

I always found another way, even if that meant being patient and suffering while I waited for the right moment.

"No!" I threw my head back and released a half scream half howl.

The wildness rushed through me, spinning me around and around, and the churning black sea pulled me into darkness again.

BISHOP

I GENTLY ROCKED AUDREY IN MY ARMS AS SHE SOBBED uncontrollably, praying her latest dose of sedative would take effect soon.

I had no idea what was going on in her head, but I feared it didn't bode well for how she'd feel when she was fully conscious. I'd been afraid that because she was so shy about sex, she'd be horrified at what her heat had made her do, and it was looking like I was right.

We were going to have to tread carefully with her once Cyrus had decided she'd recovered enough from her exhaustion to stop sedating her and reassure her that there was nothing she should be ashamed of.

If I was smart, I'd arrange for her and Nova to talk when we got back. Audrey might not believe what a bunch of men said about her heat, but she might believe another woman.

It was such a weird thing to be upset about. Nakedness and sex weren't something members of our pack were ashamed or afraid of. But I knew from having met other races as part of my education in becoming one of the pack's alphas that that wasn't the case with everyone. And while Audrey was a shifter, her pack was vastly different from ours and we couldn't treat her like one. Not for this.

"We need to pick up our pace," Cyrus said, glaring at the southern horizon before turning his glare on me.

My wolf bristled, taking his expression as a challenge and I nuzzled the top of Audrey's head with my cheek, a subtle reminder to the beast half of my soul that we had more important things to worry about and that Cyrus wasn't challenging us. He'd been glaring at everyone and everything since having sex with Audrey.

Her sobs turned to drowsy tears, her body still trembling against me with her distress and my chest squeezed so tight it was hard to breathe. I wanted so desperately for her to be okay, to not worry about anything, but I suspected she was afraid of what we now thought of her.

She was probably also afraid of her permanent relationship with Knox. Even unconscious, her soul would be able to sense that the mating bond had been sealed, and that was another huge thing for her to be afraid of.

"For fuck's sake," Cyrus snapped as he ran his hands down his face. "Just hold her, Knox. The sedative is about to take over and she'll be out for at least five hours. She needs her fucking mate to steady her soul."

Knox tensed. His gaze, like it had been for the last two days, was locked on Audrey, and a wave of longing washed through our twin bond along with a stomach-churning mix of emotions: need, anger, shame, horror, hope.

He'd been a mess since we'd left Kelna, clinging to her for almost all of the first day, his emotions flipflopping between panic and satisfaction when she snuggled close and terror when he realized he was preening at her unconscious attention.

He'd refused to let me or Cyrus carry her until we let the sedative partially release her in order to coax some food into her and she'd started coming to and had begun to cry.

Then he'd really panicked and shoved her into my arms and refused to take her back.

"I don't know what to say to her," he said, rushing down a steep incline as if I were going to throw her into his arms that instant.

"She's unconscious." Cyrus hopped down after him while I took it slowly, mindful of my precious cargo. "No witty banter is required. Hell, no banter at all. Right now, she's perfect for you."

Knox released a sharp growl and leaped at Cyrus, slamming him against a boulder and ramming his fist into Cyrus's stomach.

"Take that back," Knox snarled, his eyes flashing dark for a second as his wolf strained to break the collar imprisoning him.

"Take on your responsibilities," Cyrus spat, shoving Knox off him with a powerful push that sent my twin stumbling backward.

"I am." Knox tensed, readying to leap at Cyrus again, and I shoved my way between them knowing Audrey's unconscious presence would automatically stop the fight.

"She needs her bonded mate steadying her soul." I glared at Knox. "She needs to know she'll be loved and accepted for what's happened even if she's unconscious."

Knox huffed but didn't retreat or resist when I pressed her against his chest and she snuggled up against him.

The motion made my throat tighten and my wolf rise to the surface in a strange mix of relief that she'd accepted him — even if she wasn't fully aware of him — and jealousy. It didn't matter that I logically knew having Knox hold her would be best for her. I didn't want to give up comforting her.

"And you!" I wrenched my glare to Cyrus once I'd made sure Knox had a solid grip on Audrey and had forced myself to step away from them.

"Me what?" Cyrus demanded back as he squared his shoulders in a not-so-subtle reminder that he was bigger than me.

A ripple of his power escaped his control and I raised an eyebrow, knowing I didn't need to point out that he was being an asshole. Something I sure as hell wanted the reason for but wasn't stupid enough to ask about at the moment.

I'd ask him later when his wolf wasn't riding him so hard.

I knew he cared about Audrey, but I would have thought his mood would have improved now that her fever was gone.

He wrenched his power back and pushed past me. "I want to get to the edge of the next forest by nightfall."

The forest that was still so far away we only knew it was there because of the map and the fact that we'd passed through it on our way north. We were going to have to really push our pace if we were going to make it there before the sun set.

But that meant we'd be that much closer to Stonehaven and help for Audrey, help I prayed she wouldn't need.

Maybe when she finally regained full consciousness, she'd have already cried out all of her negative emotions.

Except I knew it didn't work that way. Even if she acted fine and said she was fine, she might not be. I needed to keep an eye on her since Knox had no experience with women and wouldn't have a clue if something was wrong, and Cyrus was hopeless with them and would probably say something to make it worse.

AUDREY

THE NEXT TIME I SURFACED, BISHOP WAS SETTING ME ON A FOLDED blanket on the ground, a large boulder at my back to help me sit upright.

"There she is," he said, his eyes lighting with warmth. "How do you feel?"

He brushed a lock of hair from my face, and I dragged my wavering gaze from him to the fire behind him, my thoughts moving in slow motion. The flames danced merrily, crackling and snapping as Cyrus slowly turned some kind of animal on the spit above it.

Behind him, I could make out hints of rocky landscape, a thick shrub covered in leaves and small white flowers, and a dark sky with only a hint of light at the very edge of the horizon, indicating that the sun had just set.

"Where are we?" We weren't in the death god's lands — the ground hadn't been this uneven and the shrubs shouldn't have had leaves let alone flowers. That, and I felt like we'd already returned to Kelna, that we should have still been there.

But my thoughts were too fuzzy, swirling around and around, too soft to properly catch, and I couldn't get past when we would have gotten back to Kelna in the first place. The spell at the death god's temple had failed... I'd been too cold... I—

Realization stole my breath and I pressed my hands over my heart. The bond.

"Your heat turned into a fever," Bishop said, his brown eyes searching mine looking for... I didn't know what. Recognition? Remembrance?

There was something there, but it felt so far away, pushed down beneath a viscous sea of darkness.

"The only way to break the fever was to seal the mating bond," he added.

Yes. I nodded slowly, my cheeks burning as some of the memories filtered back in and my stomach twisting with the thought of that horrible dream.

"But don't worry." He sat beside me and pulled me into his lap. The warmth of our shifter connection swelled within my chest, soothing and steadying me. "As soon as you're strong enough, we can bond."

And then I'd be in a second mating bond with a guy I barely knew.

My throat tightened at that. I didn't know why. I felt safe with Bishop, was attracted to him, and knew he'd love me. But that didn't negate the whirling mess of emotions inside me for Knox or the nagging doubt from my nightmare.

My soul said Knox was my mate and always would be. I couldn't just bond with Bishop and forget about him... even if that was what Knox wanted.

The shrub rustled and Knox stepped out from behind it, carrying an armful of branches for the fire.

My gaze instantly jumped to his and I was drowning in the brown depths of his eyes. Even in the darkness with him standing at the edge of the fire's light, I was pulled into those depths.

The heat in my chest billowed stronger as if he were holding me like Bishop was, and the realization that he could affect me like that without touching me stole my breath.

I ached for him. But it wasn't the desperate consuming need that I'd fought before. This was a sadness, a recognition that he wasn't rushing to my side, and a knowing that he still wanted to put distance between us.

But if I looked deep — or perhaps that was if I *sensed* deeper into our bond — I could also see uncertainty.

Of course, he had lots of reasons to be uncertain about me. He was probably still angry that I'd forced the bond on him and that to save me — and hence save himself — he'd had to complete it.

Cyrus huffed, breaking the spell between me and Knox, and handed a canteen to Bishop.

"Drink," he said, shooting me a stern look along with a ripple of power that thankfully wasn't strong enough to compel me.

I raised my hands to take it from Bishop and realized they were trembling and weak. In fact, all of me was weak and worn out. Was that from the fever? How—? "How long did it last?"

"Your heat fever?" Bishop asked as he helped me drink. "Nine days."

"Nine days?" I gasped. "I've been out of it for nine days?"

"Longer," Cyrus replied without looking away from the fire while Knox took up position opposite me and broke apart the branches into fire-appropriate pieces. "Do you remember? You passed out before we'd even gotten out of the death god's lands. Then it was seven days in Kelna and three more after we left."

"Those last three were aided by a sedative," Bishop said. "The fever exhausted you and you needed to recover."

I motioned for Bishop to help me take another long sip of water, unsure what to say to that.

"So, we're a week away from Stonehaven?" I asked instead.

"Closer to half a week," Cyrus replied. "About five days. We've been pushing our pace."

I guess I really had been slowing them down. And given how weak and shaky I felt, I doubt they were going to let me walk anytime soon.

Not that I was going to be insisting they let me. I'd already embarrassed myself enough during the fever.

The memory of begging Bishop for sex flashed through me and my cheeks heated.

"Hey," he said softly. "None of that." He hooked his finger under my chin and drew my gaze up to his. "Fevers are the worst case scenario for heats. Don't be ashamed of whatever you remember. You couldn't control it and none of us judge you for it."

I glanced at Cyrus, who was now watching me, his expression hard.

"Even if you and Bishop had been mated, Nova still would have sent you to the heat clinic," he said. "It's a miracle he got you through as much as he did."

"And sealing the bond was the only way?" I turned my attention to Knox, but he'd slipped back into the darkness beyond the campfire.

It looked like nothing had changed between us. He was still avoiding me, and while his rejection didn't threaten my sanity, it still hurt, and I still had a feeling we'd come crashing back together if we didn't work something out.

Despite being exhausted, I stayed awake long enough to eat a full serving of dinner — which consisted mostly of meat and fresh greens that the guys had picked up while walking.

Then I drifted off, wrapped in a blanket and Bishop's arms, and was tossed through a lurching montage of having sex with Bishop — sex that wasn't like our soft sweet joining that had been perfect for my first time.

The dreams ended with Knox capturing my mouth and body and sealing our bond with a golden blaze, a resounding gong, and a soul-shattering orgasm.

AUDREY

With a gasp, I jerked awake. A soft, warm throbbing radiated from my core and for a sudden, fearful heartbeat, I was afraid my heat wasn't over.

But the throbbing was a whisper of what my heat had been before, even when I'd first thought my heat was over. The throbbing now was more like my body remembering what had happened, the sensation spurred on by my dreams.

I didn't know if I should be grateful that those were my only dreams and I hadn't had a repeat of the nightmare or not.

Before me, the fire had burned down to embers and a pot now hung on the spit. Cyrus sat on the other side from me, packing his blanket and three of our four eating bowls into his pack, while Bishop crouched by the fire, stirring our breakfast.

Hints of pink still edged the horizon, indicating dawn hadn't been that long ago, but I was still a little surprised we hadn't broken camp and headed out already.

Whatever the reason, I was grateful I wasn't going to have to eat breakfast in the early dawn gray, although given that Cyrus was just about ready to go, I was still going to have to rush.

Groaning, I sat up, my muscles still weak and achy from whatever it was that I'd gone through.

"I was hoping you'd wake for breakfast," Bishop said with a heart-melting smile.

He scooped oatmeal from the pot into the last of our eating bowls and handed it to me along with a spoon.

"Thanks," I replied, taking it just as my stomach let out a loud, long growl.

Cyrus sighed at the noise, but it didn't sound like a huff of frustration, more like one of relief, which was very un-Cyrus like.

As I ate — oatmeal with last night's leftover meat and spinach — Knox returned to camp with our canteens, the outsides wet from having just been refilled.

Once again our gazes locked, the moment stealing my breath, and I was falling into eyes so much like Bishop's and yet so very different. Where Bishop's brown depths were warm and inviting, Knox's were filled with something deeper and darker. Longing? Confusion? Frustration?

He opened his mouth and his eyes narrowed. I could tell he wanted to say something and prayed it wouldn't be more rejection. We needed to figure out what was next because whatever it was, we had to do it together.

And as much as that broke a piece of my heart and made me want to scream, it was our inescapable reality.

I didn't want to be mated to someone who didn't want me and would forever hate me for trapping him, but there wasn't anything that could be done about it. We just needed to suck it up and move forward.

And I wasn't going to acknowledge my deepest fear that my nightmare was correct and they were just using me.

The strange look in Knox's eyes deepened and he jerked his attention to Cyrus. "Are you done with the pot?" he asked, setting the canteens beside Cyrus's pack.

"Yes." Cyrus dumped one of the canteens on the fire then handed it back to Knox who took it and the pot and disappeared around a large, rocky outcropping.

"He should have waited until you were done," Bishop said with a sigh and he unwrapped the blanket from around me and shoved it into his pack.

"I'll clean her bowl," Cyrus replied. "You get started, and Knox and I will catch up."

Right. Because I was going to be painfully slow getting moving this morning. I scraped my bowl clean and handed it over to Cyrus, trying hard to not think about the fantasies I'd had about him while in that strange dream-state for the last few days.

I didn't know how long the images were going to be dancing in my head, but I sure hoped they would stop soon. I was already mated to Knox and soon to be mated to Bishop. I didn't need all three brothers. Two was more than enough.

And if I really thought about it. I should focus on figuring things out with my first mate before adding another one.

Bishop slung his pack over his shoulders, and with a groan, I staggered to my feet. The world lurched with the movement, and I clung to the boulder to steady myself, not to mention keep myself standing on my shaky legs.

What the hell had happened to me? Why was I so weak?

"If you're feeling up to it," Bishop said, sweeping me into his arms. "We'll get you walking for a bit after lunch."

"Yeah," I replied, grateful I wasn't expected to start hiking right away. Walking after lunch sounded like a good idea, although I had no idea if I'd feel stronger in a few hours or not.

Even just waking up, eating, and now standing seemed to have sapped all my strength.

"Weakness and exhaustion is a side effect of a heat fever," Bishop said. "It doesn't let you sleep or eat much until the fever is broken."

"And my fever only broke when Knox and I sealed the bond."

He'd said my heat had lasted nine days and I'd been unconscious or out of it for all of that. How many of those days had I been suffering with the fever? I doubt Knox would have jumped on the idea of sealing our bond right away. Hell, had they even known that was the only way to break the fever?

"Your fever went on longer than normal," Bishop said, answering my unspoken question as he quickly picked his way over the uneven ground. "We didn't know the mating bond was affecting the fever until it should have been over and wasn't. But it's done now and you're safe. I'm sure you'll be back to normal by the time we get to Stonehaven."

Given how weak I felt, I wasn't sure about that, especially since I didn't heal like a regular shifter. But that wasn't my greatest worry.

"So what now?" I asked, my voice frustratingly small.

Except that was how I felt. Small and weak and frustrated.

We'd suffered walking for ten days for nothing, and while I wanted to cry and yell at Knox and tell him how much he hurt me and how much it hurt that he didn't really want me — even though we didn't know each other — I was far too weak even at my strongest to make demands of an alpha. I was going to have to submit and accept whatever Knox decided.

A growl bubbled in my throat. I was tired of submitting, of trying to go unnoticed for fear of retribution.

"Now?" Bishop said. "I bond with you and we return home."

"Just like that?" I asked unable to keep my disappointment from my voice. We weren't going to bond because we were in love, but because we had to.

"Hey. I choose to bond with you because I want to, but if you aren't ready—"

"We don't really know each other and I—" My throat tightened. "I —" How could I say what I felt without sounding ungrateful?

"You wanted to be courted," Bishop finished for me as if he could see into my heart and knew how disappointed I was that he wasn't going to court me like he'd promised.

"Yeah," I confessed. "I never had a boyfriend. No one was ever interested in me and I never got... you know." God, it felt so selfish to say it.

"You never got the courtship gifts? The fancy dinners? The

romance?" Bishop asked. He set me on my feet and cupped my cheeks in his palms to make me meet his gaze.

"You're allowed to ask for things," he said, his voice tender, his soft expression making my heart flutter with a mix of hope and fear. "Which would you like?"

"Well... I...?" I tried to look at my feet, my cheeks heating with embarrassment, but Bishop kept a firm grip on my face.

"You can say it," he urged. "You want all of it?"

"Yeah," I forced out. "I want to know what those first magical days of being in love feel like. I want to feel..." Like I mattered, like someone loved me for me not because an accidental bond was making them. And I felt like Bishop did, but I also felt like if we rushed our mating I'd miss out on all those romantic dreams and jump straight into the real life of being mates. "I want to feel like you want to mate with me because of me, not because you have to."

"I do, beautiful. I swear I do." He brushed his lips against mine, a whisper of a kiss that sent teasing sensual warmth sliding through my body. The kiss wasn't hungry with desire, not like his kisses when we'd first had sex or like the kisses floating around my foggy memory from my heat, but it still sent my heart soaring because it was a promise. A promise that I *did* deserve to be loved and that he'd prove it to me.

AUDREY

BISHOP CARRIED ME ALL DAY AS IF I DIDN'T WEIGH ANYTHING, ONLY pausing when we stopped for lunch and for half an hour where I tried to walk on my own. And while I was feeling better, I was still shaky and weak, and it was obvious that my pace was a lot slower than the guys'.

Both Cyrus and Knox — once they'd caught up to us — stayed a good ten feet ahead of us. I doubted it had anything to do with wanting to offer us privacy since from that distance they could still easily hear our conversation with their better-than-human hearing, but I wasn't sure why they were giving us space.

Well, Knox, I knew was pointedly ignoring me because he still couldn't accept our bond, but I had no idea why Cyrus was.

Although maybe Cyrus wasn't outright ignoring me. He was just going about his business as usual. He hadn't paid that much attention to me when we'd walked north. It shouldn't surprise me that nothing changed on our way back south.

Except I couldn't shake the feeling that there was something more going on, something connected to my fever that I couldn't remember.

Also strange was the fact that Knox hadn't shifted.

Everyone had made it clear that he preferred his wolf form and he'd remained as a wolf for almost the entire walk to Kelna. I hadn't even known he and Bishop were identical twins until a few days ago... Well, I guess it was more than a few days now since I'd been unconscious for over a week. But it still felt like a few days to me.

We made camp as the sun was setting, the sky dark reds and oranges. Cyrus picked another campsite that was protected on three sides with rocky outcroppings, one of which had an overhang that would shelter us against the weather. We were about a hundred yards from a forest and the closest we'd ever set up camp to the river. If it hadn't been for the uneven ground and the bushes, I would have been able to see the fast-moving water from my seat near the overhang.

"Bishop, firewood. Knox and Audrey, fill the canteens," Cyrus said as he dropped the two packs he'd been carrying — mine and his — and yanked off his shirt.

"I can fill the canteens by myself," Knox replied. He dropped his packs — his and Bishop's — and unhooked the canteens.

"It's not far and she needs to rebuild her strength." Cyrus dropped his pants, exposing all of his powerful, muscular body, and my breath hitched.

The yearning from before didn't swell within me, I wasn't desperate for sex with anyone I could get ahold of, but I did warm up. I might not be in heat anymore or aching to seal my mating bond, but Cyrus was a handsome man — in a dangerous bad boy kind of way — and I was still a living, breathing woman.

"The water is moving too fast," Knox replied not bothering to look at the river. "If you want her up and walking, have her pace the campsite."

"The campsite is flat. The way to the river isn't and it'll be better for her," Cyrus said, a hint of his power rolling off him, the only indication his temper was rising.

"And *she* is standing right here," I shot back as I heaved myself to my feet and used the nearby rocks to keep my balance. "She's capable of making her own decisions."

"So, are you going to stay here or be useful?" Cyrus demanded, his words stinging, a reminder that I'd been a burden to him and his brothers since I'd stumbled into this realm.

"I'm going to help with the canteens." I might be weak, but I wasn't useless and I refused to let anyone take control of my life again. With the bond sealed, leaving was no longer an option, but I would prove to Cyrus and everyone else that I deserved the same respect as anyone in his pack.

Cyrus huffed, shifted into his massive black wolf, and bounded toward the forest to hunt for our dinner. Bishop shot me an encouraging smile and followed him.

"So…" I turned to Knox. This was the first time we'd been alone since we sealed the bond and a churning mix of emotions swept through me.

"You're staying," he growled, grabbing the other two canteens.

"I'll be fine. It's what? Fifty? Sixty feet to the river?" I shuffled a few steps toward the river, staying close to the outcroppings just in case I needed to catch my balance.

"I don't need your help." His gaze flickered to me then jerked away as if he couldn't stand looking at me.

"So, this is the way it's going to be?" I asked, unable to keep my grief and frustration from my voice.

If I was smart, I'd bottle it all away and not give him more ammunition to hurt me, but I'd always been terrible at keeping my emotions in. Sterling had seen through any front I'd put up and knew exactly where and how to strike.

I didn't want to go back to a life like that and yet sealing our bond hadn't seemed to change anything between us.

"It's the way it has to be," Knox replied.

"Why? I know this isn't what either of us wanted, but we're—" We were what? Going to have to figure something out? Make things work?

There wasn't a *we,* no matter what our bond said. And I'd never been able to *make* anyone do anything.

"Just mate with Bishop so we can move on," Knox growled.

"You mean so *you* can move on," I said, a new realization hitting me. "Is that what you're waiting for? Me to bond with Bishop so you can bond with someone else?"

The thought made my chest tight. I didn't want him to mate with anyone else. He was mine. But if I mated with Bishop it would only be fair. Maybe there was someone he loved and that was why he'd fought so hard against our bond.

Except I could feel the pull of the bond inside my chest, warm and comforting, locked around my heart, and knew even if we did bond with other people we wouldn't be able to move on from each other.

"Just bond with him," he snarled, not answering my question.

My chest squeezed tighter. He *did* have someone. I'd suffered for days feeling like I was going to shatter with all the ice he was shoving into our bond when he could have just said something at the start. I would have understood.

"It's what's best for you," he added.

"What's best for me?" Shock snapped through me. I couldn't believe he just said that.

Merrick used to say that as well, particularly when he'd first taken me in and I hadn't been as obedient and submissive as I should have been. He'd said Sterling hurting and belittling me was good for me. It would make me stronger.

But the second I showed an ounce of strength, I was punished, locked in the basement for a day without food, extra cleaning duties at his betas' houses on top of cleaning Merrick's, or forced to kneel in the snow or blazing sun for hours without moving, the alpha's power crushing me into submission.

It had never been anything that would leave a mark — although I had no idea why. No one in the pack would have challenged him if he had. But in some sick way, I think he actually believed what he was doing was best for me, and that made it even worse.

And now Knox was spewing the same shit. How dare he!

Anger burned in my veins, but instead of swallowing it back like Merrick had always demanded, I embraced it. Submitting had never saved me and I didn't care if it could save me now. How dare Knox try to crush me through a sacred bond and then tell me it was for my own good. Even if he was in love with someone else, that was no excuse for how he'd treated me.

"This has never been what's best for *me*," I snapped at him. "It's always been about you."

"We left our pack responsibilities to walk you to the death god's temple on the slim chance that we could break the bond. Don't tell me I didn't do this for you."

"Right," I said, my voice thick with sarcasm. "Because yelling at me that you didn't want me, rejecting the bond so thoroughly it felt like my soul was shattering, and being reminded every second of every day that I'm weak and worthless and no one wants me was all for me. You're so self-centered you think doing a favor for yourself is a favor for me. Well, fuck you!"

He tensed and his lips curled back in a snarl.

"What are you going to do? Punish me?" I demanded, opening my arms in invitation.

My frustration and fury screamed through my veins, hot and violent. It was so strong it felt like it was rolling off my body in waves and my pulse *thu-thudded* hard in my chest, powerful and ferocious.

"You can take your *best for me* and shove it up your ass, you selfish coward," I snarled. "If you hadn't wanted to walk for twenty fucking days you should have tried to figure something out, tried to come up with some kind of arrangement because this bond was permanent before you fucked me without my consent."

I jerked a step toward him, my body no longer shaking from weakness but from rage, a rage that made me feel powerful for once in my God damned life.

"You go fill the canteens by yourself and keep avoiding me. But this bond will pull us together whether you want it to or not, and I swear to God, now that my fucking heat is over, my strength of will is stronger than yours."

A low growl rumbled in Knox's chest and I jerked forward another step, the *thu-thud* inside me pounded louder, turning my fury into an inferno.

His eyes widened and something flashed across his expression too fast for me to recognize.

Yeah, he didn't expect me to advance, thought growling at me would scare me and make me retreat.

Well, fuck you!

Then he stomped up to me so close I had to strain my neck to look up at him. Power rolled off him in a crushing wave, stealing my breath, making my knees weak, and snapping electricity across my skin.

But I gritted my teeth and stood my ground. And I was going to stand my ground for as long as possible.

He could have had sweet, submissive Audrey if he'd actually made an effort, but now she was gone. She'd been hurt too deeply for too long and she'd had enough.

"You'll come begging to me," I said, my voice strained against the crush of his power. "You, the alpha, begging the weakest shifter in existence, and I'll make you wait. But don't worry. It'll be what's best for you."

His chest heaved and his breath rushed across my face in powerful, angry gusts. Our gazes locked — his with only just a hint of his wolf darkening his eyes even though I could see his anger — and I vowed I would *not* look away first. I would *not* submit to him.

Then his gaze flickered to my lips, sending a whisper of desire curling around my core.

Oh, no!

Oh, hell no!

I'd just told him I was stronger than him. I wasn't going to back down and I sure as hell wasn't going to let him kiss me, no matter what the mating bond wanted.

"No." I shoved him as hard as I could.

He stumbled back a step, moved only because I'd caught him off guard, and I pointed in the direction of the river.

"Go!" I commanded. My anger *thu-thudded* hard and fast, rolling off me in a great wave, and with a snarl, Knox stormed off.

I stomped around the sheltered campsite fuming. How dare he say it was best for me. How dare he!

Except telling him off had been stupid. We still had five maybe six days of traveling together and I knew once my adrenaline wore off, I'd regret screaming at him. I was going to have to live with him one way or another for the rest of my life. I couldn't escape him, and he was so much stronger than me.

But for right now, my body thrummed and I felt good. I felt powerful.

KNOX

Fuck.

I dropped the canteens on the rocks by the water's edge and strangled the scream threatening to rip from my throat. My cock was so hard it hurt, and I was furious and confused and grief stricken and—

Fuck! Fuck fuck fuck!

I grabbed a rock and shattered it against a boulder with my palm.

Audrey practically glowed with her fury and strength, a radiant, vengeful goddess, and I'd wanted to claim her all over again.

Except I also wanted to beat the shit out of myself.

If anyone else had hurt her as much as I had, I would have ripped their throat out.

Fuck. How had I not seen it? I knew she'd been struggling, knew freezing the bond hadn't been good for her or me, but that pain in her eyes when she was yelling at me crushed me.

I had done that to her in my fight to avoid trapping both of us in a bond that I now knew in my soul was fated.

I'd thought it had been her heat making her struggle, or at least part of it. I hadn't realized just how deeply my rejection had hurt her.

And now I had the gall to be pissed when she wouldn't even

consider kissing me. I'd barely even thought the thought before she'd shoved me away.

What the fuck was wrong with me?

I shattered another stone and another, my throat tight from keeping my screams of frustration bottled in. But I was too close to our camp and I knew letting go would scare her.

I'd seen the fear of retribution in her eyes even as her temper got the better of her. I'd also seen the resignation, the acceptance that letting me know how she really felt would end in punishment. She was so angry with me, she was willing to face my fury.

She was so angry, I'd felt power, true alpha power like the power I'd felt in our shared dreams, rolling off her for just a moment.

It had rushed against my power, taunting, teasing, tempting, and my wolf had clawed and heaved against the collar. He wanted her just like how he'd had her in the dream, wanted that energy crackling against ours in a battle of dominance and seduction.

But she hadn't released her power in sexual challenge. Hell, she hadn't even knowingly released it, and I was sure she wasn't even aware she had it.

It had stuttered, the flow uneven, probably a match to the mix of rage and fear boiling over inside her, then it had flared sudden and strong, compelling me away from her, before vanishing.

I was worse than the asshole everyone thought I was. I'd hurt my mate so deeply the rage she kept locked within herself for fear of reprisal had burst free. She no longer cared if I punished her. Not that I ever would. But that didn't matter. I'd already done all the damage to our mating that I could.

I sagged to the ground, my smothered screams squeezing my chest until I couldn't breathe.

This was why I'd never be a good mate for her, why I'd fought so hard against the bond.

Except that was a lie.

I hadn't fought the bond because I thought I was terrible mate material. I'd fought it because I was afraid.

Fuck.

I had to fix this.

I just had no idea how.

I hadn't even known what to say to her when she'd been yelling at me. Normally I didn't care. I said what I thought and ignored and avoided those who didn't matter.

But Audrey mattered. She was the only one who mattered and, even if I had any idea what to say, being blunt wouldn't make her feel better and the thought of avoiding her forever made my soul scream.

She was right. She'd always been right.

The bond was inevitable and even if I stayed away from her, it would pull us back together.

I was a selfish asshole for not even considering that we'd have to figure out how our relationship would work. Even if she bonded with Bishop that wouldn't absolve me of my responsibilities to her and our bond.

I shoved a canteen into the river to fill it.

It had felt so good, so right carrying her while she was unconscious for those first few days after we left Kelna.

I'd been so sure I was going to have to let her go to embrace her relationship with Bishop that I'd clung to her every possible second until it looked like she was going to wake. But then I hadn't known how to say goodbye or deal with her sobbing, so I'd avoided her.

I couldn't have been a bigger idiot and now I needed to figure out how to fix it.

Except I had no idea how to fix a normal relationship let alone one as fucked up as the one I'd made with Audrey.

Hell, I didn't even know how to start one.

Movement downstream caught my attention and Cyrus pushed around a bush to get to the water's edge. He saw me and came closer to crouch a few feet away.

"I told Audrey to help you," he said, setting his catch — a skinned and gutted fox — on the rocks beside him, before shoving his bloody hands into the water.

"You should have minded your fucking business," I snarled. He'd made the order on purpose to force us together.

"And you should have taken the gift offered to you," he snarled back. "She's your mate and you've already fucked it up. She's shy and uncertain, but even a cornered mouse will bite back."

No shit. And she was hardly a mouse. She'd just been trained to act like one by the assholes who'd raised her.

"You don't deserve her," Cyrus said, his voice a low rumble, his wolf pushing to the surface. It almost sounded like Cyrus wanted Audrey as well even though he'd vowed to put the needs of the pack first.

"Then you do your fucking chores with her," I spat back, a sudden jealous rage surging inside me.

She was mine. Mine.

"I'm not the one who needs to build a relationship with her. You've avoided her from the start. Any idiot can see she doesn't trust you."

I huffed. She didn't trust me and she outright despised me.

And I deserved it all.

AUDREY

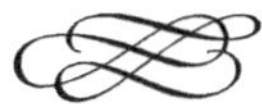

Over the next two days, I regained my strength enough to walk at the guys' pace for half the morning and ride Bishop in wolf form for most of the afternoon. I pointedly ignored Knox, and Cyrus didn't tell me to help him with his campsite jobs again. Instead, I helped Cyrus or Bishop — whoever wasn't hunting — with filling canteens, foraging for wild fruit and vegetables to supplement our meat, or gathering firewood.

The tension between Knox and I was palpable, and my fear of reprisal for yelling at him squeezed my insides, but I was determined not to back down. For once in my life, I was going to stand up for myself.

Knox had purposely hurt me and I couldn't just pretend to shrug that off. He could glower and avoid me or hell, even yell and hit me, but I had to stand firm. I couldn't run away from him like I'd wanted to run away from Merrick and Sterling, and I wouldn't go back to a life of always being afraid.

But God, it was so hard not to curl in on myself and try to make myself invisible.

"Tomorrow night we'll be camping just outside Darkweald," Bishop said as he helped me down a steep slope.

"At this pace, we'll probably reach the campsite by midafternoon," Cyrus replied, glancing up at the sun even though we'd just stopped for lunch half an hour ago, at noon. "We're making good time."

I bit back a sigh. Bishop had said our slower pace north hadn't been because I'd been walking and that we'd only made great time this time because the guys had pushed themselves while I was unconscious and when they were carrying me.

But I didn't really believe him. Yes, they looked a little more worn out than before, but I was pretty sure they'd have been able to handle the faster pace when we'd first headed out.

Except according to Bishop, they'd gone at the slightly slower pace — and he insisted it had only been *slightly* slower — because they'd thought we were going to be walking for the full twenty days. The rest at Kelna had been a welcome surprise... well, the rest that hadn't involved my body going crazy with a heat fever.

Cyrus skirted a copse of trees and hopped down another incline into a ravine that wound through the rocky landscape. I remembered it from when we were going the other way and it really did mean we were getting closer to Darkweald. Beyond the ravine lay a dense forest, then a more or less flat stretch of ground, and then the forest where the malicious god slept. We *were* almost home.

The thought sent mixed emotions swirling through me. I'd only spent a few days in Stonehaven and I already thought of it as home.

Except that wasn't entirely true. The guys referred to it as home so that's why I thought about it that way. Not because I had an emotional attachment to the place. Although I hoped I soon would.

I hoped the other pack members, if they couldn't accept me, would ignore me. That was probably the best outcome I could wish for and was a step up from my previous pack.

I stumbled down the second incline, falling into Bishop's arms, and flashed him a smile of thanks.

He'd been giving me longer and longer stints of walking and I was starting to feel stronger. Almost as strong as when I'd first started this journey.

"Want me to carry you?" he asked, his voice gruff.

"Half an hour more?" I asked, pulling out of his embrace.

"It'll be good for her," Cyrus called over his shoulder. "She's still too weak."

"I'll always be too weak for him," I mumbled, hopefully soft enough that he couldn't hear me. He was a good twenty feet ahead of us, so the odds were fifty-fifty.

"He pushes everyone," Bishop replied with a wry smile. "It's how he shows he cares."

He offered me his arm like a gentleman escorting a fine lady and I took it.

"You should have seen him after our mother and fathers died. He was an angry, growly, obnoxious beast," he said as we followed along the ravine after him.

"And if that's what gets you to combat practice and keeps you alive, so be it," Cyrus shot back.

A cloud swept over the sun, throwing us into shadows for a second. When it scuttled away, the sunlight caught in streaks of gold in Cyrus's light brown hair, streaks I hadn't noticed before.

The image of his eyes, filled with concern, his irises dark with his wolf's influence, swept through me. Then he dipped forward, wrapped his arms around me, and pulled me into a tight embrace as he plunged into me again and again and—

I shoved the fantasy aside even as a part of me questioned if it actually was a fantasy.

Had that actually happened?

Everything about my heat fever was so foggy and incomplete...

Which meant it was just another of my messed-up dreams. Just like the dreams I'd had of having sex with Knox, dreams that I hadn't had since we'd sealed our bond, or the shame dreams where a nasty voice called me names for what I'd done during the fever.

Cyrus wasn't interested in me, he'd made that clear, and I was mated to his brother. That was the only reason he was being some-what nice to me.

Another cloud covered the sun for a second and then another as a gust of wind swept down the ravine.

"We need to pick up the pace," Knox said from behind us.

I glanced back, unable to stop myself from looking at him even though I was determined to give him just as cold a shoulder as he was giving me. But he wasn't glaring at me for being too slow like I expected, he was glaring at the rapidly darkening sky.

"I remember there's a cave halfway down the ravine," I said as the first drops of rain splattered on the ground, darkening the rock.

"No," Cyrus replied, shooting down my suggestion without giving it any thought. "We need to go up. Get out of here."

I swept my gaze at the rocky walls on either side of us. They stood a good fifteen feet high and the bottom half was worn smooth.

Oh, shit.

Water smoothed rock meant the water in the ravine rose to above my head, and while we were in summer and could be standing in a dried riverbed, the more likely answer was that the ravine was a naturally occurring floodway during storms.

A heavy drop of rain plopped on my face and then another and another.

"I think there's a fallen chunk of rock a short way down," Bishop said.

Cyrus gave him a sharp nod and took off as Bishop scooped me into his arms and raced after him.

The fat drops quickly multiplied into a stinging, cold torrent, and the wind picked up with sharp bursts that stole my breath and made the guys stagger and fight against the force to keep moving.

I was drenched in seconds and forced to hide my face against Bishop's shoulder to keep the downpour from my face.

We reached the rock, an enormous chunk of stone that had broken off the ravine's side and slid to the bottom. Cyrus hopped up it with ease despite the blinding rain and turned back to us.

I'll get to the top and pull Audrey up, he said in my head, not bothering to yell over the roar of the storm.

Hurry it up, Knox shot back, his gaze on the steady stream of water running down the center of the ravine, now deep enough to cover his feet.

Bishop hefted me up as high as he could, and I scrambled the rest of the way up the rock to the top, while Cyrus jumped and grabbed the top of the ravine wall.

But just as he was about to haul himself up, a jackal leaped to the edge and snapped its sharp teeth at him.

My pulse jerked as he dropped back down and landed beside me, crowding me to the side and making my foot slip. With a yelp, I wind-milled my arms, fighting to keep my balance, knowing it was a losing battle even if the wind hadn't just gusted and pushed me over.

Fuck, Cyrus snarled and jerked forward, seizing my arm and yanking me up against his side, sending a flash of my fantasy rushing through my head.

But the heat vanished as quickly as it appeared. The rain picked up into a near-blinding torrent, the water level on the ground suddenly rising to Knox's ankles, and above us, half a dozen jackals stood at the edge, snarling and snapping blocking our only escape.

AUDREY

*W*E *NEED TO MAKE A PATH THROUGH THE JACKALS,* CYRUS SAID.

Toss training? Bishop asked.

Yep. See, showing up for combat practice is important. He turned his attention to me. *Bishop and I are going up first then Knox. He'll help you up. When you get up, run. Don't hesitate. Don't try and help. Just run. We can handle a bunch of jackals if we're not worrying about you.*

Because of course, I was a hindrance.

His words stung, but I couldn't deny them. I'd barely survived two fights with grimalkins, and while jackals were smaller, there was probably a whole pack of them just like the last time. And the last time Knox had been seriously injured to the point where shifting wouldn't immediately heal him.

I swiped rain out of my eyes and nodded. "I'll follow the ravine for as long as I can."

"Good girl," he praised, and he lowered me off the rock into Bishop's arms.

"Be careful," I told Bishop, squeezing him tight for a second. I didn't know what toss training was, but I knew climbing over the edge of the ravine would make him vulnerable and I couldn't bear the thought of losing him. Not when I'd just found him and things between us were filled with possibilities.

Bishop handed his pack to Knox then climbed onto the rock.

On three? he asked as Cyrus braced his back against the ravine wall and laced his fingers together.

On three, he replied.

Bishop placed his foot on the step Cyrus had created with hands, quickly counted down, and on three leaped as Cyrus propelled him into the air.

I rapidly blinked rain from my eyes, fighting the torrential downpour to keep watching.

With his incredible strength, Cyrus threw him into the air, the feat astounding since I doubted that Bishop, being almost as tall as his brother and packed with sculpted muscles, was lighter than the average man.

Bishop shifted in mid-air, the magic that let him shift destroying his clothes, and he landed on top of one of the jackals that was hanging over the ravine's edge snarling and snapping at us. With a growl, Bishop sank his teeth into the back of the beast's neck and wrenched his head, breaking its spine and killing it.

The other jackals lunged at him, but he bounded off the jackal he'd just killed and tore out the throat of another one before the fight took him out of sight.

The jackals on the ravine's edge raced after him, their yips and snarls still loud, indicating that they hadn't gone very far. Despite that, Cyrus hopped up, grabbed the edge, and hauled himself up.

A jackal snapped at him, but he rolled out of the way — and out of sight — and a second later a dead jackal landed with a heavy, wet thump on the ground a few feet away... ground that was now almost completely covered in water, the gathering rain no longer contained within a narrow stream running down the center of the ravine.

Come on, Knox said, grabbing my hips and hoisting me three-quarters of the way up the rock in preparation of climbing out. *When I pull you up, remember to run.*

Right, I replied as I tried to scramble up, but my grip slipped on the wet rock and Knox had to set his hands under my ass to catch me. Then he shoved, boosting me high enough to get my chest over the top, and I dug my fingers into a narrow crack, scrambled for a decent foothold, and hauled myself up.

Gasping, I carefully stood and clung to the ravine wall to keep my balance and make room for Knox. The rain was now coming down so hard it was hard to see even a few feet in front of me and the gusting wind threatened to toss me off my precarious perch.

Knox easily climbed up beside me as if it wasn't pouring then jumped and grabbed the ravine's edge.

A jackal leaped at him, but Cyrus appeared, his fingers extended into claws and his expression fierce, and he tore out the beast's throat before it could sink its teeth into Knox.

Get moving, Cyrus snarled as two more jackals raced toward him.

He caught the first one and tried to slash at the other as it raced past him, but it twisted out of the way, narrowly missing his claws. It dove at Knox who, already on his knees, ducked low, catching the beast's stomach against his shoulder, and tossed it over the edge.

The jackal landed on the ravine floor on its feet, only momentarily stunned from the fifteen-foot fall before jumping and snapping at me, trying to reach me on top of the rock.

Audrey, Knox barked, jerking my attention away from the snarling beast intent on eating me. *Grab my hand.*

He lay on his stomach and reached for me. Rain poured down his arm, splattering on the ravine wall and adding to the water stinging my eyes.

I reached for him, my fingertips barely brushing his. I wasn't tall enough.

Come on, he growled as I stood on my tiptoes.

More of our fingers brushed, but it still wasn't enough to get a proper grip.

You have to jump.

I dropped my gaze to the uneven, slippery rock beneath my feet. If I missed, I'd fall off and then have to figure out how to climb back up without help.

The jackal below me leaped again, his teeth snapping close to my foot, making me jerk away. The movement threw my balance off and I clutched at the ravine wall, desperately holding on, praying I wouldn't fall.

Getting back up would be the least of my worries if I couldn't grab Knox's hand.

Audrey, please!

The desperation in Knox's voice snapped my attention back to him. Fear filled his expression, a look I'd never seen in his eyes before, and his gaze kept darting up the ravine and back to me.

What was he looking at?

I turned to look and time stuttered into slow motion. A massive wall of water rose at the far end of the ravine, roaring its way toward me.

I had to jump. Now. And I only got one attempt.

My pulse pounding, I leaped. Somehow my feet didn't slip out from under me, and Knox wrapped his large hand around my wrist.

But as he was hauling me up, the wave of water slammed into my legs.

I tried to hold on, tried to tighten my grip and futilely cling to the ravine wall, but the force of the impact yanked my hand from his.

Cold water engulfed me, the shock stealing my breath, and I was wrenched under. I fought to find the surface, but the current was too strong, tumbling me around and around.

Pain exploded through my head and sliced across my shoulder, and I belatedly realized I'd hit the ravine wall. I scrambled to find a handhold, but the water had already swept me away.

Another explosion of agony in my knee, my shoulder, my knee again, around and around. My lungs screamed for air and darkness swam across my vision. I flailed, fighting to find the surface or something to hold onto, but I could barely see what was around me and everything was moving too quickly.

AUDREY

THE WORLD HEAVED IN A WRITHING, FROTHING MASS OF DARK WATER, and my lungs burned. What little breath I had was almost gone. Then something snagged my ankle, wrenching me against the torrent, and a strong arm wrapped around my chest.

Warmth billowed around my heart, strong and sure.

Knox.

Knox had jumped in after me... because of course if I died, he died or went insane. Not because he actually liked or was interested in me. Just like my nightmares had reminded me.

We crashed into the ravine wall, the impact shooting agony through my shoulder. Somehow he grabbed it with one hand and hauled us up enough for me to draw in a gasping, desperate breath before immediately coughing it and a whole bunch of water out.

Hold on tight, he snarled in my head, pulling me tight against his chest. *I need both hands.*

I wrapped my arms around his neck, hooked my ankles behind his back, and clung to him, my body trembling and exhausted and throbbing with pain.

With a growl, he dug his claws into the rock and hauled us up high enough that he could shove me over the edge.

Coughing and wheezing, I scrambled out of the water and collapsed on the hard ground, my body trembling from the effort, cold, and shock. The rain still pounded down in a painful torrent and the wind yanked on my wet hair and clothes.

Knox climbed up beside me, drew in a few deep breaths then picked me up, cradling me against his chest, and marched toward... I had no idea what. I could barely see anything more than dark mounds that, once we were close enough, turned out to be rocky outcroppings and boulders.

Somehow, he found us a sheltered crack that was barely wide and deep enough for the two of us if we huddled close together but would keep us out of the wind and rain. With a groan, he set me down and crouched in front of me.

"How badly are you hurt?" he asked, capturing my chin and turning my head to the side to look at what I could only assume was a cut at my temple.

My head throbbed, but it wasn't a migraine, and save for a pain in my knee whenever I twitched and my lungs still complaining about the water I'd breathed in, I didn't feel too bad. That and *I* wasn't the one in immediate danger. Bishop and Cyrus were.

"I'm fine." I tried to pull out of his grip but he held tight.

"You're not fine. You're bleeding and you almost drowned." He pressed a finger against my temple, sending pain shooting through my skull, and I sucked in a sharp breath that turned into hacking coughs.

"I'm fine enough," I choked out. "You have to go back and help Bishop and Cyrus."

"My brothers can take care of themselves," he replied, his voice gruff, and he turned his attention to the rip in my pants.

"It took all three of you to deal with the jackals last time," I insisted.

I didn't know how many there were this time, I hadn't gotten much of a look over the ravine's edge, but it seemed like every time Bishop or Cyrus killed one, two more had appeared. And while Knox hadn't needed an elixir for the last fight, he'd still been seriously hurt.

If this new pack was bigger than the last, Bishop or Cyrus could be killed. It wouldn't matter if, as shifters, they were stronger than the jackals. There were only two of them and they were surrounded.

Knox made the rip in my pants bigger, revealing nothing more than a skinned knee.

"See? Fine. I can hide here and wait for all three of you to get back." They had to come back.

Fear tightened my chest. It was selfish, but I didn't want to lose Bishop. He was the first man to ever show any interest in me and a part of my soul wept at the thought of him dying... a part that felt far too similar to the part that was certain Knox was my mate.

"You have to go." My pulse *thu-thudded*, picking up speed.

"I'm not leaving you." Knox grabbed my arm and pulled me forward. Blood stained my shirt indicating that the cut on my shoulder that I couldn't feel was worse than my skinned knee. Still, It wasn't pouring down my body, so it couldn't be that bad. I'd survive. Bishop and Cyrus might not.

I wrenched out of his grip and shoved him back. "They're your brothers."

"And they're not my priority right now."

"Well, they are mine." My pulse *thu-thudded* again, harder, a pressure growing in my chest fueled by my worry.

Knox gritted his teeth. His power rolled off him, a great wave that stole my breath, but vanished a second later as if he'd changed his mind about forcing me to submit.

"Bishop is fine," he said, his voice gruff but not angry.

"You don't know that."

How could he be so calm?

He, Bishop, and Cyrus had been all about protecting each other and they'd made it clear they'd sacrifice me to do so. I couldn't imagine the mating bond would drastically change Knox's priorities in such a short time.

"I'm not stupid enough to wander around by myself," I told him, "and I'm not bleeding to death."

"You hit your head. You need someone to keep you awake and I still don't know how bad the cut on your shoulder is." He held out his hands, silently asking for me to show him. "And I do know Bishop is fine. If he was seriously hurt, I'd feel it. Our twin bond is stronger than a mating bond."

Stronger? What could be stronger than a bond that deepened the love and soul connection between two people?

If he knew when Bishop was seriously hurt, that meant he could feel what Bishop was feeling, something I couldn't do with Knox — and something I hoped he couldn't do with me because if he knew what I was feeling, he was an even worse man than I thought he was. That also meant Bishop could feel what Knox was feeling. Could he tell which were his feelings and which were his brother's?

"No," Knox said, tugging me forward and ripping my shirt a bit more to get a better look at my shoulder.

"No?"

"You're thinking Bishop only cares for you because of our mating bond. That our twin bond is influencing him," he said, taking off his shirt and ripping it into strips. "It isn't."

"How do you know?" I knew I shouldn't have asked, but I couldn't help myself. I wanted *real* love. Not love influenced by a bond I couldn't control.

"We've sealed our bond and the pressure is gone. The need to be with you isn't anywhere as powerful as it was before. If it had been influencing Bishop, his feelings for you would have changed. They haven't. Turn around."

I blinked at him, the order such a sudden change in the topic that I needed a second for it to register.

He motioned turning around with his finger and I turned, not worrying about whether I remained sheltered from the rain while I did so. I was already soaked and wasn't going to get dry anytime soon. Getting wetter now wouldn't matter.

"Bishop is still going to court you and I'm not going to stop him." He wrapped a strip of his shirt around my shoulder and another high around my chest.

"I'll also try with us," he said, his voice soft and gruff. "But I can't be a proper mate. That's why I was trying so hard to break our bond."

"You don't even know what I want in a mate."

"I'm barely a brother and I'm not a friend," he replied, pulling me into his arms, placing a folded-up strip of shirt against my bleeding temple, and inching us as deep into the crack as he could get so we were both out of the rain. "I doubt I can be a mate."

Heat from his body sank into me and warmth radiated around my heart. I wanted to argue with him about making assumptions and not bothering to talk to me, but I was too exhausted to fight.

I'd never been good at standing up for myself. It was always easier to give in. I still didn't want to let him off the hook for hurting me, but I could fight with him later.

Silence didn't necessarily mean submission, it just meant I was biding my time.

I huffed a soft laugh and leaned into his warmth, resting my cheek against his bare chest. Biding my time made it sound like I knew what I was doing when really I was groping around in the dark like I always did.

AUDREY

"Hey," Knox said, giving me a soft shake as the storm raged around us. "You're not supposed to fall asleep."

"Pretty sure that's a myth," I replied even as I forced my eyes open — eyes I hadn't realized I'd closed. "At least in my realm I think it's a myth. For all I know brains work differently in this realm, like hormones."

"I wouldn't know about that. I just know you're not falling asleep until sunset."

I looked out at the gloom unable to see more than a couple feet beyond our dry little crack. "Will we even know when it sets?"

"It'll get even darker," he replied dryly. "But I'm hoping the storm will pass soon."

"It did come on us suddenly." The sky had been bright with only a few clouds moments before the rain had started... or maybe I'd just missed the signs. We'd been in the ravine and hadn't been able to see the horizon. The storm still had to have been fast-moving since there hadn't been any cloud on the horizon when we'd entered the ravine just after lunch, but it might not have been as magically sudden as it felt.

Knox, however, didn't elaborate and I didn't want to pry answers out of him. I'd ask Bishop about it when he and Cyrus found us.

The rain continued to pour in a steady rush, picking up in pitch and volume every time the wind gusted. I watched a bush that was barely visible through the torrent thrash against a boulder. It jerked this way and that, unable to escape and forced to endure.

That was me now.

I couldn't escape Knox. I had to endure and make the best of my situation, but I also couldn't roll over and submit — like my screaming instincts insisted.

That would only lead to a lifetime of subservience and I was never going to go back to that. Ever.

It wouldn't matter if I also had Bishop as a mate. I couldn't let Knox think he could push me around again, even if he thought it was best for me.

But God! Just the thought of standing my ground again made my pulse race and my insides squirm.

"Bishop is still fine," Knox said, his tone still gruff, but his words surprisingly comforting.

Even if I hadn't been panicking about Bishop being in danger, Knox had sensed my worry and was trying to calm me.

"When do you think he and Cyrus will find us?" I couldn't imagine them finding anything in this downpour, but Knox had found this crack and they were real shifters who could see in low, to almost no, light.

"Tonight at the earliest," Knox replied. "The flash flood was moving quickly and we could have easily gone a few miles in a few moments. We were also swept past the slope where we would have exited the ravine and headed away from the river, which means we're past the split and they're going to have to find a way to cross it or wait for the water to go down."

The split was another ravine that joined the one we'd been following that had crossed our path. It had been easier to slide down the only available slope and follow the ravine leading north until we found another easy-to-climb slope farther along instead of trying to scale the almost sheer rock face on the other side.

"Do you think that other ravine flooded?" I asked.

"Probably."

Again, I waited for him to say more, creating an awkward silence between us, but he still didn't elaborate.

Swell.

"I guess that means we're even closer to Darkweald."

"We're in Darkweald."

"We're what?" I tried to jerk upright, but he tightened his grip, clutching me to his chest.

I couldn't believe the water had raced so quickly that we'd travel a whole day's worth of walking. But then I hadn't known how long I'd been in the water or where either ravine had gone to. I'd have thought they'd have both gone to the river, but the one had clearly branched away from it. Regardless—

"We have to get out of the forest," I said. There were dangerous spirits in Darkweald and from everything the guys had told me, they were most active at night. We had to leave before the sun set.

"Calm down," he snarled, a wave of his power rolling through me and making me go limp.

"Don't you dare!" I snapped at him, fighting his command.

"Then act reasonable."

"I am. The last time we were in Darkweald, flying snake monsters tried to kill us. If everything you guys have been telling me is true we need to get out of Tzanagoth's sphere of influence before sunset."

"I'm not dragging you back into the storm to hide for who-knows-how-long just to get out of Darkweald. It's bad enough you're bleeding and I can't make a fire to warm you up. Darkweald is a big forest and isn't all within Tzanagoth's influence. And even if we are within his influence, we'll be fine if we don't do anything to draw attention to ourselves."

"And you know this for a fact?" I demanded.

"I do."

Silence. Again.

Jeez. And I'd thought Cyrus was stingy with sharing information.

But as much as I wanted to know more, I sure as hell wasn't going to beg him for it. I couldn't escape — his grip around me was too tight — and even if I could, I didn't know where I was going and I could barely see. For all I knew, I'd stumble deeper into the forest.

We sat in a long, awkward silence until I couldn't keep my eyes open any longer and I let them slide shut. I wasn't completely recovered from my heat and I was exhausted, not to mention sore and my head was really starting to pound. The heat from Knox's body along with his smoky scent and the warmth around my heart from our shifter connection was too much and I soon fell asleep.

I woke with Knox's arms still wrapped around me and his warm breath gently caressing the side of my face. Sunlight streamed through a thin canopy of trees and that eerie stillness I'd felt the first time I'd stepped into Darkweald wrapped around me.

Knox hadn't lied. We'd been swept all the way into the forest... well, from the wide open area that lay beyond a few tree trunks in front of me, it was clear we were *just* inside the forest.

I wasn't sure how much time had passed, but it didn't look like it was close to sunset, and my gut told me the shadows were going in the wrong direction. Which meant it was the next day. Knox had let me sleep through the night despite what he'd told me about needing to stay awake, and there, about sixty feet away, were Bishop and Cyrus walking across the rocky ground toward us.

Relief flooded me. They were all right. Thank God they were all right.

"Thought you'd try to get ahead of us," Bishop said as he knelt in front of me and flashed me his panty-melting smile.

I tore myself out of Knox's grip and threw myself against Bishop's chest despite my body complaining from having slept cramped against my mate and what I was sure was a stunning collection of bruises from my watery trip down the ravine. I wrapped my arms around him, and he chuckled as he hugged me back, the sound melting the last of the frozen fear sitting heavy in my stomach.

"You're okay?" I asked, pressing my nose into the crook of his neck and inhaling his fresh-cut grass scent. Our shifter connection swelled around my heart and tears stung my eyes at how comforting it was. He was, and would always be, my soul's home.

"We're fine," he murmured, holding me tight before placing his hands on my shoulders and leaning back to look at me. "Better than you."

He brushed his fingers against my temple, sending pain spiking through my skull.

"It's just a few bruises and scratches." I shrugged, feeling every single bruise in that slight movement.

Cyrus huffed, drawing my attention to him. He was shirtless and his pants were ripped and bloody. Three red welts sliced across his chest, indicating just how deep the jackals' claws had cut into him that they couldn't be healed right away with a quick shift.

Bishop, on the other hand, looked fine. But then he'd destroyed his clothes when he'd shifted and had to put on new, clean ones that hid any remaining evidence of the fight.

"She has a nasty bump on her head, a deep cut on her shoulder, and a skinned knee," Knox told him. "Little more than a few bruises and scratches."

"Not enough for an elixir," Cyrus replied. "Come on. We're on the eastern-most side of Darkweald, about as far as we can get from the patrol shed and not the three-quarter day hike we would have had if we'd camped where we were supposed to."

Aaaand somehow our change of camping location had become my fault.

Jeez. I couldn't win with Cyrus. Not that it mattered. He wasn't my mate and wasn't interested in becoming my mate like Bishop was. He was just my brother-in-law and my pack alpha. Someone I was going to be connected to for the rest of my life.

AUDREY

Cyrus led us deeper into Darkweald, following what looked like a game trail — and at times no trail at all — and we passed through the forest without incident.

We also, thankfully, avoided Anakar, the temple complex where I'd first arrived in the realm. I didn't want another run in with Sterling or Royce since they'd already proven they didn't need to be in the same realm as me to control me and threaten my life, and I didn't need another reminder.

And while it would have been nice to know the rip between this realm and mine was gone, I was sure someone would report what was going on with it sometime soon to Cyrus. I could ask him about it later.

We walked all day and reached the patrol shed just after the sun had set. It surprised me that there was no one around. If they were investigating the rip, the shed was the most logical place to make camp. It had a well for clean water, was guaranteed shelter against the elements and any beasts in the area, and was out of Tzanagoth's influence where his spirits couldn't reach them.

Of course, if the rip was closed, there'd be nothing left to study and everyone would have returned to Stonehaven. Either that, or after the flying snake spirit incident, they decided it was too dangerous to stick around.

Cyrus and Bishop got to work building a campfire with the wood piled against the side of the shed, while Knox, much to my surprise, took my Cyrus-assigned duty for the night and filled up the water bucket.

I didn't argue like I would have, like a part of me screamed I had to so I could prove I wasn't worthless. I might have shrugged off my near-death experience in the ravine when talking with Bishop, but my aches had only gotten worse the longer we'd walked, and I was grateful for Knox helping me with anything. I also didn't have high hopes I'd feel better tomorrow.

Tomorrow night, however, I'd sleep in a real bed, be able to have a real shower, and not have to walk any great distance ever again. Hopefully the day after tomorrow, or the day after that, I get back to feeling like myself.

Just one more day to go and this whole, horrible ordeal would be over.

Except it wouldn't be because I was now permanently mate bonded with Knox.

I bit back a sigh, wrapped my thin blanket around me, and snuggled closer to Bishop. One more day and then, good or bad, the rest of my life would begin.

The next morning, Knox took my pack without saying anything, and he and Cyrus led the way back to Stonehaven. I stayed about fifty feet behind them with Bishop even though my heat was over and I no longer needed to keep my distance from them.

"I can't decide if I want to spend a week soaking in a bath or sleeping," I said as I finished my lunch of more dried rations and heaved myself to my feet.

Bishop chuckled. "You could do both, but I don't recommend it without supervision."

I glanced at him, but his back was turned to me and I couldn't tell if he was being literal and serious or flirting with me.

It had to be flirting, right?

"Is that an offer?" I asked, my voice suddenly husky and my cheeks burning with the embarrassed fear that I was wrong.

"Absolutely," he replied, flashing me a smile that made my pulse stall for a breathtaking moment. But then his smile quickly faded. "We're going to have to wait a few days for that though. Even with Nova and Deacon running things, work will still have piled up." His gaze jumped to Knox who was already on the road headed to Stonehaven.

My mate hadn't said anything to me today, but I hadn't gotten the sense he was avoiding me or angry with me like he'd been for most of our journey. It felt more like he didn't know what to say. And while I could sympathize with him, I wasn't going to let him off the hook.

I'd vowed I wouldn't break first and I wasn't going to. No matter how uncomfortable it felt to make an alpha apologize to me.

"I'm going to be busy for the next few days, maybe a week," Bishop added. "But you should take it easy and stay close to the Residence. You've been through an ordeal. You deserve time to recover."

"Yeah." Sour disappointment oozed through me and I pushed it back. Bishop wasn't brushing me off. He was saying he just needed time to take care of pack business.

Besides, I had my relationship with Knox that I had to figure out, along with what I was going to do with the rest of my life. If Cyrus was also busy with pack stuff and didn't demand I make myself useful right away, I could take a few days to decide some things. Things like if I wanted to stay in the Residence, what job I wanted to do, and what I needed to do to become literate — since the magic of this realm let me speak and understand their language but didn't let me read it.

I didn't like the idea of being all on my own, especially when some of Cyrus's and Bishop's betas didn't like me, but I doubted they'd do anything to outright hurt me. This wasn't my old pack after all. If I kept to myself and didn't draw anyone's attention, I'd be fine.

I huffed a bitter laugh.

That plan hadn't worked with my last pack. Was I foolish enough to think it would work with this one?

"But I'll still see you at dinner every night," Bishop continued, his words reigniting the warmth around my heart from our shifter connection even though he wasn't holding me. "Even if you weren't Knox's mate, you'd be welcome at dinner."

Yeah, I thought to myself. I *was* foolish enough to hope everything would work out. I might even be right this time.

Stonehaven came into sight just after dinnertime, and I took in the buildings sprawling down the mountainside, those closest looking like modern buildings and those farther away surrounded by a thick, Medieval-looking stone wall.

If I pretended the older buildings didn't exist, I could have been back home in Oregon. At least until I tilted my gaze up and looked at the two moons, one that looked like the regular moon and one smaller and pinker, reminding me I wasn't in my realm.

As much as I was grateful to be here with an alpha who wanted to protect me and not own me, I still had a lot of confusing emotions about not being on Earth. Emotions that I'd been ignoring because they were insignificant compared to everything else that was going on.

And in reality, even though I was now more or less safe, and my mate bond with Knox had been dealt with — even if the outcome had been disappointing — how I felt about being in this new realm still didn't matter. I couldn't do anything about it and wouldn't go back to Sterling and Royce even if I could.

Although if those two psychopaths weren't a part of the equation, would I feel differently?

There were things I really missed from my realm, like cars and coffee, and my realm had so many things that I wanted to show Bishop. He'd been excited to learn that I'd seen a real angel. How would he react to TV or cell phones? The internet would probably blow his mind.

Hunh.

I didn't know exactly how most things worked, but I knew of things that didn't exist in this world. Perhaps with Whil and some of the pack's inventors and engineers I could share some of humanity's ingenuity and they could figure out an equivalent for their realm. There wasn't electricity here — that I knew of — and I wasn't going to introduce them to fossil fuels, but they had a lot more magic than my realm did. It was literally sleeping in the ground around us.

Maybe I wasn't so useless.

Once Bishop had taken care of his piled-up work, I'd talk to him about sharing what I knew.

Cyrus and Knox — who was still, much to my surprise, in his human form — left the road before we'd made the final turn and crested the last hill to reach the town.

I raised my eyebrows at Bishop once they were out of earshot and he just shrugged.

"Pack business," he said. "We've been gone long enough that once word gets out that we've returned, we might get swarmed, and there are few things they need to take care of before that happens."

I shrugged back. I didn't know what that could possibly be, but then I'd never been an alpha or privy to any of my previous alpha's business.

I pondered Bishop's words as we walked the rest of the way, doing the math on how long it had actually been. When I woke from my heat, the guys had said there were five days left to reach Stonehaven, and yep, we'd walked for five days.

Before that, I'd been unconscious for three days of walking and nine days with my heat. That was seventeen days just to get home, plus the ten it took us to get to the death god's temple.

My pulse lurched. I'd been traveling for almost a month.

I'd been in this realm for a whole month.

Which meant my birthday was in a month. I'd turn twenty-three, and my wolf would still be asleep. If I even had a wolf.

My shock at having been in this realm for a month along with all my fears and uncertainties soured the thought of my upcoming birthday. Not that birthdays had ever been a time for celebration. They were always a reminder that I was lacking, and Merrick and Sterling made sure I was aware of that.

Of course, since I'd only had Mila and no other friends or family, it hadn't really mattered if I'd been able to celebrate my birthday or not.

But shockingly, a part of me had hoped that being away from my old pack this year might be different, that there might be a few people who'd want to help me celebrate the way I'd seen everyone else celebrate.

I glanced at Bishop through my lashes, wondering if I should tell him? Were birthdays something celebrated in this realm? Did I want to draw attention to myself like that?

AUDREY

I WAS STILL FLIPFLOPPING BETWEEN TELLING BISHOP ABOUT MY BIRTHDAY and hoping for some kind of celebration or keeping my mouth shut so I wouldn't be disappointed when we reached the first building at the outskirts of town.

A lanky man about my age, maybe a little younger, stepped out of the shadows, stopping us.

"You're back!" he gasped. Then his wide green eyes swept around us and narrowed with worry. "Where are Cyrus and Knox?"

"They're fine," Bishop assured him. "Taking care of some business before the betas swarm us. Are you our welcome party?"

"Sort of. Deacon set up extra watches since there was a grimalkin attack and told us to keep an eye out for you. You've been gone so long, I was starting to get worried, but now you're back," he replied. "Did you find what you were looking for?"

I shot a glance at Bishop. I didn't know how to answer that and wasn't the wolf in charge. It wasn't my place to say anything.

Bishop shook his head. "Unfortunately, no."

"Well, that sucks." The young man huffed, his gaze jumping to me, his expression brightening. "At least you look better than the last time I saw you," he said as he held out his hand. "I'm Zavier."

I reached to shake it, but Bishop released a low, dangerous growl along with a snap of power, and I jerked my hand back, my pulse pounding. It had been years since I'd heard it, but Merrick used to growl like that. Just before he'd punish me.

I didn't know what I'd done wrong, but it had to be something about shaking Zavier's hand, which reminded me that I couldn't assume things in this realm were the same as mine. For all I knew, I was now off limits for every other man because I was mate bonded.

Except that didn't make sense, especially since the guys had told me they'd have sent me to the heat clinic to have sex with strangers which was a lot more intimate than shaking someone's hand.

Zavier's eyebrows jumped up beneath the hair flopping over his forehead, showing he was just as surprised by Bishop's reaction as I was. Then his gaze dropped to his feet and he took a step back. "Forgive me, alpha. I didn't realize—"

"No," Bishop said, his power vanishing. "Forgive me. It's been a difficult few weeks."

"I mean there's gossip about Cyrus and the outsider, but I—" Zavier began. "I mean I thought— But of course you both can—" His face turned bright red and I didn't know if I should laugh or cry.

If Zavier was a gossip, everyone was going to know before tomorrow morning that Bishop was interested in me. Which was true, but I didn't know how public he wanted to be about us, especially if it came out that I was also Knox's mate.

Except that shouldn't be a problem because he'd already told me that monogamy wasn't a requirement for wolves in this realm.

Cyrus on the other hand was going to be pissed that people were still talking about an *us* that didn't exist. We'd been gone almost a month and whatever he'd said before we'd left hadn't been enough to squash the rumors.

"The outsider's name is Audrey," Bishop replied, saving Zavier from any more incomplete sentences. "And she's no longer an outsider. She's pack." He placed a possessive hand on my shoulder and a whisper of power slipped his control.

Zavier bobbed his head and shifted back another step. "Understood, alpha. Welcome to the Stonehaven pack, Audrey."

His tone was overly formal, and his gaze focused on my right ear as if I were an alpha and he didn't want to make eye contact and challenge me.

Swell. I could see other members of the pack being pissed that a shifter who couldn't even shift was being treated like an alpha. I could only pray that Zavier wasn't a gossip and he wouldn't tell everyone how he thought they should behave around me.

I also prayed that Bishop got ahold of himself. I didn't even know what had set him off. It wasn't like Zavier had been rude to me.

Two guys a few feet up the street spotted Bishop and waved. He nodded in response, placed a hand on my lower back, and urged me forward up the busy main street and away from Zavier and the awkwardness.

More people looked at us and nodded, smiled, or waved but thankfully didn't approach. I was too tired and sore to put on a brave face around strangers and was suddenly uncertain about where I stood with Bishop.

"So, ah... What was that about?" I asked once we were far enough away from Zavier. I tried to keep my voice steady but couldn't help the sliver of fear creeping into it. Bishop had seemed so relaxed and kind, and I'd never seen him throw his alpha power around like that.

Of course, that was a reminder that I barely knew him. I'd only been in Stonehaven a few days before it had just been the four of us walking through the wilderness. For all I knew, he had all the undesirable alpha traits and I just hadn't seen them yet.

"Sorry," he mumbled as he palmed the back of his neck and looked sheepish. "He was checking you out and I just got... angry."

Angry? I bit the inside of my cheek to stay silent. It was best to keep my mouth shut. Looking embarrassed for overreacting was the behavior I'd expect from Bishop. But being angry for no reason wasn't like him. I'd been in that conversation, too, and Zavier hadn't been checking me out. Who'd want to check out someone like me? That kind of response was more like Knox.

My pulse stuttered.

"Could your twin bond be influencing you?" I asked, my voice frustratingly small because if it was the twin bond, that could mean no matter what Knox had said about Bishop's feelings for me, they weren't real. They were just from my mating bond with Knox.

"Probably," Bishop said with a sigh, making my throat tighten.

What he felt for me wasn't real.

"Hey, no." He tugged me to the side of the road, hooked his thumb under my chin, and tipped my head up, forcing me to look at him. "Not like that. What I feel for you is all me. It has nothing to do with my connection with Knox. He's stressed right now and he expresses that with anger which sometimes puts me on edge." His expression softened and he huffed a soft laugh. "I never expected it'd make me possessive."

"Never been jealous, hunh?" I tentatively teased.

"Oh, I've been jealous about a lot of things, like how Cyrus always seems to have it together, or how Knox is the best hunter in the pack and I'm not even in the top twenty." He flashed me a wry smile and offered me the crook of his elbow. "But I've never been jealous over a woman. What she does is always her choice and only my business if it involves me."

I hooked my arm around his and let him continue to escort me up the main road. "So, I can shake hands with any guy I want?"

"You can do more than shake hands." He rumbled again, the sound low and soft in his chest, and he released another sigh. "My wolf would prefer if you just stuck with shaking hands."

So, he wouldn't control me, but his wolf, the most primal part of his being, wanted me for himself. Or at least, himself and his brother... brothers?

The thought sent warmth rushing through me. His wolf wanting to control what I did should have bothered me, but instead it sent a thrill rushing through me. He *wanted* me. No one had ever wanted me, and I trusted that Bishop had enough control of his wolf that he wouldn't let him abuse our relationship.

"So, no conversations?" I asked, more confident in my teasing. "What about brief eye contact? Should I avoid other women as well?"

"All of the above," he said with overexaggerated seriousness. "I decree that only blind, mute servants shall attend to you and everyone will have to wear blindfolds when you wish to walk about the town."

"Everyone, hunh?" I laughed with him. "That seems dangerous."

"Seriously, though. Even if Knox is around, you can do and say what you want with whoever you want. You don't belong to him or me or anyone."

I squeezed his arm in thanks. "There might still be some social rules that I don't know about and inevitably mess up," I replied, turning serious. "You behave like everyone back home — better even — and I understand your language and you don't have an accent. Sometimes I forget this is a different realm and a different culture. I don't know what I don't know, and you don't know it, either, so you can't help me avoid it."

"That's a lot of *don't knows.*" He bumped my shoulder with his, drawing my gaze up to see the warmth and affection in his brown eyes. "It'll be all right. You're not alone anymore, Audrey. You've got me." His wry expression deepened, his eyes sparkling with laughter. "And believe it or not, you've got Knox. His social skills suck, but for what it's worth, he won't betray you."

Because the bond wouldn't let him.

But that thought didn't ring true. Knox was harsh and gruff and might not like me for putting us in an unwinnable situation, but I knew in my soul he'd never purposely be cruel. Not like Sterling had been for all of my teen years and not like Royce when he'd tricked me into thinking we were fated mates.

"Speaking of having your back," Bishop said as we passed through the open, unguarded gate in the thick stone Old Town wall. "We all agreed that you can't keep staying in the guest room."

"So where will I be staying?" After the conversation we just had, I didn't think they were going to throw me out of the alpha's residence to fend for myself, but I did fear that they were going to move me in with Knox, something I wasn't at all ready for.

"A guest suite. You need more space to call your own to figure out what you want to do. Something a little less temporary. The suite has a bathroom, bedroom, and a sitting room."

"I'm pretty sure I can think just fine in the bedroom you've already given me," I instinctively replied, years of declining big *gifts* that were really traps having taught me to say no to everything. No matter how much I wanted it, it was always safer to turn it down even if that meant being reprimanded for being ungrateful.

"It's already been decided. By now Cyrus has already had someone move your clothes."

Clothes that they'd also bought me.

"I can't keep taking advantage of your good will."

"You're not just pack now. You're family," Bishop said. "Hopefully soon you'll be family twice over when you accept me as a mate as well."

My pulse fluttered in anticipation of the thought, even as a whisper of fear curled in my stomach. I wanted so desperately to believe him, believe everything was as it looked to be, but I couldn't kill that sliver of worry that I was wrong and I was going to go back to living in a nightmare.

We reached the gate in the stone wall surrounding the Residence and passed through. Beyond, the Residence was highlighted by a band of sunlight streaming between two mountain peaks as if the realm were putting the building on display. And it was worthy of display, looking like a spectacular, enormous Medieval castle with multiple turrets and wings and a grand front door.

"You belong in the Residence with your mate," Bishop said.

But that was only if my relationship with Knox had been normal, if I'd actually been chosen. At the moment, I was his dirty little secret.

My throat tightened at the thought. "Is he going to acknowledge me?"

The muscles in Bishop's jaw flexed.

That was a no.

"It's okay," I replied, even though he hadn't actually said anything, the sting of being rejected yet again making my eyes burn with tears I didn't want to cry. "Our mating wasn't because either of us wanted it. Best not to let the pack think there's more between us than there actually is."

"He doesn't want the mating to create trouble for you until the pack knows you. He'd never willingly mate with someone, so there's going to be questions."

"Not ever?"

Bishop shrugged as we entered the Residence, stepping into the grand front entrance with its enormous glittering chandelier, thick red carpet, and sweeping staircase. The staircase started with stairs on either side of the entranceway then joined halfway up to create a grand archway over the doorway to a large ballroom before splitting again and leading to the wings on either side of the building.

My room had been up the stairs, to the left, and a few doors down, but instead of taking the stairs, Bishop led me down the righthand ground-floor hall and along a series of other halls.

"I'd like to think he would have found someone on his own eventually, but I know I was just fooling myself. He'd been withdrawing more and more, not coming back to us like we hoped," he said, and I could tell there was more behind his words than he was saying. Knox had left them for some reason and it didn't sound as if he'd willingly returned. "But then you came, and I've seen more glimpses of my real brother than I ever did before... well... everything. It's not your place to heal him and I don't expect you to, but just being in his life has helped."

We stopped at a wooden door carved with sweeping scrollwork and a shiny silver doorknob. It was much fancier than the door of my previous room.

"Audrey," Bishop said, his voice low, sending a shiver of attraction slipping down my spine.

I raised my gaze to meet his and fell into his warm brown eyes, mesmerized by the bright green flecks. God, he was so beautiful and kind. I had no idea how I'd gotten so lucky that I'd just fallen into his life and he accepted me. If someone else had found me, my time in this realm could have been very different.

The memory of him pushing into me as I begged for more more more rushed through me along with a wave of heated embarrassment.

After what had happened, it could have been really awkward between us, but while I still felt flashes of embarrassment, Bishop had never made me feel uncomfortable.

"I'm glad you came to us." His gaze dipped to my lips and my pulse fluttered with anticipation.

We hadn't done more than cuddle since my heat. I hadn't felt as if I was ready for more and he hadn't brought it up, somehow just knowing I needed space.

But now my insides were warm, the heat sinking lower and lower, and the embarrassing memories were also exciting.

"I'm glad you came to *me*," he said, his voice husky, sending shivers of anticipation racing down my spine.

AUDREY

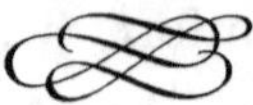

My pulse pounding, half in fear of rejection and half in hope, I rose onto my toes and brushed my lips against Bishop's. It was a test to see if the connection I felt between us was still there after my heat and not my imagination.

A rumble rattled in his chest again, the vibration somehow hotter and more sensual than his angry growl, fueling my confidence.

He felt it, too, the need, the yearning. The attraction was still as strong as ever and with a soft moan, I tangled my fingers in his hair and tugged him closer so I could deepen our kiss.

Without hesitation, he dipped in and captured the back of my waist with his arm to steady me but let me stay in control of the kiss until both of our breaths came too fast and my body was hot and tingly.

Then he took over, pinning me against the door and plundering my mouth with a desire that stole my breath and left no doubt about his intentions.

"Audrey," he groaned as he jerked away and pressed his forehead to mine. "If I didn't have to check in with my betas—" He brushed his thumb over my cheek then took a jerky step back. "What just happened here, between us— It's a promise for more to come."

My pulse throbbed, my body aching with the need for more but I nodded instead and didn't press for more. Desire and disappointment warred inside me, but strangely no sadness. He wasn't rejecting me. He was saying 'not right now.'

And God! I couldn't wait for him to fulfill that promise, couldn't wait to be with him again when I was conscious enough to enjoy it.

"Take a bath and relax. I'll have dinner brought to your room." He cupped my cheek, his attention on my lips as if he were going to kiss me again before pulling even farther away. "Sleep as long as you like. You deserve it, and there's no need for you to be on any kind of schedule until you've decided your future."

He quickly strode away as if walking too slowly or looking back would break his willpower.

I watched him go until he stepped out of sight, then sighed and opened the door to my new room.

Inside was an opulent room done in creams, tans, and browns with gold accents. A large fireplace sat against the lefthand wall with a mantle covered in scrollwork that matched the door.

In fact, everything was covered in matching scrollwork: the couch and matching chairs' wooden frames, the dark wood four-person dining room table with its matching chairs, and everything else that could be ornamented. It had to have taken a craftsman months, possibly even years to complete such detailed and extensive work.

The plush couch and chairs faced the fireplace, creating a conversation area, while the table sat at the back and to my right, leaving room for the French doors — which I doubted were called French doors in this realm — that led onto a small patio made private by a flowering hedge and planter boxes.

The room was easily three times the size of the bedroom I'd originally been in, and I hadn't even stepped into my new bedroom or attached bathroom.

That thought sent a mix of pleasure and discomfort rushing through me. I liked the idea that Bishop wanted to pamper me, but I also felt like I was drawing attention to myself, and being noticed was dangerous.

My new bedroom was just as opulent as the sitting room with a large canopy bed, the mattress big enough that it would have been considered extra king size in my realm, a full-length mirror that could show two people standing side-by-side, and a large wardrobe.

It sent more mixed palpitations rushing through me. When Bishop had said I needed more space, I hadn't expected it to also come with an upgrade to first class.

My few pieces of clothing had been hung in the wardrobe, barely taking up any space, and I vowed *I* would be the one to fill it. Not Bishop. I needed to start doing things on my own. I *wanted* to.

And now I could. Here, in this new realm, I was my own person and I'd been given a second chance. I didn't want to let it go to waste by becoming dependent on Bishop. I wasn't afraid of hard work, and I was sure I could find a way to earn my place in this pack in a way that wasn't just as Knox's and Bishop's mate.

The bathroom was similar to the one I'd used before — except this one was private, not shared with the other rooms in the hall. It had shiny chrome fixtures and white marble everything: floors, counters, and tiles. A tub, larger than the previous one, sat at the back, looking just as welcoming even though it didn't sit in a bay window overlooking a garden, and the stand-up, glassed-in shower was also larger, big enough for three people.

Just like the other bathroom, it was fully stocked, and I turned on the water to fill the tub and dropped in some bath salts that smelled fruity and sweet.

With a groan, I pulled off my boots and peeled away my filthy shirt and pants. My skin was mottled with scratches and bruises from being swept away in the flashflood, and I was so dirty, I felt as if I should peel my skin off, too, and throw it on the floor with my clothes. I really didn't want to get in the bath while covered in filth. That would just be gross.

New plan!

I slowed the stream of water filling the tub, hopped into the shower, and scrubbed away all the grime that had built up from having walked for almost a month with only two showers and a handful of cold dunks in the river.

By the time I'd scrubbed down and washed my hair twice, the tub was full, and I sank into its sweet-smelling warm embrace and let my mind go blank.

But as I sat there half staring at the marble tiles and half drifting off, an uneasiness grew in my chest. The weight slowly getting heavier and heavier, twisting into something cold and sour.

I shifted, hoping a change of position would relax me, but the uneasiness continued to grow.

It had to be the room. That was the only thing that had really changed in the last little while. It couldn't have been returning to Stonehaven. I hadn't felt like this for the few days I was here before we left for the death god's temple.

No. It had to be the new *suite*. It was too much, too luxurious. Someone like me wasn't given a room like this without it being a trick or a mistake and I felt like it was going to be ripped away any second and I was going to be banished to the basement. Or rather, since this was a castle, the dungeon.

Did Cyrus even know Bishop had moved me to a suite? Bishop had said they'd all agreed, but upgrading someone with almost no useful skills didn't seem Cyrus's style. I didn't deserve a room like this. I barely deserved the room I'd originally been given.

Except that was something Merrick and Sterling would tell me, and Bishop wasn't like them. Cyrus and Knox weren't like them, either. They might not have welcomed me or thought highly of me, but they hadn't tricked or punished me.

Yet, a small voice whispered inside me, even as my heart and soul assured me it would never happen. The mating bond might let Knox reject me and be angry with me, but it would never let him be purposefully cruel.

And while Cyrus was tough and didn't sugarcoat things, he didn't strike me as cruel either. Without a doubt, all of them would eventually do things to hurt me, but their intent would never be malicious.

Which meant I just had to get over myself and accept the fact that someone wanted to do something nice for me with no strings attached.

Really.

Except the sense of unease didn't diminish with my certainty that the guys weren't screwing with me. It was going to take a while to let go of all the doubts and fears Merrick had driven into me for far too many years, and telling myself things were different wasn't what would help. I needed proof. I needed Bishop and Knox and Cyrus to keep treating me differently until it finally sunk in. My own words to myself didn't matter.

And neither did soaking in the bath.

I was still too worked up. I could spend all day in the warm water and it still wasn't going to relax me.

With a sigh, I climbed out of the tub, dried off, and wrapped myself in the big, fluffy robe hanging on the hook behind the door.

While I'd been in the bath, someone had entered my suite and set a large silver tray with my dinner on the table in the living room. That only added to my unease. I didn't like that anyone could just come and go from my suite. I should have thought to lock the door, but I'd been distracted by Bishop's kiss on top of being tired from our long journey.

Had that been Bishop's intent? To distract me?

No. Just no!

I couldn't start doubting him. He'd taken care of me and been kind and sweet for the entire journey. I had to break the cycle of mistrust and doubt.

But the unease kept growing, twisting in my chest, making me twitchy.

What the hell was wrong with me?

I hadn't been afraid like this in the entire time we'd been traveling and there'd been times when I'd be in serious danger.

But my current fear wasn't because my life was being threatened. It was the fear that the safety and comfort I felt with these men in this realm wasn't real, that it was all a trick, just like my mating bond with Royce.

I paced the room, hoping movement would burn away the tightness that was slowly squeezing my chest, but it didn't help. I picked at my meal, a pasta in cream sauce with a side salad but couldn't bring myself to eat much despite having been ecstatic about not eating camp food when I'd first returned to the city.

Jeez.

I collapsed on the bed and buried my face in a pillow. Sleep — if I could fall asleep — was my last option before I broke down and ran screaming through the halls.

With a groan, I rolled over and pressed my hands against my chest. It was so tight now that it was hard to breathe, my unease blossoming into full anxiety.

I could only pray sleep would reset my brain and I'd no longer be freaking out in the morning.

AUDREY

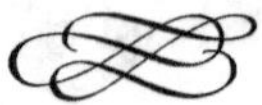

A LOW, MENACING CHUCKLE WHISPERED OVER ME, AND I WRENCHED around, searching for whoever was laughing, my pulse racing.

Once again, I stood in my old pack's sacred grove, surrounded by undulating red mist. And while logically I knew being back on earth was impossible and I had to be dreaming, the rest of me was too afraid to care. The monster was coming and this time it would eat me.

I bolted into the thick underbrush, running like I had that horrible night, barely able to see in the darkness. I didn't care when the shrub and tree branches sliced at my skin or I bashed my shins or bare toes against rocks, I ran as hard and as fast as I could. I had to get away. I couldn't get caught.

Lightning lit the forest around me, a shocking burst of light that passed too quickly for me to tell where I was before plunging me back into darkness. A second later, the menacing laugh returned, now a rolling thunder and part of the storm closing in on me.

"You can't escape," a voice hissed.

"I can. I did," I yelled back, fighting to be heard over another roll of thunderous laughter. "I'm in a different realm. You can't get me."

Ahead, a hint of soft light glowed through the thick branches and my pulse leaped with hope. The way out of the forest and this nightmare.

With a growl of determination, I picked up my pace, shoving through a dense bush with sharp thorns, and ran back into the sacred grove.

No.

I twisted to look behind me. The bush I'd pushed through was gone and had become the familiar path between the two towering oaks that the pack used to enter the grove.

How did I get back here?

It was easy to get lost and turned around in the forest, but I couldn't have run in a wide circle. Not without hitting a recognizable landmark first. And the bush I pushed through. It had just disappeared.

Because it's a dream, my logical voice cried, barely audible against another burst of thunder.

"It's because you can't escape me," Sterling replied, his voice echoing around me, sending shivers of fear rushing down my spine.

"You can't escape *us.*" Royce stepped out of the darkness, his expression filled with the same worry he'd had when he'd tricked me into starting the mating vows despite his ominous words.

"I did escape you," I insisted even as my body took a step toward him.

"You can't escape fate." He held out his arms and my body stepped into his embrace, despite my mind screaming at me to run the other way. *Now. Run now!* "You belong to me."

He tugged me closer and captured my lips in the same scorching kiss from before. It was just as powerful and overwhelming, but instead of igniting a dizzy desire, it ignited fear. Now I knew the truth, knew that what I'd felt had all been a manipulation of magic, a trap I'd blindly jumped headlong into.

"No," I gasped against his lips, trying to shove him away. "I refuted you. I don't belong to you."

"You said the vow," he sneered, his fingers tangling in my hair and painfully jerking my head back, exposing my neck. "You practically threw yourself at me, so desperate for someone to love you."

"No."

"Yes." With a growl, he nipped my lips with wolf-sharpened teeth, drawing blood and a flicker of pain, tighten his grip around my waist, and ground his hard length against my belly. "You bound your soul to mine, Audrey. You belong to me."

"That's not true. I'm bound to Knox." Even before Knox and I had sealed the bond, I'd known I was bound to him. I felt nothing for Royce and I never would.

Royce shoved his hand down the front of my dress and roughly palmed my breast as his teeth grazed over my collarbone.

"You could fuck their whole pack, but you'd still be mine." He pushed the top of my dress down and sucked on my nipple with a force that shot a gut-churning mix of pain and desire to my core.

"I don't want you. I never wanted you." I shoved at his head, trying to get him away from me, but he sucked harder, and the pain turned into liquid need. It burned through me like the feverish heat I'd just survived and my knees buckled.

"You do want me." He tightened his grip in my hair and bit down hard on the flesh about my nipple, his sharp canines drawing blood.

More pain sliced through me and my core clenched in anticipation.

"No." No no no.

This wasn't me. I didn't want him. He was manipulating me just like he'd manipulated me that horrible night.

I heaved in his grip. He was a psychopath. I couldn't be attracted to a psychopath. I couldn't be bound to one.

And I wasn't.

I was *not*.

Because this was some sick nightmare, all my worst fears coming true, and I couldn't make myself wake up or break free.

"Stop," I begged, tears blurring my vision. I clawed at his face and hands, anything to get away from him, but my nails just skidded over his skin, not even drawing lines on his flesh. "I'm bonded with Knox. Not you."

"But you're a greedy cunt," he sneered. "You want his brothers, too. You want anyone. You want me."

"I don't want you!" I screamed, slamming my fist as hard as I could against his temple.

With a roar, he shoved me and my knees slammed onto the hard ground. I scrambled away from him, my body screaming in pain, my transformation dress ripped down the front and my chest bleeding from Royce's claws just like that horrible night.

"I'll never want you. You're a monster!"

"But I have you." His lips curled back in a vicious smile and tendrils of black smoke lashed around my body, seizing my arms and legs and pinning me to the ground.

The inky tendrils raced around my waist digging into my skin and pinching my nipples, but — thank God — my body didn't heat with desire and betray me this time. Only pain and fear roared through me, making me tremble and tightening my chest until I could barely breathe.

"I'll never be yours," I gasped, heaving and snarling, determined to be free, despite the panic roaring through me. "If I ever see you again, I'll kill you."

Royce threw his head back and howled with laughter. "You won't even be able to touch me."

The tendrils oozed up my neck and started to tighten.

"I will," I gasped, heaving and thrashing. "I'll kill you." I wrenched one hand free and clawed at the smoke, tearing into it as if I had claws, the wildness from my dreams with Knox rising up within me, giving me a crazy, manic strength.

"I'll never be yours," I screamed. "I'll kill you!"

AUDREY

I JERKED AWAKE, MY PULSE RACING, MY BODY STICKY WITH SWEAT AND ugly red scratches up and down my arms and around my neck from where the sticky black smoke had captured me in my dream. The unease sat tight and heavy in my chest, worse than before I went to bed, and tears rolled down my cheeks.

Furious, I wiped them away. I was done with him, done with all of them. They couldn't reach me and I was finally safe.

I. Was. Safe.

God, why couldn't I make myself believe that?

I dragged my bleary gaze to the window, the curtains still open since I'd collapsed on the bed and hadn't bothered to shut them.

Dawn was just starting to lighten the sky, which meant I'd slept for most of the night, but I didn't feel like it. I was still exhausted, and the unease still seethed inside me and made me tremble.

With a groan of frustration, I got out of bed and slipped into a dark blue, backless dress with a high neckline that hid the scratches at my throat and was made from a material thick enough that it wouldn't show off my nipples. Not that I had to worry about being perpetually turned on now that my heat was over.

Normally I would have preferred a shirt and pair of pants, but for some reason I balked at the idea. I wanted to look pretty just in case I came across Bishop, and he'd spent the last month watching me get dirtier and dirtier in a shirt and pants. I didn't want to remind him of that. I wanted to remind him of the woman in the pretty dress he'd made love to the night of the wedding in Kelna.

Trying to remind myself that I likely wouldn't see Bishop until dinner and that I shouldn't get my hopes up, I headed down the quiet halls to the kitchen.

Inside, two women — one middle-aged and the other about my age — were making morning pastries. The young woman sang and danced as she worked while the old woman was more restrained and just hummed along with her. They were still in the early stages of their work with the young woman filling a pan with what looked like cinnamon rolls and the older one working on a batter that I guessed was intended for the empty muffin tray on the counter beside her.

Breakfast clearly wasn't ready, but I suspected if I asked, there'd be fruit and bread in the fridge.

Except, even though I hadn't eaten a lot last night, I wasn't hungry. The unease was like a vise around my chest, making it hard to breathe, and it fed an angry irritation that was sure to get me in trouble if I talked to anyone.

And since I still wasn't entirely sure where I stood with Cyrus and the pack, I didn't want to risk pissing off the wrong person. In my old pack, the wrong person had been everyone except my friend Mila. I had to assume until I knew otherwise that it was the same here.

Which meant it was best to step away before one of them saw me.

And here I was being terrified of reprisal from everyone once again.

The thought made me want to scream and I hurried out the front door, hoping that being outside would help.

But the crisp air and the peaceful early morning silence did nothing to diminish the unease and frustration and anger — so much anger — boiling inside me.

Jeez. What was wrong with me?

I'd never been so angry in my life.

But maybe it was about time. I'd barely stood up for myself when I was a child and Merrick had punished that away within a year of living with him. Now I was free from him and his son. Perhaps all the rage and fear I'd kept bottled up all the years had finally broken free.

If that was the case, I needed to figure out how to get rid of it before I yelled at the wrong person. Just because I was Knox's mate and Bishop was romantically interested in me, didn't mean I had immunity from bad behavior.

Sure, shifters tended to be more volatile in nature than other supers, but losing it for no apparent reason was still bad.

I marched around the Residence's grounds. My emotions roiled inside me and my thoughts were a jumble, searching for a reason for why I'd finally broken. Then my thoughts jumped to my horrible childhood then to the terrifying moment when that monster had started to eat Merrick while he'd still been alive then back to the beginning again. Around and around and around I went.

It wasn't fair.

It just God damned wasn't fair.

And while logically I knew life wasn't fair, I couldn't get my emotions under control. All that blood, all of my *father's* blood, splattering the bathtub tiles, all the punishments, all the fear about when Sterling would attack next, building and building until I couldn't breathe. All the hope Royce had given me in the blink of an eye before crushing it completely.

How dare they! How dare all of them.

I'd been trapped in my life through my naivety and my position in my pack, and I was still trapped. I was trapped in my bond with Knox and I was trapped in my own body, my wolf form locked away forever.

A ferocious wildness rose inside me, and I threw my head back and screamed, desperate to release the pressure crushing my chest.

Tears of heartache and frustration and emotions I couldn't even recognize streamed down my cheeks. I could be brave for Bishop, and I could hold out until Knox apologized for hurting me, but I was always going to be broken. Always.

The sudden need to escape crashed over me. It consumed every other thought and feeling, propelling me into a wild run out the Residence's gates, through Old Town's narrow winding streets, and out into the newer part of Stonehaven. I ran and ran and ran as if I could run away from the hurt and fear and shame inside me.

As if I could run away from who I was and become someone else.

I ran until I was straining for breath, covered in sweat, and my whole body trembled from exertion, and then I sagged against an alley wall damp with morning dew.

The wildness still churned inside me, desperate to escape, furious at being trapped, the emotions so strong they felt like they belonged to someone else. Weak little Audrey would never feel anything so deeply. She'd never scream and run like a mad woman.

But maybe that was what I was now. A mad woman. Maybe I'd finally lost it, my soul broken, just like my father's. Just like my nightmares had whispered to me.

I raked my hands through my hair, pushing it away from my face, and sucked in deep breaths, determined to steady myself.

Each inhalation hurt my chest, the pressure and unease still clawing inside me, and the urge to run still made me twitch, but both sensations started feeling foreign as if they weren't mine as if they belonged to—

Knox.

My pulse stuttered. The need to escape and the blinding white rage were Knox's emotions, and they were fueling my own insecurities.

Something was happening with him, something that was making him feel so strongly he was influencing my emotions through our mating bond.

I pressed my hands over my chest as if that would somehow focus my connection on our bond. I needed to distance myself from him and regain control. It was bad enough he could physically control me with his alpha power. Now he could make me feel things I wasn't really feeling through our bond.

But the second I thought that, I knew he wasn't doing it on

purpose. He was in trouble and the only way to stop the onslaught of unwanted emotions was to help him. Now. Now now now.

Except I had no idea where he was.

Hell, I didn't even know where *I* was.

I hurried out of the alley and looked down the street. From the street's width and the large stone paving tiles, as well as the smaller brick on the two- and three-story buildings on either side, I had to be in a newer part of town.

I didn't recognize any of the buildings and from where I stood I couldn't see the Old Town wall. There were about a dozen people on the street. Most were carrying bags and heading somewhere — off to work maybe? — while a few were setting out sandwich boards and turning on lights in the nearby stores.

From the angle of the shadows and the mountains looming to my right, I guessed I was facing southeast, and since I couldn't see Old Town, that meant it was behind me. But when I turned to head the other way and return to the Residence, the pressure of Knox's emotions surged, stealing my breath and filling me with a desperate urgency.

I jerked back to the southeast and the pressure turned into a sharp pull, yanking me forward a few steps before I realized what I was doing.

I hadn't been running blindly through town. Knox's emotions were pulling me to him... because he needed me. Whether he knew it or not, his overwhelming emotions were a call for help. One that, even if I wanted to, I couldn't deny.

I took off, letting the pull lead me down the street. The path drew up close to the mountainside before opening into an enormous courtyard blocked in by the mountain and two-story buildings on either side.

Pillars had been carved into the side of the mountain framing half a dozen large openings and the pull led me through the closest one into a dimly lit hall. The pressure surged again and I ran down the hall, faster and faster. The rage that had consumed me earlier threatened to take over and I knew if I didn't get to Knox soon, I'd lose myself to it again.

Knox was inside and the sense of urgency squeezed tighter.

I bolted down the hall. Large faintly glowing stones placed every twenty feet along the wall at head-height offered barely enough illumination for me to see with my practically-human vision, but it was enough to keep from tripping and to spot the tunnel leading deeper into the mountain.

This way. Hurry. Hurry. Run. Fight. Kill.

More light, brighter than what was in the hall, shone from the end of the tunnel, and I raced toward it, straight to a closed metal gate.

Shit.

I grabbed the cold bars and heaved, but the gate wouldn't budge. It was locked.

No! I had to keep going. It was the only way to stop the emotional onslaught before it took over again.

Beyond the gate lay an arena lit well enough to see everything in the center, but not so bright it was blinding. It had been built in an enormous cavern in the heart of the mountain and had a polished stone floor, a wall about a foot taller than me surrounding the "field," and two dozen rows of bench seating surrounding it.

Knox, in his wolf form, prowled the arena floor, snarling and baring his teeth. Pools of blood darkened the floor with a ripped piece of clothing lying in the center of the largest one. He looked as if he were a real wolf trapped in a cage and not a shifter, his movements jerky and wild.

I pressed a hand against my chest, clinging to the gate with my other hand to keep standing, and focused on the pressure inside me. This close to Knox, the pull felt like it was tearing my soul from my chest, and a rage and primal wildness that needed to rip everything apart threatened to seize me.

I wrenched my eyes open and strained to suck in a steadying breath. The emotions coming through the bond had exploded into a vortex that tore at my insides and likely tore at his as well.

For whatever reason, the primal core of his wolf was devouring the human half of his soul, and if it succeeded, I'd lose my mate forever.

I had to get in there. I had to save him.

The lock on the gate required a key that I didn't have, so I swept my gaze around, looking for it or a way up to the arena's seating, anything that would help.

There. About ten feet behind me. A passage I hadn't noticed because I'd been focused on the gate and the light beyond it.

I rushed into the passage, up the short set of stairs into the first row of benches, and climbed over the edge of the wall determined to get into the arena as fast as possible. If I hung from my fingertips, the fall was only a foot or two, but the stone was smooth and I'd barely gotten turned around and over the edge, when my fingers slipped and I crashed to the arena floor, landing on my butt.

A low growl jerked my attention up and I locked gazes with Knox as he bolted toward me with no glimmer of recognition in his eyes.

My pulse stuttered.

He wouldn't hurt me. I was his mate. If I died, he died. But did his animal half understand that? He was so angry, so determined to kill everything.

"Audrey!"

A wave of power crashed over me along with the sudden need to run away. I wrenched my gaze around the arena, searching for a way to escape even as a part of me screamed that the impetus came from someone's alpha power, not me.

On the far side, Cyrus and Deacon leaped over the wall to the arena floor their expressions filled with panic and raced toward me.

Both guys looked like they'd already fought with a feral wolf and barely escaped with their lives, and if all the unease churning inside me came from Knox then that meant they'd been fighting with him since last night.

How had it gotten so bad? And why hadn't they shifted out their injuries? Unless, of course, they were bad enough they feared the shift would exhaust them and they wouldn't be able to keep doing whatever they were doing with Knox.

Cyrus, who still wore the pants he'd worn yesterday morning indicating that he and Knox had gone straight to this arena when we'd returned to Stonehaven, had lost his shirt and held one arm against his stomach. Blood smeared his chest and ran from beneath his arm and down his legs, soaking into his pants, while Deacon's whole right side was bloody. He held his right arm to his chest, blood leaking from long gashes that ran from his shoulder to his elbow.

Behind them, Bishop lay on a bench, not moving, and my pulse lurched with a new fear. I couldn't see if he was injured, but I also couldn't see if he was breathing.

Oh, God! Had Knox done that?

"Run!" Cyrus roared at me and another burst of power made my muscles tense.

But there wasn't anywhere to go and the command only added to the emotions crushing my chest. I couldn't climb back up the wall. It was too tall. The closest gate was locked. And there was no way in hell I'd be able to outrun a wolf.

And now I was no longer certain that Knox wouldn't hurt me.

He'd mauled Cyrus and hurt Bishop and they were his brothers. I was just some weak little girl who'd forced a mating bond on him.

AUDREY

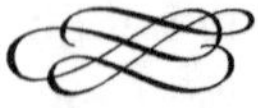

escape wasn't working.

An enormous wave of power slammed into me, Cyrus willing to freeze me in place to control his brother, and I dropped to my knees before I could even think of doing anything else.

But Knox kept running straight for me, his eyes wild and his teeth bared, Cyrus's power not affecting him.

"I. Said. Stop." The pressure of Cyrus's power increased, and darkness swept across my vision, narrowing it down to a pinprick where I was focused on the massive black wolf barreling toward me.

"Knox," I gasped, his name a whisper on my lips as he crashed into me.

God. This was it. He was going to kill me.

The impact knocked me onto my back, and he pinned me down with his front paws and clamped his teeth around my throat.

My pulse *thu-thudded*, straining against Knox's physical and emotional weight along with the weight of Cyrus's power that crashed again and again, stronger and stronger, with his desperate attempts to control Knox.

But Knox didn't move, didn't even raise his head to look at his brother, who was clearly more of a threat than me. His hot wet breath huffed against my throat and he released a low growl.

Mine, his wolf snarled in my head, his voice filled with rage.

Black specks danced across my vision and I fought to breathe even as my body shook with fear. With a snap of his jaw, Knox could kill me.

Mine mine mine. Knox's wolf released my throat and jerked his attention to Cyrus and Deacon, stopping them a good sixty feet away from us with a low, dangerous growl. *Mine.*

He looked ready to attack, his teeth bared, his body tense.

Mine.

"Let her go, Knox." Cyrus took another step closer, his claws extending from his fingertips, and the muscles in Knox's back legs bunched.

He was going to attack, and while Cyrus and Deacon were two of the most powerful shifters I'd ever met, they were already bleeding. A lot. I didn't want to think about the damage Knox's wolf would do if he thought they were trying to take what was his.

Bishop had said wolves in this realm weren't possessive, but I wasn't sure that applied to Knox, or at least Knox's wolf.

Mine, he roared again, adding a suffocating wave of his own alpha power to the already suffocating mix.

"I am," I gasped, praying that he wanted to protect and not hurt me and cupping his furry cheek with a trembling hand.

The touch drew his attention away from his brother and Deacon and back to me, and his dark eyes, filled with vibrant green flecks, captured me, stealing my breath and flooding me with his emotions: rage, fear, yearning... hurt.

I didn't know why he hurt, but I recognized that he, too, was broken in ways others didn't see or understand. I also felt his acceptance, or what had been his acceptance of how he thought he was before I'd come along, and the agony that he wasn't worthy of having a mate.

I bit back a bitter laugh. *I* was the one who wasn't worthy in our relationship. I couldn't even shift.

He growled, his wolf pushing back his human emotions and insecurities and replacing them with a blinding fury. Those emotions would never get in the way again, not so long as his wolf was in control.

But that wasn't good for him or me or anyone. The wolf half of a shifter's soul was his primal half. It didn't understand complex emotions or the need to sometimes sacrifice those emotions to protect someone.

Like protecting a girl who didn't know he was broken.

The realization of what had happened hit me, and I brushed both hands into his thick fur, urging him to keep looking at me. He hadn't taken his wolf form since before I'd had sex with Bishop, a form I'd been told — and had seen for myself — that he preferred. Which meant he'd been actively suppressing his wolf.

If his wolf was determined to keep me as a mate, then it would have taken everything he had to keep that half of his soul from taking over while I'd been suffering through my heat. He might have even had to collar his wolf to keep him contained.

And now his wolf was pissed, had taken over, and was never letting go of their body.

"I *am* yours," I repeated, praying his wolf could sense my sincerity. "But I'm also his."

I wouldn't be able to have a relationship with him without his human form, and while his wolf might even be strong enough to shift into a human, we still wouldn't be able to connect in a way only our human souls could connect.

He huffed, his dismissal of his human half clear in that snort.

"He hurt both of us," I said, "but you know it was to protect me."

Out of the corner of my eyes, I saw Cyrus creeping closer. I needed to hurry and convince Knox's wolf to let me go and agree to the natural balance found in all shifters' souls. Because if Cyrus attacked, Knox's wolf was going to go completely feral and do something he wouldn't be able to come back from, like kill his brother.

"You know he did it because he was afraid."

He'd said he'd done it for my own good, but now I knew it wasn't because I was weak, but because he thought he was broken beyond repair.

Maybe he was.

But maybe so was I.

That didn't mean we could avoid what fate had forced on us.

"You know it in your heart." I slid my fingers through his soft fur, keeping my movements slow and soothing. "You know he thought he was doing the right thing for me."

He huffed again, the sound softer and some of the tension eased from his body.

"I'll always be yours. I need you to show me how to be strong. But I also need him. He's as much my mate as you are. Can you let him go? Please?"

Mine, he rumbled, but all the rage and possessiveness were gone. In its place were love and wonder and a little bit of hurt, not because I'd hurt him for asking for human Knox back, but because Knox had forced him away and resisted what his wolf had known was fate.

Whether we liked or even knew each other, accidentally mate bonding with him hadn't been a mistake. We were fated mates. Neither of us could deny it.

Audrey? Knox, the human, gasped in my head, and the churning unease that had been squeezing my insides since last night vanished.

The green flecks in his wolf's eyes brightened for a second before he collapsed on top of me, his body shifting from his heavy wolf to his almost equally heavy human form.

"What the hell are you doing here?" Cyrus roared as he stormed toward me. His rage rolled off him in waves of uncontained power, making my pulse race and my mind whirl.

"What?" I didn't understand why he was so mad. I expected him to be relieved that I'd brought Knox back.

But he was furious with a rage I'd never seen before, one that reminded me too much of Merrick and Sterling.

"Did you follow Bishop, thinking because he's interested in you the rules don't apply to you?" he accused.

"No." I shrunk back from him, instinct screaming that I make myself smaller and hide because I couldn't get away. "I just—"

"You just what?" He rolled Knox off me, fully exposing me to his furious glare. "Deacon, take Knox to the grove before he wakes up here and freaks out," he commanded without looking away from me.

Deacon dropped his kilt, shifted from human to wolf and back again, turning the gashes in his arm into not-as-bad but still bleeding cuts, then resecured his kilt. He shot me a concerned look as he hefted Knox onto his shoulder, except I couldn't tell if he was worried for me or concerned that I was what Cyrus was accusing me of: someone who thought the rules didn't apply to her.

"We don't know how long he'll be out," Cyrus said with a snap of power. Then he frowned and Deacon raised an eyebrow as if he expected an answer.

The muscles in Cyrus's jaw flexed, his fury sinking into a simmering rage, and Deacon nodded. The beta's expression was still concerned, but he obviously wasn't concerned about me because he turned on his heel and carried Knox out of the arena, leaving me alone with Cyrus and his now partially contained fury.

I curled in on myself, my arms wrapped around my stomach, trembling at the thought of what was going to happen now and trying to be as small as possible. Even if Cyrus had pulled in his temper that didn't mean anything.

"You just what?" he repeated, his voice low and dangerous.

"I—" I squeaked.

No, damn it. I didn't want to be small. I wanted to be strong.

"I felt—" I said, struggling to sound more confident.

I tried to scramble to my feet, but only got halfway up before the force of Cyrus's wrath pushed me to my knees and consumed that flicker of determination that had told me to stand in the hope that he'd gotten his emotions under control.

But this was just like what had happened with Merrick in those early years. There'd been times when he'd calmed down for a moment, usually when there was a witness, but as soon as the witness was gone...

It didn't matter if I had a good reason or not for jumping in and saving Knox, I knew what came next. The alpha was always right and always punished those who disobeyed him.

I was a fool to think I was anything other than what I was.

I clenched my jaw, fighting the urge to look down, and failed, my gaze dropping to the polished stone floor in submission. As much as I wanted to be strong, to be someone new in this realm, and as much as I'd momentarily lost my mind and tried to goad Knox into punishing me for talking back to him. I was weak and I'd always be weak.

"You can't go sneaking around. Ever. It's dangerous. Knox could have killed you and we would have lost both of you. You," he growled, his tone growing darker with each word, his control vanishing. "You are not exempt from the rules. You might be mated to one of the pack alphas but you are *not* an alpha. You can't just do what you want whenever you want."

"Yes, alpha," I forced out, hugging myself, desperate to stop shaking. "I'll learn my place, alpha."

Remember your lessons, I told myself, my throat tightening and my eyes burning with tears. *Stay calm. Stay small.*

Cyrus growled, the sound a precursor to violence, and I squeezed my eyes shut. I couldn't let him see me cry. Crying was weak. Crying wasn't submitting to the will of my alpha and accepting my situation.

Just stay small. He'll do whatever he'll do and then it will be over.

Until the next time.

He threw his head back and roared, the sound echoing through the arena, and I flinched, anticipating a strike.

But instead of hitting me or ordering a punishment, he stormed away.

Tears rolled down my cheeks and I fought to stay silent. I couldn't let him hear me. I couldn't risk bringing him back.

For whatever reason, he hadn't vented his anger on me and I needed to keep it that way. He was so much stronger than Merrick or Sterling, both in alpha power and physical strength. He could easily hurt or even kill me. I didn't stand a chance against him.

God! I didn't know what had happened. I didn't understand how

Cyrus could turn on me so quickly, but maybe I'd been wrong about him. Traveling together had been extenuating circumstances and this was what he was really like when he was leading his pack.

Except that didn't match with how he'd been at dinner with his betas and how they'd all been comfortable joking and disagreeing with him.

But none of that really mattered. I'd forgotten myself. I'd let my guard down because I'd thought I was safe when my whole life was proof that I was never going to be safe. Bishop had seemed sincere in his promise to court and mate me, but that didn't mean I was safe from Cyrus.

A sob broke through and I slapped my hands over my mouth to muffle the ones that were sure to follow.

I'd really thought things were different, but I was even more trapped here than I was in my old pack. The only thing I could do was keep my head down and make myself as small and as invisible as possible.

CYRUS

With Bishop's unconscious form over my shoulder, I stormed away from Audrey as fast as I could before I did something stupid like grab her, drag her up to my bedroom, and lock her inside so I always knew where she was and she was never in danger again. I'd never been so furious and so terrified in my life.

She'd fallen into the arena and Knox, little more than a feral wolf at that point, had charged her.

My heart had completely stopped and I was certain he was going to kill her.

If he'd been completely feral and he'd killed her, he wouldn't have died or gone insane because of their broken mating bond.

How the hell had she even found us? She had to have followed Bishop after he'd shown her to her new rooms... which didn't explain why she'd waited until the morning to jump in or didn't come running when Knox was trying to kill us or react when Bishop's last attempt to use his twin bond with Knox had knocked him out.

Sisters! Knox had been going crazy all night, slipping further and further into feralness, and had attacked us as if he hadn't recognized us. We'd been trying to pin him down long enough for Bishop to calm him and use their twin bond to bring him back like he'd done the last time, but Knox was more ferocious than I'd ever seen him.

Deacon had almost lost an arm and I'd almost had my stomach ripped open. We'd been unable to shift to heal ourselves, since Knox would have seen that as an act of aggression, and none of us wanted to leave the others alone in the arena to go outside. That and I wasn't sure if shifting would fully heal us. It certainly wouldn't have left us with enough strength to battle Knox.

Then Audrey had shown up, naive and vulnerable like she always was. It didn't matter that he hadn't hurt her, that she'd been exactly what he'd needed to regain his humanity. She. Could. Have. Died.

I didn't know how to get that through to her. I hadn't meant to yell at her, not like I had with my power raging out of control.

Deacon had even warned me to calm down — thankfully through a telepathic link because embarrassing me in front of her would have completely set my wolf off — but I couldn't calm down.

If she'd just stayed where she was supposed to, she wouldn't have been in danger. I needed her to understand that, understand that seeing her in danger, seeing her die would turn *me* feral.

But she hadn't heard what I was trying to tell her. She'd shut down, shrinking in on herself, staring at the floor, and trembling, which only made me angrier. Angry that her immediate response was to become fully submissive. I knew she had more fight in her than that, I'd seen it during our journey to the death god's temple.

Except whatever fight she'd been born with had been trained out of her. The shivering, small woman who'd just cowered in front of me was what her previous alpha had made her.

And now she thought I was the same as that monster.

I bit back a howl but wasn't strong enough to fully contain the wave of power rolling off me. I needed to get away from her, from everyone, and calm the fuck down.

I didn't want her to look at me like she was terrified ever again.

And yet... maybe it was for the best. If she hated me, there couldn't be anything between us.

Because there *couldn't* be anything between us.

And I couldn't stop thinking about her.

The memory of pushing into her tight, slick heat and holding her small soft body was burned into my brain.

I wanted more than a fevered desperation that she didn't fully remember. I wanted the smiles and heated looks she'd given Bishop after her first time with him. I wanted to protect her, lift her up, and show her she could do anything.

I wanted her.

But the pack might not see what I saw. They'd see a shifter who couldn't shift and I wasn't going to risk putting her through that. Mating Knox and Bishop would be what was best for her, and I needed to forget all about her.

Hell, she didn't even remember having sex with me. I suspected what she did remember she thought was just a fevered dream, which was why she kept glancing at me, looking confused and blushing, and a part of me prayed she'd always believe it was just a dream.

It was the coward's way out and I hated being a coward, but she'd cried for days while partially sedated and still blushed when she looked at all three of us. Knowing we'd all seen her naked and begging and that we'd all slept with her would mortify her. Just knowing we could smell her arousal and that she was going into heat had embarrassed her. I wanted to save her that pain.

And yet, I'd just traumatized her by yelling at her.

Bishop couldn't wake up fast enough. He was the only one who could patch up my complete fuck up, because it wasn't just me she was afraid of. I'd seen her shrink away from Deacon as well and suspected she was going to be that way with everyone until they proved to her she was safe.

Fuck.

I reached the top of the narrow stairs carved into the heart of the mountain that connected the Residence with the arena and opened the heavy wooden door. It opened into a hall in the storage area of the castle near the kitchens, and I took one of the many back staircases up to Bishop's suite.

Nova, I called out to her as I approached Bishop's door. There was a chance she wasn't in the Residence or even on the Residence's ground, and while I had the greatest telepathic reach in the pack, I still wouldn't be able to reach her if she were at the hospital.

Thankfully, as I opened Bishop's door, I felt her feathery mental touch indicating she'd heard me.

Where do you need me? she asked in her Nova-the-physician voice, which still, every time I heard it, surprised me. She'd been more mischievous than Deacon and Bishop combined when we were growing up.

Bishop's suite.

He hurt Bishop? she gasped, and I could just imagine the shock then deep worry flashing across her face before she was back in control of her emotions.

No. Knocked him out through their bond. I strode through Bishop's sitting room to his bedroom, past the clutter of finished and half finished paintings, painting supplies, and musical instruments.

What about you and Deacon?

A shift and a good night's sleep will suffice, I replied gruffly. I'd be exhausted for a couple of days but I'd be fine. I was more worried about Bishop. Knox had never knocked him out before and I was worried the mental blow had seriously hurt him.

The last time Bishop had pulled Knox back from the brink of going completely feral, he'd been exhausted and had a headache for a week.

Of course, the last time, Knox's wolf hadn't been furious with me and Bishop. He'd ended up surrounded by a crowd with no easy way out and had panicked. This time, his wolf had taken over because we'd collared him. To protect Audrey.

I bit back a growl at how stupid I was as Nova hurried into Bishop's bedroom.

Knox's wolf had wanted Audrey from the start. Even feral, the chances he'd hurt her were slim.

Nova set her medical bag on the floor by her feet, sat on the bed beside Bishop, and went to work checking him over.

"His pulse is strong, his breathing normal," she said, pulling out a detection stone. It was mined near the underground lake where we got the water to make our elixirs and was imbued with some of the healing god's power as well. It didn't tell Nova what was wrong, but it did light up any area of the body that she needed to focus on. "Help me get him undressed."

"If there's nothing wrong," I said pulling Bishop into a sitting position so Nova could take off his shirt, "can you wake him?"

Because he needed to wake up and fix what I'd fucked up with Audrey. Yes, she needed to hate me, not flash me shy, heated looks that made both me and my wolf want to claim her, but she didn't have to be afraid of anyone else.

"I don't know if I can, but it would be best if we let him wake naturally. I've never had a patient unconscious because of a soul bond."

Swell.

"Then after this, check on Deacon—"

Her eyes narrowed to the bloody mess I was still making of my pants and now Bishop's bed.

"Fine. Check me out after I shift, then Deacon, then check on Audrey. I might have—"

"Been yourself when it comes to women you're romantically interested in?" she asked in her driest possible tone.

"I'm not interested in her."

Her expression didn't change.

Yeah, I didn't believe myself, either.

AUDREY

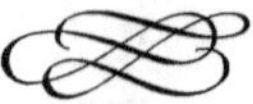

I knelt on the hard arena floor and cried into my hands, muffling my sobs, until I couldn't cry anymore. My eyes and throat hurt and my chest felt hollow like it had when Knox had rejected our bond.

A small voice inside me begged me to get up, do something, stand up for myself, but I had no idea what to do. I was permanently bound to Knox. I was trapped in Stonehaven and in this pack with no hope of escape until I died.

Was this how my father felt? Had he felt trapped in his nightmares? Had he known the only way to escape and end the horror was to die?

I didn't want to accept that killing myself was my only option, but there wasn't any other way to end my awful reality. I couldn't run away and there was no point in waiting for something to change. Nothing ever changed.

A part of me couldn't reconcile the Cyrus who'd just yelled at me with the Cyrus who I'd walked with for a month. How could he have suddenly turned into an alpha like Merrick or Sterling?

No. He was worse than them. He'd hidden who he really was for our entire journey north and back. Sure, he hadn't been the most welcoming, but I hadn't thought he was a typical alpha. I'd thought we could have eventually become friends.

The memory of my fevered fantasy rushed through me and more tears threatened to fall.

I'd greedily fantasized that we could have been more than friends, even if I was mated to his brothers.

God, I was such an idiot. Such a stupid, foolish, naive little girl.

Even if I trusted that Bishop wasn't trying to trick me like Royce had, he wouldn't be able to protect me from Cyrus. Cyrus was the alpha. His word was pack law unless someone challenged him and won. But only a powerful alpha would be able to stand a chance against Cyrus and if I learned anything from this horrible lesson, it was that all alphas were the same.

Except Bishop was an alpha...

Which meant my nightmares had been right. He was using me and once he'd had his fun, I'd see the real Bishop just like I'd seen the real Cyrus.

I rasped a strangled sob, my eyes burning, too sore and dry to cry anymore.

It couldn't be true. That wasn't who Bishop was. That wasn't even who Cyrus really was. They were the men who'd made sure I ate when I was exhausted, who held me when I was tired, and who told me I had a future with their pack and with them. They weren't monsters like Merrick and Sterling and Royce.

But it didn't matter how much I wanted something to not be true. It didn't even matter if there was a chance it wasn't true. I couldn't let my guard down, couldn't be so stupidly trusting like I'd been for the last month. I had to stay quiet and stay small. For the rest of my life.

Which was no life at all.

Voices echoed in the vast arena, coming from the gated passage behind me, and I scrambled to my feet.

Stay quiet. Stay small.

Stay invisible.

Cyrus and Deacon had left on the far side of the arena where one of the gates was unlocked, and I bolted toward it. The voices behind me grew louder and the metal gate clanged open.

A masculine voice called out as I reached the passage and slipped into the darkness beyond. Thankfully, he didn't order me back and didn't release any alpha power to stop me, and I hurried down the passage into the wider hall.

The hall was still dimly lit and I prayed whoever was behind me wouldn't follow me. I probably shouldn't have fled and just faced whatever punishment they were going to give me. They were going to report what they'd seen to Cyrus, and he'd know I'd stayed where I wasn't supposed to be after he'd left.

But I hadn't been able to ignore the compulsion to flee. I was prey, after all, and running was what prey did.

The thought filled me with a bone deep exhaustion, and the small burst of energy that had propelled me out of the arena drained out of me, weighing me down.

Aimlessly, I followed the hall that turned out to be one large circle ringing the arena and returned to the large front entrance. Sunshine blazed in the courtyard beyond, an almost blinding light compared to the shadowy hall, but I didn't care. I wasn't sure if I cared about anything anymore.

If Cyrus wanted to find me, he'd find me. Once Knox woke, he'd be able to find me even faster since our mating bond was so strong I could feel when his emotions were raging out of control.

Despite that, I didn't want to go back to the Residence, didn't want to go back to the fancy suite. The door might not have been locked, but it was still a cage, and now I knew the truth. I was something to be toyed with until I was no longer entertaining, and I refused to be entertainment for an alpha ever again.

Which brought me back again to ending it all. It was the only thing left in my control.

My pulse lurched at the thought and my chest clenched as a voice within me, the one that wanted desperately to believe that being with Bishop hadn't been a lie and that gruff and distant Cyrus wasn't really a monster, begged me to reconsider.

There's another way. There's always another way. I'm just too tired to find it.

But my exhaustion and my grief were stronger, and I now knew the truth. That voice was just the last of my foolish hope, a hope that would have me continue to suffer.

Too tired to pay attention to where I was going, I stumbled into a narrow, shaded alley that reeked of rotting food and piss. At the end, sat a large wheeled bin with its lid hanging open and garbage spilling out. Someone had painted an uneven white circle on the bin's dented metal side and the ground in front of it was littered with broken bottles and ceramic jugs.

Guess even in this realm there were alleys like this. Not that I'd ever been to an alley like this in my realm. I'd only seen them on TV and the internet.

I turned to head back out onto the street, but the sight of the light at the end of the alley and the idea of taking another step was too much. I was exhausted just thinking about moving one more step. I just wanted to close my eyes and sleep.

Maybe when I woke this nightmare would be over.

I huffed to myself.

Who was I kidding? It would never be over and it didn't really matter where I stopped anyway.

I slid down the alley wall, hugged my knees to my chest, and closed my eyes. Staying here with the broken and discarded things was fitting for a broken and discarded shifter.

AUDREY

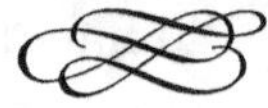

A DARK, MENACING LAUGH REVERBERATED AROUND ME AND SOMEONE screamed in agony. Merrick. Merrick was screaming. The monster was eating him alive and I was next.

Panic stole my breath and I ran. Tree branches clawed at my face and arms and tore into my dress more viciously in my dreams than they'd been in reality. Blood poured down my chest, stark against the shredded white fabric, while agony blazed through my body and my mind spun.

I had to get away. Had to—

The menacing laugh grew louder, a deep roiling sound with Merrick's screams a terrifying descant that made my soul tremble with fear.

"You can't escape," Sterling said, making me wrench my gaze around the dark forest, desperate to find him.

I was back in my old pack's sacred grove. Alone. My heart threatening to pound out of my chest.

With a lurch, I realized I was dreaming. Again. But that did little to ease the panic threatening to consume me.

"You're pathetic," Royce added. "So weak your only use is to be a sacrifice."

"No." I jerked around, trying to find them even though I knew I wouldn't until the dream wanted me to.

Were they behind me? I couldn't tell, couldn't see them, could barely see anything in the gloom.

The laugh roared through the glade, deafening me, making the trees and ground tremble, and stirring up a frozen wind that stung my skin.

"No one wants you," Sterling taunted.

"That's not true," I gasped. Bishop wanted me.

Except I didn't know that. Cyrus hadn't been who I'd thought he was. Bishop could be the same. My previous dreams could be right and everyone was just using me.

"You're a convenient cunt," Sterling laughed. "You begged for it and soon you'll go crawling back to them and beg some more."

"I won't," I insisted. I could be strong. But the second I thought that, I knew it wasn't true. I wasn't strong. I'd never be strong.

"Of course you will, because that's all that you're good for. Fuck toy or sacrifice." Sterling's laugh crescendoed, pressing in and oozing against my body as if it had physical mass even as the wind picked up and the trembling ground threaten to knock me over.

I tried to wipe the laugh away, but it clung to me, crawling over my skin and digging into the gashes Royce's claws had carved into my chest when he'd torn open my white transformation dress.

"I can't believe you were stupid enough to think I was your fated mate," Royce added, his voice suddenly right behind me.

I jerked around, my pulse roaring in my ears, bile burning my throat, but he wasn't there.

"Fate would never match me to someone like you," he hissed. "Fate wouldn't match you to anyone."

Not even to Bishop.

I knew that now. I'd seen the truth. I wasn't worthy.

But he'd promised—

And Royce had made me believe he'd wanted me, too.

I was so stupid. My throat tightened with tears. I'd fallen for the same trick in less than a month because I *was* desperate. Desperate for hope and love and all the things someone like me didn't deserve.

Except that doesn't make sense, a small voice whispered inside me, barely audible over Sterling's roaring laugh and stinging wind.

Of course, it didn't make sense. Nothing made sense. Because this was a dream.

Except even when I was awake my life didn't make sense. It never had.

"Because you're not supposed to be alive. You're supposed to bleed," Sterling hissed, his voice coming from the right. "*He* desires your screams." No, Sterling was to my left.

I whirled around, jerking this way and that, but couldn't see anyone in the darkness and couldn't seem to make myself stop looking. If I had night vision like a normal shifter, I'd have been able to see him... maybe. No. I *would* have.

"Scream little wolf," Royce growled, his voice right behind me, making me lurch, my heart in my throat.

"No," I squeaked. "Never."

But I knew they could smell my fear, knew I'd finally come to realize that fighting them, fighting everything, was futile. It just prolonged my suffering.

"If you won't scream, then you'll bleed," Sterling snarled and dozens of flying snake monsters swarmed around me.

I batted my hands at the closest ones, slapping them away, but there were too many and they moved too quickly. Their sharp teeth tore into my flesh, while their tails wrapped around my arms, slowing my movement, and one wrapped around my throat, cutting off my air.

Another blast of laughter roared around me and the ground lurched beneath my feet. I heaved and squirmed, agony burning with every bite, each breath a desperate gasp. I had to get them off me, and I *had* to keep my balance. If I fell, I'd never get back up again.

"Scream, prey. Scream and cry and beg and feed Tzanagoth," Sterling howled, as the snake around my neck vanished and the agony in my body roared into an inferno, igniting every inch of me inside and out. "Scream and bleed."

"No," I forced out, tears streaming down my cheeks, as blood poured down my arms and chest. My white transformation dress was soaked and every time my blood splattered on the ground it exploded into a ball of red mist and birthed another snake.

I clawed and swatted at them, yanking one hand free, then the other only to be captured again. My heart pounded, threatening to tear out of my chest. I had to get them off me, had to run, had to escape.

But just as I heaved both arms free and wrenched away the snake around my neck and turned to flee, something seized my hair and jerked me back.

Royce.

He tightened his grip in my dirty blond locks, just like he had that horrible night, and he used it to haul me up until my bare toes skimmed the ground. Pain lanced through my scalp, and I heaved and clawed against his hold, uselessly repeating everything I'd tried the night of the transformation ceremony.

"You're supposed to scream," he snarled, raking his claws down my chest, ripping open my dress, and slicing into my flesh as if it hadn't just been ripped and bloody moments before.

I squeezed my eyes shut, praying I'd wake up.

It was just a dream. Just a dream.

"Waking won't be any better," Sterling laughed. "You're still an alpha's whore and they're going to use you until you die."

They wouldn't. I wouldn't let them. Please. I couldn't.

But I was nothing compared to them, compared to everyone. They could take what they wanted and they would. They were alphas.

"No," I begged. "Please." Just the thought of seeing Bishop with Sterling or Royce's malicious expression hurt. He wasn't a psychopath. He couldn't be. He'd never use me like that... wouldn't he?

"Of course he won't," Royce growled. "I won't let him, because you're mine. You're my whore and I didn't get to fuck you."

Royce's black smoke lashed around my body, binding me to the ground, and the flying snakes latched onto me with their sharp teeth.

"You belong to me," he sneered as the snakes started burrowing into my skin.

Pain roared through me and I heaved against the smoke. They were going to take over, possess me. I could feel their sickening evil, born of violent blood sacrifices, oozing through my veins.

"No."

"Oh, yes," Sterling crowed.

"Please, no." I had to get free, had to get them off of me, out of me. I had to. I had to. They were going to take over, consume me from the inside out, and empower the malicious god that Sterling and Royce had tried to summon.

With a strength I didn't know I had, fueled by a panic that consumed all other thoughts, I wrenched one of my hands free and clawed at the snakes sinking into my skin.

"Get out. Get out!" I didn't belong to them. I didn't belong to anyone. Not even Knox. And I sure as hell wasn't going to let Tzanagoth consume me.

My hand hit a rock with a sharp edge and I seized it, slicing at the snakes trying to crawl under my skin. I'd kill them all. I wouldn't let them possess me. I wouldn't let anyone possess me, not Knox or Sterling or even a god.

I controlled my own fate no matter how lonely or pathetic it was.

Frantic, I slashed and swatted and fought. I freed my other hand and the smoky darkness tried to capture me again, but I writhed and twisted, avoiding its sticky grasp as more snakes tore at my skin.

Sterling stepped out of the grove, his eyes bright with a wicked smile, ghostly red rams horns curling from his temples like the depiction of Tzanagoth in Anakar. The terrifying power I'd sensed when he'd tried to get me to step into the rip and burn myself up, howled with the wind, suffocating and crushing, stronger than even Cyrus's alpha power.

"Yes," he cackled, his eyes bright with manic glee. "Bleed for me. Bleed!"

The snakes tore into my flesh and I screamed and screamed and—

— jerked awake.

Oh God.

It was a dream. Just a dream.

The reek of rotting food and piss hit my nose, then the metallic tang of blood. My head felt heavy, my body numb, even as my pulse pounded hard and fast.

I stood at the end of the alley, brandishing a broken bottle edged with blood, confused about how I'd gotten there and why I held the bottle.

Something plopped on my sandaled foot and I dragged my gaze, my thoughts working in slow motion, down down down my body.

Blood soaked my dress and rushed down my mutilated left arm. Everywhere there'd been a snake trying to possess me there were dozens of ragged slices, so many slices, so much blood, so—

Sterling's wicked laughter roared through me even though I was awake and the horror of what just happened stole my breath.

"Took you long enough," he taunted. "The sacrifice is now complete."

WOLF DISTRESSED

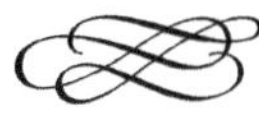

ENSNARED BY THE PACK: BOOK 4

KNOX

I woke with a start, shifting into my wolf form before I was fully conscious. I'd passed out after my mate had saved me from my furious wolf and, just like the last time my wolf had taken over, my brothers had left me in the private sacred grove behind the Residence to recover.

Except this time, instead of waking groggy and exhausted, a burning urgency screamed through my veins.

Audrey was in trouble and I had to get to her. Her emotions roaring inside me were stronger than Bishop's when he was upset, but I didn't know how that was possible.

A mating bond didn't connect two people like my twin bond connected me and Bishop. Mates were more attuned to their partners, but not to the extent that they felt each other's emotions like they were their own.

Surely, I would have noticed something before now, especially during that moment when she'd yelled at me for hurting her. She'd been conscious for five days, angry with me, and almost drowned, and I hadn't noticed more than a hint of emotions that weren't mine or Bishop's. The emotions couldn't be hers...

Except I knew in every fiber of my being that the panic and pain coursing through me was Audrey's.

It didn't matter if it made sense or not, I had to go to her.

She was the piece of my soul that I hadn't realized was missing until I'd thought she was going to drown in that flash flood. Even if we hadn't been bonded and her death wouldn't have affected me like it did now, I'd go after her.

She was mine. My fate. My mate. My responsibility to protect.

My wolf had known the truth the moment he'd caught her scent, and he was still furious that I'd denied him for so long. And while I didn't know exactly what had happened in the arena, I knew he'd have completely taken over if she hadn't begged him to release me.

I didn't deserve her kindness. She'd have survived fine if my wolf had completely taken over, probably lived a better life than the one she was facing now. He'd never hurt her, not like I had, and surely would in the future.

I had to make it up to her, had to figure out how to be a good mate. Except I wouldn't be able to do that if she died, and I feared, from the emotions coursing through me, that that was about to happen.

I didn't know why I believed that. I could only feel her fear and heartache. But something about that fear, how it ran so cold and deep, cutting into my soul, told me she was in immediate danger.

Bishop, I said, reaching out to him mentally as I bounded out of the grove and followed the pull on my soul, praying it would take me to Audrey.

Knox? His mental voice was groggy as if he was barely awake. Then he registered the urgency in my voice and I felt our connection strengthen. *What's wrong? How are you—? I—?*

A confusing muddle of emotions and half thoughts rushed through me but I couldn't understand why he was confused.

Of course, I also didn't remember anything after Cyrus and Bishop released the collar containing the wolf half of my soul and before I was staring down into Audrey's wide brown eyes with the knowledge that she'd asked my wolf to give me back to her. Anything could have happened. I didn't even know how long my wolf had possessed me.

And none of that mattered.

Audrey is in trouble.

A flash of panic snapped through our twin bond, now second in strength to my bond with Audrey, something I hadn't thought possible. *Where? How?*

I don't know, I growled back, frustrated that I couldn't answer those simple questions.

The pull on my soul compelled me through the Residence's gates and into Old Town, and my frustration grew stronger. *Why the hell isn't she in the Residence?*

She isn't—? Cyrus? Bishop asked, adding our older brother to our telepathic conversation. *Where's Audrey?*

I— He paused for too long and even though I didn't have an emotional connection with Cyrus like I did with Bishop, I knew something was up.

What did you do? I demanded, the pull taking me out of Old Town and drawing me north, following the outside edge of the towering Old Town wall.

Nova, Cyrus said, not answering my question. *Where's Audrey?*

She wasn't in her suite, the grove, or the gardens. I figured she didn't want to be found right now, Nova replied. *I told Finn to keep an eye out for her. She's probably exploring her new home and wants a little space.*

Why would she want space? Bishop asked, his worry growing.

You know— Nova began but I released my connection with them, not bothering to hear whatever excuse they were going to come up with. If they didn't know where she was, they couldn't help her.

Clearly, she was outside the Residence walls, and it looked like she was in the northern part of Stonehaven, a part that despite all our initiatives was still a seedy part of town. It was closest to the road connecting the town to the mountain pass and was near to the market and housed the warehouses and cheap inns and bars that poorer traveling merchants liked to visit. Foreigners weren't restricted to the area, but most of them stayed where the food and lodging wouldn't eat into their profits.

Finn, I barked, praying he was within reach of my telepathic ability.

I was a strong alpha so I could communicate with someone farther away from me than most shifters, but I still wasn't strong enough to talk to someone on the other side of town. Not even Cyrus could do that, and he'd worked to extend his ability beyond what anyone else in the pack could do.

Knox? Finn asked, surprise coloring his mental voice.

Yeah, I didn't usually communicate with the pack's betas except for Nova who was really more like a sister than a beta. Technically they were my betas as well, not just my brothers', but I never wanted the responsibility of being one of the pack's alphas. I was the person least suited to the job because I didn't want to talk to anyone.

Except if it saved Audrey, I'd talk to the whole damn pack and deal with the emotional fallout later.

Anything to protect her.

And the first guy who might know something was the beta in command of the town's watch.

Audrey, I said. I couldn't let his surprise pull him off topic and I needed to know where she was. Now. *Where's Audrey?*

Nova mentioned something, Finn replied. *Why—?*

Where is she? Do any of the watchmen have eyes on her? I asked and a burst of alpha power escaped my control and blasted out around me.

The half dozen people on the street, some barely in sight at the far end, dropped to their knees in submission while Finn groaned, my power reaching through our telepathic connection.

Fuck, Knox, Cyrus snapped. *Pull your power back. You just dropped everyone in the kitchen.*

The kitchen? He was still in the kitchen? Why wasn't he looking for Audrey?

Fury roared through me and another blast of power broke through my control.

What the fuck are you still doing in the Residence? I demanded, not caring that my power slip was big enough that it reached all the way to the Residence. *You should be looking for her! Audrey's in trouble and she's somewhere in the north end of town.*

Where in the north end? Cyrus asked.

I don't know! I didn't know anything. I didn't know what kind of trouble she was in or if she was already hurt.

All I knew was that she needed me and I had to go to her.

Vida says she saw her near Jaxon's smithy about an hour ago, Finn said. *I'll send a team to bring her in.*

You're not arresting her, I snarled.

Sending a team would scare her. Even I could tell people in authority made her nervous, especially if it looked like she was going to be accused of something. Anyone who'd spent two seconds with her would know that, and I was furious that Finn automatically jumped to the conclusion that she'd done something wrong.

I doubted she'd put up a fight, not in her current emotional state, but that would still erode the trust Bishop and Cyrus had built with her during our journey to the death god's temple. She'd be afraid again and I couldn't stand to see her afraid.

I'll get her myself, I added before Finn could ask any questions. I didn't want to have to explain why I cared about Audrey. Sure, we'd traveled north together, but everyone knew I didn't like people and wouldn't express even a casual interest in a woman.

The terror racing through our mating bond surged, stealing my breath, and I ran as fast as I could, narrowly avoiding running into people and carts.

It didn't matter that I was making a spectacle of myself, that these pack members were seeing me for the first time in years. I had to get to her.

I barreled around a corner and climbed half a dozen stairs to the northern terrace, following the pull on my soul.

The reek of alcohol, rotting food, and piss was strong, and the street was lined with refuse. The two inns, three bars, and one brothel that took up this block still hadn't kept their part of Stonehaven clear. It was an ongoing cycle where Cyrus fined the owners, they did their part for a month and then slacked off again.

If any of them had been shifters, he could have compelled them, but the inns and bars were owned by humans and the brothel by a Dedearc — a being supposedly originating from the mythical dragons and demons — and our alpha power didn't work on them.

The pull jerked me toward a narrow alley between the last bar on the row and a blocky two-story building with a clothier on the first floor.

There. Audrey was there.

I raced to the alley's mouth afraid of what I'd find—

Fuck! It was worse than I could have imagined.

She stood at the back of the alley beside a dented garbage bin, screaming and sobbing, and swinging a broken bottle as if she were being attacked.

Blood poured from her body and pooled beneath her feet. Her left arm had been cut so many times it was impossible to tell if her injuries were a few deep cuts or dozens of shallow ones. More cuts sliced through her dress over her left breast and across her right thigh as well as a few shallow ones close to the artery in her neck that turned my panic into frozen horror.

"Get out," she cried, tears leaking from her closed eyes as I raced to get to her. "Get out, get out, get out."

With a scream, she slashed the broken bottle across her already bloody left forearm then jerked as if she'd been struck and sucked in a sharp breath. Her eyelids fluttered open, her expression dazed, then her gaze slowly dragged down her body to the bottle, her ruined dress, and the too-large pool of blood around her feet.

"Sterling," she gasped, saying the name of one of the monsters from her old pack who'd tried to kill her.

Horror flooded our bond then her eyes rolled back.

"No!" I leaped toward her, shifting into my human form, and caught her before she crumpled to the ground.

There was so much blood. Too much blood. I could feel her life draining out of her as I clutched her to my chest.

My mate was dying. I didn't know what had happened, but I'd failed her.

I'd. Failed. Her.

BISHOP

A HEART-STOPPING MIX OF RAGE AND PANIC SHOT THROUGH MY BOND with Knox, making my knees buckle. With a growl, I slammed my shoulder against the alley wall and managed to stay upright while only staggering up the remaining uneven steps to reach the top of the northern terrace then kept running.

Knox had said Audrey was in trouble, his worry so strong he'd let his full power slip — or maybe even released it on purpose — something he never did. Eloise and Kira, our cook and her assistant, had dropped to their knees from the force of his power, and I had a feeling so had everyone in a two-hundred-foot radius from Knox since Cyrus had then been inundated with telepathic questions about what was going on.

Another full blast hit me, compelling me to hurry and help, and Knox screamed in my head.

"Oh, Sisters," Nova gasped. "Was that—?"

"Knox?" I said. "Yeah."

"Finn says he sees them. Northgate Road. Nova," Cyrus barked with a leak of power. "You need to shift and meet them at the closest med pack."

"Corner of Northgate and Menders," Nova said as she shifted into her small, white and reddish-brown wolf, not even pausing to take off her dress. Then she raced out of the alley and onto a narrow, unnamed street heading toward Northgate.

I shifted as well and ran after her. While we'd traveled to the death god's temple, the betas had set up medical packs in secure locations all over town — the majority on the perimeter — and started voluntary first aid classes for anyone who wanted to know how to use what was in the packs. We'd lost too many people in the grimalkin attack and Nova had sworn it wouldn't happen again.

I could only pray that Finn had been in one of the first few classes, or that there was someone else nearby who could help since Knox didn't know a whole lot of first aid and, from the panic racing through our bond, was barely holding it together.

What the hell had happened? And why the hell had Audrey been roaming Stonehaven alone?

For the most part, the town was safe, but she was a very weak, very pretty female and even in the nicest parts of town she could have drawn males too eager for her attention and unwilling to listen to her soft, shy requests to be left alone. That she'd ended up on the north side of Stonehaven, the shadiest part of town with the foreigners not beholden to an alpha, had me even more worried.

Knox, I called out, praying I was close enough to reach him.

She's dying, he screamed back. *She— Bishop, I can't— It's just like when we found her in the river.*

Someone attacked her? My wolf rose to the surface and seized control. We'd kill whoever had hurt her, tear him to pieces and bathe in their blood.

I don't know. There wasn't anyone around. She wasn't even awake when she hurt herself.

She hurt herself? How—?

I. Don't. Know! he roared, his desperation and panic crashing through me, propelling me faster.

With my longer legs, I passed Nova even though I had no idea which building had the Northgate Menders med pack.

But it didn't matter. Knox's fear was a physical, impossible pull on our bond, drawing me to him — something that had never happened before. I wasn't even sure how it was possible, because there wasn't a bond strong enough to tell someone where the other was.

I sped out of another narrow no-name street and climbed the shallow steps onto Menders, a wider street that joined the northern terrace with the rest of the town. I passed a group of people frozen from the power pouring off Knox, caught in the opposing compulsions to help and to get away. Beyond them, I could see Knox at the next intersection. Menders and Northgate.

He knelt on the ground, clutching a limp Audrey to his chest while Finn knelt beside him, pulling stuff out of a bright yellow duffle bag. Blood darkened the ground around them in a too-large pool and there were already two elixir ampules lying discarded on the ground.

I slid to a stop beside them and shifted into my human form, taking a handful of gauze from Finn and clamping it down on Audrey's mutilated left forearm.

A second later, Nova appeared and nudged me to the side so she could get at Audrey.

"Save her," Knox growled, clutching Audrey tighter.

"I will," she said, meeting Knox's dark gaze, her expression tight with worry and determination. "I promise. But you have to put her down."

Knox trembled and the muscles in his arms flexed. Power rolled off him, commanding me to save her, now now now, and the panic in our bond stole my breath.

"I can't," he gasped. "I can't. Nova, please."

"I've already given her the pack's two elixirs," Finn said.

"Who did this?" Cyrus demanded, his own power vibrating at the edge of my senses, his control on the verge of slipping.

He was going to kill whoever had hurt her. It was clear in his eyes. But there was also something deeper, darker in his gaze. I couldn't recognize the emotion, but it made my already churning insides cold with dread.

Nova peeled back the gauze, revealing the mess of Audrey's arm then slapped the gauze back down and moved to the gauze Finn held over her chest and thigh.

"I don't know," Knox replied, his attention locked on Audrey's pale face, his body trembling. "I saw her cut herself. She was standing and crying and cutting herself with a broken bottle."

All the color drained from Cyrus's face and he jerked a step closer.

Knox tensed. "Too close," he growled, his voice low, his breathing suddenly sharp and ragged, the surge of fear that marked a panic attack bursting through our bond. "You're too close. All of you are too close!"

Cyrus heaved himself back, and Finn and I inched as far away as we could while still holding the gauze in place. No one wanted to risk Knox's wolf losing it, and while Finn didn't know we'd just barely saved him from going feral a few hours ago, he sure as hell remembered how vicious Knox had been the last time.

Knox sucked in a sharp breath then another and squeezed his eyes tight. I could feel him struggling to not let his fear overwhelm him. Even his wolf was helping, fighting against the most primal part of its nature to stay in control because that was the only way to help Audrey.

"I think she was asleep," Knox forced out. "She looked so surprised."

"I need to stitch most of this," Nova said as she taped the gauze around Audrey's forearm then ripped the front of Audrey's dress so she could tape gauze there as well. "But I want to do a thorough cleaning first. The elixirs will help, but I'd rather she wasn't also fighting an infection on top of trying to heal this degree of damage."

Another burst of panic swept through our bond and Knox's grip on Audrey tightened.

"I need to be with her," he said.

Finn's eyebrows shot up at that announcement but he thankfully didn't say anything. As it was, people were going to be talking. Knox had frozen every shifter in the immediate area, locking them in his fear to avoid crowds and his desperation to save his mate.

Before the day was done, everyone was going to know that Knox and Audrey were mate bonded. There was no other logical explanation for his reaction. And everyone was going to be wondering how and why it had happened. The wolf that didn't need or want anyone now had a mate. One who couldn't even shift and live the same lifestyle as him.

"We'll set up something outside her suite," Cyrus assured him. "Finn. Run ahead until you're close enough. Tell Whil to meet us in the gold suite and get Zavier to set up a mattress on the patio. Last time I saw him, he was with Lucius in the library."

"Yes, alpha," he said, thankfully without asking the questions that I could see in his confused expression. He yanked off his shirt, dropped his pants, and raced away, shifting mid-step.

"You think there's more going on?" I asked Cyrus, as he gathered up Finn's clothes and shoved the gauze, tape, and empty ampules back in the med pack. There wasn't any other reason for him to summon Whil.

"She didn't sleepwalk the entire time we were traveling. I don't know why she'd start now," he replied, leading us back toward the Residence. "She was caught up in a spell that ripped a hole between her realm and ours, and her heat was a lot stronger than it should have been for someone so weak."

Nova shot him a dark look. "And trauma can do strange things to a person. She's in a mate bond she didn't expect, just survived a dangerous and exhausting journey, and doesn't yet know her place in this pack. Anything could have been the last straw for her. Any *sharp words* could have pushed her subconscious over the edge."

Cyrus stiffened at that. Something had happened, and if I knew Cyrus, she'd done something to make him panic — like she'd done for most of our journey — and with the stress of Knox going feral, he'd lost it.

Sudden fury blazed through my bond with Knox.

"You did this?" he demanded, his eyes dark and his canines extended as his wolf took over. "You made our mate hurt herself?"

A crack of his power made me and Nova stumble while Audrey whimpered and the rage in the bond jerked back to fear.

"We'll find out what happened and we'll deal with it," Cyrus said.

We ran through the Residence's main gate and skirted around the castle, not bothering to navigate the maze of hallways to get to Audrey's suite. Zavier and Lucius had already set up a mattress with pillows and blankets on the small, semi-private patio that was sheltered by some tall shrubs and planter boxes. Beside it, was a white sheet and a low table with the medical supplies Nova needed to clean Audrey's wounds, stitch them up, and rebind them.

Knox sat on the white sheet, laying Audrey so her head was cradled in his lap. It still wasn't the space Nova needed to work, but it was better than clutching Audrey to his chest, and Nova didn't comment on the position.

Nova had cornered me when I'd first gotten back to Stonehaven and demanded to know what had happened between Audrey and Knox, and I'd told her they'd been forced to seal the bond.

I could only assume since Deacon had known about the mate bond and that we'd been traveling to the death god's temple to break it, that he'd told Nova, since the only other person who'd known about it when we'd left town, was Whil, and she'd sworn to keep it a secret.

Of course, now it didn't matter. Everyone knew and everyone was going to be talking about it.

Nova got to work cutting Audrey out of her dress and cleaning the gashes on her left breast, right over her heart.

What had she been trying to do? Cut her heart out? Cut out her bond with Knox?

She'd been so strong for the journey to the death god's temple and I'd thought, even though she'd been shaken by the heat fever, that she was all right. She'd been upset and shyer than she'd been when we'd first met, but I hadn't thought she was suicidal, not even on an unconscious level.

Maybe Cyrus was right. Maybe, somehow, she'd been influenced by magic.

Whil and Finn hurried around the shrubs, and Knox tensed at the additional people before Finn, Lucius, Cyrus, and I stepped back.

"What happened?" Whil asked, her bright green gaze sweeping over Audrey and taking in the blood and gauze and her still too-thin frame.

It broke my heart to see her so fragile because I knew she wasn't fragile. Someone had just convinced her she was. And while I didn't know the extent of what she suffered in her previous pack, I knew enough to know she wouldn't have survived if she'd truly been fragile. She also wouldn't have survived the attack that had brought her to us, the journey to the death god's temple, or a heat fever.

"We're not sure," Cyrus replied, making Knox growl, the sound low and threatening. The muscles in Cyrus's jaw flexed and his spine straightened just a little bit more, revealing his discomfort. "We need you to check her for magical influence."

"I didn't notice anything when I checked her when she first arrived," Whil said as she sat on Audrey's other side and placed a hand on her forehead. "Oh, Sisters!"

Cyrus flinched as if he wanted to get closer then remembered that we needed to give Knox space. "What?"

"She's tethered to someone," Whil replied.

"Who?" I asked.

"I don't know. They're far away. I swear the tether wasn't there a month ago." Whil closed her eyes to concentrate and her magic brightened enough for me to see the golden glow around her hand even in the bright sunlight.

"It's that asshole," Knox said. "The one that tried to kill her. It has to be."

"And he could have made her hurt herself with this connection?" Cyrus asked.

The glow flared, washing out Audrey's already pale face and Whil frowned. "It could make her do lots of things," she replied. "But she'd have to be vulnerable to start with. This isn't strong enough to possess her. She'd have to already have emotions toward whatever they wanted her to do and then they could amplify it out of proportion."

Which meant Audrey might not have been stressed and depressed enough to hurt herself, but the seed had been there.

Cyrus hissed a curse and ran his hand over his face, his "alpha-in-control" mask sliding over his expression. Her being connected to someone had more repercussions than just her hurting herself.

What if she got mad at one of us? Could whoever it was influence her into hurting someone else? Maybe even kill them? Now it was a matter of protecting not just Audrey but the whole pack.

"Can you cut the tether?" Cyrus asked, his voice gruff.

"I—" Whil's expression tightened and her body tensed.

The glow from her magic surrounded Audrey's head, making it difficult to make out her features, and a second later, Audrey cried out and started writhing.

"Whil!" Knox snapped, holding Audrey's head and keeping it in his lap, as Nova threw herself over Audrey's body to keep her still, and I grabbed Audrey's legs.

"Just— I—" Tears rolled down Whil's cheeks, her body clenched with effort, and the light started to stutter, sharp, piercing strobes that sliced into my brain.

Please let her cut it. Please let Audrey be free. I could protect her from a lot of things and I wanted to with all my heart, but I couldn't protect her from someone in her head. Even if we were mate bonded, I wouldn't be able to do that.

"I can't," Whil gasped as she threw herself back, leaning against the side of the mattress gasping for air as Audrey went limp again. "I've blocked it, so whoever it is can't influence her again, for now, but I can't sever it. I'm not strong enough."

Cyrus gave a tight nod and Knox's emotions soured inside me.

Yeah, I didn't like the "for now," either.

"I'll need to check the block regularly to keep it intact," Whil said.

"For how long?" Knox asked.

Her expression turned grim. "Indefinitely."

Which meant that monster was going to be haunting Audrey for the rest of her life.

<h1 style="text-align:center">AUDREY</h1>

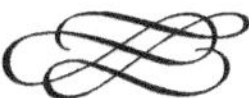

I woke groggy and sore and strangely at peace. Warmth radiated around my heart and every breath was filled with the comforting scent of wood smoke.

For some reason, I was outside on a soft mattress bundled in blankets that smelled smoky like Knox, but I couldn't figure out why. In front of me, I could see French doors that looked a lot like the doors in my suite, but it was too dark — the sky barely lightening with dawn — for me to tell if I was actually on the patio outside my suite or not.

Behind me, something big and heavy and warm pressed against my back, like how Bishop used to curl around me when we cuddled around the campfire, but there weren't any arms around me so it couldn't have been a person, and I was too woozy to bother moving to see what it actually was. I just wanted to lie there, wrapped in the warmth, feeling safe.

But the memories flooded in.

The fear and rage of Knox's emotions through our mate bond as his wolf tried to consume the human half of his soul. The terror when I'd fallen into the arena and he'd charged at me, and my relief when his wolf finally released him. Then Cyrus had yelled at me, shown who he really was, and proven I wasn't safe in Stonehaven. I wasn't safe anywhere.

Except was that really true?

Cyrus had been gruff and looked down on me for not being able to do much of anything, but he'd never been cruel. Even when he'd been yelling at me, I'd seen the worry in his eyes... I just hadn't realized I'd seen it at the time.

I'd been so focused on the similarities between him and Merrick when Merrick had first taken me in, and I'd been scared that my nightmares had been right, that the guys were using me, that I should be ashamed for how I'd behaved during my heat. That I was worthless and trapped.

My throat tightened, the fear and shame swelling and threatening to strangle me.

I thought I was stronger than that, that I could wait and plan and stay unnoticed. I thought things had finally changed.

No. They *had* changed.

Without the pressure of Knox's emotions and being exhausted from traveling for close to a month, the bleakness that had overwhelmed me when Cyrus had yelled at me was gone. How could I have thought Bishop was using me?

Because I'd trusted the false mating call and believed Royce would love me. I couldn't trust my own judgment. I was too easily tricked and manipulated.

No.

I squeezed my eyes shut and sucked in more deep breaths of Knox's comforting scent.

I'd been manipulated because of magic. No one would have suspected Royce and Sterling would have hired a witch to fake a mating call. No one would have suspected anyone of doing that.

I could trust Bishop, and even though Knox had really hurt me when he rejected me, the bond was sealed. I could trust him. Even if we weren't in love now, we would be... eventually. The bond would see to that. It didn't matter if I feared that he couldn't possibly love me. That fear was wrong. He'd said he'd try with us and I believed him... or did I just want to believe him?

Gah! This was so frustrating.

I. Could. Trust. Them.

Neither Bishop nor Knox were psychopaths. Cyrus wasn't one, either. Everything Cyrus did was to protect his pack. Knox had already hurt him, Deacon, and Bishop and was on the verge of completely losing his humanity. Even *I'd* feared that he was going to hurt me when I'd fallen into the arena.

Except even if Cyrus had been rightly afraid for me, that didn't negate what he'd said afterward. People said what lay deep in their hearts when they finally snapped, and Cyrus had looked like he'd completely snapped. He'd meant it when he told me I couldn't just do what I wanted, that I needed to remember my place.

He might not be cruel like Merrick, but he was still an alpha, and somewhere during our trip north I'd forgotten that, forgotten how I was supposed to behave. Even if he and his brothers hadn't cared while we'd been alone, we were back in the pack and I was the newest weakest member. My place was to be seen, not heard, and obey commands from my superiors — which included everyone in the pack.

I couldn't let my guard down around anyone until they'd proven without a doubt that I could trust them and that I was safe with them. Which meant for the time being, I could only relax around Knox and Bishop.

The realization about my safety, or lack thereof, made my thoughts jump back to Sterling and how he'd tortured me for half of my life. Even in my nightmares, I hadn't been able to escape him.

Was he always going to be stuck in my mind?

I hadn't dreamed of him when I'd first arrived in this realm. Instead, I'd had intense sexual dreams of Knox. But after the spell to break our bond had failed, my dreams of Knox had turned into night-mares of Sterling.

My thoughts stuttered. His words at the end of my latest nightmare, just before I woken and realized I'd cut myself over and over again with a broken bottle, shuddered through me.

The sacrifice is now complete.

That was what he'd wanted all along. My only use for him as a member of his pack and as a person was to feed a monster and make him more powerful.

Except I wasn't dead.

Had I somehow screwed up his plans by surviving that horrible night when I'd escaped into this realm?

I'd thought when I'd confronted him at the rip and his skin had turned red and ghostly ram's horns had appeared at his temples just like the monster that had tried to eat me, that he'd gotten the power he'd wanted. But maybe I was wrong.

The monster had eaten Merrick, but he hadn't been the one whose incomplete mating bond had been used to power the spell.

That thought made my lips twitch with a vicious smile. Weak little me might have fucked up Sterling's plans.

But my smile quickly slipped away with a new horrible realization.

If my nightmares were more than nightmares — and a big part of me felt that they were — then Sterling wasn't done with me.

I'd thought I was safe from him in this realm, that the rip was gone or too small for him to get to me, but what if I was wrong?

I might have been in a different realm when he'd used his alpha power through the rip to control me, but my dreams were different from standing within sight of him. I hadn't even been close to the rip. It was over a day away in Anakar.

Except he'd been able to control Tzanagoth's spirits, creating those flying snake things to attack us. He had powers he'd never had before and there was no telling what else he could do. He could have used them to make me dream and think those horrible things in an attempt to kill myself and finish his ritual.

The heavy pillow behind me huffed and hot breath washed over the back of my neck.

Oh, shit. Not a pillow. I'm in bed with someone.

The panic of being in bed with a stranger squeezed my chest, and I lurched onto my back to stare into the dark brown, green-flecked eyes of an enormous black wolf.

Knox.

He nuzzled my throat, his wet nose cold against my skin and my sudden panic vanished, leaving me achy and exhausted from my ordeal. With a whimper, I rolled closer and dug my fingers into his soft fur.

I still wanted to be mad at him for hurting me when he rejected our bond, and I was determined to keep my word and make him beg for my forgiveness, but I also needed to be comforted by my mate. I was scared that Sterling could still get to me, and with Knox — just like with Bishop — my soul felt steadier, stronger.

With him, as conflicted as I was, I felt safe.

But was I? If Sterling was in my head making me dream things— hell, making me *think* things, I wasn't safe anywhere.

It wasn't you, he said, his mental voice gruff. But it wasn't gruff with anger. It was gruff with worry. And the second I realized that, I could feel his concern seeping through the bond.

"It was Sterling," I told him.

Yes. He sighed, his relief breezing through me that I realized the truth and wasn't still trying to kill myself. *He was influencing you through a magical connection.* Then he drew back to look me in the eyes. *May I hold you?*

Ahhh...?

"You're my mate. Aaaand we're already lying in a bed together." Except he wasn't in his human form which put a certain amount of distance between us.

You needed me to help you heal, he said, as if that explained why we were in a bed, outside... which it sort of did. At least the "in bed together" part. Just not the "outside" part.

But I— His gaze shifted to the edge of the hedges, but I couldn't tell if it was because he'd heard something or couldn't maintain eye contact. *I didn't know if you'd want me to hold you.*

I do, I said, my voice not nearly as strong as I wanted it to be. I needed him and I wasn't going to think too hard about it. "I'm still upset at you, but I—" Now it was my turn to look away. "Sterling is in my head. I'm afraid I'm never going to be free of him."

Knox shifted into his human form, revealing his lean-muscled, sculpted body before sliding under the blankets with me and pulling me to his chest.

"Whil couldn't break the connection, but she did block it."

"So I'm safe?" I asked, shivering at the feel of his body pressed against mine.

"Yes," he replied, but I could feel his hesitation through our mating bond.

"It's not just yes, is it?"

He frowned. "So you can feel my emotions, too. It's not just me?" he asked instead.

"It's not just you and don't change the subject." I didn't want to make demands of an alpha. I couldn't force him to tell me anything even if I was his mate, but I needed to know what he wasn't telling me. "I need to know."

"Whil will need to regularly reinforce the block," he said.

"How regularly?" And for how long?

Except I had a feeling I already knew. It was going to be for however long Sterling or I lived.

"She doesn't know. But it's not a mating or soul bond in any way. There will be ways to break it," he replied, tightening his grip around me.

"Swell." I felt like I was back where I started a month ago, with a connection I needed to break and no easy way to do it... because if there was an easy way, Whil would have done it already.

"I promise," Knox said, his grip around me tightening as if he could keep me safe from my own head by just holding me tighter. "You'll be free of him even if I have to find a way to your realm and kill him."

A surge of violent determination swept through the bond. Yeah, a part of me wanted to go back to watch that, but according to everything Whil and Bishop had told me, returning to my realm was impossible.

"Whil is confident you can have a normal life," Knox insisted. "Do what you want... with who you want."

A shiver of desire swept down my spine and Knox groaned, reminding me that we could feel each other's emotions.

"I'm sorry," I murmured, embarrassment heating my cheeks.

"You don't apologize," he growled. "*I* apologize."

He brushed his lips against my jaw, the tenderness of his touch surprising and feeding the warmth of our shifter connection around my heart. With the exception of when we were huddling together for warmth after he'd rescued me from the flash flood, all my interactions with Knox — at least all that I could remember — were brusque, distant, or angry.

Nothing between us had been tender like it was between me and Bishop. Even the Knox in my dreams had been wild and ferocious. And while Bishop and Knox were identical twins with only a few subtle differences to tell them apart, I knew in my soul Knox was the one kissing me, not Bishop.

Except now that I focused on his kiss, it felt less tender and compassionate and more careful, as if he were afraid of hurting me... or me rejecting him.

AUDREY

"Knox—" I began, but I didn't know what to say. My soul yearned to reassure him, remind him that we were mates and that I'd never reject him. But my brain was still angry at him for doing exactly that to me.

"You almost died," he said, his lips brushing across my jaw to find my mouth. "I wasn't there to protect you and you almost—" He growled, the sound a low rumble in his chest. "Never again. I'll figure it out. Somehow. You're mine and I protect what's mine."

Ah. So he wasn't being tender because he was afraid of me rejecting him. He was afraid because I was so weak.

I wanted to yell at him that I wasn't weak, but Sterling had once again proven that I was. Even my mind was weak, easily manipulated.

God, I was so sick and tired of the same thoughts running through my head over and over again. I didn't want to be weak. I might not have any power and might not be able to shift, but I could be strong. Humans were strong, or at least stronger than me. They didn't have any magic and weren't simpering doormats. Some of them knew how to stand up for themselves and I wanted to be like that. I yearned for that.

Except every time I tried something, I was slapped back down and reminded of my place. And I couldn't afford to forget that, not now when I couldn't escape this pack.

Knox deepened our kiss, his desire and determination seeping through our mate bond, and he skimmed his hand down my throat, under my blanket, and along the top of my right breast, so close to my nipple and yet oh so far away.

A shiver of need pebbled the tiny bud, making him smile into our kiss, and I felt his pleasure at my pleasure swell between us. It was a complete circuit, both of us feeding off each other, our need building with each stroke of his tongue against mine and each brush of his fingers over my aching flesh.

Except I wanted to be strong about something. Anything. And giving in to Knox the second an intimate moment present itself wasn't standing up for myself.

I'd told him I was going to make him beg. If I gave in now, he'd know he could always get what he wanted with a kiss and a gentle touch.

"Knox," I gasped, pushing his mouth away from mine. "I'm not giving you sex."

He stared at me, his gaze capturing mine, concern sliding through the desire coming from him along with a hint of surprise as if he didn't understand why I'd pushed him away.

"I'm still mad at you for hurting me."

"You should be." He frowned and for a second it felt like he was reaching through our bond and sifting through all my emotions. "But you're not. You're determined."

He rose onto one elbow to better stare into my eyes and his hand on my breast shifted, the edge of his fingers brushing my nipple and sliding soft heat to my core.

"And you want me to keep touching you," he said slowly as if he couldn't understand my emotions.

"I told you'd I'd resist you. That—"

"That you'd make me beg," he said, cutting me off. "Even if it goes against what you want?"

"Not having sex won't hurt me," I huffed, even though a part of me was starting to ache for him, for the glorious sensations that made all the other complicated, painful emotions, go away. "You thinking you can always get what you want does hurt me. I've already lived that life, trapped with alphas that didn't care what I wanted. I won't go back to that." I swallowed at the lump in my throat. "I can't." Not with my mate.

My voice broke on the last word and Knox pulled me into his arms, hugging me to his chest, his tenderness surprising me... but then he'd held me after I'd almost drowned as well, giving me strength through our shifter connection and our mating bond.

"You won't go back to that. I promise. I didn't mean to hurt you," he said, his voice gruff, his desire softening and turning into something heartbreakingly sad. "I'm broken. I didn't want you stuck with me."

"I know you were trying to protect me." But I'd only realized that truth when I'd begged his wolf to let the human half of his soul go and figured out that he'd gone so far as to collar his wolf to keep us apart. It would have been so much easier, and hurt a lot less, if he'd just come out and told me. So much heartache could have been avoided.

"There's a reason we're outside on a mattress and not in the big bed in your suite. And it's not because it's a nice night," he said, his voice soft. "You were badly hurt and you needed me to steady your soul as much as I needed you to steady mine." The muscles in his jaw flexed and a whisper of panic ghosted through our bond. "But I can only be inside for a few hours. Less if I'm stressed."

The panic grew stronger as if just thinking about it scared him.

"I can't do crowds, either," he added, his fear making my breath pick up and my stomach churn. "I don't really like most people, with or without a crowd. I can't be a good mate. I can't give you a mating ceremony or spend the night with you. I can't hang out with your friends or go to events with you. That's no way to live."

I wasn't sure what to say to that. I'd thought he didn't want me because I was weak and couldn't shift, or because he was in love with someone else or afraid of commitment.

Hell, he *was* afraid of commitment, just not the way I expected.

He didn't want to commit because he thought he couldn't. And from the fear bleeding through our bond it wasn't a matter of him not wanting to do those things. He actually *couldn't*.

If we were back in my realm, he'd have access to therapists and psychiatrists — if he could be convinced to see them — and medication. In this realm, his only option for dealing with his phobia was avoidance.

I'd be a horrible person, let alone a terrible mate, if I demanded him to change. I was afraid I couldn't change from being a weakling, no matter how much I wanted to. I couldn't expect him to change, either.

This was the reality of our relationship and we were just going to have to figure it out since breaking up wasn't an option.

"It's okay," I said. "I don't need those things."

He huffed. "I know you do. I can feel it in our bond. I felt your hurt when I said we couldn't have a mating ceremony."

I wanted to deny those words, but I couldn't, and with him being able to feel my emotions, there was no point in putting up a false front.

A mating ceremony was a proclamation to the pack that we were mated. It told everyone that he wanted me and even though he was trying to protect me from unwanted questions by not having the ceremony — if he could even stand being in that type of gathering with the least amount of people possible — it still hurt. It felt like he was rejecting me all over again even though I knew he wasn't.

"It hurts because it reminds me of your rejection." My throat tightened to the point of burning, and I slid my gaze to the two moons, still visible in the lightening sky. The one moon looked like the regular moon in the mortal realm, while the other was smaller and pink, a constant reminder of everything that had happened to me and that I wasn't home and never would be.

"It's a hurt that's going to stick around," I told him truthfully even though I was afraid of his reaction. "There's a lot mixed up with it, like how sometimes I'm still that little girl who thinks no one wants her."

Knox's grip tightened and he pressed his lips against the top of my head, breathing in my scent.

"I thought it was the right thing to do." He released a shuddering breath that washed warm over my forehead and cheeks. "And I was scared. You weren't anything I planned for and it happened so fast and I can't even come close to the mate you deserve. You should have bonded with Bishop."

"But I didn't."

"You didn't," he murmured. "I'm sorry I hurt you and I swear I'll try."

His emotions churned, his fear growing stronger, but mixed in with the fear was determination and worry and a hint of surprise.

"I don't deserve you," he said, "and I don't expect you to be anyone other than who you are." The fear in his emotions churned stronger. "But you need to talk to me. I don't want to find you like that —" The muscles in his jaw flexed and more worry slid through the bond. "I don't want to find you like that again."

"It works both ways," I told him, making him frown. "The talking part. You need to talk to me, too."

KNOX

I drew in another deep breath of Audrey's scent and held her close. I couldn't get enough of her, of the warmth around my heart from our bond and our deep shifter connection, or the feel of her tiny, fragile body protected against mine. I also couldn't get enough of her good feelings, her hope and determination and desire.

Our stronger-than-normal mating bond was an incredible blessing… but also a curse.

It went both ways and neither of us could hide from the other — since I'd already tried blocking it, like I could block my twin bond with Bishop, and failed.

For good or bad, we'd always know what the other was feeling.

The thought that I'd never be alone even in my own head worried me. I liked being alone and needed quiet even from my own thoughts. But I also liked this direct connection to Audrey's emotions. I'd never have to guess if I made her happy and I'd know right away when I screwed up.

Given how I had trouble reading subtle emotional clues, along with how Audrey was sometimes afraid to speak her mind, our bond was the only way to know when she was truly happy and content.

And speaking of happy…

I wanted to go back to the warmth of her desire. She was worried again and sad, and while Whil had said she'd blocked that asshole's influence, I didn't want a repeat of yesterday morning. The best way to prevent it was to strengthen her positive emotions so she couldn't spiral into depression and be coerced into anything again.

I slid my hand back under the blankets to her right breast — since her left was covered with gauze — and traced my fingers over her flesh, circling closer and closer to her nipple. She'd liked that before and I was rewarded with her growing desire radiating soft and warm through our bond.

"Knox, please," she said, frustration edging her voice and seeping into her emotions.

"I'm not asking for sex." Even though my wolf and my cock thought that was a great idea. "I'm *giving* you sex."

"Giving me sex, gives you sex."

"Not if you're the only one having orgasms."

She huffed and the frustration flickering through her desire bled away. She ached for me as much as I ached for her and only part of that was due to the mating bond's influence. Or at least, it was in her case.

In my case, the bond had almost nothing to do with it. She was everything my wolf desired despite his desires being contradictory. She was strong, even though it was a quiet, persistent strength that she and others didn't recognize, *and* she needed me to protect her.

The urge to wrap her in my arms and never let her go surged and she responded with a flutter of comfort, knowing, even if it was on a subconscious level, that she was safe with me. And now that I'd gotten my head out of my ass, she always would be.

She turned her head to look me in the eyes, our emotions feeding off each other, my satisfaction growing at her comfort and my desire surging with hers.

But there was still uncertainty in her eyes. It was so soft, I wouldn't have felt it in our bond if I hadn't seen it in her stunning golden-brown orbs, and all I wanted was to make it go away, to reassure her completely.

You know what we need to do, my wolf said, his need to mate with her, to feel her coming around our cock, rising to the surface.

We could probably tease her into giving us sex, but she'd said no and I intended to honor that. I needed to rise her up and give her confidence to stand against the assholes she'd inevitably come across, just like she had when she'd yelled at me on our way back to Stonehaven. Going against her wishes wouldn't accomplish that.

Then make her scream our name.

My hand dipped lower, jumping straight to her mound, and I directed it to her thigh before my wolf could plunge our fingers inside her.

Slowly. We need to go slowly, I insisted, even as her desire spiked.

She'd been unconscious for almost a whole day, and while the elixirs would have mostly healed her injuries by now, she wasn't a hundred percent. That, and as much as my hard-as-hell cock hurt, I wanted to prove myself to her and worship her.

At least let us taste her, my wolf whined, thankfully not pushing me because he, too, knew Audrey needed to be loved, not fucked.

A taste was a great idea. Her scent was soft and sweet, her arousal would be the same. I just had to remember to take it slow, prove to her that I wanted to spend my time on her and that she was worth it... something I'd never done, and never felt, for a woman before.

My fingers inched higher up her thigh, dipping from the top of her leg to the inside, and I pressed my palm against her flesh to stop myself.

Slowly, I reminded my wolf as I tenderly brushed my lips along her jaw.

She turned into the kiss, her lips seeking mine, the uncertainty still a barely-there whisper in her emotions.

I feared no matter what I did, it would always be there, an ugly insidious seed her previous alpha had planted in her soul when she was a child.

Then our lips connected and she released a soft sigh, her desire strengthening, making my soul sing. I'd done that. I'd made her forget her worries even if it was only for a second, and I was determined to make her feel and forget so much more.

With a control I hadn't thought possible given the wildness of my wolf, I kissed her softly, reverently with gentle sips that, much to my surprise, built up a heated need within her.

Moaning, she leaned into me, pressing more of her body against mine, her lips growing insistent, begging me to deepen the kiss. Hints of the power locked deep within her flickered against my skin, teasing out my own power like it had in our shared dreams.

But unlike the dreams, our powers didn't fight for dominance. They swirled and danced, curling around each other, merging together then breaking apart, building building building into a heady, aching heat.

"Knox," she begged, her ache at just being kissed shocking me. I hadn't thought something so soft could be so sexual.

But then, I realized it wasn't the softness building up her need, it was the tease and our whirling emotions.

My fingers were still firmly pressed against her thigh, but if I moved an inch I'd be at the crux between her leg and mound. Less than an inch more and I could be playing with her wet heat.

My kiss had inflamed her desire for more, possibly for everything despite her earlier insistences, and my cock throbbed at the thought, precum slicking against my stomach. Except if I took advantage of her now, she'd never trust me.

I'd fucked everything up right from the start and that trust was going to be hard won. I deserved to work for it, and I would.

With a soft growl, I deepened the kiss, plunging my tongue inside her mouth and stealing her moans. Her glorious desire tingled around my heart and made my balls painfully tight, and I reveled in the sensation. I wanted her not because of the mate bond but because she was persistent and brave and kind. She'd tried to be kind to me and I'd been too blinded by my fear to accept her.

Never again. I swear by the Sisters. Never again.

I let all my desire for her pour through our mating bond, not wanting her to have any doubts about how I felt. It was just a fraction of what I needed to do to make it up to her, but it was a start and better than just talking to her.

I kissed her until she was breathless and trembling, then swept my lips down her neck to my mating mark, a shimmering white scar on her shoulder where I'd claimed her and sealed our bond.

It should have been the only scar on her body and not just because shifters healed fast enough to not scar with the exception of a mating mark, but because she shouldn't have had to suffer like she had.

I swept my tongue over the mark and was rewarded with a full body shiver than raced from her head to her toes along with a billow of heated need through our bond.

"Knox," she gasped, bucking her hips, trying to get me to move my fingers up her thigh. "You're killing me."

Her words brought a feral grin to my lips that I hid by dipping down to her breast and flicking my tongue over her nipple. I was beginning to understand why Bishop liked foreplay so much. It hadn't made sense to me or my wolf, but with a direct link to Audrey's emotions, I could feel her growing need, the achy, squirmy desire getting tighter and tighter, and knew I could make her see stars without pushing my cock into her.

And gods, I wanted her to feel so good she did see stars.

I doubled my effort on my teasing, sucking her nipple into my mouth and laving it with my tongue while inching my fingers closer and closer to her core. I concentrated on her, listening to her breath pick up then start to catch, feeling her body twitch and shiver, and feeling her need in our bond turn into an inferno before pulling away.

"Knox, please," she gasped, digging her fingers into my hair, her arms trembling. But it was like she couldn't decide if she wanted to hold me closer to her breast or push me away.

I decided for her and kissed my way down her belly, teasing my tongue into her belly button and nudging her thighs with my palms, asking for entrance.

She accepted me with a trembling sigh, her legs falling open, and

I settled between them, drawing in deep breaths of her scent. It was sweet and heady, thickened by her desire and captured under the blankets with me, and as much as I wanted to be cocooned in her scent, I wanted to see her face when she came more.

I pushed the blankets off my head and shoulders, exposing Audrey's pale flesh, tight nipple, and the patch of gauze tape to her chest covering her other one to the early morning sun, watching for signs that she was uncomfortable being exposed.

But she was too caught up in her desire. There wasn't even a flicker of unease in the bond, and her gaze, now molten gold in the light, captured mine, making my breath hitch.

Sisters, she was so beautiful. I didn't know which sleeping god or goddess I'd pleased to have such a stunning mate, but I would spend every day worshiping Audrey in thanks.

Her body trembling in anticipation, I nuzzled into the soft hair covering her mound and swept my tongue over her folds, carefully avoiding her clit. But she still jerked like she'd been zapped with lightning and the desire in our bond roared into a burning frenzy.

Her fingers dug into my scalp and my wolf flashed her a satisfied grin at the possessive move.

Mine. Mine mine mine.

And hers. Forever.

I trailed my tongue over her again and again, teasing and sucking, flicking her clit and pushing inside her. Her desire was the sweetest nectar, coating my tongue and filling my nose and her gasps and moans the sweetest music.

The whirl of her need propelled me forward. It was like a drug. If I licked here, she'd shudder and moan. If I backed off for a moment then licked again, her moan would be louder. I brought her to the edge of climax again and again, building the tension within her until she was begging for release.

"Knox, please," she moaned, her body strung tight, hanging on the precipice.

With a growl from my wolf, I pushed my tongue inside her, fucking her even higher, then sucked on her clit.

Audrey screamed and white-hot pleasure shot through the bond. Her body convulsed, her eyes squeezed tight and her mouth hung open. The pleasure filling her expression was glorious.

I came hard, shooting hot jets of cum onto the mattress, and didn't care. Audrey had seen stars. I didn't need to ask. The emotions rushing through our bond told me everything, and I'd never been so satisfied to not have gotten my cock wet in my life.

AUDREY

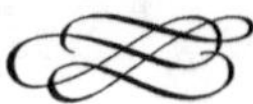

I woke to a gentle hand on my shoulder and Nova's soft voice calling my name.

"Hey," she said as she sat on the edge of the bed and I blinked sleepily at her. "How are you feeling?"

Amazing. Boneless. Thoroughly satisfied. I hadn't orgasmed so hard in my life.

And to know my pleasure had also brought Knox pleasure was empowering. I'd feared knowing what he felt would be distracting or worse, overwhelming by not knowing where my emotions ended and his began. But it had enhanced everything, a feedback loop that had just kept building and building with glorious pleasure.

After I'd seen stars and the universe and everything, Knox had carried me inside, saying he could handle a few hours before the walls closed in on him. He'd helped steady my boneless and still-trembling body as we cleaned up in the shower then held me until I fell asleep.

He'd warned me that he wouldn't be able to stay and he hadn't. The space behind me where he'd been was cold which meant he'd been gone for a while.

A whisper of disappointment that I was alone in bed curled

within me but I shoved it down. It wasn't his fault. I'd felt his growing unease as we'd cuddled even though we hadn't been inside for very long, and I could tell he was trying to hide it from me.

That was just who he was and I had to accept that, just like he had to accept I was a shifter who couldn't shift.

Except that wasn't what Nova was asking me about. She didn't know Knox had given me an earth-shattering orgasm or that we'd cuddle in bed until I passed out. She was asking about my new scars, the ones that had been under the gauze patches that Knox had peeled away in the shower.

How *was* I feeling?

Better and yet not better.

Most of the weight and shame and grief since waking from the heat fever was gone, although not all of it. I didn't doubt that Bishop cared for me and the fear that he was using me and would throw me away when he was done was also gone.

But I was still wary of Cyrus and every other pack member... including Nova. Not because I thought Cyrus would hurt or punish me to the extent Merrick or Sterling had, but because there was still a chance he would reprimand me with more than just words next time. That, and he'd made it clear he didn't like weaknesses and I was a weakness.

It would be best if I just stayed out of sight and not remind him that I was permanently bound to his family, as well as keep a low profile from the rest of the pack, let them know I knew my place at least until I'd proven that I wasn't worthless. Hopefully, everyone would just leave me alone.

On the other hand, I was ashamed and embarrassed that Sterling had manipulated me again. How long had he been whispering poison into my soul? And how long until Whil's magical block broke and he was influencing me again?

Except the only thing I could do about it was to pay attention to when my thoughts turned dark and ask Whil to remake the block.

I sighed. Always being on guard and hiding from everyone was no way to live, but, at the moment, it was the only way I had.

"I'm okay," I told her hesitantly, deciding okay was the safest, least complicated response I could give her.

She raised an eyebrow at that.

Guess "not complicated" wasn't a satisfactory response.

But what else could I say? Nova had been kind to me, but she'd grown up and was close friends with Bishop, Knox, and Cyrus. I needed to be careful what I said to her. At least until I was certain I could trust her.

"I ah... I spent a month walking and the spell failed, and I ah... have a mate who's..." How did I politely sum up Knox yet still sound truthful? I couldn't lie to her. She knew better than me that Knox had issues.

"Complicated?" Nova supplied as she motioned for me to sit up. "You have a complicated mate."

"Sure. Let's go with complicated." And hot and moody and fierce and good with his mouth and difficult. "I have a mate bond neither of us wanted and I'm... ah... not sure how I can be useful to the pack."

I sat up, holding the sheet to my breasts to keep myself covered even though I knew she wanted to look at my injuries. Thankfully she didn't comment on the fact that I hadn't told her anything about my situation that she didn't already know or about my modesty. From what I'd seen of this pack, nudity wasn't something to be embarrassed about and most shifters weren't.

Only my pack, which had cursed ourselves generations ago to prevent us from shifting before after our eighteenth birthday had human-levels of modesty. And since my wolf hadn't awakened and I'd never shifted, I'd never been nude in public before.

"So, yeah," Nova replied with a wry smile. "Okay. Sounds about right." She looked at the new, pink scars on my left breast and on my left inner arm. "These have healed nicely. You should soak in the bath for a few minutes so it's easier to take the stitches out."

And then it'd be back to how it was when I'd first arrived: me needing to figure out my place in this pack and prove my worthiness. Except I needed to be careful how I went about doing it, certainly more careful with how I interacted with people than before.

Which wasn't entirely true. I was now fully mated to Knox and Bishop had promised to court me. I wasn't back to nothing.

Still, I didn't want my identity to revolve around the men in my life. I could be more than just someone's mate, no matter what Merrick or Sterling or all the others said about me.

"So, Cyrus mentioned you might be interested in joining a first aid class," Nova said as she hurried ahead of me to the bathroom and started filling the tub. "He said you knew the basics and didn't panic at the sight of blood."

I glanced around for a robe but didn't see one and didn't want to grab something from the wardrobe and change when I was only going to undress again as soon as I got to the bath.

"It wasn't anything special," I said, contemplating wrapping myself in the sheet then deciding to just suck it up.

Nova wouldn't care that I was naked *and* she was a doctor, so I clenched my jaw, trying to keep my insecurities from overwhelming me, and shuffled on still slightly weak legs to the bathtub.

"Your ability to shift eliminates the risk of infection so there isn't a lot to worry about," I said. I'd bandaged a few of Knox's deeper wounds after our first fight with a pack of jackals, but it hadn't been anything anyone else couldn't have done.

"Still, if you're interested, I have a class in a few days that's going through how and when to use everything in the emergency medical packs we've placed all over town. I wouldn't say no to anyone who wants to learn about them."

Worry darkened her expression and I could just imagine what she was thinking. Too many people had been seriously hurt and killed when that pack of grimalkins had attacked the town. She wanted anyone and everyone able to help save lives if it ever happened again.

And so did I. Maybe someone could have saved those children the grimalkin had killed. I'd managed to save four of them, and the other two had looked dead, but maybe they hadn't been. Maybe some of the pack's magical elixir would have saved them.

"Sure." I sank into the tub, letting the warm water lap up to my chin to ensure the stitches on my chest were submerged while Nova perched on the edge of the large tub and thankfully looked away to give me privacy. "I'll take the class."

I just hoped this was a hands-on class and didn't involve a textbook like the classes back home since I couldn't read their language. Which was something else I was going to have to take care of sooner rather than later.

But Bishop had said he'd help me with that so now I just needed to remember to bring it up whenever I saw him next.

"Knox said you weren't aware that you'd hurt yourself," Nova said. "You want to tell me what happened?"

Not really. But she'd asked and not answering her could make her angry since she was my superior in the pack, something I should have been thinking about from the moment I'd first met her a month ago.

"I'm not really sure," I replied, trying to keep the hesitation from my voice.

Except that was only half the truth. After our shower, while snuggling in bed, Knox had told me that Sterling had manipulated my dreams and he'd been able to make me hurt myself because I'd already been afraid and sad and desperate. But I wasn't sure how much I wanted to confess to Nova. If she knew about my weaknesses, she could use them against me.

Except that had been true in my previous pack. It might not be true with this one.

Thinking both packs were the same was Sterling's doing. Nova had already been kind to me, and while I didn't have definitive proof I could trust her, I wanted to give her a chance.

I wanted to give everyone a chance.

Which was ridiculously naive of me, but I couldn't help myself. My old pack had decided I was useless before I'd even had a chance to prove myself. I didn't want to make the same mistake.

"I'd been having bad dreams since I woke from the heat fever," I told her, my heart racing as I studied her profile for any hint that I'd revealed too much.

But Nova's expression didn't darken or turn pleased. It didn't even stay the same as if she were trying to keep her emotions hidden. Instead, her lips pressed tight, her brow furrowed in concern, and a hint of her power slipped her control as if she were upset, but not necessarily angry at me.

"Cyrus mentioned the only way to break your heat was for you and Knox to seal your bond. I'm sorry for that. I know neither of you wanted it."

"What else did Cyrus tell you?" Had he talked about how I didn't know my place or that I couldn't do anything?

"Only medically pertinent information," she replied. "That your heat turned into a fever and went longer than normal and way beyond what was safe. We're going to need to watch out for that in about six months when you have your next heat just in case it wasn't just the bond affecting you. He also said that you got some new scars on your shin from fighting a grimalkin and that you almost drowned. You seem to have bad luck when it comes to beasts, monsters, and fast-moving water."

That was an understatement. So far, I was 0-2 for falling in rivers and nearly drowning and 2-5 in the monster department with only two wins because I hadn't actually fought any of the jackals.

Or was I 2-7? Did psychopathic Sterling count as a monster? I mean, I knew he was a monster, but physically he was just a shifter.

"Yeah," I agreed, dropping my gaze in case she looked at me.

"We're going to have to keep an eye on you," she added

I didn't know if she meant that in a caring way or a controlling way, and the thought sent a shiver rushing down my spine.

"Audrey," Nova said, her posture tensing as if she'd seen my shiver. "It's understandable that you've had bad dreams. You're from another realm. Things work differently here and you're alone and surrounded by strangers. I'd be shocked if you didn't have doubts or fears that haunt your dreams. It's understandable that someone magically connected to you could amplify them." She stood and grabbed a large towel from the rack near the tub, her tone softening.

"No one is upset at what happened. We're just worried about you and want to keep you safe."

That was something Merrick had said when he'd first taken me in, but I didn't get the sense that Nova meant it in the same way he had. She sounded like she was genuinely concerned about me.

"So you know I'm from another realm?" I asked, hoping she wouldn't notice that I'd changed the conversation to something less personal.

She handed me the towel without looking at me. Gratitude swelled within me that she was respecting my shyness even though she probably didn't understand it.

"Deacon got the guys to talk your first night out, and he told me when he, his hunt team, and Whil returned from Anakar," she said. "Wrap yourself in the towel and lie down on the bed so we can get those stitches out."

"Does everyone know?" I asked, obeying her instructions. Would it be good if everyone knew or would people somehow take advantage of me? It certainly would make me look like even more of a freak than I already was.

Nova grabbed her medical bag from the floor near the bedroom door and sat beside me. "Just me and Deacon and whoever else you've told."

"So only you two, Bishop, Cyrus, Knox, and Whil," I said as she pulled out her supplies then turned my left arm so it was resting comfortably on the bed and she could easily remove the stitches.

"Your hedging when I was trying to get your family history with heats makes more sense now."

"I wasn't hedging. Heats in my realm aren't like heats here." But I also hadn't told her the truth because I didn't want to become a science experiment or for her to think I was crazy and lock me up in an institution or wherever it was they locked crazy people here.

"I'd like to take some blood and monitor you," she said. "If heats don't get serious in your realm, and your first heat rose to a fever then other changes could be happening to you. It's best to try to stay on top of it."

And with one little statement, all the positive feelings I had about Nova during this conversation vanished.

"How closely do you want to monitor me?" I asked, trying to keep my fear from my voice.

"Just vitals and blood. You're not going to be an experiment," she assured me as if she knew that was one of my fears. "You have a life and a new mate who, let me tell you, is going to be a handful." She rolled her eyes at me, a lifetime of knowing Knox and his ways making her expression wry.

"He will be. But I think we'll figure it out. He's already agreed to try to make our mating work, which seems like a big deal for him."

"It's huge," she replied. "Enormous. Knox hasn't tried anything with anyone since he was a kid. For a while there, he wasn't even speaking with Cyrus and Bishop. Just basic communication with Deacon to get his solo hunting assignments."

Which didn't surprise me. Even before I'd felt the whisper of panic through our bond when Knox had mentioned he couldn't stand crowds, I knew he didn't like them. His avoiding me hadn't just been because I was an unwanted mate. It was because he didn't like social interactions with anyone.

Speaking of—

"Do you know if he's waiting outside for me?" I didn't expect him to be waiting, but if he was, I didn't want to waste his time.

"Knox had to meet with Deacon, but he told me to tell you he'd find you after lunch," Nova said. "Don't let him take you on a long walk outside of town. You're still recovering from your injuries, your heat fever, and all that traveling. And don't let Bishop march you all around town, either. You're to stay on the Residence's grounds for the next four days, eat three meals a day plus snacks, gain some weight back, and take it easy."

She leveled a hard look at me, meeting my gaze and holding it in a show of dominance. A flicker of her power washed over me, not enough to compel me to do what she'd ordered but enough to remind me that she could.

"No leaving the Residence, eating more, and taking it easy," I repeated. "Got it."

I hadn't planned anything for the next little while. Hell, at the moment I didn't have plans for anything, not my future, or what to do about Knox and Bishop, or if I wanted to face Cyrus again or just avoid him as best I could for the rest of my life.

Staying put for the next four days was okay. Hopefully, by then I'd come up with some answers.

AUDREY

Nova finished removing the stitches from my body then waited in the living room for me to get dressed so we could go to the kitchen together and have lunch. She said it was after the usual lunchtime, but too far away from dinner to just have a snack, and given how my stomach had grumbled when she'd mentioned food, I had to agree with her.

Except now I stared at the clothes in the wardrobe, determined to ignore my reflection in the two-person, full-body mirror sitting beside it.

I had more scars and they were ragged and thick, ugly pink patches marring the flesh above my heart, my right thigh, and my left forearm. I also had new scars at the base of my neck and a few more along my ribs.

Thankfully, those ones were thin and would be less noticeable once they faded. But the other scars were always going to be obvious, just like the thick claw marks across my chest and the puncture wounds in my back and chest from the monster's claws when it had grabbed me.

Even if I could have hidden my lack of shifter power, the scars would always mark me as an anomaly. Shifters didn't scar. They healed too quickly.

Only mating bites scarred, and those were rare in my realm, and from what Bishop had told me, they were pretty rare in this realm as well.

Which meant, as much as my essence said I was a shifter to those who could sense essences, I shouldn't call myself one. I was, for all intents and purposes, a human.

Maybe if I thought of myself like that, I'd find peace. I hadn't met a lot of humans before I'd walked into Kelna, but I hadn't seemed weaker than them. In fact, if I just gained a little self-confidence, I'd probably make a decent human.

Of course, that didn't address the fact that I was still surrounded by shifters. I could be the strongest human in the realm and I'd still be weak and pathetic compared to them.

But the point was not to compare myself to them. I'd never get close and I needed to leave all the ugly things Merrick had beaten into me behind. I had a mate and another man interested in me, and I had a fresh start. People in this pack would talk and look down on me and probably hurt me just like my other pack, but I wasn't alone anymore.

I just needed to find my own path and keep out of everyone else's way.

Which was easier said than done, but true, nonetheless.

I pulled on a loose cotton shirt and pants similar to what I'd worn traveling. From what I'd seen, the outfit wasn't as common as the long, backless dresses most women wore, but I didn't want to show off more scars than necessary and I wanted to feel comfortable.

Besides, I wasn't competing with any of the women in the pack. Even if Bishop changed his mind about me — which would hurt, but wasn't something I'd fight — I still had Knox. Our relationship was still rocky, but it was permanent. The warmth radiating around my heart and the strong, sure emotions seeping through our bond reassured me.

In time, everything between us would work out. We just needed to be patient with each other.

Holding on to those feelings to keep my tentative new confidence strong, I left the bedroom.

Nova sat at the dining room table, writing in a black leatherbound notebook, but she quickly put the book and her pen into her bag and didn't keep me waiting. Beside her, the French doors were open, letting in a soft warm breeze scented with the flowers in the planter boxes and a hint of something sweet mixed with wood smoke... Knox's scent. The mattress with its rumpled blanket still sat in the middle of the small patio, and heat warmed my cheeks with the memory of what Knox and I had done last night.

"So," she said, flashing me a mischievous smile that made me smile in return despite my embarrassment. "You and Knox really are trying to make your mating work."

"We don't really have a choice," I mumbled, the heat in my face burning into my scalp and down my throat.

With her heightened senses, she could probably smell our lovemaking. There was no hiding anything from shifters.

"You don't have to have sex if you aren't sexually interested in each other... but he is handsome." She waggled her eyebrows at me, the action surprising me and making me giggle.

"He is," I replied with a sigh. "I also think once he lets his gruff standoffishness go, he'll be really sweet. I've already seen glimpses of it."

"He's just trying to protect himself," she said, leading me out of my suite and down the hall. "Also, he probably doesn't know what to do with you."

Socially, maybe. But he'd known exactly what I'd needed last night and hadn't asked for anything in return.

"He told me he's never had a relationship before."

"And very few friendships outside of his brothers. But that doesn't mean he's a bad person," Nova replied, a hint of sisterly affection seeping into her tone, reminding me that even though she wasn't technically his sister, they had grown up together and were close.

"I know. He's just shy. I can feel it." I pressed my hand over my heart. "Our bond is stronger than I expected. I can feel his emotions and he can feel mine."

"Really?" Nova's eyes widened in surprise.

A sudden flash of panic raced through me and I fought to school my expression. Had I said too much? If I'd said that to Merrick, he would have found a way to use that information against me. I didn't know how, but he would, and if Nova wasn't as trustworthy as I hoped, she could, too.

"If I hadn't thought I needed to monitor you before," she said, "I know now. Mate bonds aren't supposed to be that strong. Are they that strong in your realm?"

"No. But—" Shit. I had to tell her something. "It could be the unusual way our bond formed. And I didn't notice his emotions until we returned to Stonehaven and then on that first night Knox…" I trailed off, not sure how much more I should share. Almost going feral seemed like a really personal thing and Knox was a very private man.

"And Knox almost went feral," Nova finished for me. "A high stress situation can strengthen a bond. It's why Bishop and Knox are so deeply connected."

I waited for her to say more, but she didn't. Guess whatever happened to the twins to deepen their connection wasn't Nova's story to tell and one of them would either tell me himself or not at all. I wasn't going to push the matter. It sounded like it was serious and life-altering and I didn't want them to relive their trauma.

Sometimes it was better to just leave the past in the past.

Nova led me out of the maze of halls through the Residence's grand foyer with its sweeping staircase and massive crystal chandelier and to the kitchen. She'd mentioned that it was past lunch so it didn't surprise me that there wasn't anyone preparing food like there'd been yesterday morning.

What did surprise me were Bishop and Velora sitting at the kitchen table with open file folders, leather-bound books, and an explosion of loose papers covering the surface.

"Audrey!" Bishop exclaimed the second I stepped inside. "How are you feeling?"

He rushed around the table to reach me and cupped my cheeks with his large palms. His warm brown gaze locked with mine as if he were seeing into my soul and learning whatever was wrong with me without me telling him. Warmth and joy rushed through me — and not just because of our shifter connection.

He was genuinely pleased to see me and concerned about my well-being.

Of course, he'd always been pleased and concerned when it came to me. I didn't know how I'd doubted his intentions.

Except I did know.

I was afraid I was unlovable.

My life so far had proven I was unlovable, and to have someone like Bishop, someone beautiful and powerful, to express interest in me went beyond my wildest dreams.

I might not be able to trust anyone else in the pack, especially not his oldest brother, but I could trust Bishop.

"I'm okay." I leaned into his touch and let my eyes drift shut. Our shifter connection blended with the heat from my mating bond, swelled around my heart, and flooded my chest.

"She's healed, but she's still recovering," Nova said, her tone stern. "That means no tromping around town and wearing her out. She's to say on the Residence's grounds for four days."

"I can carry her," Bishop shot back. "She won't have to walk anywhere."

"It's only four days and there's plenty to do around the Residence that doesn't risk exhausting her." A hint of Nova's power leaked from her control, not-so-subtly telling Bishop how serious she was about me resting. "She can look at the gardens or meditate in the sacred grove. Whil would probably appreciate a little company from someone who isn't asking for something and there are all the public rooms in the Residence that she can explore. The library, the music room as well as the sauna and pool on the lower level."

"We also have a gym," Bishop added.

"Which you won't use until your four days of rest are over," Nova told me.

"I'm sure I'll need more than four days to see everything," I assured her. That and I needed to do some serious thinking about my future. I needed to figure out how I could be useful and be worthy of being mated to one — maybe two — of the pack's alphas... I just wasn't sure how to do that because it needed to be really good to make me stand out.

"But first," Nova added. "Lunch."

She turned toward the fridge and cupboards, but Bishop cleared his throat and stopped her.

"I've already got lunch covered. I was just waiting for you to wake up," he said as he dipped close and brushed his lips across my forehead.

Nova crossed her arms and glared at him. "It better not involve taking her into town."

"It doesn't," Bishop replied, beaming at her, clearly pleased with his lunch plans. "Grab the picnic basket from the fridge, will you?"

"Bishop," Velora said, tapping her pen on the papers in front of her and shooting me an angry glare. "We need to get this done. The summer festival is only six days away."

"It's waited most of a month," he replied as Nova got a wide wooden basket with a short handle out of the fridge and he grabbed a blanket from a cupboard in the corner. "It can wait a few more hours. Deal with what we've already finished or take a break."

"The sooner we get it done, the sooner we can slow down," she replied.

"We appreciate how hard you work for us, Velora," he said, slinging the blanket over his shoulder and taking the basket. Then he wrapped his free arm around my back to my hip and tugged me to his side. "But don't forget you have a life, too."

"Of course." She dropped her glare to her work as he turned to face her.

"Come on, Audrey. I want to show you something. Oh, and speaking of life..." He led me out of the kitchen's back door into the herb garden and the bright, hot summer sunshine. "I want to take you to the summer festival. You'll love it, there'll be food and games and dancing."

As we turned to head deeper into the garden, I couldn't help but glance back into the kitchen. Nova flashed me a warm smile then turned her attention to inside the fridge, while Velora raised her gaze and returned to glaring at me.

The look sent a shiver of fear sliding down my spine. Shae, Sterling's girlfriend had worn a similar look when she thought that me moving in with Sterling and Merrick meant I was going to steal him from her.

Velora also hadn't been overly kind to me the night I'd arrived in Stonehaven and had dinner with Bishop, Cyrus, and their betas. I'd thought her dislike was because I was a weak shifter who was clearly keeping secrets along with me not being able to control my desire for Bishop and filling the room with the scent of my arousal.

Now I wasn't so sure.

Now it felt like she was angry Bishop was spending time with me and not on a professional, they needed to get work done, level.

I could guess with the way Bishop unconsciously flirted and the looks other women gave him that he had a trail of broken hearts in his wake. What I didn't know was if Velora was one of them or was still hoping to catch his eye.

And really, who wouldn't want Bishop's attention? He was kind and funny and gorgeous. He was also a powerful catch. Anyone who mated with Bishop got as close to being a pack alpha as they could get. A woman could only get closer if she mated Cyrus, the primary alpha. But with his hurtful gruffness, he wasn't as desirable a catch as Bishop, no matter how bad-boy beautiful Cyrus was.

Velora probably wanted a rise in position in the pack along with the most eligible bachelor between the three brothers. But as far as I could see, Bishop hadn't shown any interest in her. Not at the dinner and not from the glimpse I'd just seen of them working together before he'd known I was in the kitchen.

And now I'd made an enemy of Velora.

She wasn't going to be able to obviously hurt or shame me like Shae and Sterling had done unless she got Cyrus's support which I doubted Knox or Bishop would allow. But that didn't mean she wouldn't try more subtle attacks.

I was going to have to be careful, especially when I was alone.

I'd already known I needed to watch myself and stay in my place until I'd quietly proven my usefulness, but this was more than that. Velora wouldn't be waiting for me to screw up, she'd attack regardless and when I least expected it.

BISHOP

"Lots of foreign merchants come to the festival and there's a ton of strange and interesting things to buy and eat," I said as I took Audrey's hand in mine and led her around the back of the Residence. I was excited to not just show her my favorite spot on the grounds but at the prospect of showing her the year's best festival. "It starts in six days, *after* you're done resting for Nova. Say yes."

She'd said she wanted all the things that came with courting, and that said to me that she wanted someone to make her feel special and desired. What was more special than a picnic in the gardens and a day dancing and laughing and eating and playing games at a festival?

She deserved all of it and more. It made me furious that no one had ever made her feel that way. And while Knox — once he got his head out of his ass — would be a dedicated mate and would protect her from everyone and everything, he wouldn't know how to make her feel like she was special. That was going to be my job and I was happy to do it.

Even if Knox came to me for advice — which he would when he realized the truth about our mate and that he had no idea how to give her what she deserved — I'd still be the mate to spoil her and treat her like a true alpha queen.

Because that was my job. I could protect her but not as well as Knox. I might be able to challenge her, but again, Cyrus was better than me at that.

Of course, first I had to get Cyrus to accept he had feelings for her. Which had been obvious even before he'd panicked over her being coerced by a magical connection and hurting herself. But he was determined to do right by our pack like our parents had taught him, and very few people in our pack would accept Audrey as an alpha.

They'd accept her as mine and Knox's mate, but not the mate of the primary alpha. At least not until they got to know her and realized her power didn't come from aggression and alpha strength, but determination and kindness.

With what she'd gone through, she could have been angry and hateful toward alphas and other shifters. She could have turned her determination into figuring out how to burn down the world — and I had no doubt she'd figure it out if she put her mind to it. Instead, she was soft and shy and tried to protect those who couldn't protect themselves to the detriment of her own safety despite her lack of power.

I squeezed her hand and glanced at her, and she responded with a soft warm smile.

"Say yes," I said.

Her warm smile faltered. I could see her insecurities starting to take over, insecurities that had only gotten worse since her heat fever and that monster's influence on her emotions.

Even with Whil's magic blocking him, the emotional wounds he'd insidiously inflicted on her heart and soul were still there, and it was going to take time for them to heal. It made me furious and broke my heart at the same time.

Audrey deserved to feel free to be herself, to do what she wanted without fear of anything.

But that confidence didn't happen right away, not with a lifetime of being abused. Going out, having fun, and seeing that my pack wasn't like her old pack would help. Everyone would be curious about her, the woman who mated Knox, but by going out they'd see she was perfect for us and fall in love with her, just like I had.

I fluttered my eyelashes at her and offered her my most innocent smile, drawing out her smile again with my goofiness. "Say you'll go to the festival with me."

She giggled and rolled her eyes. I could still see some hesitation in her expression, but I could also see her battling her insecurities. She *wanted* to go to the festival, to have fun.

"We'll have so much fun..." I batted my eyelashes again and added my flashiest smile, making her laugh.

"How can I say no to that?"

"So you'll go?" I asked.

"Of course I'll go," she laughed. "Now, where are you taking me for this picnic?" she asked as I led her past the small orchard with various fruit trees toward a towering hedgerow.

"To the prettiest place on the Residence's ground this time of year!"

"To Whil's greenhouse library?" Her lips quirked up at the edges and a hint of a mischievous glint danced in her eyes, telling me she'd already figured out we weren't anywhere near Whil's cottage.

"Nope. Prettier *and* more private." I waggled my eyebrows at her, happy to play her game, and was rewarded with a soft, musical giggle, one I wanted to spend the rest of my life hearing.

"What could be prettier than the gardens outside Whil's house? I bet those flowers bloom all year long despite the season."

"It's a side effect of her being summer fae," I said, leading her through a wrought iron archway set in the hedgerow and into the partially dead, partially evergreen winter garden. "She says unconsciously feeding the plants with a small but steady stream of magic isn't common among her people but does happen sometimes."

"She can't stop it?" Audrey asked, her gaze sliding over the flowerbeds that would be vibrant and alive in winter.

"She can't. At least it doesn't drain her and just happens."

"I'm guessing it's only in a close vicinity to where she lives," she added. "Or these plants would be a lot happier."

"This is the winter garden. There's an assortment of evergreens and plants that flourish in the colder weather," I told her. "It's stunning with a light blanket of snow."

"But not where we're picnicking?"

"Nope. We're going to the summer garden... because it's summer," I replied taking her through another wrought iron arch in the hedgerow on the far side of the garden.

"Of course we are," she laughed then abruptly sucked in a sharp breath as she took in the summer garden.

Everything was in bloom in a cacophony of colors, shapes, and sizes. Purple, pink, and red clematises as well as purple wisteria and yellow honeysuckle climbed over the connected archways in the middle, creating a shady oasis where I was going to lay out the blanket for our picnic. I knew from all the hours I'd spent in my mother's garden that the grass was soft and the hush of the wind through the vines relaxing.

Surrounding the flower-covered shelter were rose bushes, daylilies, and daisies of various colors. There were also flowering shrubs covered in flowers, some big, others small as well as hibiscus, fragrant lavender, and dozens of other types of flowers.

"You're right," she said her eyes wide with wonder. "This place is stunning."

"The season gardens were my mother's passion when she could spare time from leading the pack. Our head groundskeeper and I have been keeping them blooming in her memory even though only a few of the Residence's residents come here."

"Why wouldn't they come?" she asked as I walked her to the vine-covered arches and laid out the blanket. "It's amazing here and so peaceful."

"A lot of people are busy." I urged her to sit and started setting up our picnic, beginning with the bite-sized appetizers and the wine.

This morning I'd begged Eloise, our cook, to put a romantic picnic together for me with the hopes that Audrey would be feeling better and wouldn't mind taking a short walk. Eloise had been more than happy to do it once she learned it was for the shy woman who'd been seriously hurt yesterday.

Apparently, the kitchen staff had noticed Audrey during the two nights she'd stayed with us and decided they liked her. She was quiet but very polite and gracious when they'd served her. A lot of strangers — like the foreign dignitaries who visited along with some of our pack members — looked down on them because they'd chosen to be of service to the alpha. But they weren't lesser than anyone else. We paid them a good wage and treated them with respect.

Audrey had lived through the same disparaging looks and remarks and had been looked down on, too, and I couldn't help wondering if the kitchen staff had seen a kindred spirit in her.

Regardless, they were going to be shocked when they learned that she'd mated Knox. Everyone would be shocked. But everyone would also know soon since Knox had lost his mind when she'd been hurt and hadn't cared who'd seen him or who he'd influenced with his power. And I had no doubt word was already racing through the pack about them.

That said, the kitchen staff were also going to be thrilled about Audrey and Knox mating because it meant she was staying.

"Wow, you're really going all out on this picnic," she said as I handed her a glass of wine. "*Hors d'oeuvres and* wine and it's only just after lunch."

"What does the time of day have to do with anything?" I frowned. "And what's an *hors d'oeuvres?*"

She pointed to the mini appetizers. "That's an *hors d'oeuvres.* Guess the magical translator stuck in my head doesn't translate French."

"That's another language in your realm? But not one you're fluent in?"

"Yeah." She sipped at her wine, her expression thoughtful. "I wonder how this translator actually works. It didn't translate TV or movie because you don't have those things in your realm. But it also didn't translate *hors d'oeuvres.* Which is a word that didn't originate in my native language but is still in common use. Most people in my realm who speak my language probably know what the word means."

"So that means it's common for people from different cultures to communicate with each other?" It was the only reason a word from a foreign language could become common use.

The thought astounded me. We had messengers and so did the neighboring packs, kingdoms, and city states, but it took days, sometimes weeks or even months to reach them.

A dialogue between our pack and other communities, especially those we didn't share a language with was slow and infrequent. There were only a few people in the pack who'd learned a second language and no part of those languages had become common use in ours, especially if we had our own word for it.

"My realm has more technology than yours," she said. "I've told you about TV, movies, and photography. We've also discovered the telephone, which, now that we've set up a whole bunch of wires, lets us talk with anyone around the world. Close to the time we discovered the telephone, we also discovered radio waves which can be used to communicate with someone within the waves' radius..." She frowned and sighed, the look so adorable I wanted to kiss the little wrinkles in her forehead.

"I can't remember how big it is," she said after some thought. "But it doesn't require wires. Then we made cell phones which are phones that connect to a tower without wires, kind of like a radio but I'm not sure if they use radio waves or some other kind of wave. That wave connects with towers that relay the signal and sometimes relay that signal to a satellite in space so you can reach someone on the other side of the planet. Oh, and then we have the internet which is a bunch of computers that people can connect to with their own computer. Through that, we can talk to anyone anywhere with email or in chat rooms."

I took a big gulp of my wine, thrilled that the tension she'd had when she'd stepped into the kitchen was relaxing, but also overwhelmed with everything she said. There was so much information in that little speech, most of which I didn't understand, and the idea of communicating with someone anywhere in an instant was astounding.

Audrey sighed, her expression turning sad. "I thought maybe I could work with the pack's scientists and engineers and share what I have in my realm, but I don't know how any of it works. I just know what it does."

"But you know *of* these things," I assured her, squeezing her hand and hoping to bring back her smile. "Even if we can't make all of it, we might be able to make some of it. Hell, even if we can't make any of it, I love hearing about it. Your realm sounds incredible."

A shadow of fear swept over her expression.

Shit. Not what I wanted to do.

"Not all of my realm is great," she said, her voice too soft.

"Not all of my realm is great, either, but there are some incredible things within it, like our healing elixir, this garden, and—" I pulled Audrey into my lap and hugged her. "— you. You're incredible."

"Bishop," she admonished, her cheeks turning pink, but she didn't try to push out of my hold. Instead, she leaned into it, pressing her nose against my neck and drawing in a deep breath of my scent.

"Your idea is a good one," he said. "Once you're no longer restricted to the Residence's grounds, I'll arrange a meeting with our chief scientist, chief engineer, and Whil since she might know of something magical that would help with your new inventions."

"Well, they're not *my* inventions," she murmured against my neck.

"In this realm, they will be." I pressed my lips to the top of her head. Sisters, she smelled so good. I could hold her and be wrapped in her scent forever. In fact, I wanted to.

But I needed to take it slow, prove to her that I was in love with her not because her bond with Knox was influencing me — which it wasn't — but because she was everything I wanted in a mate and so much more.

"Our history books will tell the story of a brave young woman who brought the ideas for our technological advancement. And," I added, a new realization flashing through my mind. "You'll bring economic prosperity, too. We'll have things no one else will have. We could sell them to get more water for our elixirs instead of sending hunters to work for our allies. We could also sell them to get more of that sedative Kelna makes. Nova hasn't stopped talking about it since we showed it to her. We could also—"

"Alright," Audrey giggled, grinning at my enthusiasm. "I get the point. I'm not as useless as I thought I was. I know things no one else does."

"And there's more to you than just that." I hooked my thumb under her chin and urged her to look at me.

She turned her brown eyes, almost gold in the streams of brilliant sunlight cutting through our leafy canopy, and mesmerized me, stealing my breath. She was so beautiful, so fragile, yet also incredibly strong. I'd do anything to make her mine, to convince her she belonged in this pack with me and Knox.

"You'll find your place in this pack and people will see you as I see you. Kind, compassionate, gorgeous, and strong," I said.

She opened her mouth to protest, but I brushed my lips against hers, silencing her.

"There's more to strength than physical prowess, alpha power, or being a good fighter," I whispered against her mouth. "You've been afraid and confused and heartbroken, yet you've risked your life to protect those who couldn't protect themselves. You've been beaten down, but you always, quietly get back up. You don't give up and you don't make a big deal about it. You just do it. If you decide something needs to be done, especially if it involves children, I have no doubt it'll get done."

"I don't want any child to go through what I went through."

"And on your watch, it'll never happen. You're incredible." I brushed my lips against hers again, aiming for another soft, sweet kiss, but she tangled her fingers in my hair, held me close, and deepened our kiss.

My wolf howled in pleasure, and I could feel, at the very edge of my consciousness, Knox's wolf howling back. This was where I belonged, where *we* belonged, loving this incredible woman and helping her to see in herself what we saw.

AUDREY

I kissed Bishop with everything I had, trying to match the passion in his eyes, while desperately wanting to believe his words. I wanted to be as strong as he said I was, but I couldn't even pretend he was right. I never stood up for myself, it was always too dangerous, and that made me a coward.

Even now I wasn't willing to stand up to Cyrus. It was always best to be as unnoticed as possible.

And while I had fought those two grimalkins, both times it had been a fluke, an impulsive decision and a bad one at that. I hadn't thought it through, just reacted, just like I'd reacted when Knox's wolf had taken control of his body and refused to let go. I might have been exhausted and vulnerable and partially manipulated by Sterling at the time, but that didn't make what Cyrus said to me any less true.

Bishop cupped the back of my head and returned my passion, his tongue raking against mine, his breath picking up like mine.

Heat gathered low within me and the desire I'd always had for Bishop electrified my nerves, proving that my yearning for him had never been my heat. He made my soul sing with his kindness, compassion, and warmth. His stunning face and sleek muscles didn't hurt, either.

I brushed my hands down his shirt then dipped under it, tracing the hard lines of his abs with my fingers and drawing a soft moan.

"So we're playing dirty," he said, his voice deliciously gruff.

"This is dirty?" I trailed my fingers higher, sliding them along the bottom ridge of his pecs.

"You know it is," he groaned. "Now all I want to do is touch you back."

"So why don't you?" I purred, hoping and praying he'd touch me like I was touching him... except lower.

"Because groping isn't something a person does on a first date."

"I'm pretty sure we're beyond first date rules. We've already had sex." Fire burned my cheeks at the memory of my heat... or at least the erotic flashes that I could remember. "A lot of sex that I don't really remember."

"Heats don't count and I promised I'd court you. That starts with dates and perhaps a little kissing."

"That's how it works, hunh?" I raised an eyebrow and gave him my driest look. I didn't just want kisses, I wanted more, I wanted what we'd had our first night together in Kelna, and I didn't want to wait any longer. "Those are *your* rules. There's nothing that says I can't grope you."

I swept my hands up his chest to his collar bone then slowly dragged my nails down his skin to the waistband of his pants.

Bishop groaned but didn't pull my hands away. "Audrey, you're killing me."

"You should probably do something about that," I said, my voice husky. I didn't know where this flirtatious woman had come from or how I was so confident in this moment, but I liked it. For just a moment, I felt powerful, able to bring this incredible alpha in front of me to his knees with desire.

With a growl, he captured my lips again in a searing kiss that stole my breath, a kiss that was more like my dream-Knox than the Bishop I knew.

His tongue plundered my mouth and his hand in my hair tightened, controlling my head, while his other hand pushed under my shirt and swept a blazing line to my breast.

Moaning, I arched into his touch, urging him for more. For everything.

But he broke off the kiss, his breath heaving, expanding his broad chest with every quick inhalation. Then he grabbed the bottom of my shirt, pulled it up over my head, and tossed it to the far side of the blanket. His heated gaze raked over my skin, starting at my waist, rising to my breasts, and stopping at my face.

The desire in his eyes tightened my core and made my blush burn hotter, sweeping down my neck to the top of my chest. I dropped my gaze to the ground, unable to meet that intensity and maintain eye contact.

Except that was a mistake and I now had a perfect view of his thick erection straining the front of his pants.

"You're so beautiful," he breathed, making me suddenly self-conscious.

I wasn't beautiful. I had too many horrible scars.

I crossed my arms over my chest, but it was a futile attempt. I couldn't cover my nudity and all my scars at the same time. There were just too many of them.

"None of that," he said as he brushed his lips over the new scar at the top of my left breast. It sat right over my heart and the whisper of his touch sent desire shivering down my spine. "I think you're gorgeous and I intend to convince you that I'm worthy to be your mate."

"You are worthy." He'd always been worthy from the moment we'd first met and he was kind to me when he'd made my first time having sex wonderous and beautiful. I was the one who wasn't worthy.

"I'm still going to court you. This is the first of many dates. I want to show you all the best places and all the best people in Stonehaven. I want to watch sunsets and sunrises with you that don't involve hiking across the countryside all day. And I'm definitely taking you dancing. At the festival and afterwards." He punctuated each item on his list with a gentle kiss, inching lower and lower until his nose nuzzled against my arm covering my nipple, begging for access.

I hesitated a moment. Did I really want to do this? Only a few seconds ago, I'd thought I did, but we were still outside, and despite Bishop saying no one visited this garden, someone could still see us.

Of course, I'd probably been more out in the open when Knox had gone down on me last night and that hadn't bothered me, but I'd also been caught in mine and Knox's emotions. I wanted our mating to work so badly, I couldn't have said no if I tried.

This time, I didn't have another set of emotions urging me on and I *still* wanted him. I wanted the confirmation that he wanted me — even though logically I knew he did and wasn't lying.

"It's not fair if I'm the only one naked," I murmured, a small spike of fear stabbing through my chest at my bold words.

"You're still wearing pants," he said, his lips brushing over my skin, sending hot need racing to my core. "You're not naked."

"But I will be," I moaned, my voice breathy with desire.

"Your wish is my command." He slid me off his lap then yanked his shirt and pants off and settled back on the blanket beside me.

I stared at him, stunned at how quickly he shed his clothes, but also at all his mouthwatering muscles — along with his already thick cock, fully engorged and standing at attention.

With a grin that told me he knew he'd stunned me — I was probably drooling, too — he leaned forward and kissed me.

The kiss was tentative at first as if he were afraid that stripping naked was too much for me. But when I didn't pull away and teased my tongue against his lips, he opened with a low, delicious growl and wrapped his arms around me, pulling me back onto his lap.

Desire coursed through my system, reigniting my yearning and pooling hot between my thighs. All doubt about being naked out in the open was gone, all that mattered was the incredible man kissing me and hopefully about to do more.

I tangled my fingers in his hair, holding him close. I'd never get enough of Bishop's kisses or his body.

And yes, I recognized how weird that was since Knox and Bishop had the same body. But to me they were different, completely separate individuals. I didn't see them as two versions of the same person. Bishop was Bishop and Knox was Knox. Both attractive in their own way.

Bishop kissed me until I was breathless and squirming. Then he set me back on the blanket, kissed his way down to my breasts, and ran his tongue slowly, oh so slowly, over my nipple.

I moaned, the heat within me surging, and he repeated the sensual lick then sucked the tight bud into his mouth.

"Bishop," I gasped as my back arched, pressing my breasts closer to him.

He pulled off with a pop, flashing me another wicked smile, and turned to my other breast, giving it the same agonizingly slow lick.

I tightened my grip on him and held him close, letting the pleasure rush through me and spin me tighter.

"Fuck, Audrey. I want you so much," he groaned against my breast.

"Then have me." I lay back, more confident than I'd ever been in my whole life, and propped myself on my elbows to maintain eye contact. "Please."

AUDREY

I LET MY GAZE, FILLED WITH NEED, SLIDE DOWN BISHOP'S BODY TO HIS cock. He was so hard for me the head was an angry red, and thick veins stood out along his length. Precum already glistened at his slit, and as I watched, a drop broke free and trailed down, disappearing into the thick hair at his base.

I licked my lips, unable to help myself, and brought my gaze back to his. His eyes widened for a split-second as if he were surprised at what he saw, then his pupils expanded and darkened, making the green fleck stand out.

With a growl that heightened the desire racing through me, he surged forward and kissed me again. This time the kiss was wild, his tongue tangling with mine, his hands finding my breasts and kneading them. No more soft sweet kisses. This was Bishop unraveling, sinking into his need for me.

My breath picked up and he kissed his way back to my breasts, sucking on each nipple before going lower. He licked around my belly button and teased the skin just about the waistband of my pants, making me tremble, desire swirling like lava through my veins and pooling low.

"These have to go," he growled at my pants.

"Yes," I agreed breathlessly. "Please."

He quickly undid the tie that held the fabric up, hooked his fingers in the waistband, and pulled them down. Somehow, he regained some control and drew them down so... damned... slowly that I was panting with anticipation before he'd gotten them to my ankles.

Once they'd joined my shirt on the other side of the blanket, Bishop slid his hands up the insides of my thighs, and I let them fall open in invitation.

His eyes darkened even more, his wolf rising close to the surface, and he drew in a deep breath then hummed it out in pleasure.

"One taste is never enough," he said, replacing his hands with his lips and kissing higher and higher up my thigh.

"I'm pretty sure you've tasted me more than once," I replied with a shiver, my breath turning short and sharp. I had disjointed flashes of him going down on me during my heat, but nothing was clear.

"Heat fevers don't count." He blew a warm breath over my folds, the sensation adding to the building heat in my core. But he didn't put his lips where I wanted them and kissed down my other thigh to my knee. "Fevers are medical emergencies. The sex was necessary, not romantic. This..." he purred, kissing his way back up to my core. "This is romantic."

He blew another warm breath over me then flicked his tongue out. It was just a quick touch, not even close to my clit, but sensation jolted through me and my breath hitched.

"You taste so good. So sweet and perfect," he groaned before sliding his tongue through my folds with a slow, sensual lick. "So much like home."

My breath caught again and I dug my fingers into the blanket, needing to hold on to something, but not sure what.

Bishop ran his tongue over me again and again, building up my desire without even touching my clit.

Oh, please. Oh, please please please.

But he avoided touching that sensitive nub, spiraling my need so tight that I was gasping and moaning and not caring if someone could hear us. My desire had grown into an inferno and I couldn't catch my breath. The ache in my core told me I was close, so close, and yet not close enough. If he'd just touch my clit.

"More," I gasped, bucking into him, my whole body trembling. "Please, more."

He grabbed my hips, holding me still, and pressed closer, raking his tongue inside me and nuzzling my clit with his nose with the lightest of touches. Despite that, I still jerked against his grasp.

Oh, yes!

I just needed a little more pressure on that sizzling bundle of nerves. I was sure that was all I needed to go tumbling over the edge.

Bishop rumbled in pleasure, the sound vibrating from my core and up through my body.

Oh, please, I mentally chanted. *Please please please.*

Then he sucked hard in my clit and stars exploded behind my lids.

"Oh, yes!" I cried as pleasure rushed through me, stealing my breath.

"That's my girl," Bishop purred, licking at my release for a moment before crawling up my body and capturing my lips in a searing kiss.

His cock nudged at my entrance and before I'd fully come down, I was rocking up into him, brushing my sensitive, soaked folds against his tip.

"You're so beautiful with your hair wild and your face and chest flushed."

He pressed his cock at my entrance and slowly pushed inside, giving me lots of time to adjust to his girth. But I was so wet and relaxed from my orgasm that there wasn't even a whisper of pain, just the glorious feeling of being full and having every nerve in my channel bursting back to life.

We were both panting by the time he'd pushed all the way in and my walls were already fluttering, ready for another release. Then he started moving, slowly sliding out and pushing back in, rebuilding the needy ache inside me, and my thoughts scattered.

My body matched his rhythm, rocking my hips and urging him deeper as more bliss built inside me. The feel of him sliding in and out and raking against already sensitive flesh, while his body bumped my clit over and over again soon had me spinning. My pleasure wound tight and hot in my core and my breath turned ragged.

Bishop picked up his pace, soft grunts and growls escaping his lips, as his eyes darkened. They were almost fully black with only a few specks of green remaining, and that meant I was no longer just making love to Bishop.

His wolf had risen high enough to take over. So far, I didn't think he had, but it wouldn't have bothered me. His wolf was a part of him and it was natural for the more primal part of a shifter's soul to join or take over during moments of passion.

His rhythm started to falter, his hips working faster and faster, his thrusts snapping harder and harder into me. I moaned, my pleasure still building, an electric tingle at the base of my spine that was almost there, almost to the edge of an earth-shattering release, but not quite.

Once again, I was so close, and while it was selfish to want another one when Bishop hadn't had any, I couldn't help myself. The pressure and ache and the electricity racing through my veins felt so good. I didn't think I'd ever get enough of how Bishop made me feel.

In his eyes, I was beautiful despite my scars, and I was safe. I knew in my heart he'd always be there for me, and even though I ached for another orgasm, I also wanted this moment to last forever.

"Fuck, Audrey," he growled as he roughly rubbed his thumb against my clit.

Sparks burst through my body and the pressure inside me exploded. Every muscle in my body contracted, and a scream was ripped from my lips. More stars flooded the darkness behind my lids, brighter and sharper than before, and I spun around and around, gasping and shivering as the sensation overwhelmed me.

Bishop groaned his release, his body locked inside me as all his muscles contracted, too, and we held each other, spinning on brilliant, bone-melting bliss.

Then after a long moment of gasping for breath, he pulled out, and we resettled, lying on the blanket with me in his arms, my back to his chest.

"That was not how I expected our picnic to go," he said, sounding dazed and sleepy. "It was so much better."

He grabbed his shirt and helped me into it, warming my heart with his consideration for my discomfort at being naked in public, then wrapped me in his arms again.

The sound of his heartbeat and the warmth from his body, along with the summer heat and the sounds of insects and birds and the gentle breeze in the garden soon pulled me into a satisfied sleep.

When I woke, Bishop was gone. I was still in his shirt, but Knox, in his wolf form lay beside me, sending a rush of uncertainty racing through me.

There was no way Knox didn't know I'd had sex with Bishop. I was covered in his scent and the scent of sex, was wearing his shirt with no pants, and — I bit back a groan — he would have felt us having sex through the mating bond.

He'd wanted me to also mate with Bishop... but did he really or had that just been when he hadn't been willing to work on our relationship?

AUDREY

THE SECOND I THOUGHT KNOX WOULD BE ANGRY WITH ME FOR SLEEPING with Bishop, he woke and I was flooded with contentment. Not even a flicker of anger or jealousy. He really did want to share me with his brother, which was so unlike the wolf shifters in my realm it made my head spin.

Worry seeped into the bond and he nuzzled closer to me.

What's wrong? he asked.

"Nothing," I replied, sitting up and tugging Bishop's shirt down to ensure I wasn't flashing him or anyone who walked by.

You're confused and worried. Did Bishop do something? Did he hurt you?

"Did it feel like he hurt me?" I murmured, not wanting to rub in the fact that Bishop and I had been intimate again when Knox and I had only had intercourse once and I barely remembered it.

It felt like you wanted it and enjoyed it. But that doesn't mean you don't regret it now.

"I'd only regret it if it makes you angry at me and your brother. But it was just a silly thought." I pressed my hand over my heart. "I know it isn't true."

I already told you I wanted you to mate with him. He sounded genuinely confused about why I'd even think such a thing as well as a little hurt and those emotions radiated through our bond, making my insides squirm.

"It was just habit. Wolves in my realm are possessive of their mates," I told him. "And I know you told me you wanted me to mate with Bishop, but that was before you agreed to work on our relationship. I didn't even think that being with Bishop might upset you until I found you here, beside me."

You have nothing to worry about. Bishop and his wolf want you, and he'll be able to offer you things I can't, he said. *It's only an issue if you don't want him. But it sounds and feels like you do.*

My cheeks heated at the thought of what Bishop and I had done... outside... where anyone could have seen us. But even though I was embarrassed, I wouldn't have changed what we'd done. I'd loved every second of being with him.

Contentment from Knox radiated through our mating bond, igniting a spark of hope inside me. Maybe it would all work out.

I liked Bishop a lot and was relieved Knox wasn't going to demand we stop seeing each other. I could also feel my affection for Knox growing. He wasn't ignoring me, being terse or rude, or making demands like before. Maybe I was finally free. Maybe, so long as everyone else left me alone, I finally had a life with people who cared about me.

It smells like you didn't finish your picnic, Knox said, sniffing the basket.

"Barely even started." More heat bloomed across my face and I tried to get my blush under control. I had nothing to be embarrassed about. Bishop was going to be my mate, too. There was nothing wrong with having sex with him.

Then we should finish it. Knox's body turned to liquid, and in the blink of an eye, he'd shifted into his human form. "We wouldn't want all of Bishop's hard work to go to waste."

I gaped at him, unable to stop my gaze from sweeping over the contour of his chest and arms and down to his rippled abs and his partially erect cock.

The blush I'd been trying to control burned over my scalp and down my neck onto my chest.

"Could you—" I jerked my attention away, realizing even if I asked him to get dressed, he couldn't. He hadn't brought any clothes with him, and Bishop had taken his pants when he left.

Jeez. Nudity wasn't a thing with shifters, but I couldn't seem to get past it.

Of course, it didn't help that he was gorgeous.

And now I couldn't stop thinking about how amazing his mouth had felt when he made me come.

He grunted — but I couldn't feel any frustration in our bond — and grabbed my shirt on the other side of the blanket, using it to cover himself.

"Let's see what Bishop left us," he said, not addressing what most shifters thought was a ridiculous reaction to being naked.

He tugged the basket closer and pushed aside the cloth that was protecting the food. "Mini appetizers, three different types of sandwiches, two with wild mountain blackbuck cheese, sweet red berries, and two types of confection." A thread of worry seeped into the bond. "I should have thought of this."

"I feel like this isn't your thing," I told him, trying to send my burgeoning love for him through our bond.

"But it makes you happy."

"And I'll be happy with whatever you think will be an enjoyable date. You're your own person. You don't have to do what Bishop does. That, and I get the feeling that Bishop has had a lot of experience with this kind of thing." I gave him a wry smile and picked up one of the four remaining *hors d'oeuvres* and offered it to him. "I wouldn't have thought of it, either."

With a tentative smile, he took it and popped it into his mouth, his pleasure at what he tasted flowing through our bond.

Over the next couple of hours, we finished off Bishop's romantic picnic and chatted... which turned out to be a little awkward since I wasn't very good at casual conversation and Knox was terrible.

Still, it made me feel special to have Knox open up a bit to me. I suspected there were very few people he'd have an hour-long conversation with, let alone two hours — even in an enormous, open field. I could feel in our bond that he genuinely wanted to talk with me and that he was trying to make an effort, as promised.

"We should do something tomorrow," I suggested as I pulled on my pants. The more time we spent together, the more we'd figure out our relationship.

But Knox frowned in the middle of packing everything back into the basket as if he hadn't expected me to propose another date, and uncertainty rushed through our bond.

My own uncertainty rose to meet his. Had I been too bold? I'd thought we'd been getting along, but maybe that had all been in my head. Maybe Knox had been humoring me, which wasn't like him and I hadn't felt it in our bond, but I still couldn't shake the fear that I was wrong. Again.

Knox's eyes widened and his uncertainty switched to fear. "What are you thinking? What did I do wrong?"

I opened my mouth to tell him "nothing," but with our ability to sense each other's feelings he'd know right away I was lying.

"You don't want to see me again," I replied instead, fighting to keep my tone neutral even though I knew he could feel my churning emotions. "That's fine. I'm disappointed," I added because I definitely couldn't hide that from him, "but we can go at your pace."

"That isn't—" He pressed his hand over his heart, realization flooding his expression and our bond.

"We can't hide anything from each other," I said, saying what I knew he had to be thinking, "even if it's to protect the other's feelings."

"Fuck," he hissed, raising his gaze to meet mine. "I do want to do something with you tomorrow. Being with you is easy. Like being with my brothers, or Nova and Deacon."

"But..." I prompted. I could feel his sincerity and see it in his eyes. He did want to spend more time with me, but I could also feel the "but" hiding in the wings, waiting to come out.

"But I leave in a few hours on a hunt. That's why I'd originally come looking for you and found you asleep on Bishop." His gaze slid to the basket between us and a hint of shame curled through the bond. "I didn't want to reject your suggestion. I've done too much of that already. But I didn't know how to tell you I couldn't spend tomorrow with you."

I couldn't decide if I wanted to laugh or cry at the ridiculousness of the situation. I'd gotten so worried and he'd gotten upset because he didn't know how to decline a suggestion... probably without being brusque and rude like before.

Being able to sense each other's emotions was a dangerous thing, especially since we still didn't fully trust each other.

"I have to work tomorrow, Audrey," I said, providing him with the appropriate response.

He frowned, confused. "That's it? You'd accept that?"

"You and Bishop have responsibilities to the pack. I hope I'll have some soon, too. Working or just needing a little space because this is too much peopling or because you've got some other engagement is a perfectly acceptable answer. I understand that you have a life and we don't know how I fit into it yet."

"But I promised I'd try." Worry colored his voice and rushed through our bond, breaking my heart for him. I wasn't sure exactly what had made him completely change his behavior with me, but it was obvious he wasn't used to it, just as it was obvious he meant what he said. He wanted to make our relationship work and I knew he wouldn't use his work as an excuse to avoid me.

"You can continue trying when you get back from the hunt," I told him. I cautiously reached for his hand and met his dark gaze. "I'll look forward to your return."

A tentative smile curled his lips, softening his usually hard expression, while relief and surprise filled our bond. "It'll only be four or five days."

I matched his smile. "Then I'll see you in four or five days. Which will be perfect because I'll be finished my doctor-mandated period of rest in four days."

Knox grunted, the happiness I'd felt when we'd been chatting returning. With his soft smile growing a little more, he finished loading the basket, handed me back my shirt, and shifted into his wolf.

I'll take this back to the kitchen, he said. *And I'll see you in four or five days.*

I opened my mouth to tell him that I had to return to the kitchen to figure out how to get back to my suite and I could take the basket with me, but he was already at the metal arch in the hedgerow, trotting with ease despite the basket handle in his teeth.

With a sigh, I laid back, propping myself up on my elbows, and looked up at the interwoven vines, their flowers a cacophony of color curling over the pergola. Soft beams of sunlight cut through foliage softly *shushing* in the breeze.

It was so peaceful here. Bishop had picked the perfect place for our picnic, and while I was a little sorry we didn't get to eat it together, I wasn't at all sorry for what we'd done instead.

A shiver teased down my spine with the memory of how good Bishop had made me feel, how loved. There was no doubt in my mind that Bishop was telling the truth when he said he was going to court me, and if this was the beginning, I couldn't wait for more.

I drew the collar of his shirt up to my nose and inhaled his fresh-cut grass scent, my smile deepening. God, I loved how he smelled. Crisp and bright and fresh. I could wrap myself in his scent forever and never get tired of it.

I could also wrap myself in Knox's deep, rich smoldering wood smoke scent. He was a warm, thick blanket and a hot chocolate on a winter's night, and despite our rocky start, I wanted to keep cuddling with him.

Things wouldn't be automatically easy between us, but today — and last night — had been a good start. Being able to feel his emotions also helped. I could tell he genuinely wanted to try to make our relationship work and that he felt guilty for how he'd treated me.

Of course, I still wasn't going to let him off easy.

As much as I knew how he felt, I wasn't ready to trust him with my body, not completely. I wanted to know him better, figure out how we could make a life for ourselves even if it wasn't the life either of us had wanted.

With that said, I was going to have to figure out how to be useful to the pack. Bishop had seemed excited about me sharing ideas from my world. If I was really going to do that, I needed to get my thoughts together and write down what I did know about things. Especially things that the pack might find useful. Which meant I needed a pen and some paper.

I sat up, considering who I might ask for them. I doubted I'd run into Knox before he left and Bishop could be anywhere. I certainly didn't want to go wandering about the Residence unescorted until I knew for sure if Cyrus would allow it.

Sure, Nova had suggested it, but she wasn't the alpha. She was someone else who might loan me writing stuff, but again, I didn't want to go hunting for her.

Maybe there was something in my suite. I hadn't explored my new rooms since they'd been given to me... yesterday evening...? The day before yesterday evening? Yeah, I guess that had been the day before when we'd gotten back from our trip north.

I'd been too tired and fidgety to check things out, then I'd woken upset, had that catastrophic moment with Knox and Cyrus, and Sterling had tried to get me to kill myself. I hadn't even gotten a chance this morning when Nova woke me and hurried me out to get food.

So, check the room first, then find the one person I trusted or the other person I sort of trusted... or wait for them to find me.

That was probably the safest option. If I just stayed where I was, eventually one of them would come looking for me.

With that decided, I glanced at my shirt, decided I didn't want to take off Bishop's shirt, and headed back to the kitchen so I could find my way back to my suite.

Thankfully, I didn't meet anyone on the way there, and when I entered from the herb garden door, the two women I'd seen working in the kitchen earlier — the older woman and the woman about my age — offered me big smiles and more food while telling me supper would be in a couple of hours.

Despite declining, I still left the kitchen with a bowl filled with grapes, a hunk of cheese the size of my fist, an apple, and two large dinner rolls. It was almost as if they were worried that I wasn't eating enough.

I supposed I'd lost weight during our trip and from my unnaturally long heat, but I hadn't thought I looked that bad. Of course, when I'd looked in the mirror this morning, I hadn't been able to see past all my scars to really pay attention to my figure.

Food in hand, I stepped into the hall, reminding myself to stay small and quiet and not to make eye contact and challenge anyone. If I just minded my own business and went straight to my room, everything would be fine.

Really.

My pulse picked up and I strained to slow it down. This was the first time I'd been alone since I'd woken up and it was hard to ignore my worries that I couldn't relax and be myself.

I'd felt so safe with Bishop and even Nova and now I felt exposed and vulnerable.

Still, I couldn't look afraid. I squared my shoulders, raised my head, and plastered on the calmest, most submissive expression I could. I needed to look like I accepted my position as the lowest ranking member in the pack and was happy about it. That's what alphas wanted.

I was halfway across the grand foyer, the lights glittering in the enormous crystal chandelier and peppering the red carpet with mesmerizing rainbow flecks of light, when one of the massive front doors opened.

Calm and accepting and unobtrusive.

Except I was in the center of the foyer and couldn't duck out of the way as Cyrus stepped inside.

Shit.

I froze in place, pinned by Cyrus's stern glare and unable to escape to the shadows so he could forget about me. I wasn't ready to run into him yet and I certainly hadn't wanted to face him for the first time since he'd yelled at me while I was alone.

And even while my body trembled — much to my mind's frustration — afraid he'd reprimand me again or do worse, the image of my fantasy flooded my mind's eye. Cyrus naked, all his powerful muscles on display as he held me gently, carefully, and slowly pushed inside me.

"Audrey," he said, his voice gruff as stuttering waves of power rolled off him as if he was trying to hold it back but was too upset to manage it.

"Alpha," I said, dropping my gaze to the floor, my cheeks heating with an unwanted blush despite my nervousness.

"You're going to ruin your dinner with all that." The front door shut with a thud, a finality that echoed through the room.

I opened my mouth to explain I hadn't wanted the food but also hadn't wanted to disrespect members of his pack by declining twice, then I remembered that was an excuse.

No excuse was ever good enough.

"Yes, alpha."

"Audrey," he huffed and another wave of power, this one sharp and stronger, jerked my head up to look at him.

Damn it. I didn't want to look at him, didn't want another glimpse of his bad-boy beauty, large, muscled figure, and the hard look in his moss green eyes. But I couldn't help myself. Just like his brothers, seeing Cyrus stole my breath.

A little more than a day's worth of scruff covered his square jaw, and the shaved sides of his head were longer as well as if he hadn't had time to shave in a while. The rest of his brown hair was tied back in its usual thick braid that reached the nape of his neck and I couldn't see any of the golden highlights that shone bright in the sunlight.

Audrey, remember your place! I snapped at myself and quickly yanked my gaze to a spot on the door behind him.

"Dinner really is in a couple of hours. Do you remember your way to the dining hall or should I send someone?" he asked.

From his curt tone and choice of words, that hadn't been a request. It was an order.

I didn't think it was a trap to get me in front of his betas so he could reprimand me again. That didn't seem his style, but I was still going to have to watch myself. Just because he didn't plan it to be a trap, didn't mean it couldn't become one.

Small. Quiet. Invisible.

With luck, if I kept to myself and he didn't see me with Bishop, he and everyone else would forget about me... at least until I'd proven my worth.

"I can find my way, alpha," I replied, trying to keep my worry from my expression.

"Good."

He marched down the hall toward the kitchen and I hurried in the opposite direction, realizing that I had no idea when exactly dinner was since a couple of hours was still somewhat vague, or how to tell if a certain amount of time had passed.

CYRUS

I PACED MY OFFICE UNABLE TO CONCENTRATE ON MY WORK EVEN THOUGH stacks of reports and requests covered most of my large wooden desk. I'd been trying to concentrate for two hours now and hadn't gotten a thing done.

Seeing Audrey in the foyer had been the first time I'd seen her conscious since I'd yelled at her yesterday morning and she'd retreated into her shell. She was even more withdrawn than she'd been when she'd first arrived and I knew it had nothing to do with being manipulated into hurting herself and everything to do with me.

The thought squeezed my chest, making it hard to breathe, and I clenched my jaw against howling out my frustration.

I had to stay in control. And in better control than when she'd dropped her gaze in the foyer. My frustration at her retreating into herself and my guilt for hurting her enough that someone could have influenced her into her hurting herself were just too strong, and I'd been unable to fully contain my power.

No one could know how I really felt about Audrey, how I desperately wanted to go with my wolf's instinct, to say to hell with pack responsibilities, and court her like Bishop was. My wolf was determined to have her and all but the responsible side of my human half agreed with him.

Except it wasn't possible. She couldn't be mine. I had to remember that.

Why couldn't I remember that? Why couldn't I stop thinking about her, about how she'd worked so hard during our trip north, how she made something in my chest warm when she was near or smiling or relaxed, and how much I'd needed to protect her when she'd been suffering through her heat?

I'd thought her hating me would kill those thoughts and help me stay detached, that it was for the best for us to keep our distance from each other. It probably still was the best way to go about it. But that didn't stop all the air from being sucked out of the foyer when I'd stepped inside and she'd looked at her feet.

The air hadn't returned when I'd accidentally let my power slip and forced her to look at me. Her eye contact had been so brief, I couldn't help wondering if it had really happened before it slid to somewhere past my shoulder.

And then — of course! — I had to be me. I commented on the first thing I noticed, the bowl piled with fruit and bread.

Dinner really had been in two hours, but she hadn't needed to be reprimanded about it. Eloise had probably told her when dinner was when she'd handed Audrey the bowl of food.

Knowing our head cook, the grandmother had taken one look at Audrey, decided she was too skinny, and wouldn't take no for an answer. Without a doubt, Audrey hadn't been able to decline the food.

And with me playing the villain in order to not let my attraction to her take over and keep her away from unnecessary scrutiny, she didn't want to explain that to me.

A growl slipped past my clenched jaw, the sound low and dangerous, and I was grateful there wasn't anyone around to hear me.

She'd shut down when I'd lost my mind with fear and yelled at her. She hadn't reacted the way I'd expected but I'd have thought she'd have regrouped by now. She was so determined about everything, it drove me crazy seeing her so submissive.

I could only pray her submissiveness was only with me and not everyone in the pack.

She obviously wasn't that way with Bishop. I'd overheard him asking Eloise for a romantic picnic and it looked like it had worked. She was wearing Bishop's shirt and had his and — much to my surprise — Knox's scent coating her like a second skin.

That, at least, was promising, especially if she was accepting Knox... unless, of course, I'd scared her so much she'd lost all her fight and was giving in to Knox's demands.

No. That couldn't be true. She was so determined to make him grovel, and after having the shit scared out of him and nearly losing her, I knew my brother would do everything in his power to make her happy... even if he didn't understand it.

Even without a bond between us like Knox had with Bishop, I'd felt Knox's terror. Hell, everyone in a two-hundred-foot radius had felt it, and without a doubt, the whole pack knew Knox had mate bonded with Audrey.

That was another issue that I wasn't sure how to deal with. How much did I interfere in Audrey's life? If I showed her too much favoritism rumors would start.

I huffed a bitter laugh. Rumors had already started from the moment we brought her to Stonehaven. I'd thought everyone would have gotten bored of the idea of me and her during the month we were away, but no. People were still talking about how I'd stormed into Nova's office to get a dress for Audrey, and now that she was here to stay, people would keep talking.

Damn it. I didn't know how to fix this. And I *really* wanted to fix this.

But fixing social problems was Bishop's job, and I had to stay out of it and be patient or I'd make things worse.

I slammed my fist against my desk, pulling back at the last minute so I didn't break it. I used to be good at patience, but it was getting harder and harder to stay in control.

I'd been the one who'd weakened her mental defenses so that asshole could convince her to hurt herself, and *I'd* been the one to make her afraid of me.

Her being submissive was all my fault and I hated myself for it.

Someone touched my mind, asking permission to talk to me, and I mentally touched them back, letting them know they weren't interrupting.

I've notified Audrey that dinner will be ready in ten minutes, Eloise said.

Thank you, I replied, as I ran a nervous hand over my head and silently prayed, *Please, let her submissiveness just be with me. Please, don't let me have fucked this up for her.*

I'd asked Eloise to notify Audrey about dinner since I had no idea if anyone had pointed out the clock on the mantle over the fireplace or if she even knew how to read it. I'd tried to ask Bishop to get her, he'd been the most obvious choice and the least likely to startle her, but he'd had to leave the Residence's grounds, and while I'd been able to reach him, he didn't have the telepathic strength to reach Audrey.

I headed out, knowing I'd get to the dining room early, but I couldn't continue to pace in my office. I'd check in with Eloise to see how she and Kira were doing. Eloise had a new grandchild — number two — who'd been born a few weeks before we'd left for the death god's temple, and Kira was studying foreign cuisine with a visiting Dedearc chef who'd been invited to take over the fanciest restaurant in town until the fall.

Except as I rounded the corner and strode into the wider hall where some of our small public rooms were, I saw Audrey, and all the air vanished again, from the hall, my lungs, from everywhere.

She sat on a bench in an alcove, leaning into the corner where the shadows were the deepest. But they weren't enough to hide her. Even tucked away, someone standing at the right angle — like I was — would be able to see most of her.

It also didn't help her that she'd worn a dark green dress. From her nervous posture, I suspected she thought it would help her blend into the background, but all it did was contrast with her pale skin and her blond hair and drew my attention to her hazel eyes and soft pink lips as if they were the only sparks of color on her black and white canvas.

She looked even more fragile than she had in the foyer and certainly before I'd yelled at her, and I couldn't stop staring at her. My heart hurt looking at her.

The memory of pushing into her warm hot sheath, her body too weak and exhausted, swept through me. I'd needed so desperately to protect her then, just like I needed to now. Except I had no idea how to do that and keep my distance.

CYRUS

BECAUSE YOU CAN'T PROTECT HER AND KEEP YOUR DISTANCE AT THE SAME *time*, my wolf growled at me, fighting to take over and go to Audrey.

I mentally tightened my grip on him, willing him to calm down. *I have to.*

She's ours.

She can't be, I growled back at him, startling Audrey who turned wide eyes toward me before jerking her gaze to her feet.

Shit.

"You're early," I said, my voice gruff despite my effort to act natural... which clearly didn't work because she tensed, making me realize that my words, once again, could be a reprimand. "Punctuality isn't a bad thing," I added.

"Yes, alpha."

I cringed at her response. Talking about punctuality could be a reprimand as well or be interpreted that if she was ever late, I'd punished her.

Sisters! How the hell did Bishop talk to women? This was a quagmire just waiting to swallow me whole.

"Cyrus," Finn called from down the hall, saving me from having to figure out what to say while also frustrating me that I hadn't fixed the situation. "Have you had a chance to look at the new watch schedule?"

"Yes," I said, forcing myself to turn away from Audrey so I could lead my watch commander away from her and into the dining room. "I like the extra shifts you've added, but I think we need at least two more men at the market. We can't risk endangering our economy by not having enough protection."

"I'll need to recruit more watchmen," Finn replied, taking his usual seat at the table. "We're stretched thin already. Unless you can recall ten of them back from Ciliran or Lais."

I sagged into my seat at the head of the table and sighed. "I wish I could, but we'd need to renegotiate our treaty with them since we can't replace the watchmen with hunters."

"If we could just get the beast population back under control," Finn added.

"It's not like we're not trying," Deacon said as he strode into the room. "We've got a dozen hunters in the hospital with serious injuries and are stretched thin as well."

"We might be able to do something about that," Lucius added, and I leaped from my seat and drew him into a hug.

"Welcome back." I squeezed a little tighter and held on a little longer than proper but I didn't care. I'd been back for two days now and our schedules had kept us too busy to talk before now.

Lucius had been a beta for my parents since I was little and his presence always steadied me. He was the rational, experienced one between me, my brothers, and our betas, and while Thane, our chief of finance, was rational to the extreme, he lacked Lucius's empathy that allowed him to offer logical *and kind* options for difficult decisions.

I released him and he took his usual seat as Thane and Velora entered followed by Bishop and a pale Audrey wearing a soft, bland smile that didn't reach her eyes.

"The discussion was good at the Mountain and Sea Alliance emergency meeting. But we weren't able to finalize anything because it really is something you should weigh in on," Lucius said. "Speaker

Jundar, King Gower, Representative Folmar, and Pimryl will be coming here in three weeks to continue talks, and they've reported that they're in talks with merchants who have new weapons that are effective against any beast, even grimalkins."

Deacon whistled as Audrey took Knox's usually empty seat beside me, offering me a too-polite nod of acknowledgment, and Bishop sat beside her.

"I'll believe there are weapons that strong when I see it," Deacon said.

"His Majesty King Gower says he's seen them in action and can attest to their power. We'll know more when everyone arrives." Lucius sat back down and turned his attention to Audrey. "I see there's someone new joining us tonight. I'm Lucius."

Audrey's gaze flickered to mine as if asking permission to speak, putting a slightly too-long pause in the conversation before Bishop said, "She's Audrey."

"Knox's mate," Velora added a little too cheerfully.

She'd been interested in Bishop since we'd been kids and had thought being promoted to beta had assured her a place at his side, but he'd never expressed or shown an interest in her. I couldn't tell if she was relieved Bishop wasn't mated to Audrey or concerned they were still sitting too close together just to be polite like the last time we'd all had supper together.

"So the rumors are true," Lucius said, confirming my suspicions that the pack was talking about Knox and Audrey.

Audrey nodded, her gaze still on Lucius's right ear and the soft smile that didn't reach her eyes firmly in place.

Eloise and Kira came out with salads, warm rolls, and bottles of wine, and Audrey quietly thanked them whenever they set something in front of her. But she was so withdrawn, Eloise's smile quickly turned to a frown and the Residence's cook shot me a worried look.

I couldn't have agreed with her more. This wasn't the Audrey who'd had dinner with us a month ago, and it wasn't even close to the woman I'd seen in the final few days of our journey.

"I want to know how it happened," Velora said once Eloise and Kira had left. "We all thought Knox would never mate."

Again Audrey's gaze flickered to mine, making me squirm in my seat even if it made sense to look for my permission this time. The question involved more than just her and I doubted she wanted to say anything that might upset me or Knox.

Except whatever she said would be fine. It was her life and her mating and she had the right to tell as much or as little of it as she wanted. Although if she spoke the whole truth, that would bring up a lot of questions that I wasn't sure she wanted to answer.

"I want to know about that as well," Thane said, filling his and Velora's wine glasses then handing the bottle to Deacon. "If we know what got Knox to mate with you, perhaps it could help us get him to open up with the rest of us."

"Or really just open up with anyone," Finn added. He'd idolized Knox almost as soon as he could walk and had been angry — perhaps still was — that Knox had shut out everyone except me, Bishop, Nova, and Deacon.

"Well?" Velora pressed, turning her full attention to Audrey. "Did you lure him in with your feminine wiles?"

"No, beta," Audrey replied, her voice soft and bland like her expression, and her gaze locked on the far wall.

Velora huffed. "It's got to be something."

"It's complicated," Bishop said, an edge in his tone that I was sure only I heard because we were brothers and I'd known him all his life.

"What does that mean?" Thane asked, a small line forming between his brows, the precursor to a frown. Out of all our betas, he was the most curious and also the most socially oblivious.

Audrey's eyes flashed to Bishop for a second, the movement so subtle I wasn't sure if anyone else noticed, and she gave a tight nod as if Bishop had said something to her telepathically. It was rude to have a mental conversation with someone while at the table, but I wasn't going to call her or Bishop out on it. She needed the reassurance only Bishop could give her... because she needed to stay angry with me.

Except she wasn't angry. She was afraid of me and everyone else, just like I'd feared.

"It's complicated because they're fated," Bishop said, answering for her. Then he took a bite of his salad as if that statement answered everything, even though we both knew it wouldn't, not for Thane and not for any of our other betas.

Deacon and Nova didn't react since they already knew the truth, and thankfully they didn't correct Bishop about how Knox and Audrey weren't really fated. Although maybe they were and we were too upset to see the truth. That would explain why her incomplete mating bond had latched on to him and not Bishop.

Thane, however, frowned in full, while Finn and Velora looked shocked.

"You mean *fated* fated?" Velora stammered. "That's impossible."

"I'd have to agree," Finn added. "True fated mates are a myth."

"Clearly, they're not. It's the only logical explanation for why sweet Audrey here is mated to the grumpiest member of our pack," Deacon said, rolling his eyes at Thane.

The hint of Deacon's usual mirth curled his lips but didn't reach his eyes. He was trying to lighten the situation but was just as worried as I was about how the others were reacting. They were supposed to welcome her warmly, just like they had for her first dinner, or feel compassion for her for being mate bonded to Knox. But instead, they were suspicious and that agitated my already agitated wolf even more.

Thane's frown deepened. I could practically see the wheels in his head turning as he tried to solve the mystery of why Audrey and Knox were mated. "The most recent mention of fated mates was three hundred years ago."

"That's the only one mentioned and we don't know how accurate it is," Velora said.

Nova ripped a piece off her roll and gave Velora her driest, least impressed look. "Whil wrote the book you're talking about. Why don't we go ask her if she made it up."

"Doesn't mean Knox and Audrey are true fated mates," Velora

shot back, unwilling to back down, surprising me. If Knox and Audrey were fated, that would mean there was a greater chance she could have Bishop... unless, of course, she believed the rumors that because Knox and Bishop were twins, they were going to share a mate.

Of course, anyone close to Bishop — which didn't include Velora — knew it wasn't just speculation. Bishop had been saying to me and a few select others that he felt he'd share a mate with his twin since he was a teenager.

Nova raised an eyebrow, shooting me a questioning look, and ate her piece of dinner roll.

Yeah, I'd seen it, too. Velora was far too interested in Bishop and therefore Audrey. And because they both lived in the Residence, Velora could make Audrey's life more difficult without anyone else knowing.

Well, without anyone but Knox knowing. That would inevitably end with Velora pushing Knox too far and the pack demanding Knox be banished because he was too dangerous. And while people would be understanding that Knox was defending his mate, everyone was still afraid he'd snap, turn feral, and start killing people.

If I'd thought when we'd first promoted Velora to beta that her crush on Bishop would have turned into a problem, I'd have picked someone else. It wouldn't have mattered how organized and efficient she was.

But once again, I'd misread a romantic situation.

"They're mated now so it doesn't matter if they're fated or not," Thane concluded. Then he turned his attention to Audrey, his eyes bright with curiosity. "I have so many questions for you, like how far away is your old pack? You weren't comfortable in our loose clothing. Does that mean your environment is colder, or do you feel the cold more than we do?" He turned to Nova. "We should run a study. I'd be interested to know if there are biological differences between us and if so, does that mean her pack didn't originate from the Original Pack?"

"And then you'll want to know her exact height and weight and when she had her last heat," Deacon mocked.

"Oh! Yes! That's good information, too," Thane replied, completely oblivious to the fact that Deacon was making fun of him, while Audrey shrank deeper into her chair, embarrassment and worry starting to dampen her bland smile and seep into her eyes.

"We're not hounding Audrey with questions," Bishop insisted, his arm moving closer to her, his hand, hidden by the table, likely on her thigh to reassure her and steady her soul.

"No," Finn said. "Thane has a point. We know nothing about her and she's mated into the pack's alpha unit. She could be dangerous."

CYRUS

Bishop growled at Finn's words and power slipped from Deacon's control.

"Audrey isn't dangerous," I said, fighting to keep my voice even, while the urge to tear into Finn for making such an accusation squeezed my insides. "And just because she's mated into the alpha unit doesn't make her an alpha."

Audrey flinched and my stomach churned, threatening to expel what little I'd eaten of dinner. I hadn't meant to remind her about what I'd yelled at her in the arena, but I needed to stop my betas' worry and accusations before it got out of hand.

I didn't know how the conversation had twisted into them thinking Audrey was dangerous, and while I could understand my watch commander being suspicious, I hadn't expected Velora to be so outwardly hostile.

I'd always encouraged our betas to question decisions with logical arguments so Bishop and I could get different perspectives on a situation, but it was driving both me and my wolf crazy that they were questioning my judgment when it came to Audrey.

Out of the corner of my eye — my glare still on Finn — I watched Audrey raise a trembling fork to her mouth as if she were trying to hide her discomfort by eating. But the fluttering piece of lettuce at the end of the utensil only made her shaking more obvious and she quickly set her fork aside and clasped her hands on the table.

Sisters, I needed to protect her, hold her, reassure her.

But I couldn't. I had to keep my distance.

"She's not an alpha," Finn agreed, "you're right. But that doesn't mean she can't influence you. I mean look at Bishop. He's obviously taken with her and we all know how he feels about women in distress." Finn drained his wine and set the glass on the table to punctuate his words. "She won't tell us where she's from or anything else about herself. You found her in Darkweald after that wave of power and then our hunt team found that strange magic in Anakar. How do we know she's not connected to that? How do we know she's not a spy or whether she intends to hurt the pack? She's already made all three of you leave for a month."

My wolf heaved at Finn's accusations and how Velora was nodding in agreement and Thane was looking thoughtful, actually considering Finn's words.

Come on, Audrey, I mentally begged, struggling to keep my thoughts to myself. *Tell him to fuck off. That it's none of his business. Prove you can stand your ground.*

Sisters, I wanted to tell them all to fuck off, but that wouldn't help the situation. Everything would get worse if they started thinking I was interested in Audrey, too. She needed to speak up and prove that she might be powerless but she was still a person and deserved respect. But gods, my wolf was on the verge of taking over. How dare they question her and talk about her as if she wasn't even in the room!

"She didn't make us leave for a month, Knox did," Bishop said, his posture growing tense. "We all know how he felt about mating. *He* didn't want a bond and Whil had found a spell that might have helped."

"But it didn't," Finn pressed.

"Maybe Audrey found a way to force the bond on him," Velora said, catching Deacon mid-sip.

He sprayed wine across his salad and roll, his expression shocked, while Bishop's eyes narrowed, and my wolf howled and heaved inside me.

"If she was going to force a bond on anyone, why the hell would she pick Knox?" Deacon sputtered.

"Because she's too stupid to know Knox isn't really a pack alpha," Velora shot back.

Her words hit like one of Knox's punches to my chest, shattering what little hold I had on my emotions and my wolf. No one called my mate stupid because she sure as hell wasn't stupid.

"Enough!" I roared, a blast of my power snapping through the room.

My betas sat up straighter and stared at me with wide eyes, while Audrey shook even harder and paled to the point I was afraid she was going to pass out.

She wasn't even bothering to keep up her meek, bland mask, and she probably thought I was angry with her even though this conversation and my loss of control was my betas' fault.

Fuck. Fuck fuck fuck.

"Audrey is a member of my family," I growled, my wolf rising to the surface but not taking over.

Somehow, he understood that if he took over, my betas would accuse me of desiring her and not thinking straight, but he still wanted to show my betas— hell, show everyone, that he agreed with me. Audrey was family. Audrey was mine. This wasn't just something my human half felt strongly about. All of me felt this.

"You *will* respect her." I glared at Velora, making her tense.

Then I slid my gaze over everyone else to let them know it wasn't just Velora I was pissed at. Finn swallowed hard while Thane bobbed his head in agreement and Deacon and Nova looked concerned. Lucius on the other hand tipped his head in acknowledgment, pride lighting his eyes. He agreed with me defending Audrey. Hell, he could probably tell what everyone was thinking — which was why we'd made him our diplomat — and knew Audrey was exactly what she seemed: a lost scared young woman with too many scars on her body and soul.

"I'd still like to know more about her," Thane insisted, his curiosity undeterred by my growl and power slip, because of course, he didn't see hounding Audrey with questions as disrespectful. "We could learn more about what lies beyond our territory and that of our neighbors."

"Thane," Deacon hissed, loud enough for the whole table to hear, including Audrey with her practically human hearing. "Stop while you're ahead."

Thane frowned. "But I'm not ahead. I still don't know anything new."

My huntmaster groaned and looked skyward. "Sisters, help me!"

Thane looked even more confused and Deacon burst out laughing.

If I hadn't been so angry about my betas interrogating Audrey, I might have laughed at Thane being Thane, too.

"This isn't funny," Finn insisted. "We don't know her intentions. She just shows up one day and is fated for Knox? I find that suspicious."

"Pup," Deacon groaned. "Just because you dated out of the pack and she turned out to be a lying manipulative bitch, doesn't mean Audrey is."

"But—" Finn protested.

"Whil already confirmed when Audrey first arrived that she has no ill intent and that everything she told us is the truth," Bishop said, while Audrey continued to tremble and stare at her plate.

Please. I tried to will her to look up and challenge my betas. *Say something. Stand up for yourself. Show them what you showed me and my brothers while we were traveling. Show them what I see in you.*

But she didn't move, just took it like she'd been taught, which only made me angrier.

A growl rumbled in my chest again and more power slipped my control. "This conversation ended a minute ago. It will *not* continue and will *not* be heard again."

But that only made my three suspicious betas frown.

"She's from another realm," Bishop said with a huff of frustration. None of us had wanted to reveal that until Audrey was ready because we knew she'd be inundated with questions.

And sure enough, Finn and Thane opened their mouths, but Bishop raised a hand and glared, silencing them.

"Whil has confirmed this is also true. Which means Audrey has no ulterior motives towards our pack. She didn't even know we existed until we found her."

"Then she knows—" Thane started.

"No," Bishop snapped.

He wrapped a protective arm across Audrey's shoulders and drew her to his side, doing what I wanted to do but couldn't without creating a mutiny among my betas or without sending Audrey the wrong signals... or maybe the right ones that I couldn't accept.

The thought twisted around my heart and made my wolf claw at my insides, and I struggled to remind myself that it was best if Audrey didn't like me.

"If or when Audrey feels comfortable talking to you about it, she will," Bishop added. "Until then, leave her alone."

He pushed out his chair, helped Audrey stand, and led her out of the dining room.

Well, that went well, Nova said, her mental voice dry as Velora and Finn shoved back their chairs and left and Thane looked confused.

"You understand why Cyrus told you to back off, don't you?" Lucius asked him.

"Because I can be overwhelming when I get excited?" our chief of finance replied, making it sound like a question instead of a statement.

Nova nodded. "We're all curious. We just need to remember that Audrey doesn't know us and we might make her nervous."

As if that hadn't been obvious from the beginning. But Thane was worse than Knox when it came to reading body language and hadn't clued in on her distress.

Thane nodded. I'm not sure if he understood exactly what Nova meant — I wasn't sure if he ever did — but he knew enough that if we told him someone was upset or scared, he'd wait until we'd told him they were better.

We ate our main course discussing what went on with the pack while we'd been gone, Lucius's observations about the members of the Mountain and Sea Alliance, and the upcoming summer festival until Thane left.

Then Deacon poured himself another glass of wine and sagged back in his chair. "What the fuck, Cyrus? I leave you alone with her in the arena for ten minutes after you assured me she'd be fine and somehow the woman who walked with us to patrol shed twelve a month ago is completely gone. Did you do that after she saved Knox from going feral, or was that a build up from your entire journey north? She's clearly afraid of you."

"She was afraid of everyone here except Bishop," Lucius stated. "She was even wary of Eloise and Kira."

"Which she wasn't before," Nova added, grabbing the wine bottle in front of Deacon.

I ran my hands down my face, wanting to scream with frustration while also wanting to find her, grab hold, and never let her go.

This was all my fault. If I'd just talked to her instead of yelled, everything would be fine and she might not have nearly killed herself, but—

"She almost died in the arena," I insisted as if that was a good excuse for me losing my temper.

"So you decided to put the fear of the alpha in her to stop her from doing something else?" Nova rolled her eyes at me. "Well it worked. She was even nervous around me this afternoon when I checked in on her. I think she's more afraid of everyone than when she first arrived."

"I know that," I growled. "I can't fix that."

"Sure you can. You go up to her and apologize." Deacon took a long sip of his wine, waiting for me to agree. "I know you can do it. I've seen you apologize before. I've even seen you do it after you became primary alpha."

"It's not that simple," I shot back, even though I knew it was exactly that simple.

"Audrey, I'm sorry." Deacon glanced at Lucius and Nova. "I believe that was three words?"

Nova nodded in agreement. "I believe so."

"I concur," Lucius added.

I groaned and glared at Lucius. "Not you, too?"

"But if we need someone to count," Nova continued, "we should ask Thane. He's the genius when it comes to numbers."

"Come on, guys," I begged. "You know it's not that simple. The pack can't think I have any interest in her. They'll be worse to her than Thane, Finn, and Velora were."

Nova quirked her eyebrow again. "That would suggest you're interested in her."

"It doesn't matter if I am. You know how the pack gossips." And it would be worse if they knew that I really did want her, too hell with her being too weak to shift or anything else. "The only people who can fix this are you and Bishop. I don't want to confuse her."

"Why would she be confused?" Deacon asked as realization flashed across Nova's expression.

"Her heat. You said it turned into a fever that went on for nine days. You had to have sex with her."

"And sex means something to her, even if she doesn't remember," I said, mumbling the last part. "I crossed that line and now I have to put that line back."

"I'm pretty sure you have." Deacon downed the rest of his wine and shook his head at me. "You've built a whole chasm between you and she'll never look you in the eyes again."

Which was exactly what I'd wanted and made my chest so tight I could barely breathe.

AUDREY

I CLUNG TO BISHOP, DESPERATELY HOLDING ONTO HIM AND THE WARMTH of his soul steadying mine. He'd rushed me out of the dining room before I'd even known what had happened, brought me to my suite, sat on the couch, and cradled me in his arms.

"You don't have to do that again. Ever," he said. "If I could, I'd demote them for scaring you."

"They don't know me and are trying to protect you and the pack," I forced out.

I didn't want to defend them, but I also didn't want to make them any angrier with me than they already were. And from the look on Velora's face, she was already furious and I suspected it'd be easy for her to convince Finn that I couldn't be trusted.

Thane on the other hand just seemed obsessively curious. I didn't even think he knew what he and the others were saying was scaring me, and God, did it scare me.

They talked about me as if I wasn't there, something Merrick did all the time, and just like my old alpha and his betas, they could do whatever they wanted to me. They could turn me into a test subject, lock me up forever, or turn the pack against me, just like Sterling had done with all the other kids in my old pack.

I'd thought I could just sit there and keep my expression neutral, but I should have known they wouldn't have ignored me, not with the look Velora had given me earlier when I'd left the kitchen to have lunch with Bishop.

And while Cyrus had defended me and told his betas that I was family, I had no doubt some of his anger was still directed at me. It was my fault they didn't listen to him and hounded me. If I hadn't been there, they would have had a perfectly normal conversation, and that had made me even more nervous.

This was his house and his pack. He couldn't let such disobedience go without punishment and without a doubt, that would mean punishing me for making his betas question him.

The punishment might not happen right away because I was currently with Bishop, but I doubted Cyrus would forget about what had happened. He'd made how he felt about me perfectly clear with his hard expression in the foyer when he'd told me to come to dinner and again when he'd commented on my punctuality — something I was pretty sure had been a threat.

And yet I still thought he was gorgeous and my body craved his arms around me. As much as I wanted to, I couldn't shake that fantasy I kept having about having sex with Cyrus. I should hate him for reminding me where I belonged and how much power he had over my life, and I did. But thoughts and feelings were two frustratingly different things and no matter what I tried, I couldn't get them to agree.

"We'll have dinner tomorrow in the summer garden," Bishop cooed, running his hand along my hair in slow, soothing strokes.

"Cyrus will expect you to dine with him." I wasn't sure if Cyrus's temper would extend to his youngest brother, but I didn't want to find out, even if I didn't want to be alone.

Except I couldn't ask any more from him. He'd spoken up for me when I knew no one would believe me.

And why would they? I was a nobody, a nothing, and they were already suspicious. There was no point in drawing more attention to myself by denying their accusations.

But they hadn't backed off, even when Bishop lied about Knox and I being fated for each other or when he'd revealed the truth about where I'd come from.

I hadn't wanted everyone to know that I was from another realm, not until after I'd started working on bringing things from my realm into this one with Whil and an engineer's help, but I'd prayed — like Bishop probably had when he'd asked me if he could tell them — that knowing the truth would shut them up or at least make their questions less aggressive and more compassionate.

Except it had only made things worse, and now I wasn't sure if it was safe to be alone in the Residence.

And I would be alone at some point.

Probably most of the time, because Bishop had work to do and Knox was on a hunt for the next three or four days and would get more hunting assignments in the future.

Given that I hadn't felt Knox's emotions since before dinner, he had to have left right after returning the picnic basket and was too far away for us to connect the way we had before.

"Cyrus will understand," Bishop said.

"He might not if it's every dinner."

"He will," Bishop insisted. "But if you're worried about it, Knox will be back in a couple of days and I suspect Nova and Deacon wouldn't mind avoiding Finn and Velora for a while." Bishop pressed his lips against the top of my head. "If you're comfortable with that."

"I ah... I don't know," I murmured.

Nova had been kind to me, even after Cyrus had yelled at me in the arena and had undoubtedly informed his betas about how I didn't know my place. She also hadn't questioned me or seemed suspicious.

In fact, she'd looked upset when Finn and Velora had started accusing me of being dangerous. Deacon had looked upset as well. Both of them knew I was from another realm, and neither of them had questioned me or suspected my intentions before or during the dinner.

Although, I hadn't really talked with Deacon. He seemed easygoing, but feralness and power radiated off him despite the laugh lines around his eyes and mouth. He could be dangerous if he wanted to be. Hell, he was the pack's huntmaster. He hunted down and fought the wild beasts in the area to help keep the pack safe. The question was, was I safe with him?

"So, want to tell me what happened?" Bishop asked after a long pause. "I thought you were getting comfortable around us."

"I am." With him and Knox. "I just— I forgot who I was when it was just the three of us. Now we're back with your pack and I needed to remember where I belonged."

"You're exactly where you belong," he said, cutting me off. "You're Knox's mate and you're going to be mine."

"I know that." I pressed my face against his chest, drawing in more of his scent to stop the tears burning my eyes. Even in the face of his betas' disapproval he still wanted me, and I couldn't thank fate enough for bringing him into my life. "I still need to remember that I'm not an alpha and never will be."

A growl rumbled in Bishop's chest. "It doesn't matter if you're an alpha. Finn, Velora, and Thane aren't alphas. Velora and Thane aren't even close, but they still have something to offer the pack. Audrey—" He nudged me back so he could look me in the eyes. "You're perfect the way you are."

My pulse stuttered and my breath caught at the affection in his eyes. It was softer than the looks he'd given me in the garden, but just as warm and soul deep, and made more tears threaten to fall.

I had no idea how I'd caught the interest of a man so kind and generous and sexy, and a part deep in my soul, a part that had momentarily grown stronger when I'd been standing in the natural stillness in the field beside the patrol shed a month ago, rose again. It brushed my consciousness for a split second, so fast I almost didn't sense it, before settling back within me.

It didn't care about the how or why Bishop was attracted to me. It just knew it was right.

"Knox, Cyrus, and I trust you and that should be more than

enough for them. You won't be punished for telling them to fuck off," he assured me. "Our pack isn't like your old pack."

He kissed the tip of my nose then pulled me back to his chest. "Thane might need more than one fuck off, but he doesn't mean to badger you. He just doesn't know when his curiosity is too much for someone."

"I kind of got that impression." I closed my eyes, Bishop's steady heartbeat even more calming now that it was mixed with the feeling in my soul that being in his arms was where I belonged. "He might actually be a good person to talk to."

"He'll ask you about everything and it'll be hard to get him to stop," Bishop warned.

"But he wasn't suspicious. He was excited. He didn't care that I came from another realm or that I was mated to Knox. He just wanted to know more about all of it." And now that I said it, I realized it was true.

I'd been nervous of Cyrus and his betas at the beginning of the meal, and that nervousness had grown to fear when they'd started accusing me of being a... spy? A danger? An I-don't-know-what-but-it-had-to-be-bad and that meant being punished.

But Thane hadn't made me feel like that at all. He reminded me of a puppy and knowledge was the bone he eagerly begged for. I just hadn't been prepared for his onslaught of questions.

"Thane has a pretty set routine and chaos ensues if you break it, so you wouldn't be able to talk to him until mid-afternoon," Bishop said, and my fear fluttered back, making my throat tighten with frustrated tears.

I wasn't supposed to be afraid. I was just supposed to be cautious until I knew I was safe with someone. And while I still wasn't sure about Nova, Deacon, or Lucius — who'd barely spoken a word — I knew without a doubt, I wasn't safe with Velora or Finn.

I also wanted to believe that I wasn't safe with Cyrus, everything told me he was dangerous, but a traitorous part of me still believed I could trust him.

Gah!

"I don't think I'm quite ready for Thane's... intensity just yet." I wanted to be brave. I desperately wanted it, but that dinner had been another reminder that I had to remain cautious. I couldn't let my guard down around someone until I knew for sure I could trust them, despite my gut instinct telling me Thane wouldn't pull rank on me.

What I needed was to prove myself. Then they'd have to respect me, or in the very least stop suspecting me.

"Bishop?" I said, suddenly too tired to care that his shirt muffled my voice. I didn't want to move from his embrace. I wanted to lie there forever, safe and warm and loved. "Is it possible to get a pen and a notebook?"

"For you, anything is possible," he replied, his words not just sounding like he'd get me what I'd asked for, but that *I* could do anything, that it was all possible.

I just needed to be brave enough.

AUDREY

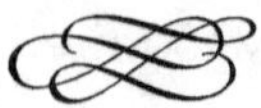

I woke the next morning in my bed, wrapped in a soft sheet, and completely alone. I vaguely remembered Bishop carrying me into the bedroom, lying down with me, and holding me until I fell asleep, but I didn't notice him getting up.

A small twist of disappointment tightened my stomach, but I pushed it back. Bishop had pack responsibilities and from the bright sunlight streaming through the partially closed bedroom curtains, it was well past dawn.

As much as I wanted him to, I couldn't expect him to stay in bed with me all day. He'd needed to get to work, and so did I.

I quickly showered, changed into a cream-colored shirt and tan pants, and braided my hair. The braid made me feel like I was ready to get to work and I hoped the bland clothing would make me less noticeable — since the dark green dress had done nothing to avoid Cyrus's attention. I didn't want to slink about the Residence, but I wasn't completely safe here and the more I blended into the background, the better.

With my stomach growling, since I'd barely eaten anything at dinner, I knew my first step was to find food. After that, I needed to find Bishop and get the notebook he promised, something I wasn't looking forward to.

I didn't want to aimlessly wander the Residence and possibly get in trouble, but I also didn't know who I could ask who'd know where he was.

Trying to figure out the safest way to accomplish what should have been simple goals, I strode into my sitting room to see the answers sitting on the dining room table.

I'd placed the bowl of fruit, cheese, and rolls that the older cook had insisted I take yesterday on the table, and beside it sat a leather-bound notebook and three pens.

Bishop must have brought them to my room while I was sleeping — and I wasn't going to think too hard about how I'd been alone and unconscious with my suite door unlocked.

He'd also left me a small satchel big enough for the notebook and pens and a few other things like a wallet, which reminded me of how much I didn't have and just how dependent I was on him.

I didn't feel safe wandering around town. Lucius had said last night that the pack was already talking about me and Knox, and I didn't want to risk the rest of the pack reacting like the betas had. But even if I did feel safe, there wasn't much I could do. I had no money so I couldn't buy myself food or even just a trinket that made me happy.

And while Bishop hadn't used money with the shopkeepers when he'd bought me clothes, other people had exchanged coins for their purchases. The alphas probably had free rein over what they wanted or they had expense accounts and the bills were sent to the Residence. It wasn't like everyone didn't know where they lived or something.

I didn't want to stay dependent on Bishop, Knox, or anyone else, which meant I needed to come up with good information soon and get Bishop to convince Cyrus to pay me for it.

That thought left a sour taste in my mouth. Would Cyrus even consider paying me? Or would he say I cost them money walking to the death god's temple and was paying off my debt?

It was going to be like living with Merrick all over again. Cyrus was going to say I needed to work for him to pay him back for living at the Residence, and I'd never earn my own money.

I bit back a growl of frustration. I'd sworn I'd never go back to that and I wouldn't. If Cyrus was going to demand my labor for room and board without any extra compensation, I'd find a cheaper place to live. It might even be safer than staying at the Residence.

Knox would be pissed, of course, but I could probably convince him it was for the best, especially if I found a place near the edge of town where we could spend time together.

I might even be able to convince Bishop it was what I needed, too. I'd never been on my own before, never been free.

My heart sank. All of that was only if Cyrus allowed it and he'd never allow it.

What was the point of even trying? He'd never let me go all in the name of protecting his brothers. If I begged, would Knox and Bishop even be able to get Cyrus to listen to them?

And the God damned frustrating part of me that was somehow attracted to Cyrus and fantasized about him didn't want to leave at all.

Damn it! A week ago, I wouldn't have had this fear. Cyrus had asked about my plans for the future, had seemed to care about me. Then in a flash, he'd acted like Merrick and all that confidence in him and the others vanished.

I trusted too easily because I didn't want to believe all alphas were like Merrick, Sterling, and Royce. On TV, alphas were heroic and protective. And yes, it was foolish to think there was any truth in a TV show, movie, or book.

But just like I'd foolishly hoped there was someone out there who'd love me for me, despite all my weaknesses, I'd hoped I'd find a pack where I wasn't the alpha's slave.

And I *had* found it. The first part at least. Bishop wanted me for me. But that only kept a glimmer of hope alive for Cyrus and the idea that if I proved myself, he'd accept me. He'd respect me.

He'd care about me.

Praying that proving myself would set me free, I bit into one of the apples, opened the notebook to make notes, and tapped my pen on the paper. All the things I thought the pack might find useful rushed through my head and I realized I had no idea what the pack knew and didn't know.

I knew they didn't know about photography and movies, but did they know about electricity — even on a basic level — or what about light and sound waves?

It didn't look like they had a whole lot of sophisticated medical equipment — which as shifters they didn't really need — but did they know about blood pressure or the spinal cord or near-sightedness?

If they didn't know about vision problems, did they know about concave and convex lenses that could magnify things or help them see things far away?

The list went on and on, and I was going to have to talk to someone and figure out what they did and didn't know. Bishop wouldn't have the time, not with how much I needed to know and how fast I wanted it. But would anyone else help me?

My thoughts jumped to Whil. Maybe she'd be willing to help. She'd been nothing but kind to me. Although after Cyrus had turned suddenly into Merrick, I had more evidence that I couldn't trust my own judgment of people.

I'd approach her cautiously. If she reacted badly then I'd know she'd talked with Cyrus and agreed with him.

If not, spending time with her, even if it was just drinking tea while she worked, would ease my too-on-edge nerves and help me think. I'd gotten the impression not a lot of people visited her cottage library greenhouse at the back of the Residence's ground. That would limit the nasty looks I'd get from people or the fear that someone was going to teach me a lesson.

Someone knocked on my door, startling me and making my pulse lurch then race at a furious pace.

"Audrey?" Nova called through the door. "Are you up?"

I released the breath I hadn't realized I was holding. Nova, for now, was safe. She could still turn on me, but nothing in her behavior suggested she would and she was even polite enough to knock and ask first before opening the door.

"I'm up," I called as I hurried to answer the door.

"Are you hungry?" she asked, her critical gaze sliding over me.

Worry fluttered through my chest for a second, but quickly vanished. I didn't feel like she was judging me, not like Velora and Finn had at dinner last night. It was more like she was assessing my health.

"The other betas have left the kitchen so I thought now would be a perfect time." Her attention jumped past my shoulder to the table. "But I see you've already found food."

"The older woman in the kitchen gave me the bowl last night." But confessing that only reminded me of Cyrus's comments about it. "She wouldn't take no for an answer," I mumbled.

Nova chuckled, clearly hearing everything I said with her better-than-human hearing.

"Yeah, Eloise is like that," she said, affection warming her voice. "If you'd like a warm breakfast, I have no doubt she'll want to cook something for you."

That had been my impression of the older cook as well as the younger one. They'd also seemed concerned for me at dinner last night.

I glanced at the barely eaten apple in my hand and the bowl of food on the table. If I had something more substantial now, I could save what was in the bowl for when I really needed it.

"Come on," Nova said. "I have half an hour before my next meeting. I'll keep you company."

"Thank you." I instinctually dropped my gaze and Nova huffed, making me cringe.

"Head up, Audrey," Nova scolded. "You're Knox's mate and you have more right to be here than they do."

I shoved my notebook and pens into the satchel, grabbed the apple I'd taken a bite out of, and forced my gaze to meet Nova's.

In return, she offered me a brilliant smile and held the door open.

"There's something you need to know about Cyrus," she said as we headed down the hall to the kitchen. "About all of the brothers, actually. They're extremely powerful alphas."

I nodded even though any idiot would have been able to see they were powerful.

"I have a hypersensitivity to alpha power, so I can feel how powerful they are even when they're controlling it." Her gaze slid to mine. "I suspect you can feel it, too."

For a split-second I contemplated denying it, but it didn't matter if Nova knew I could sense someone's power level or not and it would be a small way to test her sincerity. I didn't know how she or anyone could use the information against me, but Sterling would have figured out a way, which meant someone else could as well.

"I can," I replied softly.

"Alphas with that amount of power have a stronger connection with their wolf and it makes it harder to control their instincts."

Ah, so this was the excuse for her alpha's behavior conversation.

"And no, this isn't an excuse," she continued as if she could read my mind. "It's an explanation. Bishop deals with his wolf freaking out by being the life of the party, Knox doesn't deal with it at all, just lets it take over, and Cyrus fights so hard to regain control he sometimes hurts the people around him. I know Cyrus yelled at you and I can assume he said some pretty awful things."

"I'd forgotten my place and he reminded me. It won't happen again."

Nova sighed. "Knowing Cyrus, it probably will, but it has nothing to do with your place in this pack. It's all about Cyrus and his wolf freaking out because he failed to protect you."

We turned down the hall toward the kitchen, its door twenty feet away, and Nova grabbed my arm.

"You did nothing wrong," she insisted.

"I didn't think."

"Your mate was in danger and you did what your instincts told you. You didn't step out of line because there isn't a line like that in this pack. You're not a servant or slave or lesser than anyone else."

I opened my mouth to protest that part, but she cut me off.

"You're not lesser and if you can sense power like I think you can, you have an ability that very few in this pack have." Her expression turned wry. "Cyrus will apologize. It'll be long after you've gotten over it and moved on, but he'll get his head out of his ass eventually."

I nodded, not sure what to say to that or if I even believed it.

Regardless, I still didn't have proof that it was safe enough to let my guard down around him or almost anyone else.

Nova's wry expression softened with affection and a hint of sadness. She could tell I didn't completely believe her. But she didn't press the matter, likely knowing I needed concrete evidence and that would take time to get.

AUDREY

Nova stayed and chatted with me while Eloise made me an omelet and the younger cook, Kira, poured me a glass of sweet, pink juice and cut my apple into pieces. We talked about the pack, the things I could see and do in town — once my doctor-appointed rest was complete — and where I should get Bishop and Knox to take me.

I learned the pack was almost completely self-sufficient and its primary exports were hunters and the healing elixirs, both of which were in short supply. They didn't mass produce anything, and I didn't know if that was because they didn't want to, didn't know they could, or couldn't.

Time ran out before I could ask Nova about medical equipment and she hurried off to her meeting, leaving me with Eloise and Kira who were happy to talk about their kitchen and how they prepared food.

They were so warm and friendly and excited about their work that I didn't realize it was lunchtime until Deacon walked in, startling me.

"You're still here," he exclaimed to Eloise and Kira as I tried to subtly shy away from him. "Shouldn't you be on break or shopping?"

"We were telling Audrey about our kitchen," Kira replied with a brilliant smile as if no one had asked her about her work before.

Deacon's gaze slid to mine, and I plastered on my most submissive expression and found a spot on the wall beside his head that I could look at. I didn't want to risk my gut instinct being wrong about him. Better to err on the side of caution.

"I didn't realize it was lunchtime," I said. "Excuse me. I don't want to disturb you." And I really didn't want to still be there when Finn and Velora showed up.

"You're so quiet, I doubt you'd disturb a mouse," Deacon replied.

I glanced at Eloise and Kira, who were frowning.

"Thank you," I told them.

"You better come back tomorrow," Eloise said. "I was just about to give you a tour of the herb garden and show you my favorite recipe." Her worry bloomed into a warm, inviting smile, the kind of smile a mother might give her child, something I'd seen but never experienced before.

"I will," I assured her and rushed out the back door into brilliant hot sunshine, buzzing insects, chirping birds, and fragrant air. For a moment, I'd felt free and safe and comfortable. Eloise's and Kira's excitement over cooking was contagious and I wanted more of that feeling.

Hoping I'd receive the same welcome with Whil, I followed the path through the herb garden, past the Residence's private sacred grove to Whil's greenhouse-English cottage-library.

Trees and bushes and all manner of flowers crowded around the strange building. It didn't seem to matter that it was summer, tulips and irises bloomed beside daisies and daylilies and fall chrysanthemums and dahlias.

Much to my surprise, Whil, the most beautiful woman I'd ever seen with her long golden hair, delicately pointed ears, and perpetual soft golden fae glow, was outside picking berries from a bush near the back.

I walked toward her, my pace getting slower and slower, my nerves making my heart race.

She wasn't pack so she might not feel the same way about me as other shifters.

Please, let that be true.

"Audrey!" Whil's face brightened the moment she saw me, flooding me with relief. "You've got to try these. They're the closest I can get to a berry I loved in Fairy and this is the only bush in the area."

The bush wasn't very big, standing as high as my waist and only a few feet wider than me. It was heavy with small, bright pink berries but they were still only enough to make three, maybe four pies, and likely wouldn't even fill her medium-sized bucket.

"If you love them so much, why wouldn't you grow more?" I asked as Whil lifted the basket, offering me her precious fruit.

"A merchant brought the plant to Stonehaven from a much warmer land about two hundred years ago, and trust me, I've tried to make it grow bigger, tried to grow cuttings, tried everything I could think of."

I popped the berry in my mouth, letting the juice coat my tongue before swallowing it. It tasted like strawberries and cream, and I couldn't hold back a soft moan. "It's so good."

"I told you," she said with a grin. "I think the only reason it's alive is because it's here and I unconsciously make things grow in a fifty-foot radius around my cottage despite the weather."

"Does it make berries all the time?"

Whil sighed. "Only twice a year so I make sure I pick them before any of them go bad. Come! I have the perfect tea for these."

She led me back to the entrance to her greenhouse library and its inside garden, just as vibrant as the flowering garden outside. The strange combination still astounded me with the bookshelves crammed with books and scrolls and jars, making secret nooks and standing among a cacophony of colorful flowers, even though the ceiling and walls were glass like an ordinary greenhouse.

As she led me farther across the uneven flagstone floor and past the strange steps that went nowhere in the middle of a small gurgling pool, the glass turned into a mix of glass windows and stone walls and the ceiling became a normal ceiling. More bookshelves lined the walls, creating more secret little nooks partially hidden by foliage and begging to be explored.

Whil took me to the back to the mismatched seating area consisting of two simple wooden chairs, a stool, a chair with thick cushions, and an old-fashioned couch with only one arm. Piles of books littered the area, and I couldn't tell if she'd moved anything from when I'd first visited her greenhouse a month ago.

She set the basket of berries on the table between the various seats and hurried around a corner into the cottage part of her house, the dimmer light making her golden glow more obvious.

I sat on the old-fashioned couch stunned. I'd planned to approach her cautiously and find out how she felt about me. Instead, she'd welcomed me like a long-lost friend and now I was sitting in her home awaiting tea so I could eat her precious berries.

Had Cyrus not talked to her?

It was possible, which meant the next time I visited, I might not be so welcome. But then again, maybe not. Maybe Whil liked me like Eloise and Kira did.

"Here we are," Whil announced as she reentered carrying a silver tray with two tall glasses and a pitcher filled with a pale green liquid.

She set the tray beside the basket, filled both glasses, and sat on the floor opposite me surrounded by uneven stacks of books.

"You've had quite a journey," she said. "I'm sorry the spell didn't work and you had to seal your bond with Knox. And I'm sorry Cyrus was an idiot and lost his temper."

So she did know what had happened. But did she know what he'd actually said or how he really felt about me?

She must have seen something in my expression because hers softened and she pushed the basket of berries closer to me.

"Cyrus comes from a long line of protectors and sometimes they can mistake overbearing for protecting." She took a long sip of her cold tea and studied me. "It doesn't excuse what he did. He owes you an enormous apology. I just hope knowing this helps you see that it wasn't your fault."

I nodded and took my own sip of tea to avoid saying anything, surprised at the sweet minty taste of the beverage. Nova had said something similar and while I could see overprotectiveness being Cyrus's reason for yelling at me, it was safer to assume I'd displeased him and try not to do it again in the future.

"I'm sure you have questions about the tether and the blocking magic I used to prevent whoever is on the other end from influencing you," she said changing the conversation.

A shudder swept through me. I'd been so worried about Cyrus, I'd forgotten that Sterling could make me dream horrible things and manipulate me.

"Bishop said the block wasn't permanent." That was the biggest thing I was worried about. How sturdy was the block? Would it fade away or just vanished leaving me susceptible to Sterling's manipulations?

"Correct, it isn't permanent," Whil replied, her expression turning grim. "I'm not sure how long the block will last so I'd like to check it regularly so we can get an idea of the tether's strength. Thankfully the tether isn't a true bond so there are other ways to break it besides going back to the death god's temple."

"There are?" I leaned toward her, a small flicker of hope bursting to life inside me.

I could finally be free of Sterling.

"I found some possible options while I was looking for a way to break your mating bond."

Except Bishop hadn't mentioned anything about breaking the tether yesterday, which meant Whil hadn't told him or he'd decided not to tell me. Either option indicated that these ways to break the tether were long shots, just like breaking the mating bond.

"Would you let me take a closer look at the tether? I was in a hurry when I blocked it and I doubted Knox would have let me stick around after you were safe. I'm actually surprised about the number of people he let help you." Whil chuckled softly. "The power of a sealed mating bond, I guess."

"I guess so," I replied, the sudden mention of Knox making my chest ache. He hadn't even been gone a full day and I already missed the feel of his emotions whispering through our bond.

"So…" Whil popped two more berries into her mouth. "Can I look at that tether?"

"Please." If it finally got Sterling out of my life for good, I'd do just about anything.

Whil sat on the old-fashioned couch beside me and placed her palms against my temples. Warmth radiated from her skin and into my head, and a gold light filled my vision.

"Take a breath," she ordered, making me realize I'd been holding it. "This won't hurt. It'll probably make you drowsy. Just relax."

I drew in a deep breath and slowly let it out, sinking into the warmth and golden glow of her magic. A soft haze muddled my thoughts and I knew I was completely helpless against Whil or anyone else who entered the greenhouse library.

But I also knew in my soul that I was safe with her. It was as if her magic connected me to her, and just like I knew I was safe with Knox and he was my mate, I could tell Whil didn't have ill intentions toward me. In fact, she saw me as a kind of kindred spirit. We were both outsiders to the pack in our own way, separated from our homes, and didn't fit easily into the pack's hierarchy. The realization let me fall deeper into her golden warmth.

A moment later, the warmth withdrew and I opened my eyes. Except I wasn't sitting on the old-fashioned couch anymore, I was lying on it and Whil sat on the floor near one of her bookcases with a large tome open on her lap.

"Good," she said. "You're awake just in time for dinner."

My pulse lurched and I jerked upright.

Dinner? I slept all afternoon?

And hell, dinner! I didn't want to have dinner in the dining room again. Bishop had promised I wouldn't have to, but I didn't know where he was, and if he hadn't talked to Cyrus, I'd get in trouble for not showing up.

I tried to suck in a calming breath. I really really didn't want to go, but it would be safest to dress, present myself, and suffer through another meal. Now that I knew I had Bishop, Whil, and possibly Nova on my side, I had a better chance of keeping my expression pleasant when interrogated by the others.

"Bishop said to meet him in the summer garden," Whil said, sending a blast of relief flooding through me before it jerked to panic.

Bishop wanted to see me again in the summer garden. We'd had sex there the last time and I really hoped it meant we'd have sex again, but I wasn't ready. I was in a shirt and pants again, not a pretty dress and—

I ran a hand over my hair.

Yep, half of it had fallen out of my braid while I'd slept.

I had to look like a complete mess.

"When do I need to meet him?" Maybe I could run back to my room to freshen up.

"He said whenever it got close to dinner time or you woke up."

"So now?" I squeaked. I didn't know why I was suddenly so nervous. It wasn't like we hadn't had sex before *and* while I'd been wearing the exact same outfit. "I could have slept through the night."

I quickly rebraided my hair. I had to get ahold of myself. I was making too much of his invitation. He might not want sex. He might just want to eat a meal with me.

"Calm down," Whil chuckled. "I'm pretty sure he's already madly in love with you."

"What? He's not— I— You can tell?" Could everyone? I knew he hadn't made an attempt to hide his intentions, but—

But nothing. He wasn't hiding and neither should I.

I thanked Whil for the tea and berries and, with my heart racing in anticipation, I rushed to the herb garden near the kitchen so I could find my way to the summer garden.

AUDREY

Bishop wasn't there when I arrived, but he'd told Whil he'd meet me there and he'd never broken his word to me, so I sat underneath the pergola and all its gorgeous flowering vines. A gentle breeze *shushed* through the foliage, easing the summer heat and making the bands of early evening sunshine dance on the soft grass around me.

The bright yellow glow of a summer afternoon had deepened into a rich gold, edged with oranges and reds, and for a moment, it felt like summer back on Earth. The cicadas were buzzing, the air was warm and thick, and the soft breeze brought quick breaths of contrasting coolness.

Except I'd never felt as at home there as I did here. Even with my worry about Cyrus and the rest of the pack, I felt like this realm was where I belonged.

Footsteps crunched on the gravel path and I tensed, my gaze jumping up to watch Bishop stride through the wrought iron arch. Just the sight of him stole my breath, and his radiant smile when he saw me sucked all the air from the garden.

He was happy to see me. Me. Awkward, weak me.

I didn't think I'd ever get used to that.

The smile turned heated the closer he got and I could hear the handle of the wicker basket in his grip creak as he tightened his hold.

"I promised myself we'd eat first this time," he said, his voice gruff, sending a shiver of desire racing down my spine.

"Do you have anywhere else to be after dinner?" I asked, my tone just as husky and filled with invitation.

"No."

"Then it doesn't matter when we eat." I mentally gaped at my words. I didn't know where I'd found the confidence to flirt with him like that again, but I liked it.

Bishop dropped to his knees. He captured my lips in a demanding kiss and the shiver of desire he'd inspired when he'd stepped into the garden exploded into desperate need.

Oh, yes. This was what I hadn't realized I'd been craving all day right from the moment I'd woken in an empty bed.

I tangled my fingers in his jaw-length hair and kissed him back just as wildly. Our tongues fought for dominance, our teeth clacked together in our passion, and his hands were everywhere. They tugged at my hair, stroked over my breasts, and slid to my ass. Arms, thighs, back, neck, stomach as if he couldn't get enough of me. It ignited every nerve in my body until I was aching and panting and desperate for him.

"I've been thinking about you all day," he gasped, pulling up for air and pressing his forehead against mine. "Haven't been able to concentrate on anything."

His hands swept under my shirt, teasing up my already sensitive flesh until he reached my breasts, where he palmed them roughly. Hungry for more contact, I arched into his touch. I needed more, needed him, needed everything.

It had surprised me the first time Bishop had kissed me with almost the same wildness as my dream-Knox. I'd always thought he'd be a gentle lover all the time, and I loved how careful he was with me. But I also loved when he let go. It made me feel like he couldn't be without me, that he needed me with the same overwhelming desire my dream-Knox had needed me.

I nipped at his jaw, drawing a low rumble in his chest that sent wet heat rushing to my core.

"Fuck, you smell so good." He yanked off my shirt, his eyes fully dark as if his wolf was taking over, and raked his gaze over my naked breasts.

The urge to cover my nudity and my scars dampened my desire, but it only lasted a second. Bishop didn't look at me with disgust or pity. He never had. He looked like he wanted to devour me and couldn't figure out where to start first, and my reaction was just an old habit that I really hoped I'd break soon.

With a groan, he dipped down and swept his tongue over my right breast with a heavy, slow stroke. My nipple instantly hardened and my breath caught as desire zinged through me.

"Mine," he growled, his voice so much like Knox's that I realized it wasn't Bishop pleasuring me, but his wolf... which was more than fine with me. We'd never be able to have a lasting relationship if his wolf didn't want me and I really wanted a relationship with Bishop.

He scraped his partially extended canines over my sensitive flesh then sucked the aching bud into his mouth. The pull verged on painful and yet the throbbing in my core intensified and I could feel my desire leaking down my thighs.

Moaning, I clung to him as he nipped and sucked one nipple then the other, the rumble in his chest getting louder and louder, vibrating with delicious pleasure straight to my core.

The ache within me swelled and I was on the verge of a climax with just him sucking my nipples. But he pulled away before I fell over the edge.

I groaned with disappointment but he quickly undid my pants, yanked them to my knees, and buried his face between my legs.

Oh, yes!

My orgasm swelled right to the edge, and I trembled as if I was about to crash into bliss. But I needed one more lick or suck or something.

"Bishop, please." I bucked my hips, trying to get the friction I needed on my clit to throw me over the edge.

But he clamped his hands on my hips instead, holding me still and making me writhe and whine in frustration.

Just a little more. Please.

The ache inside me just kept building. Why wasn't he doing anything? Why was he just breathing in my scent like he needed it to survive?

"Mine," he growled as he glanced up at me.

His canines were fully extended and hints of his wolf sharpened his features. The wildness in his eyes set off a mini orgasm, just a tease of what I knew was coming, not enough for relief, and his lips curled into a smirk. He knew exactly what he was doing to me.

In that moment, he looked like Knox, but I knew I hadn't mistaken the twins for each other. I knew he wasn't my bonded mate. I couldn't feel this man's emotions. I could only see them in the intensity in his eyes. And his eyes said that this was one hundred percent Bishop's wolf, the primal nature of his soul, and that his wolf was hungry for me.

"Yours," I told him and in my heart, I knew it was true.

I belonged with Knox *and* Bishop. Somehow, I just *knew* they were both my mates. And while yes, I wanted to wait on mating with Bishop so he could court me and make me feel loved and special, I'd also already fallen in love with him. I'd fallen the moment he'd held me in Kelna and swore he wanted to mate with me even if I was weak and couldn't shift and was already mated to Knox.

The look in Bishop's eyes turned into a victorious gleam and he roughly licked my clit, sending stars shooting across my vision.

The orgasm was violent and quick, but he didn't let up, licking and sucking me straight into another orgasm and another. My mind spun with pleasure, my breath was ragged, and I didn't care what noises I made or who could hear them.

Bishop's wolf was relentless, turning me into a moaning, gasping mess. He flipped me to my stomach and yanked my pants off before I'd even fully realized we'd changed position. Then he jerked my hips up and plunged his cock into me in one ferocious thrust.

The impact of our bodies colliding rattled down my spine and pushed me hard into the ground, but I didn't care. The rush of him inside me, the force of his need, just made this moment even better.

He withdrew and slammed into me again and again, faster, harder, wilder, claiming my body with his delicious, merciless attack.

I strained to catch my breath, stars flashing behind my lids with the promise of an earth-shattering release. The heated need that I'd thought was satiated from all the oral sex, roared into a raging inferno of desperate desire.

I clawed at the ground, digging my nails into the grass and dirt, and screamed with every ferocious thrust. It created a wildness within me that I'd only felt during my dreams about Knox, and I shoved my ass back, meeting Bishop's thrust, submitting to its need. And it needed to claim Bishop as my own, needed him deep within my body, fucking me until I couldn't see straight.

"More," I gasped at Bishop's wolf. "Harder."

The wildness surged and so did my pleasure. This was what I wanted. What I hadn't *known* I'd wanted. To be completely claimed by Bishop, to have his body mark mine, if not with a bite, then with a wonderful ache that would last for days. "More more more."

I hadn't thought I was ready for rough sex like I'd had in my dreams, not with how big Bishop's cock was, but half a dozen quick orgasms were enough to make me slick and ready, and I never wanted it to end. I wanted to fly on this high forever. I wanted to seize my power, a power that had this incredible, strong shifter, unable to control himself.

With a growl, Bishop clasped a hand around my throat and arched my back, his cock hitting a new spot within me that made electric need zap through me, stealing all breath and sight and sound.

"Yes," I screamed.

"Mine," he snarled and he pinched my clit with a sharp, painful twist with his free hand.

I completely shattered, screaming my release like a wild animal, the sensation too strong to keep in. Every muscle in my body clenched tight, pleasure flooding into my very essence and I whirled on violent flashes of light and ecstasy.

Bishop stiffened and howled with his own release, the sound more like a wolf than a man, and his canines grazed my neck. It was on the opposite shoulder of Knox's mating marks, the only scars I should have had as a shifter.

Yes, I mentally begged. *Make me yours forever.*

In that moment, I didn't care that he'd barely courted me. I wanted him more than I'd wanted anything in my life.

Somehow, he managed to control his wolf and not bite me, sending a sliver of disappointment oozing through my bliss.

"Soon," he murmured, his voice human again as he clutched me tight.

A violent aftershock swept through me, burning away my disappointment, and I collapsed against his chest

"Soon," I agreed and his wolf rumbled his pleasure.

Soon this powerful alpha would be mine. Just like he was supposed to be. Just like fate demanded.

AUDREY

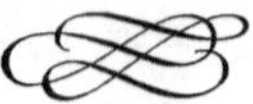

THE NEXT FOUR DAYS WERE PLEASANTLY SIMILAR TO THE PREVIOUS ONE. Nova or Bishop took me to breakfast after the other betas had eaten, then they headed to work. I stayed and chatted with Eloise and Kira, learning more about the pack, its recent history, and what living in Stonehaven was like.

The pack was more alive and vibrant than my old pack, and that wasn't just because I'd been ostracized or because it was a quarter of the size. The Stonehaven pack had more than two restaurants and a single bar. It had six restaurants and seven pubs, a couple of dance halls, a theatre for plays, and a community center that always had something happening morning, afternoon, and evening. There was also the arena that hosted events that the whole pack would be interested in like traveling musicians or acting troupes or sporting events among the pack.

It was clear by how she talked about the pack that Eloise loved it and the people. Kira loved it as well, but I could sense every time she mentioned something outside the pack that she wanted to see new sights and sounds and, more importantly, learn new dishes.

As we talked, I helped wash the breakfast dishes or prepare the informal lunch that those working and living in the Residence could eat whenever their schedules allowed it.

Then, before the betas arrived to grab their lunches, I headed to the back of the grounds to Whil's cottage where she studied the tether — usually knocking me out for the rest of the day — or answered my questions about what scientific and engineering discoveries the pack had made and about their magical items.

I had no doubt that they used magic for more than just their lights and discovered their fridges and freezers had magical cold stones and every faucet had hot and cold stone chips to heat or cool the water temperature.

My evenings ended with dinner in my suite. Much to my disappointment, Bishop couldn't eat with me the first two nights, but Nova and then Nova and Deacon kept me company, and neither of them looked at me with suspicion or made me feel threatened.

Last night, I'd had Bishop all to myself again and we mostly ate our spicy chicken and pasta dinner before falling into my bed and making love.

Now I stood at the open gate to the Residence's grounds waiting for Bishop to take me to the community center — which also happened to be Stonehaven's school — where Nova was teaching her first aid class.

It was just past lunch and I shifted from foot to foot, unable to hold in my nervousness. On one hand, I was excited to finally be able to explore the town and was eagerly awaiting Knox's return sometime today.

On the other hand, I'd started feeling safe in my quiet, reclusive routine. I'd managed to successfully avoid running into Velora, Finn, and Thane, and, most importantly, Cyrus.

A shiver of desire skated down my spine just like it always did when I thought of Cyrus and the fantasy of having sex with him flooded my mind.

God, when was it going to go away?

I couldn't believe I was still thinking about it even after having three glorious sexual encounters — not to mention numerous orgasms — with Bishop.

I wanted to scream in frustration. I was happy with Bishop, and while I barely knew Knox, I knew I'd be happy with him, too. I certainly didn't need to be fantasizing about their older brother.

Footsteps thudded on the flagstone driveway and I looked up, my pulse suddenly twice as fast as it had been a moment ago and my body heating.

"Bish—" I started then realized it was Cyrus who was marching toward me.

My pulse picked up even faster, no longer spurred by desire, and a cold dread sank heavy into my stomach. This was the first time I'd spoken with him since that disastrous dinner — and I was definitely speaking to him because there was nowhere to hide and from the hard set of his jaw, he'd already spotted me.

"Leaving the Residence?" he asked, his voice gruff as he approached. "Do you have Nova's permission?"

I dropped my gaze and strained to school my expression into a pleasant mask. "I do, alpha. She asked me to attend her first aid class."

"And you're waiting for Bishop to escort you?"

"Yes, alpha."

A hint of his power stuttered over me. The need to look at him seized me, but it vanished just as quickly, saving me from getting an eyeful of him and reigniting my fantasy.

But as soon as I realized that—

I shoved the fantasy as far back in my mind as I could and concentrated on all the cracks and grooves in the stone driveway beneath my feet.

I don't think he's sexy. I don't think he's sexy. God, why couldn't I make myself believe that?

He'd put me in my place and clearly didn't want to even be around a weakling like me.

"I just saw Velora ambush him with the final last details for tomorrow's festival," Cyrus said, making something sour curl around my heart. "I doubt he'll be free until dinner."

Disappointment joined the sour sensation, surprising me. I hadn't realized just how much I wanted to see Bishop or how much I didn't want him hanging around Velora. Which was ridiculous. Bishop wasn't interested in Velora. He was interested in me.

"Thank you for telling me, alpha," I said, managing to keep my voice steady. "Excuse me."

I turned to head to Whil's cottage. If Bishop wasn't coming, there was no point in continuing to wait. I'd find out when Nova was teaching her next first aid class and try to join again.

"Where are you going?" Cyrus demanded, his words freezing me in place despite him not using any of his power.

Shit. I hadn't asked to be excused and left before he'd given me permission.

I turned back to him, my gaze back on my feet and my hands clasped in front of me.

Shit shit shit.

I'd dropped my guard, just for a moment because Bishop, Nova, and Deacon, as well as Whil, Eloise, and Kira had made me feel safe. Now I'd given Cyrus a reason to discipline me.

"Don't you want to take the first aid class?" he asked.

"I..." I couldn't tell from his tone if he wanted me to say yes or no. When we'd been traveling, he'd suggested it, but that was before he'd reminded me of my position in the pack.

He huffed. "Come on. I'm meeting with some merchants here for the festival. The school is on my way."

He turned on his heel and headed through the gate, his posture rigid and a muscle in his jaw twitching.

Confused, I hurried after him. Was he trying to make me useful for the pack, or was he actually being nice?

Either way, he told me to follow, and I couldn't disobey him.

Cyrus took the most direct path into town, his pace almost too quick for me as if he couldn't stand being with me and wanted to get our walk over and done with. He followed the main road through Old

Town and halfway into the newer part of Stonehaven before taking a right onto another prominent road to a large, three-story building.

The building had decorative scrollwork at its eaves and around the windows and door as well as large bricks, suggesting it wasn't one of the newer buildings, but it also had the newer buildings' style of large windows, making it a beautiful blending of old and new.

It sat butted against a granite slope that had been carved to make long, wide steps. The steps curved around an area paved with flagstones that had a few stone benches and tables, along with three patches of white marks — each patch a different pattern — and a large white circle in the center, reminding me of a school playground. Beside the paved area lay a grassed area with a jungle gym that looked to be a mix of human obstacles and ones suited to wolf pups.

Both areas were shaded by towering oaks and both had a few large stone planters marking the edges and filled with colorful flowers.

Cyrus strode across the paved area and straight through the front door, and I scrambled to catch up with him, surprised he hadn't just left me and worried about what going inside with me meant.

AUDREY

The inside of the school/community center looked like a regular school without any people in it. There were open doors at regular intervals, revealing empty classrooms, and smaller halls breaking off from the main one to get to more classrooms.

In the center of the building was a grand foyer with a wide staircase, similar to the one in the Residence. The stairs swept up all three stories in the same meet halfway break apart to a landing on either side of the building style. It'd be a pain in the ass if you had classes on both sides of the building and had to go down half a flight and back up to reach the other, but it looked spectacular.

I could hear the soft sounds of people talking from somewhere in the building, but I didn't see anyone and could only assume it was the weekend or summer break or something since it was just after lunch and there should have been classes going.

The voices, however, grew louder the closer we got to the back of the school. Here, the rooms had more of an office look with long rectangular or wide circular tables, and more comfortable looking chairs. Or they were completely empty of furniture with large rugs on the floor instead of the polished stone in the rest of the building.

"Here," Cyrus said as he stopped at an open door and gestured for me to enter.

"Thank you, alpha," I murmured as I stepped into the room.

All conversation in the room stopped and everyone stared at me.

Then Cyrus stepped in behind me and all the eyes rose a foot and a half above my head.

"Where's Nova?" he asked.

"Got hung up at the hospital. Said she'd be here in about ten minutes," a very familiar looking young man said.

Why did he look familiar?

Oh! The guy from the road on the outskirts of town when Bishop and I had returned from our long journey north. He'd told me his name... but as much as I wracked my brain, I couldn't remember it.

"Good." Cyrus turned on his heel and strode back down the hall, leaving me in a room full of strangers. Strangers who were looking at me with an unsettling mix of emotions.

Swell.

Everyone was seated around a circular table, and, if the chairs between people were any indication, they were separated into three groups.

The group closest to me consisted of three girls and two guys. They looked to be around my age, maybe a year or two younger, and had the darkest, most unnerving expressions. But I didn't know if they didn't like me because they were friends or family of Velora or Finn, or just because I was a stranger.

The group to my left, who were older, mid-thirties, had two women and two men. From the way they were sitting together, it looked like they were two mated pairs. They looked intensely curious, reminding me too much of Thane and his barrage of questions.

The final group, to my right and closer to the back, consisted of the guy I'd met the other night whose name I couldn't remember and a tiny woman with a soft, kind, smile.

"I've got a seat right here for you, Audrey," the guy said, pushing out the chair beside him and making my cheeks heat with embarrassment because he'd remembered my name and I couldn't remember his.

"Thank you." I hurried around the table and sat, my pulse picking up as people continued to stare at me.

From the alpha power radiating off them, one of the women in the group of four and the nice guy beside me were the strongest, although neither of them were close to my guys' or Cyrus's strength. The others were still stronger than me, but not by so much that I wouldn't be able to resist their compulsion.

"Jeez, guys," Nice Guy said. "Why don't you introduce yourselves instead of staring."

One of the women in the group of five who had black hair and piercing green eyes huffed. "I want to know why the alpha personally escorted her here."

"Yeah," the guy beside her said. He had matching black hair and green eyes and was probably her brother. "He's got more important things to do, especially after taking off with her for a month."

The other woman in the group who reminded me of a slightly younger version of Velora with her dark hair and similar bone structure nodded her agreement, her stare edged with a hint of jealousy.

"I—" I started then stopped myself before I told them Bishop was supposed to have escorted me.

Given how all the other women seemed interested in Bishop and how Velora's possible sister or cousin or whatever she was had looked after I'd shown up with Cyrus, it probably wasn't smart to mention I also spent time with Bishop. Sure it was going to come out sooner or later — like tomorrow when we walked around the festival together — that Bishop was courting me to be his mate, but I'd rather make the confession with at least one person I trusted in the room with me.

"Is it true you're mated to Knox?" a bulky guy in the foursome asked.

"Of course it's true," the black-haired green-eyed guy said. "He wouldn't have lost his shit like that and run deeper into town if she hadn't been his mate."

"My uncle saw it all," one of the girls in the foursome said. She was gorgeous and curvy and I was shocked that no one in the room was giving her a second look. Perhaps it was because she seemed almost as shy as me. "He's never seen Knox act like that before and it was definitely the behavior of a bonded mate."

"So what's she doing with Cyrus?" asked Female Green Eyes from the group of five — now dubbed the Nasty group in my mind because they were the first group I'd noticed and no one was sharing their name.

"Knox is on a hunt," I said, looking up but not making eye contact with any of them. I didn't know if it was smart to offer an explanation but no one here was an alpha and the strongest wolf in the room was Nice Guy. "Cyrus has a meeting in town and said the community center was on his way."

Not-Velora frowned and crossed her arms. "But he came in and checked the room."

"I saw that too," a guy from Nasty added. He had shaggy blond hair and a slim figure, and the third girl in the group, just as skinny as him, leaned against his shoulder and possessively clung to his arm.

Nice Guy rolled his eyes. "Of course he did. One of the foreigners attacked her. He'd do the same for any of us."

Shy girl of the more neutral foursome glanced up at me with a sad smile. "My uncle said she hurt herself."

"That's what I heard," Not-Velora agreed.

"She's mated to Knox. Would you blame her?" the black-haired guy asked. Everyone stiffened and my stomach churned with the clashing urges to stand up for Knox and not draw even more attention to myself.

Nice Guy growled low in his throat, his bright green eyes darkening as his wolf rose to the surface. "He's your alpha and you just insulted him in front of his mate." The rumble in his chest deepened and he leaned forward. "If you want to get hurt so badly become a hunter or join the watch."

Black-haired Guy's eyes widened as if suddenly realizing what he'd said. "I'm sorry, alpha."

Alpha? Was he talking to Nice Guy, who clearly wasn't an alpha, or apologizing into the air just in case Knox was listening in?

Except from the way he was looking at me, he was really talking to me.

Soft Smile sitting beside Nice Guy must have seen my confusion because she leaned in front of Nice Guy and said, "You're mated to one of our alphas. It's respectful—" She shot a stern look at everyone else "—to call the alpha's mate alpha as well, especially when apologizing or acknowledging a command."

Dear, God! They couldn't call me alpha. Cyrus would lose his mind.

He'd already made it crystal clear that I was not and never would be an alpha in his pack. Surely this would push him over the edge and the punishment that I knew he was holding onto would happen. This was the kind of situation Merrick had loved: an impossible one that I had no control over.

The black-haired girl and Not-Velora shared a glance, something dark passing between them that they clearly wanted me to see. These shifters were able to communicate telepathically in their human forms unlike most shifters in my realm and they could have easily had a conversation without looking at each other.

"You're right, Quinn," the powerful girl in the group of four said. "Just because Knox is more reclusive than our other alphas doesn't mean he isn't one."

"My uncle also believes, given how Knox stays away from everyone and how powerful his reaction to his mate being hurt was that they have to be fated," Shy Girl said, offering me another tentative smile.

I returned it while everyone else stared at me again. Those in Nasty looked skeptical, everyone in Neutral was curious and nodded their agreement, while Nice Guy and the girl beside him, Quinn, looked happy and slightly amazed... because as I'd learned at dinner the other night, fated mates were just as rare here as they were back home.

Then Nova strode into the room, looked at me right away, and smiled. The tension that I'd been trying to ignore since Cyrus left me alone with strangers, eased a little, and Quinn blew out a soft breath as if she'd been tense, too.

"Sorry I'm late," Nova said as she shut the door behind her and set a bright yellow duffle bag in front of an empty chair between Nasty and Neutral. "Have you introduced yourselves to Audrey?"

AUDREY

THE MEMBERS OF THE NASTY GROUP STARTED TO NOD THEIR HEADS YES, claiming they'd already introduced themselves to me, when Nice Guy spoke up.

"We haven't. I'm Zavier. We were introduced a few days ago but you were pretty tired at the time and I don't expect you to remember."

Quinn introduced herself next, then the members of Neutral, and finally Nasty. The Neutral group did consist of two mated pairs, while the suspected siblings in Nasty were indeed siblings — twins in fact — and Not-Velora was Velora's younger sister.

After that, Nova started the class, pulling things out of the bright yellow bag and explaining what they were and how to use them. Then she started going into more detail about situations and the appropriate first aid.

My head was full by the time we stopped, two breaks and however many hours later — and from the angle of the sun shining through the large window at the back of the room, it had been at least five, probably six hours.

"That's it, everyone," Nova said. "If you feel overwhelmed, I'm more than happy to answer additional questions at any time, or you can sign up to take the class again."

"This is my second time," Zavier said to me.

"Of course it is," Not-Velora, aka Danica, scoffed as she strode out of the room, the rest of Nasty following her and laughing.

Zavier sighed and shot Quinn an exasperated look.

"Some people never outgrow school," Shy Girl, Hazel, said with a sad smile.

Her mate, the big bulky guy named Micah, hugged her against his side and pressed his lips against her temple. "It gets better."

"Yeah," Nova said with a wicked grin. "Now Zavier can give them citations."

"Probably not the smartest move to constantly cite Danica or the twins. They've both got family members in high places and don't mind being vindictive," Quinn replied.

"Spoilsport," Nova said with an exaggerated pout as she put all the medical supplies back into the duffle bag. "

The Neutral group said goodbye to all of us and left, and Nova hefted the bag over her shoulder.

"I think this calls for dinner and drinks," she said, glancing at me before turning to Quinn. "We haven't had a girls' night for over a month."

Zavier expelled an exaggerated sigh. "Guess it's back to my apartment for soup and water."

Quinn and Nova burst out laughing and rolled their eyes at him as if this was a common situation for them.

"I'm sure Nova will make an exception for you," Quinn assured him.

"Only because if we have a watchman with us, people will be less likely to corner Audrey." Nova turned to me. "What do you say?"

I wasn't sure what to say. Bishop had told me yesterday that he'd walk me to the community center and pick me up when the class was done, but he hadn't been able to get away from work to escort me and I had no idea if he was on his way right now or still tied up with Velora, a thought that made my mouth sour.

"Did I hear drinks?" Bishop asked as he walked through the door, startling me.

He rounded the table without hesitation, wrapped me into a fierce hug, and kissed me full on the lips, not caring who was in the room and what gossip he might be spreading.

I bit back a sigh. Was there any point in fighting it? Everyone would see it — or hear about it — by the end of tomorrow. Trying to keep it on the down-low was pointless.

Of course, after the looks from Danica and the rest of her group, I wasn't sure I wanted every woman in town to know that Bishop had decided I was going to be his mate.

It was bad enough when they just suspected something was going on between me and Cyrus. I wasn't prepared for every woman in the pack to outwardly hate me... which meant, as much as I didn't want to, I had to turn down Bishop's invitation to go to the festival.

I hadn't expected to be welcomed with open arms by the pack. I thought they'd be curious but respectful. But after the disastrous dinner with Cyrus and the betas, and the chilling welcome in class, I had serious doubts that they'd leave me alone.

Nova chuckled, flashing Bishop a genuine smile. "It never fails. Mention getting together and Bishop will suddenly show up."

"Hey!" he said with feigned shock. "I'm the social connection between the alphas and the pack. It's my duty to connect with everyone so Cyrus isn't forced to."

Zavier snorted and held out his hand to Quinn. "Looks like I win."

Quinn sighed, pulled out a few coins from her handbag, and handed them over. "Just because you're right, doesn't mean I'm wrong."

"About what?" Nova asked and Quinn's face turned bright red.

"I told her something was going on between you guys," Zavier said, pointing to me and Bishop. "But little miss here"— He jerked his thumb toward Quinn. "She said there hadn't been rumors about Cyrus and anyone for a few years and they started again when Audrey showed up. That had to mean something."

I bit back a groan. "There's nothing between me and Cyrus."

"Oh, there's something," Zavier said as we headed out of the room and down the hall. "He personally escorted you here and then checked the room for danger."

"He was looking for Nova," I insisted. "Trust me. Cyrus doesn't like me." Not as a friend or a family member and especially not romantically like they were insisting.

"Sorry, Audrey," Quinn replied. "He definitely checked the room for danger before he left."

"Because I'm mated to his brother."

God, I really hoped no one else in the class thought Cyrus had checked out the room to ensure I was safe before he left. Because he hadn't. He never would.

He'd been stiff and angry the whole walk down here, a clear sign that he didn't enjoy my company. But of course, no one believed me. My word was never good enough.

"Tell them," I said, looking up at Bishop as we left the community center and headed down the street.

He had his arm across my shoulders and was possessively holding me to his side. The heat of our shifter connection warmed around my heart and I relaxed into him despite my worry that being seen with him was going to cause trouble.

If he was with me, I was safe. I'd always be safe.

"Where are we grabbing dinner?" Bishop asked, not answering my question.

"Annalise's," Nova replied. "It's halfway between here and the Residence and has a mostly hidden patio. I suspect Audrey would prefer someplace quiet and not in the main square."

"The main square's too nosy to have a decent conversation anyway," Zavier agreed, although I suspected Nova had made the suggestion so I wouldn't get swarmed by people curious about the stranger who'd mated Knox and was getting far too cozy with Bishop, and I greatly appreciated it.

We wound our way up narrow streets, avoiding the main road, until we reached a three-story building a block from the towering Old Town wall. It was a triangular structure placed on a small terrace between larger ones above and below it, and a sign hung above a bright blue door announcing the business in a strange flowing script that I couldn't read, reminding me I still needed to learn.

Zavier opened the door and a gust of mouthwatering smells washed over us as we stepped into a small dining room with a dozen tables, half of which were occupied. A few of the diners glanced up to see who'd entered then did a double take, staring at me and Bishop.

By the time we'd reached the side door near the back of the dining room, everyone was staring, making my insides twist. I could see the curiosity and judgment in their eyes and wanted to beg Bishop to take me back to the Residence so I could hide in my suite.

I wasn't ready for this kind of attention. I didn't think I'd ever be ready, especially when I knew my position in the pack was precarious.

"Unbelievable," Zavier hissed as he opened the door, revealing three narrow steps leading up to the patio.

"They'll come around. They're just curious," Nova said, climbing the steps to a magical patio, or rather, a secret courtyard.

Buildings surrounded it, the rise of the land dictating their placement and shape, creating the hidden space. In the center stood an enormous tree, its branches spread wide, creating a leafy canopy over the entire area with wisteria and this realm's version of fairy lights hanging from the branches.

With the shade from the tree and the growing shadow of the mountain creeping over the town as the sun inched toward setting, I could see a hint of soft light emanating from the magical light stones and could just imagine how beautiful everything would look after sunset.

"Wow," I gasped and Quinn grinned at me.

"That's what I thought the first time I came here. I'm glad Nova picked this place."

"And only one set of nosy diners to contend with," Zavier huffed, shooting a glare at a couple sitting in a cozy corner created by the front of the restaurant and its neighboring building. "I mean, I get the girls. They all wanted to be Bishop's mate and now it's obvious he's off the market."

Quinn gave him a playful shove. "Not everyone wants to be Bishop's mate."

"Ouch," Bishop gasped, pressing a hand over his heart in exaggerated pain. "You don't want me, Quinn?"

She rolled her eyes at him. "I'm sure you'll survive."

"You bet I will," he replied, hugging me close to his side. "I've found my life's mate. There are no other women in the world."

Warmth shot through my chest at his words. I was his life's mate. He'd actually said it in front of Nova, Zavier, and Quinn. Not that I'd expected him to hide our relationship, but the only person who'd publicly declared he wanted me was Royce and that had been a trick.

"Come on, let's sit over here. They won't be able to stare through the *throver* tree." Bishop tugged me to the back of the patio to a four-person table, pulled out a chair for me, then grabbed a chair from a nearby table and sat beside me.

After we'd all settled and a waiter had come to tell us the four things the chef was cooking that night, we ate and talked and laughed.

The tension that had been coiled inside me about how people were going to treat me melted away like it always did when I was around Bishop and the few others I trusted. And Quinn and Zavier quickly joined that group. They didn't ask me questions, although I was sure they were curious about everything. They just treated me like a normal person.

The feeling was strange, but also incredible.

Maybe I could find a place in this pack other than just being Knox's or Bishop's mate. It didn't feel as if Quinn and Zavier were being nice to me because of Bishop. It felt like they liked me for me, like how Eloise and Kira made me feel.

I could live with that. Four possible friends were three more than I had in my old pack. I also had Knox and Bishop as well as Nova, Deacon, and Whil. I could happily be content with a quiet life if I had this.

Warmth radiated around my heart and for a second it felt as if my soul was creating a shifter connection with everyone at the table and not just Bishop even though we weren't in close contact. I might not have known the others as well as Bishop, but something in my soul assured me I was safe with them.

Which was crazy. I barely knew them. That, and that thing inside me was also certain that I was safe with Cyrus, which made me seriously doubt my certainty.

Except right in this moment I didn't want to. Sitting with them on the patio felt too good. It was a glimpse of what might be possible and I never wanted to let it go.

As I savored the strange feeling of peace and laughed softly at Bishop and Zavier's bad jokes, and Nova and Quinn's eye rolls, a new sensation seeped into me.

It was urgent and needy, an overwhelming desire to get somewhere. Faster, faster!

But I didn't know where and I didn't know what I was suddenly desperate about or why.

I forced a smile and nodded at something Quinn said, although I didn't fully hear her. She taught the younger kids at the school and was in the middle of telling a story about their adorable antics. I was also sure she had horror stories about them misbehaving, but so far, she hadn't mentioned any of them.

Nova added something and Bishop and Zavier burst out laughing. I forced my smile brighter but didn't try to fake a laugh. I wasn't that good of an actress and they'd see right through me. Better to stay quiet and avoid drawing attention to myself.

Except Bishop still noticed something wasn't right.

"Audrey?" he asked, his voice filled with concern.

"I'm fine." I tried to make my smile more convincing, but that only made him frown and everyone else look at me with concern.

"What are you feeling?" Nova asked. "Was it something from the meal? So far, you've been able to eat and drink everything in this realm, but we can't assume that will always be the case."

"That's not it." I pressed a hand over my heart, the urgency squeezing tighter.

Faster. Faster. Soon soon soon.

Soon it would be right, the way it was supposed to be, the way it should always be.

AUDREY

A MOMENT LATER, THE PRESSURE EXPLODED INTO RELIEF, AND A SOUL-deep love flooded into every cell in my body.

"Knox," I breathed, joy rushing up inside me to match his love. "Knox is back."

Zavier frowned. "He told you?"

"No." I turned to see his enormous black wolf mostly hidden in the shadows of an alley between the neighboring buildings. I doubted I'd have been able to see him if I hadn't just known exactly where to look.

Audrey, he rumbled in my head, and before I realized what I was doing, I raced across the courtyard and threw myself at him.

He shifted into his human form in the blink of an eye and caught me mid-leap in a crushing embrace.

Our mouths crashed together in a hungry kiss, igniting our desires since our desires fed off each other in a never-ending loop. An emptiness in my soul that I hadn't fully realized was there but had sunk into my essence the moment I'd stopped feeling Knox's emotions melted away.

"I missed you," he said, his voice low as he pulled me up, clutching me tighter.

Instinctively, I wrapped my legs around his waist, my hot core pressed against his hardening cock. With a groan, he pinned me against the alley wall. His fingers tangled into my hair and he jerked my head back and deepened our kiss with a ferocity that matched my dream-Knox.

"Sisters, I missed you," he gasped, suddenly breaking the kiss and pressing his forehead against mine.

Our breathing had turned ragged and desire zinged through our bond, but I could also feel him trying to get a hold of himself. He'd made a promise to not have sex with me until I'd forgiven him for hurting me when he'd refused our bond.

But for the life of me, I couldn't understand why I'd been so determined to put off our fate. I wanted him more than I wanted my next breath, and I'd been numb and aching without even realizing it while he'd been gone.

"I missed you, too," I replied, sliding my hands down his naked, sculpted chest to his cock trapped between us. It was already thick and hard and leaking precum, and I wanted nothing more than to have him buried inside me.

Someone cleared his throat and I jerked my gaze to Bishop and the others at the table. They were watching us with a mix of emotions. Bishop had a wicked grin as if he were getting pleasure out of Knox working me up, the thought sending more desire spiraling to my core, and Nova looked happy while Quinn and Zavier were in complete shock.

"Well, if there was any doubt about them being mated..." Zavier said. "I'd say that clears that up."

Quinn slapped him on the arm. "There never was any doubt and you should be happy for them."

A flicker of unease seeped through my mating bond and Knox's gaze darted around the courtyard as if he suddenly realized we were out in public. When he saw the only people were us — the other couple having left a while ago — the unease vanished even though his grip on me tightened.

"We're leaving," he announced, quickly turning on his heel and carrying me down the alley, before I had a chance to say goodbye.

But in that moment, I didn't care. I felt the same urgency he did, the need to re-consummate our bond again and again.

At the end of the alley, Knox shifted back to his wolf and I climbed on top and clung to him as he raced along mostly deserted back streets and alleys back to the Residence. Without slowing, he rushed through the open gate and skirted the Residence's tall wall, heading away from the castle and deep into the grounds.

He bounded over flowerbeds and bushes and leaped up hills, his powerful muscles bunching beneath me, his soft fur caressing my neck and chin as I clung to him, and his seductive wood smoke scent wrapping around me.

The air rushed through my hair and swept cool over my face, easing the summer heat as we ran. Joy surged through our bond, Knox's feeling of freedom and power flowing into me and filling me up with sensations I'd never felt before.

I whooped with joy, feeling wild as if the world was filled with amazing sights and sounds and opportunities and they were all at my fingertips.

The wildness flooded my body and my next whoop turned into a human howl of thanks to the moons, the Two Sisters of the Night.

Knox joined my howl and we bounded up a narrow path cut into a stony ridge at the back of the Residence's grounds up to a wide ledge that overlooked the town.

I slid off his back, awed at the view. Warm, inviting lights shone through the windows and in what I could only assume were public gathering areas since I hadn't been in that part of the city after dark. From this distance, they sparkled like stars, a property of the magic that made them glow.

Beyond, to my left and past another part of town I'd yet to see, stood a vast forest that climbed up into the mountains. That had to be where the pack's sacred grove was since the small one on the Residence's grounds was only big enough for a handful of people, not the whole town. Above me, stars filled the night sky, bright against the darkness even though the Sisters looked almost full.

Behind me, Knox shifted and drew me down to the ground so we could cuddle together while stargazing.

"It's beautiful," I whispered as if speaking too loudly would shatter the magical stillness enveloping us.

"This is my favorite spot on the grounds," Knox replied. "When the weather's good, I sleep up here. Not that I expect you to— I mean, I wouldn't—"

I nuzzled closer to him, taking in deep breaths of his scent, and placed my palm over his heart hyperaware that he was completely naked and I was still a little worked up. "I know what you mean. You wanted to share this with me."

"I've been thinking about bringing you here since the night I left."

Contentment and peace radiated through our bond, and a giggle bubbled up inside me from the joy and awe and love, things I'd never expected to feel. Everything in my being said this was where I was supposed to be, and tonight I wasn't going to question it or fight it. I'd never seen Knox so calm before, so at ease, but he was finally in his element with just the two of us in nature, and he'd fully accepted our bond.

"I couldn't stop thinking of you and I felt so empty," he said, tightening his grip around me and pressing his lips to my forehead. "Will you let me hold you?"

I raised my head until our lips met. Knox hadn't outwardly begged a whole lot, but I could feel it through our bond how truly sorry he was for hurting me, which was all I really needed to know. "I'd like it if you did more than hold me."

"But I promised—" I brushed my lips against his and his breath hitched. "I haven't begged enough. You swore—"

"And I've changed my mind. I missed you, too." I slid my hand over the sculpted contours of his chest. "I need you, Knox,"

Without hesitation, he captured my lips in a hungry kiss, surprise and awe rushing through the bond before being consumed with desire.

I kissed him back, just as hungry. I hadn't thought I'd give in so easily, but the mating bond was a powerful magic and connected us in a way we'd never been connected before.

I *knew* he didn't want to hold back or deny me, and I *knew* he wouldn't use this moment to hurt me.

It seemed foolish to change my mind so quickly, but the bond reassured me. Now that we'd sealed it and Knox had accepted it, I was safe with him, body, heart, and soul.

I tangled my fingers in his hair, holding him close, never wanting to let him go. With a groan, he ground his cock into the crux of my leg between my thigh and mound.

Anticipation shivered down my spine. I felt as if I'd been waiting for this all my life. I didn't fully remember the first time we'd joined. I'd been partially delirious from the heat fever. But this time would be seared into my memory. And if intercourse with Knox was anything like when he went down on me, it was going to be amazing.

He groaned again and shoved one hand under my shirt and roughly palmed my breasts. I arched into his touch, my body begging for more, knowing this wasn't going to be a gentle lovemaking. I could already feel the frenzy building inside him and his struggle to hold himself back.

"Knox, it's—"

A flash of brilliant light lit up the night sky followed by an explosive clap of thunder.

"Fu—" Knox snarled.

But before he could even finish the word, rain crashed over us in a warm torrential downpour.

I gasped at the sudden assault, my hair and clothes instantly soaked by the storm that hadn't been there a moment ago.

Knox pulled me into his arms and stood.

"What's going on?" I asked, trying to wipe water from my eyes, disappointment that we'd been interrupted souring my desire. I'd been more than ready to be with him, to join our bodies like our souls were joined, and now the moment was gone.

"It's the rainy season." He hurried off the ledge and down the uneven path to the ground. "In the summer the wind changes and the storms that roll off two of the storm gods' resting places in the south are more likely to hit us. That's why they come out of nowhere and are so powerful."

He reached the bottom and sprinted across the Residence's ground, his wolf rising to the surface and a wildness rushing through our bond.

It was the same wildness I'd felt when riding him, primal, fierce, joyful. It didn't matter that it was raining and we could barely see more than a few feet away from us. The power in the storm called to the beast within him.

And through him, I could almost imagine my own wolf rising up, riding on the energy sparking and flashing in the force of nature pouring down on us.

Thunder clapped again, sharp and explosive, rattling my bones and filling me up. With Knox's emotions riding me, I felt powerful, unstoppable. I wanted to run, too. But in reality, I'd just slow him down.

"Run with me," he— no his wolf said as if he could read my mind — and with our emotions so strongly connected maybe he could. "I know you can feel it. The power crackling all around us."

As if to punctuate his words, lightning flashed and thunder clapped again.

"Run, Audrey. Run with me."

He set me on the ground, grabbed my hand, and I had no choice but to run or be dragged behind him.

I raced as fast as I could with Knox keeping pace at my side, sprinting around trees, shrubs, and flowerbeds, the wind whipping warm rain in my face.

Exhilaration welled up inside me fed by Knox's wild joy, and once again, I howled, letting the storm devour my voice.

I hadn't liked running before, but then I'd been running to escape and stay safe. This was completely different. Just like when I'd ridden Knox, I felt free. I felt like a part of me did contain a wild wolf and by running for joy, I was letting a little piece of her out.

We rounded a small copse of trees and there in the distance through the downpour was the soft warm glow of shelter.

The light wasn't very bright, perhaps just a lamp in someone's window. Whatever it was, it only made Knox happier, which confused me. If I went inside, this amazing moment would end, and I never wanted it to end.

But a few seconds later, I realized the light wasn't coming from the Residence. It came from Whil's cottage greenhouse, the shimmering glass orb by her front door that I'd originally assumed was a whimsical decoration but was actually a light.

"In here," Knox said, guiding me to the greenhouse door.

Gasping, I hurried inside, water rushing off me into a large puddle on the uneven flagstone floor.

"That was—" I sucked in rapid breaths filled with the sweet scent of Whil's flowers and the rich wood smoke that was all Knox.

Exhilaration still raced through my veins, even though I was out of breath, more powerful than our run to the ledge. And mixed within it, was Knox's joy.

I met his wild grin, his canines extended and his eyes dark, and the exhilaration turned hot. His gaze raked down my body with so much heat my whole body was aching and strung tight with desire by the time he looked back up again.

"Mine," he snarled.

"Yes," I gasped back and we crashed together, our lips meeting in a frenzied kiss.

KNOX

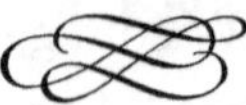

I kissed Audrey with a hunger I'd never known before, a hunger that had been growing the moment I'd tasted her the other night and hadn't been satisfied because I'd had to go on that fucking hunt.

Not that I hadn't loved the thrill of the chase and the peacefulness of being alone, but I needed Audrey more. And if it came down to it, I'd give up hunting for Audrey. I'd give up all of it.

Of course, she'd never ask that of me, even if it was to her own detriment. I was a complete idiot for thinking she'd trap me. I was the one trapping her. She was stuck with a mate who couldn't give her everything.

"Whatever you're thinking," she said, grabbing a handful of my hair and yanking it to catch my attention. "Stop it. It's not true and I need you, Knox. Now. Please."

A whine edged her tone and the force of her need swelled through our bond, consuming my doubts and insecurities while my wolf snarled at me for being stupid. I had our gorgeous, fragile mate in our arms and she ached for us. Just like I ached for her and had been for the last four days.

"Mine," my wolf snarled, itching to be the one to claim her this time.

He seized control of our body, jerked her head back by her hair, and kissed her like he was starving.

He'd told me from the beginning that Audrey was ours and I'd resisted much to his growing fury. I also hadn't let him take over when we'd sealed the bond because of her fragile state from her heat, and he was still angry about that, too.

Audrey moaned into my mouth, leaning into my embrace. Her wet clothes dragged against my naked flesh. Her hard nipples, straining against the practically see-through fabric, drew short erotic lines against my chest with every quick breath, while the rougher fabric of her pants ground against my straining cock.

Fuck. I wanted nothing more than to give in to my wolf and bury myself into her tight, slick heat. One powerful stroke and I'd be where I was supposed to be.

But Bishop had warned me before I'd left for the hunt to make sure she was ready first. Sure, she wasn't a virgin anymore and had had marathon sex during her heat, but she was still inexperienced. I couldn't let go like I had in our shared dreams when we'd first been bound together no matter what my wolf wanted.

But it was getting harder and harder to think straight with her need pouring through our mating bond.

Sisters, I needed to get my mouth on her and taste the liquid desire leaking from her pussy and perfuming the air with her seductive, sweet scent.

"Too many clothes," my wolf said, grabbing the front of her shirt and tearing it open.

Audrey's breath hitched and a blast of her need shot painfully to my cock.

Fuck me. I was going to take her right on the cold wet flagstones if I didn't do something about it. Now.

Struggling against my wolf, I picked her up and carried her the few feet to one of Whil's reading nooks. It lay in a pop-out section in the greenhouse's wall with two fully glassed walls and two waist-high walls, leaving the space open to the rest of the greenhouse. With its all-glass ceiling and only minimum foliage to block the outside, the space didn't set off my claustrophobia as quickly as other spaces. I still couldn't spend the whole night, but I could satisfy Audrey a few times before I had to get back outside.

I tossed her onto the slightly raised, cushioned floor, watching her pert tits bounce and her mouth open in a surprised "oh."

And now all I could think about were her perfect lips wrapped around my cock.

But not now. Later. Gods damned later.

She didn't remember much of her heat, so I was sure she didn't remember drinking Bishop down night after night and I wasn't going to remind her. She was shy enough about sex and I didn't want to risk her withdrawing from me.

Her half-lidded gaze raked over my body, slowly sliding down my chest to my cock, and she licked her lips.

Oh, Sisters!

Maybe I was wrong about what she remembered.

"You want this?" I asked, my voice barely more than a rumble as I grabbed my cock and squeezed the base, trying to calm the fuck down.

Her gaze dipped to my feet and a blush rushed over her cheeks and down her neck, straight to her taut nipples even as her desire in our bond burned hotter. It blazed around my heart before sinking into my throbbing groin, making me grit my teeth, desperate to stay in control.

"Do you want this?" I barked as I stepped onto the cushions.

A hint of alpha power snapped through my words, yanking her attention back to my cock. I slowly pumped up then back down my length, her attention riveted on my hand.

"Take me," I ordered, making sure to have a firm grip on my power, and was rewarded with another breathtaking blast of lust, mixed with a hint of uncertainty.

"I haven't done it—" She frowned as if she wasn't certain whether she'd sucked cock before, adding to my suspicion that she didn't remember much from her heat. "I won't be very good."

"Take me," my wolf growled again, this time with a sharp blast of power.

A whisper of her power, a power I'd been feeling since we'd run through the rain rose to meet me. It wasn't strong like it had been in our dreams or the first time I'd made her come after nearly dying, but I could still feel it. It was a swirling dancing promise, a siren's song to my own alpha power, and the truth of her soul that was hidden so deep it was almost impossible to recognize.

She rose to her knees, her breath becoming rapid gasps. In this position, her mouth was barely an inch from my cock.

"Audrey," I groaned, brushing myself against her bottom lip, leaving a glistening trail of precum.

Her tongue darted out, licking me up, and it was more than I could handle. With a growl, I grabbed a fistful of her hair and jerked hard. She gasped at the pain even as more desire flooded our bond and thickened the air, and I pushed my cock into her mouth.

"I'm going to fuck your mouth, Audrey," I snarled, my body trembling as I held myself back. "You want me to stop, you say so now, because once I start, I'm not stopping."

Not that I wouldn't stop if her emotions changed. But I also knew she wouldn't say no. She wanted this so much it hurt but she was afraid to ask for it.

I rocked my hips forward, a shallow thrust to get her started. "Last, chance."

Her eyes met mine and sucked me in deeper.

"Then hang on."

Her small hands wrapped around the back of my thighs and I withdrew from her wet heat and thrust back in again a little harder and deeper.

Her gaze never left mine, blazing with desire and fueling my need to claim every last inch of her. I firmly held her head where I wanted her and thrust again and again, making sure to keep on the right side of the edge of hard and fast.

She sucked and moaned, her desire pouring through me, urging me on, threatening what little control I had, and the air was thick with her arousal.

I hit the back of her throat, making her gag and sending arousal zinging through our bond.

"Relax," I snarled, angling her head back, pushing deeper, feeling her throat contract around my tip as she tried to swallow.

Fuck. Sex had never felt this good before. Even if I couldn't fuck her mouth fully, it was still the most incredible sensation. But then, I'd never had a direct emotional connection to a lover before.

Audrey liked a little roughness. She liked it when I took control. I just couldn't let it go to my head and push her past her limits. And I sure as hell couldn't blow my load down her throat. I wanted to come in her tight pussy, wanted to feel my seed filling her even though I knew she was on the birth inhibitor extract and I couldn't get her pregnant. Something primal inside me needed to fill her with my cum again and again and permanently mark her with my scent.

Fuck.

I yanked out of her mouth, making her whine at the loss, shoved her back against the cushions, and tore her pants from her body.

She gasped, shocked and turned on, and I buried my face between her thighs. She smelled incredible and was already dripping wet and desperate for me.

"Knox, please."

I lapped at her juices, flicking my tongue against her clit, once, twice, three times and she was crashing over the edge of ecstasy on a strangled moan.

More nectar gushed out of her — what Bishop had told me I needed to enter her — and I gripped her hips, lined up my cock, and plunged into her in a quick, powerful stroke just like I wanted. She moaned even louder, her walls fluttering around me, and her eyes rolled back in pleasure.

"Fuck me, Knox," she begged. "Fuck me hard."

I chuckled, knowing she'd be mortified in the morning that she'd said that and loving that I'd gotten her to fully relax around me and tell me what she wanted.

I fucked her until she was writhing and screaming, and the tingling up my spine and the pressure in my balls was almost too much to handle. But I still held it together, taking her over the edge again and tearing out a third climax before the second was even done.

"One more," I commanded, grinding my thumb against her clit and pumping fast and hard.

Her little tits bounced with each impact, the sound of flesh smacking flesh along with my moans and her screams filling the greenhouse. Sweat slicked her forehead and strands of her blond hair were stuck to her skin. She looked like a goddess, practically glowing with bliss and I never wanted it to stop.

"I can't," she gasped, shaking her head, even as her walls began to flutter, a precursor to her coming.

"You can. You will." My alpha power rose up, not in a command, but a challenge, and her power rose up to meet mine. It was barely there, but without a doubt, it was there. She *had* power, she just needed to realize it. It was a seductive, swirling glimmer that teased mine, wove itself through mine, and made my wolf howl, calling out to awaken the wolf half of his mate.

"Oh, God," she gasped, her body trembling, and my wolf howled again then completely took over.

I rode the building wave with him, reveling in the glorious sensation of our cock pounding into her, her body arching up to meet mine, thrust for thrust, and our pleasure feeding off each other.

More. More more more, my wolf growled, needing to feel her come again as much as I did.

"Come." My power rushed over her and her muscles contracted, tearing my own orgasm free. I howled with my pleasure as well as hers, a wild loop of sensation rushing through our bond as my hot cum streamed into her and our bodies locked in a primal battle of life and love.

Fate had been cruel to me in the past, trapping me for days, crushed under heavy rock in complete darkness, but I wouldn't change any of it if it meant I could keep Audrey. She was an amazing gift, one I hadn't known I wanted and certainly didn't deserve.

She was the other half of my dual soul, a perfect match to both human and wolf. I'd always been meant for her and I'd be by her side, protecting and loving her forever. The way it was always supposed to be.

AUDREY

I woke to soft kisses against my jaw and a growing sense of unease, even as warmth and affection flowed through our mating bond.

"You have to go," I mumbled, understanding that he couldn't stay inside any longer but still disappointed that he wasn't waking me up for more sex like he had the last time.

Of course, after the hard sex at the beginning of the night and the slower, drawn-out lovemaking when the Sisters were high in the sky, I wasn't sure my body could handle another round.

I wasn't even sure I'd be able to walk normally and not give away the fact I'd had mind-blowing sex with my mate... not that I needed to hide that, but too many people were looking at me as it was and I didn't want to give them more to talk about.

"I do," he rumbled, his warm breath feathering across my cheek as he tightened his grip around me.

I snuggled back against his chest and breathed in his rich wood smoke scent, not ready to open my eyes and watch him leave.

I wanted to stay in Whil's greenhouse forever, lying on the soft mattress covering the floor, warmed by the hot stone in a metal bowl, covered by a light sheet, and wrapped in his arms.

"I don't want you to go."

"Neither do I, but I—" Fear blossomed in our bond and I sent my love back to combat it. And somehow, even though I didn't fully know him yet, I really did love him.

"I understand," I told him. "It's alright."

Reluctantly, I cracked open my eyes, surprised to see the sky lightening and an early morning mist clinging to the gardens beyond the glass.

"You stayed the night," I gasped, rolling to face him.

"You steady my soul." He brushed his lips against mine in a tender kiss. "I can last longer in Whil's greenhouse than any other structure, but usually not more than five or so hours."

I kissed him back with more heat. "Thank you for staying the night."

"I'd stay every night with you if I could. But Whil won't agree to that."

I cringed, heat spreading across my face. I hadn't been quiet during our lovemaking, had just let go for once, too caught up in the moment. Whil had to have heard everything—

Oh my God! She had to have heard me beg Knox to fuck me harder.

My hot face turned into an inferno with embarrassment and to top it off, Knox had torn my clothes to shreds and I was going to have to do the walk of shame back to my suite in a sheet.

Except it wasn't a walk of shame. Knox and I were bonded mates. We were expected to have sex, a lot of sex, especially in the beginning when we were still getting used to the bond.

Then a new thought struck me. "Is it just Whil's greenhouse that gives you extra time indoors or all greenhouses?"

"A couple of our farmers have greenhouses," he said with a chuckle, probably laughing at the color of my face. "But I've never stayed longer than an hour in any of them."

"But could you stay longer if you had the chance?" I asked, shocked at how simple the solution was for us being together. If, of course, I could get over the fact that anyone could walk by and see us having sex.

Maybe getting the pack engineers to figure out one-way glass was my first priority. Except I had no idea what went into making one-way glass. And, on top of that, it would have to work with the lights being off *and* on, and I didn't know if even the glass in my realm could handle that or if Knox could even withstand the tinted glass like he could the regular glass.

Maybe it would be better just building a very tall garden and hope for the best. But if the pack was talking about me now, someone would surely jump at the chance to watch me and Knox going at it. Probably a lot of someones.

"We need to go up!" I gasped.

Knox huffed even as his lips quirked in a barely-there smile. "What are you talking about?"

"Building us a greenhouse." I turned my attention to the Residence's towers peeking out between the trees. "Is there access to the Residence's roof?"

But as soon as I asked that, my excitement soured. It didn't matter if we could build on the Residence's roof or not. It would cost money and I'd need Cyrus's permission. He could easily deny me as a way of reminding me of my place. Knox had been getting along just fine without a greenhouse bedroom, and I, as a weak shifter, was supposed to accept my alpha's and mate's way of life. It didn't matter that I couldn't shift and was more vulnerable to the elements.

"Audrey," Knox growled, dragging my attention away from the ruins of a possible great plan. "It's a good idea."

"But it's too much. I haven't shown anyone that I deserve it."

"What the fuck are you talking about?" he snapped.

I jumped at the sharpness in his voice and instinctively started to make myself smaller even though the action frustrated me and I knew Knox wouldn't hurt me.

"Shit." Panic swept through the bond and he cupped my face in his large palms. "I'm sorry. I didn't mean to snap. I'm not angry with you."

"I know," I replied, my voice frustratingly small. I nuzzled against his neck, seeking comfort from him to steady my soul. "It's a habit. I can't seem to break it even when I'm around you."

Probably because I couldn't break it around Cyrus and the majority of the pack.

"Bishop would say it just takes time," Knox huffed. "But I'm still waiting."

The unease radiating through the bond increased and he growled in frustration.

"Go," I told him, not wanting to be the reason he was torturing himself. "I'll be okay."

"Bishop is on his way with breakfast and clothes. I'll stick around until he shows up, then I have to report to Deacon about the hunt." He rolled away from me, got up, and strode out of the greenhouse as if he couldn't stop for a second.

I gathered the sheet around me, tapped the side of the heating bowl to deactivate the hot stone, and followed him outside.

"What are you doing?" he asked before shifting into his wolf form, all the stress and discomfort from being inside melting away as he gave into his wolf nature.

"If you're sticking around, we might as well sit together." I sat on the shallow step in front of the greenhouse's door and Knox settled beside me, a furry heater that smelled like love and safety and home.

Knox rumbled, the sound vibrating through my body, relaxing me even more, and just like our desire, our contentment fed off each other, making me feel, just for a moment, as if I were completely safe and had the space to figure out who I was.

I didn't want the feeling to end, but I knew it would the moment Knox left. "Will you come back after talking with Deacon?"

"Until you and Bishop leave for the festival," he assured me, reminding me of how nervous I was to go to the festival and how excited Bishop was to show me.

But it was bittersweet because Knox couldn't join us.

I quickly shoved that emotion back and focused on my excitement. I didn't want Knox to feel guilty about not being able to come to the festival with me. I'd promised I'd accept all of him and I would. We would have our own special moments together. Perhaps, once I'd proven my usefulness to Cyrus, we'd have them in a greenhouse bedroom where he could stay the whole night.

AUDREY

Bishop arrived a few minutes later with clothes and breakfast and Knox left to report about his hunt to Deacon. We ate and chatted, Bishop's excitement about the festival bubbling out of him.

A part of me wanted to tell him I'd changed my mind about going. When I'd agreed, I hadn't known how everyone would judge me like the nasty group in the first aid class or stare at me like they had last night in the restaurant. I didn't want to face more people like that and from the way Bishop was talking about it, most of the pack visited the festival all five days. It was going to be busy.

Except if I refused to go because I didn't want everyone looking at me, then I'd be stuck hiding in the Residence for who knew how long, a self-made prisoner. And I really didn't want that.

I wanted to go out with Bishop not just to the festival but to do other things. Kira had invited me to the restaurant where she was learning new dishes and I wanted to taste them.

If I could get through having everyone stare at me at the festival, most of the pack would learn in one fell swoop that I was plain and boring and a weakling. I wasn't a threat like Finn and Velora believed... although from the way I'd caught Velora looking at Bishop maybe I was a threat to her.

On top of that, Bishop would be with me the entire time. I had no doubt that he'd keep me safe. All I needed to do was stay close, put up with the stares and the whispered comments, and hopefully soon after that, they'd forget about how interesting I was. I wouldn't be able to leave the Residence by myself. That was just calling for trouble, but I'd hopefully be able to enjoy future outings.

A couple of hours after I'd convinced myself it was better to go than to stay hiding in the Residence, Knox returned. The three of us chatted some more until it was just before lunch.

We left Knox and returned to my suite so I could have a quick shower. That turned into a longer shower when Bishop offered to wash me and we'd ended up teasing each other with hands and lips, but thankfully didn't go beyond that since I really was sore from last night.

It also didn't feel weird like I was afraid it would. I wasn't uncomfortable knowing I'd had sex with Knox and the next day was making out in the shower with Bishop.

And it was a great distraction from my nerves about the festival.

I wanted to feel feminine and beautiful for Bishop since this was an official courting date, but I didn't want everyone staring at all my scars so I ended up wearing a green shirt that matched the flecks in Bishop's eyes and a pair of light, loose, beige pants.

Then we headed to the festival, strolling down the streets while I made an effort to not make eye contact with anyone so I wouldn't see them staring at me.

From the way the road sloped, I saw the festival before we reached it, the sight stealing my breath for a second. Even from a distance, I could tell there were going to be hundreds of things to see and do because it looked like the market on steroids.

It had at least a hundred more tents and stalls than the market I'd seen before, so many that they poured past the boundaries of Stonehaven onto the grassy plains. Flags and banners fluttered in the summer breeze, adding to the cacophony of colors from the tents and people, some wearing bright colors and others with flower crowns and necklaces, and— Oh! There were more overflowing planter boxes where there hadn't been before filled with flowers.

As we drew closer, the wind shifted, carrying a mouth-watering mix of aromas, and the voices from all the people grew louder.

I inched closer to Bishop, uneasy about stepping into the crowd with the pack's most eligible bachelor.

Maybe this was a bad idea after all.

I could already guess what everyone would think about me. The nasty group at the first aid class had made it perfectly clear.

Although not everyone had thought that. The neutral group had been curious, not judging, and Quinn and Zavier had been friendly and inviting. All I really needed to worry about was not embarrassing myself or drawing more attention than I already was and giving Cyrus or his betas more reasons to be mad at me.

We reached the crowd and those closest to us went silent.

Oh, crap.

My pulse lurched and I locked my gaze on the road just ahead of my toes. Everyone was looking at me.

"Look up, Audrey," Bishop murmured, his voice so low I could barely hear him. "You've got this."

I swallowed hard. I couldn't spend my life hiding in the Residence from the pack. Even if I could, I'd still have to hide because Velora and Finn didn't like me. I had to do this.

I *could* do this.

I raised my gaze and tried to smile but couldn't stop feeling like I was a strange specimen on display.

"Everyone. This is Audrey," Bishop announced and those farther down the street quieted and looked in our direction.

I tried to breathe through my rising panic. I didn't want to be there, didn't want people looking at me, judging me, seeing everything that was wrong with me.

People glanced at each other, a few said something, their mouths moving, but I wasn't close enough to hear them.

Were they wondering what I was doing with Bishop?

Of course they were. I was Knox's mate. I was supposed to stay in my lane and hide from the rest of the pack with Knox.

And boy, right now, I wanted to hide.

Stop looking at me, I mentally begged. *Go back to what you were doing. Please.*

This was a mistake, a horrible, terrible mistake. I shouldn't be here, shouldn't have left the Residence. But that would mean I was trapped for life and I couldn't accept that.

Except could I accept all these people staring at me?

I glanced at Bishop who was beaming at me as if he were oblivious to the awkward silence, and warmth from our shifter connection warmed around my heart.

Yes. Yes, I could. People were always going to stare at me. I was just going to have to live with that. But really, most people wouldn't care what I did or who I was with. I was merely today's curiosity and tomorrow's gossip. After that, I'd just be Audrey.

I drew in a slow breath and squared my shoulders.

I'd faced monsters and survived. I could face normal, everyday shifters.

"Someone needs some flowers," a woman with a basket of flowers said, breaking the awkward moment and everyone else burst back into action as if they'd been frozen in the moment just like me.

"Bishop, you're losing your game," another man called out making those around him laugh.

A few more people started ribbing Bishop while others laughed, and while I could see there were still a lot of people staring at me with a mix of negative expressions varying from concern to disgust and outright hate, there were those, now that the shock of the moment was gone, who were a mix of curious or friendly.

See, it isn't everyone. And a few was a lot better than none. Maybe I could have a place in this pack.

"You're Knox's mate," a teenaged girl said as she held out a crown made of bright yellow flowers.

"I am. I'm sorry," I replied, looking at the flower crown. "I don't have any money."

"Don't be silly." She reached up and put it on my head then her expression turned sad. "Mom and I heard you're from far away and all by yourself. We made this one special for you to welcome you to the pack."

My throat tightened and tears pricked my eyes.

"My mom also says—" She glanced at Bishop before looking back at me and sighing the kind of sigh girls in the movies sighed when they fell in love "—that you and Knox are fated, which probably means you and Bishop are fated because they're twins and all. It's just so romantic."

The woman with the basket pushed past a couple of men still teasing Bishop and tugged on the girl's arm. "Welcome to the pack, alpha."

My pulse lurched. Was everyone going to call me that?

"Come on, Everly, before those old men rope the alpha into something he can't get away from. I'm sure these two want to enjoy the festival." The woman gave me a warm, welcoming smile and not-so-accidentally bumped into the man beside her. "Donovan, have you gotten your wife a flower crown yet?"

"No," he replied.

"Then you should pick one now before all the good ones are gone." She gave me a wink and nudged the other two guys talking with Bishop.

Bishop grabbed my hand and gave me a brilliant smile. "See? Nothing to worry about."

"Yeah," I replied, pretending I didn't notice the others hanging back and watching me. "Nothing to worry about."

We strolled down the street, drawing attention, the same mix of concerned and welcoming looks as before. The streets were packed and a lot of people greeted Bishop. He smiled, nodded, answered quick questions, and introduced me.

But the whole thing with almost everyone staring at me and talking to people I didn't know and didn't know that I could trust started to make me nervous again. It didn't matter how hard I tried to embrace those with welcoming smiles and friendly words, my insides were getting tighter and tighter.

As if able to read my mind, Bishop stopped introducing me and held my hand, letting me shyly hide in his shadow while he talked with people. I was sure it didn't make as good an impression as me trying to smile and returning people's greetings, but it felt a lot safer.

I'd never been in such a large group before and it was getting harder and harder to ignore all the things Merrick had drilled into me about no one wanting to see me or hear what I had to say. It made me furious and frustrated that I couldn't get him out of my head, but it was also a good reminder that I couldn't break my programming in a single day.

It was going to take time and I needed to remember to be kind to myself.

We made our way down the street, looking at booths and tents, drawing closer and closer to the actual market until we reached the playground beside the market where I'd sat at a picnic table a month ago watching kids running around and playing

Three of the picnic tables that had once been scattered around the greenspace had been pulled together creating one long table. It was covered with craft supplies, and half a dozen kids of various ages sat on the benches, working away on their projects, while Quinn sat at the end, talking with one of the older kids.

A few feet away, at another picnic table, sat a handful of adults, half of them watching the kids and half chatting among themselves. Behind them, more kids enjoyed the playground, running and laughing, supervised by a few more adults, and to the side, under the shade of a big tree, was a baby and toddlers play area with a handful of teens and a few other adults taking care of the littlest ones.

It looked so idyllic, like I was in the middle of a movie. Everyone was happy and relaxed, and the kids were having a great time. And this time, watching normal children do normal children things, I didn't feel jealous and sad like I had the last time I'd been in the market. I was happy for them, happy that they were allowed to play and that they weren't afraid of the playground — which could have happened since the playground had been ground zero for the grimalkin attack.

The wind shifted and the amazing smells from the food vendors washed over me, making my stomach rumble, which made Bishop glance at me and laugh.

"I'd say that smells like lunch," he said just as Velora pushed through the crowd and rushed up to us. She flashed Bishop a saccharine smile that made my stomach churn, grabbed his free arm, and pushed her breasts against it.

"Otis and Rex are going at it again. Will you sweet talk them into behaving?" She fluttered her lashes and I was pretty sure she didn't mean the action in a sarcastic way. She actually thought it would attract Bishop and make him interested in her.

He sighed and glanced at me, a hint of frustration in his eyes that he kept from bleeding into his expression.

I forced a smile knowing everyone was watching, and at least a third of them, probably more like a half, were judging if I'd get in the way of pack business.

Velora sneered at me as if asking Bishop to do his job was a win for her and I struggled to keep my expression pleasant. If I got upset, I'd just be proving her and anyone who doubted me right. And I was *not* going to prove her right.

AUDREY

"Go," I told him as upbeat and happily as I could, making Velora's sneer falter. "It sounds important."

I dragged my gaze to the park, knowing I'd have to sit there alone until he returned, something that made me even more nervous, but then Quinn laughed at something, catching my attention, and I realized I didn't have to be alone. I could help Quinn with the kids while I waited, which would keep me busy with someone I trusted.

"I'll hang out with Quinn until you're done and then we'll have lunch," I added, not having to force myself to smile. So far, I'd enjoyed every moment I'd had with Quinn and something inside me assured me that I could trust her... and despite that something telling me I could also trust Cyrus, I was going to believe it.

Bishop glanced over my shoulder at Quinn's play station, his own smile deepening. "I won't be long."

Then he captured my lips in a quick but searing kiss that sent me reeling before he escorted me closer to the playground partitioned off for the kids.

"Hey, Audrey," Quinn called out. "Come to keep me company? My shift isn't done for another couple of hours."

I stepped off the street onto the park's soft grass and turned back to see Bishop still watching me and Velora tapping her foot impatiently while still smiling that too-sweet smile. I couldn't have been the only one to see through that smile, but no one was looking at her. They were all looking at me.

I stepped back, crossing the colorful barrier into the kids' space, and darkness flashed through Bishop's eyes as his wolf gave me a hungry look before he hurried away with Velora.

"I don't know what was hotter," Quinn whispered, fanning herself, "that kiss or that look."

I tried not to look at the crowd, who I knew were all still staring at me, as heat rushed over my face and down my neck. Both the kiss and the look were something better done in private and now the rumors wouldn't just be about me spending time with Bishop. They'd be about how Bishop had kissed me, which was juicier and would spread like wildfire through the festival.

"Come on," she said, saving me from spontaneously combusting from embarrassment. "Meet my pups for the day."

I approached the art station and all of the kids instantly looked up at me, along with the adults at the nearby table.

I strengthened my smile and ignored the adults, hoping they wouldn't freak out that I was near their children. So far everyone who'd spoken to me had been nice. Everyone who looked wary or angry had just avoided me, but I was no longer with a pack alpha. Those who'd held their tongue before might not now.

"Everyone, this is Audrey," Quinn said, drawing my attention back to the kids.

The kids ranged from four or five to nine, maybe ten, and were a mix of boys and girls. Five of them greeted me, while the sixth, a little girl with big brown eyes and curly brown hair just stared at me.

She looked very familiar and I didn't get the impression that she was staring at me because she was curious about me. It was more like she was wary and not just wary about me but about everything. I understood how she was feeling even if I didn't know why.

I returned the kids' smiles and greetings while wracking my brain, trying to remember her. Then it hit me. She'd been a part of the group who I'd saved from the grimalkin, the girl who'd been sobbing. And beside her, hovering protectively close was the other girl, the one who'd been deathly pale and silent.

"Read us a story," the youngest kid of the group said, holding out a thin book in his gluey, paint-smeared hands.

"How about I tell you a story," I offered instead. I would have loved to have read the book to them, but until I got some lessons, I wouldn't be reading anything to anyone.

"I want this story," the little guy insisted and the others voiced their agreement.

I smiled at his enthusiasm while trying to figure out a way to give them what they wanted. "It must be a great story."

The boy vigorously nodded and now I wanted to sit with them and read even more. Maybe even have them pile around me to help steady their shifter souls, especially the silent little girl because I knew about some of her trauma and ached to reassure her.

But I was a stranger. It wasn't my place to cuddle with them despite every instinct inside me screaming that I should.

"How about we finish our pieces of art first?" Quinn suggested, saving me from having to explain that I couldn't read. I wasn't sure if she'd figured that out or just thought I was reluctant to be around children.

But the kids all pouted. Even the two girls who I'd saved kept staring at me expectantly. They wanted my attention and I really wanted to give it to them, but I couldn't—

Except I could. I might not be able to read, but I could still spend time with them, and I had the perfect thing to entertain them.

I opened my satchel and pulled out the flipbook I was making to explain to Bishop how movies worked. It wasn't completely done, I wanted to draw a few more pictures to get the point across, but I was sure the kids wouldn't care.

"I think I have something just as good as a story." The little guy — still holding the book — scrunched up his face in disappointment. "I can make a picture dance."

I held up the roughly made book, catching everyone's attention. I hadn't asked for scissors and had had to rip the pages from my note-book then rip them into smaller pieces. The book hadn't been intended for anyone except Bishop, but again, I doubted the kids would care.

"Have you seen a flipbook before?" I asked them.

The kids shook their heads and they and Quinn gathered around me. The adults at the nearby bench stared at me, one with a wary expression the others curious.

Holding the edge of the book tight — since it was only held together by some string Eloise had given me — I flipped through the pages, making my stickman jump and turn and start to hop to the side.

The kids and Quinn gasped.

"Audrey, that's—" Quinn began.

"Again!" the little guy exclaimed, cutting her off, and the others picked up the call.

I flipped through the book two more times then scanned the picnic table, looking for paper. There was some, but not enough for all the kids to make their own book.

"Is it possible to get more paper?" I asked Quinn as I handed the book to the oldest kid and drew her aside. I wasn't far enough away for the kids not to hear me even if I whispered, but I was hoping the book would distract them since I didn't want to disappoint them if I couldn't get the paper.

"It's easy to make one of these," I continued, "and if the kids want, I can teach them to make one of their own."

Quinn sighed. "They'd love that, but I can't leave my post."

"I'll go," one of the adults, a woman in her mid-thirties, said as the others joined the kids to look at the book. "Gemma hasn't looked interested in anything since the grimalkin attack." She swallowed hard. "I didn't get a chance to thank you for saving my pups and here you are helping again."

"Her son and daughter were two of the kids you saved," Quinn said as she pointed to the silent little girl who still looked as closed off as before, with the exception that she was staring intently every time the older kid flipped the pages of my little book.

"Thank you, alpha," the woman said, running away before I could tell her not to call me that.

"Can you spread gossip?" I begged Quinn. "Please. People shouldn't call me that."

"Yes, they should. You're mated to Knox and from the way Bishop kissed you in front of everyone, it won't be long before you're mated with him, too."

"Still doesn't make me an alpha," I insisted.

"Kind of does," said the man who'd been looking at me warily. His expression was still guarded, but it had softened a bit as if he was reconsidering how he felt about me — which I guessed was the whole reason I was here in public, letting everyone stare at me while I freaked out on the inside. "What is that thing?"

"It's a flipbook," I said and he raised his eyebrows telling me that wasn't a good enough explanation. "If you, ah... If you create a series of slightly different images going from one position to another and flip the pages at the right speed, it'll look like the image is moving."

"Fascinating." He turned back to the kids and watched as the older kid flipped the book again.

"Felix is an engineer," Quinn said. "Bishop mentioned that you might want to talk to one. He has to know how things work or it'll drive him crazy, so I'm sure he'll be able to help you. He belongs to Owen, the one you handed the book to."

"It's a pleasure to meet you." I nodded and respectfully shifted my gaze to his ear when he looked back at me, making him frown.

"Alpha, you show me too much respect," he replied, making me cringe.

"Please don't call me that. I'm just a girl who was fated for Knox." God, if calling me alpha caught on, Cyrus was going to kill me, and it wouldn't matter if I was mated to Knox.

"I have a feeling you're more than that. Beth says you're the one who nearly killed herself rescuing her kids."

"Well, I..." I had no idea how to respond to that. I couldn't have ignored them if I'd tried. It had been stupid and terrifying and I'd do it again if I had to.

"What were some of the things you wanted to talk to an engineer about?" Quinn asked, saving me from having to come up with a response.

I shot her a thankful look and she returned a warm smile before turning to the kids and herding them back to the art table.

"I've heard a rumor that you're from another realm," Felix said, pushing his hands in his pockets and watching his kid show one of the younger kids how to flip the book. "Is it true?"

"It is." And there were only two people who could have spread that rumor. Velora or Finn. Maybe that was why everyone was looking at me strangely. Except I knew it was mostly because I was mated to Knox, the strange, reclusive alpha of their pack... and *now* because Bishop had kissed me like he wanted me.

Felix nodded his head, his expression turning thoughtful. "That's why you want to talk with an engineer."

"And a scientist. I know about things that the pack might find useful, but I—" I dug my toe into the ground. Bishop had said sharing what I knew was a great idea, but everyone was going to be frustrated with me because I didn't know how anything worked. "I just know about them. I don't know how they work and for a lot of the things we'd need to figure out some kind of power source," I said, the words coming out in a rush, my heart in my throat, waiting for him to laugh at me.

"So you don't know how the flipbook works?"

"Oh, the flipbook is simple. The brain is great at filling in little blank spots. So when you draw the stickman moving in small increments then flip the pages, your brain fills in the action between one drawing and the next. It won't work if the movement between one drawing and the next is too big, but you don't need a million pictures with microscopic differences for it to work."

He frowned at me. "Microscopic?"

Right. Shit. They hadn't discovered microscopes yet. Whil had already told me that. There were some curved lenses in the realm for correcting vision, but the quality was rough and shifters didn't have bad eyesight so the pack hadn't explored that area of research.

"Microscopic means something that can only be seen by a microscope, which is a device with a lens or lenses, I'm not sure which, that helps you see small things that you couldn't normally see."

His frown deepened, but his eyes brightened as if he was fascinated with what I was saying. "Like what?"

I told him about viruses and things like pollen and mites and that there was a whole world of things we couldn't see that affect our bodies — or at least human bodies — and the water and the soil and the air we breathed.

I was in the middle of explaining telescopes when the woman who'd run off to get the paper returned. Felix made me promise to meet with him again to hear more about the wonders of my realm and I sat at the table and taught the kids how to make their own flipbooks.

It didn't take long before the kids were hard at work creating their books, the youngest with Quinn's help and the sobbing girl I'd rescued from the grimalkins, Gemma, with her mother's.

The rest of the adults chatted amongst themselves, no longer worried about my presence, and with a sigh, I sat back, looked up at the perfect, cloudless sky, and let the kid's joyful chatter and the rush of conversation from those at the nearby booths wash over me. If I wasn't looking at the festival goers and seeing them stare at me, I could pretend I was part of all the excitement, that I belonged.

And maybe I did.

Maybe Bishop was right and his pack just needed to see me to realize how plain and ordinary I was. The kids hadn't cared that I was practically human or that I'd somehow mated their antisocial alpha, and once I'd gotten them excited about the flipbooks, their parents had stopped giving me serious looks. A few of them were still glancing over at me, but their expressions had changed to more curious than wary.

AUDREY

A FEW MINUTES LATER, AS THE NEW SMALL, HOPEFUL PEACE SETTLED inside me, the boy closest to me, Holden, sat back and held up his flipbook, looking at me expectantly.

"What have you got?" I asked, crouching beside him.

He slowly flipped through the six pages that he'd drawn. He wasn't a very skilled artist — of course, he *was* seven so that could easily change — but his incremental position changes looked great.

"That's fantastic," I praised, making him puff out his chest. "A few more pages and you'll complete the action. What do you think your guy should do after he leaps over that rock?"

"Leap on it," he replied, his expression serious as if jumping onto the rock after jumping over it was the next logical action.

"Good idea. If you want to keep going after that, you could make it look like he's running away from the rock or jumping up really high by drawing the rock farther and farther away from your guy—" I pointed at the space behind his stick figure and then a few more spots getting closer and closer to the spine of the book. "Or draw the rock getting smaller and smaller as your guy gets higher and higher."

My flipbook had been very simple, just a guy moving around, but this kid had already added a prop, and I hoped my little nudge helped him think about other ways he could work with the prop.

"Oh! I know!" he exclaimed and went back to drawing.

I straightened and let my gaze wander to the parents, praying I hadn't overstepped and that Holden's parent, whoever they were, wouldn't get upset with me.

But Felix gave me a nod of approval, making me wonder if Holden's parents had just dropped him off and hadn't stayed since Quinn hadn't indicated that Felix had more than one kid in the group.

And now that I thought about it, it was kind of surprising to see so many adults standing around watching. I'd gotten the impression this area was a form of daycare and that they weren't required to help out.

"They were about to leave when you showed up with the flipbook," Quinn chuckled as if she could read my mind, although my wondering was probably obvious in my expression. "You know she doesn't bite," she added to the others.

One of the women offered an embarrassed smile. "We didn't—"

"You're mated to Knox and—" the man beside her said.

Felix huffed. "She's obviously not like Knox. She's here talking to us, showing our pups something new and exciting."

"But Knox has to be watching," the man protested. "He flattened a third of Stonehaven just to get to her. I don't want to risk saying something wrong and have him go after me."

"He's not going to go after you," Quinn said, glancing at the kids who thankfully weren't paying attention to the conversation. "He's never seriously hurt a pack member."

"He would for his mate," the first woman said.

"Then don't threaten her," Quinn shot back as if it was obvious.

"But we don't know anything about her," the first woman said, making me cringe. It looked like I hadn't done enough to ease their worries.

"Then talk to her." Quinn threw her hands up in exasperation.

Do you need me to rescue you? Knox asked.

My gaze jumped straight to a shadow in the grasses between a red tent and a booth with yellow and green triangle flags.

Knox.

I knew without a doubt that it wasn't a grimalkin like it had been a month ago when I'd been in the same playground watching happy families being happy. It was my mate.

A hint of worry seeped through our bond and I could tell Knox was willing to leave the safety of the shadows to rescue me. He didn't want to, but he'd do it.

I shook my head and tried to calm myself. They were just talking. Felix and Gemma's mother had relaxed around me, the others would, too. Eventually.

Except it was the eventually part and how long that would take that concerned me. Which set off my worry and desire to shrink in on myself and become less noticeable.

"Excuse me," I murmured, needing to get away from them to refocus on what worries were real and what was the product of my upbringing. "I should find a table for lunch."

I clasped my hands in front of me to stop them from trembling and strolled away from the craft table while everything inside me screamed to hurry up, be invisible, just for a moment.

Are you sure? Knox growled. *You just say the word.*

I nodded yes. Then realized Knox might think that was me asking him to rescue me, so I shook my head, then huffed realizing that wasn't clear, either.

I pushed some love through our bond, trying to will him to understand that I just needed a moment and that I could stay strong until Bishop came back because his plan for his pack to see me *was* making them more welcoming.

I've finally managed to get rid of Velora and clear up the non-argument. Getting food now, Bishop said in my head.

About time, Knox huffed. *She's uncomfortable being alone.*

I left her with Quinn, Bishop protested.

And Quinn is only one person and she's responsible for looking after the pups, not Audrey.

I opened my mouth to tell them it was fine then snapped it shut. There was no point in saying anything. I was too far away from both of them to be heard and speaking into the air would only make people more wary of me.

I'd never wanted telepathic communication more than I did now, even if it was just to tell them to shut up. But I couldn't, so I just had to put up with them arguing in my head.

Straining to ignore them, I let my gaze wander to a nearby game street at the side of the park with booths that had all manner of games. There weren't as many people down the impromptu street as there'd been on the other narrow streets through the festival, but that only meant it wasn't crowded. Families played games and cheered each other on, a large group of eager-looking kids gathered around a booth with bright blue stripes, and—

A hint of gold caught in sunlight flashed for a second and I turned my attention back to the group of kids to see Cyrus stand up. He must have been hunched over or crouching in the middle of the group for me not to have seen him when I first looked because he stood easily a head taller than most of the kids.

He said something and ruffled the hair of one of the kids, making the young man beam with pride, then he turned to someone else. The kids hung onto every word he said, but I didn't get the impression it was because he was commanding them. No, they all looked excited and happy.

"So what's the plan?" Cyrus asked, making me realize I'd wandered close enough to hear him.

My heart stuttered, but I couldn't make myself walk away so I turned to face the playground, praying it wasn't obvious that I was eavesdropping.

God, it was the stupidest thing I could have done. He'd already told me to remember my place and accused me of sneaking around, but my body had frozen on the spot. In fact, something inside me was screaming that I needed to get closer.

I'd never seen Cyrus look so relaxed, so comfortable, and the kids looked at him with adoration. They clearly loved him and weren't afraid of him.

So, it's just me he hates.

But that thought didn't feel right, no matter how scared I was of him. What I saw now was a kinder softer version of the gruff man who I'd walked with for a month. The man who I'd originally thought he was.

Except that didn't fit with the man who'd yelled at me and it was always safer to assume someone was more dangerous than they might be.

"Meet your little brother or sister," a young man said, his voice cracking. "Buy them lunch and play games."

"And win a toy for them," another guy said, this one a few years younger than the first.

"And don't mention the attack," added one of the girls, making me look back at the group.

"Right," Cyrus said. "We want them to forget for a day who they've lost or who's still in the hospital."

All the kids nodded and Cyrus handed out coin purses.

I couldn't stop staring. It sounded like Cyrus had arranged for a group of older kids to help younger kids have fun at the festival, kids who'd suffered during the grimalkin attack.

That certainly wasn't the man who'd yelled at me or who said veiled threats about ruining my dinner or being on time.

My fantasy rushed through my mind's eye. He was always gentle and loving. He always held me with such tenderness and looked at me like I was the most precious thing in the world as he pushed inside me to ease the heat fever from burning me up.

For a second, it felt like it was more than just a fantasy, like the moment between us had been real.

But that was the Cyrus I wanted him to be, the Cyrus he was showing to these kids and the rest of their pack. Not the Cyrus he was with me.

The thought made my throat tighten and the fantasy slipped away.

"Don't forget to have fun yourselves," he said as they all rushed past me into the park to a group of young kids waiting on the other side.

Oh, shit.

I froze, holding my breath as if that would make me invisible even though I was standing out in the open. I didn't want to find out how he'd react to me listening in and could only pray he wouldn't want to make a scene in front of his pack.

Worry swelled through our mating bond and I pushed as much love back at Knox as I could, hoping to reassure him. I didn't want him upset enough that he'd run into the middle of the festival. That could only spell disaster.

Out of the corner of my eye, I watched Cyrus head deeper down the makeshift street and released the breath I'd been holding, relief flooding me... as well as disappointment. I didn't want to be invisible to him or ignored by him. I wanted the Cyrus of my fantasies.

But that was never going to happen.

AUDREY

"Hey, gorgeous," Bishop said a moment later from somewhere behind me.

I turned around, my heart skipping a beat with joy as I saw him *and* the heated look in his eyes.

"Hey," I replied, suddenly feeling shy, my cheeks warming.

He held up two paper bags in one hand and a large paper cup in the other. "I've got lunch. Have you found us a place to sit?"

"Sit with me," Quinn said from a nearby bench. "I've got twenty minutes and wouldn't mind the company."

"Do you need lunch?" I asked as we sat beside her. "We can get you something if you can't leave."

"Nope," she said and jerked her thumb toward the park's entrance just as Zavier hurried inside. "All taken care of."

"But I can't stay," Zavier said, rushing over to us. "My shift starts in two minutes and I need to be on the other side of the festival."

"Then what are you waiting for?" Quinn laughed, taking the bag and making a shooing motion.

Zavier huffed and she flashed him a brilliant smile, making him huff again before taking off.

"Thank you. You're the best!" she called after him and I couldn't help but wonder just what their relationship was.

Bishop pulled a sandwich out of one of our bags and handed it to me, while Quinn carefully pulled out a steaming meat pie.

"Sisters, I love these pies," Quinn sighed, staring at her food. "But they're only ever made during the summer festival."

"So, ah…" Did I dare ask? It was kind of a personal question. "That was awfully nice of Zavier to bring you one," I said instead.

"Yeah, he's the best." She glanced at me and raised an eyebrow. "And whatever you're thinking, it's wrong."

"How do you know what I was thinking?" I asked, making Bishop chuckle.

"Kind of obvious because it's what all of us have been thinking for years," he said.

"He's practically my brother," she shot back.

"But not." Bishop waggled his eyebrows at me and flashed me a wicked smile. "Zavier's family took in Quinn when her parents were killed. You guys were what? Five or six?"

"Seven," Quinn corrected, "and, no. I don't care what everyone has been saying for the last five years. He's my brother."

"But you're so good together," Bishop pressed.

"Because we're family." She pinched the bridge of her nose. "He's a watchman because his father, his uncle, his grandfather, and who-knows-how-many other relatives are. It's what's expected of him, but I know he'd rather become a hunter or a merchant or anything that will get him out of this town." Her expression turned wistful, but I couldn't tell if it was because she wanted to join him or if she was in love with him and knew she couldn't be what he needed. "I'm happy here with my kids. I'll help Zavier make his dream come true and I'll find a nice guy or—" she winked at me "—a couple of guys to settle down with to have my own pups."

I took a bite of my sandwich, a creation loaded with chicken — or the equivalent of it in this realm — a few grilled vegetables, and a delicious spread that tasted like a spicy mayonnaise, hoping it wasn't obvious to Quinn how I felt. I could see why everyone thought they'd mate. Even from the first moment I'd seen them, I could tell they were close and they both seemed to look at each other with something more than brotherly or sisterly affection. Of course, I doubt either could see that, and if Quinn was so sure that they wanted different things then nothing would happen between them.

"So, the pups really liked your flipbook," Quinn said, not even trying to hide her change of conversation. "I have a feeling we're going to be making them for the rest of the festival."

"A flipbook?" Bishop asked.

"Show him," Quinn insisted, holding out my flipbook to me.

I set my sandwich back in its bag, took the book, and flipped the pages. "I was making it for you to explain how movies work."

"That's amazing." He took the book from me and flipped the pages. "And you said the pups are making them?"

"Audrey showed them how." Quinn nudged me with her elbow. "You know if you haven't figured out what you want to do with yourself, you should consider becoming a teacher. You were so patient with the kids and they loved you."

"I, ah..." It was a kind offer and a part of me loved the idea, but another part was afraid of angry parents. Sure the parents at the craft tables had warmed up to me but not everyone would and I doubted they wanted someone like me spending all day with their children. Half an hour in the park, sure, but not a whole day at school.

"No need to decide now. Just wanted to suggest it." Quinn finished her pie, stood, and brushed the remaining crumbs from her dress. "Are you going to the dance later?"

"Of course we are," Bishop said.

"Then I'll see you there." She hurried back to the craft tables and was met with bright smiles and cheerful hellos from the children.

"Almost done?" Bishop asked me as I took my second to last bite of my sandwich.

I nodded and his smile deepened.

"Good, because there's so much more I want to show you."

For the rest of the afternoon, we strolled through the festival's winding streets, looking at all the amazing things for sale, eating far too many treats, and playing all the games.

At the beginning, I was still far too aware of everyone staring at me, but as the day wore on and people stopped asking Bishop who I was, I stopped noticing their stares. I was having too much fun with Bishop, laughing at his bad jokes, cheering him on when he tried to win me prizes, and overall feeling amazing.

I'd never felt so happy and by the time we'd made our way to a big square lit with fairy lights and lanterns, my cheeks were sore from smiling so much.

The square was filled with people dancing, others watching the dancing, and those just standing around chatting.

"Dance with me," Bishop said, tugging me closer to the dancers.

They were gathered in paired lines and were stepping and spinning and hopping in a crazy pattern that everyone seemed to know.

I slowed down, pulling back from the group. "I don't know the steps."

"It doesn't matter. Look." He pointed to a preteen who obviously didn't know all the steps but everyone around him didn't seem to care. They were all laughing and having a good time.

Alright, maybe I could join in. And really, after its initial rocky start, I was having a great day. So great, I didn't want it to end. "Okay."

Bishop flashed me a heart-stopping smile and drew me to the edge of the bystanders. Beyond the dancers, on the far side of the square, were the musicians on a raised platform. They were a mix of hand drum, some kind of flute, and two stringed instruments that looked like guitars but had more twang, and they laughed and sang while they played. The music was upbeat and folky and the drum was like a steady heartbeat urging me to move within seconds of listening.

A moment later, the song came to an end and Bishop led me to the back of a line beside an elderly couple who'd been moving just as sprightly as everyone else.

"Alpha!" the woman joyfully exclaimed, shifting to make more room for us. "I was wondering why you weren't playing tonight."

"You play an instrument?" I asked.

The man chuckled. "He plays *all* the instruments."

"But not at the same time," the woman added, making the man laugh louder.

"No," the man replied, "but that would be something to see. I'm Guthrie and this is my mate Embry."

"Audrey," I replied, my insides tightening as the conversation moved from Bishop to me.

"Are you enjoying your first festival?" Embry asked with no sign of wariness or disgust in her expression.

"I am," I told her, still a little hesitant.

The band played the first few cords of the next song telling the dancers to get ready. Bishop held both my hands, the look of happiness and love in his eyes making my shifter connection to him warm even more, and then we were hopping and spinning and laughing.

AUDREY

W E DANCED TO FOUR SONGS BEFORE THE CROWD CAJOLED BISHOP INTO playing, but I didn't mind. The last song had been the fastest yet, and I was completely out of breath so I hung out with Quinn while she waited for Zavier to finish his shift and Bishop stepped onto the stage.

He picked up one of the twangy guitars, sat on a nearby stool, and strummed a few notes.

Beside me, Quinn sighed and her expression softened. "I love this song."

Other women had the same reaction while a few people — including Guthrie and Embry — glanced my way with soft smiles.

Then Bishop slowly played the first four melancholy bars, drew in a breath, and started to sing, his gaze locked on me.

The song was sweet and sad and hopeful, about a man longing for his fated mate, knowing she was out there but never having met her.

I could see why Quinn loved it and Bishop had an amazing, emotive voice that seemed to reach out to me and warm our shifter connection even though he was on the other side of the dance floor. And the way he wouldn't stop looking at me, with yearning and love in his eyes deepened the feeling.

I ached and yearned along with him and the song, and I knew in my heart that Knox *and* Bishop were the men I'd waited my whole life to find. They were my fate... and so, according to the aching in my soul, was Cyrus.

The song concluded with the final few bars turning happy and the man finding his fated mate. Bishop held my gaze as the final notes faded, looking at me like I was the only woman in the world.

Quinn sighed, caught in the musical spell Bishop had woven, and I had to agree with her. That was the most beautiful thing I'd ever heard.

"Wow," Quinn breathed. "When Bishop wants to make a statement, he really makes a statement. He just made his intentions about you clear to everyone here."

I glanced around nervously, but while there were some women glaring daggers at me, everyone else was either happy or didn't seem to care that Bishop had basically said I was the one he'd been searching for even though I was also Knox's mate.

Then someone started clapping, breaking the silence, and everyone else joined in, clapping and cheering. The rest of the band, who'd let him have his solo performance, nodded their approval, while the drummer flashed him a knowing smile.

Bishop gave me another heated look then turned his attention back to the crowd as he strummed a few upbeat chords making all the dancers scramble to get into position.

"Dance with me!" Quinn exclaimed, and she grabbed my hand and pulled me to the end of one of the dance rows.

She easily stepped into the next move without missing a beat despite the dancing having already started and laughed good-naturedly at me as I stumbled to catch up. I laughed with her and continued to stumble through the rest of the dance like I had with all the other dances before.

After Bishop's third song, he bowed to his audience, handed the guitar back to its owner, and pushed through the crowd heading straight for me.

Heat burned my cheeks but I was determined to push through my embarrassment. He'd sung me a love song. No one had ever sung me a love song before, and I was filled with awe and joy.

"That first song was beautiful," I said as he picked me up and spun us around.

"A beautiful song for a beautiful woman." He cupped my cheeks, his eyes shining with affection, and pressed a breathtaking kiss against my lips, leaving me reeling and overflowing with joyful emotions.

For just a moment, I didn't care that people were looking at me and wondering who the hell I was to have the eye of the pack's most eligible bachelor. All I could see was the desire in Bishop's eyes and feel the heat of our connection growing stronger the longer he kissed me.

After that, we talked and laughed and danced and ate treats deep into the night until I was so tired, I could barely keep my eyes open.

"I think it's time to go home," he said as I sleepily clung to him, my head resting against his arm and my heart overflowing.

"One more dance?" I begged.

I was going to be so sore in the morning but I didn't care. I was having more fun than I'd ever had in my life and didn't want tomorrow morning to shatter the magical spell Bishop had cast over me. It was like I was Cinderella and I wanted to stop time so the clock never struck twelve.

"Your mate is waiting to give you a private dance in the summer garden," he replied, his voice deepening and sending heat rushing through me.

The memory of how Knox and I had *danced* last night in Whil's greenhouse heated my insides and now I was torn. Being with Knox and connecting with him had felt amazing and I wanted to do it again, but I didn't want to leave Bishop, didn't want this amazing day to end... of course maybe he could stay with me and Knox.

He had mentioned the possibility of being with both of them at the same time back in Kelna and the thought had turned me on.

It had also embarrassed the hell out of me, but that hadn't stopped me from thinking about it.

I hugged him tighter and opened my mouth to invite him to join me and Knox, but I couldn't make myself say it.

Blazing heat radiated from my face and I was grateful for the dim light. I was also frustrated that talking about sex still embarrassed me, but I had to remind myself that I was taking baby steps. I'd had sex with both of them and was no longer embarrassed that they'd seen me naked. Eventually I'd work up to talking about it or even asking for what I wanted.

Bishop frowned at me. He'd noticed that I'd been about to say something and then cut myself off, so I smiled at him, showing him just how happy I felt and how grateful I was that he'd given me this amazing day.

"I had a great time today," I said.

"Me, too." He led us away from the square packed with people and up the wide main road.

Ahead of us, the Residence stood tall and proud at the top of the rise, standing sentinel over the town, lit by the realm's two moons, and looking like a fairy tale. Just like how my whole day had felt.

The last upbeat song I'd heard jumped into my head and I skipped beside him, humming the tune, despite being sleepy. It was a really catchy tune and I was sure I was going to be singing it for the rest of the week, a thought that made my smile deepen.

The song was going to remind me all week of the amazing day I'd had and the hope that I'd have more amazing days with Bishop and Knox.

Then Bishop started to actually sing the song — I hadn't realized it had words — and with a whoop of joy I danced ahead of him, hopping and whirling and laughing.

With another whoop, I spun around to face him to see his eyes light up, his expression mirroring the happiness inside me. Behind him, the festival's lights lit the market, and even halfway up the road, I could hear bits of music and cheering and the roar of many voices talking. It was the most beautiful, most amazing thing I'd ever seen and I wanted to remember it forever. I didn't know how my life had gone from beaten down and despised to this, but I wasn't going to question it.

For once, something was going my way and it felt good, incredibly, amazingly good.

"You liked that song?" He sang a few more bars and I beamed at him.

"It's catchy and my last one of the night." I spun another full circle and held out my hands to him. "But I really liked the one you sang to me."

I spun again, and when I stopped, he was suddenly close, his eyes dark, the flecks of green so bright they looked like they glowed.

"I meant what I sang," he said, cupping my cheek with his palm.

I leaned into his touch, breathed in his fresh-cut grass scent, and sank deeper into his mesmerizing gaze.

"You're the one I've been searching for and I want everyone to know that I'm yours."

My smile turned wry. "Pretty sure everyone will know by the end of the night."

He'd made no attempt to hide how he felt about me all day and singing that song while never looking away from me had confirmed whatever gossip he'd started this afternoon.

And while I knew I'd made some female enemies today, right now, with my heart so full I thought it would burst, I didn't care. Bishop only had eyes for me and I felt like I was in an amazing dream.

"Then my plan was a success." He brushed his lips against mine.

It was just a whisper of a kiss, but it sent tingles racing down my spine, warming my heart and heating my core.

"I wanted everyone to know how I feel about you. If I hadn't made it obvious by singing *Fated Stars* then I'll scream it from the Residence's highest tower."

His words sparked within me and my soul soared with joy. This was right. This was the way it was supposed to be. Love. Happiness. Home.

He captured my lips in a powerful, hungry kiss. Hot slick heat raced through me, pooling low within me, and I moaned into his mouth. He took advantage of my parting lips and raked his tongue against mine, fueling my desire.

He was an incredible man, so full of joy and so accepting. Not once had he made me feel small or pathetic. Everything he'd done had been to show me that I deserved a place at his side, that I was worthy and special and wanted.

I was so in love with Bishop, I thought my heart would burst.

"You're my mate, Audrey," he growled against my lips, his wolf rising to the surface. "I love you."

AUDREY

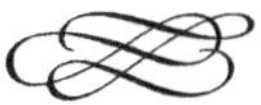

I STARED INTO HIS WOLF-DARKENED EYES, FALLING INTO THEIR bottomless depths surrounded by brilliant green stars and my heart soared at his words. He loved me.

He. Loved. Me.

No one had ever said those words to me and I knew deep in my soul that Bishop was mine just as much as Knox was.

"I love you—"

But Bishop's grip tightened, his body suddenly tense, and he shoved me to the side, hard.

I stumbled, lost my balance, and fell onto my butt as someone dressed head to toe in thick black clothing, his face hidden by a heavy hood, plunged the claws on both of his hands into Bishop's chest.

Oh, God! My heart leaped into my throat and I scrambled to my feet.

Bishop roared, the sound a mix of pain and rage, pushed his hands up between the man's arms, and shoved his claws away. The action made the man's arms fly wide, and Bishop tore the claws of his right hand through the man's side with a spray of unnaturally bright red blood.

The man screeched. The sound was barely human, sending fear

racing down my spine and chilling my blood, and for a second, I feared this man wasn't another shifter, he was something else, something dangerous.

But that didn't make sense. Underneath his bulky clothes, he was shaped like a man, and his claws, while hard to see in the dim light, looked like shifter's claws.

Bishop swiped his other hand at the man but he twisted out of the way to avoid Bishop's attack and dragged both sets of his claws through Bishop's side.

More blood splattered on the road by Bishop's feet and oozed between his fingers as the man jerked his attention to me.

Time stuttered to a halt, my pulse slow, dragging thuds, crushing around my heart. With the hood pulled low and the dim illumination from the streetlight, I couldn't see his face — all I could see were shadows — but his body language was threatening and I knew, without a doubt, that he wanted me dead.

I backed up a step, everything within me screaming to run. Run Now!

I couldn't help Bishop fight. I didn't know how to fight and I was slower than Bishop which meant I was slower than the man. I was better off screaming at the top of my lungs and finding help.

Except I knew the second I looked away, the man would jump on me.

With another screech, time lurched back to its regular speed, and the man surged forward. I scrambled back and slammed my back against the closest building, missing the alley behind me by three feet.

Oh shit oh shit oh shit.

The man raised his hands, ready to tear me open with his claws when Bishop snagged the back of his thick, oversized shirt and yanked. His claws grazed the front of my shirt, tearing the fabric but missing my flesh and before I could blink, the man had turned and rammed Bishop with his shoulder.

They both fell to the ground, the man on top, one set of claws already digging into Bishop's chest, the other about to slash open Bishop's throat.

"No!" I screamed, the sound tearing out of me, bringing the bitter acidic bite of bile rolling up my throat while sudden violent nausea erupted in my stomach.

The man froze, his attention snapping to me, and my stomach heaved as more bile burned my throat.

No no no.

Bishop raked his claws at the man's chest, but somehow the man noticed even though he was still staring at me and leaped up and out of the way. His body shuddered and Bishop lunged for him again, fast enough to tear into his calf with another spray of too-bright blood.

More bile burned up my throat and my stomach heaved.

Another shudder swept through the man's body as he dodged Bishop's next swipe and then he raced into the closest alley.

With a growl, Bishop scrambled to his feet to chase after him but staggered and dropped to one knee after only a few steps.

I rushed to his side as he sagged to the ground, trying to swallow back the bile and not throw up. Blood soaked his clothes, a mix of his and the assailant's, although the brightness in the man's blood was quickly fading and was now almost indistinguishable from Bishop's.

"Do you need a med pack?" I asked, trying to get a look at how deep the man had dug into his chest. "Where's the closest one?"

During the first aid class, Nova had mentioned where the packs were, but I didn't know any of the street names or the city's layout and had planned to ask her about it the next time I saw her.

"There's one—" He groaned and clutched his chest, making my panic spike.

Oh, God. Were his injuries so bad he actually needed an elixir?

"Can you shift?" *Please say you can shift.* Even if the shift didn't fully heal his injuries, it would still help. Except if the injury was severe enough, he wouldn't have enough strength to complete the transformation and it could kill him.

He groaned and shook his head, making my pulse spike. I had to get a vial of the healing elixir into him. Now.

"Where? Where is it?" I grabbed his arm, helping to steady him, and he raised his gaze to meet mine.

"It's—" He sucked in a sharp, sudden breath and his eyes widened.

Fear and agony raced through his expression as strange black and red veins bulged under his skin and raced up his neck.

A strangled cry fell from his lips and he locked eyes with me, making my pulse stall completely.

"Love you," he gasped. "I—"

With another cry, he lurched back onto the road and started convulsing.

Oh no. Oh no no no.

This couldn't be happening. Not now. Not after he'd told me that he loved me. Today was supposed to have been happy and wonderful. I'd been overflowing with joy a moment ago and now... now I couldn't catch my breath.

Something was horribly wrong with Bishop, more than just being beaten up in a fight, and it had everything to do with that man. The strange black and red veins meant he'd cast a spell or cursed him or... poisoned him.

That was the most logical explanation, more logical than magic even though magic was more prevalent in this realm than the mortal realm. That man had to have poisoned Bishop because if it was anything else there might not be a cure.

My breath caught in my too-tight throat. It *was* poison and there *was* an antidote. There had to be.

"Help!" I screamed, scrambling to get his head onto my lap to protect it from the stone road. I didn't know where the med pack was, I couldn't contact anyone telepathically, and I couldn't leave him to get help, not without him bashing his head on the ground.

God, no. Please. I couldn't be useless like Merrick and Sterling had said I was my entire life. I just couldn't be.

"Please," I sobbed.

Bishop was dying. It was obvious from the pallor of his skin and the way his body convulsed as the veins grew thicker, now covering his cheeks and forearms.

It had happened so fast, the attack, the poison. Everything... and just after he'd told me that he loved me, told his whole pack, really. He hadn't been embarrassed of me for being so weak I couldn't shift. He'd sung me a love song and kissed me in public and... God!

I bit back another sob and ground my teeth together.

I. Was. Not. Useless.

That was Sterling and Merrick's poison. Not the truth.

I'd killed a grimalkin. It might have been by accident, but I killed one, and I sure as hell could save Bishop. If I couldn't get help to come to me, I'd go to the help.

I grabbed Bishop under the shoulders and heaved. He was as heavy as I'd thought he'd be, which was heavier than I could realistically manage with him writhing in agony, but I *was not* going to let him die.

He convulsed again, jerking out of my grip and bashing his head against my foot. Pain shot through my toes, making me cry out, but I didn't stop. I couldn't stop. I had to save him.

I grabbed him again and dragged him farther down the street as fast as I could, my hands hurting with how tightly I gripped his shirt. It wasn't far. I could make it and I wouldn't let go again. I wouldn't let go, ever. Just a little farther and someone would hear me.

Please, God.

"Help!"

WOLF DECIDED

ENSNARED BY THE PACK: BOOK 5

AUDREY

Bishop released a strangled groan and convulsed, his violent thrashing threatening my grip under his shoulders, but I clenched tighter to his shirt, ignoring the pain in my hands and my trembling arms.

I just had to hold on a little longer, drag him a little farther, find help.

I heaved with all my might, inching closer and closer to the festival, desperate to reach someone, anyone.

Surely someone would notice us. They had to.

But the festival was still going strong even into the early hours of the morning, and while I could hear the dance music and the roar of many voices getting louder, indicating that I was getting closer, the square was on a side street from the main road we were on and a few buildings down.

No one in the square would be able to see us until we'd reached the intersection.

The black and red veins on Bishop's neck and face from the poison — it *had* to be poison because poisons had antidotes — stood out stark against his too-pale skin, and blood poured from his many wounds, leaving thick dark streaks on the ground that shimmered wetly in the moonlight of the realm's two moons.

He wasn't healing.

Not even a little bit.

He should have been healing. A wolf shifter's claws weren't that long, he should have only been seriously bleeding from the gashes in his side, but blood still leaked from his ruined chest.

"Help!" I screamed, my pulse pounding, tears burning my eyes, even as I pushed forward, determined to save him, determined to not be useless when he needed me the most.

I'd just had the most amazing day, and Bishop — gorgeous, wonderful, amazing Bishop — had just told me he loved me. Everything had been perfect and then that man had jumped out of nowhere and dug all his claws into Bishop's chest.

More black and red veins appeared on his neck and cheeks and oozed down his arms and across the back of his hands.

My panic surged, stealing my breath, as something deep within me screamed in agony at the thought of losing Bishop. He was mine. Mine! He couldn't die. I wouldn't let him.

"Help!" *Oh, God, please.* "Help!"

Someone had to know what was going on with him whether he'd been poisoned or enspelled or cursed.

And someone had to save him because I couldn't.

I couldn't shift into my wolf form and mentally call for help, and even if I did somehow have telepathy, I wouldn't be able to use it in my human form like the shifters in this realm could. That just wasn't possible for shifters from my realm.

A wave of panic crashed through me, sudden and ferocious, stealing my breath and threatening to bring me to my knees.

Knox.

Knox could feel my fear through our mating bond.

And through his twin bond with Bishop, he could feel his brother dying.

Another sob caught in my throat. There were too many emotions rushing through me, overwhelming me, and on the verge of ripping me apart. I could barely catch my breath. It was too much, too—

Audrey. I'm coming, Knox said in my head, sending a wave of love and determination through our bond. But my fear was too strong, and I couldn't stop that horrible voice in my head that said I was going to fail Bishop and Knox because I wasn't strong enough.

Because I was useless.

No, I mentally screamed back at the voice. Those thoughts weren't mine. They were Merrick's and Sterling's, beaten into me for years. I was weak. I was useless. No one wanted me.

But Bishop had proven that wasn't true.

He wanted me for me and not because of a mating bond or anything else. He'd seen me at my worst and still told me he loved me.

And I was God damned going to save him, even if all I could do was drag him down the road to someone who could help him.

Knox in his enormous black wolf form raced out of the shadows of a side street, sending a flicker of relief snapping through me. *He* could call for help. Hell, *he* probably knew where the closest med pack was.

He shifted into his human form and took Bishop from me, lifting him into his arms as if he didn't weigh anything, because, of course, with his shifter strength Bishop's weight was nothing.

"What happened?" he asked, picking up his pace and heading to the building on the corner of the intersection.

"Some guy attacked us."

A chill raced down my spine. Bishop had shoved me out of the way. I'd been right in the attacker's path, and once I was out of the way, the guy kept trying to get past Bishop to get to me.

"No," I said, unable to keep the trembling from my voice at the realization that the poison or whatever was killing Bishop had been meant for me. "Some guy attacked *me.*"

And Bishop had paid the price.

Cyrus and Nova raced into sight, Nova heading into the building on the corner while Cyrus stormed toward us.

"What happened?" he snarled, making my pulse pick up with a different fear.

Was he going to blame me for Bishop? If I hadn't wanted to go to the festival. If I hadn't danced for as long or as short as I had. If I hadn't been foolish enough to think I could fit into this pack, be mated to Knox, and also have Bishop court me without consequences none of this would have happened.

But it didn't matter what Cyrus thought or did to me if Bishop didn't make it. None of this would matter. I could already feel my heart and soul starting to crack and knew I'd forever be incomplete without him.

Which didn't make sense. He wasn't my mate yet. We hadn't taken the vows and sealed the bond. I shouldn't be feeling as if I was losing my bonded mate, which only made me worry about how bad it would be if something happened to Knox.

"Set him down," Nova commanded as she hurried out of the house with a bright yellow duffle bag.

Knox lay Bishop on the ground and grabbed my hand, yanking me to his side before taking one of Bishop's hands while Nova went to work. His fear and anger and desperation churned in my stomach and I could feel him barely holding his wolf back.

I was losing him, too.

God, this wasn't happening.

But Knox's and Bishop's twin bond was unusually strong. They could sense each other's emotions just like those in a mating bond, and I had no doubt if one of them died, the other would suffer as if they'd lost a bonded mate.

Which meant Knox would go crazy, most likely going feral, or he'd die.

Fear gripped my heart at the thought while something deep inside me, something hard and angry and wild, whispered in my soul.

Neither of them were dying or going crazy. I wouldn't allow it.

They were mine.

AUDREY

I SENT AS MUCH LOVE AND STRENGTH THROUGH THE MATING BOND AS I could, determined to anchor Knox in his body so his wolf wouldn't take over and go feral. Then I grabbed a handful of gauze from the med pack ready to get to work because there was no way I was going to just sit there and cry when I could do something to help.

Nova tore open Bishop's shirt and my pulse lurched, my breath stalling in my throat and cold dread flash-freezing around my heart.

There was so much blood. It coated his chest and side and pooled on the road around his body while more red and black veins covered his chest in a thick web.

"Fuck," Cyrus snarled his power rolling over me, making me tremble but thankfully not forcing me to do anything because I didn't have time to grovel.

I was going to save my mate... or rather, my soon-to-be mate.

I mentally shoved at Cyrus's power and pressed my handful of gauze against Bishop's side, trying to staunch the blood from eight deep gashes, but my hands weren't big enough to cover them all.

"Knox," Nova said, jerking her chin toward me, and he dropped Bishop's hand and took over with his much larger hands.

"What the fuck is that?" Cyrus dropped to his knees beside Nova and was about to reach into the med pack when Bishop gasped a sharp breath, his only warning, before screaming and convulsing.

I shoved my hands under his head as it slammed down on the road, sending agony racing through my fingers before Cyrus took over from me.

"If the streaks were all red and a fraction of the size, I'd say it's *karoose* venom," Nova said, popping off the stoppers on the med pack's two elixirs then pouring both of them into Bishop's mouth the second he stopped convulsing. "We need Whil."

"Right here," the summer fae called out as she hurried around the corner from the side street, looking like the perfect fairy tale image of a fae from Fairy.

She, like all fae, was stunning and ageless, and her perpetual golden glow shone brightly in the dim light, even with a streetlight nearby, giving her an ethereal, magical presence.

"Have you seen anything like this?" Nova asked as Cyrus handed me more gauze and together we applied pressure to the wounds on Bishop's chest.

"Not since the last of the gods were awake." Whil placed her hands on Bishop's forehead and closed her eyes. "It's *karoose* venom imbued with a god or goddess's power. The healing elixirs will help but not enough to cure him. He needs to be fully submerged in the healing pool so I can pull it out of him."

"We need to get him to the Residence," Cyrus said as Nova ripped off a piece of tape and handed it to him. "Before we draw a crowd."

He, Nova, and Whil all glanced at Knox then went back to taping fresh gauze to Bishop's wounds.

"My wolf is under control," Knox growled even as the turmoil churning through our bond grew stronger. "Bishop needs us."

"Keep it that way," Cyrus replied as he picked up Bishop and raced up the road.

Knox swept me into his arms and followed while Nova stripped, shifted, and raced ahead.

We passed through the open gate to the Residence and ran around the outside of the building until we reached a small, partially sheltered patio in front of a set of French doors that looked a lot like the ones to my suite.

Someone had set out a mattress just like when I'd woken up after Sterling had tricked me into hurting myself, and Cyrus set Bishop on it while Knox, still holding me as if I were the only thing keeping him in his body, sagged to the ground beside him.

"Tell me he at least killed whoever attacked him," Cyrus snapped as Nova rushed out my suite doors wearing a different colored dress than the one she'd left with Whil and carrying her doctor's bag.

She dropped beside Bishop and pulled out a stitching kit as Whil hurried to join her with gauze and saline.

"He got away," I stated, my voice steadier than I would have expected given how Cyrus made me nervous. He was a powerful alpha and he'd made his position about me clear. He didn't like me, thought I didn't know my place, and I'd been trying for the last few days to stay small and invisible and not do anything that would upset him.

And now, I didn't care.

Now that wildness inside me whispered to fight for my mate. Fight and win.

"Fuck," he snarled. "Tell me everything." His power roared over me stealing my breath, squeezing my insides, and drawing a whimper even as my wildness demanded I stay strong.

Knox growled low in his throat, the sound more wolf than human even though he was still fully in his human form.

"Fuck," Cyrus barked again and his power vanished, making me shudder with the sudden loss. He raked his hands through his hair pulling strands from the braid that kept his longer hair on top away from his face and shaved sides.

"The man wore thick clothes with a hood so I couldn't see his face or any distinguishing marks," I said before Cyrus could lose control of his power again and because I needed him to send out watchmen and hunters to catch whoever had attacked us.

And while the thought of catching the assailant pissed off the wildness inside me that really wanted him dead, keeping him alive meant we might get answers, like why he'd want to poison me instead of just kill me or where he'd gotten the poison.

"He ran down an alley when it looked like Bishop was going to win their fight, then Bishop collapsed," I added. "He was hurt, but not so bad that he couldn't have shifted out most of his injuries."

Cyrus's eyes narrowed and he pursed his lips, pausing for a moment, hopefully ordering the pack to find whoever it was.

"Okay," he growled a second later, more of his power rippling over me as if he couldn't fully contain it. "The pool is six days away, five if we push it. I'm assuming," he said turning to Whil, "that because you said we need to get him in it, he can last that long."

"But not much longer," Whil said.

"Nova, you and Lucius are in charge. We can't afford to take a whole team, so Deacon is coming with us." He glanced at the moons creeping closer and closer to the western horizon. "Dawn is in a couple of hours. Will that give you enough time to get ready?" he asked, turning his attention back to Whil and making that strange wildness — that, now that I thought about it had to be coming from Knox — rise in anger. It didn't matter that she needed to come. It mattered that Cyrus wasn't asking me as well and I sure as hell was going.

"I only need to pack," I replied as if he'd asked me instead of just Whil.

Cyrus's attention snapped to me, his eyes narrowed, and his power rose, a great wave on the verge of crashing over me and forcing me to submit. "You're not going."

The wildness surged from the depths of my soul, and I met his gaze, directly challenging him. "Yes. I am."

"No." His tenuous control snapped and his power slammed into me, stealing my breath and demanding I look away, bow down, and submit.

Which was *not* happening.

My mates needed me, Bishop because he was dying and Knox because he was barely keeping his wolf from going feral. Cyrus could throw everything he had at me, but I wouldn't give in.

I wouldn't even give in so I could find another way to go, which was what I usually did. Step back, submit, and shut my mouth. That was what I always did and it had kept me alive.

But now there wasn't another way. Not going with them would kill me. Maybe not right away, but if I lost them, I'd wither away to nothing. On top of that, it wasn't safe to follow them from a distance. With their heightened senses, Cyrus would know I was following them and going beyond the town's limits by myself was too dangerous.

Of course, standing my ground now meant Cyrus could punish me and lock me up, and I'd be trapped in Stonehaven unable to protect my soul's mates.

No. I wouldn't let that happen.

My pulse *thu-thudded*, hard and fast, and I fought to breathe against the pressure.

"I'm going," I insisted as another wave of Cyrus's power slammed into me.

My body started to bow, submitting to his will, as my soul screamed in fear and fury.

"No," I gritted out, straightening my back with another *thu-thud*, making Cyrus's eyes widen and his power flare stronger.

"Back the fuck off," Knox snapped, his own power adding to the crushing mix.

"It's too dangerous," Cyrus snarled back.

The devastating force I'd felt outside the death god's temple when Cyrus had made Knox submit crackled in the air and seized my muscles.

"I'm. Going."

My pulse roared, pounding hard, surging strength to my limbs, and I heaved to my feet, squared my shoulders, and glared into Cyrus's now shocked expression.

"Mine," I snarled at him, my voice sounding strange and gravelly. "I won't leave my mates when they need me and you can't make me."

CYRUS

Audrey's gaze drilled into mine in a fierce challenge. Somehow, she'd resisted my power and even had the strength to stand, completely defying my command. If I hadn't felt the ferocious force pouring off her, I'd have no idea how she'd done it.

Hell, I still didn't. I had no idea where the power had come from.

Sure, her bond with Knox was unusually strong, but that wouldn't have allowed her to channel his power. And besides, I could feel Knox's radiating from him, so he obviously wasn't giving it to Audrey.

No. This alpha power was all hers. A glimpse deep into her soul at what her ancestors had locked away with a curse.

It had only taken her bonded mate to be on the verge of going feral and her soon-to-be mate dying for it to make an appearance.

Except as soon as I thought that I knew it was wrong. She and Bishop might not have had a mating bond or even just a bonding ceremony publicly announcing their love for each other, but they were mates.

At the disastrous dinner a week ago, Bishop had said Audrey and Knox were fated for each other. It had been an easier way to explain what had happened than saying Audrey had already started a mating bond with someone else and when we'd found her close to death that bond had connected with Knox's soul.

But now I wondered if it hadn't actually been the truth. She'd brought Knox back from being feral and was now helping him hold off his panic so he could stay in control and protect his brother.

Bishop had told me the other day that Knox had been more relaxed in the one full day of being with Audrey before he'd had to leave on a hunt than he'd ever been — and more like the brother I'd known before his claustrophobia had gotten out of control.

Knox had needed to have the scare of his life when he thought she was going to die, but it had broken through the rest of his resistance to a mate he hadn't wanted and had actually been good for him. Before this attack, he'd seemed genuinely happy.

Bishop had been happy, too. Happier than I'd seen him in a long while. He'd practically glowed with happiness every time I'd gotten a glimpse of him and Audrey wandering around the festival, and he hadn't hesitated to be affectionate with her while the rest of the pack watched.

Hell, he'd sung her *Fated Stars* at the dance, which was Bishop's way of publicly announcing Audrey was the woman he'd been searching for.

He and Audrey were fated for each other, too. Their mating bond had probably already started to form even though neither of them had said the vows to awaken the magic that bound their souls together.

And it completely explained why Audrey was willing to defy me to stay with them and why the wolf locked deep in her soul was suddenly stronger than her curse. Bonded mates would do anything to protect each other.

"Nova," Audrey said, refusing to look away from me. "Do you still need my help or can I go pack?"

"I'm good," Nova replied, her voice strained with all the alpha power crashing around us which was another surprise. Normally she would have told me to grow up and pull it back so she could work, but she'd remained silent.

Was she too stunned to see that Audrey's power held its own against mine or had she wanted to give Audrey the chance to stand up for herself?

Probably a combination of both. Audrey had only stood up to me once and that was to defend her actions when she'd risked her life to save a group of children from a grimalkin.

My wolf had howled with joy at her defiance, falling even more in love with her. She was everything we'd been waiting for. She could challenge us and stand at our side in battle. She would be the mother of our pups because she was ours.

But even as I glared at her, I could feel her power trembling. She wasn't fully aware of it or her wolf, and the effort it took to push past the curse was taking its toll on her body. Not to mention the emotional toll of defying everything that had been beaten into her during her childhood along with her naturally gentle disposition.

She was holding on by her all-too-human fingernails and could lose it at any second, destroying everything she'd just shown me.

"Alpha," she spat out in acknowledgment before squeezing Knox's shoulder and marching into her suite.

"You were saying, *alpha?*" Nova said, her tone dry.

I glared at her. "Don't start. It's dangerous on the road to Savaria and it'll be even more dangerous when we leave the road to get to the pool."

"It's dangerous here," Knox growled. "That man didn't attack Bishop. He went after Audrey. Bishop was hurt defending her."

Fuck.

Her shirt had been torn open, but I hadn't thought anything about it. She hadn't been acting as if she were hurt. I'd assumed all the blood on her was Bishop's.

"We need to check her," I said as my wolf lurched against my hold. It didn't care how pissed off she was at us. He had to protect her and he couldn't stand the idea of losing both her and Bishop.

"She hasn't been poisoned," Knox replied, his tone barely human.

"Maybe she was nicked or only inhaled a bit of it and it isn't spreading as fast." Sisters, I had to protect her. Save her. Now now

now. "You might not be able to tell with your bond with Bishop going crazy."

"If I was losing them both, I'd be feral," Knox replied. "If you want to keep it that way, she'll stay with me."

"I could also use the help," Whil added. "I can keep Bishop alive without Nova's help, but a second set of hands would be helpful. Especially if we run into trouble."

"You don't need to convince me," I ground out, my insides churning. I needed to stay in control of myself and this situation, needed to make sure everyone was safe and survived this poison.

Still, I really didn't want Audrey to go with us. We might not be traveling through the northern wilderness, but everything within me screamed that it was still too dangerous, especially with Bishop unconscious and Knox barely holding it together.

I wouldn't be able to protect her the way she deserved... the way I *had* to protect her.

Except I also couldn't leave her here.

"We don't know who attacked them," I said, "so she's safest with us." With me.

I wanted to say it was a foreigner who'd attacked her and Bishop and that she'd be safe with the pack, but without Bishop to identify the culprit's scent, I couldn't assume anything. Which made my wolf even more determined to keep her close and the rest of me furious.

Were there members of my pack who were so determined to get rid of her they'd kill her? And why use poison? She wouldn't survive against any of us in our wolf form. Why not just attack her and be done with it?

I'd thought with her being noticeably nervous and submissive around me that the rumors that I was interested in Audrey would finally die, but it looked like that was a serious miscalculation.

Bishop moaned and his muscles tightened but he didn't convulse, the elixir thankfully easing the worst of the poison's effects.

Maybe I wasn't the reason Audrey had been targeted. Even before Bishop had proclaimed Audrey his soon-to-be mate, he'd showered her with affection and made no attempt to hide it.

Not that he should. Bishop could mate whoever he wanted, not like—

My thoughts stuttered. I'd been holding my wolf back from pursuing her because she was weak and I didn't think the pack would respect her if we mated.

But now she'd revealed an enormous power strong enough to challenge me and possibly win.

Of course, she was still cursed and once her adrenaline wore off, she'd be back to being a powerless shifter.

Was that how it was always going to be with her or was there a way to completely break the curse?

She'd gained strength with strong emotions, like when she'd defended her decision to sacrifice herself to save those kids, and now with her determination to stay with her mates.

If I pushed her, would I be able to get her to break through and permanently become the shifter she'd just shown me?

"Whatever you're thinking," Nova said with her uncanny ability to know when I was thinking something stupid regarding a woman. "Stop. Just stop."

And she was right. The last time I'd pushed Audrey, she'd withdrawn into herself and become so submissive it made me want to scream.

Still, there had to be a way to help her without destroying her... because I needed her at my side just like she was at my brothers' sides.

I didn't care if she was strong or not, but I didn't want to put her in a situation where my pack constantly questioned her worth or where our mating created challenges to my leadership.

I already knew how she'd take that and it wouldn't be with anger. She'd get withdrawn and submissive again and feel guilty even though it wasn't her fault.

Fuck.

This was a no win situation.

And I couldn't keep standing here. I had to meet with Lucius and Deacon, arrange for a cart to be ready at the north gate, and get someone to put supplies together for Bishop and Knox — since neither of them were in any shape to do their own packing.

Without thinking, I jerked open the doors leading to Audrey's suite and stormed inside. It was the fastest way to get to my office so I could meet with my betas and get everything done in the next two hours that needed to get done.

But the second the door closed I was surrounded by her scent, soft and sweet and soured by fear, making my wolf growl with anger. Then a small hiccupping sob sounded from the bedroom and my wolf rushed me to the open bedroom door before I could stop him.

To my horror, Audrey sat on the bed, tears streaming down her cheeks and her hands covering her mouth trying to muffle her sobs. She froze when she saw me, her eyes widening with fear and her body trembling.

Shit.

All her adrenaline was gone, she wasn't radiating a hint of alpha power, and the terror of the night had finally come crashing down on her.

I mentally cursed myself. Given that she could also sense how Knox felt, she was probably experiencing double her usual emotions, and with them so strong, it had to be overwhelming.

On top of that, she'd outwardly defied her alpha and everything she knew told her she couldn't do that, not without repercussions. And now that the moment of determination had passed, all her old fears had returned.

"I don't care what you do to me, but don't make me stay here," she begged, her voice raspy with tears, her reaction to me the complete opposite of what it had been outside. "Punish me after they're saved."

Fucking hell. I wanted angry Audrey back.

But this was just proof that I couldn't continue playing the villain. Not even if it was better for me to keep my distance from her. Just seeing me terrified her and I couldn't take it anymore. This was the last straw.

It had been hard enough to keep my distance from her and pretend I didn't see her so I wouldn't keep scaring her. And it had been even harder today when I'd kept catching glimpses of her wandering around the market with Bishop and couldn't make myself look away.

She'd been shy and uncertain at first, which tore at my heart, but as Bishop got her to relax and she stopped glancing at all the people watching her and just had fun, it was like watching a morning flower open to the first rays of sunshine.

By the time they'd reached the square with the dancing, she'd been radiant, making others around her smile because she was so happy it was contagious. Many of my pack had stopped looking at her like she was dangerous or a strange curiosity and saw the stunning woman I'd seen grow before my very eyes during our journey north.

I wanted radiant Audrey back. Needed her. Not just for myself but for my brothers and the rest of my pack. They needed to remember that strength came in many forms, and gentleness and kindness weren't a weakness, they were what kept a community thriving.

"Audrey." I stepped into the room and she shrunk in on herself, tugging her ruined shirt closed to hide her body, but I kept going until I was at the edge of the bed, close enough to touch her, then sank to my knees. "I'm sorry. I shouldn't have said the things I said to you."

She blinked, her expression still scared as if she hadn't fully heard me, and I desperately wanted to wrap my arms around her and never let go.

But that would only scare her more.

"I was wrong," I added, praying that she'd heard me. My apology wouldn't make everything right, but hopefully it was a start, the first step in proving that even if she never forgave me, she could say what she wanted and not fear reprisal. "There's no good excuse for why I yelled at you in the arena. I didn't think and I hurt you. I'm so very sorry."

AUDREY

Cyrus's words were a trap. They had to be.

I'd just defied him, challenged his authority by refusing to look away. No one did that to an alpha and got away with it.

Even if I'd only done it in front of his brother and his trusted friends, he still should have been furious with me.

Except he wasn't, and every instinct I had told me he was being sincere, that he meant his apology.

Which didn't help me figure out how to respond. Did I just accept it and pretend nothing had happened?

A minute ago, when I'd been filled with what had to have been Knox's ferocious wildness — since it couldn't have been mine — I would have said yes. But the wildness had vanished the moment I'd stepped inside, and now all I felt was a terrifying, nauseating churn of emotions that were both mine and Knox's along with a bone-deep exhaustion.

In the back of my mind, I knew it was shock. The adrenaline from the fight, trying to save Bishop, and the fight to stay with Knox and Bishop had worn off, and I was crashing. Hard.

I didn't have it in me to figure out how to respond to Cyrus.

"I'll put a pack together for you." He glanced at my wardrobe as if he could look beyond the closed doors and see that after I changed out of my ruined shirt, I wouldn't have a spare. It wasn't my fault my clothes kept getting ruined, but for any other alpha that wouldn't have mattered, and I swore to myself that once I'd made myself a valuable member of the pack, I'd pay Cyrus back. For everything.

I hugged myself tighter and tried to imagine how the wildness had felt rushing through me in a desperate attempt to keep me from getting any more submissive than I already was.

I'd liked feeling powerful, liked feeling as if I had control over my life.

I wanted that feeling back.

I wanted it to stay.

"Change your clothes and shoes," he said, his attention shifting to my feet and the sandals he'd given me when I'd first arrived in his realm. "And get back out there. They both need you, and I want Nova to give you a once over before we head out."

"So if I'm hurt you can order me to stay?" I huffed, the words slipping out on a sudden wave of frustration.

"No." He ran a hand through his hair, mussing it even more and releasing a heavy breath.

For a second, he looked as exhausted as I felt... and as heartbroken.

The urge to hold him, comfort him, and take comfort from his embrace as if he were one of my mates rose inside me like a great wave.

Both his brothers were in danger, and he, an alpha, had just humbled himself to the weakest shifter in existence. Not to mention he had someone running around town wielding a dangerous poison. He didn't just have his brothers or me to worry about. He had the whole pack.

Then his expression snapped back to serious and he stood, startling me and — much to my frustration — making me instinctively shrink back further up the bed.

"Knox and Bishop need you, and you need them," he said. "You're going with us. Whil said she wanted your help keeping Bishop stable, and you now know how to forage, find ideal firewood, and set up a safe fire. Having you along will be helpful."

His expression shifting into something I couldn't recognize, he inched closer as if he wanted to... I had no idea what. Touch me? Hold me?

But then he froze and the muscles in his jaw flexed. "We leave in less than two hours. Try to get some sleep if you can."

With that, he stormed out of my bedroom and, a moment later, I heard the door to my suite, the one leading into the hall and not outside, open and close.

I stared out my bedroom doorway into the sitting room, a heavy confusion swirling into the mix of all my other emotions.

What had just happened?

I was going to be helpful?

I must have hallucinated the whole conversation. I hadn't done anything right in Cyrus's eyes from the very beginning, and now I was going to be helpful?

Also, an alpha just apologized to me. Me! And that made strange, hopeful feelings warm around my heart.

I quickly showered off Bishop's blood, trying hard not to think about how I'd gotten it on me, changed my shirt and pants, replaced my sandals with my hiking boots, and headed back to the private patio outside my suite.

First things first: reassure Knox that I was holding it together. He'd been too caught up with his failing twin bond to register my sobbing breakdown the second I'd entered my suite or my emotions from my strange conversation with Cyrus, and I planned to keep it that way. He had more than enough to worry about.

After that, once we were on our way, I'd ask Whil about the magical block she'd cast on me to keep Sterling out of my head. I couldn't afford to be mistaken about the conversation with Cyrus and didn't want to risk having been manipulated.

Outside, Knox had shifted into his wolf form, the stress of Bishop being near death too much for him, but I could tell he was still himself. His wolf hadn't completely taken over, and he hadn't lost his mind, although I could sense both of them fighting to keep it together. Across from him, Nova was finishing up wrapping Bishop's wounds to keep them clean and Whil was gone, presumably at her cottage packing.

"Cyrus wanted me to give you a quick check," she said. "Now that your adrenaline has worn off, does anything hurt?"

I opened my mouth to say no but made myself pause. Whether the order had come from Cyrus or not, this was a genuine question and it was best to take it seriously just in case I was injured and it got worse halfway to the pool.

My hands hurt from where they'd been caught between Bishop's head and the ground as well as from gripping Bishop's shirt and dragging him down the road, and the rest of me was getting achier and achier by the second from dragging him as well as a full night of dancing. But it wasn't serious, not something worth wasting an elixir on.

My foot, however, hurt a lot more than my hands from when Bishop had convulsed and I'd dropped him.

I didn't think anything was broken, but it was best if Nova looked at it. That, and it would give her something to tell Cyrus when he inevitably asked her about me.

"I'm a little beat up," I told her, showing the bruises that were starting to form on the back of my hands, "but not too bad. My foot got the worst of it."

I took off my boot and more worry bled through my mating bond with Knox as he nudged my arm with his damp nose.

"I think it's just a bad bruise," I added, wrapping my arms around his neck and leaning my head against his.

His rich wood smoke scent enveloped me and the warmth of our bond wrapped around my heart, steadying my soul, while Nova studied my foot.

Please don't let it be broken. Please don't let this be the reason Cyrus refuses to let me go.

I didn't want to fight him again. I still felt shaky and exhausted from standing up to him. And while he'd said I was going and I'd be useful, a broken foot would change everything.

I'd challenge him again if I had to. I could feel that certainty deep in my soul. But then I'd also turn back into a shivering sobbing mess once I'd won.

Except I didn't believe I'd broken down the moment I'd stepped into my suite because I'd challenged Cyrus and was afraid of him. I'd broken down because it was all too much. Bishop had just told me he loved me and was now dying, and the roar of Knox's emotions, his rage and panic and desperation over the thought that he was losing his bonded twin, was threatening to drown me.

I'd been submerged under all that emotion once the adrenaline and wildness had rushed out of me, and it was a miracle I wasn't a sobbing ball of completely-messed-up buried between Knox and Bishop right now.

"It's just a nasty bruise," Nova confirmed, releasing my foot. She'd felt every bone and flexed every joint and now it was really throbbing. "It's starting to swell, so I've asked Eloise to bring you an ice pack. It's going to hurt while you walk for the next few days." Her gaze grew unfocused for a moment then she turned her attention back to me. "I've told Cyrus you need to ride in the cart with Bishop for the next two days. You barely weigh anything as it is, so he and Deacon won't notice you riding along."

"He and Deacon?" I asked, confused.

They'll be taking turns pulling the cart, Knox said.

"Ah." I didn't know what to say about that. It made sense, though. Knox would need to stay in contact with Bishop, and neither Whil nor I were strong enough to pull a cart with a full grown man in it. Also, Cyrus wasn't like my previous alpha... or at least he was somewhat different. He did manual labor and had done chores like everyone else when we'd travel north. It made sense that he'd take turns pulling the cart.

"You can do this, Audrey," Nova said.

She stood and gave me a soft smile as Eloise hurried around the flowering shrub that made the patio private, carrying an ice pack.

"By the Sisters!" she gasped, the sight of Bishop's bandaged body covered in horrible black and red veins making her stumble. Then her attention jumped to me. "Oh, child. He'll be alright. Nova and Whil are miracle workers. They'll save him. I'm sure of it."

She knelt and gently pressed the ice pack against my foot, making tears burn my eyes.

It was such a big thing for her to think of me while one of her pack alphas was gravely ill since no one ever thought of me. No one in my old pack would have cared that my heart was breaking, they'd have only been worried about Bishop.

Knox whined and sent confusion and reassuring love through our bond, not knowing how to take my sudden swell of emotions.

I sent love back to him. "I'm okay. Just—" I met Eloise's eyes. "Thank you."

"Come on, Eloise," Nova said. "They need their rest and we've got rations to make and pack."

"Right." Eloise offered me a smile just as soft and warm as Nova's, sending more warmth radiating around my heart.

Mine, whispered something inside me so quietly I could barely hear it. *My people. My pack. Mine.*

The voice had to have come from Knox because if I even had a wolf, she was buried so deep within me she was never waking up.

Although maybe... just maybe that wasn't completely true anymore.

KNOX

AUDREY SNUGGLED CLOSER TO ME, HELD THE ICE PACK AGAINST HER bruised foot, and passed out ten minutes later. She'd been amazing. A glorious, determined goddess standing up to Cyrus and asking for what she wanted.

I knew she had alpha power enough to tease mine, but I didn't expect it to be strong enough to fully challenge my brother. She hadn't backed down or looked away once, and I couldn't have been more proud of her and more furious that she felt she had to tear past the curse locking her wolf away to ensure she could stay with her mates.

And given the feelings coming from both Bishop and Audrey, they were mates already. They just needed the bond.

Cyrus had seen that truth even while his power had tried to get her to submit. I'd seen it in his eyes. There wasn't any other reason for Audrey, who'd become far too nervous around him while I was away on a hunt, to defy him. That kind of determination, and that kind of power, only manifested when a mating bond was in danger of being broken, and I'd felt that it hadn't just been our bond she was fighting for.

Which was good and a relief in a way. She'd just demonstrated that she was an extremely powerful female alpha which meant her heat fever might not just have been because we hadn't sealed our bond. Powerful females had powerful heats and often instinctively took multiple mates because of that.

Bishop was her second mate, but she'd probably need at least one more.

And somehow, that idea didn't piss off my wolf. It knew she needed more mates to keep her safe and it was good with anything that protected Audrey.

I shifted into my human form, my wolf having settled enough to allow the change now that Audrey was cuddled against us. I pulled her into my arms and settled against Bishop's side with Audrey between us, and the agony screaming through my twin bond eased a bit, our souls steadying him, reassuring him that we were doing everything in our power to save him.

This. This was how it was supposed to be.

Bishop had been so sure that we'd share a mate, but I hadn't believed him. I couldn't imagine any woman willing to put up with me and all my broken bits.

And yet, here she was, beautiful and kind and smart and perfect.

I'd never felt so comfortable in my human skin before and my wolf had never felt steadier. None of his primal wildness had vanished. In fact, it felt stronger, energized, as if Audrey physically strengthened us, but now all that power was focused on her, protecting her, cherishing her, loving her. Our mate.

She was the one we'd been waiting for our whole life. She was love. She was comfort.

She was home.

And when I found whoever had tried to kill her and poisoned Bishop, I was going to tear him limb from limb. I didn't care if it was a member of our pack or not. Bishop and Audrey were mine, and I protected what was mine.

Somehow, I managed to doze with her, waking when Deacon stepped onto the semi-private patio outside Audrey's suite.

"We're just about ready to go," he said softly, thankfully not waking Audrey since I could still feel her exhaustion radiating through our bond. "How's she holding up?"

My wolf grinned at his question. It meant, unlike some members of the pack, he'd accepted her. While I'd been skulking in the shadows at the festival, daring to get as close as possible to keep an eye on her, I'd heard whispers and seen the dark looks thrown at Bishop and Audrey when their backs were turned.

Not everyone was happy she was in the pack. Most didn't seem to care that she was my mate, but Bishop was another story. She wasn't good enough for him, wasn't strong enough.

If only they'd seen her challenge Cyrus. If only I could help her wolf fully wake.

But she was just as broken as I was and a lot more fragile. Whether she wanted to or not, she cared about other people, and that meant it hurt her when they were cruel to her. I didn't care. If you were an asshole then I ignored you. Hell, if you were a person, I mostly ignored you. But Audrey didn't want that. She wanted a pack. I think she even needed one to feel fulfilled in her life. She needed to help people.

Bishop was the mate who could give that to her. He could introduce her to the people who could help her satisfy that need.

"She might not look it." And she might not believe it. "But she's tough," I whispered back.

"Oh, I believe it. Did Nova tell the truth?" he asked. "Was she part of that alpha power battle that woke up the entire Residence?"

I stiffened at that. "Who else knows?"

"No one. Nova only told me. Everyone thinks it was you losing your shit over Bishop."

"So they know he's poisoned?" Fuck. Were they going to blame Audrey for that? I didn't understand how people reacted, but I knew people would look for someone to blame and at the moment Audrey was an easy target. She looked like prey in a whole town of predators.

"They knew there was trouble." Deacon's expression turned grim, something that looked so out of place on him it made me sit up, worry rushing through me.

Audrey groaned in her sleep, and I brushed my hand over her head, hoping to soothe her back to sleep. If the pack was blaming Audrey, I didn't want her to hear this conversation. She was already shaken up by the attack and by standing up to Cyrus... something that shouldn't have terrified her but did.

"Tell me," I growled. "Who do I need to protect my mate from?"

"Whoa." He raised his hands and crouched beside me. "Now's not the time to wolf out."

My wolf took over and deepened our growl. "Tell. Me. Why is Audrey afraid of Cyrus? Why did she feel she had to fight him to stay by my and Bishop's side?"

"Cyrus isn't who she has to worry about." Deacon sighed and rolled his eyes, his expression turning wry. "You know how he gets when he isn't in control of the situation."

I narrowed my eyes. I knew all too well that Cyrus would do anything, say anything to protect his pack, and I'd seen him growl at Audrey for the entire walk to the death god's temple. He'd been freaking out over the fact that she had no wilderness skills and that if we got separated, she'd die.

"What did he do?" My fury as well as my wolf's was starting to boil over, and Audrey, while still asleep, somehow knowing I was upset, rolled over and wrapped her arms around me.

My wolf huffed, the warmth of our connection and her love calming some of our anger. We couldn't go on a rampage, no matter how much we wanted to beat the shit out of Cyrus. That would leave Audrey unprotected.

"She really is something, isn't she?" Deacon sighed.

"Don't change the topic."

"Wasn't trying," he said. "Just amazed by your mate. Not even Bishop can calm you like that. She pulled you out of a near-feral state, you know."

"I remember."

"That scared the shit out of Cyrus." Deacon ran a hand over his face making me wonder if he'd gotten any sleep. Yesterday had been the first day of the festival, the day when everyone danced until dawn.

"I told him not to, but he lost his temper and yelled at her. I was already taking you up to the sacred grove so I don't know what he said to her, but she turned into a complete mouse, afraid of everyone and everything."

My wolf started growling again, and Audrey nuzzled closer, drawing in a deep breath of my scent, settling him again.

"Nova and I helped Bishop reassure her that she was safe, and I think she was starting to regain her confidence, at least with a few of us, but Finn and Velora are particularly suspicious of her and I suspect they've been spreading rumors." He sighed. "The fact that she was with Bishop when he was attacked—"

"When *she* was attacked," I corrected.

His eyes widened in shock. "She was the target? Fuck. Of course she was. No one has tried to hurt any of you in your life. Audrey is the only thing that's changed."

"I have to keep her safe," I told him. "I won't hesitate to protect her, but that could be bad for her." I could be thrown out of the pack.

If enough people told Cyrus I was dangerous, he'd have no choice but to throw me out or face who-knew-how-many challenges to his leadership. And that would mean Audrey would be packless with me.

Of course, I wonder what people would say if Bishop left the pack as well. Would they change their minds?

"Just point me in the right direction," Deacon said, his wolf rising to the surface and his enormous alpha power slipping out of his control for a second. "They'd never question my judgment when it comes to protecting the pack. And she *is* pack."

He stood, a wildness in his eyes I'd never seen before. He was always joking, always laughing, but when it came to Audrey, he was dead serious. My shy, gentle mate had won over a man who kept everyone at arm's length with a well-placed quip.

"The cart at the north gate is waiting for us. Cyrus sent our packs and supplies ahead so we just need to get there." His gaze dipped to Audrey. "Do you want to wake her, carry her, or have me carry her?"

AUDREY

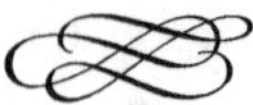

KNOX WOKE ME WITH A SOFT MENTAL NUDGE AND A KISS TO MY forehead. His wood smoke scent filled my senses first, warm and comforting, then I opened my eyes and fell into wolf-darkened orbs flecked with brilliant shards of green.

Mine. My mate.

Then everything came crashing back. The attack, Bishop being poisoned, and the sea of emotions threatening to drown me. My throat tightened even as I tried to control my emotions for Knox's sake.

"It's time to go," he said his voice gruff. But I knew he wasn't upset with me. Beneath the drowning sea of desperation and fear was his love for me.

We could do this. We could save Bishop. We *would* save Bishop.

"Right." I sat up and moved out of the way and put my boot back on as Deacon and Knox dressed Bishop in a shirt and pair of pants.

I wasn't sure when Deacon had arrived, but it made sense for someone to help Knox or in the very least someone to bring clothes since I doubted Knox could leave Bishop's side at the moment, even if he wanted to.

It also made sense that it wasn't Cyrus since he had to get

someone ready to take over running the pack while he was away, for which I was grateful. I still had no idea how to react to Cyrus after he'd apologized, and I still wasn't one hundred percent sure it hadn't been a stress-induced — or Sterling-induced — hallucination.

"Ready?" Deacon asked as he handed Knox this realm's equivalent of a kilt, something the huntmaster only ever wore. I'd never seen him in anything else and even though we'd had dinner a few times while Knox was away hunting for the pack, it was still a struggle not to ogle him.

How could I not? The man was built, each muscle mouth-wateringly defined, and the kilt put almost all of it on display. He also radiated a sharp feral quality and was constantly releasing a trickle of alpha power, unable to fully contain the force within him that was just as strong as Bishop, Knox, and possibly even Cyrus.

All of that equaled a magnetic pull that made it hard to look away... well hard if he hadn't been standing beside Knox.

Knox was a pull on my soul that I couldn't deny and didn't want to. It didn't matter that he was gorgeous, his body just as beautifully defined as Deacon's, his face the picture of a dark angel. I'd have loved him regardless of his stunning looks because he was mine, but having a handsome mate certainly didn't hurt.

Knox wrapped the kilt around his waist then pulled Bishop into his arms, easily lifting him.

"You good?" Deacon asked, turning his attention to me, the deep laugh lines around his eyes crinkling and his lips quirking as if he'd thought of something amusing but wasn't going to share with the class. "Need me to carry you?"

Knox groaned and glared at him, making Deacon chuckle and me feel like I'd missed part of a conversation.

"You know I had to offer," Deacon said with a shrug.

"You know she'd have asked for help if she wanted it," Knox huffed.

"*You* know she wouldn't," Deacon shot back.

"And you both know I'm standing right here," I cut in before the conversation continued as if I weren't around. "I'm fine for now, thank you," I told Deacon. "And I'll ask for help if I need it. I learned the first time after not mentioning my blisters."

Deacon cocked an eyebrow, drawing my attention to his golden brown eyes that were bright with curiosity. "Blisters?"

"She walked north until her feet bled and didn't tell anyone. Not even Bishop," Knox replied as we hurried away from my semi-private patio toward the Residence's gate and the town beyond.

My foot throbbed with every step, and I gritted my teeth, trying to keep my gait as even as possible while acknowledging the irony of the conversation. Knox and Bishop needed me to be strong and I couldn't afford for Cyrus to think I was too weak to travel with them even if he'd said I was going and had apologized for his earlier behavior.

He could still change his mind and I'd fight him again if I had to, but I'd rather not. Looking like I was going to be useful and not a burden was the best place to start.

"I was trying to not be a nuisance," I said, somehow finding myself half walking half jogging between Bishop and Deacon because of their much longer legs.

"And not trying to prove you could keep up with experienced hunters," Deacon chuckled, ruffling my hair as if I were an annoying little sister. "Sure you were."

"Hands off," Knox growled.

A possessive anger rushed through our bond, and his wolf fully darkened his eyes, taking over.

"You bet." Deacon took a step away and raised his hands. "But you know you're not the one in charge. She is."

"And if she wants you to touch her, she'll tell you," Knox's wolf snarled with a sharp glare before turning away from the main road and taking a dark, narrow alley even though the light was still the pre-dawn gray before the sunrise and the streets were empty.

Despite the lack of people around, I could still feel the tension building inside Knox, the one that screamed too close, too tight, not enough space and sky and air.

Of course, I had no idea if this was how he always felt walking through Stonehaven or if the current circumstances were exacerbating his claustrophobia. Which didn't really matter. He needed me to get through this just like I needed him.

I placed my hand against his arm and sent as much love as I could muster with my own emotions going crazy.

With a groan, he sucked in a deep breath, some of the tension melting away as I helped steady his soul, and we hurried forward, rushing down dark alley after dark alley, Deacon not saying a word about our route.

A moment later, we reached a main road leading up to a large square only fifty feet ahead where Cyrus, Whil, and Nova waited beside a cart big enough to fit Bishop and Knox and our supplies.

The cart was plain — no decoration or even a coat of paint — had four wheels so whoever was pulling didn't also have to hold up the front, and a push bar that had been wrapped in fabric to cushion the pusher's hands.

Someone had laid out a pile of blankets on the cart bed, and Knox laid Bishop on top of them. Just above Bishop's head were five travel packs, and two sturdier packs that were, without a doubt, waterproof and likely held Whil's books and supplies.

"Up you go, Audrey," Cyrus said his voice strange, still gruff but also strained as if he didn't know how to speak to me anymore.

He gestured to the cart without hesitation and a tension that had blended in with all the other things worrying me eased. I wasn't going to have to fight my instincts and work up the nerve to argue with him again.

"Stay off your foot for two days. Give it time to heal," Nova said as Whil climbed into the cart with me, and Knox stepped to the side and held Bishop's hand.

"The pack is yours and Lucius's," Cyrus said to Nova. He ducked under the cart's push bar and got into position while Deacon tossed his kilt into the cart and shifted into his large gray wolf. "Keep an ear on the rumor mill."

Nova gave him a knowing look and nodded her understanding.

If I hadn't been so worried about saving Bishop and keeping Knox sane, Cyrus's comment would have renewed my uncertainty about being accepted by the pack. Sure there'd been nice people at the festival, but there'd still been those who'd felt brave enough to give me dirty looks even while I was with Bishop. Which meant there were others who'd smiled at me because of Bishop but still didn't like me.

Which wasn't a problem to worry about. Not until we'd saved Bishop.

Nothing else would matter if he died.

AUDREY

We traveled all day, not stopping for lunch because Whil and I were the only ones who needed it and we ate in the cart. Bishop's convulsions started increasing in severity and frequency by mid-morning, and I helped Whil pour another elixir into his mouth and held him steady until I was sure he'd swallowed it.

Tension filled the air and Knox's worry churned with heavy dread inside me. It also didn't help that the road, while wide enough for two carts to pass side by side, was boxed in with rock walls that grew taller and taller the farther we went, adding his claustrophobia to his fear of losing his brother.

No one said anything until just before sunset when we reached a tall, wide but shallow cavern in the rock big enough for half a dozen carts to mostly stay under the shelter of the rock overhang and four or five more beyond it. At the back, protected from the elements on three sides sat a squat stone building with a metal door and two windows framed by metal shutters.

"This is our stop for the night," Cyrus said, pushing the cart halfway to the building and securing the front two wheels with a nifty locking system that involved the lock on the wheel and a wire running up to a locking handle built into the push bar.

Behind me, Deacon shifted back into his human form and shut a large metal gate, securing the enormous alcove from outside threats while Whil grabbed one of her waterproof packs and hopped off the back of the cart.

"This is a major road," she said, answering my unspoken question about why there was a house and a protected shelter beside the road when there wasn't anything or anyone else around. "There are three shelters along it before it comes out of the mountains."

I nodded my understanding and turned my attention back to the house. It was guaranteed shelter and it had a chimney, which meant not sleeping outside in the slightly cool summer night. And while it was easily twice as big as the patrol shed between Stonehaven and Anakar, nothing would be big enough for Knox the stay the entire night.

"Knox, Bishop, and I aren't staying in there," I said. It would tear Knox up having to fight his claustrophobia and his need to stay with his twin at the same time, and I wasn't going to allow that.

"Of course not," Cyrus said, pointing ten feet away to a scorched hole in the ground edged by fist-sized rocks. "We'll make camp here. Whil and Deacon can stay inside if they want."

"Nah," Deacon said at the same time Whil replied, "I'm staying with Bishop in case anything changes."

"Do you think something will?" I asked, suddenly not wanting to leave Bishop's side, not even to just hop off the cart despite knowing I needed to move so Knox could carry him closer to the fire pit to keep him from getting cold during the night.

Pushing past that urge, I shifted to the edge of the cart to hop off.

"Stop!" Cyrus barked with a snap of power.

My pulse lurched and my muscles twitched, his power freezing me in place and sending a blast of instinctual fear racing through my body.

I squeezed my eyes shut, fighting my reaction before Knox lost it.

Cyrus apologized... maybe. He's not going to hurt me. He's not Sterling.

But damn, none of that, no matter how logical, could break a lifetime of conditioning, and I couldn't completely get rid of my concern.

"Nova said to stay off your feet for two days," he said as he hurried to my side. His voice was almost as gruff as Knox's, and his power softly stuttered as if he were trying to hold it in but couldn't, not completely, giving me a sense that he wasn't angry with me.

Without warning, he picked me up, and our eyes locked, my plain brown to his deep, dark mossy green, and my breath caught in my throat.

The fantasy of him holding me as if I were precious and slowly pushing into me rushed through me, heating my cheeks, and for a second, the fantasy felt like so much more than just a dream. It felt real, like a memory I couldn't quite grasp, slipping between my mental fingers as I desperately tried to cling to it while that thing in my soul that said I could trust Cyrus, had *always* said I could trust him, fluttered, a barely-there warmth around my heart.

His eyes widened as if he felt it, too, and something pulled between us, some strange magnetic force that made me want to bury myself in his arms and wrap myself in his warm earthy scent.

It had to be the stress of the situation. My soul needed steadying, and I couldn't get that from Bishop or even Knox since my mates needed steadying more than I did. I was still wary of Cyrus... wasn't I? One apology that I wasn't even sure had happened didn't make up for terrifying me and then leaving me afraid of him for days. The only reason I'd connected with him in any way was because I was desperate for a stable, emotional foundation.

Which only made a part of me mourn the Cyrus I'd lost, the one who, when we were almost at the death god's temple, had encouraged me to think about my future. Even the one who, after the spell to break my bond with Knox failed, had tried to convince me that being mated to Knox wasn't the end of my world.

I wanted that Cyrus back.

Was that the real Cyrus or was the alpha who'd yelled at me in the arena been the real one?

His gaze dipped to my lips, turning my embarrassment at thinking about having sex with him into desire.

No! Bad, Audrey. I wasn't supposed to want that from Cyrus. He'd made it perfectly clear he didn't want me, and I was supposed to be happy with my strange fantasy despite that small, barely audible voice inside my head that said he was mine, too.

Stress. It was stress, God damn it.

I didn't trust him.

But it was just so hard to remember that, not with his strong arms around me and him looking at me with a confusing mix of emotions that I couldn't quite recognize but was certain none were anger or disgust.

Then he jerked his attention away, shattering the moment and leaving me strangely breathless while wondering if we'd really shared a moment or if it had all been in my head again.

He carried me to the fire pit, set me on the ground, and straightened, his stern in-control alpha mask firmly back in place.

"Deacon," he growled before clearing his throat and making his voice sound more human. "Get enough wood from the shelter so Audrey can start a fire then go out and collect more in the forest. I'll get us something to eat."

Deacon raised an eyebrow at Cyrus, his lips quirking, but I couldn't figure out what was so funny.

"I need the run," Cyrus added before turning his back to me, pulling off his shirt, and stepping out of his pants, giving me a spectacular view of his powerful muscles and his amazing ass before he melted into his massive black wolf.

Whil opened the metal gate for him and he ran out, while Deacon pulled a pack from the cart, handed it to me, and went into the house.

A minute later, Whil had the blankets from the cart on the ground for Bishop, a pile of a few more blankets for the rest of us, and Deacon had returned from the house with an armful of wood, all while I sat there and watched, feeling selfish for not helping.

Except Cyrus hadn't let me get off the cart by myself and I was sure neither Whil nor Deacon would let me get up and walk around.

And really, just thinking about moving made me exhausted. It didn't matter that I'd sat in the cart all day. I'd barely gotten any sleep last night, an hour if I was lucky, and trying to keep it together to help Knox keep it together was beyond tiring.

Inside I was a screaming crying mess, clinging to myself with my mental fingernails while Knox's emotions threatened to drown me, adding to my own fear and heartache and grief.

All I wanted was to hold Bishop tight and never let go. He was mine. He'd told me that he loved me and I hadn't gotten a chance to tell him back.

I wanted that chance. I wanted to stop being so selfish by demanding that he court me and just mate with him. We belonged together and there was a chance he wouldn't make it to the pool or that Whil's spell at the pool wouldn't work.

My throat tightened and tears burned my eyes, but I gritted my teeth and swallowed down my grief.

I had to stay strong and in control. Knox was counting on me. Through our bond, I could feel his grip on his human self weakening, and I could feel a fury that went beyond the most primal aspect of his wolf threatening to take over.

That was his true feral nature. It wasn't just his wolf, it went deeper, rooted in fear and a need to protect his human soul, whatever the cost, even if that meant burying his human half inside his wolf forever.

I didn't want Bishop to wake up to that, didn't want him to find his brother fully feral without anyone able to get him back.

I sent more love and confidence to Knox, knowing he could still feel all my worries but hoping that by showing him that I was being brave, he and his wolf could control his fear. Then I made a fire in the fire pit and used the starter in my pack to start it.

Deacon left through the gate and shut it behind him. The latch that could be opened from either side — if you had an opposable thumb — clicked into place and for a second there was nerve-racking silence only disturbed by the crackling fire.

"So," Whil said as she grabbed the second sturdy waterproof pack from the cart and sat beside me. "How are you doing?"

"I'm exhausted and sore."

Knox huffed, worry for me and not just Bishop swirling into the mix of emotions coming through the bond.

"Stay awake for dinner. You'll need your strength," he growled.

"I know," I told him.

I had no doubt that if I dozed off, Cyrus would use his power to wake me and make me eat, something I'd rather do on my own. But that thought didn't stop me from glancing at the blankets around Knox and Bishop and longing to just crawl under one and cling to my mates.

But food first!

I slapped my cheeks, forcing myself to stay awake and praying Cyrus caught something fast and it didn't take long to cook.

"From what you told me of your bond, it makes sense that you'd be exhausted," Whil said. "And I suspect it's not going to get much better."

"Swell."

"You should get Deacon or Cyrus to help you once we leave the road. I doubt you'll be able to keep Cyrus's pace all day." Whil huffed a soft laugh. "I'm not sure I'll be able to, either, but time is of the essence here."

As if to prove her point, Bishop groaned and his body went stiff, making my chest tighten. It wasn't a full blown convulsion, but it was the sign that the elixir was starting to wear off again.

Whil had explained the last time we'd given him an elixir that it was only a stopgap. All of its power was going toward slowing the poison, which meant it couldn't cure him — no amount of elixir would be able to remove it from his system — so there was no point in wasting an elixir by giving him more than one or two at a time. Even that wasn't enough to completely slow the poison down, which meant we were going to have to be giving him more elixirs closer and closer together so he could make it to the pool.

"Knox, help hold him," Whil said as she opened one of the packs, revealing that it was packed with elixir ampuls and lots of padding to ensure nothing broke.

Once Whil had given Bishop the elixir, we returned to an uncomfortable silence. It felt like everyone's worries were pressing down on me which made me acutely aware of my worry that Whil's block on the magical tether connecting me to Sterling had weakened. The last thing we needed right now was for me to go crazy.

"Whil." I shivered with a sudden chill and added another log to the fire. "After dinner, would you be able to check your block?" Because if she checked it now, I was guaranteed to pass out just like the other times she'd checked.

Knox stiffened at that. "You think that asshole might be influencing you?"

I squeezed his hand in reassurance. "I think I'm under a lot of stress and want to make sure the situation can't get worse."

"I checked it a few days ago and it was fine," Whil said. "But you're right. Better safe than sorry."

A few minutes later, Deacon returned with more firewood and Cyrus returned with a skinned and gutted animal the size of a large raccoon and a plucked and gutted bird the size of a chicken.

Just like when we'd been traveling north, I pretended our dinner hadn't been alive when Cyrus had caught it even though I knew it was silly and that I should have been used to it by now what with all the camping I'd already done.

On top of that, I was supposed to be a predator and I'd probably have no problems with killing an animal in wolf form. But unless a miracle happened, I'd never be a wolf, and I doubted I'd get over the idea of killing something.

Cyrus put the bird on the same collapsible spit we'd used the last time and Deacon set the firewood nearby then dropped his kilt — giving me an eyeful and making me hope the fire wasn't bright enough for everyone to see me blush. Then he shifted into his wolf and settled between Whil and Cyrus, resting his head in his paws and making me wonder if he was going to spend the night like that.

Which was a ridiculous thought. Why wouldn't he? His wolf was more comfortable in the elements, and he wouldn't need a blanket to keep the evening chill away... if there was much of a chill tonight. It was, after all, still summer and the temperature was still more or less comfortable.

Somehow, I managed to stay awake long enough to eat some dinner, then I snuggled in between Bishop and Knox and let Whil check the magical block in my head.

I knew I was supposed to close my eyes and just relax, but I couldn't stop looking at Bishop while she worked. He was so pale, his skin nearly white against the black and red veins covering his body. Sweat slicked his brow and his breathing was quick and shallow, which I supposed was better than convulsing and not breathing at all, but not by much.

The memory of dancing with him, of the joy and freedom, of having him whirl me around and around until I was breathless, clawed up to the front of my mind. Again, my throat tightened and tears burned my eyes. I tried, but this time I couldn't stop them from slowly leaking from my eyes.

He'd been so happy. The look in his eyes when he'd told me he loved me had stolen my breath, and he'd looked at me like I was amazing and beautiful, like I was the only woman in the world.

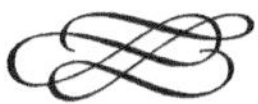

My eyes closed for a second, or at least I thought it was a second. But when I opened them, I was no longer snuggled between Knox and Bishop, I was in the middle of the Residence's sacred grove.

Groggy, I sat up.

How had I—?

Right.

A dream.

I just hadn't had a dream like this since before Knox and I had sealed our bond.

Of course, it wasn't quite the same. The grove was only a few trees deep and beyond was a shimmering white wall. I glanced around. The wall was everywhere, even above me, which meant I was in a dome. The dream world, unlike all my previous dreams, was only as big as the shimmering bubble.

That, however, was the only thing that had changed from my sexy dreams with Knox, and once again I wore my white transformation dress with my hair flowing loose around my shoulders and down my back.

Out of the corner of my eye, it looked blonder than it really was, with hints of shimmering gold when it was really just a drab dirty blond, and my skin was also brighter, as if I were summer fae and had a perpetual soft glow like Whil.

Rustling in the trees around me caught my attention, and I jerked my gaze away from my glowing skin, my heart racing. Having sexy times with Knox hadn't been the only thing that had happened in my dreams. Sterling had also invaded them, laughing at me, hurting me, convincing me I was worthless and an unwanted whore.

But instead of Sterling or Royce, Knox stepped into the grove—

No, not Knox. Bishop.

His expression was softer than Knox's and he didn't radiate that same amount of feral energy as his brother, so it had to be Bishop. And he looked healthy, no sign of the horrible discolored veins, his complexion warm and vibrant.

"Bishop!" I jumped to my feet and threw myself at him.

With a laugh, he caught me and spun me around, just like he had at the festival. And then just like the festival, he caught my lips in a searing kiss, making me feel his overwhelming love for me as if we were bonded like I was bonded with his brother.

It was so dazzling and wonderful, and so clearly a dream, that tears leaked from my eyes.

"Hey, beautiful," he murmured, pressing his forehead against mine and wiping my cheeks with his thumbs. "None of that."

"But you're dying, and I didn't get a chance to tell you that I love you." And I needed to. My heart would break if I didn't.

I leaned back so I could look into his warm brown eyes with their mesmerizing green flecks. He brushed a lock of hair away from my face, his expression gentle as if he knew how much I was hurting.

"I love you so much," I said.

I just wished I could tell him in person... not that I wasn't going to be able to tell him when Whil healed him because he'd survive this. He would. I just had to stay strong for a few days and then I could tell him and show him and do what I should have done with him from the beginning. Mate with him.

He'd shown me time and time again that he wanted to be my mate, but deep within me, I hadn't completely believed him, hadn't thought I could be worthy of the love from such an amazing, kind, generous man.

Maybe this Cinderella did have a prince... or rather two princes. They were night and day in their personalities but they were without a doubt mine.

"The moment you're awake, I'm telling you," I told dream-Bishop.

"You're telling me now." He cupped my cheek with his large hand and I leaned into his touch, savoring the heat from his body and the warmth that radiated around my heart from our shifter connection.

It had only been a day, and I already missed this physical connection with its sense of affection and certainty and protection.

"I'm just telling a dream." My throat tightened, despite my determination to stay strong. "You're a figment of my imagination and I haven't told you anything yet."

"Audrey," he said, my name on his lips teasing desire down my body from my head to my quickly heating core. "I don't think this is a dream."

"I'm pretty sure I'm dreaming." And now I was arguing with my subconscious.

"No, I mean, it *is* a dream, but not in the way you think." He squeezed my hand and a red low-back couch with thick plush cushions appeared beside him. "This is *my* dream."

"How can it be your dream?"

He pointed to the shimmering dome above us. "My consciousness retreated into my mind and created a bubble in my dream world to keep out the pain of the poison. If we were in your dream world, the bubble wouldn't be there. You're sharing my dream."

"I just want you back. That's why I'm dreaming this." It was the only explanation that made sense.

"You know that's not true." He sat, pulled me into his lap, and wrapped me in a warm, protective embrace. "Knox and I often share dreams, usually when he's hunting and beyond the reach of our twin bond. With you mate bonded with him, it doesn't surprise me that you're able to join us."

But then that would mean the wild sex with Knox that I'd

dreamed about when I'd first arrived in this realm hadn't just been my fantasy.

It had been Knox's as well.

Oh, no.

He'd known about us having wild dream sex. Hell, he'd started all of it as if he hadn't been able to control himself and he hadn't said a thing to me.

A branch cracked behind me, drawing my attention as Knox stormed into the grove. His eyes were dark and he radiated the same kind of barely contained energy he'd had in our previous dreams.

"Took you long enough," Bishop said, patting the seat beside him.

"We're on guard," he growled. "I don't want to be here." His gaze slid to mine, his expression turning hungry. "Mate."

With a snarl, he was on me, tangling his fingers in my hair and kissing me like I was his only source of oxygen. Heat erupted in my body, pooling between my thighs, and I was aching and ready in an instant.

My soul cried out for him, for his strength and our connection, and I grabbed the front of his pants and yanked on the tie holding them up, not caring that I was in Bishop's arms or that this was the real Knox in my dream—

Crap.

"You didn't tell me we were having shared dreams," I gasped trying to shove him away and failing.

"Would you have fucked him if you knew?" Knox— no, his wolf asked. "You. Are. Mine." He yanked on my hair, sending more pleasure rushing through me. "I wasn't giving you up because he was afraid. And I'm not stopping because you know the truth."

He dipped in and nipped my neck. Another bolt of pure lust soaked into my dress and I squirmed in Bishop's lap.

I wanted him. I wanted *both* of them, and my body didn't care I was supposed to be upset with Knox for lying through omission.

"Fuck, Audrey," Bishop hissed as he shifted his hips, his hard length digging into my thigh. "You like him like this?"

I opened my mouth to deny it but couldn't. Even if this was a dream, I was sure both of them could smell how turned on I was.

"Answer him," Knox barked, a burst of his power snapping into me and making my own dream power rise up and snap back. "Do you like when I take over his human body and fuck you senseless?"

I nodded, my voice gone and my mouth dry in anticipation.

"Tell him." Knox's wolf tightened his grip in my hair and shoved a hand inside the front of my dress. "Tell him."

"I do," I gasped.

He squeezed my breast adding another point of pressure verging on pain and my breath picked up with need.

"Tell him."

"I love it," I moaned. Because I did. I loved the wildness, the fierceness, and the passion.

When Knox's wolf fucked me in our dreams, I felt overwhelmed in the best way and yet also powerful. Powerful because I made this ferocious man wild with lust, and powerful because he brought out a ferociousness in me that I'd never had in real life.

Not before I'd yelled at Cyrus last night... hunh?

"And you're going to love it when *both* of your mates fuck you," Knox said, jerking my attention back to him.

Did I want to have sex with both of them?

My body quivered in anticipation.

Hell, yes I did.

AUDREY

I WANTED THEM BOTH IN THIS DREAM *AND* WHEN I WAS AWAKE. I wanted it all with them. Forever.

Mine, that small voice in my head growled.

Yes. They. Were.

I tore open the front of Knox's pants, something I could only do because this was a dream. His hard cock, thick and long, jutted proudly from his body and my mouth watered at the memory of taking him in my mouth in Whil's greenhouse library.

Somehow he'd known exactly what I'd wanted *and* what I'd needed to get past my insecurities. Of course, he'd already experienced me without any inhibitions in our shared dreams. He knew what I looked like when I ached for him and knew I loved it when he overwhelmed me.

I teased my fingers over his tip, dragging them through the precum gathering at his slit, then pumped my hand down his length.

He groaned, the sound long and low and growly, going straight to my core.

"Damn that's hot, beautiful," Bishop purred, his warm breath washing over my cheek and neck, teasing already hypersensitive nerves. "Can you make him come with just that?"

Knox huffed. "Maybe my human but not me. I'm saving it for when I'm buried in her hot pussy. But you—" He narrowed his eyes, capturing me in their bottomless dark depths. "You're denying your other mate. He wants to eat you out."

"He does, does he?" Bishop asked with a chuckle, even as his pupils dilated with desire.

Knox's wolf sneered back at him. "Don't you? All that dripping nectar going to waste? Unless you want to bury yourself in her. She doesn't need a warm up in our dreams." His sneer deepened and he tore my dress from my body. "And she'll come all night."

Bishop's gaze jumped to my breasts then sank lower to my curls and he drew in a deep breath. "I want to bury my face between your thighs, breathe in your scent, and make you come on my tongue."

His words sent the tremor of an orgasm racing through me. "Yes." *Please yes. God yes!*

The couch turned into a bed and Bishop fell back so he was lying down.

Knox, with his grip still in my hair, turned my head, forcing me to look at him. "Straddle his face." Then he gripped my hand around his cock, squeezing tight but not making it move. "And don't you dare stop."

I shifted so I straddled Bishop, and he grabbed my hips with his large hands and dragged me up his body. With a groan, he shoved his nose in my curls and breathed in my scent then released his breath, teasing my sensitive folds.

I shuddered at the sensation, my breath already ragged with anticipation.

"Audrey," Knox growled with a tug on my hair, and I realized I wasn't moving my hand.

Damn. This multiple partners thing was harder than I anticipated and we'd barely begun.

Somehow, I managed to heave my attention away from Bishop still just teasing me with his breath, and slowly dragged my hand up to Knox's tip, dampen it with more precum then pumped back down. Hard.

"That's it," he purred, his voice rumbling low in his chest. "Don't stop."

"Yes—"

Bishop teased his tongue through my folds and I forgot what I was going to say.

Sensation flooded me, his tongue teasing and licking and dipping inside me. My thighs burned with the effort to hold myself up and not suffocate him, and Knox's hard length somehow grew harder and bigger with each stroke of my hand.

I tried to keep my hand moving, but couldn't maintain my concentration, not with the tingling heat building in my core.

"Mate." Knox's wolf tugged on my hair and a shiver, not quite an orgasm, but heading in that direction, teased and tormented me.

I heaved my attention to him, but Bishop flicked his tongue against my clit and my thoughts scattered.

Oh, fuck.

My eyes rolled back as I reached the precipice. But instead of taking me over the edge, Bishop drew back and the feeling slipped away, making me whine in disappointment.

"Mate," Knox growled.

I dragged myself back to him and he captured my jaw, forcing me to look at him.

"You keep stopping," he snarled. "Open up."

My pulse lurched then leaped into a wild tattoo and I eagerly opened. The bed magically shrank, getting lower into the perfect position, and Knox smeared his precum over my lips with a teasing slide of his tip.

Before I could lick it away, he yanked on my hair, angling my head back as far as it would go, and held my chin in place, forcing me open.

With a snarl, he plunged inside with a thrust more powerful than any he'd made the other night. His cock hit the back of my throat then went deeper, blocking my breath for a nerve-racking, thrilling second before he jerked out.

Wild desire burned in his eyes and his canines extended.

"Audrey?" Bishop asked, brushing a finger across my cheek. "Are you okay with this?"

I nodded and Knox slapped his cock against my lips.

"Use words," he commanded. "Do you want me to fuck your mouth in a way that can only happen here? Do you want us to make you see stars?"

"Yes," I moaned, and Knox plunged back into my mouth while Bishop continued to tease me with his tongue, bringing me to the edge again and again but not letting me fall over.

I gasped and moaned, unable to concentrate on anything except the desire building inside me, grateful that all I had to do was let go and let the guys bring me pleasure.

A small part of me, the part that was raised in the mortal realm that was shy about sex and nudity, wondered if I should be feeling used, especially by Knox who was fucking my throat with a wild fury that made it nearly impossible to catch my breath and had tears spilling from my eyes and drool leaking from my mouth.

But it felt too good. I could feel Knox's wild passion even though the emotions from our bond were muted in this dream world. I could also feel his power rising, teasing and taunting mine into a ferocious dance of longing and lust.

I did that. *I* made him wild and hungry.

He wanted me so much, desired me so deeply, that he couldn't hold himself back.

Then Bishop flicked his tongue on my clit, heaving my attention back to him. He wasn't as wild, the human half of his soul still in control, but I could feel an intensity radiating from him, more powerful than any I'd felt before.

He wanted me just as much as Knox did. But where Knox lost control, Bishop took it, possessing my body, refusing to let me come until he decided I could.

"Mate," Knox snarled, his eyes completely black, his power crackling over my skin. "Fuck."

He jerked out of my mouth and Bishop shoved two fingers inside me and sucked on my clit.

Fireworks exploded inside me, stealing my breath and sending bone-melting bliss racing into every cell in my body. The world went bright white, and I spun around and around and then found myself face down on the bed.

A slightly out-of-focus Bishop aimed a wolfish grin at me as strong hands seized my hips and jerked me up to my knees.

"Scream for me, Audrey," Knox growled, plunging his hard-as-steel thick cock inside me with a powerful stroke.

He bottomed out, the impact driving me into the bed, knocking the air from my lungs, and sending the tremor of another climax tingling up my spine.

"Who's your mate?"

My eyes rolled back with pleasure. I didn't know why it turned me on so much when Knox fucked me like a maniac and demanded I name him my mate.

In real life, I didn't want to submit to him or anyone even though my instincts kept me doing it. I'd spent too much time living in fear and cowering, but in this dream world — and while I was awake, if I was being honest with myself — I wanted to submit to Knox during sex. I wanted all his ferocious power and desire claiming me as his, wanted his strength and wild power protecting me. Wanted to always be his.

"Who." He slammed into me again. "Is." Another thrust that had me seeing stars and my core tightening in anticipation. "Your. Mate?"

"You," I gasped, power roaring up inside me, whirling around and through Knox's in a wild primal dance not of dominance or submission but of lust and competition between equals.

"Who?" His pace turned wild and he reached around and rubbed violent circles against my clit, lighting me up, driving my need higher and higher.

Oh, God.

The pleasure that had roared back to life the second he'd thrust into me tightened, lighting up every nerve in my body and the precipice was suddenly there. Right there.

Then, with another thrust, I careened over the edge.

"You," I screamed. "You are, Knox."

With a roar, he slammed home, wrapped his body around mine, and sank his teeth into my shoulder. His muscles jerked with the force of his release and he filled me with hot jets of cum and power and light and oh!

Stars snapped behind my lids and again I was whirling, glowing, floating on a consuming bliss that stole all sight and sound, leaving me with only amazing sensation.

AUDREY

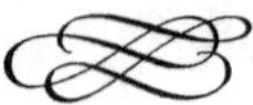

THIS TIME, WHEN I CAME TO, I WAS STILL LYING FACE DOWN ON THE mattress and looking into Bishop's warm brown eyes. Knox was still buried inside me, his tongue laving the wound he'd made in my shoulder and his body still vibrating with power.

"Hi," Bishop said, and he brushed a lock of sweaty hair from my forehead. Lust still filled his eyes, but it was softened with a breath-taking love.

My heart swelled, the warmth I felt when I was with him building, filling me with certainty. Just like wild Knox with his even wilder wolf was mine, so, too, was gentle, generous Bishop.

"Kiss me," I told him.

Knox nuzzled my neck then pulled out and helped me roll over and lie on my back while keeping a hand on my stomach.

Bishop didn't seem to care that Knox was still touching me. He settled himself over me, holding himself up on his elbows and dipping close until our foreheads touched, creating a private cocoon for just the two of us.

"As my mate commands," he said, his voice soft and reverent, and he slowly pressed his lips against mine.

Warmth billowed around my heart and seeped outward, sinking deep into every nerve, fiber, and cell in my body.

Home.

This was home. Everything about Bishop reassured me that I was finally safe, finally loved, finally home.

Knox was my freedom, my primal wildness that only appeared in my dreams, and Bishop was my shelter in the storm.

"You're so amazing, Audrey," Bishop murmured against my lips. "So beautiful and determined and brave. I knew the minute I saw you that you were special. I love you so much."

"I love you, too," I said, my eyes burning with tears. I'd waited my whole life for someone to say those words to me and I never wanted to let him go. I wanted to stay in this dream forever, making love to Bishop and Knox.

But that wouldn't help save him. If I didn't wake up, it would only make things more complicated and I *had* to save him.

"Hey," he said, nuzzling my cheek as if he could sense my shift of emotions. "It's okay. We can just cuddle for the rest of the dream."

"No." Never. I wanted him closer, *needed* him closer. The compulsion surged within me, and I tangled my fingers in his hair and drew him down so I could kiss him again.

"I want you to make love to me," I told him. I wanted the awe and tenderness from our first time together.

"Always," he whispered, his expression filled with a soul-deep affection. "Forever."

He captured my lips in a passionate kiss and slowly pushed inside me, drawing out my aching yearning until finally — finally! — he was deep inside me.

Our shifter connection deepened and for a second, I felt as connected with him as I did with Knox when I was awake.

Then he started to move, a slow slide out and a just as slow push back in. Each stroke dragged against my hypersensitive channel, rebuilding the heat he'd ignited with his tongue before Knox had made me see stars and sinking it deep inside me, strengthening our connection.

In and out.

Slow and steady.

Driving me higher and higher, making me breathless with anticipation.

"Bishop," I moaned, my hips bucking into his thrust, desperate for more friction.

My core ached with a deep thrumming desire, my whole body tense with the buildup of his sensual strokes despite his agonizingly slow pace.

"So beautiful," Bishop said, sitting back and grabbing my hips to hold me still, taking full control of my pleasure. "Let me make you feel good."

He withdrew to just the tip, and my inner muscles fluttered with his withdrawal, needing him back inside me, filling me. Then he thrust back in, a little harder than before, sending desire shivering through me.

A moan escaped my lips and my eyes rolled back as I gave in to him. I focused on where our bodies connected, on the sensual thrusts igniting every nerve in my core and the warmth around my heart.

The wildness I sometimes had in these dreams lazily rose from deep within me and Bishop matched it. Our dream-powers caressed and entwined in a slow primal dance. It filled my senses with everything that was Bishop, power and affection and comfort.

"Sisters, Audrey," Bishop groaned, his pace picking up, his control starting to slip.

I dragged my eyes open and met his gaze, falling into a bottomless brown warmth filled with green stars. I could feel his desire on the edge of breaking free of his hold as well as his love and pride and awe.

The feelings astounded me. People didn't feel things like that for me. I was weak. I couldn't shift. I could only dream that someone as powerful and handsome as Bishop would want to be with me.

But it wasn't just a dream. He wanted me in real life. It wasn't a trick and I wasn't imagining it.

He wanted me and he was *mine*.

The thought made my soul sing and my power billowed stronger, igniting around my heart and rushing into every part of my body.

God, I loved this man. I loved him with the very depths of my soul.

He pumped harder and faster into me, and my desire spiraled higher.

"Yes, Bishop," I moaned. *Yes yes yes.*

His hips jerked, and his rhythm stuttered as he struggled to maintain his pace. The brown warmth of his gaze darkened as his wolf rose to the surface and the feelings rushing between us turned molten, everything else forgotten. All that remained was our overwhelming need.

An inferno roared around my heart and my muscles shook. I squirmed in his grip, unable to control myself, desperate to buck up to meet him, and couldn't catch my breath. Our dream-powers writhed, swirling faster and faster, building higher and higher, and I couldn't look away from him.

I was on fire, desperate for a release and yet desperate to hold on as long as possible even as the pressure threatened to burn me up.

And then he rubbed my clit and pleasure exploded through my body.

Oh, God.

He roared his own release and every muscle in my body contracted, locking us together and capturing me in a blazing inferno of bliss. The pleasure spun me around and around, green stars flashing across my vision, and a deep booming gong roared through me.

It dragged my essence into its consuming reverberations and brilliant golden light surrounded us. I fell deeper and deeper into his eyes, his soul, his very essence, spinning around and around, our powers— No, our souls, merging into a blazing golden tapestry.

Mine.

The tapestry flared, locking into place and connecting my soul to Bishop's.

Yes, yours. Always.

CYRUS

AUDREY WOKE WITH A SHARP GASP, JERKED UPRIGHT, AND PRESSED HER hands over her heart, her eyes wide.

"Audrey." I scrambled to my feet to get to her on the other side of the campfire. I didn't know what had shocked her awake — probably a bad dream — all I knew was that I had to reassure her. Her other mates were still unconscious which meant it was up to me—

My thoughts stuttered at that.

Not *other* mates.

That would imply I was also her mate.

Her mates were still asleep. She only had two.

Whil sat up as well, though not nearly as quick to react as me. Still, she was closer. She'd been dozing close to the three of them since she and I had given Bishop his late-night dose of elixir. I should let her comfort Audrey or whatever the hell she needed.

But my wolf was determined and there was no way I was going to be able to fight the compulsion.

"Oh, my," Whil gasped as she squinted at Audrey with her head cocked to the side.

"Oh my, what?" I asked as I reached for Audrey. "Audrey, what?"

So far neither Audrey nor Whil looked upset, suggesting nothing horrible had happened to Bishop, but still— They were both stunned.

"Audrey," I pressed, capturing her chin with my fingers and forcing her to look at me, my pulse racing. Was she hurt and too stunned to register it or had something else happened? "What?"

"I..." Myriad emotions flashed across her expression: confusion, longing, shock before setting on nervous and she pulled away from my touch.

My wolf snarled at the loss of contact, especially because it looked like she was afraid of us, but I managed to stay where I was and crossed my arms so I wouldn't touch her again.

But then I realized that made me look angry at her.

I dropped my arms to my side but that didn't feel right, either.

Fuck. How was Bishop always so relaxed around her? If I was courting her, I'd be holding her tight and never letting her go, which of course, would only piss her off and damage her grown confidence and desire for independence.

Fuck fuck fuck.

"I suppose I shouldn't be surprised," Whil said.

"Surprised about what!" I barked, my power snapping out of my control and waking Knox and Deacon who both tensed, ready for danger.

I hated surprises. I couldn't protect her if there was something I didn't know. Everything within me screamed that I needed to fix whatever had happened. Now now now.

Whil flashed me a bittersweet smile. "She just mate bonded with Bishop."

"She—" I wrenched my attention back to Audrey, who was shrinking in on herself before Knox wrapped his arms around her and tugged her close. "You—"

How could she have mate bonded with him? He wasn't even conscious and I'd been on watch for the second half of the night. I would have noticed if Bishop had woken up.

Well, if I hadn't believed in fated mates before, I do now," Deacon said in my head, his wolf chuffing with wolfy laughter.

"That's impossible," I spat out, still stunned.

Shit. I hadn't meant to say that.

Just because we thought her mating bond with Knox formed because of her incomplete bond didn't mean that was what really happened.

In fact, she'd already proven that deep down, locked away — possibly for good — were strong alpha powers. She was an alpha, and that could mean with the curse she had all of the downsides and none of the advantages. She could have mate bonded with Knox and Bishop because she needed to. At her power level, she'd need three mates at the minimum to get her through a heat without her developing a fever.

Except bonding with Bishop now was a disaster. She was in even more danger than before and there wasn't anything I could do about it.

"I didn't mean to," she said, her voice soft but her spine straightening. "But I don't regret it."

"Of course you meant it," Knox growled, glaring at me. "You and Bishop are meant to be mates."

"But if we can't save Bishop, you'll die," I snapped.

"I'll keep her safe," Knox snarled back.

"You'll be fucking insane!" More of my power stuttered out of control and Audrey winced but didn't shrink in on herself like before.

Fuck. I hadn't meant to say any of that, either.

Sisters, I needed to stop talking. I'd been certain their bond had already been forming when she'd stood her ground and somehow awakened her alpha power to defy me and stay by his side. I should have expected that she wouldn't need the formal declaration to awaken the magic in a shifter's soul that created mating bonds.

Why the hell was I freaking out about it?

But the thought of losing my brothers *and* Audrey made my heart race. Yes, I was determined to save Bishop, but I couldn't guarantee it. Not everything was in my control — no matter how hard I tried to control everything.

Hell, at the moment, it looked like any control I possessed was pure fantasy.

"It still needs to be sealed," Whil said to Audrey. "But we're only four or five days away from the pool. I'd suggest waiting until we're back in Stonehaven and have more privacy, but that's probably not reasonable with how your incomplete bond with Knox set off your heat."

Audrey's eyes widened and her breath picked up as panic tightened her expression. "You mean I could go into heat again even though it's only been about three weeks since my last one and I'm not supposed to have my next one for another five months?"

"A strong mating bond can set off an early heat," Whil said, not easing any of Audrey's fears.

My pulse lurched. I couldn't let her go into heat again in the middle of nowhere. Sure, she wouldn't put off dealing with it like the last time, but the chances of her having heat fever again with her alpha power level and only one conscious mate, me, and Deacon to help were too high — since non-bonded mates weren't as effective at keeping the heat fever at bay.

Everything that could go wrong with Audrey had, and she could still end up in the same dangerous situation she'd been in with her first heat because of her incomplete bond with Bishop.

And fuck me, the signs of her heat had started showing her first night in Stonehaven, two days after we'd found her. With her luck, it would hit just as fast and harder now.

Fear squeezed around my heart. If Bishop died, she wouldn't be able to seal her bond. Would she end up stuck in a heat fever until it killed her?

"Bishop and I will get you through it," Knox reassured her, nuzzling her neck in an attempt to get her to relax.

Except that was only if her heat didn't start until after we reached the pool and if Bishop survived.

But you can help, my wolf snarled at me. *Like you did last time.*

Still a terrible option, I huffed back. *We're not going to be able to walk away from her and that makes her a target. We can't be with her until the pack can see her for who she really is.*

And then?

The memory of being captured in her gaze when I'd lifted her out of the cast last night flashed through me. She'd been so soft and warm, and her sweet scent had enveloped me, seeping into my soul. The urge to kiss her had been overwhelming and it hadn't just come from my wolf. *I* wanted to wrap myself around her, plunge inside her, and bind my soul to hers.

She was mine. She'd always be mine.

I just needed to be patient and wait for my pack to fall in love with her, too. Then I'd be free to court her.

Except I was a disaster at courting women. I didn't know what to say and my responsibilities to the pack took up a lot of my time.

But even that thought couldn't snuff out the tiny spark that had ignited in my soul at the idea that one day Audrey could be my mate.

I ached for her smile, her caress... her everything, and I'd been torturing myself by trying to make her hate me while keeping my distance from her.

It had taken everything within me to not look at her or stand close to her when I'd shown her to the community center for Nova's first aid class the other day, and my control had slipped when I'd had to ensure the room was safe for her.

I hadn't been happy that Danica and her followers were in the class but knew Zavier and Quinn would protect Audrey. Micah and Hazel wouldn't have been as aggressive in Audrey's defense as Zavier or even Quinn, but they, too, would have stood up for her.

I wasn't going to last until everyone in my pack had gotten their heads out of their asses. Except I had to, especially if it had been a member of my pack who'd tried to murder Audrey... a thought that made me furious and one I really didn't want to accept.

I couldn't believe that anyone in my pack was capable of murdering the mate of one of their alphas. They had to know Knox would go feral and we'd never get him back if Audrey died. Not to mention if Knox lost it, there was a chance Bishop would lose it, too.

Were there members who were so disgruntled with our leadership that they wanted to destroy us?

If so, they had to be serious in their hate, enough to get an extremely rare magic poison.

Was it one person? More?

I shoved those thoughts aside. So far there was no proof the man who'd attacked Audrey and Bishop had been a pack member, and there was nothing I could do about it right now. I had to get Bishop to the pool and save him then pretend to not know when he and Audrey sealed their bond and not be jealous about it. Which was another impossibility I doubted I'd be able to control.

When we got back, I'd ensure Audrey was safe, even if I had to be by her side all day every day... except that could only happen if she didn't go into heat and if Bishop survived and sealed their bond.

AUDREY

CYRUS'S EXPRESSION TURNED HARD, AND A WAVE OF HIS POWER ROLLED over me, squeezing my chest and compelling me to submit. But I ground my teeth together and resisted everything within me screaming to make myself small and get as close to Knox as possible.

Cyrus had apologized for saying those horrible things to me and Whil had confirmed her magic was still keeping Sterling out of my head. Which meant my instinct that I could trust him came from within me.

And so did that damn fantasy that I couldn't get out of my head.

It had flared to life the moment Whil had mentioned the possibility of another heat, and I tried to shove it out of my mind, but it was stuck there, on replay. Cyrus holding me like I was precious as he pushed inside me. Kissing me like he cared for me.

Damn it. I shouldn't be thinking of Cyrus. I should be thinking of my mate— *mates.* That shared dream had been so hot, my cheeks were flaming with embarrassment. Knox had taken me like he always had in our dreams, wild and ferocious, claiming my body like no one else could. And then Bishop—

God, Bishop. He was so sweet and sensual. Sex with him had been the complete opposite of Knox but just as sexy. It made my heart swell with love, and I felt our new impossible bond pulsing with warmth and spikes of pain.

Somehow, the connection we'd made in our dream, the overwhelming sense of belonging and claiming, was real.

But that wasn't possible. It had just been a hot as hell dream. Even if we'd said the vows to each other, a bond shouldn't have formed because we'd been asleep.

Of course, my bond with Knox shouldn't have been possible, either.

And yet I'd known the moment Bishop had been hurt that I couldn't live without him, that something inside me would shatter and I wouldn't be able to recover.

Had that compulsion been our bond? Had it already started to form before we'd been attacked? And how the hell had I done it without saying the words or even being conscious?

And it had to be me. I was the only common denominator between bonding with Knox and bonding with Bishop.

Did that mean my soul would randomly bond with anyone?

Cyrus sat back on his heels and pulled back his power. His expression was still hard, his gaze unfocused as if he were thinking about something serious. But despite that, my memories of the dream jumped back to my fantasy of him.

A shiver swept down my spine. Would whatever was broken inside me bond with anyone I was attracted to?

I couldn't let that happen. I couldn't accidentally mate bond with Cyrus. He'd despise me for the rest of our lives, and it wouldn't matter if the bond was supposed to make him fall in love with me or not.

He'd made it perfectly clear he didn't want me, and even if he'd apologized, that didn't mean he was suddenly in love with me... or that he even wanted to be my friend.

Congratulations, Deacon said in my head from where he sat on the other side of the campfire, still in his wolf form. *Bishop will be ecstatic with how your bond formed. Now no one can deny that you're meant to be together.*

"Oh, I'm sure someone will complain," Cyrus replied, indicating that Deacon had spoken to everyone and not just me.

The muscle in Cyrus's jaw flexed and he ran his hands through his mussed hair. The braid running from the top of his head to the nape of his neck had almost completely fallen apart and most of his hair hung loose in silky brown waves that would make any girl jealous.

"I have no doubt someone will accuse her of having unnatural magic and that she imprisoned Bishop in a bond against his will," he added.

"Of course they would," I groaned. People were assholes and I'd just taken the pack's most eligible bachelor off the market.

Which only firmed my determination that there was no way in hell I was going to risk accidentally bonding with Cyrus.

Knox's emotions churned stronger through the bond, his anger rising to the surface as he battled to stay in control of himself and not let the feral nature of his wolf take over.

"I won't let them hurt you," he— no, his wolf snarled. "I'll challenge anyone who says you and Bishop aren't fated for each other. They might have forgotten that I'm their alpha, but I am. They won't disrespect what's mine."

"And I won't stop you," Cyrus replied, a strange look flashing in his eyes before disappearing behind his usual hard mask. "But before we do that, we need to make sure Bishop lives." He glanced at the sky that was now just starting to lighten with dawn. "Let's have breakfast and head out. I want to get to the next shelter early so we're well rested for the days after. The remaining days won't be easy."

With that, he grabbed the water bucket and headed to the house while Deacon shifted into his human form and gave me an eyeful before putting on his kilt and following him.

Whil grabbed our travel pot, which sat close to the fire with last night's leftovers, and got to work preparing breakfast.

I glanced around, looking for something to do so I wouldn't be useless even though my soul screamed to stay with Bishop and Knox and steady our souls.

Knox tightened his grip and buried his nose in my neck, drawing in my scent, and a violent flash of panic crashed through our bond, threatening to drag me under. He must have noticed my uncertainty about staying where I was or proving myself to Cyrus and the thought had shattered his control.

"I need you with me," he rumbled, his grip crushing me against his chest.

"It's okay," I gasped, trying to focus on pushing love and certainty to him, but a spike of Bishop's pain shot through our bond and I lost my concentration.

Knox growled, the sound low and dangerous, making Whil's eyes widen.

"I'm not going anywhere."

Concentrate. Push it out. Block it off. Something.

Incomplete thoughts whirled through me. Knox's fear and determination and love had had me clinging to myself and holding myself together when Bishop had been hurt, but add in Bishop's pain and it was too much.

"Knox," Whil said and my mate's gaze snapped to her. "She's got two bonds now. She's feeling what you're feeling from Bishop *and* all your emotions."

"Fuck," he snarled, and the whirlpool drowning me pulled back just enough to let me catch my breath. "I'm sorry, Audrey. I'm sorry." He relaxed his grip around me and nuzzled my neck in an attempt to soothe me. "It's just so hard. My wolf is freaking out. *I'm* freaking out."

"I know," I murmured back. "It'll be okay. We just need to hang on for a few more days and Bishop will be safe."

AUDREY

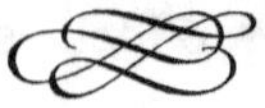

WE ATE BREAKFAST, CLEANED UP OUR CAMPSITE FOR THE NEXT travelers, and repacked our travel packs. Once again, Cyrus wouldn't let me walk — even to go to the bathroom in the house at the back of the shelter, and I had to sneak a moment when his back was turned to stand on my bruised foot to see how it was doing.

It was still achy, but not nearly as bad as yesterday morning. Although I had no doubt it wouldn't be happy hiking for three or four days. Perhaps it would feel better tomorrow morning after another full day of being off it.

Cyrus opened the heavy gate protecting the shelter from monsters, and we got into our traveling positions with me, Whil, and Bishop in the cart, and Knox walking beside us, holding Bishop's hand. Much to my surprise, Cyrus took the job of scouting ahead and looking for trouble in his wolf form, leaving Deacon to push the cart.

I'd have thought Cyrus would have wanted to leave the scouting to his huntmaster and stay with his brothers like he had for most of yesterday, but I wasn't going to complain. He probably had a lot on his mind, and I was still concerned about how upset he'd gotten when he learned I'd unconsciously formed another mating bond with one of his brothers.

If he wasn't near me, he couldn't yell at me and add to the stress I was already drowning under, and I couldn't accidentally mate bond with him.

Of course, he wasn't going to stay away forever, and I was going to have to figure out what to do about that.

I turned my attention to Bishop and swept a lock of hair away from his sweaty forehead, refocusing my thoughts on him. His complexion was ghostly and tinged with gray, not a good sign, and the ugly black and red veins covering his body had thickened while we'd been asleep.

My heart thudded hard, the weight of everything crushing inside my chest.

I *was* going to save him. I'd walk until my feet bled to get to the pool as quickly as possible because he was mine. My mate. He'd always been mine and always would be and I knew, even if he was unconscious, that he wanted to be my mate. He'd told me before we bonded that he loved me and again during our sexy shared dream.

The thought made my heart sing. I wasn't worried about figuring out our relationship — although we were still going to have to figure a few things out. There wasn't any resistance with Bishop. Not like there'd been with Knox. The biggest complication was going to be balancing my time between him and Knox, since there were situations where Knox wouldn't be able to be with us.

Of course, that only mattered if we got Bishop to the pool in time and Whil could magically pull the poison out of him.

"He's strong," Whil said as if she could read my thoughts when she was probably just seeing all my fears written on my face. "He'll make it."

"He will," I replied. He had to.

But the nagging voice of fear inside me, the one made stronger with the flood of Knox's emotions, worried that he wouldn't make it.

He'd said the shimmer surrounding the dream-grove had been his subconscious holding back the pain, but I'd seen thick black cracks in it just before I'd woken up. That mental protection was going to shatter and then he'd be in agony, even while he was unconscious.

Although maybe that had just been my imagination. I'd just had the most amazing dream sex and felt so connected with him that I'd somehow created a real mating bond between us.

Maybe seeing those cracks was my dream mind showing me a glimpse of my deepest fear because I was unable to truly trust my happiness. People didn't treat me the way Bishop did. I was weak and pathetic and—

No.

I lay down and snuggled against Bishop, suddenly needing all the physical contact I could get to strengthen our shifter connection and to push out those horrible thoughts that had been with me all my life.

The thoughts weren't true. Bishop wasn't the only one who was kind to me. Knox was kind, but it had taken him a while to get there so he didn't count. But Eloise and Kira and Zavier and Quinn had been kind from the moment they'd met me. So had Whil, Nova, and Deacon.

There wasn't something fundamentally wrong with me even though I couldn't shift. There was something fundamentally wrong with my old pack, especially my old alpha, his son, and their friends.

Everyone else in the pack I might be able to excuse for their lack of kindness and support because they were afraid. But the others had no excuse. They were cruel because they were horrible, heartless people.

I could see that now.

Bishop and the others had shown me time and again that I was more than what Merrick and Sterling had said I was and that there were people out there who we kind and caring even to strangers.

Perhaps other things were a lie, too.

Perhaps I *could* trust my happiness. Or rather the happiness I'd have once we saved Bishop.

At lunch, we stopped long enough for everyone to eat some rations and for Deacon and Cyrus to switch duties.

Thankfully, I hadn't been watching when Deacon yanked off his kilt and shifted or when Cyrus shifted into his human form and pulled on his clothes. It was safer if I only ogled my mates. Two was good enough for me. It was two more than I ever expected I'd have.

Cyrus stepped close and grabbed the cart's handles, his power stuttering in and out of his control, sending shocking zaps rushing through my body and drawing my attention.

Knox grunted, but he wasn't in any position to complain about his brother's lack of control. His power was a constant, grating vibration against my skin, and even if I hadn't been able to sense the turmoil raging inside him, I would have known keeping it contained to a low steady stream was the best he could manage.

"Hey." I sat up and wrapped my hands around his hand that still clutched tightly to Bishop's and tried to focus on steadying his soul by pushing strength and love through our bond.

We traveled all day, needing to give Bishop six elixirs to stop his convulsions, which was two more than yesterday, and reached the roadside shelter late in the afternoon.

It had a similar construction to the first one with a heavy iron gate, a wide open area scattered with the stone circles indicating fire pits as well as a rocky overhang protecting half the space. At the back was another squat stone building with a metal door and two windows framed by metal shutters.

Cyrus again pulled the cart under the overhang to protect us from any nighttime rain as Deacon in his wolf form, stepped into the mouth of the sheltered area with a small, deer-like creature in his jaws. It looked like he'd already hunted down our dinner while he'd been scouting ahead.

"Good," Cyrus said as he locked the cart in position. "That'll be enough for dinner and breakfast. We can leave the leftovers in the cold cupboard in the shelter for when we come back. I'll get these guys set up and then meet you outside the shelter to help you butcher it."

Cyrus strode around to the back of the cart and held out his hands to me.

"Last time I'll force you to do this," he said, his voice gruff. "But I'll expect you to say something if you're struggling to keep up."

I slid my butt to the edge of the cart, my eyes flickering to his on their own volition.

His expression was strange. It wasn't angry or hard like it usually was, but it was tight with tension mixed with something softer, something heartbreaking.

"I will," I murmured back, that thing in my soul urging me to get closer, to comfort his soul as well. He was just as worried about his brothers as I was... and he was mine.

No. Not mine. Never mine, and I had to pull myself together and stop thinking those kinds of things so I didn't accidentally trap him in a mating bond.

I gritted my teeth and leaned into his embrace so he could lift me off the cart. One arm hooked under my thighs, the other behind my back, and his powerful deep earthy scent enveloped me. Warmth and certainty blossomed around my heart, sending a surge of panic shooting through me.

Not. Mine.

I squeezed my eyes shut until he set me on the ground. But as soon as I opened them, they instantly jumped back to Cyrus and the hurt in his eyes.

Then his alpha-in-control mask snapped into place, leaving me wondering what the hell had just happened.

Except I didn't have the mental strength to figure it out right now. Everything within me was focused on sending assurance and calm to Knox while ignoring the sharp flashes of agony coming through my bond with Bishop. Which was something I wasn't going to outwardly react to because it would make it even harder for Knox to stay in control and Cyrus would question my ability to keep up.

And I was damn well going to keep up.

There were only three or four days left to get to the pool. I'd hiked for a lot longer while fighting my heat. I could do this while fighting the onslaught of overwhelming emotions and a little pain.

AUDREY

For the first day, I was right. I'd woken after a fitful night where we'd had to give Bishop three elixirs, disappointed that I hadn't had another sexy shared dream with my mates and worried for both of them.

Despite that, I'd felt strong and determined, ready to save Bishop. It was as if a glimmer of Knox's powerful feral nature, the strength he'd lent me to stand my ground against Cyrus, had sparked to life inside me. My foot had still been a little tender, but I wasn't going to complain about it because... I. Could. Do. This.

We'd left the cart in the shelter, secured the metal gate to keep out beasts, and marched down the road until midmorning where there was a break in the rocks and a steep, but manageable, slope up into the forest.

Then we'd hiked across the rocky, uneven ground just like we had on our journey north until dusk and set up camp.

Cyrus had commanded I go with Deacon to fill our canteens while Deacon gathered firewood and I'd hopped to it, surprised my legs were barely sore when the last time I'd hiked across the wilderness they'd started to hurt before lunch on the first day.

The next morning, however, was a different story.

I'd gotten even less sleep with Bishop's pain growing stronger inside me and his body twitching and shaking all night despite giving him four elixirs. Knox's worry and rage were also building, crushing inside me, making it difficult to draw in a full breath, *and* I hadn't gotten another sexy dream!

It was ridiculous to be upset about that. Everyone was too stressed to think, or even dream, about sex and yet my soul now ached with need.

God, what was wrong with me?

I bit back a groan, determined to not draw Cyrus's attention, and stretched my achy muscles.

There was nothing wrong with me. I had an incomplete mating bond and just like the last time, it didn't give me any time to adjust. I needed to seal my bond and I needed it now.

Swell.

"All right, ladies," Deacon said as he doused the fire. "Ready for another day? Or do I need to carry you?" The laugh lines at the edges of his eyes crinkled and he flashed us a bright smile.

"I'll be good to get to the pool," Whil replied, rolling up her blanket and securing it in her pack. "I'm using a bit of magic to fortify my body."

Panic and rage exploded through my bond with Knox, stealing my breath.

"You're wasting magic?" he roared, his eyes going completely black as his wolf took over. "You need your magic to save Bishop."

Whil raised her hands in defense and Deacon stepped in front of her, blocking Knox from getting to her.

"Knox," I gasped, grabbing his arm and pushing as much of my body against his as I could, trying to get him to calm down.

He growled at Deacon, and his claws and canines extended as the feralness within him surged.

Oh, shit. This wasn't good. We were so close. He couldn't lose it now. If he went feral, he could kill Bishop's only hope of survival.

"Stop." My pulse *thu-thudded* hard, and that spark of power exploded from my body, sudden and sharp and gone just as quickly as it appeared.

Knox froze, every muscle in his body tightening, and his claws and canines retracted. He turned his attention to me, his eyes still dark with his wolf.

"It's three more days at most," I murmured, pushing love through our bond.

"He's in agony," his wolf growled at me.

"I know."

He stared at me, his body trembling with his raging emotions, emotions that threatened my grip on myself. But I rode the violent waves, waiting for his wolf to realize the truth. He couldn't protect Knox from the next three days. If he took control and gave in to his primal fear it was all over.

And it couldn't be over. I needed both of them sane and conscious, not surviving on pure animalistic instinct. My reasons for needing Knox and his wolf hadn't changed since I'd pulled them back from the brink of feralness. I needed his wolf to show me how to be strong and I needed Knox's fierce love.

He'd completely changed after Sterling had tricked me into hurting myself, and I could feel his commitment to me and our bond — even if it was barely noticeable underneath all the other emotions right now. He was my ferocious protector. He didn't care about politics or other people's feelings. If I was in trouble, he'd do whatever it took to protect me. His wolf would, too.

Which was why I didn't push, didn't make his wolf think I was attacking him. I stayed stalwart in my certainty in us, praying that would anchor him back in his body.

And slowly, after an agonizingly long moment of just holding all his emotions without trying to change them, his wolf reached through our bond and found my reasons.

"Whil would never jeopardize Bishop," I soothed as the blackness faded from his eyes, revealing dark brown orbs flecked with brilliant green.

"I know that," he gritted out. "It's just so hard to focus and he's getting worse."

I offered him a soft smile, praying it looked hopeful and he didn't notice just how worried I was about Bishop. "He has us. He's strong. Just three more days."

A burst of Bishop's pain shot through my chest, but I kept my smile soft and breathed through it, determined not to let anyone see how much I was struggling.

I had to be strong for the both of them, and I would be.

"Well then," Deacon said, putting his hands on his hips. "What the hell are we waiting for?"

"That's what I want to know." Cyrus huffed, hooking the now-clean cooking pot to his pack.

"We were waiting for you," Whil said to Cyrus.

"Yeah," Deacon replied. "You need to volunteer more in the kitchen. How long does it take to wash a pot and a couple of bowls?"

CYRUS

I ROLLED MY EYES AT DEACON, PRAYING HE WOULDN'T NOTICE THE REAL reason I took five times longer to wash the pot and bowls than usual, and started marching toward the pool assuming everyone else would follow. I'd tried to shift out the evidence, but Deacon had a sensitive nose that he liked to stick in other people's business and he wasn't as distracted by Bishop's condition as Knox was.

Jeez. This was what I'd become. It was like I was a pup again, hiding in the mountains to jerk off so no one knew.

But early this morning, while I was sitting on watch, Audrey's scent had started to change. Her sweet fresh scent had deepened with desire even while she was unconscious and my wolf had lost it.

He wasn't going to let Audrey suffer through another heat fever and he was determined to stop it before it even started... despite the fact that her changing scent might not indicate another heat and could just be her incomplete mating bond compelling her to seal it.

As it was, I'd escaped camp with the morning dishes, praying no one had noticed my cock tenting my pants, washed the dishes as fast as I could, and then shucked my clothes — since I couldn't afford to have them smell like my arousal.

With a groan, I'd fallen to my knees and grabbed myself. My cock was already painfully hard and leaking precum thanks to my wolf's eagerness to claim Audrey and the realization that maybe, one day, I could.

That crack in my determination to never mate with her had been enough for him to take a little more control of our body. Thankfully, that crack wasn't enough for him to come on to Audrey — we both knew that wouldn't go over well given the current situation — but it was enough to make me need a release.

I huffed a bitter laugh.

I was just kidding myself. I didn't need my wolf to make me hard for Audrey. I hadn't even needed to see her glorious and radiating alpha power to defy me. I'd wanted her from the moment I'd seen her, a small, broken warrior defying death himself.

But I'd just been so determined to do right by my pack.

Except my pack would eventually come around and I'd expel any from the pack who wanted to hurt her. I just needed to be patient, needed to find the right moment where my pack would accept her and she'd accept me as her mate.

I squeezed my cock, knowing the only way to get it to calm down was to come, and my thoughts had jumped to our one time together. It had been terrifying and heartbreaking, and I hadn't been able to stop thinking about it, about how tight she was, how warm, how fragile. I'd needed to protect her, care for her, love her, and that feeling had only grown stronger the more I tried to avoid her.

I'd roughly jerked my hand along my length until hot jets of cum had poured into the stream where I'd washed the pots. Then I shifted into my wolf and back to human, destroying the scent of my cum as much as possible.

Now I was hiking downwind of her — because that was the direction we had to go — her scent pure torture and pure ecstasy as each tiny gust dragged it over me.

"We need to pick up our pace," Deacon said, his voice low, as he stepped up beside me.

His attention flickered back to the others behind us and his expression turned serious. "You can smell that, can't you? Audrey's need? It's subtle, but it's there."

"You think it's subtle?" I choked out. I was damn near drowning in it.

He glanced down at my crotch where I'd secured my hard-as-hell cock under the waistband of my pants so my condition wasn't so obvious — and something I'd needed to do less than ten minutes after jerking off.

"Ah," he said, that one word filled with knowing. "Nova would say you're hyper-attuned to her scent after watching her suffer through a heat fever for so long."

"What would you say?" I wasn't sure I wanted to know, but he was a good friend and my beta. He knew the whole situation and wouldn't let his friendship with Audrey get in the way of telling me the truth. I trusted him, even if I looked like an idiot.

"That it's too soon for Audrey's incomplete bond to start affecting her and we need to save Bishop and get them to bond before it's more than just a little desire. Oh, and—" He flashed me a crooked smile, his eyes bright with laughter even as he managed to keep it in and not laugh out loud. "Nova's right."

"Not always," I huffed.

He cocked an eyebrow at me. "Nova is always right."

Yeah, Nova was wrong so few times it didn't count.

"I think your instincts are telling you something about Audrey, but you've made a royal mess of it before it could even get started."

"The pack needs to accept her first," I insisted. "I won't put her through that scrutiny and hate."

"She's stronger than you think she is," Deacon replied.

"No," I corrected. "She's stronger than *she* thinks she is, and I won't put her in front of the pack as my mate until she realizes that. I won't be cruel to her."

"Again," Deacon said, the laughter melting from his eyes, his expression turning serious. "You won't be cruel to her *again*."

"Yeah." I ran my hands over my head, fearing the damage was already done. Putting her in front of my pack as my mate was pure fantasy. It meant she'd have to accept me first, and I wasn't sure I'd ever be able to convince her that her heart, not just her body, was safe with me.

KNOX

My insides were a suffocating twisted knot. We were going too fucking slow. And yet that thought twisted me up even more because faster meant more strain on Audrey. She was keeping up — because my mate was strong — but I feared it wouldn't last. Even the strongest shifter could break with enough stress and she was under so much.

And I could still feel her stress despite my wolf freaking out while I fought the threatening feralness inside me.

She was fighting to be strong for me, sending a near-constant stream of love and determination through our bond, but the emotions were edged with fear. A fear I couldn't do anything about because I couldn't shut off my most primal nature and get my emotions under control.

I was also pretty sure she was feeling some of Bishop's agony. She didn't seem to be experiencing the constant stream of pain slicing into her soul like I was, but I saw her flinch whenever the pain surged. And on top of that, her scent had changed, deepening with need like when she'd first started fighting her heat before we'd even left Stonehaven to go north.

Back then, it had been her incomplete bond with me setting her off, so I was certain it was her bond with Bishop doing the same thing now.

Her scent, however, hadn't changed this quickly before. Her bond with Bishop was less than a day old, and I feared she was going to have a heat fever again, possibly before we even reached the pool.

All of which she was trying to hide from me because she didn't want me to worry.

Except all I could do was worry, since I couldn't hold both her and Bishop, and I *had* to hold Bishop. His soul was the weakest right now, and if I let go for too long, I'd lose him.

As if thinking about losing him to the poison gave it strength, agony burst through my twin bond, blacking out my vision for a second. Bishop moaned and tensed, the precursor to a convulsion.

"Whil," I growled, and she pulled out an elixir without me having to say more while I had to watch Audrey stumble and couldn't do anything to help her.

"Shit," Cyrus hissed, grabbing her before she fell, his body almost as stiff as Bishop's.

His nose twitched and his eyes squeezed shut for a moment, but Audrey didn't notice, her worried expression locked on Bishop.

So, he could smell it, too.

Was it as potent to him as it was to me? Was her need so strong because I was attuned to her and was partially feeling it through our bond, or could everyone smell her?

A growl bubbled in the back of my throat.

Mine.

She was mine, and my wolf didn't want anyone else to know she needed sex, especially when I couldn't satisfy her right this minute.

"We have enough elixirs to make it to the pool," Whil said, mistaking my growl for worry for Bishop. "I'm not letting him die."

I huffed and gave her a tight nod, the pressure and wildness inside me squeezing so tight I could barely breathe.

Audrey took a big step away from Cyrus, her cheeks just a little too pink. "I can make it to our next camp without stopping for lunch. How about you, Whil?"

"No," Cyrus barked with a snap of power that made Audrey tense. "Neither of you can hike on two meals a day. I won't have you slowing us down because you're hungry." His power stuttered again, slipping out of his control, and Audrey squared her shoulders and glared at him.

"It's only three days. I've survived worse for longer."

More power snapped from Cyrus and my wolf growled.

She'd suffered without food for longer than three days?

If her previous alpha wasn't already dead, and I could get to her realm — which I couldn't — I'd kill him for making her suffer.

"I doubt you were also exerting yourself at the same time."

"And we're losing time arguing about it," Deacon said with a snap of his power, what little control he had also slipping.

My wolf seized our body and I jerked forward. "Mine."

Deacon's eyes widened and more power snapped from him. He threw his hands up and backed away from Audrey even though he wasn't even close to her.

"Yours," Audrey assured my wolf, wrapping her hands around my biceps. "Always yours."

Love flooded our bond, easing the crushing tension in my chest, and I nearly dropped to my knees with relief.

"But Deacon's right," she added, looking exhausted for a split second before her sweet, soft smile returned. "We have to keep moving."

"And you have to eat," Cyrus insisted as he started walking at a fast pace.

"I'll eat and walk," she shot back.

"You'll choke," he growled.

"I won't choke."

He shot her a hard glare. "You tripped over nothing on the completely flat death god's lands. I'll just consider it a miracle if we get to the pool without you breaking something."

"The rest of the way to and from the death god's lands was just as rocky as here." She swept out her hand, gesturing at the rocky, uneven landscape.

Trees, thick with leaves, as well as evergreens, crowded close, creating a thick cool shade, blocking the summer's heat, but that also made the jagged landscape and fallen trees slippery with moss and rot.

"You *just* tripped." He jerked his thumb over his shoulder to where we'd stopped a moment ago.

"Bishop was about to convulse. I was distracted," she huffed. Then her eyes widened and a new worry trembled through our bond. "I'll stop long enough to eat a granola bar and an apple."

What the fuck? Why the hell had she just submitted to him?

The worry quickly turned into frustration as if she were angry at herself for not standing her ground.

"A wise wolf knows how to pick her battles," Deacon whispered to her even though both Cyrus and I could easily hear him. "He's too stubborn to see sense right now. There's no point going up against that brick wall unless it's absolutely necessary. Stopping for a quick snack is a good compromise. Well done."

Surprise and pleasure leaped through our mating bond, and she dropped her gaze to her feet, her cheeks turning pink again.

For a second, I thought she was reciprocating Deacon's flirtations until I realized she was actually reacting to his praise.

She practically lit up at a simple well done. Of course, if I praised her, it would come out all wrong. That didn't mean I wasn't going to try, but the best mate for that was Bishop and I was sure as hell telling him that little fact about Audrey.

I'd make sure he praised her as much as he told her she was beautiful. We just needed to get to the damned pool first.

AUDREY

A COUPLE OF HOURS LATER, I WAS STILL RIDING THE HIGH OF DEACON'S simple "well done" when we stopped for our lunchtime snack. Whil and I ate as fast as possible so we could keep moving while Knox clung to a now-constantly trembling and moaning Bishop. Deacon tried to lighten the mood with funny stories about growing up in the pack with Nova and the guys — even though he was more than fifteen years older than the twins — and Cyrus spent the time glaring into the forest.

A part of me was furious at myself for realizing that I'd been talking back to Cyrus and had gotten nervous, while another part was furious that I'd submitted to his wishes without much of a fight, my fear of angry alphas raising its ugly head once again.

I'd thought I was doing better. I'd been worried about his reaction to me while we traveled, but not afraid that he'd yell at me like he had in the arena. There were even times when I felt comfortable with him, that sense of trust deep within me overriding all common sense.

Not to mention, he had to be under horrible stress. I was kind of surprised he hadn't yelled at me yet. Sure, he'd huffed at me to do things, but he hadn't cracked like he had in the arena when Knox was about to go completely feral, and he wasn't giving me the cold shoulder. A lukewarm shoulder, but that was a big improvement from before.

Although I still got the impression that he didn't want to talk to me. That, however, I could live with, especially since I needed to keep my distance from him. I didn't want to accidentally mate bond with him despite that strange part inside me insisting I needed more, that he was mine like Bishop and Knox were.

We hiked until after dusk and found a cave where we'd be out of the elements. So far, the weather had been perfect, but that didn't mean it would stay that way.

Knox had told me the summer was their stormy season when violent storms suddenly appeared from magic that had built up over the resting places of a couple of storm gods.

The cave would also protect us from beasts, although they, too, hadn't been a bother. I hadn't even really sensed their presence like I had on the journey north.

But, as Deacon explained, the pack regularly hunted the most dangerous beasts in the area around the road to keep the trade route open as well as around the pool to protect those guarding and tending to it.

The Kingdom of Lais considered the pool a sacred resource that needed to be nurtured and protected, especially since Whil could create powerful healing elixirs from its water, and the pack and kingdom had strengthened their once weak alliance because of it. All of which could fall apart if something happened to the pool.

"Deacon, dinner," Cyrus commanded, setting down his pack as Knox sat at the mouth of the cave with Bishop — which was as deep into the cave as he could go without setting off his claustrophobia. "Audrey, grab the canteens and stick by me while I gather firewood."

"I'm not going to trip," I mumbled under my breath, setting my pack beside Knox's and brushing my lips across his in a quick, reassuring kiss.

Except that was a mistake, and the whisper of our lips touching made need swell low within me.

Knox's eyes darkened while his expression turned pained, and I tried to focus on anything other than sex. I wasn't nearly as needy as I'd been last time... but it had only been two days since I'd formed my incomplete bond with Bishop and my desire had been steadily growing despite being hungry and tired and worried.

"Of course you're going to trip," Cyrus replied, having heard me with his god-damned wolf-enhanced hearing. "It's after dark and you don't have night vision. I'd tell you to stay here but—"

But Knox couldn't leave Bishop and Whil was better at sensing the magical poison and knowing when it was time for another elixir. Whoever was gathering the firewood might have been able to fill the canteens as well, but everything was faster with more people helping.

I grabbed the canteens and followed Cyrus out into the darkness where he led me to a river. Unlike when we set up camp going north and pretty much followed the river the whole way there, this river was farther away. I doubted we were within screaming distance of the camp even with Knox's enhanced hearing and there was no way I'd have been able to find it myself.

I also didn't want to admit that there was a good chance I'd have tripped and hurt myself on the way here if Cyrus hadn't been with me.

With the exception of a glade at the bottom of a steep ridge, the trees had crowded close, blocking out the moonlight, and there'd been a few terrifying moments when I'd been almost blind and nearly lost my footing. But I did successfully get to the river without tripping.

One point for me.

None for the grumpy overbearing — far too sexy — alpha.

Shoving that thought to the back of my mind, I filled the canteens while Cyrus gathered firewood.

My desire for him was just the desire from my incomplete mating bond that was making me more attracted to him than I was.

Except I knew that wasn't true, and every time I tried to pretend I wasn't aware of his powerful body nearby or how he'd helped me navigate the uneven ground in the darkness, that stupid fantasy flashed through my mind.

Cyrus holding me, pushing into me, and kissing me like I meant something to him. Like I was precious and wanted and—

Stop. Just stop.

"You done?" Cyrus asked, making me jump.

Shit. I'd been so caught up in the fantasy — and denying the fantasy — that I hadn't heard him approach.

"Ah..." I pulled the canteen I was holding from the water, secured the lid, and reached to grab the next one.

Except all the lids were screwed on. They'd all been open when I'd reached the river, so somehow I'd filled the canteens while daydreaming and hadn't even noticed.

Jeez. I hadn't been this distracted by my heat when we'd traveled north. Of course, I also hadn't been under this much stress. My body ached for a release and I was crazy frustrated that I stopped having sex dreams with my mates. On top of it, I was terrified I was going to lose both Bishop and Knox but had to stay calm to keep Knox from going feral.

I should probably be surprised I wasn't a sobbing mess by now. Getting distracted from a sexy fantasy that was never going to happen was the least of my worries.

"Come on," he said, his voice gruff. He jerked his chin the way we'd come, his hands full of firewood, and started leading the way back.

I followed, weighed down by the now-full canteens, and carefully picked my way across the uneven ground, my pace so slow Cyrus kept stopping to gather more firewood, not so subtly waiting for me to catch up. But I was determined not to trip and with my hands full, it wasn't as easy to catch myself if I lost my balance.

We climbed up a shallow slope, rounded a tall chunk of rock jutting up from the ground, and stepped onto the ridge overlooking the glade.

Moonlight filled the glade, illuminating our path, and I breathed a quick sigh of relief. We still had three-quarters of the way to get back to camp, but at least for this stretch, I wouldn't have to worry about not seeing where I was going.

I picked up my pace, eager to catch up to Cyrus who stood at the center of the ridge, waiting for me. But I'd only managed to get halfway to him when the ground gave way beneath me.

With a yelp, I lurched to the side and knew I couldn't save myself. I was rolling down that steep incline to the bottom whether I wanted to or not.

Cyrus's eyes flashed wide, realization hitting him, and he dropped his firewood and lunged at me, grabbing my wrist.

But it was already too late. My fall was inevitable and he had to stretch to reach me, throwing him off balance, too.

Together, we tumbled over the edge, crashing through small shrubs and over hunks of stone, the world spinning around me so fast I had no idea which way was up or down.

We landed with a heavy thump, heaped together at the bottom on a cushion of moss and fallen leaves. Somehow, Cyrus had managed to pull me to his chest and turn so I ended on top of him with his hard body wrapped protectively around mine.

Mine, that annoying little voice in my head whispered as a surge of desire swept through me.

I scrambled off him, falling onto my butt and bashing my elbow on a tree trunk. This was *not* the way tonight was supposed to go. I was supposed to have proven to Cyrus that I wasn't a klutz and not ended up in his embrace.

"Damn it," I huffed, slapping the ground with my frustration. "I was determined I wasn't going to trip."

Cyrus huffed back — it almost sounded like a laugh. "Rest assured, you didn't trip. The ground gave out beneath you. Obviously not your fault."

I rolled my eyes at him, surprised he pointed out the difference. "Are you sure? You're not one to sugarcoat anything."

"You're not a disaster, Audrey." He leaned forward, his moss green eyes locked on mine as he plucked a leaf out of my hair.

Except he didn't lean back when he was done.

The heat from his body teased across my skin. He was close. Too close. And yet I didn't have the willpower to put space between us.

Except I *had* to put space between us.

The ache between my legs was growing stronger every second I was captured in his gaze, and that awful voice was getting louder.

Not mine. Never mine, I insisted. I couldn't accidentally trap him in a mating bond.

"But you scared the shit out of me," he confessed, reaching and pulling another leaf from my hair, the motion drawing him even closer.

So close that if I dipped forward, our lips would touch.

I squeezed my eyes shut, trying to think of something else, anything else. But it was like I could feel his alpha power caressing inside me, not with a command, but a plea. I wasn't even sure he was aware he was doing it.

"Audrey," he breathed. "Are you hurt?"

"I'm fine," I immediately replied.

"Audrey." He captured my chin with his hand.

My eyes flew open at the sudden contact and I was caught in his gaze again. He was commanding and strong, his alpha power rolling off him in soft, almost teasing waves that made all of me tingle. He was the most powerful member of his pack, the ideal mate, and that made the stupid primal something inside me giddy from his attention.

Which was stupid stupid stupid.

He didn't want me and I didn't want someone who didn't want me.

It was bad enough when Knox had frozen our mating bond and nearly broken my spirit. Cyrus would crush me, probably without even trying.

"Are you hurt?" he asked again.

This time I dragged my attention away from him and focused on my body, that stupid primal nature wanting to please him.

Nothing hurt bad enough to be worried about it. I'd gathered a few new bruises and scrapes but that was all.

"Just a little beaten up. I can make it to the pools."

A low growl bubbled in Cyrus's throat and he captured my head between his palms. "That wasn't what I was asking about. I'd have happily carried you to the pools all the way from Stonehaven. I'm worried about *you*."

"I'm not going to die and endanger your brothers."

The growl came out in full, the sound vibrating through my body and sending more heat rushing to my core instead of scaring me.

"Not worried about that, either, Audrey," he rumbled. "This, here and now, is all about you. My worry is all about you. No one else."

"Me?" I squeaked, his words sending me spinning while making something in my heart swell.

I had to be unconscious and dreaming. Cyrus's worry had always been about my connection to his brothers... or had I just assumed that?

"I—" I didn't know what to say. "I—"

"You, Audrey," he insisted and dipped forward, capturing my mouth in a searing, breathtaking kiss.

AUDREY

Hot aching need exploded in my core, and I grabbed the front of Cyrus's shirt and kissed him back. All the reasons I had for keeping my distance from him vanished.

Except they'd been good reasons.

They'd been...

What had they been?

He tangled his fingers in my hair and deepened the kiss, his tongue battling with mine, his free hand still carefully cupping my cheek. It was just like the fantasy I'd been having of him from the moment I'd woken from my heat fever.

Cyrus held me as if I were precious, like he loved me, but this time the kiss wasn't soft and sweet, it was deep and passionate. Whatever wall he'd locked his heart and all his emotions behind had broken open, turning him into the man I'd hoped he'd be, the man I wanted him to be.

Because he. Was. Mine.

That voice inside me that wanted the impossible howled with joy, and I let it. I didn't care about the consequences—

I mean I did. They were really important. But—

What were they again?

"Audrey," Cyrus groaned, pulling away to look me in the eyes. "You're the most frustrating person I've ever met."

But there wasn't a hint of frustration in his eyes. Instead, they were dark with his wolf and hungry.

Need shivered down my spine and Cyrus sucked in a deep breath, drawing in my scent. The hunger deepened and so did my desire. I ached like I'd ached when I'd been battling my heat, just before I succumbed to a heat fever and lost all awareness.

I'd always been attracted to Cyrus. He was just as handsome as his brothers but edgier. Not dark and brooding like Knox, but fierce and commanding. Everything about him screamed bad boy... or hardened warrior — which was more likely the case.

He made the rules and everyone else obeyed.

And I *wanted* him this very minute in this moonlit glade, cushioned by a soft bed of moss and leaves. Fireflies had even come out, little spots of light dancing around us, making the moment feel magical, and every nerve, every cell in my body, ached for him.

"You don't have to do everything by yourself. There are people around you who want to help. *I* want to help."

And from the longing in his eyes, his "help" was to make me come, screaming his name.

"Yes," I breathed. "Please."

I tightened my grip on his shirt and we crashed back together, kissing as if we needed each other to breathe.

His hands were everywhere, clutching my hair, pushing under my shirt, palming my breasts, sliding into my pants. I arched into his touch, my body begging for him for more as I dragged my hands over him.

I couldn't get enough. He was so strong, so powerful, so stunningly beautiful in his edgy bad boy way. He wasn't loving like Bishop or wild like Knox, but there was something overwhelming about him. He possessed me with his mouth and hands, made me gasp and moan, building up my need until I ached for a release.

"Cyrus," I begged. "I need— I need."

I clawed at his shirt, and he pulled back long enough to grab his collar with one hand and haul it off.

Eagerly, I swept my hands over his chest, savoring the feel of his bulky powerful muscles. I was so small, so fragile compared to him. He could attack me and I wouldn't stand a chance, and yet in this moment, I felt completely safe.

Cyrus would protect me. He'd take care of me. He'd satisfy my needs. He—

There was something wrong about that. He wasn't—? I shouldn't—?

With a groan, he pushed me onto my back and smashed his lips against mine, his tongue demanding entrance.

My desire surged and my thoughts scattered.

Yes. Yes more. I needed this. Needed him.

Needed to relieve the pressure building up inside me before I went insane.

I clawed at his back and bucked my hips up, hitting his erection and making him growl. His gaze darkened with desire, sending shivers of need rushing through me, and I bucked up again, showing him with my body what I needed.

Except instead of grinding down against me or yanking down my pants, he frowned.

There was something I was supposed to remember—

But the emotion disappeared as quickly as it appeared and he shoved his hand down the front of my pants, once again scattering my thoughts.

Oh, yes. This was what I wanted.

Two of his fingers swept through my folds and plunged inside me, and I moaned my pleasure.

Thank God he wasn't going to tease me. I didn't think I'd survive if he wanted to draw this out.

I rolled my hips, taking his fingers deep within me, savoring the feel of them driving into me hard and fast, setting every nerve on fire.

In seconds, I lit up and screamed his name. Pleasure roared through me and I didn't care that I'd come so quickly. Quickly meant he'd plunge his cock inside me sooner, and his cock was what I really wanted, what I needed to break the desire threatening to burn me up.

"Yes," I moaned. "More." More more more.

I rose up and kissed him but instead of returning the kiss, he jerked back, and gave his head a hard shake.

What the—?

"Cyrus?" My throat tightened.

Why wasn't he—?

Because this is wrong, a tiny voice in the back of my mind said, barely audible against the roar of my desire.

Not wrong, that strange wildness inside me roared back. *Mine.*

"Fuck, Audrey. No. I'm sorry." He drew back even farther, sucked in deep breaths as if to steady himself, and ran his hands through his hair, not seeming to care that he had my cum all over his fingers. "This isn't us."

Mine.

Except something about his words rang true, like I agreed with them despite desperately needing him.

I squeezed my eyes shut.

The voice inside me that claimed he was mine had always been wrong. He wasn't mine and wasn't interested in being mine, except...

God, why was it so hard to think?

He cupped my cheeks, his touch making my eyes fly open, and I was drowning in the heat and hunger in his gaze.

"We're being influenced by spirits," he forced out, worry seeping into his desire.

"Spirits?"

That didn't make sense. I'd wanted him before this moment... but I'd never have acted on it.

Oh, shit.

One of the fireflies zipped close, drawing my attention, and I stared at it, stunned, unable to understand what I was looking at.

It wasn't a firefly.

It was a fairy — the kind from fairy tales, not the fae who'd come to earth to join the fight against Michael. The little creature screeched at us and tossed a surprisingly large handful of glitter with its tiny hands.

I gasped in surprise and the glitter caught in the back of my throat and up my nose.

"No, Audrey," Cyrus said, jerking me forward.

Except instead of protecting me from the spirit, his lips crashed against mine again.

Oh, yes. Yes yes yes.

Now we could finish what we'd started.

I ran my hands down Cyrus's muscular chest, from his pecs and the rippling female fantasy of his abs to the waistband of his pants.

"Audrey," he groaned. "Fuck, I want you. I've wanted—" He jerked away, the muscles in his jaw flexing as he fought the fairy's magic.

"I want you, too." And I did, but...

He didn't really want me. He'd made that clear.

The spirits. Damn it.

Another fairy darted toward us and I slapped it away. We had to get out of there. It was bad enough that Cyrus had kissed the hell out of me and made me come with his fingers. We couldn't let it go to the next step.

I could accidentally mate bond with him.

That was it! That was what I'd been forgetting!

I didn't want to trap him in a mating bond.

AUDREY

"Cyrus!" I shoved him back, catching him by surprise — since that was the only way I'd be able to move him. "We have to get out of here."

His body tensed and his eyes squeezed shut then they flew open and captured me. They were black. His wolf was in control and he wanted me.

I froze, knowing if I made a move, he'd think I was fleeing and pounce.

Two more fairies buzzed around us, and his face partially shifted into a snout. He snapped at the spirits, devouring them with a desperate, high-pitched scream and a stomach-churning crunch.

"Mine," he snarled.

"Not yours," I forced out, the words tearing something in my soul.

He doesn't want me. He doesn't want me. He doesn't want me.

And yet I ached for him, body, heart, and soul. I was incomplete without him, just like I'd been incomplete without Knox and Bishop.

No. That was the fairy glitter speaking. It wasn't true.

I should be God damned happy with the two mates I already had.

"Cyrus." This time I barked the words, my pulse *thu-thudding*, and he jerked back as if I'd slapped him. "We have to get out of here."

If we didn't leave now, whatever hold I had on myself would shatter, and I'd succumb to my glitter-induced desire.

He grabbed me, stood, and tossed me over his shoulder.

With his free hand, he slapped two more spirits out of the air before rushing to the rise we'd fallen down.

The fairies screeched as he scrambled up the rise and tossed more glitter at us. For a second, I was surrounded in a thick cloud of glitter, the grit rushing up my nose and into my mouth and making my eyes water.

I *loved* Cyrus. I *needed* Cyrus.

My desire turned to lava, pouring through my veins. I couldn't breathe, couldn't think. I *needed*. Oh, God, I needed him.

I squirmed in his grip. "Cyrus," I begged.

He crested the ridge and set me on the ground where I promptly yanked off my shirt.

"Audrey—"

I grabbed my breasts, desperate for relief, but pleasuring myself wasn't what I wanted. I wanted Cyrus. We belonged together.

He. Was. Mine.

"I need you," I pleaded. "Please." I rose on my knees and grabbed the waistband of his pants.

"It's the spirits' magic," he said, his voice gruff as he grabbed my wrists, stopping me from undoing his pants.

"I know it is." God, I knew he didn't want me and that I wasn't in love with him, and yet that small voice of reason in the back of my mind was being devoured by my need. "Please. I love you."

He crouched, still holding my wrists. "You don't love me. That's the spirits," he said, his expression strained.

My eyes burned with tears that I didn't want to cry, but his rejection was breaking my heart.

This was ridiculous. I didn't love him. I was still partially afraid of him.

And yet...

And yet it felt as if there was truth in those words. How long had the niggling voice in the back of my mind been telling me he was mine?

My desire flared, stealing my breath and arching my back. My breasts were so heavy, needy, and I'd soaked through my pants.

"Audrey." He cupped my cheeks, urging me to look at him. "This isn't a fever. You're not hot. We'll get you to Knox and—"

Another jolt of desire twisted me tight.

"Look at me, Audrey," he commanded.

I dragged my eyes open, not realizing I'd closed them.

"The magic will wear off but— Fuck." His expression turned pained. "I'll get you off again and then get you to Knox."

"Where everyone will watch us have sex," I told him. Sure I'd liked it when Knox had watched me have sex with Bishop and vice versa, but Deacon and Whil...?

The thought made my stomach churn. I had to have sex now and it had to be with Cyrus.

God, what was wrong with me? Why was I so adamant to have Cyrus relieve my need? "Why won't you have sex with me?"

The words came out choked and tears leaked from my eyes.

"You're being influenced by magic." He gathered me in his arms and cradled me against his chest, the sensation so comforting, so right... so... familiar.

I gasped, drawing back so I could look him in the eyes. "We've had sex before. It wasn't a fantasy. It really happened."

"You were dying and Bishop couldn't—" The muscles in his jaw flexed. "It was just your heat. It didn't mean anything."

"And it doesn't mean anything now," I lied. "This fairy glitter isn't easing up. Every time I move or twitch, or hell, even breathe, I ache. I can't take it anymore and we both know if Knox saw me like this he'd lose his shit."

"He's going to lose his shit over me having sex with you," Cyrus huffed as he helped me stand and slid my pants off my hips and down my legs.

With a groan, he grabbed my waist and drew me close, pressing his nose into my curls and drawing in deep breaths.

That wasn't the action of a man who didn't want to make love to me.

Except he'd also been affected by the spirits' magic. He might not have gotten that final, enormous face full that I had, but he'd still been dosed enough to kiss me like he loved me and make me come.

I had to keep remembering that.

And I *had* to keep remembering that this was just the same situation as my heat fever. I needed someone to fuck me and he was the only one present who could.

Another tear trailed down my cheek, and I tipped my head back just in case Cyrus looked up.

He nuzzled lower, sending shivers rushing down my spine, then flicked his tongue against my clit.

Sensation zinged through me, tensing my muscles then melting them with liquid need. Now I wasn't holding my head back to keep him from seeing my tears, it was thrown back in ecstasy.

He flicked again and again, and more shivers rolled down my body. I was already so worked up that a few more flicks had me coming.

I let out a long, satisfied moan as hot relief flooded my body and leaked from between my thighs.

Cyrus clutched me tight as I rode the wave, bliss washing through me, languid and hot.

But the ache returned, urging me to squirm, pressed my breasts into his face, or even push him back down to lick me clean.

"Damn it," I hissed. Not that I expected a quick little orgasm like that to bleed off the spirits' magic.

"I've got you," he murmured, just like when he'd helped me with my heat. "I've got you."

He undid his pants and pushed them to his knees, before pulling me down to straddle him.

My hips rocked forward, eager for more, painting my release over his large cock.

So big. Larger than Knox and Bishop. And I had to still be under the spirits' influence because that didn't scare me at all. Instead, it made more need rush from my core.

Everything within me screamed to take him. Take him now. I needed to be filled by him, loved by him, because he was mine.

He kissed me tenderly, like how he'd kissed me in my fantasy— No, not my fantasy. When we'd had sex during my heat. And my heart broke a little more.

It doesn't mean anything to him.

And I still needed him with my heart, my essence, my very soul.

I forced those thoughts from my head and gave into the lusty haze from the glitter. I grabbed his cock between us, spreading around my release, not needing to do anything to work him up. He was hard as steel and precum wept from his slit. The urge to slide from his lap and take him in my mouth swelled up inside me, but Cyrus held tight with both hands on my hips, his fingers nearly spanning my waist, refusing to let me go.

Then, with a low growl, he lifted me up and eased me down his length slowly, being oh so careful as his girth stretched me to the edge of my limit, verging on painful.

But the spirits' magic didn't care if he was too big for me or if I needed to relax more. The desire surging within me needed to be satisfied.

This was what it wanted. What deep down, *I* wanted.

Possessed by the glitter, I begged for him to go faster, harder, fill me, now. My hips rocked, and I dug my fingernails into his shoulders, straining against his hold on me.

His breath turned as ragged as mine, his control driving me crazy until finally — finally! — our pelvises met and he was completely buried inside me.

"Cyrus," I moaned, rocking my hips, savoring the feel of him. "You feel so good."

My head rolled back and he nuzzled my neck, teasing soft kisses along my jaw, his body trembling... and not moving.

"Cyrus?" Uncertainty wormed its way into the haze. Was he regretting this?

Oh, God. I'd fucked up. I'd fucked up so bad.

Then he grabbed the nape of my neck and braced his other hand behind my back and slowly slid out.

My muscles twitched with pleasure. He felt amazing. Just like how Knox and Bishop felt. His large cock raked against my channel, igniting already hypersensitive nerves, and sending me spinning.

Carefully, he pushed back in then withdrew. He repeated the process again and again, driving me crazy.

Making love to me.

This wasn't a quick fuck. I could feel the emotion in every stroke, every groan slipping from his lips. He drove me higher and higher, his pace getting faster and faster as he built a glorious peak then sent me flying.

Every muscle in my body clenched, my channel seizing him as he fucked through my orgasm to his own release. With a long low groan, he came hard, clenching me to his body and turning my amazing orgasm into something glorious.

The world went white and I spun around and around, pleasure rushing through me. Tremors rolled aftershock after aftershock through me, capturing me in breathtaking bliss.

Mine. He was mine.

"Maybe one day," Cyrus murmured against my temple, so softly I could barely hear him. "One day."

Cyrus held me as the heat of the glitter-induced desire cooled and our breathing returned to normal. "Are you okay?"

I nodded but kept clinging to him, afraid to look him in the eyes. I didn't know what to say or how to feel.

Disappointment and frustration twisted in my gut, and I could only hope Knox was too distracted by his own emotions and Bishop's pain to notice... because I had no idea what to say to him, either.

In the moment, I'd been so sure Cyrus was mine and I had to have him and I sure as hell couldn't have made it back to camp without having sex. But I hadn't formed a mating bond with him, which meant that horrible voice inside me that insisted he was mine was wrong.

And now I had no idea how I could ever look him in the eyes.

Except I was also frustrated that I felt that way. Sure, I was attracted to him and I had fantasies about him — which actually hadn't been fantasies but memories — but that didn't mean there was something between us.

Hell, I still didn't completely trust him despite what my instincts were telling me.

It was exactly what I'd told him before we'd had sex. It didn't mean anything.

He'd been helping me out like he'd helped me out during my heat. We'd both been influenced by the spirits and their magical glitter and it was never going to happen again... no matter how much that stupid voice inside me wanted it.

"Come on," he said as he carefully lifted me off his lap and set me on the ground. "We have to get back to camp."

I grabbed my pants — they were the closest — and stood on shaky legs to put them on.

Inside me, Knox's emotions continued to crush around my heart, adding to my own confusing mix of emotions. I was going to have to talk with him about what had happened. We were mates and I'd had sex with someone else. I wasn't going to try to hide it.

I mentally rolled my eyes at myself. Even if I wanted to — which I didn't because that was wrong — there was no way I'd be able to hide it. I could scrub myself down in the stream where I'd filled our canteens and Knox still would have been able to smell his brother on me.

I finished getting dressed while Cyrus pulled up his pants and retrieved four of our six canteens scattered across the top of the ridge. The other two, along with his shirt, were at the bottom in the glade, sacrifices to whichever god or goddess of sex or love or whatever slept in the land below.

He handed me the canteens, gathered a large armful of firewood, and we hiked back to camp.

Deacon glanced up, the first to see us, and his eyes widened. "What happened?"

Everyone else looked up at his words and I hunched my shoulders, curling in on myself, not wanting to deal with questions or judgment even among people I considered friends.

"Aphrodite's lands have expanded," Cyrus huffed as if that explained everything. And maybe it did. We'd been overcome with lust and it had been a battle to stop ourselves long enough to get away.

"Are you okay, Audrey?" Deacon asked, his expression growing concerned even as his nostrils flared, not-so-subtly drawing in the scent of mine and Cyrus's mixed releases.

"I'm fine." I set the canteens near our packs and started to sag to the ground beside Bishop, nervous about Knox's reaction.

But before my knees hit the cavern's floor, Knox grabbed me, pulled me into his lap, and clung to me as if he were afraid I was going to run away. "You're not fine."

"I had sex with your brother. I didn't mean to, but I'd wanted to and I..." Guilt twisted in my gut.

"Did he give you what you need?"

I nodded, afraid to speak.

"Then that's all that matters."

Love and certainty cut through the other emotions, and I leaned into him, clinging to the sensation. This time, he was sending me reassurance and I knew in my heart he didn't think I'd done anything wrong. Still, it had been extenuating circumstances and I couldn't let it happen again.

No matter how much that voice in my head was certain Cyrus was mine.

"Once we've saved Bishop, the three of you are going to have to talk about Audrey taking more mates," Cyrus said, his voice gruff as he added more wood to the fire.

"What?" I gasped as Knox tensed and Deacon choked mid-sip of his canteen, spraying water into the flames.

That strange primal feeling inside me jolted as if Cyrus's words confirmed that he was mine even though it was clear he wasn't.

"You couldn't have waited until she bonded with Bishop then gotten Bishop to bring it up," Deacon groaned.

"It's obvious she's feeling guilty," Cyrus shot back. "She needs to get over that or she's going to be in trouble when her next heat hits."

"I'm sure two mates will be more than enough," I insisted, my cheeks burning with embarrassment.

The muscles in Cyrus's jaw flexed. "You need to prepare yourself. You formed mating bonds with Knox and Bishop without the vows and your last heat turned into a near-deadly fever just like a powerful female alpha without enough mates."

"That was because of my incomplete mating bond. I'm so far away from being a powerful female alpha it's laughable. I'm not going to need more mates."

Deacon opened his mouth then snapped it shut, and Cyrus looked at me like I was being stupid.

I turned to Knox, but even he was giving me a strange look.

"You resisted the full force of Cyrus's power and almost had him submitting to you," Knox said.

"That was your power," I told Knox. "I was channeling it through our bond."

Knox shook his head and my heart stuttered.

It hadn't been his power?

It had been *my* power?

That ferocious wildness that had roared through me was mine? It wasn't just a dream?

Impossible.

A hysterical laugh escaped my lips and I shook my head. I was weak. I'd always be weak. If I was an alpha, why hadn't my wolf woken? Why was I still... me?

"Your power might only be able to break through your curse when your mates are in danger," Cyrus said. "But that doesn't mean you won't have the side effects of being powerful. For all we know, unlike alpha females from this realm, you'll claim the mates you need like you claimed Knox and Bishop." His gaze jumped to Knox. "Bishop will understand, but you need your wolf to be okay with that."

"Whatever protects Audrey," Knox growled, his eyes darkening with his wolf.

"So you'd just be fine with me being with other men?"

"If they're worthy, yes," he replied.

I wasn't going to ask what made someone worthy in Knox's eyes. It was all too much. Knox was agreeing to share me with someone, maybe multiple someones, even though I could feel his possessiveness toward me. And somehow, beyond my wildest dreams, I was an alpha. Except I could only reach my power when I was freaking out and even then, I had no control over it.

I hugged myself and curled into Knox's embrace. I really wanted Bishop. He'd know what to say to make sense of everything.

Was Cyrus right? Would I just claim whoever I needed whether I knew them or not? I didn't want to be mate bonded with a stranger again. Would fate be so cruel a second time or should I trust it? Things had worked out with Knox and I knew in my soul that he was mine, just like Bishop was mine.

I let my gaze wander to Cyrus who turned his attention to rotating our dinner on the spit.

My soul said he was mine, too, but I hadn't bonded with him.

I probably wasn't ready… or Cyrus wasn't. He'd made it clear he wasn't interested in me. Would that change?

And was there any point in worrying about it?

Fate was going to do what fate was going to do. Right now the only thing I did have control over was saving Bishop, and I damn well was going to do that.

AUDREY

I woke early the next morning, bleary-eyed after a restless sleep, my body aching from walking for two days straight and my core throbbing with need. Bishop's pain shot through me like agonizing zaps from an electric fence, more powerful and persistent than last night, despite the six elixirs we'd given him.

Only two more days.

We'd be at the pool in two days and then I'd have Bishop back.

"We're closer than that," Knox said, reading my thoughts with his telepathy as I eased out from between him and Bishop.

Except the moment I was no longer in contact with Bishop, his pain surged, stealing my breath and making my knees buckle.

His muscles contracted and a strangled moan escaped his lips, the precursor to a convulsion.

"Shit," Knox snarled, cushioning Bishop's head. "We just gave him an elixir two hours ago.

Whil scrambled for her pack and pulled out the small vial containing the only thing keeping Bishop alive, and I sagged back to the ground and pressed my hands against his cheeks. Instantly some of the tension released from his body, giving Whil enough time to pour the elixir down his throat.

Whil sat back on her heels and turned to Cyrus. "This is progressing faster than I expected."

"Then it's a good thing we're only a day away," Deacon said.

"But only if we leave now, push our pace, and keep walking after sunset," Cyrus replied, grabbing four ration bars from his pack and tossing them at me and Whil. "No time for breakfast."

I expected Deacon to make a joke about me walking and eating at the same time, but his expression remained serious which meant if I hadn't known it already, the situation was bad. Deacon always looked like he was trying not to spill an inside joke. And while he hadn't been as chatty as he'd been when I'd had dinner with him and Nova back in the Residence, he'd made an effort to keep us — probably just me — from having a complete breakdown.

Now he wasn't even trying.

I shoved my blanket into my pack and tried to stay in control of my emotions while Knox's were crashing through me.

It wasn't even two days now.

Sometime tonight we'd save Bishop.

If he lasted that long... and if Whil could actually pull out the poison.

She'd been confident when we'd left Stonehaven, but the veins in Bishop's flesh were thicker now and some of the larger veins had started weeping thick, black pus.

Bishop's pain surged again, making me stumble, but thankfully he didn't break out into a full convulsion. He trembled and moaned in Knox's arms, the few visible patches of skin left on his face gray, and sweat slicked his forehead.

God, was this the best the elixir could do for him now?

My once vibrant and powerful mate was weak and barely alive, and my heart broke just looking at him.

And there wasn't a damn thing I could do.

Even if I was as powerful as Cyrus, Knox, and Deacon seemed to think and I could actually access my alpha power, I still wouldn't be able to save him. Alpha power didn't work that way and neither did our soul bond. Unlike angelic mating bonds, shifters couldn't share life forces.

I was just as useless as I'd always been.

But that wasn't true. Just touching Bishop had helped ease his pain. Between Knox and I, we might have been slowing the progression of the poison with our souls' connections.

Another burst of pain made me stumble and Cyrus huffed.

"You seemed so confident yesterday that you could eat and walk," he said, scooping me into his arms.

I sighed. "Bishop's pain wasn't as bad yesterday."

"You can feel it?" He glanced at me, his expression a mix of pain and concern.

"You don't have to carry me," I said, dragging my attention to the forest in front of us before I fell into his moss green eyes and that stupid voice said he was mine.

"If we're going to make it to the pool tonight, I do."

"I could carry you," Deacon offered, a hint of mischievous mirth crinkling around his eyes.

"Fuck off, Deacon," Cyrus snarled, his voice dropping an octave into a sexy ramble and sending a shiver of need rushing down my spine and heating my core.

His nostrils flared at my arousal and my cheeks heated.

Stupid incomplete mating bond.

And stupid magical sex fairies. Now I knew what it felt like to be with Cyrus, to have his powerful arms hold me while his thick cock plunged into me again and again and again.

"Whatever you're thinking," Cyrus growled, "you need to stop."

Right. Because last night hadn't meant anything and he didn't want to be my mate... he just wasn't going to let Deacon carry me or me walk on my own.

"Then put me down."

"Finish your breakfast and I will." But his grip tightened as he spoke.

Was he lying? Had last night meant something?

Now I was just imagining things. We didn't even have a friend-ship. A relationship was pure fantasy.

Some of the sex glitter had to still be in my system. It was the only explanation for such a ridiculous thought, and I was only thinking it because I desired him and he'd brought up the multiple mates thing. My stress was through the roof and once again it was just us and a few others in the middle of nowhere.

I was confusing Cyrus's gruff kindness and practical suggestion for more than it really was. Everything would return to normal once we got back to Stonehaven and he had to become the pack alpha again.

If he really was mine, he was going to have to make his intentions clear. I'd drive myself crazy trying to figure out any subtle meaning behind his words and actions and expressions when they all said different things at the same time.

Except could I ignore that voice inside me?

Yes. Yes, I could.

If I didn't, it was only going to hurt.

Cyrus carried me for most of the morning and I'd never been so grateful to be distracted by the feel of his arms and his solid chest against my side or the barely-there warmth around my heart from our shifter connection. All of it managed to help me ignore Bishop's pain and Knox's emotions enough to stay more or less focused on my surroundings.

When the sun was high in the sky, he set me down, and I managed a few steps across relatively flat terrain before Bishop convulsed and the pain dropped me to my knees.

"Fuck," Cyrus snarled, grabbing me again and pressing me against Bishop to ease the convulsion so Whil could give him an elixir.

After that, he only set me down long enough for bathroom breaks. And as much as I wanted to do it on my own, I knew I wouldn't have been able to keep up even without Bishop's pain. The pace the guys set was just shy of a jog, and even Whil, with her magic enhancing her body, was barely keeping up.

Almost there, Knox said in my head as the sky started to turn dark gold with the beginnings of the sunset.

His emotions were hard, desperate, and icy as if he were trying to freeze our bond like he had when it had first formed. But this time it wasn't to keep me out. It was to protect me.

He grunted, and I glanced over Cyrus's shoulder at him as he caught his balance while Bishop thrashed in his arms.

We'd just given him an elixir less than an hour ago, but from the look of it — and the feel of his pain — he was going to need another one.

"How many elixirs do we have left?" I asked Whil.

"Two after this one," she said between gasping breaths.

"We have four hours to the pool," Deacon added. "We're not going to make it."

"Then we move faster." Cyrus stopped and turned so I could touch Bishop. "Whil, give him another. Deacon, take Whil. We're upping our pace."

A spike of fear surged through my bond with Knox.

"Can you handle that?" I asked him.

"Yes," he grunted as his fear grew stronger. His arms had to be tired. Even with his shifter strength, he couldn't keep carrying Bishop, especially with his constant small convulsions.

Knox's eyes narrowed and determination swept through the fear.

"Let's get moving," Cyrus snapped as Whil gave Bishop another dose of elixir.

Deacon swept her into his arms before she'd finished securing the clasp on her pack and started jogging.

Cyrus and Knox matched his pace. They ran until just after the sun sank below the horizon and a flickering light amongst the tree trunks ahead of us grew bright enough for us to make out a clearing with a person-sized statue of a woman pouring water from a large jug.

"Thank the Sisters," Knox groaned, relief cutting into his raging emotions.

We'd reached the pool with no time to spare. Thank God.

AUDREY

The clearing wasn't big, just wide enough for a couple of carts, and it was sheltered on two sides by naturally towering rock walls. The ground had been leveled and paved with flagstones and those flagstones narrowed along the far rock wall into a road that quickly turned into uneven ground with wheel ruts that led through the trees and off into the darkness.

"Alpha," a woman said as she stepped out of the shadows made by a recess in the closest rock wall.

She was a moderately powerful shifter radiating more than the regular level of feralness like Knox and Deacon and carried herself as if she were ready for a fight. But I didn't get the impression she was going to fight us, just that she was alert and prepared for danger.

"Alphas," she corrected herself. "What are you—" Then her gaze dipped to me in Cyrus's arms before sliding over the rest of the group.

"Thora, where's your Laisian partner?" Cyrus demanded as he set me down on shaky legs.

"Lewis is inside taking a piss." Thora jerked her thumb over her shoulder, making me realize the recess was actually the mouth of a cave with a wooden wall — complete with door — blocking it off.

As if speaking of him made him appear, the door opened and a middle-aged human warrior — wearing a leather jacket covered with metal rings — stepped out. His eyes widened when he saw us just as pain shot through my bond with Bishop and he released a strangled groan.

My knees buckled and Cyrus grabbed my arm and held me upright.

"We're using the pool," Cyrus growled, his alpha power pouring off him, making Thora gasp, but not affecting Lewis because he was human.

But Lewis didn't question or hesitate. He also didn't look scared about having to defend the pool against a powerful shifter. He just stepped aside and opened the door wider, allowing a soft band of warm light to spill across the flagstones.

"Don't worry," Deacon said as he strode inside. "We won't tell your king you just let us in."

"I don't really care if you do. Your hunters have kept us humans alive out here and he—" he pointed at Bishop, writhing in Knox's arms. "He doesn't look good."

"Thank you," Cyrus replied, heading toward the door with me in tow.

But a wave of panic crushed over me, stealing my breath and making me jerk away from him and cling to the doorframe.

Knox stood a few feet away, staring at the entrance, his breath suddenly too fast and his jaw clenched tight.

"I can take Bishop," Cyrus said as Whil stepped past us.

Pain tightened Knox's expression and frustration blended with his fear. "I can't let go."

My throat tightened, my heart breaking for him. He was so angry and afraid and now not just because Bishop was dying.

The only way to save Bishop was to take him inside, and we both knew the second Knox stopped holding him, he'd start convulsing, and we were out of elixirs.

"Knox," I said, shuffling the few feet to him and pressing my hands against his forearms to establish a physical connection.

He released a ragged breath and a hint of peace whispered through his emotions.

"You can do this." I shoved up my sleeves, adding more flesh to flesh contact while I fought to steady myself.

Somehow, I had to find the strength to reassure Knox, despite my own fears, and steady his soul so he could get Bishop to the pool.

But Bishop's pain was a constant burning in my limbs, Knox's emotions battered me from the inside, and I couldn't push past my own writhing emotions to focus. It was all a vortex pulling me under, suffocating and crushing me. It hadn't been as powerful this morning, but then Bishop's condition was quickly deteriorating.

I sucked in a ragged breath and squeezed my eyes shut, but that only made me more aware of everything raging inside me.

Damn it. Focus.

We were running out of time.

"Knox," I ground out, meeting his gaze.

Darkness filled his eyes, making the green specks stand out in sharp contrast, and I let myself fall into them. He was my ferocious mate, my strength and my protector, and I needed him now more than ever.

No. I *needed* his wolf. I needed to reach that primal part of his soul to push past his fear and do what needed to be done. Because if Bishop died, I'd lose both of them, and I didn't think I'd be able to survive that.

"Protect me." My pulse *thu-thudded*, hard and jarring, and jerked my whirling thoughts into focus. Nothing mattered except saving my mates and to do that I needed to steady Knox's soul.

Knox's eyes went completely black and his canines extended, his wolf taking over as I shoved love and certainty through our bond, steadying his soul.

He rumbled low in his throat, his power rolling off him, not in a demand of submission but in support, and I moved to his side and pushed my hands up under the back of his shirt to maintain contact.

Together, we marched through the door.

Inside, lit by magical glowing stones was a thirty by thirty room, half of it a living room with old, worn furniture, a fireplace, and a kitchenette, and the other half a storage area with stacks of wooden crates. It wasn't at all what I expected and there wasn't a pool in sight.

A door by the kitchenette stood partially open, revealing a toilet and sink, while another lay directly ahead of us. Deacon had his hand on the handle of that door, watching us enter, his expression tight.

"How long can you last?" he asked Knox as he opened the door, letting a wave of warm wet air wash over us and giving me a glimpse of the top of a large cavern with stalactites but not much else.

"As long as my mate needs me," his wolf growled back.

"Good," Cyrus said.

Beyond the door was a rock landing about ten feet off the ground and a shallow ramp that led down to the cavern floor. A shallow pool, the water glowing a soft blue, lay at the bottom of the ramp, and beside it was a deeper one.

Whil led us down the ramp and along a narrow, slippery path to the slightly deeper pool, set her pack on a ledge, and pulled out a thin, leather-bound book.

"We need to strip him and get him into the pool," she said, wiping sweat from her forehead. "You too, Knox and Audrey. You'll be able to get more flesh to flesh contact that way and I'm not taking any chances with this. I want your soul bonds steadying him."

"Right." I nodded, focusing on what needed to be done... because if I thought about stripping in front of everyone, I was going to panic, and I couldn't afford to panic. Not with Knox's tenuous grip on his claustrophobia.

Besides, getting naked in front of others was a natural shifter thing to do. Really.

And maybe if I kept telling myself that, I'd believe that I actually was a shifter and would stop being embarrassed about someone seeing me naked.

I could do this.

Just power through.

I pulled off my clothes as fast as possible and hopped into the

water without making eye contact with anyone, especially Cyrus —
even though he'd already seen me naked and I hadn't cared before.

The water was warm, verging on too hot, and the edge of the pool
quickly sloped into the deeper water so I only needed a few steps
before it was up to my shoulders.

Cyrus and Knox quickly stripped Bishop and, with Cyrus holding
his head out of the water, they submerged him in the glowing liquid.

He groaned, his muscles contracting and releasing again and
again with wave after wave of agony. The red and black veins pulsed
like a too-fast heartbeat, churning my stomach, and the black pus
oozing from the veins billowed around him, clouding the clear, shimmering water.

Please let this work, I prayed. *Please God or the Sisters or whatever
gods or goddesses can hear me.* I needed him alive and well. I needed to
tell him how much I loved him.

I pressed my body against his side and clung to his arm to avoid
getting bashed in the face. Knox hopped in a second later and took
over holding Bishop's head while also pressing himself against Bishop's side, pinning him between us.

A shuddering breath escaped Bishop's lips and the muscle
contractions slowed down but didn't stop.

Whil knelt on the rock above his head, not stripping or getting in
the water, and opened her book. "Whatever happens, just keep as
much of him in the water as you can."

That didn't sound good.

KNOX

I clung to Bishop, wishing I was also in physical contact with Audrey because my insides were squeezed so tight I could barely breathe.

The cavern was bigger than the ballroom in the Residence where I could have spent an hour with only four other people in it, but it could have been as big as the arena and it still would have been too small right now. There weren't any windows and the only way out was the door where we'd entered and that led to an even smaller, windowless room.

My soul hadn't been steady since Bishop had been poisoned, and the only reason I hadn't shifted into my wolf and raced outside was because my brother and my mate needed me.

It was actually a miracle I was even in the cavern, but my smart mate had known exactly what I needed to fight through the fear threatening to crush me into nothing.

She'd called on my wolf's need to protect her. He would go through anything, *do* anything whether I wanted to do it or not to keep her safe, even if that took us to the edge of losing our humanity. And we were barely holding on.

"Make it quick," I growled at Whil as my wolf surged even

stronger and pushed me farther back into my consciousness which also pushed back the primal feralness that would completely take over if he released even a fraction of his hold on me.

"That's the idea," Whil replied, scanning the book's pages.

Bishop groaned, his already twitching muscles contracting tight, arching his back, and pushing his chest out of the water.

More of the horrific black and red veins burst, oozing thick, viscous pus that clouded the pristine water, making me grit my teeth. All I could do was hold him. I hated that was all I could do while everything else was up to Whil.

"Come on, Bishop," Audrey murmured, pressing her forehead to his. "Just a little longer. Please." Her voice cracked, making both me and my wolf furious.

She shouldn't have to go through anything like this. Not now. Not ever. Yes, she'd proven she was strong — in her quiet, persistent, always-gets-back-up way — but if my wolf and I had anything to say about it, she'd never have to endure heartache and fear like this again.

It didn't matter that she had a powerful alpha locked inside her. Even if she finally broke her curse, I wouldn't allow her to suffer.

"Okay." Whil handed Deacon the book, knelt by Bishop's head, and placed her hands on his forehead while Cyrus crouched beside her.

"If things go wrong," he said, glancing at Deacon, "you grab Whil. I've got Audrey."

Whil gave him a tight nod, her perpetual golden glow growing brighter as she focused on gathering her magic.

Blue light flickered in the water around us in response, cutting through the growing cloud of black pus. Then she closed her eyes, whispered a prayer to Ninti whose power imbued this water with magic, and light burst from her hands.

Bishop's head jerked back, threatening my grip, and a desperate howl of agony tore from his throat and ripped through our twin bond.

"Oh, God," Audrey gasped, her face suddenly white, her expression tight with Bishop's pain.

For a second, he was trapped in that horrible scream, his body locked in agony, then the pain flared stronger, whitening out my vision, and he thrashed with the full strength of an alpha shifter.

"Hold him still," Whil cried.

I tightened my grip and blinked my vision clear just in time to see Bishop slam his elbow into Audrey's face.

Her head snapped back and panic, stronger than Bishop's pain, shot through my bond with her. It vanished a second later and she went limp, unconscious.

"No," I lurched forward to rescue her.

"Stay!" Cyrus commanded with a blast of power, keeping me in place, and he grabbed Audrey's arm and hauled her head out of the water.

Blood poured from her nose, and I grabbed both of Bishop's arms and pinned them to his sides before he could accidentally hit her again. Thankfully, Deacon leaped in and secured Bishop's head so I didn't have to worry about drowning him.

"Come on, Audrey," Cyrus said, pushing Audrey's wet hair out of her face. "Your mates need you."

She groaned, her expression dazed for a moment before her eyes finally focused on Cyrus. Then realization, horror, and pain swept in before turning into determination.

She shoved out of Cyrus's arms and threw herself on Bishop as best she could with me in the way.

More blue light flashed through the water and Whil's breathing turned ragged. Sweat slicked her skin, soaked her shirt, and dripped into her eyes, but she kept her hands pressed against Bishop's forehead even as he bucked and twisted in my grip. The red and black veins pulsed, hard and fast and more of them burst, sending more black pus into the water.

Bishop screamed and gasped for what felt like forever but was probably only a few seconds. Then his flailing started to slow and his breathing grew labored. But the veins still covered him and they weren't going away.

He was losing strength, losing the fight against the poison. I could feel the exhaustion and agony in our bond weakening his body and soul.

He wasn't going to give up and stop fighting. I could feel that, too. But he wasn't going to be able to go on for much longer and break my mate's heart.

"Fight it," I snarled at him. "Don't you dare fucking die." I shoved him against the stone slope. "Fight it. Don't. You. Die."

He groaned and his eyelids fluttered as if they were finally going to open after five days of unconsciousness. But instead, he sucked in a shallow breath, gurgled it out, and stopped breathing.

"No," Audrey gasped. "No. Please."

"Whil," Cyrus barked.

"Almost there," she ground out.

"He isn't breathing!" Cyrus snapped. "He—"

Audrey lurched forward and pressed her lips against Bishop's with a final kiss that made me want to scream.

This wasn't happening. No way in hell would this be their last kiss.

Except instead of actually kissing him, she breathed into his mouth.

"Audrey," Cyrus said, his voice breaking on her name, his alpha-in-control mask gone and his affection for her clear in the pain in his eyes.

"We'll save him. We just have to keep him alive long enough." She pulled back and felt for a pulse. "Too slow. I need him on a flat surface."

"He has to say in the water," Whil gasped.

"Fine," Audrey said, her expression fierce with determination. "Knox, start CPR. I'll keep doing the breathing."

Deacon shot her a wild look. "What the hell is CPR?"

"You don't—?" Her eyes widened then narrowed. "Knox, I'm teaching you CPR. Move aside. Hands here." She clasped her hands together, one on top of the other, and placed them on his chest. "Lock your elbows and push hard and fast, like this. Fifteen times. You're pumping his heart for him. Now show me."

I repeated her movements fifteen times and she gave Bishop a breath.

Another fifteen.

Another breath.

The golden glow around Whil's hands flared, and blue sparks jumped out of the water and sank into Bishop's face. More blue light flared around us, the flickers snapping faster and faster and I pumped my brother's heart while Audrey gave him breath. Again and again. Fifteen. Breathe. Fifteen. Breathe.

More of the black and red veins burst, except this time they didn't stay or get bigger, they drained their horrible pus into the water, shrinking until they were ugly black and red bruises under his skin.

"Come on, Bishop," Audrey said over and over again like a prayer, tears streaming down her cheeks while blood still oozed from her broken nose. "Please. Please. Come on. Please"

"Almost there," Whil gasped, her body trembling, her glow faint and flickering. "Just a little more."

Bishop gasped and his eyes fluttered open then closed again.

"Oh, God," Audrey cried, cupping his face and looking desperately at his closed eyes. "Tell me he's okay. Tell me he'll live."

"Tell me, please," I begged, trying to will Bishop into consciousness. He had to live. The thought that this wouldn't work, that we'd hiked as fast as we could and still failed was soul-crushing. It was worse than walking all the way to the death god's temple and failing to break my bond with Knox.

Whil's glow flickered bright for a second then completely vanished, and she collapsed against Deacon who held Bishop's head above the water.

My pulse lurched. She was out of magic and Bishop still hadn't woken up.

"No," I insisted, "just a little more. Please, Whil."

We were so close. Most of the veins had already sunk under his skin, but I could still see the poison lying like dark, horrific bruises under his flesh. She needed to get rid of all of it, every last stain to ensure he was safe.

My throat tightened and more tears streamed down my cheeks. If Bishop died, I didn't think I'd ever stop crying.

More blue light snapped through the water, dancing over Bishop, wrapping around his torso before sinking into him.

He gasped and pain lanced through our bond as streaks of blue raced to each poisoned bruise. His muscles contracted, but Knox held on tight, stopping Bishop from hitting me in the face again.

"Come on, Bishop," Knox growled. "Fight."

The blue light glowed brighter than the bruises and spread until his entire body glowed and I could barely look at him.

The pain from our bond sparked, little zaps that made me jolt, but they were getting weaker and weaker.

Finally, with a brilliant flare of blue that forced me to close my eyes, the pain vanished.

"What—?" Bishop groaned, the words making my heart lurch with hope.

A second later, I realized the agony that had been a constant presence from the moment I'd bonded with Bishop was gone. All that remained was my relief and Knox's.

My eyes flew open, locking with Bishop's gaze and I was falling, falling, falling into a sea of warmth and love flecked with brilliant green stars.

"Audrey," he breathed and a giant wave of love crashed into me.

I gasped, shocked that I could feel Bishop's emotions so strongly before we'd even sealed our mating bond.

Then Knox's relief and concern swelled, crushing inside me, swirling and churning with Bishop's, becoming a giant whirling vortex. I was exhausted and confused and relieved and worried and afraid and everything at once.

It was too much. So much more than what I'd been fighting before.

I'd thought Knox's emotions had been overwhelming, but this was a tsunami, inundating me from all sides. I couldn't figure out what emotions were mine and which were theirs, unable to push through the onslaught from my mates.

I clutched my head as if that would help me focus and differentiate where they ended and I began, but their worry slammed into me, tearing at what little hold I had on myself.

The worry exploded into fear and someone reached for me, but I jerked away. I couldn't let them touch me. Physical contact would only make it stronger.

I needed space. I needed to breathe. I needed all the emotions to stop before I lost myself completely.

"Audrey," Knox growled, his fear roaring through me.

I pushed away from the slope, farther into the pool.

Get away get away get away.

Please.

"What's wrong with her?" Cyrus demanded.

"She's panicking but I don't know why," Knox replied as I fought to breathe and keep my head above the water.

More fear roared through me. I was going to drown, emotionally and physically, if I didn't pull myself together.

But was that my emotion or Knox's or Bishop's?

I grasped onto the emotion and tried to concentrate on it but couldn't tell where it had come from. Desperate, I tried to connect with my bonds. Maybe if I found them, I'd be able to tell which emotions were theirs, but I couldn't find my bonds in the consuming vortex inside me.

My head dipped into the water, shattering my concentration, and the vortex whirled stronger.

No. Please.

I flailed, heaving myself up long enough to break the surface and suck in a quick breath, before dipping back under.

Nothing was working and now all I could feel was panic. It made me thrash even when a barely audible voice in the back of my head knew if I just stayed calm I could tread water.

But everything was happening so fast, crashing around me, crushing my insides, and—

Strong hands grabbed me, hauled me up, and pinned me to a wide muscular chest. Heat swelled around my heart, my shifter connection latching on to whoever held me.

Except it was more than just a fellow shifter. The connection was strong and steady, drawing me out of the vortex of emotions for a second, long enough for me to find a spark of myself and cling to it. It was someone my soul aligned with as if he were a mate or family... except the connection wasn't from Bishop or Knox.

"Can't take you anywhere," Cyrus rumbled and he cupped the back of my head with his hand and pressed my face into the crook of his neck, soothing me with his scent. "I should have asked if you could swim before I let you jump into the pool."

"I can swim," I groaned, hyperaware that I was completely naked and not caring that I was or that he didn't want me the way my soul wanted him, the way our shifter connection said we belonged together.

He carried me back to the edge of the pool and lifted me out of the water, setting me on the edge before pulling away. Except the loss of our connection let the vortex of emotions crash over me, twice as strong as before.

"Bishop, Knox, you need to try to block your bonds," Whil said with a weak voice.

"I'm not blocking my bond," Knox snarled as he reached for me. "Never again."

But the second he touched me, his emotions roared stronger, sending me spinning into darkness.

I heaved out of his grip, my heart breaking at the hurt in his eyes. "I'm sorry. I just— It's so hard to concentrate."

Cyrus hopped out of the water and clutched me to his chest again as I squeezed my eyes shut, sucking in ragged breaths and concentrating on the warmth around my heart from my shifter connection with him.

"I'm not letting you hold her all night," Knox spat. "She's my mate."

"And right now, you're overwhelming her with your bond," Whil said.

Knox growled. "I wasn't before. Not like this."

"She didn't have two mating bonds before," Whil huffed back. "You don't have to block it permanently, just until she can regain her bearings, and then you can carefully open it again. With both you and Bishop completely open to her, you're flooding her with emotions. Audrey—" Small hands grasped mine and I cracked open one eye to look at Whil.

She looked exhausted, her complexion was gray, and all of her golden glow was gone.

"Once you find your center, restrict the flow of their emotions. Just enough so they stop overwhelming you."

I nodded and leaned into Cyrus, needing all the steadiness I could get from his soul.

Slowly, the roar of emotions from Knox and Bishop eased, getting quieter and quieter until I could recognize my soul bonds with them and which emotions were theirs.

The heat around my heart grew and so did a warmth in my core. I was completely naked in Cyrus's powerful arms, my body pressed against his naked, muscular chest, and my soul ached for him to recognize that we were meant to be together.

Which was not what I was supposed to be thinking about.

I dragged my attention away from him and concentrated on turning down the volume on both Knox's and Bishop's emotions.

"That's it, beautiful," Bishop murmured.

He stared at me, his love and desire surging through our incomplete bond, not overwhelming me like before, but igniting a suddenly wild, primal desire within me.

The sensation exploded through my body, searing my nerves, turning them instantly hypersensitive, and making my breasts and core ache. My breathing turned ragged, and I trembled in Cyrus's grip, desire leaking from my core, my body instantly ready for what it wanted.

BISHOP

NEED FOR AUDREY TORE THROUGH ME, ALL CONSUMING AND WILD. MY cock went instantly hard and my wolf took over.

Mine. Audrey was mine.

I could feel it in my soul, in the incomplete mating bond wrapped around my heart. Somehow, even though it had only been a dream and neither of us had said the vows, Audrey had claimed me as hers. And completing the bond was the only thing I could think about.

I'd deal with what had happened, where the hell I was, and why it felt like I had cracked ribs later. Right now, I needed Audrey, needed to bury myself deep inside her and sink my teeth into her and complete the bond. And then, after she was fully mine, I needed to punch whoever had broken her nose.

"Wouldn't you rather someplace more comfortable?" Whil asked, placing a hand on my shoulder, but I jerked away and snarled at her.

No one was taking me away from my mate.

"Come on, Whil," Deacon said, urging her away from me. "His wolf is in charge right now, and from Audrey's scent, she's practically in heat."

My mate's face turned red, adorably embarrassed that Deacon was talking about her body signaling me that she wanted to mate.

Except my human half knew I should take care of her and not claim her on the stone floor of... where was I? A cavern? The healing pool?

Mine. Now, my wolf snarled.

He'd wanted to claim her from the beginning and had patiently waited while I courted her. But no more. She'd almost died when that man— no, that *thing* had attacked her. It hadn't smelled like a shifter, a human, or any other race I was familiar with. My wolf wasn't going to wait a minute longer.

And while my wolf wasn't nearly as wild as Knox's, he was still a primal, ferocious predator.

I can't stay, Knox said in my head, his telepathic connection drawing my attention to our twin bond and his emotions.

He was relieved that I was safe, but also barely hanging on from going feral, the fear of being inside a vise around his chest.

I turned to him. His expression was tight, and I grabbed the back of his head and pressed our foreheads together.

She's safe with me, I assured him.

I know, he replied. *I just want—*

What we had in the dream, I finished for him.

But your claiming should be just you two, he added, knowing my thoughts.

With a snarl, he jerked away from me. "Don't you dare leave her unsatisfied."

He stormed over to Audrey, still clutched tight in Cyrus's arms, and kissed her with a claiming ferocity that made the scent of her arousal spike and flood the air.

Then he jerked back, making her whimper, her lips chasing his, desperate for more.

"Next time," she breathed, watching him shift and race out of the cavern. Then her gaze jumped to me and her pupils dilated with lust.

"Mine," she growled, the sound low and dangerous, making my already hard cock harder.

Sisters! She was the sexiest woman I'd ever seen, and I liked this confident side of her, even if it was only her need riding her hard.

The tip of her tongue flicked out, wetting her lips, and she pulled out of Cyrus's embrace and crawled toward me.

A rumbling purr rattled in Cyrus's chest, there one second then gone so fast I might not have believed I'd heard it if his hungry gaze wasn't locked on her pussy. Her position put her on full display to him, but from her intent gaze on me, she had no idea what she was doing to him.

Sucking in a sharp breath, he shoved to his feet, as if he hadn't just reacted to her, and pretended the massive tent in his soaked pants wasn't giving him away.

He wanted our mate.

How long was he going to use the excuse of pack responsibilities to ignore what was obvious — or at least obvious to me?

I could see him being a complete idiot and trying to ignore it for the rest of his life... although maybe not.

When I'd regained consciousness, he'd been holding her as if they belonged together. There hadn't been any hint of him holding himself back and overthinking the situation like he usually did with women he was attracted to. He'd been acting on instinct, which told me his wolf had already decided. Audrey was his mate.

Hopefully, it was just a matter of time before his human half accepted the truth.

"We'll be outside," he said, his voice gruff as he pulled out a shirt and pants from a travel pack and set them beside a pile of smaller clothing haphazardly thrown on the ground near the cavern wall. "Come on."

He stormed in the same direction Knox had fled with Deacon and Whil close at his heels, leaving me and Audrey alone.

"Come here," I commanded, giving my wolf full control. Audrey and I had had our sweet bonding in our shared dream and now it was my wolf's turn.

A snap of my power broke free of my hold and compelled her to obey. But instead of being upset that I'd used my power on her, the hunger in her expression deepened. In fact, it didn't seem as if my power had affected her—

No, that wasn't right. It *had* affected her, but it hadn't commanded her. Instead, it awakened a power within her, something that I'd thought had just been a part of our shared dream, and not something that could happen in reality.

It was radiant and strong, stronger than it had been in our dream, and it rolled over me, a hot wave challenging my power and bringing it to the surface as if I wasn't the one in control of it, shocking me.

My wolf rumbled with pleasure, sucking in deep breaths of her arousal, waiting for her to come to him. Then, when she was mere inches away, he pounced, ignoring the pain in our chest. He grabbed her and rolled until she was pinned against the slope in the pool with our body.

"Mine," we snarled and she tipped her head back, exposing her neck.

"Claim me, alpha," she moaned, her hips already rocking up, rubbing her heated core against my cock.

I took her lips in a ferocious kiss fueled by my wolf's need to mate her and she kissed back, just as needy. Our tongues battled and our teeth clicked. Her fingers dug into my shoulders, and she ground herself against me as if she'd been aching with need for too long and was desperate for a release.

It was beautiful torture, her body begging for me, the whisper of her lust teasing through the bond making my wolf crazy.

I roughly palmed her breast, kneading her soft flesh and drawing a moan of pleasure. Her nipple tightened and I dipped into the water to suck on it.

Her lust coming through our bond swelled, swirling with mine. My heart raced and my soul strained toward her desperate to complete what we'd started in our dream.

I needed her more than I needed to breathe. My soul was incomplete without her. It always had been, and I'd always known I was waiting for someone amazing, someone who saw my twin for who he really was, who'd accept both of us.

I thrust forward, grinding down and hitting her clit. Her hips twitched, the jerky movement rubbing just where she needed, making her shiver and moan but not taking her over the edge.

I could feel the tension building in her through our bond as well as her frustration.

"Bishop, please," she begged. "I need you in me. I need to seal our bond."

My wolf released a snap of power, and her body shook. A throaty moan escaped her lips and her breaths turned ragged. She teetered on the edge, aching with a need that sent tingles racing up my spine. Every fiber of her being strained for more, for me, for our bond to be completed.

With a snarl, my wolf drew back our hips, drawing a whimper of displeasure from our mate, then plunged inside her with one powerful stroke.

Her walls fluttered around our cock with a whisper of the orgasm I was going to give her, and she released a cry of pleasure.

"Yes," she moaned, her head tipping back and turning to the side to expose her neck. "Make me yours."

"You've always been mine," my wolf snarled. "Always been fated for me."

My canines extended as I pounded into her with wild, ferocious strokes. I overwhelmed her with pleasure, making her moan and gasp, and the feeling of her desire roared through me.

Mine. Always mine.

She clung to me and bucked her hips, meeting me stroke for stroke, our bodies crashing together in a primal dance, our souls entwining tighter and tighter. Her channel quivered, its grip straining my hold on my release. But she needed to come first, always first — and multiple times once our bond was sealed.

She moaned my name, repeating it over and over again like a prayer, and strained her neck, tilting it as far as it could go.

Then her muscles clamped down hard on me and she screamed her release. That threw me over the edge. With a final thrust, my cum erupted from me, filling her up, satisfying my wolf's need to mate, and I sank my teeth into her neck just above Knox's mating marks.

Sensation roared through our bond, bliss, satisfaction, joy, and love, so much love. It flooded my soul and radiated warmth across my chest. It sank deep into every fiber of my being and locked into place. We were finally connected the way we were supposed to be, the way it had always been meant to be.

"I love you," she murmured. Her words were slurred, and I could feel her exhaustion rushing in.

"I love you, too," I whispered back as she passed out. "Always."

AUDREY

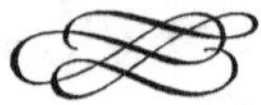

I woke in Bishop's arms, lying on a futon and covered with a light, soft blanket. We were in a small room with exposed thick stone blocks along the back wall and small blocks making up the other walls. Sunlight poured through a narrow window above our heads, and at our feet stood a plain wooden door. My whole face throbbed and I could barely open my right eye, but I'd happily pay the price of a broken nose again to ensure Bishop survived.

"There you are," he rumbled, the sound vibrating in my chest and setting off a soft, delicious warmth between my thighs. It wasn't a desperate need like it had been before and it certainly wasn't anywhere near the level of my heat. It was just me reacting to being naked in the arms of a sexy naked man who loved me.

"I could feel you waking up through the bond but it took you a minute to open your eyes," he said, pressing his lips against the top of my head and squeezing me tighter. "That's going to take some getting used to. I'm not even that connected with Knox and our twin bond is unusually strong."

"It is weird and there are some downsides to being able to sense each other's emotions," I told him. "We can't keep anything from each other, even if it's a lie to spare my feelings."

"Not much of a downside if it means I'll know when you need me and what you need."

I snuggled in closer, breathing in his bright, fresh-cut grass scent. He was alive and safe and mine, and I could feel through our bond that he was thrilled to be my mate. His love shimmered bright and warm around my heart and, just like I felt with Knox, I felt like I was home with Bishop.

Of course, I'd always felt like I belonged with Bishop. Not once had he made me feel unwanted or weak or unworthy. Everything Bishop had done had been to build me up, to prove I deserved love, and that there wasn't anything wrong with me, even though I couldn't shift.

But I also knew, if I'd bonded with him first, I'd never have bonded with Knox, and my soul needed Knox as much as it needed Bishop. I wasn't sure how I knew that or if I really was as powerful as they said and that was the reason I needed both of them — and Cyrus, too, if I was being honest with myself — but I felt more settled and at peace with who and where I was than I'd ever been before.

Bishop stroked a gentle hand along my cheek, his fingers skimming too close to my broken nose, spiking pain through my throbbing face and making me wince.

"Sorry." He jerked his hand away and leaned back so he could look me in the eyes. "Cyrus said I'm the one who hurt you."

Shame flickered through our bond and I responded by sending him more love.

His eyes widened in surprise. "*That's* going to take some getting used to, too. Can I do that?"

The shame vanished, replaced by curiosity. Then a massive wave of love and desire flooded me, making my heated core ache with need.

"Oh!" he gasped, then his voice lowered and his pupils dilated with desire. "I see. I've left my mate wanting."

With a sexy groan, he captured my lips in a long, sweltering kiss that stole my breath and left me gasping. His desire spun around and wove through mine with a heady rush of emotions that both of us could feel, drawing another sexy groan from him.

"You mentioned the disadvantage of the bond," he purred, teasing his lips down my neck and flicking his tongue against his mating mark.

Sensation jolted through me, rushing straight to my core and making me moan.

"But you didn't mention the advantages," he added.

He teased his lips to my breasts and sucked on one nipple then the other, working them into tight buds, before pushing the blanket aside and moving lower.

His need and love and awe roared through me before shifting into a ferocious hunger. He settled between my thighs and buried his nose in my curls, breathing in my scent.

Tremors of anticipation fluttered through my core, and he hummed in satisfaction, now knowing — because of our bond — how much I wanted him.

"Bishop," I moaned, tangling my fingers in his hair. "Don't make me wait."

"As my mate commands."

He swept his tongue through my folds in a slow, sensual stroke, sending shivers rushing up my spine. I moaned again and sank into the sensation. His desire and mine swirled together and grew stronger as he worked me to the edge.

I clung to him, riding the building wave, my hips bucking into his mouth. He pushed a finger inside me and sucked on my clit, drawing me closer and closer.

Right to the edge.

Then he pulled back before I could come, making me whimper in disappointment.

"I've got you, Audrey," he said, crawling up my body and kissing me, filling my mouth with the flavor of my desire.

The head of his cocked pushed at my opening and slowly — so damned slowly — he pushed inside me. My breath picked up, my pulse racing with anticipation while he bottomed out then held still, fighting to control himself.

"You feel so good and with our bond, it's even more intense." He met my gaze, capturing me with his warm brown eyes and the mesmerizing bright green flecks. "So perfect."

His love flooded me and he began to move, his pace getting faster and faster and my desire spinning tighter and tighter, taking me higher than he had before, and sending me spiraling over the edge.

My satisfaction sent him over the edge as well and together we whirled in bliss, his and mine mingling, feeding each other, before slowly releasing us.

A moment later someone knocked on the door.

"Well that sounded satisfying," Deacon chuckled through the door, making my face burn with embarrassment. "Wish I could give you more time, but our mighty leader wants to head out."

"Tell him Audrey needs to rest," Bishop replied.

Deacon snorted. "That didn't sound like resting."

"We've just bonded," Bishop insisted. "You know we're not going to be able to keep our hands off each other."

"You couldn't keep your hands off her before," he laughed. "But if you want more time, then you'll have to tell him yourself."

Bishop tipped his head back and groaned. "How long did it take us to get here?"

"Five days, and yes, Cyrus plans a slower pace so six or seven days back," Deacon replied.

"And the alliance meeting in Stonehaven will only be a few days after that," Bishop groaned. "That doesn't give us much time to prepare."

"Exactly. The bathrooms are at the end of the hall to your right, the stairs to the first floor beside them," Deacon said. "You probably have enough time to clean up and eat breakfast before Cyrus starts getting agitated. Oh, and watch your nudity. There are humans around."

Bishop sighed. "Looks like we should get up."

"If we don't, the next person at our door will be Cyrus, and I doubt he'll knock," I replied.

A small shiver of desire rushed down my spine at that thought but thankfully Bishop didn't comment on it. The bond didn't tell us where the other person's emotions were coming from, although sometimes it was pretty easy to guess.

Someone had brought our packs to the small room, leaving them in a neat row by the door, and Bishop grabbed a pair of pants while I wrapped myself in the blanket — not wanting to put on clean clothes until I'd bathed.

It wasn't a walk of shame if you were doing it with your mate.

"Sisters, you're so beautiful," Bishop groaned, his gaze raking down my body. "When we get back—"

"You'll have the meeting with the alliance members to prepare for." And I had no doubt Bishop was necessary.

Cyrus could conduct business and negotiate the best deal for the pack, but he needed Bishop's social finesse to put the alliance members at ease.

"There'll be times when I can get away. And besides—" He wiggled his eyebrows at me. "You do have another mate to keep you satisfied." He grabbed our packs before opening the door, gesturing for me to step out into a narrow, windowless hall lit by glowing stones. "Then after the meeting, you're all mine for at least a week."

"Just a week?" I asked with a chuckle, turning right and heading to the bathroom while pretending not to see the three men at the end of the hall staring at us. "Pretty sure we're mated for life."

"The week is just for us," he said, leaning close and dropping his voice to that sexy low rumble that always turned me on. "After that, I'll share you with my brother."

Heat blossomed across my cheeks and in my core, making both of us groan.

One of the men at the end of the hall gave us a knowing look before ushering the other two — who looked surprised — down the stairs.

"Damn," he said, clutching his chest in mock agony. "Teasing you now teases me. That's not fair."

I laughed at him. "I'd say that's only fair."

"Nothing is fair with you, beautiful. You can slay me with a smile and I'll always die happy."

"Yeah, well," I said, trying to get my blush under control. "Hold off on the dying for... I don't know... close to a century or so."

His expression softened and he pulled me into a warm embrace. "I promise. No dying. I'll never leave you, Audrey."

"I know." My throat tightened with all the fear I'd been fighting since he'd been poisoned.

"You'll never be alone again," he murmured as he pressed his lips to my forehead. Then he released a soft huff. "But we now have to change the conversation. Knox just yelled at me for making you upset."

I squeezed Bishop tighter, savoring his fresh green scent, and sent love to Knox to reassure him that I was fine.

This was going to be a very strange relationship, but I wouldn't change it for anything. I was with the people I was supposed to be with and loved by two incredible men.

AUDREY

BISHOP AND I SEPARATED AND WENT INTO THE APPROPRIATE BATHROOMS — Bishop having to point out which door said woman. Inside the women's bathroom was a long counter with three sinks and a wide mirror reflecting just how bad I looked.

My hair was a mess, my skin too pale from barely getting any sleep and overexerting myself, and my face was a swollen, bruised mess.

Thankfully, it didn't look like my nose was completely out of shape, so at least when it healed, I'd look more or less normal, but both of my eyes had blackened.

I couldn't believe Bishop had made love to me while I looked like a raccoon or called me beautiful. But I guess that was what it meant to be in love. I'd make love to Bishop no matter what he looked like because he was mine and we were meant to be together.

Across from the counter were three toilet stalls and tucked around a corner was an area with a bench, another counter, and three wide shower stalls. At the far end of the counter was a rack with fluffy towels and a half-full bin with used towels.

I quickly cleaned up, got dressed — ignoring my reflection in the mirror — and returned to the hall where Bishop was waiting for me.

We took the stairs down one flight to the first floor and stepped into a cafeteria.

The room wasn't big with half a dozen long tables and benches, but it looked warm and inviting. The whole left side was filled with tall, wide windows letting in streams of sunlight and looking out onto a square with grass and flowerbeds and benches.

A cluster of tall trees shaded half the square and with the rocky ground rising up in front and to the right, it gave the square a feeling of peaceful seclusion. A couple sat on one of the benches chatting while another woman was weeding one of the flower beds.

Inside, opposite the windows was an open kitchen where a stout, older man stood at the stove cooking something that smelled amazing, and at the far end sat the three men who'd been watching us.

"Morning, alpha," the cook said. "I'm just cooking up some extra sausage for you because I know how much meat you wolves like to eat." He winked at us and rolled half a dozen large sausages onto a platter then set it on the counter behind me. "There's also fruit and pancakes."

"Thank you," Bishop replied with a huge smile. "Everything smells incredible."

I took half a sausage, a couple of pancakes, and an orange — something I hadn't seen a lot of in Stonehaven — and we sat at one of the tables and ate. A few minutes later, Cyrus, Deacon, and Whil joined us.

"Sisters," Deacon breathed, looking at my face. "It didn't look that bad last night."

"It can take a while for bruises to form," Whil replied. "Here." She handed me a large cup filled with water. "Drink this."

Blue light flickered in its depths reminding me of the healing pool last night, and I raised my eyes in question. She'd pulled the poison out of Bishop and released it in the pool, not to mention none of us had cleaned up before we'd hopped in and Bishop and I— Well, I was pretty sure we defiled it by completing our mating bond.

"The pool purifies itself and it was clean when we woke this morning. All trace of poison and anything else was gone," she said.

"This isn't as refined as an elixir, which is why you have to drink so much, but it should help with your nose."

"Hopefully, you won't look like you lost a fight by the time we get back to Stonehaven," Cyrus said, his voice gruff.

"Hopefully," I repeated. I hadn't thought about what returning to Stonehaven would be like, especially if it looked like I'd been beaten up.

I was now mated to two of the pack's alphas, and while it was obvious I was weak, I didn't want it to be painted on my face. Who knew what I'd be up against when we returned. Velora and anyone else who had their heart set on being Bishop's mate would be furious with me, not to mention I'd been with Bishop when he'd been poisoned. Those who didn't like me before were probably spreading rumors that I was somehow responsible.

Except, wasn't I?

That man had been trying to poison me, not Bishop, and had only run away because Bishop would have killed him before he could touch me.

And there wasn't anything I could do about that. I couldn't convince people to like me. I'd never been able to convince anyone of anything. I just had to be careful, stick with the people I could trust, and live my life.

I drank Whil's not-elixir and finished my breakfast while the others talked about our return trip. When we were done, we returned our dishes to the cook and thanked him again then headed out of the building — which was built flush against a tall rock wall — into the outside square, and around to a set of wide steps.

The steps were carved into the rock wall beside the building and led up to the courtyard I'd seen last night with the statue of the woman pouring water and the entrance to the sacred pool. Knox, in his wolf form, lay by the statue watching the stairs.

He bounded over to me the second he saw me, and I wrapped my arms around his neck and nuzzled my face in his soft fur, breathing in his rich, wood smoke scent. Relief and love rushed through our bond and I sent relief and love back to him.

Bishop joined us in the hug and warmth billowed around my heart, our shifter connection aligning our souls, comforting and assuring us: this was who we were supposed to be with.

I wanted to be with you, Knox said, his emotions indicating he'd wanted to be close not necessarily have sex. *But Bishop needed you more and you deserved to sleep on a bed.*

"Thank you," I told him. "I love you and I promise, I'll work on getting us that greenhouse bedroom."

"A greenhouse bedroom?" Bishop asked.

"Knox and I spent the entire night together in Whil's greenhouse, which means he can be inside, it just has to be a glass room," I replied.

She wants to build it on the Residence's roof, Knox replied with a chuckle.

"So no one can see us naked!"

"What's this about naked?" Deacon asked, laughing as my face turned red. He'd seen *everything* last night and I had a foggy memory of maybe flashing Cyrus my privates... but I wasn't a hundred percent sure on that. The need to complete my bond with Bishop was all that I really remembered after saving him.

"She wants to build a greenhouse bedroom for Knox so they can spend the night together," Bishop said.

Deacon's eyes flashed bright, but it wasn't with amusement. It was with surprise and happiness. "That's a brilliant idea."

"And something we'll deal with once we get back to Stonehaven," Cyrus growled. "Let's get moving. I'm setting an easier pace but that doesn't mean we should waste time."

"Yes, alpha," Deacon chuckled, making Cyrus frown. "What? You *are* the alpha."

"But you only call me that when you're being a pain in my ass," he grumbled. "You and Nova."

Deacon's smile grew bigger. "It's our job. But you are right. Whil, can I carry your pack?"

"Absolutely," she replied, handing it over.

AUDREY

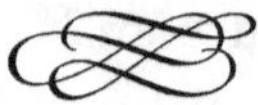

WE LEFT THE HEALING POOL AT A SLOWER PACE THAN WE ARRIVED, FOR which I was grateful. I wasn't as sore as I'd been walking north, but I was still sore. Bishop held my hand while Knox, in his wolf form, kept brushing up against me, and my heart couldn't have been fuller.

On top of that, a gentle breeze whispered through the forest and the sun shone brightly, turning into brilliant specks of dancing light with the fluttering leaves and branches.

Even Cyrus looked more relaxed. He and Deacon chatted about the upcoming alliance meeting and their thoughts about the merchants with the weapons powerful enough to take down a grimalkin.

"If they do what Gower claims, this could change things," Deacon said.

"Yes, we'd suffer fewer casualties but we have to weigh how this will also affect our alliances, not to mention anyone who wants to hurt or conquer us," Cyrus replied.

"You know I hate it when you bring a good thing down," Deacon huffed.

"But you know he's right," Bishop replied. "If Gower buys enough of these weapons he won't need our warriors, and our warriors and Whil's elixir are our primary export."

"Not until Audrey works her magic with her new technology," Deacon said, flashing me a teasing smile.

Cyrus slowed his pace to fall into step with Bishop. "New technology?"

"I might not have anything soon," I replied, glaring at Deacon, who just kept smiling at me. I hadn't been sure if Deacon, Nova, Whil, or Bishop had mentioned to Cyrus my plan to tell the pack's scientists and engineers about stuff from my realm, but it was clear they hadn't. I'd been planning to keep it a secret and not draw attention to myself until I actually had something to show Cyrus. I wanted him to see I was valuable to the pack, and I couldn't do that without proof.

"What kind of timeline are we talking about?" Cyrus asked.

"I don't know."

He frowned at me, but instead of wanting to shrink away from him like I used to, I just felt frustrated. I hadn't even started working with anyone, and I was still learning what the pack knew and didn't know.

Sensing my frustration, both Knox and Bishop hit me on both sides with a wave of confidence and determination. The emotions were so strong, I stumbled, needing to clutch Bishop's hand and lean against Knox to keep my balance.

Cyrus groaned and looked skyward. "We aren't even walking that fast."

Deacon's shoulders shook, and he clamped his jaw shut then slapped his hands over his mouth then gave up, releasing a deep laugh. The sound was contagious and soon all of us were laughing and I'd just couldn't stop.

It was like the final wall I'd put up to protect myself from the stress of trying to save Bishop had shattered, and all the worry and fear came rushing out in a laugh. The situation hadn't even been that funny.

"Really, though," Bishop said, sucking in deep breaths and trying to get himself under control. "That was our fault. You were frustrating her and we both sent support through our bond at the same time." He palmed the back of his neck and looked sheepish. "Next time, I won't be so forceful."

Me, too, Knox said.

"I don't mind," I assured them. I'd rather be knocked off my feet with love and support than anything else. That, and I liked how determined they were to show me that they had my back. No one else had ever been so certain. Not even Mila, who'd been my only friend in my old pack.

Sure, she cared for me but not enough to stand up against our alpha for me, and I wouldn't have expected that from her, either. She had a medium level of shifter strength but that still wasn't enough for Merrick to respect her. I wasn't sure if Merrick respected anyone.

Cyrus huffed and rolled his eyes. "I'm not criticizing or stopping you. I want to help and I need to know where you are in the process so I can provide the proper support."

Warmth fluttered around my heart at his words, a hint of a shifter connection forming even though we weren't touching. Or was that something else? The connection my soul was determined to make with him that I doubted he'd ever accept.

"I'm at the 'I don't know what I don't know' stage," I said, making him frown again.

"We've been spending time together," Whil added, "and I've been answering her questions about our realm and our pack."

"For example, lenses," Deacon said. "And I've talked to a few different human merchants and still don't know if they've figured out how to correct bad eyesight or not."

"What does human eyesight have to do with anything?" Cyrus asked.

"If they've figured out what concave and convex lenses do," I told him, "they'll have invented glasses to help people see better as well as magnifying glasses and telescopes."

A wrinkle formed between Cyrus's eyebrows. "I have no idea what those are. Those words sound weird."

"They sound weird to me, too," Deacon said and everyone else nodded, even Whil who had more experience traveling beyond the pack's lands.

"I guess that means the magic that lets me understand and speak to you can't translate the words." Which suggested that for whatever reason, no one had discovered those things.

"So like *hors d'oeuvres*," Bishop piped in.

Cyrus threw his hands up and groaned. "What the hell is an *hors d'oeuvres*? A new technology as well?"

"It's a mini appetizer," I told him. "But the magic doesn't translate it because it's not my native language."

Deacon looked at me as if he'd never seen me before. "You speak more than one language in your realm?"

"No," Bishop said on my behalf, eager to share what he'd learned, but then looked at me, his expression — and his emotions from the bond — guilty for answering when he didn't actually know if I spoke more languages or not.

I smiled at him and shook my head, sending him encouragement through the bond so he'd keep going. We'd had the conversation days ago during a picnic lunch and he was still excited at the idea of me helping the pack with what I knew.

"They have ways of communicating long distances so some foreign words have become common use."

"That's incredible," Deacon replied. I'd mentioned the lenses during one of our dinners together when Bishop was away, but I hadn't talked about all the other things from my world.

"What would be the fastest and easiest thing to make?" Cyrus asked.

"The lenses," I replied without hesitation. I'd been thinking about what needed the least amount of learning since I'd started seriously learning about this realm. "They require creating perfectly clear glass which you already have on some of your windows and creating the glass with a curve... and I'm not sure the best way to go about doing that."

Cyrus pursed his lips, his gaze traveling into the woods ahead of us as he thought. "When we get back, I'll set you up with Isac. He's our best glassmaker. He should be able to make what you need."

His attention jumped back to me, his eyes bright with determination, something I'd never seen from him before. The look made my heart flutter and a sliver of the warmth in my chest slipped down to my core. That annoying voice inside me started to speak up, but I shove it aside, not wanting to shatter the moment.

Except he must have seen something in my eyes, because he grunted and looked away, shattering the moment.

"The faster you make something, anything," he said, his voice gruff. "The faster the reluctant members of our pack will accept you."

BISHOP

I couldn't stop looking at Audrey. Even with both her eyes bruised and her face slightly swollen, she was still the most beautiful woman I'd ever seen. She practically glowed with relief, and the sense I got through our mating bond was that everything was right... well, almost right. *Almost* right because of my surly, obstinate older brother.

But now I knew why he was holding back *and* that he'd realized a solution. He wasn't going to die thinking he had to mate with a woman the pack would accept. He just had to make the pack accept the woman he wanted.

We hiked until the sun reached the horizon, moving at an even slower pace than the one we'd set for Audrey after her heat, and I was still exhausted when Deacon found us a campsite.

We'd even stopped for a longer than normal lunch, Cyrus making sure Audrey had eaten everything before moving on — apparently there'd been something about walking and choking while I'd been unconscious, and Cyrus was his usual overprotective self — which I wasn't going to complain about.

Audrey was everything to me, and while I knew I shouldn't treat her like glass and she wasn't going to break, I couldn't calm my need to keep her safe.

Part of that came from Knox, his wolf riding him hard after all the stress from the last couple of days, but the other part was all me.

The poison that had nearly killed me with my more powerful healing had been meant for Audrey. And the *thing* that had attacked us hadn't smelled natural.

Cyrus ordered Knox to hunt, Deacon to gather firewood, and Whil to find berries and greens to supplement our dinner. Then he grabbed our canteens to fill them at the nearby river, leaving me alone with my mate since we'd woken up this morning.

"How are you feeling," Audrey asked me, gathering enough wood from the surrounding forest to start a fire.

"Tired," I confessed.

"You feel tired." She stacked the wood like I'd taught her and pulled a starter from her pack. "I remember when Cyrus asked me if I could start a fire without a starter as if everyone could do that."

"Most of us can," I replied. "We learn as pups, but the starter is faster and more consistent."

She rolled her eyes at me, a soft smile tugging at her lips and the feeling of a groan teasing through our bond — and not the sexy kind of groan, the kind made when Deacon told a bad joke.

"I'd like to see him in my realm." She lit the kindling and gently breathed on the flames, encouraging them to grow. "Tell him to turn on a smartphone and make a call. We all learn *that* as children."

I snorted a laugh. "I have no doubt Cyrus would be lost in your realm, and I doubt he'd be as gracious learning all the things he'd need to know to survive as you were."

"Yeah, I could see a whole bunch of broken phones. God, I can't imagine him behind the wheel of a car. All the other drivers doing crazy driver stuff would drive him crazy."

I sighed, my chest aching with longing. "I really wish I could visit your realm, see you in your element."

Her gaze dropped to her hands, an action born of years of abuse that she probably wouldn't be able to completely get rid of.

"I wasn't that impressive there, either."

"You weren't given a chance to be impressive," Whil said as she stepped through the underbrush about twenty feet away. "And I wish I *could* open the gate, allow you and the boys the share each other's realms. I think I've figured out how to recreate the spell that brought you here, but..."

"But it involves an incomplete mating bond," Audrey replied as her expression darkened, probably remembering the horrible events that brought her to our realm.

"Yes and I'm not willing to do that to someone." Whil set her foraging down — a collection of wild spinach and mushrooms that would go well with whatever Knox caught — and started pulling the collapsible rotisserie and everything else we needed to make dinner out of our packs.

"You shouldn't," Audrey said, settling in my lap and cuddling against me.

Her scent flooded my senses, sweet and fresh, as warmth billowed around my heart and contentment radiated through our bond.

I wrapped my arms around her, drawing a soft sigh, while trying to ignore my hardening cock. She wouldn't want everyone watching, or even just hearing us have sex, and really, we were both too tired for it.

A few minutes later, Deacon returned with an armful of firewood, then Cyrus came back with our canteens. A few minutes after that, Knox returned with a perfectly skinned and gutted goat... in his human hands and not his wolf's teeth.

Deacon raised his eyebrows in surprise.

"What?" Knox huffed, handing him the goat.

Deacon continued to stare in disbelief as Knox stormed to my side, sat, and pulled Audrey into his lap.

A part of me wanted to protest that she was mine and our bond was still new, but the rest of me knew he needed this. He'd been under extreme stress and hadn't gone feral, but also hadn't been able to hold Audrey because he'd been holding me, keeping me alive.

"Audrey, you *are* a goddess," Deacon said in exaggerated awe, drawing a growl from Knox. "I've rarely seen him choose to be human."

"Don't poke him," Cyrus warned. "I won't stop him if he wants to pick a fight."

"I'm happy to help him let off steam," Deacon shot back. "But he's not going to."

Knox growled again but didn't move and I felt Audrey's pleasure at knowing that Knox would rather cuddle with her than let the feral creature inside him take over and fight Deacon.

We ate and chatted as the sun sank below the horizon, and it felt right, comfortable. Even Cyrus relaxed and I laughed at a few of Deacon's bad jokes. Whil, whose glow was weak — indicating she'd completely drained her magic saving me — turned in early, and Audrey dozed off in Knox's lap soon after.

We need to talk about what we're returning to, Cyrus said in my head. *Your campaign to show Audrey off at the festival worked on most of the pack, but not all, and Audrey was with you when you were attacked.*

When she *was attacked,* Knox corrected.

Pretty sure the rumor mill will have it twisted around by the time we get back, Deacon replied, and I hated that he was right.

Some of the pack seemed to think so little of Audrey that I doubted it would even occur to them that she had actually been the target. They'd chalk it up to a foreigner attack and not even consider that it could have been a pack member.

Of course, it *hadn't* been a pack member, but it also hadn't been a foreigner, not one I could identify.

I think we might have a bigger problem than the rumor mill, I said, making everyone look at me. *Whatever attacked me and Audrey didn't smell like anything I've ever scented before.*

The closest scent I could compare it to was a grimalkin with its foul, almost rotting scent. Except it hadn't been quite the same, and the thing that had attacked us had fought like a man. It had hidden in the shadows waiting for us and there'd been an intelligence in its attacks that went beyond that of a beast's instincts.

I shuddered. Had the grimalkins gained the ability to shift? The idea seemed impossible, but in a realm where powerful beings leaked their magic into the ground where they slept, anything was possible.

We need Whil looking into whatever it was, I said, even though I knew it was going to be impossible. Without the creature, she had nothing to study, and all we could do was wait for it to make another appearance.

Still doesn't address how we're dealing with Audrey and the pack, Deacon said, knowing as well as I did that Whil couldn't do anything with the current situation.

She's my bonded mate. My fated *mate,* I said. *They're just going to have to get over themselves. You and Cyrus might be more powerful than me, but that doesn't mean I can't defend Audrey or my position in the pack.*

But as soon as I said it, I knew that wasn't what Deacon was really talking about. Not everyone would take a direct path to expressing their dislike for the situation, and that meant Audrey wasn't safe being alone. And trying to convince everyone Audrey and I were fated for each other wasn't going to be easy, either. Velora had already accused Audrey of using magic to trap Knox. She was going to lose her mind when she learned I'd mated Audrey as well.

"Fuck," I hissed. *Velora is going to be a problem.*

She'd been not-so-subtly trying to catch my eye for over a year now, and I'd been trying to keep her at a professional arm's length.

Do you have someone to replace her as beta? Knox asked, jumping straight to the heart of the matter.

Yes, Cyrus replied. *Zondra knows most of what Velora does.*

But it's not that easy, I added, having already had this conversation about replacing Velora with her assistant with Cyrus since she'd been less than welcoming of Audrey. *Her fur is already bristled thinking Audrey is stealing me away. If we release her from her position, we won't be able to keep as close an eye on her and she'll be able to spread rumors.*

More rumors, Deacon corrected. *She hasn't left proof, but I'm pretty sure she's spreading them already and with us gone, I'm sure they've gotten worse.*

Cyrus ran his hands down his face. *She was such a good beta in the beginning.*

Deacon snorted. *She's always had her eye on Bishop and a spot as one of the alpha's mates.*

Well, we all know I'm shit at dealing with situations like this, Cyrus said with a growl of frustration, knowing as we all did that this situation needed to be handled carefully. He couldn't just demote her. *Figure out the best way to approach this,* he said to me, *then tell me what you need me to do.*

I nodded and reached for Audrey's hand, the urge to touch her swelling inside me. I needed to figure out the right way to handle the situation or I'd make everything worse for her.

And while I knew all four of us would fight whoever disagreed with the fact that Audrey was my mate and therefore an alpha of the pack, she'd feel guilty and embarrassed, and I wasn't sure if I could convince her to be angry about it instead. Not yet.

The problem was, I wasn't sure if there *was* a good way out of this.

AUDREY

Six days later, soaked and tired, we returned to Stonehaven. It had started raining just after lunch with the steady stream of a normal storm and not the downpour of a magically enhanced one — thank God. But with no good place to stop on the road between the shelter and Stonehaven, we'd just kept walking.

Well, Cyrus, Deacon, and Knox had kept walking. Whil, Bishop, and I had ridden in the cart... and had been riding in the cart since yesterday morning at Cyrus's command, something I hadn't complained about. I was tired, and my face, while feeling better than when I'd woken after saving Bishop and sealing our bond, was still tender, and my feet hurt.

Thankfully, my mating bond with Bishop hadn't set off another heat, and I hadn't slowed us down or embarrassed myself by jumping my mates or Cyrus and demanding sex for five days straight.

Deacon pulled the cart into the large courtyard where the road led into town, released a heavy sigh, and wiped water out of his eyes. "Home sweet home."

"If you need anything," Whil said, gathering her packs and hopping out of the cart, "ask me in a few days. I plan on sleeping."

"Of course," Cyrus replied scowling at the cart while crossing and uncrossing his arms if he were angry— No, not angry... uncertain?

"Cyrus!" Zavier called out as he rushed across the courtyard.

"You're on duty?" Cyrus asked, his shoulders relaxing as if he knew how to handle *this* situation and was relieved to not have to figure out whatever had been bothering him.

"Just changing shifts with Vida." He jerked his thumb over his shoulder at a woman standing in a security guard box. "I can take care of your cart."

"Thanks," Cyrus replied.

"Also, the delegates from the Mountain and Sea Alliance arrived yesterday. They've probably just started dinner if you wanted to see them tonight."

"Fuck," Bishop hissed as he hopped off the cart and extended a hand to me to help me down. "So much for having a day or two to get organized."

"Alsoooo..." Zavier's gaze jumped to me then jumped away.

Knox growled and jerked closer to me and Bishop, and Zane's eyes flashed wide.

"It's got something to do with Audrey?" Bishop asked.

"There's a rumor going around that Audrey was responsible for Bishop getting hurt."

My throat tightened, a wave of worry and guilt churning in my stomach, and Bishop pulled me into his arms. I couldn't deny it. I *was* responsible for Bishop being poisoned.

"Quinn and I have been spreading the rumor that Audrey and Knox and—" He drew in a sharp breath and squared his shoulders. "And Bishop are fated mates. Quinn thought it best to push the romantic side after you sang *Fated Stars* at the dance." He met Cyrus's gaze head on in a direct challenge to the more powerful alpha. "Quinn just came up with the idea. I'm the one who spread it around. Don't blame her."

"Zavier," Cyrus huffed. "You know I hate rumors."

"I do," Zavier replied, his gaze locking with Cyrus's.

"But I'm glad you and Quinn are working to counteract them."

"And your rumor isn't a rumor," Bishop added, drawing Zavier's attention. "It's true. Just like with Knox, Audrey and I bonded without having to say the vows."

"I knew it!" Zavier fist-punched the air, his gaze flickering to Cyrus so fast I almost missed it.

I wondered if he still had a bet with Quinn that Cyrus was interested in me. Was he hoping Quinn was right and Cyrus would be next? Or was he worried he was going to lose the money he'd won betting on me and Bishop?

"How about you add that Audrey saved Bishop to your rumor repertoire," Deacon suggested. "Whil did the magic, but if it wasn't for Audrey, he would have died."

"Deacon," I hissed at him. "That's not true."

The huntmaster gave me a dry, *"you didn't really just say that"* look. "What would you say that CPR thing was? He'd stopped breathing and Whil needed more time."

"It's true," Whil added, offering me a soft, exhausted smile. "Without your CPR, I wouldn't have been able to save him."

"He stopped breathing?" Zavier's eyebrows hit his hairline. "I want to know all about it, but Quinn will kill me if I hear it first. I'm already in trouble knowing you two are mate bonded."

"That and it's raining?" Deacon replied, the skin around his eyes crinkling with laughter.

"Fuck! Shit! Ahhh!" Zavier sputtered, realizing we all looked like drowned rats and the rain was still pouring down on us. "I'll take the cart. Go! Go!"

Deacon's smirk deepened. "You're giving your alpha commands now?"

"No, I—

"Stop teasing the kid," Cyrus said, shaking his head at Deacon.

"Not a kid," Zavier mumbled as he hurried to the push bar at the front of the cart.

"No, you're not," Deacon chuckled. "When are you going to mate that sweet little schoolteacher?"

"Deacon!" Cyrus barked with a snap of power that did nothing to diminish Deacon's grin.

"You're horrible," I hissed at the huntmaster as Zavier hurried away with the cart.

"Come on," he groaned. "Everyone can see it but those two."

"And they both *just* turned twenty-one," Bishop said, hefting his pack as Knox took mine and his in one hand and slung them over his shoulder. "They're still young. Give them time."

"They'll realize it soon enough," Whil added, wiping water out of her eyes. "The more you push, the longer they'll resist it."

"True," Deacon sighed. "I remember being an idiot at twenty-one, too."

"You're still an idiot," Cyrus said with a laugh, making me stare at him in surprise.

"Oh my God, did Cyrus just tell a joke?" I whispered to Bishop, knowing Cyrus could still hear me with his wolf-enhanced hearing.

"Yep," Knox replied at full volume.

"Mark it on your calendar," Bishop added, making Cyrus groan and march down the street a little faster.

"Come on," he said over his shoulder as we followed. "You need to get your mate out of the rain and I need to clean up and figure out how to schmooze."

"I'll do all the schmoozing," Bishop said with a sigh. "You can just look important and in charge."

I leaned into Bishop, feeling how tired he was and how much he didn't want to go to dinner tonight and play politics.

"*You*," Cyrus shot back, "are going to Audrey's suite to spend the night. You're both tired, and I'll need you tomorrow when the real schmoozing and politics start. Both of you."

"Both of us?" I squeaked.

This was a trap, a way for Cyrus to make me embarrass myself so he could—

No.

That wasn't how Cyrus did things. He wasn't Merrick.

Still, all those people looking at me, judging me, wondering why the hell I was with the alphas. I wasn't ready for that. I—

Knox's grip on my hand tightened and a wave of support washed through the bond.

"You're mated to two of the three pack alphas," Cyrus said as if he could read my mind. "You're an alpha of this pack, Audrey, and you deserve to be involved in pack business."

"And I want you by my side if you're up for it," Bishop said, his love flooding through our bond, warm and heady. "You're mine and my pack will know it."

"But these talks are important and I don't know your culture let alone your politics." And there'd be so many people staring at me, judging me, wondering why a weakling—

No. Stop thinking that. Stop repeating Merrick and Sterling's poison.

I shoved those horrible thoughts aside, and pride washed through both of Knox's and Bishop's bonds.

"You don't know all our culture or politics," Cyrus said, stepping out of a narrow alley, making me realize we'd stayed to narrow, near-abandoned streets and alleys for Knox — who was still in his human form — and onto the main road leading into Old Town. "But you're very good at being quiet and observing."

"Good idea," Deacon said as if he just realized Cyrus's plan. "Audrey, you're perfect. You won't be able to understand anyone speaking in their native tongue, but you can still see who talks to who and study their body language when they think Cyrus and Bishop aren't paying attention."

"So I'm a spy?" A small glimmer of hope sparked in my chest. I didn't necessarily like the idea of being a spy, but this was a chance to prove my usefulness to the pack.

"You're an observer," Cyrus corrected, "and only if you want to."

"I do. I'll do it." All those years of being beaten into submission and of trying to stay small and unnoticed might actually become good for something.

AUDREY

We separated when we reached the Residence, Cyrus and Deacon entering through the front door, Whil heading across the grounds to the cottage, and Bishop, Knox, and I walking around the castle to my suite's French doors. We were already soaked so a few more minutes in the rain wouldn't hurt us, and I wasn't ready to leave Knox just yet or have Bishop taken away on pack business by someone, especially not Velora

The mattress that had been set on the small patio when Bishop had been poisoned so Knox could stay with him was gone, but Knox didn't hesitate — there was barely a flicker of fear in our bond — as he followed me and Bishop inside.

"Let's get you cleaned up and warm," Bishop said, a hint of seduction in his voice but not enough to overcome my exhaustion or the exhaustion I knew he was feeling.

Even after seven days and having shifted every day to speed up his recovery, he still didn't have the stamina he used to have, and I feared he'd never get it back.

All because he'd protected me.

And while I could feel in our bond that he didn't blame me and would do it again if it meant protecting me, I still felt guilty.

"She's tired," Knox said, his voice a low growl as he and Bishop ushered me into the bathroom.

"Yeah," I mumbled, not resisting them when they positioned me in front of the shower.

"You'll be happier after you sleep." Knox turned on the taps, the sudden *shush* of water startling me as if I'd dozed off for a second.

"I don't like where your thoughts go when you're tired," Bishop said, grabbing the hem of my shirt and peeling the almost see-through fabric up my torso.

Jeez, I must have been tired if I hadn't even noticed that my thin shirt clung to my chest doing nothing to hide the fact my nipples were pebbled from the chilly rain and the fabric hugged the curve of my breasts like a second skin.

"Audrey, whatever you're worried about, we'll face it together. The three of us," he said.

Knox grunted in agreement, and Bishop cupped my cheeks with his palms, urging me to look at him.

The warm endless night of his gaze captured mine, suspending me with the certainty of his love, and I floated among brilliant green stars. In his eyes, I was precious and desired. Neither Bishop nor Knox blamed me for what had happened, something I already knew. But it was harder to fight my demons when I was tired. When all three of us were tired.

I pushed love through the bonds, hoping to give them strength, but Knox growled and a snap of his power broke my concentration.

"But I—" I protested. I wanted to help them, *needed* to help them.

"It's our turn, mate," Knox huffed. "You held me together the whole walk to the pool when you were suffering too—"

"And sent me support to keep my strength up the whole walk back," Bishop finished. "Yeah, we're all tired. But you're exhausted, Audrey, and you can't even see it."

"And when you're exhausted," Knox said, "the shit those assholes fed you while you were growing up gets louder.

"Are you listening to my thoughts now?" I asked. It was rude to eavesdrop on people's thoughts and no shifter that I knew about could do it consistently — although it wouldn't surprise me if Knox, Bishop, and Cyrus could.

"Don't need to," Knox huffed as he knelt in front of me and pulled down my pants. "It's so obvious, even I can figure it out."

"Hey," I huffed back. "Don't insult my mate."

He rolled his eyes at me, grabbed my hips, and buried his nose in my curls.

You're mate still can't believe he's yours, he said in my head. *And I'll spend the rest of my life worshiping you to make amends for hurting you in the beginning.*

"You *were* an asshole," Bishop chuckled. He pressed his lips against mine, his tongue teasing the seam of my mouth, asking for entrance.

I opened and let him in for a long, languid kiss full of tongue, while Knox licked and sucked just as slowly at my entrance.

The fire of need grew slow and steady, building and building until rolling over me. It wasn't the biggest orgasm either of my guys had ever given me, but it was still perfect. Hot and flowing, dragging tension I hadn't noticed I had from my body.

It was exactly what I needed to let go of the worry and adrenaline that I'd clung to in order to stay strong for them.

"That's it," Bishop purred, and together he and Knox drew me into the shower, cleaning me with loving and gentle attention.

They kept me relaxed, not giving my mind a chance to return to my worries with soft, flesh against flesh teasing but not building my desire any tighter.

It was perfect. All of us were too tired for much more, and after I was clean and bundled in a warm fluffy towel, I climbed into bed sandwiched between them.

At some point in the night, Knox left, his claustrophobia forcing him outside. He lasted longer than he said he could and had only just started to get uncomfortable, suggesting maybe, with love and patience, his time indoors could be extended.

I drifted back asleep, my heart warm with their bonds, and when

I woke with brilliant morning sunlight streaming through the windows, the warmth was still there.

My lips curled into a soft lazy smile. I lay in my mate's arms, my back pressed against a firm, muscular chest, safe and secure and loved.

And then I realized who held me, and my smile grew into a goofy grin.

Knox.

He'd come back to bed.

"Bishop had to take care of pack business before breakfast," Knox rumbled in my ear, his hot breath washing over the back of my neck.

"So you thought you'd keep me warm?" I turned in his arms and nuzzled my nose into the crook of his neck, breathing in his rich wood smoke scent.

"Always. I came back an hour and a half before Bishop had to leave," he said and I couldn't even feel a hint of anxiety from him.

"Thank you."

He huffed his acknowledgment, the love in the bond saying more than words, and brushed his lips against mine with the beginning of a kiss, but stopped and groaned a second later.

"Asshole," he hissed, rolling away from me onto his back. "Bishop says breakfast will be here in five. He wants me to wake you, ensure you've eaten and changed into the dress he's sending with our meal, and have you outside the Residence's front doors in twenty minutes."

"We could still…" I said, sliding my hand down his chest.

But he grabbed my wrist before I could reach his cock. "You can't be late and you can't look recently fucked. Cyrus and Bishop are taking the alliance members on a tour of the city."

And the whole point of me being there was to not draw attention to myself, something that would definitely happen if I was late.

"Bishop promises some of that later," Knox said with a wolfish smile sending heat rushing to my core. "He's going to have to wait his turn."

AUDREY

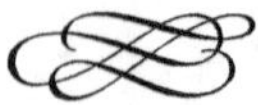

THE DRESS WAS A BEAUTIFUL EMERALD GREEN, THE SAME SHADE AS THE flecks in Bishop's and Knox's eyes with flowers embroidered on the bodice in golden thread.

It was a similar design to the dresses that were popular in the pack with a tie securing it around my neck and another mid-back to give it shape. But instead of being completely backless, the fabric tucked around me at the middle of my back, hiding two of the four large puncture-wound scars marring my skin and the tie around my neck was also slightly different. It was thinner than the usual design, revealing more of my neck and shoulders, and ensured both Knox's and Bishop's mating marks were clearly visible.

No one would be able to question if I was mated to them with the very permanent and uncommon bite-mark scars out in the open. And while I was thrilled at the idea that my mates weren't embarrassed by me and wanted their whole pack to know I belonged to them, it also made me nervous. Not everyone would like that I mate bonded with Bishop, and I needed to be wary and on my best behavior to avoid causing problems.

"Stay close to Bishop or Cyrus," Knox said, his gaze locked on his mating mark as lust oozed like lava through our bond. "I'll keep an eye on you as best I can, but part of the tour involves the market and there are too many people there."

"I'll stay close." And I wouldn't cause a scene. Although I knew that wasn't what Knox was worried about.

Whoever had attacked me and Bishop was still out there. I doubted they'd outright attack me while surrounded by dozens of witnesses, but those same people could act as cover for a secret attack, like a nick with one of his poisoned claws. It would be as easy as someone bumping into me.

A shiver rolled down my spine and Knox pulled me into a tight hug.

"I won't let anything happen to you."

"I know," I said against his chest as I nuzzled closer and drew in a breath heavy with comforting wood smoke. "I trust you."

"Good. Now go before I rip this dress off you and fuck you senseless."

A wave of need slammed into me and I groaned as I stepped out of his embrace.

"When this is done..." he promised.

He yanked off his shirt, dropped his pants, and shifted into his enormous black wolf.

I bit back another groan. This tour couldn't end fast enough.

You coming, Audrey? Bishop asked in my head, sending more need rushing through me. *The tour is about to start.*

Oh, she'll be coming. Tonight, Knox replied, making Bishop groan and me shiver in anticipation.

"Stop with the sex comments. I'm going to smell like I'm in heat again," I huffed, trying to think of ice-cold showers.

Only the other members of our pack, the gryphons, and the Dedearc will notice, Knox replied.

"That's two-thirds of the tour group."

Knox chuffed with wolfy laughter. *More like half. There's a human kingdom and a human independent state in the Alliance.*

"Still doesn't make me feel better."

But the embarrassment of smelling like I needed sex cooled some of my desires, and I hurried out onto my patio before either of my mates could work me up again.

Knox followed beside me until we reached the edge of the Residence and our next turn would make us visible to whoever stood in the front courtyard. He sent a wave of love and confidence into the bond and stepped out of sight behind a hedgerow.

I squared my shoulders determined to appear confident despite the voice from my past insisting that I didn't belong and rounded the corner.

Close to three dozen people gathered in the center of the courtyard near the fountain with the two enormous wolves on either side of a woman pouring water from a large urn.

As Knox said, half of them were human with varying degrees of sun-kissed skin, from golden tan to rich dark brown, and three-quarters of them were men. About half of the men wore military style uniforms and by the looks of them, represented two different militaries. The other men wore clean, tailored clothes while none of the human women wore military uniforms. They all wore dresses, some elaborate and some quite plain.

Beside them were two men and five women who looked human — the same height and build as the others — but they weren't. They gave off a predatory, shifter vibe that I didn't recognize and wore clothing similar to our pack's clothing. They had to be the gryphons, a type of shifter everyone in my realm thought was just legend like all the other fairy tale shifters: dragons, hydra, unicorns, and elementals.

To the right of them, a few steps away from the humans, were six enormous lizard-like people. The Dedearc.

I'd seen a few of them the last time I'd visited the market and hadn't wanted to stare, so I hadn't gotten a good look at them. But now, standing a good fifty feet away, I had a chance to study their unique features.

They reminded me of some of the demons I'd seen on TV. They had human-shaped bodies that were covered in scales — black or dark red or blue on their back and shifting to cream or white on their front. They had a lizard-like tail and a reptile-like head, and a few of them had short horns at their temples like incubi or succubi, reinforcing my suspicion that they were a type of demon or at least had demon ancestors.

They all wore the same loose clothing made from a shimmering silky fabric that was cut to accommodate their tail but didn't give me a hint to their gender. Of course, for all I knew, their species might not have a gender.

Lucius and another wolf shifter, a woman I didn't recognize, talked with the shortest of the Dedearcs who still stood half a head taller than him, which meant all the Dedearc were at least a head — and a few even head and shoulders — taller than the humans and gryphons, while Bishop talked to a Dedearc a head taller than him and two of the humans in military uniform.

Nearby, Deacon talked with three human men wearing fancier clothes. Their complexion was fairer than the other humans and their facial features sharper and narrower. All three of them would have been handsome if they hadn't been giving me an ever-so-slightly creepy vibe.

Even from where I stood at the edge of the Residence, I could sense — either from their body language or from whatever small wolf instinct I had — that they didn't belong with any of the other humans and were trying too hard to be nice to everyone.

Sterling had played that game with me too many times when I'd first moved into his house, and I'd learned my lesson not to trust anyone who's too friendly or too helpful. They wanted something. And the moment they didn't get what they wanted, their fake friendliness vanished and I'd be punished.

The Residence's front doors opened, and Cyrus walked out, drawing everyone's attention. His arrival probably marked the beginning of the tour, so I hurried toward the group.

I got halfway before Velora stepped out from the shade of a tree and grabbed my wrist.

"Where do you think you're going?" she hissed. "You don't belong here."

I tried to wrench free of her grip, but with her shifter enhanced strength, I didn't stand a chance.

"You go right back to that suite you don't deserve and stay there until the Alliance meeting is over."

My instincts to shrink in on myself and look at my feet in submission screamed at me, and I fought with everything I had to keep my head up. "Let me go."

"Not until you're where you belong."

She yanked on my arm, making me stumble, and marched back the way I'd come, not waiting for me to catch my balance.

"Velora," Bishop snapped from behind us, his voice quiet, low enough that the Alliance delegates wouldn't hear, but edged with steel.

"Bishop," she purred. She spun around, jerking me off balance again, and gave him a heated look. She even battered her eyelashes at him as if that would make her more attractive.

A growl bubbled in my throat. She was trying to take what was mine and that ferociousness trapped deep inside me didn't like that. Not. One. Bit.

But before I could foolishly attack her, Bishop snarled, her attempt at flirting hardening his expression and making my ferociousness preen with satisfaction.

"What are you doing with my mate?" he ground out.

"Your mate?" Velora hissed, her eyes flashing wide.

She jerked her attention back to me, her gaze jumping from one mating mark on my shoulder to the other and back again.

Something ugly passed across her expression then disappeared as she turned back to him, returning to overly flirty. "Congratulations, Bishop. You should have told me you'd picked your first mate."

"My *only* mate," he replied, making my soul sing with pride and pleasure while the cautious part of me cringed.

I didn't want Bishop to lead Velora or anyone else on, but there was no wiggle room in his declaration. There was no reason for her to pretend to be nice to me anymore.

"She's mated to two of the pack's alphas." Bishop held his hand out to me and I took it. He tucked me against his side, reinforcing his claim on me. "She belongs at our side, especially during political events."

"Of course, alpha." Velora dipped her head in submission but managed to glare at me through her lashes. "I'll make sure she has a place at the alpha's table at dinner tonight."

"It's already taken care of. Come on, Audrey," he said, and he turned his back on Velora. "The tour has already started. We need to catch up before we fall behind."

We hurried after the group of delegates as they stepped through the open gate separating the Residence from Old Town. I kept my focus ahead of me, knowing Velora was trying to burn a hole in the back of my head.

I didn't want another confrontation with her, especially without Bishop, Knox, or Cyrus nearby, and I could only pray with Bishop claiming me and not leaving room for doubt, she'd finally move on.

But I'd never been so lucky before and I doubted my luck would improve now.

AUDREY

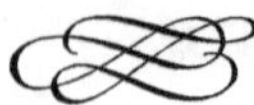

THE TOUR MARCHED DOWN THE MAIN ROAD THROUGH OLD TOWN AND into the newer part of Stonehaven. Cyrus took the lead and talked with the King of Lais, His Majesty King Gower, who was a tall, broad-shoulder man in a crisp military uniform.

The king would have looked imposing if he hadn't been walking between Cyrus — who was taller and broader — and Pimryl, the imposing female leader of Ocasha, a Dedearc colony on the coast north of the Kingdom of Lais who stood a head and a half taller than him.

Just behind Pimryl's shoulder walked the smallest Dedearc of the Dedearc representatives who I was told was the only male in the party. He repeated everything Cyrus and King Gower said to Pimryl in a soft, unobtrusive voice.

"This is our school," Cyrus announced, pointing to the large, three-story building where I'd attended Nova's first aid class. "It's mandatory for all pups when they turn five to attend the school for ten years."

"Starting at age five, all children must attend school for ten years," the male Dedearc repeated.

Pimryl nodded, keeping her attention on Cyrus and the school.

"No wonder your warriors are so tenacious. You start training them at such a young age."

"It's impressive that you train your warriors for so long," the male Dedearc said to Cyrus even though Cyrus kept looking at Pimryl.

"Not just warriors," Cyrus replied, leading the group back to the main road and continuing our slow journey to the market where we were going to stop for lunch. "Scientists, engineers, artists, musicians, writers, philosophers. The first six years include every subject. After that, pups can pick a specialization or not. They can also voluntarily study for more than ten years."

"We have a similar system," Representative Folmar said. She was a stocky, middle-aged woman and the leader of the gryphons shifters.

The male Dedearc repeated what both Cyrus and Folmar said, and Pimryl nodded. It was as if she didn't understand what the others were saying.

I turned my attention to the other group of humans from the Independent State of Ciliran and the three merchants who were hoping to sell their grimalkin killing weapons to the Alliance.

Jundar, who was the representative from Ciliran and the Speaker of the Alliance — kind of like the Speaker of the House — had a young woman repeating everything, while the merchants didn't. But there were times when the merchants said something to each other and no one seemed to understand them.

Well, shit, I mentally huffed at myself as realization hit me so hard Knox sent worry through our bond and Bishop jerked his attention away from what he'd been saying to Folmar to look at me.

What? Bishop asked in my head, drawing us to the side of the group as Lucius pointed out another building of interest.

"Those two—" I whispered, pointing at the male Dedearc and the human who repeated everything. "They're translators, aren't they."

Bishop frowned. "It's taken you this long to figure that out? They're obviously speaking different languages."

"Not to me."

My thoughts lurched to the memory of being at the death god's altar and Bishop reciting the spell to break my bond with Knox. He'd read the spell off a piece of paper but it had been as if he'd forgotten how to speak. His pronunciation had become weird and the words had been broken into syllables.

I rolled my eyes at myself. "What language was the spell to break my bond in?"

"An ancient dialect. Whil assured me my pronunciation was good, but I've wondered if I was the one who screwed up the spell."

"If that's what happened, I'm glad you did screw it up," I said, leaning into him. As much as Knox and I'd had a rocky start, I knew in my soul that being mating to him, just like being mated to Bishop, was the way it was supposed to be.

"Why the questions?" he asked.

"Because I understood what you said for the spell, and I understand what Pimryl and Jundar are saying before their translators translate for them. It's all English to me."

Bishop's eyes widened. "The magic that helps you understand us, lets you understand every language?"

"Looks like," I replied as we slowed to walk behind the group of delegates and their aides.

Cyrus, you need to know this, Bishop said with his shifter telepathy.

Cyrus gave an ever-so-slight nod and gestured for Lucius to explain the next point of interest.

What? Cyrus asked.

Audrey doesn't need a translator.

Because of the magic that lets her understand us? Cyrus asked, instantly jumping to the same conclusion Bishop had.

Exactly, Bishop replied.

Stay near the middle of the group, Cyrus commanded without any additional questions or hesitation, sending a strange sensation rushing through my chest.

He trusted me. He had no doubt that I was telling the truth, and it felt weird to not have to submit to questions and criticisms and disbelief.

When the tour is done, Cyrus said, *you can tell me if you overheard anything that we should be worried about.*

Especially from the merchants, Bishop added, his agreement with Cyrus's order to double down on my spying assignment and the confidence that I could do it flooding through our bond. *I've got a bad feeling about them.*

Me, too, Cyrus confessed before turning to Folmar and answering her question without missing a beat, giving no indication that he'd just had a mental conversation with us.

Then Cyrus stopped in front of a long, squat building on the corner of the main street and a narrower one and explained that it was Stonehaven's public works building, giving me and Bishop a chance to ease into the center of the group.

Jundar, the representative from Ciliran, asked a question that was word for word translated by the young woman standing slightly behind him, and Bishop answered.

"So there's no private construction?" One of the merchants asked. He was a lanky man who was almost as tall as Bishop but half of Bishop's weight and wore a silky robe with thick, complicated embroidery at the neck, cuffs, and hem.

"What I really want to see is their armory," another merchant with a similar build in a similar robe replied.

The third merchant, the shortest and stockiest of the group, nodded to Merchant Two but no one else reacted, and Jundar's translator didn't repeat his words.

One of the Ciliran men in military uniform gave the merchants a quick glance before jerking his attention forward and following the people in front of him as Cyrus turned off the main road, heading to the market.

"You can glare at them all you like," the soldier beside him said, his voice low enough that the human merchants wouldn't have heard him, but all the shifters — and me, who was right behind him — still could.

"I don't like them," he replied. "If their weapons are as powerful as they say, we have no choice but to buy them at the price they're selling them at. We can't even negotiate. If we do, they'll either sell them to a hostile country or outright attack us."

"That's why the whole Alliance has twice as many soldiers as usual for this meeting."

I frowned. It looked like Cyrus, Bishop, and I weren't the only ones who had bad feelings about the merchants.

"Trying to learn Cilirinian?" A broad-shouldered gryphon shifter about my age asked.

Ferocious feralness radiated off him, and I could sense an enormous alpha power within him ... which was impossible. I should have only been able to sense a wolf's level of alpha power, not that of another shifter.

"My mother's been trying to learn it for years," he said, jerking his chin toward Folmar who was deep in conversation with Cyrus and Pimryl. "I'm told the trick is to listen to the pitch as well as the words." He flashed me a chagrined smile as we strolled into the heart of the market, people making way for our larger group. "But I'm tone-deaf, so I really can't say."

I had no idea how to respond to him. I couldn't tell him I'd been eavesdropping. That would ruin my advantage over everyone who spoke a different language.

"Does it frustrate you?" I finally asked after too long a pause, making him frown. "Being tone-deaf, I mean."

"You have no idea," he said with a groan and a self-deprecating smile. "One-third of our courtship rituals involve singing."

"What are the other two-thirds?" I asked.

"Displaying our feathers and a little primal chasing." He dropped his voice into a conspiratorial whisper. "Thank the Sisters they gave me beautiful feathers and a love for the hunt, or my mother would have completely given up on me."

His expression soured with his last words, and I opened my mouth to ask him about what he meant when a terrified scream tore through the mix of voices from the market.

My pulse lurched.

Oh, no. Please, no.

Then a wave of panicked people rushed our way followed by six enormous grimalkins.

WOLF DEVOTED

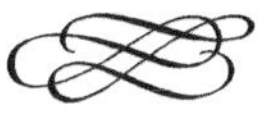

ENSNARED BY THE PACK: BOOK 6

AUDREY

"IF YOU'RE NOT FIGHTING, FOLLOW LUCIUS AND AUDREY," CYRUS yelled as he yanked off his shirt, revealing his broad, muscular chest and powerful arms.

And at any other time, I'd have appreciated his physique — despite him not being romantically interested in me — but with the panicked people rushing closer and the deadly grimalkins right behind them, all I could think about was saving as many lives as I could.

Except that only added frustration to my fear. I couldn't fight the grimalkins, not without a wolf form. Sure, I'd fought them twice before, but only because I'd had no other choice, and I knew just how lucky I'd been to make it out alive.

Which meant the best I could do was help ensure the Mountain and Sea Alliance delegates and their aides were safe. The last thing this horrible situation needed was a political incident on top of it.

"Stick with Lucius," Bishop said to me as he, too, pulled off his shirt. "Make sure no one gets separated."

"Cohnal," Representative Folmar said to the gryphon shifter beside me. "Watch their backs."

Then she shifted into her gryphon form, not caring that she destroyed her clothes in the process.

For a second, no longer than two quick pounds of my heart, I stared at her. In my realm, everyone thought gryphon shifters were extinct or had never existed, but about a dozen feet away stood a majestic creature with the body of a lion and the wings and head of an eagle.

With a piercing cry, she spread her massive wings and leaped into the air, skimming over the heads of the fleeing people and landing on one of the grimalkins.

Cyrus extended his claws from his fingertips and howled, calling his warriors — the sound strange coming from his human throat — then he plunged into the fray. Without hesitation, Bishop followed him, and I could feel his ferocious determination to protect me and his pack racing through our mating bond.

"This way," Lucius called out as he waved toward an alley beside him that sat between some of the semi-permanent market stalls.

He was an older man, his hair gray and deep laugh lines around his eyes and mouth, but I didn't doubt he was still the warrior he'd been when he retired as huntmaster to become the pack's top advisor and diplomat.

A third of the Alliance delegates rushed to follow him, while the others drew their swords or extended their claws, or — in the case of the Dedearc who were covered in scales, already had claws, and were all bigger than Cyrus — just rushed to stop the grimalkins.

But even as everyone ran forward, more grimalkins appeared.

The wave of terrified people surged around the warriors who twisted and turned, trying to move against the flow, and a second later, the wall of people was headed toward me.

Audrey, Lucius said in my head, jerking my attention back to the delegates and reminding me of my duty.

All of them were in the alley, and while I could hesitate for another few moments and let some of the men, women, and children fleeing the grimalkins go ahead of me, that would separate me from the delegates, and my alpha had given me an order.

I scrambled after the group and Cohnal hurried after me.

The alley wasn't long, only six stalls deep before we raced onto a slightly wider road. But that only meant everyone who'd run through the various alleys between the stalls converged on the street, turning into one big horde.

Children screamed and cried, some half shifted unable to control their form while afraid. Men and women who weren't taking care of terrified children or teens, ran with their claws extended, watching for danger to protect those who couldn't protect themselves.

Still, even with an eighth of the horde calm and on guard, it was chaos. A literal human stampede. One wrong move, one trip, and someone would be crushed to death before anyone could stop it. And while the road was relatively smooth, Stonehaven was built on the rocky slopes at the bottom of a mountain. There were ramps and steps everywhere.

Beside me, a lanky teen boy, probably around fourteen or fifteen, who was desperately trying to carry a much younger child whose form kept shifting between toddler and wolf, tripped.

Cohnal grabbed the back of his collar and yanked him up before he could be knocked completely to the ground by someone else. Except the child shifted into her wolf at the last minute and tumbled from the teen's arms just as he righted himself.

"Jolie!" the teen screamed.

I lunged for the child who tried to jerk out of the way of someone else's feet and ended up getting kicked deeper into the mob.

The child yelped, tiny, heartbreaking noises that I could somehow hear over the pounding feet, screaming, and crying. My pulse lurched as she tried to avoid getting trampled and I heaved against the flow.

Someone slammed into my side, twisting me around and bumping me into someone else. I jerked out of the way before crashing into another person, but everyone was too close together. Heavy feet smashed my toes, while more bodies bumped into me, ricocheting me like a pinball.

Somehow, I cut sideways and reached the child, who'd curled into a tight ball in a desperate attempt to protect herself. Fury and fear churned in a nauseating mix in my stomach as I scrambled to pick her up.

Someone ahead of me screamed and a large man slammed into me. He fell, creating some space in the horde, and I grabbed a handful of fur and yanked the child into my arms.

"You—" he snarled at me as he leaped to his feet. Then he saw the wolf pup in my arms and he gave me a tight nod.

He moved to step closer, possibly to protect us, but the crowd surged, suddenly changing direction, and forced us apart. More screams sounded, desperate and afraid, and a massive gryphon leaped into the air.

Shit. Everyone was running in every direction, slamming into each other, desperate to get away from the grimalkin that I couldn't see but knew was about to have a gryphon attacking it.

I jerked my attention around, trying to find the delegates, but I wasn't tall, a little shorter than average in height, and couldn't see anyone.

Shit shit shit.

The pup in my arms, still curled in a tight ball, whimpered. My first priority was the child's safety. I needed to find the fastest way out of the crowd, and it didn't matter if that brought me closer to or took me farther from the delegation.

A woman carrying two wailing babies slammed into me, heading the way we'd come, and I curled protectively around the pup as I stumbled after her. But someone else hit me from behind, shoving me hard. I lost my balance and the crowd surged around me.

Someone tried to help me stand but was bumped away by others. Another person tripped over me but managed to keep her balance before righting herself. She didn't even turn to look at who she'd tripped over. She just kept running.

The wind suddenly shifted, and the heavy, foul stench of a grimalkin washed over me, along with the cloying reek of blood. The beast was close. I had to move. Now.

I elbowed a man about to crash into me, earning an angry glare, and heaved to my feet.

The grimalkin roared, the sound so close I was afraid to look behind me. Then two more answered, just as close.

Cohnal screeched and one of the roars turned desperate, but I didn't know how powerful a gryphon was. I'd seen firsthand that one grimalkin was challenging for a couple of shifters unless they were powerful alphas. The black dog-like creatures moved like tigers and had feline-sharp claws. Cohnal might be able to take down one, since his alpha power was strong, but I wasn't going to bet that he could take down three by himself.

I heaved to the edge of the crowd and slipped into one of the extremely narrow passages between some of the wooden market stalls, praying that this time a grimalkin wouldn't be hot on my heels. The space was so tight I had to turn sideways and hold the pup above my head to squeeze through, and there was no way I was going to be able to turn my head to see if one of the monsters was behind me.

My pulse pounding, my breath short sharp gasps, I hurried to the thin rectangle of light ahead of me, careened out the other side, and almost crashed into the rear end of a grimalkin.

AUDREY

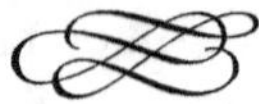

I skidded to a stop at the last minute before I hit the grimalkin, the pup in my arms whimpering, just as a large gray wolf as big as Knox lunged at it.

"Audrey!" a feminine voice screamed.

I scrambled away from the fight and scanned the area. I stood at the edge of a small courtyard similar to the one where I'd found a grimalkin toying with those kids in my first grimalkin encounter.

But unlike that one where there were two ways in and out, this courtyard only had one — since squeezing between market stalls didn't count. However, this one had buildings that faced the court-yard, offering not just a place to hide but a possible back door leading to a different, safer street.

Quinn stood at the open door of a squat, one-story building with an older man ushering a group of children inside.

The wolf fighting the grimalkin dug his teeth into the beast's throat, making it howl and rake its claws through the wolf's stomach. But the wolf—

No, Zavier. Somehow, I could tell by the feel of his stuttering, straining alpha power that Zavier was the wolf.

Zavier held on despite the blood rushing from his stomach and spilling onto the stone ground. He viciously wrenched his head to the side and tore his teeth through the grimalkin's throat.

The beast collapsed, but so, too, did Zavier.

Quinn screamed and raced toward him, and so did I.

"Get them inside," she yelled over her shoulder at the older man as she dropped to her knees beside Zavier. "Don't shift. It's too serious."

I knelt at her side. "We have to get him inside, too."

I didn't know if grimalkins were attracted to the scent of blood or not, but I wasn't going to risk it.

"I have an elixir," the man called out.

Tears streamed down Quinn's cheeks and her breathing had turned short and sharp. She scrambled to put pressure on Zavier's wounds, but they were too big for her small hands — hands that were even smaller than mine.

"Quinn!" I barked, my pulse *thu-thudding* softly. "I can't move him by myself."

Her gaze jerked up to mine, her bright blue eyes watery and filled with fear.

"We just need to keep him alive long enough for help to get to us," I said, and I put down the pup and turned my attention to the quivering child. "Get into the house with the others. I'm right behind you."

The pup darted across the courtyard and I dug my fingers into Zavier's thick fur, grabbing one of his front legs as close to his torso as I could. I didn't want to hurt him any more than he already was, but he was as big as Bishop and Knox in their wolf form and probably just as heavy.

"Sorry," I murmured to him as I braced my legs to start dragging him.

Tell Quinn... he gasped in my mind. *Tell her...*

"Tell her yourself," I hissed. "No one is dying today."

"Right!" Quinn replied, sudden determination hardening her expression, and she grabbed Zavier's other front leg.

Together, we hauled him across the courtyard, leaving a sickeningly large blood smear on the ground, pointing directly to our hiding spot.

Once inside, the older man shut the door and locked it then hurried to a tall metal cabinet and pulled out an elixir.

Quinn and I dragged Zavier to a corner in the back of the room underneath a large metal worktable and fed him the elixir. It wouldn't work quickly, but hopefully, it would be enough to help his shifter-enhanced healing stabilize him long enough for him to get medical attention.

"I don't have a lot of clean towels here," the man said, taking a small stack from a nearby shelf and handing them to Quinn.

"It's all right," Quinn replied, placing them over Zavier's wounds. "Thanks, Jaxon."

"Anything for you, sweetheart," he replied.

She applied pressure, making Zavier huff in pain, and, much to my surprise, a few of the braver children added their tiny hands, helping her to put pressure on most of his injuries.

With Zavier taken care of as best as possible, given the situation, I straightened and took stock of what was around, not wanting to bet we were safe with only a wooden door and the glass in the windows keeping the grimalkins out.

The building was a single-room smithy without a back door. A blazing-hot fire in a blacksmith's forge burned on the opposite wall from us and close to it were two large anvils and three sturdy worktables. The rest of the space was filled with raw ore, and metal everything: cabinets, stools, a handful of knives and daggers, hoes, rakes, shovels, pots, pans, a plethora of tools, and two dozen wrought-iron fence posts. All of the fence posts were an inch round and half of them had points attached to one end.

It looked like I'd found another makeshift spear, and if the soldering or whatever Jaxon the blacksmith had done to secure the tips held, the fence posts would make better spears than my stick with a point.

I grabbed a post from the rack at the back of the room then

pressed myself against the cool stone wall beside one of the front windows so I could peek out and watch for danger.

"You're definitely living up to the rumors, alpha," Jaxon said as he took a similar position at the other window.

His voice was firm, and his medium-level alpha power rolled off him in small, stuttering waves, revealing his heightened emotions, but I didn't get the impression he disliked me. In fact, for a second, I thought I saw respect in his eyes before he turned his attention out the window.

I wasn't sure if he'd always felt that way, or if seeing me, a shifter who couldn't shift, grab a weapon and stand ready to fight to protect Quinn, Zavier, and fifteen kids under the age of ten had changed his opinion of me... and I wasn't going to ask him about the rumors. Even if there were a few good ones, I was sure most were bad.

"Just trying to do the right thing," I replied, scanning the courtyard.

It was empty, but somewhere out of sight, people screamed and yelled, and it felt more like the calm before the storm.

My pulse pounded, and waves of determination, anger, and fear roared through my mating bonds, making me pray that my guys were safe. I tried to keep my bonds locked tight, not wanting my own fear to distract them. In a fight like this, just a flicker of a distraction could be deadly.

Then the sides of the two wooden stalls I'd squeezed through to get to the courtyard shook and a small, terrified wolf bolted out from between them. My muscles tensed, my body about to jump to the door to let the wolf in.

But before I could move, the stalls burst apart. Wood pieces, bright material, and books flew everywhere and two grimalkins pounced on the wolf.

The first sank its teeth into the wolf's back, drawing a desperate, terrified howl, while the other dug its claws into the wolf's side, trying to wrench it away from the first one. They snarled and roared at each other, their fight tearing the wolf in half before I could even think to scream.

I clamped a hand over my mouth, afraid to make any noise that might attract the monsters. Bile burned the back of my throat and tears stung my eyes. It had happened so fast. Logically I knew I wouldn't have had time to save whoever it was, but my soul screamed with fury that I'd been useless.

That had been a member of my pack — *mine!* — and the wildness deep inside me howled that I needed to protect what was mine.

One of the children started crying. She might not have been able to see what had happened — thank goodness — but she'd heard that wolf's death cry and the grimalkins' growls.

"Shh shh shh," Quinn hissed, her gaze darting to mine, her eyes wide with fear, before she turned to the child and tucked her against her side. "We have to stay quiet."

All the children nodded, tears rolling down their cheeks, their bodies quivering, and half of them clamped their hands over their mouths, trying to stifle their sobs.

I jerked my attention to the horror in the courtyard as the beasts fought over the wolf's corpse. They snarled and swatted at each other, then the larger one batted the slightly smaller one hard, sending it skidding across the courtyard toward the smithy.

I sucked in a sharp breath and held it, my rushing pulse filling my ears.

Don't look our way.

Don't notice us.

Don't notice the blood leading straight to our door.

Please.

The smaller grimalkin leaped to his feet, shaking off the blow, and turned away from the smithy.

Yes. That's it.

Both of you leave and run into a pack of hunters.

The large grimalkin snarled at the smaller one and a heavy, skin-crawling wave of power — far too similar to the ominous power I'd felt in Anakar — slammed into me as the smaller grimalkin shrank back.

My pulse stuttered with realization.

Holy shit!

The grimalkins had alpha power... and somehow, I could sense it?

One of the kids whimpered, making me wonder if she, too, could feel the strange power, and the smaller grimalkin's head, which had dipped in submission to the bigger one, snapped around. Its gaze locked on the blood trail and its ears tipped forward. That drew the larger one's attention and in unison, they both zeroed in on the door.

Oh shit.

AUDREY

With a roar, the large one charged past the smaller one and slammed itself against the door, the wood cracking with the impact. Desperate, I shot my gaze around, looking for something to block the entrance.

Another crash and wood flew everywhere. I jerked away to protect my face from the shrapnel, right in the direction of the shattering window.

Flicks of pain burst across my face, neck, and arms, and my pulse lurched. I wrenched my spear up before I'd fully opened my eyes, the tip skimming across the smaller grimalkin's rough hide, not even drawing a scratch.

The beast roared, its foul scent flooding my nostrils, and bounded toward Quinn, Zavier, and the children.

"No," I yelled, my pulse *thu-thudding*, my wildness roaring to the surface.

The children screamed, the group shrinking and pressing closer to the wall as if that would protect them, and Quinn leaped to her feet, her fingers extended into claws.

I didn't know how much fighting experience she had, but I

doubted it was a lot. She was a schoolteacher and was going to get torn apart like the dead wolf in the courtyard.

I rammed my spear into the grimalkin's side, breaking flesh and drawing blood. With a howl that sounded more angry than hurt, the beast turned to me, wrenching itself free from my spear.

Fuck me.

Fear tore through me but so did my wildness. I'd killed one of these monsters before and I could do it again. I had to. Quinn and those children were counting on me.

More heavy skin-crawling power crashed over me as the grimalkin leaped at me, but my own power surged, batting it away as if it were nothing, and I aimed my spear right for the monster's mouth. It had worked the last time with just a broken stick and it was going to work now.

But the beast wrenched his head to the side at the last minute, and my spear skidded uselessly across its hide — because, of course, the damn tip was only more or less sharp at the point since it was a fence post and not an actual weapon.

Its head slammed into my chest and sent me tumbling across the room, right into the fight between the larger grimalkin and Jaxon, who'd shifted into his wolf form.

The large beast swiped at me, and I rolled out of the way, slamming into a table leg and sending a box of thick nails crashing to the floor.

Jaxon charged at the beast, trying to bite its throat, but the grimalkin swatted at him, forcing him to twist mid-air to avoid its claws. Except he wasn't fast enough and the beast slashed Jaxon's side.

Too-bright blood stained his pale gray coat and he howled as the grimalkin attacked.

My heart pounded hard, fear and ferocity surging through my veins. Screaming, I grabbed my make-shift spear — which had tumbled from my grip when I'd landed in the middle of Jaxon's fight.

The grimalkin swung its large blocky head toward me, its foul breath filling the space between us as it surged toward me. I wrapped my fingers around the fence post, wrenched the weighty piece of metal around toward the beast, and shoved the pointed tip inside the monster's mouth.

Just like the last time, the spear hit something then *popped* through. Blood gushed from the grimalkin's mouth, its eyes glazed over, and it crashed on top of me.

Hell, yes!

One down. One more to go.

I half shoved half squirmed out from under the grimalkin that was larger than Cyrus in his wolf form and wrenched on my spear.

Stuck.

I couldn't even get it to budge.

Something crashed on the other side of the room, and I yanked my attention to Quinn and the kids. With her enhanced shifter strength, she'd pushed over the heavy metal table the children and Zavier had been hiding under, creating a short wall, and now stood in front of it, blocking the smaller grimalkin's way.

Except even with her claws and canines extended, it was ridiculous to think she could stand her ground against the monster. She wasn't even five feet tall and probably didn't weigh a hundred pounds.

The beast lunged at her, and Jaxon flew past me, ramming his body against the grimalkin and knocking it off balance.

I scrambled to my feet, raced to the rack at the back of the room, and grabbed another fence post.

With a roar, the grimalkin swatted at Jaxon and he stumbled to the side, more bright splashes of blood staining his fur, making my pulse stutter.

Quinn leaped forward and slashed her claws across the grimalkin's snout, drawing its attention back to her. Its heavy skin-crawling power rolled over me, making my stomach churn, and the muscles in its back legs bunched, preparing to attack.

I wasn't going to get to it in time to distract it from attacking Quinn... Except that was all I needed to do. Distract it. I only needed a second, long enough to join the fight and help them.

I threw my fence post. It hit the stone floor with a clatter a good three feet before it reached the grimalkin and skidded forward, stopping between its feet.

Swell.

But at least the beast wrenched its head toward me instead of attacking Quinn. I grabbed another spear and barreled toward it. Except before I reached it, another grimalkin and a large gray wolf flew through the already shattered window, knocking more shards from the frame and sending them flying in all directions.

The two of them rolled midair — the wolf with its teeth in the grimalkin's throat and the grimalkin trying to get its claws in the wolf's belly.

With a *thud,* they skidded across the floor, the grimalkin on top using its weight to bear down on the wolf and drive the wolf headfirst into an anvil.

Stunned, the wolf's grip on the grimalkin's throat released and the grimalkin rose to tear into the wolf with its claws.

The wildness inside me roared to the surface. I howled a war cry and charged at it. The beast jerked its head up and I rammed my spear into its eye.

Roaring, the grimalkin leaped away from the wolf— No, Finn. The dazed, bleeding wolf on the floor was Finn, Stonehaven's Watch Commander.

I scrambled out of the way of the beast's claws and slammed into the side of the other grimalkin.

Thankfully, Jaxon snapped at the smaller one's throat, making it swipe at him. He barely managed to get out of the way, but without a doubt he'd saved my life.

The new grimalkin lunged for me, and I heaved to the side, desperate to avoid getting pinned between the two monsters. But the grimalkin kept pressing its attack, forcing me to scramble out of the way, knocking over stands and buckets, scattering tools and metal things, and not giving me a chance to fight back.

That made the wildness inside me furious. My pulse roared and my heart pounded violent thuds that reverberated through me.

Finn groaned and the eyelid of his one visible eye fluttered. Blood trickled onto the floor by his stomach, but it wasn't gushing. Which meant he wasn't about to die, and if Jaxon could fight with worse injuries, so could Finn... because there was no way I was going to get lucky two more times and kill both of the grimalkins myself.

"Finn!" I barked, my wildness crashing through me.

I rolled over a worktable, the grimalkin's claws tearing the bottom half of my dress to shreds.

Fuck fuck fuck.

"Finn!" I barked again as the beast leaped over the table, forcing me to scramble out of reach.

My back hit the wall beside the forge, the stone searingly hot against my bare skin, and I jerked away, knocking over a bucket of ash. My thigh bumped a metal poker, its tip in the fire, and I grabbed it. I smashed the poker against the grimalkin's nose and raced back around the table.

The beast roared with pain and its horrible stomach-churning skin-crawling power slammed into me.

This grimalkin was a lot more powerful than the one I'd killed, and my knees started to buckle in submission.

But my wildness surged out of me in response, overwhelming the grimalkin's power. The beast shrank back with its teeth bared, red light flashing in its eyes, and fury pouring from it as its alpha power battled mine.

My stomach roiled and bile burned the back of my throat. Behind me, a wolf howled in agony and Quinn screamed.

"Get. The. Fuck. Up. Finn!" I roared and he lurched to his feet, his eyes wide, the expression almost cartoonish on a wolf. "Help me."

Without hesitation, almost as if he were being controlled, he threw himself at the grimalkin attacking me, giving me a chance to hurry around to the monster's side for my own attack.

But as I got into position, movement in the courtyard caught my attention. Two more grimalkins were barreling toward us.

"You've got to be kidding me," I hissed as my wildness tore through me, bringing with it a ferocious anger.

Mine. This pack was mine and everyone in this smithy was getting out alive.

The grimalkins needed to leave now or die. I didn't know how I'd kill them, but my wildness didn't care about the details. It would tear them to shreds and bathe in their blood.

Furious, I threw the spear at the smaller grimalkin that was about to tear into Jaxon. The weapon miraculously slammed into the beast's eye, tore through its head, and embedded itself in the stone wall behind it.

Power rolled off me in violent ferocious waves and my stomach heaved with something darker... something angrier.

Finn clamped his teeth around the other grimalkin's throat and tore it out with a rush of foul-smelling blood, and I turned my attention to the two grimalkins outside.

They were almost at the smithy. A few more steps and I'd be forced to fight them. Instead, that dark power surged. My stomach cramped with sudden, painful nausea, and the biting acid burn of bile rose up my throat.

The grimalkins' gaze leaped to mine, and I squared my shoulders despite my body's desperate plea to curl inward and protect the agony churning in my stomach.

"Come on, assholes," I snarled under my breath, sending the burn racing over my tongue and out of my mouth in a whisp of black smoke — that could only be from my imagination because of how angry I was.

And right now. I didn't care if I was hallucinating. Whatever kept me strong and ended the threat to the people who were mine.

"I will fucking kill every last one of you." Another whisp of black smoke curled out of my mouth and my stomach cramped, forcing me to suck in rapid breaths before I puked on my feet.

The grimalkins jerked to a stop. Skin-crawling power slammed into me, and I surged my wildness in return, matching their wave with my tsunami. I would crush them, rip them to shreds, and dance on their corpses. Vengeance would be mine, and I'd feast on their flesh and bathe in their blood.

I. Was. Done.

I was done with these monsters terrorizing this pack, hurting the people I'd grown to love, and terrifying children. And I was done with being weak and pathetic. I'd already killed two of these fuckers today. Two more was easy.

I blindly reached behind me, grabbed a fence post, and stormed out the front door to face them.

The grimalkins hunched almost as if they were going to pounce, but then the smaller one shifted back a step.

That's right. Fear me! the something dark and powerful screamed within me. *Die!*

With a roar, I rushed forward, my wildness— No, my *alpha* power pouring off me in giant waves, my stomach cramping, and wisps of black smoke rushing from my mouth.

The bigger grimalkin also hunched, its back legs bunching as if to attack. But that only made me grin... because somehow, I'd lost my mind. Somehow, I was furious enough to believe I could take on two more grimalkins by myself.

"Run or die," the darkness inside me hissed, and, as if I'd actually commanded them, the two beasts bolted away. "That's right, fuckers!"

Oh, my God!

I'd scared off two grimalkins!

My stomach cramped, wrenching me to my hands and knees, and I threw up a burning mix of bile and black smoke.

KNOX

Audrey collapsed onto her hands and knees and threw up. Her green dress and pale skin were soaked with blood as if someone had thrown a bucket of it on her, making it hard to tell at a distance how badly she was hurt.

Surely not all of it was hers! But the beautiful gift Bishop had given her to wear when she met the delegates and aides from the alliance was ripped to shreds, so she couldn't have gotten through the fight unscathed.

I'd found her just in time to watch her brandish a fence post, scream, and rush toward two grimalkins like a wild woman. Her alpha power had poured off her in great, destructive waves, nearly flattening me in my wolf form into submission, and I could feel her determination and rage pounding through our mating bond. But I knew none of it would affect the grimalkins. They weren't wolf shifters and our power only affected those of our kind.

My heart had clenched with fear, and my wolf seized control of our body, shoving me so far back into our consciousness it felt like I was looking at the horrific scene in front of me from the end of a long tunnel.

With a ferocious wildness that verged on going feral, my wolf raced toward them even while knowing he wasn't going be fast enough to save her. Except instead of attacking, the grimalkins turned tail, their eyes wide with fear, and bolted toward me. I tensed, but they didn't even look at me. They kept running down the street as if their life depended on it.

My wolf rushed us to Audrey's side, shifted into our human form, and curled protectively around her, clutching her to our chest as she heaved again and spat bile and breakfast onto the ground.

Her pounding power and burning rage shattered into body-shaking horror as her adrenaline vanished and her breath turned into short, sharp gasps, making my wolf growl with rage. Our mate was sick and trembling and those grimalkins were still alive. He needed to tear them apart to ensure her safety... but he also couldn't let her go.

Mine, he snarled over and over again.

Mine and I'd failed her. I hadn't been here to protect her. She'd had to face those two grimalkins—

No, three. A dead grimalkin lay on the other side of the courtyard near the torn-up corpse of one of our packmates. She'd had to deal with three grimalkins and watch that massacre.

And while both my wolf and I recognized that our mate was powerful, she was still soft and sensitive. She shouldn't have had to face those monsters. I should have been by her side the whole time, not slinking through the shadows, unable to keep her in sight all the time because of the crowded market.

"Audrey," a female called from behind me.

My wolf jerked us around, snarling and baring our human teeth at Quinn as she rushed out of Jaxon's smithy — and my wolf didn't stop snarling when we recognized the woman.

I heaved against my wolf's control, terrified the need to protect our mate would consume both of us and send us into feralness. With the stress of almost losing Bishop so strong in my wolf's memory, it was impossible to keep hold of our base instincts.

Mine.

Mine mine mine.

"Knox, it's okay," Audrey gasped, her small body still trembling in my arms.

"It's not okay," my wolf growled between clenched teeth.

Must protect. Mine.

More footsteps pounded on the ground behind me. More people. More danger.

And while my wolf recognized that the mix of human and wolf steps meant pack and not more grimalkins, it didn't calm him. He raged within my human skin, desperate to shift and take his proper form but also desperate to keep holding her, something we could only do with human arms.

Must protect. Always.

"Knox," she murmured, her voice weak and shaky, making my feralness surge.

She wasn't well. She needed protection. She'd thrown up and that meant something was wrong. Even her emotions were hard to feel, and it wasn't because my wolf was a primal beast walking the edge of becoming a mindless animal and only understood basic emotions. No, she was blocking us out.

The realization squeezed around my heart.

She was blocking *us* out.

Which meant she was hiding something, and with everything I knew about her, it was some kind of injury or weakness.

My wolf wrenched our attention to the road as Nova, two medics, and three hunters in their wolf form raced toward us.

My snarl deepened despite knowing Nova would help.

"Is she hurt?" Nova asked while still a good ten feet away.

"Yes," my wolf growled.

"I'm fine," Audrey said even though she was too pale. "Zavier and Jaxon are inside."

"No," my wolf barked, my power snapping and freezing everyone in place.

A mix of hot emotions flashed through our mating bond too fast for me to recognize any of them, and Audrey shook her head.

"Zavier and Jaxon first," she insisted.

But my wolf wouldn't release them from our power. He needed them to ensure Audrey's safety... but he also didn't want any of them closer.

The dueling emotions roared within us. Must protect. Must help. Must keep safe. Must care for her.

Fur rippled down my arms and across my cheeks, and my face started to shift, my mouth and nose extending into a snout.

Audrey shook in my arms even while I could sense through our bond that she was trying to get ahold of herself and not set me off.

"Knox," she murmured as she turned into my embrace and pressed her face against my neck. She drew in a deep breath and the comfort she felt from my scent rolled through our mating bond. "You have to let them do their job. Zavier is hurt."

A whisper of fear bled through a crack she'd formed in the block between us, and my chest tightened with both my and my wolf's emotions.

Still ten feet away, Nova and her team trembled in my control.

Safe. I had to keep Audrey safe.

"Please, Knox." A whisper of Audrey's alpha power teased over our skin, not with a demand for my submission but a reassurance that she was strong enough to wait.

My wolf's hold on our body trembled. I surged my consciousness forward, seized control, and released Nova and her team.

"Iris check out Audrey," Nova said, making eye contact with me.

I gave her a tight nod, shoved my nose against the top of Audrey's head, and huffed her scent like an addict in a desperate attempt to stay in control and not rip Iris's throat out.

"Cora with me," Nova finished as she, Cora, and Quinn rushed toward Jaxon's smithy.

"Zavier, Jaxon, and Finn all need medical attention," Audrey said. "I can wait. Iris, go with Nova."

My wolf surged, but Audrey's power grew stronger as well, pushing him back and urging me to calm the fuck down.

"You're hurt." She threw up for fuck's sake. Something was wrong with her.

"Nova, go," Audrey said, her voice stronger. "I've got Knox."

Nova and the medics hurried inside while the three hunters stood guard, watching the narrow road and the destroyed vender stalls. Nova immediately rushed to the back of the building— with Quinn at her side — while Iris and Cora split in opposite directions. Children started to cry and Audrey leaped to her feet.

Blood rolled down her thigh from three deep gashes, and my wolf saw red and surged forward.

"No." He seized her wrist and slammed our power into her, freezing her in place.

"Knox!"

Before she could counter with her own power, he tore the ruined dress from her body and pulled her close to examine her. She had thin cuts on her cheeks and arms, most that had stopped bleeding, a deep slice against her ribs, more on her calf, and half a dozen shallow ones across her back like she'd narrowly escaped the grimalkin's claws.

But before we could drag her to the ground and lick her wounds, Nova yelled to two of the hunters for help. They hurried inside, then the first hunter, Brody, carried out Jaxon, still in his wolf form. He was awake, but his panting was too fast and he'd already bled through the bandages they'd wrapped around him, while Iris, the medic, helped Finn — in his human form — limp into the courtyard. Rough bandages wrapped around my Watch Commander's torso and one thigh, and he too was still bleeding.

A second later, Quinn, her face wet with tears despite her forced calm expression along with fifteen children hurried out followed by Nova and Wade who carried Zavier. He hung limp in Wade's arms, blood dripping from the bandages they'd wrapped around his wolf form, and Audrey's power surged against mine, breaking my hold on her.

"Zavier," she cried out, even as my wolf in our human body pounced on her and pulled her into my arms.

"Stop moving. You're hurt," he snarled.

"I'm fine."

"You're not." I tugged her off her feet and clutched her to my chest.

"If she can stand, she's good enough to get to the hospital," Nova snapped at me. "Come on, we can't waste time."

CYRUS

Folmar pinned another grimalkin, and I sank my teeth in the beast's neck and jerked my head before it could break free. The reek of rotten flesh, mixed with the coppery tang of blood, rushed across my senses, making my stomach heave, but I didn't pause to react, just swung my head to the side, searching for the next grimalkin.

The beasts had been ferocious in their attack, toying and torturing, this pack more aggressive than the pack that had attacked before — not to mention five times the size.

I hadn't seen so many grimalkins in one pack in my life, not even when I'd joined the hunting party to clear out the pack that had threatened Stonehaven five years ago and was responsible for killing my mother and fathers. And these grimalkins smelled and tasted worse than any of the others I'd fought.

The thought tightened my chest for what that meant, for the safety of my pack, and for the safety of one member in particular, and I struggled to stay focused on the job at hand.

But the grimalkins were everywhere. Finn and Deacon were fielding reports from all over the eastern half of the city, and Nova had put out a call for more help, asking anyone with even basic first aid training to go to the hospital so she could pull nurses to her field hospital. We didn't have enough people trained in medicine to deal with this kind of attack. Shifters didn't get sick often, and we healed relatively quickly unless the wounds were too severe or the illness something our natural healing couldn't handle.

And Audrey was in the middle of this disaster.

My wolf threatened to take over and go after her, but I managed to hold him back. She was fine. Lucius wouldn't let anything happen to her.

Except in chaos like this, anything could happen.

Lucius, I mentally called to him, not bothering to be polite and touch his mind first. *Are the delegates safe?*

Was Audrey safe?

We're almost at the hospital, he replied. *Minor scrapes and bruises.*

Good. I clenched my jaw before I could ask about Audrey. She wasn't my mate, not yet, and I had a priority to the pack and our guests.

Audrey got separated from the group, he continued as if he knew that I desperately needed to know something about her. Except his words sent panic rushing through me. *Cohnal made sure she got away, so I'm sure she's fine.*

But you don't have eyes on her?

Except I already knew he didn't and didn't know of anyone else who did or he would have said so.

Fuck.

My thoughts lurched to mentally connecting with Audrey, but I couldn't. She didn't have telepathy like the rest of my pack. Even if I could speak into her mind, she wouldn't be able to answer me back.

Cyrus, Folmar barked in my head.

I wrenched my attention to her as she tried to leap into the air. But a grimalkin launched itself at her, forcing her to twist out of the way toward another grimalkin.

I tensed, my muscles bunching to rush in and help when one of the merchants shot his lightning weapon.

A blast of terrifying electric power roared from the device, skimming the side of the grimalkin and exploding into a wooden market stall with blankets and towels. Fabric and wood flew everywhere, and small fires littered the area where the stall had been.

The shot at least distracted the grimalkins enough for Folmar to take flight, and I dove for the injured one, snapping my teeth into the softest — but still not that soft — part of the grimalkin's hide, its throat.

The beast roared and dug its claws into my shoulder, but I locked my jaw and hung on, twisting as best I could to avoid its flailing strikes.

I had thirty seconds before the idiot merchant could shoot that nightmare weapon again, and I wanted these two grimalkins dead before he could blow up more of my city.

And fuck me, there were two more of those merchants wreaking havoc out there, fighting alongside the other alliance members.

The grimalkin got a claw into my stomach, raking through my flesh with burning agony, and I wrenched hard with my head. With a pain- and fury-filled roar, the beast shoved me with his shoulder, trying to force me onto my back.

I sank into a low crouch, ignoring the pain screaming through me from the myriad wounds I'd gotten since the fight had begun. I was the alpha.

I. Would. Not. Surrender.

Not even if the monster outweighed me, which this one did.

Folmar screeched, my only warning before she dug her claws into the grimalkin's back, giving me a chance to wrench to the side and kill it.

Folmar, check in with your son, I commanded. *Is he with Audrey?*

Folmar tilted her eagle head to the side, her lion's tail flicking fast and hard against the ground.

I can't reach him.

Bishop. Knox. Where's Audrey? I asked, panic making me pant.

I shouldn't have let her out of my sight. I should have insisted Bishop stay with her instead of helping the fight. From Finn and Deacon's reports, the grimalkins were all over the east side and she was probably sacrificing herself right now to protect the pack's children.

You can't find her? Bishop asked, his mental voice tight. *She's... It's hard to tell. She's blocking me. All I'm getting are flashes of... fear... and determination.*

Of course, she was determined. That was our mate to a T.

Except she wasn't *our* mate.

Not yet.

Knox, I mentally snapped, desperate to stay focused.

No response.

Knox! I shifted into my human form. I needed to find her. Now! And I couldn't do that as injured as I was.

Exhaustion swept over me, making me stagger because I should have stayed in my wolf form and given my body more time to heal before trying to finish the job with a shift.

Fuck, Knox. Where the hell are you?

He's almost feral, Bishop replied.

Is she alive? Bishop, please. Tell me she's alive. I didn't care if I was showing Bishop how much I needed his mate. To hell with my pride and anything else. She was all that mattered.

Mine, my wolf growled and he surged forward, shoving my consciousness to the back of our body.

Hospital, Knox finally snarled, his mental voice filled with anger and frustration. *I can't go inside, there are too many people. She says she's fine but—*

A shuddered of alpha power swept over the market.

My wolf jerked me forward, but somehow, I managed to stop us from abandoning our comrades. *Folmar!*

It's clear, she said as if already knowing what I wanted. *Find your mate.*

She's not—

She leveled an unblinking golden eye at me. *I'm old. I'm not dumb.*

With a snarl, my wolf regained control of our body, shifted us into our wolf form, and we bolted down the street. It didn't matter to my wolf that we, the alpha, was racing to the hospital for a woman we hadn't publicly claimed as our mate and wouldn't be able to until we'd squashed the horrible rumors about her.

In that moment, Audrey was all that mattered.

She was mine, the alpha I'd never known I was looking for to help lead our pack. I had to know she was safe.

Sisters! Nova had taken her to the hospital and Knox was all riled up. Audrey was even blocking her emotions from Bishop. That couldn't be good. She had to be hiding something to protect her mates, something she feared would distract them from the fight with the grimalkins.

It didn't matter that I'd done exactly what I suspected she was trying to avoid. I'd abandoned my position, trusting Folmar when she said the area was clear of grimalkins, and was running at full speed.

What the fuck was wrong with me? My mother and fathers had taught me better. Even Audrey knew better. I was the alpha. I had to lead the pack. But my instincts were screaming at me. I had to ensure my mate was safe.

CYRUS

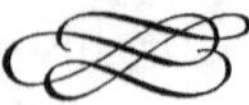

Nova, I mentally called, grateful that I'd spent all that time working to extend how far my telepathy reached.

Busy, she snapped back.

Audrey, I snarled, skidding around a corner and nearly barreling into two of the pack's watchmen.

She's with Molly.

"Not you?" my wolf wanted to roar, but I managed to hold him back, leap over the other wolves, and continue running. If Audrey was in serious condition, Nova would have been with her. Since she wasn't, it meant she felt Audrey's condition was good enough that she could delegate.

Except that thought didn't calm my wolf. Our mate was in the hospital and Knox was freaking out. *Something* had happened to her.

Molly, I said, feeling her mentally jump with surprise. *Audrey.*

I ducked down a side street purposely avoiding Nova's field hospital, my paws pounding on the smoothed-stone road. If Knox said he couldn't go inside that meant Audrey was at the building, not in Sisters Square.

I leaped up five stairs in one bound and rounded another corner, running onto a wider street, the large two-story hospital straight ahead.

Straining my body, I picked up my pace, racing toward the emergency room doors only to find it packed with people.

Fuck.

Alpha, Molly replied. *She said she's a slow healer.*

My heart lurched. Did Molly not believe her? Was necessary medical attention being withheld from my mate.

What haven't you done? I snarled as I reached a side door, shifted, and yanked it open. My alpha power snapped off me, and I knew I'd just hit everyone in the hospital with my lack of control.

Nothing, Molly squeaked. *I mean, everything? I'm treating her like a human. She said it was how I was supposed to.*

Where is she?

In the staff locker room cleaning up so I can finish, Molly replied and I could feel her submitting her will to me even through our telepathic link.

Cleaning up? Did that mean she wasn't hurt that badly? Or was she being stubborn and Molly didn't want to argue with the mate of two of the pack's alphas?

I hadn't spent a lot of time with Molly, but she'd struck me as a quiet and sensitive nurse. There was no way she'd have stood up against Audrey if my mate had made up her mind about something. Even if Audrey hadn't released her massive alpha power, all she needed was the idea that children were in danger and no one would be able to stop her.

Well, no one except me... maybe.

I raced down the halls toward the locker room, not caring that I was completely naked, and managed to avoid the busier parts of the hospital so I wouldn't be stopped by anyone. The need to get to her and ensure she was okay, that she'd received the right medical care and wasn't going to turn around and do something stupid, overwhelmed all other thoughts.

I barged into the staff locker room, not caring who might be inside. The room, with three rows of lockers and benches, was empty, everyone dealing with the grimalkin emergency. But I could hear a shower running in the shower room and smell Audrey, along with the coppery tang of blood.

Mine, my wolf growled inside me.

He was tired of waiting, tired of having gotten a taste of her twice but denied more. He didn't want to wait until Audrey had shown the rest of the pack what we already knew: that she was our mate and more than strong enough to help lead the pack.

He also didn't think we needed to be careful because someone had tried to kill her and that *someone* could be a member of our pack.

If we claimed her now, it wouldn't draw unwanted attention. It would protect her. Everyone would know not to fuck with what was ours. Claiming her wouldn't paint a bigger target on her back like our human half feared, and so what if someone challenged us to be alpha? We'd force them to submit. We'd force anyone who opposed us because Audrey was mine.

We stormed into the shower room — a single white and blue tiled room with six showerheads — to see our prize partially standing in a stream of water, her eyes shut and her expression tight with worry.

Scratches and bruises covered her perfect body, and two neat rows of stitches curled up her right calf along with another row across her right ribs. Pink water swirled around her feet before running into the drain, and she was going to need to bandage up the wounds that still wept but weren't deemed deep enough for stitches once she'd dried off.

Still, she was the most gorgeous woman I'd ever seen, her features sculpted by a master: delicate cheekbones, small nose, and eyes that could— no *had* captured my soul. Her torso and waist were still too thin from the journey north and her near-deadly heat, but her small breasts and hips were perfect. Hips that would bear me and my brothers the most beautiful babies.

My cock hardened, standing at attention and pointing to my mate.

Mine. Always mine, my soul breathed, and I strode toward her.

"Cyrus," she gasped, curling in on herself, one hand dropping to cover her mound, the other over her pert breasts.

"Don't you dare," my wolf snarled as he seized her wrists, jerked her hands up, and backed her against the tiled wall. "Don't you dare hide from me."

My wolf didn't wait for a response and smashed my lips against hers. She froze, her body tensing as my human half screamed and struggled against my wolf's control. He wanted her submission, wanted to dominate and control her. He wanted to fuck her until she saw stars and screamed with pleasure.

With a growl, he transferred her wrists to one hand, easily holding them, and tugged, stretching her until she was on her toes. Then he grabbed a handful of her wet hair and jerked her head back.

The move drew a throaty gasp and her arousal flooded around me.

So, she liked it a little rough, liked to be dominated. Good.

Of course, that also didn't surprise me. Given how Knox reacted to her, he was probably unhinged when they had sex, and she hadn't run screaming from him yet.

"You like that?" my wolf growled, breaking our kiss and capturing her gaze with mine.

"Cyrus," she gasped again, her pupils fully blown with desire.

My name on her lips, that look in her eyes, and the scent of her arousal threw my wolf into a frenzy.

We smashed our mouth back to hers, yanked her hair, and shoved our tongue into her mouth when she groaned with pleasure. Our other hand raked up and down her body, roughly kneading one breast then the other before pinching and plucking her nipples.

She moaned and panted, kissing me back with a fever that matched my own even while she struggled to break free.

"Cyrus, I want— I want to touch you," she begged.

"No," I snapped and ground my leaking cock against her stomach. "*I'm* in control. Ask again and I'll find a better use for your mouth."

She sucked in a breath. I didn't know if it was to speak or not, but my wolf snapped our power around her and dropped her to her knees.

I slapped my cock against her lips and more arousal thickened the air as her power flickered against mine, teasing and not resisting.

"Open," I commanded.

She obeyed, and I shoved my cock into her, hitting the back of her throat and making her gag. But even then, she didn't fight me, moaning in pleasure instead. She fully submitted, letting me hold her wrists above her in an iron grip and fisting her hair to jerk her head back farther.

My wolf fucked her mouth with hard, fast strokes, and there wasn't anything I could do to slow him down or soften his thrusts. He needed to brand himself on her body, mind, and soul. He didn't care that she hadn't claimed him with an unprepared mating bond like she had with Knox and Bishop. *He* was going to do the claiming this time because... She. Was. Mine.

Tears rolled down her cheeks and saliva oozed down her chin, but the scent of her arousal kept thickening, turning the mist from the hot shower still running beside us into a heady, enveloping cloud.

She moaned around me, her eyes rolled back in pleasure. I couldn't get enough of her, of her scent, her desire, and I sure as hell couldn't get enough of the feel of her tongue stroking the underside of my cock and the pressure from her swallowing around me while she tried to suck me down.

Hot tingles spread up from the base of my spine and I knew I was on the verge of coming.

With a snarl, I wrenched Audrey up, spun her around, and bent her forward. I seized her hips and plunged my cock into her dripping pussy, the same one she'd flaunted when she'd crawled across the uneven ground beside the healing pool so she could fuck my brother.

She released a throaty moan that went straight to my balls, making them tighten, her breathing ragged pants of need.

Sisters! I'd spent every night since that night in the pool dreaming of fucking her like this and nothing I imagined came close to how it actually felt.

I pulled her down to her hands and knees, pressed her forehead against the wet tiles, and sat back, savoring my mate in full submission with my cock buried inside her.

Mine. All mine.

Then I jerked my cock out and pounded back into her, drawing another moan of pleasure.

Tremors raced through her body and her walls fluttered around me. She was close. Which was good, because my wolf didn't want to wait for her pleasure. He wanted to pump her full of his seed now now now.

We thrust in and out, again and again, our pace wild and demanding. She gasped and moaned, her trembling growing to the point where she couldn't match my strokes with bucks of her own, but I didn't care. I'd get her there. My wolf might want to breed her and brand our body to hers, but I wanted her soul.

I shifted my angle and hit a spot inside her that made her scream and shake, each stroke taking her higher and higher until every muscle in her body contracted and she wailed her release.

Her cry sent me over the edge and I thrust hard, burying myself as deeply as I could and I erupted inside her. I groaned so loud I was sure anyone in the locker room, hell, probably even the hall beyond would have heard me.

My canines extended and my wolf surged forward, capturing her small body under us, but panic seized my human half.

We hadn't talked about me claiming her. It wasn't right. No matter how much my wolf and I knew she was ours, there was a proper way to claim her as a mate and this wasn't it. In the very least, we needed her consent, and a thoroughly satisfying fucking wasn't consent.

I clamped my mouth shut, but stayed over her, making it impossible for her to move as I spurted more cum into her. All the while my wolf snarled, pissed that we hadn't bitten her and marked her for everyone to see.

Soon, I promised him... and myself.

Soon she'd be ours and not because all members of my pack had accepted her, but because, after everything I'd put her through, I'd prove to her that I was a worthy mate and she'd accepted me.

AUDREY

I GASPED FOR BREATH, CAPTURED BENEATH CYRUS'S MASSIVE, POWERFUL body, every muscle within me turned to jelly. His cock jerked and more of his heat pumped into me, sending tremors of bliss rushing through me.

That had been—

I had no idea what that had been.

Shocking? Confusing? Amazing?

My soul wept because once again Cyrus and I had sex and I hadn't formed a mating bond with him despite everything within me screaming that he was mine.

The rest of me, however, was a confusing mix of boneless bliss and frustration. I'd seen the look in his wolf-darkened eyes, knew his wolf had taken over, and a mindless primal part of me had instantly submitted. He was the alpha. He was the perfect mate: powerful, strong, and commanding. He was going to fuck me until I couldn't walk and that matching wild primal part of myself *wanted* that. She wanted it so badly that it didn't matter that I still had no idea how he felt about me.

Sure, his wolf wanted to fuck, but that didn't mean he wanted me like my soul wanted him.

I'd sworn to myself that I wouldn't chase after him, but the second he looked at me, I presented like a bitch in heat.

An aftershock of my amazing orgasm rolled through me and my breath caught in my throat. His arms around me tightened and he released a low, purring rumbled, the sound vibrating through my body, relaxing me even more.

Even with everything that had happened between us and with him pressed over top of me, making it impossible for me to move let alone escape, I felt safe. And right now, I ached for that safety. Fighting the grimalkins had been scary, but using my alpha power to make them run away and breathing black smoke had been terrifying.

I didn't know what was happening to me. I'd been fighting to keep my fears away from Knox and Bishop while they were battling the grimalkins and protecting the pack and then from Knox when he was freaking out about me being hurt.

And while I'd tell Bishop and Knox soon, I also hadn't wanted to risk distracting them when their lives were in danger or when they had responsibilities to the pack.

My life wasn't the only one in turmoil right now. Once again, people had lost loved ones and children had become orphans. There were also the delegates from the alliance to think about and any political fallout that came from the attack, especially if someone important had been hurt or killed — which I really prayed hadn't happened.

Being confused because I wanted Cyrus to prove he cared about me while still letting my primal instincts take over could wait.

I could wait.

It was the responsible thing to do.

"Audrey," he murmured, his gravelly voice shooting heat straight to my core. "I—" He froze and raised his head as if hearing something. "Fuck," he snarled. "I have to go. I—"

He jerked back, his cock sliding out of me and leaving me cold and empty despite the steam filling the shower room.

"Once Molly has wrapped your wounds, have Knox take you to your suite," he said as he stood.

My throat tightened at his hard expression even though I'd already decided that I wasn't the priority right now. His pack was in the middle of an emergency and from his expression, whatever news he'd just gotten was grim.

"I— We need to talk," he said, his tone firm as if he'd made a decision.

And with those ominous words, he stormed out of the shower room.

Swell.

Logically I knew from the past few days that he wasn't the same man who'd yelled at me in the stadium. Even if he was sometimes sharp with me, it didn't feel like it was because of me anymore. It felt more like his anger or frustration or whatever it was that made him close everyone off and demand obedience was because of himself.

Except right now, the stress of the attack and my fears that something was wrong with me, not to mention the fact that he didn't want to talk about it until all the other important things had been taken care of, was making me emotionally sensitive.

Leaving me after fucking me like he was trying to one-up my dream-Knox didn't mean he regretted it or was disgusted by me. It just meant that things were happening and he needed to be the pack's leader, not my lover.

But knowing that and *feeling* that were two different things, and despite wanting to be a strong, independent woman, I felt abandoned... something I couldn't let slip through my mating bond with Knox. He wouldn't understand and would probably try to kill Cyrus the second he saw him.

I stood on still-shaky legs while trying to shove those fears to the back of my mind. I had more important things to worry about, like letting Molly bandage me up then finding Quinn and seeing how Zavier was doing before hurrying out of the hospital to calm Knox down.

And the sooner I did that, the better.

Knox's emotions were roiling, fear and anger and frustration barely contained within him and only partially kept back from flooding our bond. But I could also sense that he was trying to keep it together. He knew I'd needed to go inside and he'd let me go without a fight even though his instincts were telling him to hold me tight and not let go.

I washed off Cyrus's cum and limped out of the shower room. All my aches and pains that Cyrus had momentarily made me forget about flooded back in, and with a groan, I grabbed a towel from the rack just outside the door.

As promised, Molly was waiting for me on the bench around the corner with a med pack, and she quickly got to work bandaging my wounds.

Thankfully, she didn't comment on the fact that Cyrus had just stormed out naked or that the room smelled like sex — because even if I couldn't smell it, I had no doubt it did. And while I was grateful that she didn't say anything, I had no doubt people were going to find out sooner rather than later that I'd had sex with Cyrus.

My insides tightened at the thought of having to deal with more rumors along with the realization that I was alone with the closest of my guys being Knox, who couldn't enter the building.

Sure, I'd killed two grimalkins and scared away two more, but I wouldn't be able to fight members of my new pack like that, not if I wanted to fit in. I already had enough enemies. I needed to make more friends and prove myself worthy.

But first thing first, I had to find people I trusted—

No, I had to check in with Quinn and Zavier. Then I needed to get back to Knox before he completely lost it.

AUDREY

MOLLY TIED THE LAST BANDAGE AND HANDED ME A LOOSE SHIRT AND pants — the pack's version of hospital scrubs. She'd already checked me over with a glowing stone that would indicate if something was wrong with me other than my scrapes and bruises and found no explanation for my queasy stomach.

"Fear, anxiety, and shock," she'd said. "Those grimalkins are terrifying, and Nova said there were three dead ones in Jaxon's smithy. I'm surprised you aren't in deeper shock right now. You should get ahold of me if your symptoms get worse. We're too busy, and we don't have enough beds to keep you here for observation. But you should contact me if your stomach gets worse or you start showing other signs of shock."

She reminded me of the shock symptoms I needed to look out for: increased heart rate, breathing problems, being too cold, dizziness, etcetera. Then she gave me directions to where Quinn might be and I hurried out of the locker room.

As instructed, I turned left and headed down the long hall. Molly was pretty sure Quinn would either be in one of the waiting rooms, or in the room they were going to give to Zavier once his injuries had been treated, and since I had to pass through one of the waiting areas to get to the stairs to the patient rooms, I decided to check there first.

As I hurried, the rumble of many voices grew louder and louder, but I expected that. I was racing out of the staff-only area into the public areas, and the pack was in the middle of a crisis. It made sense that people would gather at the hospital.

What I didn't expect was to round a corner and step into a wide hall packed with people.

Shit.

The waiting area had to be full, with those who couldn't fit gathering in the hall, and I really didn't want to push my way through the crowd and draw everyone's attention. Especially if Quinn wasn't here.

Whoever had attacked me on the first night of the summer festival and had ended up poisoning Bishop was still at large, and I knew there were people in the pack who didn't like me.

"Excuse me," I murmured to the closest person, a young woman holding a sleeping baby.

Every instinct I had screamed to make myself small even though I knew that was from years of being scared and helpless. I didn't have to be small anymore. I should have *never* had to be small even when I'd been powerless.

But I still wanted to be cautious because I had no idea how these people would react to me. Not drawing undue attention to myself was always the safest plan, especially when I wasn't with my mates or friends.

"Alpha!" the woman exclaimed far louder than I'd hoped, making everyone nearby look at me.

"Alpha," another woman said, the title making me cringe. Cyrus was the alpha. Bishop and Knox were as well. I was most certainly *not* a pack alpha.

"Yes, thank you," someone else said.

"Alpha—"

"My babies—"

"My pups—"

"I can't thank you enough—"

Everyone started talking at once and crowded closer. A few of the kids who'd been with Quinn and trapped in the smithy with us pushed through the crowd to stand in front of me. For a moment, warmth swelled around my heart, a whispering shifter connection in my soul with everyone in the hall even though I wasn't touching them, wasn't emotionally close to any of them, and barely knew them.

Then my chest tightened with my old fear that there were too many of them and I'd drawn attention to myself. I wasn't supposed to draw attention.

Knox's emotions heaved inside me and I clamped down on our mating bond. I couldn't risk him running in here to protect me from his own people.

"I was so scared, alpha," a little boy from Quinn's group said to me as he tugged on my burrowed scrubs to get my attention.

"Me, too, alpha. Me, too," others chimed in.

"You were very brave," I told them, squatting to be at eye level, focusing on them and their worried faces and not the crowd of adults all around us.

"But I cried." The little boy's grip on my scrubs tightened.

"That doesn't mean you weren't brave." My heart broke for him and all the other children who'd experienced today's horrors. No child should ever be terrified or see the horrible things they'd seen. I wanted to hold all of them and protect them. I wanted to figure out how to stop the grimalkin attacks for good.

Except I had no idea if that was even possible. It seemed like grimalkins attacked Stonehaven on a semi-regular basis. More than semi-regularly if my experiences with their attacks were anything to go by. I'd only been in this realm for two months and the grimalkins had already attacked twice.

"Being brave doesn't mean you aren't afraid. I was afraid too, and I wanted to cry," I told them. "It means you do what needs to be done despite being afraid. And I saw you— I saw all of you being brave. You tried to be quiet when we needed to be quiet and you helped Quinn with Zavier when she needed help. You were all very brave, and I'd be proud to defend the pack with you at my side."

I had no idea where the words were coming from, especially since I wasn't really an alpha, and a part of me cringed that I was saying alpha things. But how I felt didn't matter. What mattered were the children, and I watched pride and self-confidence bloom in the eyes of the little boy who'd confessed to crying.

In fact, all the kids looked more determined, as if me just saying a few words helped them feel safer and more in control of their circumstances.

And while yes, I wanted them to know that it was okay to be afraid and sad and all the other emotions, it felt good to give them something I'd never experienced as a child. The knowledge that an alpha of their pack thought they were good enough.

"Della and Jake," Felix, the engineer I'd met at the summer festival, spoke up. A thick white bandage had been wrapped around his head. "Give Alpha Audrey some space." He stood from one of the few seats against the wall and motioned for me to sit.

I offered him a grateful smile because I was exhausted and my stomach was still queasy. "Thanks, but I need to find Quinn first. Does anyone know where she is?"

"She's waiting for Zavier in his room," an older woman replied, her grim expression souring the satisfaction I felt from consoling the children. That didn't look like Zavier was in good condition. "Take the stairs at the end of the hall and go to the second floor. She'll be somewhere on that main hall."

She pointed in the direction I'd originally been going, indicating I needed to push through the entire crowd.

"Thank you." I straightened from my crouch and pushed through the people, a strange mix of pride, happiness, and embarrassment churning in my stomach.

All of these people looked at me like I was someone. For the first time I was being seen. I had value and respect, and people cared about me. But on the other hand, people were *looking* at me and my lifetime of trying to be invisible made me uncomfortable with being the center of attention.

More people thanked me, some regarded me with awe, others with respect, and I tried to keep my head high while quietly acknowledging their thanks and comments.

The crowd parted to let me pass, and I kept my pace even as I walked to the stairs, even as the churning in my stomach grew stronger.

I didn't know how to behave. All I knew was that fleeing would make me look like prey and I was done with being prey. That, and an alpha didn't flee. And if everyone was calling me alpha, I had to live up to the role whether I wanted to be one or not.

AUDREY

I found Quinn in the sixth patient room on the right, sitting in a chair beside the bed and holding Zavier's paw. His fur had been shaved from most of his body and large white bandages encircled his torso as well as three of his four legs. His eyes were closed and his breath came in short sharp pants, indicating that even while unconscious, he was in pain.

"Audrey," Quinn cried when she saw me, and she sprang up and rushed the few feet to me, wrapping me in a tight embrace. "Thank the Sisters you're all right."

"Thank the Sisters *you're* all right," I replied, hugging her back.

I'd been terrified for Quinn and the children during that fight, and it was such a relief to see she only had one bandage around her forearm and no other injuries.

Zavier whimpered, drawing her attention, and worry squeezed around my heart. He didn't look good, and Quinn looked wrecked. Even if I was wrong and there wasn't anything more than sisterly affection for her adoptive brother, the two of them were still close, and it would destroy her if he died.

"You were amazing, you know," Quinn said, her voice soft, her gaze locked on Zavier. "Thanks to you none of the children were hurt. Not even a scratch."

I tightened my grip around her, hoping physical contact with me would help steady her soul even as I selfishly used my shifter connection with her to steady mine.

My insides squirmed with the need to help her, help those children. Help my pack.

"So what happens next?" I asked even though I was sore and exhausted.

There were people hurt worse than me and just as tired, and I was sure they were doing their duty.

"After all the grimalkins are dead and the injured are taken care of?"

I nodded.

She swallowed hard. "After that come the funerals."

My throat tightened as if I could feel her grief and fear. Her parents had died when she was young, probably because of a grimalkin attack or something just as horrible, and now there was a chance the not-brother she loved was going to die too.

"Then we rebuild and—" Quinn said as Nova stepped into the doorway of the hospital room and gave me a stern look.

"You're supposed to be resting and letting the elixir do its thing," Nova said. "Go. Rest. The pack is still hosting a formal dinner for the alliance members tonight, and Cyrus and Bishop will want you there."

"They're still going to hold it?" I asked even though this was my first time hearing about it, although I was sure Bishop would have mentioned it once the town tour for the delegates and their aides was over.

"More than half of the work is already done," Nova said.

"Yeah, Eloise and Kira have been working on the dinner for over a week now," Quinn added.

"But a lot of the alliance members stayed to fight," I insisted. "Some of them will be hurt." Or dead, but I didn't want to say that out loud.

"Everyone still needs to eat." Nova's expression turned grim. "They'll also want to discuss what happened, possibly blame Cyrus and Bishop for not providing enough protection. Having a meal while they talk about it will partially distract them. Hopefully, that will help them keep an honest perspective on this. We've lost far too many people in the last few months to grimalkin attacks."

And while a part of me wanted to argue with Nova and say I could help, the rest of me was exhausted and worried. Somehow, I'd controlled those grimalkins and threw up black smoke. Getting to the bottom of that was as important as helping out, possibly more so.

For all I knew, I was dangerous. Sterling had already influenced me into hurting myself. What if the smoke was connected to him... what if the grimalkins were?

He'd been able to control those shadow snake monsters through the rip between my old realm and this one. What if he could somehow control the grimalkins? Their alpha power felt a little like the heavy ominous power in Anakar, and that power came from Tzanagoth.

I was probably grasping at straws, searching for an explanation for something that had no explanation. Grimalkins were mindless beasts. They attacked because they attacked not because of some evil magic seeping from the ground.

Except I couldn't make myself believe that. Even animals in my realm had reasons for attacking an obviously more powerful pack. Sure, the grimalkins could take a single shifter one on one, but not the whole pack. Something had to have made them think this attack, and the one that had happened when I'd first gotten here, was a good idea or at least the better of two terrible options.

"Go," Nova insisted, a whisper of her power rolling over me, not enough to make me submit but enough to tell me she was serious. "You need your rest."

Nova directed me to stairs at the back of the hospital so I could leave the building without being swarmed again, and I hurried outside to reunite with Knox before he lost control of his wolf— or rather lost control of the primal wildness at the core of his wolf's soul.

"Nova says there's nothing wrong with you," Knox said as he yanked me close and held me as if I was the only thing keeping him in his human form, which I probably was.

Given how much stress leaked through our mating bond, I was surprised he hadn't shifted into his wolf.

"I still feel like I've gone ten rounds with a grimalkin," I replied, sinking into his embrace and savoring the heat of our shifter connection warming around my heart.

"Then you're not going to the formal dinner tonight." Knox swept me into his arms so he cradled me against his chest and headed up a deserted narrow street toward the Residence, completely naked.

"I have to," I said, pressing my nose into the hollow at the base of his throat and breathing in his rich wood smoke scent.

I also *wanted* to go. If I was there, I might notice or overhear something important. And despite the positive reception I'd just received in the hospital, I still needed to feel useful, still needed to prove my worth to this pack.

Besides, I had an ability no one else had. I could understand every language in this realm because of the magic in the rip between this realm and mine, not just the one spoken by the pack. I was the only one who could fully observe the Mountain and Sea Alliance delegates and their aides and, more importantly, the merchants.

I hadn't seen the merchants or their powerful monster-killing weapons after the grimalkins attacked. All I knew was that none of them had fled with the aides and translators who couldn't fight, and a part of me screamed that I needed to find them and find out what they were up to.

Because they were up to something.

It had been chaos when the grimalkins attacked, but if I thought back to that first moment, only one of the three merchants had looked surprised. The other two had worn strangely blank expressions as if they were trying to hide what they were feeling.

Of course, Cyrus, Representative Folmar, and King Gower hadn't looked surprised, either. They'd all looked angry. But they'd at least had an expression.

Knox growled, the sound rumbling in his chest. "I don't want you to go." Then he huffed. "I don't want to go, either."

"To the dinner?" I asked, surprised. There was no way Cyrus would demand Knox go inside the Residence and be surrounded by anyone, let alone all of the delegates and aides. That was the fastest way to get him to snap and Cyrus knew that.

"No," he snarled. "I don't want you to go to the dinner, and I don't want to leave you for a hunt."

He blew out a heavy breath then pressed his nose to the top of my head and inhaled my scent.

"We have to send hunters— hell, send anyone still able to fight to scour the area around town for more grimalkins," he said. "Deacon's only given me enough time to ensure you get back to your suite. Then I have to go."

My heart stuttered with a ridiculous fear for him and for how long he might be gone. It was silly. Hunting was his job in the pack, and he needed to make sure there weren't more grimalkins out there waiting to attack.

I knew of at least two grimalkins that were still alive and had no idea how long they'd obey my command... if I'd actually commanded them.

No, I *had* commanded them. And as much as I wanted to crawl into bed and nurse my aches and pains until the formal dinner, I needed to talk to Whil and find out what was wrong with me... or possibly right. Controlling the grimalkins may have made me sick, but it had saved everyone in the smithy.

Knox carried me down the narrow streets and alleys, avoiding the main roads and anyone who might be on them. He hurried along the winding Old Town streets and through the open main gate of the Residence.

It had been eerily quiet after we'd gotten a few blocks from the hospital and even farther away from the market and the chaos, and it was still quiet on the Residence's grounds despite that the Residence would be hosting a diplomatic dinner in four or five hours.

I still couldn't believe Cyrus was going through with the dinner, despite Nova's perfectly logical explanation.

Knox rounded the side of the large castle complete with multiple wings and turrets to the French doors leading into my suite.

"I want to stay," he said, his voice low as he slowly lowered me, letting me slide down his naked body.

Worry and yearning and anger radiated through our bond, and I pushed as much love and confidence back to him as I could.

"I'll be fine. I'll have Bishop whenever he's done with whatever he's doing." Although whatever that was, it was upsetting him. He'd almost completely blocked his emotions from me and what little that was seeping through our mating bond was anger and grief. "You need to protect our pack."

"Our pack?" he asked, his pride swelling into me despite his expression remaining hard.

"Yes, our pack," I repeated.

I'd thought the pack was mine when I'd been defending, Quinn, Zavier, and the pups in the smithy, and I felt it even more now. Whether I was actually an alpha or not, this pack and these people were mine.

"Alpha." Knox tangled his fingers in my hair, drew my head back, and captured my lips in a searing kiss.

It wasn't as wild as his usual kisses, I could tell he was trying to be mindful of my injuries, but it burned with passion and need. It claimed me as his, always his, and I happily submitted to him.

Deep in my soul, I knew I was safe with Knox. We might have had a rocky, unwanted start, but love and commitment roared through our mating bond. He'd do whatever it took to protect me and love me, and I loved him for that. I especially loved that the emotions in our bond didn't feel insincere, like they were all his and the mating bond wasn't compelling him to love me. He'd more than made his peace with being mate bonded with me, and he loved it. He loved me.

With a groan, he jerked away and shifted into his massive black wolf, his head reaching to the middle of my chest.

Must go, he growled in my head before bounding away and leaving me with my breath a little too fast, a warm ache in my core, and my lips tingling for more.

Love you, I thought at him even though I didn't have telepathy. I still needed to tell him. *Stay safe.*

AUDREY

I waited for a few seconds on my suite's patio to make sure Knox had a good head start and would hopefully be off the Residence's grounds by the time I walked around the front of the castle.

If he saw me, he'd insist I go to bed, and if I told him about the black smoke and controlling the grimalkins, he'd freak out. And that wouldn't be helpful at the moment. Searching the area around Stonehaven and ensuring everyone in the pack was safe, not just me, was important. Without a doubt, he was the most powerful hunter they had, and they needed him. I didn't want to get in the way of that.

And while I didn't want to hide anything from him, I also couldn't distract him from his duties. Once I'd talked to Whil, I'd have a better idea what was going on and I'd tell Bishop. It was a bit of a cop out, but Bishop wouldn't freak out and he'd know how to talk with Knox to keep him from losing it.

With that decided, I summoned my strength, pushing through my exhaustion and aches and went to Whil's greenhouse library cottage. The building was tucked against a large protective wall at the back of the grounds. Bushes and trees and vines were all in full bloom regardless that it was summer and some of the plants bloomed in the spring or fall. They crowded around the half English cottage half greenhouse structure giving it a whimsical, magical feel, which was fitting for the home of a summer fae.

I knocked on the wooden doorframe to the greenhouse. "Whil?"

No answer.

"Whil?" I tried again as I took a few steps inside.

Still no answer.

Maybe she was in the cottage half of the building.

I headed deeper into the greenhouse, walking through a garden bursting with brilliant flowers and vibrant leaves. Bookshelves crammed with books and scrolls and knickknacks hid amongst the greenery, growing more predominant the farther I walked.

I followed a path that was half wide flagstone and half moss or short grass, and up a step or two, then back down again, or down then back up with no noticeable reason for the steps, until I reached the seating area at the back made up of mismatching pieces of furniture. Beyond the sitting area stood an archway heading into the cottage proper.

"Whil?"

But before I'd even spoken, I knew she wasn't home, or if she was, she was sleeping or concentrating on something. The cottage and greenhouse felt too still, too empty.

Of course, now that I thought about it, it made sense that she wasn't home. She might not have been a shifter, but she was still a member of the pack and even with her minimal sorcerer's ability, she could still help.

Swell. I'd have to wait to get answers and I'd walked to the back of the Residence's grounds for nothing.

With a sigh, I marched back to my suite and collapsed on my bed.

Loud knocking and someone calling my name woke me, and for a second, I couldn't remember where I was.

Then it all came flooding back. I was in a realm with two moons and dangerous beasts. The son of my previous pack's alpha and his friend had tricked me into starting a mating bond and then tried to sacrifice me to a monster. I was mate bonded with two of three pack alphas — and wanted to be mated to the third as well — and now I was breathing smoke and controlling grimalkins.

"Audrey," Quinn called, her voice muffled with my door and my suite's sitting room between us.

"Coming," I called back, realizing I hadn't undressed out of my borrowed scrubs or even crawled under the blankets. I'd just collapsed on top of my bed.

I hurried out of my bedroom, surprised that I wasn't as sore and achy as I would have expected after the fight. I rushed across the lavish sitting room with its handcrafted everything, unlocked the door, and opened it.

"What are you doing here?" I asked. "You should be with Zavier."

Quinn offered me a weak smile and held up a garment bag and a handbag as if that explained everything. "Whil put him into a magical sleep so he can heal without pain, and I'd already promised Bishop I'd help you get ready for tonight."

"I'm sure Bishop would understand if you wanted to stay with Zavier," I told her even as I stepped back to let her in.

"Zavier won't wake until tomorrow and I couldn't keep sitting there and crying. I *know* he'll recover. It's just going to take a while." Her weak smile turned into a fierce one that looked anything but happy. "It could be worse. Last I heard, twenty pack members had died and two dozen were injured like Zavier."

I swallowed hard, the wildness rising within me at the thought that I'd lost twenty shifters and even more were hurt. They were mine to protect and I'd failed them. Even if I couldn't have been there to help them, I'd still failed them somehow.

"Five humans, two gryphons, and three Dedearc died as well," Quinn continued as she walked through my sitting room and bedroom and into the bathroom. "More were hurt, but Representative Folmar's son is the worst."

"Cohnal?" I asked, relief sweeping through me. He might be hurt, but from how Quinn mentioned him, it meant he was still alive after fighting three grimalkins by himself.

"He lost half of his leg, was blinded in one eye, and I'm told his beautiful feathers were shredded. Sit here," Quinn said, pointing to the edge of the tub. "Let's see how many scrapes and bruises I have to cover up."

I huffed and sat. "I wouldn't bother trying. You'd have to wrap me in a full bodysuit with a mask to cover up the fact that I went toe to toe against a grimalkin."

Although it could have been worse. Poor Cohnal had lost his leg, and his feathers had been damaged. I didn't know if they'd grow back because I knew nothing about gryphons. Up until this morning, I thought gryphon shifters were only a myth.

"You mean *many* grimalkins, not *a* grimalkin," Quinn said her expression daring me to argue with her. "You killed two grimalkins without shifting, and your alpha power..." She barked a harsh laugh and started pulling jars and bottles and tubes from her bag. "I don't think Finn even knew what he was doing until he killed that grimalkin. You must be amazing at blocking your power because it feels like you don't have any."

"Right now, I don't," I confessed. "It only shows up when I'm upset and that only started happening recently."

Quinn frowned at me so I told her about my pack and how my ancestors had cursed themselves and future generations so we could hide among the humans. I also told her how the curse was broken on the summer solstice after our eighteenth birthday, how mine was still in place, and how now it didn't matter if we were shifters or not. The archangel Michael had proclaimed war on all humans and every supernatural being had stepped up to save them.

Quinn did my makeup while listening, and I went on to tell her about Sterling and Royce betraying me and me hopefully fucking up his plans by still being alive.

"I'm glad your pack doesn't have to hide anymore, but I can't believe someone tried to exterminate a whole realm," she said, motioning for me to turn around.

"Some people are like that. Greedy, hungry for power," I said, obeying her and turning. "They'll crush anyone who's weaker than them to get what they want."

"There's something wrong with them if that's the way they are," she huffed as she gathered strands of my hair, twisting and braiding them into a complicated updo that only required six simple pins to keep it in place.

After she was done, we returned to my bedroom and she unzipped the garment bag. The dress inside was similar in design to the one I'd worn this morning with a thin neck strap and a higher back, except this one was gold with delicate green embroidery.

"Where's Bishop getting these dresses?" I asked. "They fit perfectly and hide half the scars on my back."

"He ordered a bunch of them specially made for you just before the festival," Quinn said. "And he's got great taste. You look amazing."

Quinn turned me so I could see myself in the two-person wide full-length mirror. My breath caught in my throat. Somehow, she'd made me beautiful.

The makeup was soft and subtle, just enough to highlight my eyes and hide the worst of the cuts and bruises, and my hair was twisted and curled with tendrils framing my face and accentuating my neck. The dress clung to my barely-there curves, but still seemed to cover the fact that I hadn't gained back all the weight I'd lost during my heat fever and even my bruises and cuts — those that could be seen — seemed paler, as if they were a few days old instead of a few hours. Molly must have given me an elixir from a particularly potent batch.

"Your alphas won't be able to keep their eyes off you," Quinn said.

At her words, the memory of Cyrus kissing me like he wanted to claim me, his eyes hungry and dark with his wolf, shuddered through me.

Not my alpha.

And once we had our *talk,* I was sure he was going to make that clear.

Except my stupid soul didn't want to listen to reason. He was mine, just like Bishop and Knox.

AUDREY

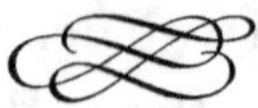

QUINN PACKED UP HER BEAUTY SUPPLIES LOOKING EXHAUSTED AND emotionally raw. Doing my hair and makeup had been a slight reprieve from her worries, but only that. They weren't going to go away until she knew Zavier had pulled through.

"You'll have to tell me about the party tomorrow," she said with a weak smile. "To distract me."

"I will," I promised. "Are you going home to rest?"

"I'm going to try," she replied, but she was probably going to toss and turn for a few hours then go to the hospital and try to sleep in the chair beside Zavier's bed. "Bishop said he has to schmooze and couldn't escort you, but he promised he'll stick by your side the entire night."

That was a relief.

Although I still wasn't sure how I was going to handle being in a room full of powerful people and not give in to my urges to shrink in on myself or find a way to slip away.

Quinn left and I sucked in a deep breath to steady my nerves. Bishop and Knox loved me and Bishop believed in me. That, and I'd just killed two grimalkins. I could face the dignitaries and aides.

They at least, wouldn't be trying to rip me to pieces.

With my back straight and my head held high, I marched down the halls inside the Residence to the grand front entrance and the main doors to the ballroom.

Standing at the threshold between the hall and grand entrance, I couldn't see into the ballroom, but I could hear the voices of people as well as soft music coming from inside. Before me, tiny rainbows shimmered on the thick, red rug, reflections of the bright lights in the crystal chandelier, and the grand staircase framed the doors to the ballroom. It started split at the bottom, curled up to a landing, creating a balcony, before splitting again to rise to the next floor.

But my gaze stalled on the landing and didn't follow the curving stairs all the way to the top.

Finn, looking tired and pale from his battle with the grimalkins, stood at the top of the stairs staring at me.

I squared my shoulders. He and Velora were the two betas who'd accused me of seducing both Knox and Bishop to gain the power and privilege of being a pack alpha, and I'd essentially taken control of his body with my alpha power, something that probably pissed him off even more.

Well, fine.

Finn could yell at me all he liked for using my alpha power on him when he was a beta and I wasn't really an alpha, but I refused to feel bad or even guilty. I'd done what needed to be done to save those children and everyone else in the smithy, and just like how I'd stood up against Cyrus for saving those children after the first grimalkin attack, I'd stand my ground against Finn now.

What I didn't want was to be reamed out in front of the doorway to the ballroom where all the dignitaries and aides could see me.

I pulled my attention away from him, about to hurry inside. After the day I'd had, I didn't want to have to deal with his or Velora's shit. Surely Finn wouldn't want to make a scene in front of everyone.

Except he called out my name and hurried down the stairs.

Shit. Did I rush to find Bishop? He'd said he'd meet me in the ballroom. Or did I look for some place more private?

But the thought of being alone with the big beta made my insides churn. It didn't matter that I'd been able to control him with my alpha power. My power wasn't predictable. I might not be able to summon it to protect myself since all the times it had manifested was in defense of someone else.

I also wanted witnesses. In my old pack, it wouldn't have mattered if someone watched one of the betas yell at me, but here it did. Here, I had people willing to stand up for me and protect me.

I strode toward the ballroom.

"Audrey, wait." Finn's power snapped over me but wasn't enough to stop me. "Alpha," he added as he leaped over the railing eight steps from the floor to land in front of me.

"Beta," I replied, uncertain if he'd called me alpha or someone in the doorway who I now couldn't see because of his broad frame.

"Alpha, please." He dropped to his knees in front of me and lifted his chin while tilting his head, baring his throat in full submission to me. To. Me. The weakest shifter—

No. Not anymore. My power might only come out when I needed to protect someone, but I wasn't weak. Not anymore.

Behind him, the people in the doorway noticed, and a hush fell over the ballroom. My stomach churned with all the attention but I held my ground. If I wanted to win over those reluctant to accept me as an alpha, I needed to act like one.

"I beg you, alpha, forgive me. I was wrong to suspect you were anything other than a gift from the Sisters to our pack," he said as he clasped his hands behind his back. "I treated you unfairly and am ashamed to confess I didn't keep my feelings about you to myself. You shouldn't have had to prove yourself to me, and I didn't deserve your kindness when you saved me."

I didn't think I'd been particularly kind to Finn during the fight with the grimalkins. I'd needed his help and had forced him into action, but I also wasn't going to argue with him.

"I failed as a beta and the Watch Commander," he continued. "I can recommend a few good men and women who can replace me. I only beg you let me remain in the pack."

Replace him? Remain in the pack?

What the hell?

I wasn't going to kick him out or try to convince Bishop and Cyrus to replace him. It wasn't my place to make that kind of decision... or was it?

I was pretty sure calling me alpha was a courtesy because I was mated to Knox and Bishop. I didn't want the responsibility of leading the pack—

Except I did want to protect it. I wanted everyone to know their loved ones would come home at night, and I really wanted every child to feel safe and loved.

Did that mean I wanted to be alpha?

Knox and Bishop were already my mates and a part of my soul was certain Cyrus was too — despite us having sex three times now and still not forming a mating bond like I had with my other mates.

"Finn," I said softly, my instincts screaming to stop drawing attention to myself because that had been my reality all my life until a few months ago. "A suspicious Watch Commander isn't a bad thing. I won't asked Bishop or Cyrus to replace you. But you also need to realize that kindness and understanding are not weaknesses. You should have tried to get to know me before making up your mind."

He frowned. "I asked you questions."

"You interrogated me and made accusations."

He dipped his head forward, his expression contrite.

"Yes, I didn't want to tell you about my origins. I was afraid," I continued. "If you'd shown me kindness, I would have opened up more like I did with Bishop."

I probably still would have been hesitant and he would have needed patience, but I'd become more comfortable with Nova, Deacon, Eloise, and Kira and they'd easily seen that I was scared and lonely.

"You also didn't take into consideration your alphas' opinions about me before making up your mind," I added.

"I promise, I'll do better," he replied, his volume just as low as mine.

"I know you will." I offered him a soft smile. It was still going to take a while for me to trust him, but I didn't like the idea of him being afraid of me. I wanted allies not enemies.

Cyrus strode out of the ballroom and placed a hand on Finn's shoulder.

"Beta," he said, his gaze locked with mine, his expression soft and strange until I realized he'd heard our conversation with his enhanced shifter hearing. Then the strange expression sort of looked like pride? "Time to get back to work."

"He's still recovering," I blurted out.

But Cyrus didn't snap back at me. There wasn't even a flicker of his power indicating I'd upset him. Instead, the probably-pride shifted to something else, something strange and hard.

"No, the alpha is right," Finn told me. "Deacon and I haven't fully confirmed all the grimalkins are dead."

Finn ducked his head and hurried back up the stairs.

I turned my attention to Cyrus. "He looked tired and pale."

"He's not doing any hunting, just coordinating," Cyrus replied. "He'll be fine. Everyone who can needs to step up."

He raked his gaze down my body, and a flash of dark hunger filled his eyes before the hardness returned.

So, he craved me, but was going to tell me it could only be sex. That was what he wanted to talk about.

I raised my chin and swallowed back my disappointment, even as my insides heated at the memory of him pounding into me.

"You have a job to do, too," he said with a pointed look, his voice gruff. "Come on."

Right. Eavesdropping on the merchants and other members of the alliance.

Cyrus stepped aside, gestured for me to enter the completely quiet ballroom, and my heart pounded. Everyone stared at me and it took everything I had not to shrink in on myself.

It's not like my old pack. They aren't staring, waiting for me to be humiliated—

Although from Velora's barely veiled death glare, I was sure *she* was waiting for the right moment.

She hadn't been happy when Bishop had told her we were mated, and she was furious when she realized I had two mating marks. That proved Bishop and I hadn't just mated with promises. We'd actually completed the rare, sacred vows and sealed our bond with a bite.

And it didn't matter that neither of us had said the vows to create the magical bond between us. She didn't need to know that.

Especially since she wouldn't recognize that we were fated mates like almost everyone else did. She'd argued that I'd manipulated Knox and she'd argue again that I manipulated Bishop in the same way.

I heaved my attention from Velora, knowing I needed to ignore her and be brave... and, if I was smart, remember to keep my guard up.

BISHOP

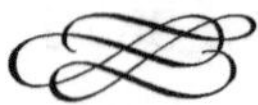

Every time I looked at Audrey, she stole my breath. I'd arrived in the ballroom a few moments ago, expecting to find her already here and had been worried when I hadn't seen her. But her entry now made that momentary burst of fear that her injuries were worse than expected worth it.

She was a goddess stepping through the open double doors into the brightly lit room. Her makeup was delicately done, hiding all but the shadows of the scrapes and bruises on her face, accentuating her beauty but not erasing the proof of her courage, and her hair twisted over her head in a stunning, complicated style. Flecks of shimmering gold caught the light in her blond strands, adding to her divine etherealness, and the golden dress I'd had made just for her clung perfectly to her scant curves — curves I intended to grow with good food, peace, and love.

My mate would never have to fear for her life — at least once we'd dealt with the grimalkins and caught whoever or *whatever* had tried to kill her — and she'd never wonder when she'd get her next meal.

She was flourishing before my eyes, bravely facing everyone in the room with her head held high and not afraid to make eye contact.

That never would have happened when she'd first arrived. Hell, she'd been looking at the ground and shrinking into herself two weeks ago.

She was still nervous — I could feel it crackling through our mating bond — but she didn't look it. I could even feel a hint of her alpha power softly rolling off her as if after standing her ground against Cyrus to go to the healing pools and fighting with the grimalkins, it hadn't fully retreated back behind her curse.

Knox had mentioned the same thing when he'd told me she was okay and that I had to keep watch over her while he hunted. But whether the curse was crumbling or not, it didn't matter. I fell in love with her when she didn't have a speck of power. If her alpha power never manifested again, I'd still love her.

Although it did feel as if things were changing for her. Just like she was breaking through her fears and claiming her place and her worth in this pack, her alpha power was breaking through her curse.

Soon everyone would be able to see what I saw, that she belonged at my and my brothers' sides.

And while I knew Cyrus was still fighting with himself because he thought our pack wouldn't accept her, his body language, the fact that he stood too close to her, told me he'd accepted the truth— or rather, his wolf had fully embraced the truth. Audrey was his mate.

Now all I needed was for his human half to catch up and stop making life confusing and stressful for Audrey.

I loved my brother, but his need to control everything while also sacrificing himself to the pack made me want to strangle him. He deserved to be happy, too. Hell, he'd probably be a better alpha to our pack if he was happy.

He, however, wasn't going to change overnight. I needed to be patient and wait for the right moment to give him that final push to tell Audrey how he feels.

I just hoped to the Sisters that it would come soon. The sexual tension between them was driving me crazy.

Plastering a pleasant smile on my face, I slipped through the crowd, and joined them just as they reached Jundar.

"Audrey, this is Speaker Jundar, General of the Ciliran forces," Cyrus said. "Speaker, this is my brothers' mate, Audrey."

Jundar, a stocky man with white short-cropped hair that stood out sharply from his dark skin, smiled at Audrey even before Yara, a small woman with large dark eyes and long wild hair, had finished translating Cyrus's words in to Cilirinian, not because he understood our language, but that it was clear Cyrus was making introductions.

Jundar's smile deepened as he bowed his head and said something back.

Audrey waited for Yara to translate, a blush already forming on her cheeks, though I doubted anyone but me and maybe Cyrus noticed.

Then she opened her mouth, looked at Jundar instead of the translator as was proper, and said two short words in Cilirinian.

Both Jundar's and Yara's eyes widened in surprise. A glower flickered over Cyrus's expression before he schooled it back to something still hard but more pleasant while my pulse lurched.

I hadn't wanted to reveal Audrey's ability to understand every language in this realm and not just because it let her listen in on conversations we couldn't understand. Our allies would ask questions that I didn't want Audrey to have to answer, not until she felt more secure in this realm and our pack.

Jundar said something, and panic snapped through our mating bond.

Thankfully, Audrey's expression remained neutral before shortly slipping into a frown when Yara didn't automatically speak, pretending she hadn't understood Jundar.

Yara glanced at Jundar, who gave a slight nod, telling her to translate.

"The speaker didn't realize you could speak Cilirinian," Yara said.

Audrey opened her mouth then snapped it shut, her gaze jumping to mine.

"She's only learned a few niceties," I replied for her as I joined their group while praying Audrey had only said thank you or something similar in Cilirinian. "She's far from fluent."

"Too bad," Yara translated. "I like Yara—" A smile pulled at Yara's lips. "But speaking through her still makes for an awkward conversation."

"Maybe next time the Alliance meets Audrey will know more." I tugged Audrey closer to my side and nuzzled the top of her head to breathe in her scent. "Will you excuse us? I haven't talked to my mate all day."

Jundar and Yara gave us knowing smiles, and I drew Audrey away from them to our table. No one else was near, they were all gathered on the dance floor talking and waiting for dinner to officially start.

"Thanks for that," Audrey said as I pulled out a chair for her. "I hadn't even realized I'd spoken in Cilirinian until I saw their expressions."

She sat and I sat beside her, my wolf urging me to move our chairs closer together. "I kind of got that from the panic rushing through our bond."

"But you covered for me perfectly and set me up to be able to speak Cilirinian the next time we see the speaker," she said.

"It's your decision when or if you want anyone to know about your fluency in languages." I brushed my lips against hers, savoring their softness as well as the love billowing through our bond. "I'll always have your back."

"I know you will." She leaned closer and deepened our kiss, filling it with a promise of something more later tonight.

Which was good. Knox and I had plans for her, and while I needed to remember to be gentle because of her injuries from the fight, I wasn't going to be able to keep my hands off her. Our bond was still so new and we'd finally gotten back from the healing pools to some privacy.

"Ah, the newly mated," Deacon laughed, his voice right in my ear.

Audrey jerked back, her face a brilliant red, which only made Deacon laugh harder.

"Sorry, alphas," he said, "but you've drawn a bit of an audience."

Horror seeped through our bond as she glanced at the dance floor from where almost everyone stared at us.

"Something joyous to celebrate in the middle of such heartache," Folmar said. "To the newly mated alphas! May you be blessed with many healthy cubs."

The rest of the room joined her toast, and Audrey's blush rushed down her neck and spread, her darkened skin highlighting the shimmering twined bond marks on the side of her throat. A throat I couldn't wait to bite again.

Sisters, I couldn't wait to get her alone.

AUDREY

I sat through dinner smiling and nodding and letting Bishop answer any direct comments to me from anyone who used a translator for fear of speaking in a language I wasn't supposed to know. Again.

God, I couldn't believe I'd done that, but it made sense. My brain thought everyone was speaking English regardless of what language they were really speaking.

I also couldn't believe I'd forgotten I was in a room full of people and kissed Bishop like I wanted to have sex with him… which I did, but now wasn't the place or time.

It was like I'd lost my mind or something. I'd experienced a little bit of power, and I'd forgotten everything that had been beaten and scolded into me.

Except it wasn't my alpha power and killing those grimalkins that made me more confident. It was everyone else. Bishop and Knox's love, the uncomfortable praise I'd gotten from the people in the hospital, and even Finn recognizing I just wanted to belong with the pack.

Sure, there were still lots of people who look down on me, but now I knew their opinion, just like Merrick's, Sterling's, and Royce's, didn't matter. That and it was almost impossible to keep my hands to myself.

Bishop and I were newly mated, and the urge to drag him out of the ballroom and lock ourselves in my suite was almost overwhelming. We'd had sex to seal our bond and again the next morning after we'd saved him, and that had been it since our time at the healing pools. Over a week with my mate and only a few teasing touches and kisses because I really didn't want to embarrass myself in front of Deacon, Whil, and...

A shiver of desire rushed through me along with a flashback of me and Cyrus in the shower room.

Yeah, I wanted Cyrus to watch me having sex with Bishop and Knox, wanted to see a possessive heat burn in his eyes.

Except I had a feeling that was never going to happen. He'd said we needed to talk and that was never a good sign.

I'd thought we were building something. I'd felt the way he'd looked at me during our march back to Stonehaven from the healing pools. Even more telling, he'd made an effort to be nice to me, encouraging me and asking instead of commanding.

But he had serious responsibilities being the primary alpha of the pack, and I had no doubt he couldn't take a mate just because he wanted to.

The thought turned the wine in my mouth sour, and I swallowed it down against the lump forming in my throat.

Damn it. I was used to disappointment. It shouldn't bother me that Cyrus might desire me, might want to have sex with me, but didn't want to mate with me.

Except my soul was certain he was my mate and it hurt thinking that he was going to reject me.

"Wow," Bishop said as he leaned close. "That was one hell of a mood swing. Don't worry, the dinner is almost done."

His warm breath caressed my cheek and teased down my neck. Desire blossomed within me and I struggled to think of chilling thoughts before I blasted the room with my arousal and a third of everyone in attendance knew I wanted to jump Bishop.

He hummed, the sound a low rumbled, and smiled. "That's better."

For him, maybe, but not for me. Now I couldn't stop thinking about dragging Bishop back to my room and having my way with him.

The dessert dishes were cleared away and then the speeches began. Cyrus welcomed the delegates and their aides to Stonehaven and spoke the grief everyone felt, since every delegation had lost someone. The other leaders each stood and thanked Cyrus for the welcome as well as acknowledging our pack's grief.

After King Gower, who was a charismatic speaker, I tuned out the other leaders and let my gaze wander, trying to not stare at the merchants for too long. One of the merchants had the strange, flat expression that I'd seen just before the grimalkins had attacked, making me think he was trying to hide his reaction, the other two looked serious.

Except, even with the serious expressions, it felt like they were anticipating something. Which made sense. After this morning's tragedy as well as the evidence of the effectiveness of their weapons, they had to feel certain the alliance would agree to buy their lightning guns.

The whole situation was a very convenient coincidence for the merchants, and while I doubted they were responsible for bringing the grimalkins to Stonehaven, something still felt off about them.

After the speeches, Eloise and Kira set up evening sweets and drinks on a long table at the side of the room, and the musicians — the group who'd been playing at the summer festival — started playing dance music. These dances were still choreographed numbers where everyone knew the movement, but they were slower, more stately, than the ones at the festival.

Bishop grabbed my hands and I stiffened. I didn't want to embarrass him or Cyrus in front of everything, and I would if I stepped onto the dance floor.

"Don't worry," he murmured against my cheek, sending a shiver racing down my spine. "I've got something better planned than dancing."

"Something more private?" I breathed, as his desire swelled through our mating bond and enflamed mine.

We slipped out the door to the kitchen to avoid notice, hurried past Eloise and Kira and the dozens of other people who were helping with the party, and raced out into the herb garden.

Bishop's grip on my hand tightened. "This way."

We rushed around the back of the Residence then headed deeper into the garden, away from the building. The second I saw the hedgerow in the distance, I knew where we were going.

The summer garden.

We'd had our first date there and instead of eating the picnic we'd made love. It seemed every time we went to the summer garden, we forgot why we'd gone there and ended up having sex.

And from the anticipation and need rushing through our bond, we were going to make love again.

Feeling freer than I'd ever felt in my life, I ran with Bishop through the winter garden and stepped through the wrought iron arch between the gardens into magic.

The summer garden had been transformed into a nighttime wonderland. Night-blooming flowers that had secretly been hidden among all the glorious daytime blooms shimmered pale white, blue, and pink in patches through the whole area, and a night-blooming vine twisted among the clematises, honeysuckle, and wisteria, climbing up and over the top of the pergola in the garden's center.

Soft light emanated from trays of little white stones inside the pergola, and in the center were dozens of pillows all white with gold trim and a soft-looking dark blue blanket.

"It's beautiful," I breathed.

I couldn't believe Bishop had done this for me or where he might have found the time to set it up with everything he'd had to do in the aftermath of the grimalkin attack.

"*You're* beautiful," he said as he stepped close behind me and teased his lips along my jaw.

With a sigh, I tipped my head back, resting it against his chest, and sank into the warmth, love, and desire rolling through our mating bond.

"Just because we're mated now doesn't mean I'm going to stop courting you," he murmured in my ear, his hot breath sending need racing straight to my core. "I promise to show you every day how beautiful you are and how much I love you."

His fingers brushed down my bare arms, drawing another blast of need, adding to the heat building between my thighs. I ached for him like I always ached for him.

He was my first love, my first real kiss, the first man to be kind to me, my first... my first everything, and I knew I wasn't in love with him because he was kind to me when everyone else had been cruel. I was in love with him because he filled my soul with certainty and comfort. He was my confidence and passion.

He was home.

He'd always been my home. I'd just needed to run through a rip in the realms to find him.

A large black wolf strode out of the shadows to stand in the middle of the blanket and pillows in the pergola. White light shimmered in his thick coat while lust and pride swelled in my mating bonds.

Knox.

My ferocious, wild mate. He was my courage and fierceness. When we made love, I felt powerful. Despite his need for submission, now that he'd fully committed to our bonding, I never felt lesser or weaker with him. I felt like an equal.

A hint of alpha power swirled around me, but I couldn't tell if it came from Knox or Bishop or even myself. It just filled the air like fog rising from the ground, getting thicker and thicker until my skin buzzed with it.

Come here, Knox commanded in my head.

A snap of power crackled across my skin, but instead of making me go to him, it made my own strange power rise up in challenge as if this were a dream and not real life.

"Make me, alpha," I challenged.

His power snapped stronger, zinging along my nerves.

I gasped, the sensation sending heat rushing through my veins, and Knox's desire crushed through our bond.

Behind me, Bishop groaned, the sound a low, sexy rumbled that vibrated in his chest and against my back.

"Audrey," he purred. "He promised he'd be gentle with you because of your injuries. You might not want to tease him."

He skimmed his fingers up my sides, brushing the swell of my breasts and setting off my already sensitive nerves.

My breath caught on a moan and Bishop's need crashed over me, swirling with Knox's into a heady drug that had me instantly wet and aching.

"Teasing him teases you and me, and I'm not sure you're ready to handle both of our wolves when we're awake."

That thought sent more heat rushing to my core and my moan escaped.

"Not tonight," Bishop groaned, his voice strained. "I know you're sore and you're going to feel worse in the morning."

"Not if both of you fuck me," I breathed, feeling bold and confident. These were my mates and they wanted me. I could feel it whirling and teasing inside me, building my own need into an achy fire just waiting to explode into an inferno.

AUDREY

 into his human form so he stood mere inches from me, gloriously naked, his cock full and proud. "We're not going to fuck you. We're going to make love. Tonight. I need to protect you, make sure you're safe."

"I *am* safe. I'm with my mates."

"I know you are," he growled back. "But still—"

He dipped forward and captured my lips in a soft kiss. I could feel his wildness and need rushing within him and stuttering through our mating bond, but I could also feel his need to protect me, even from himself.

"You're hurt and I won't hurt you more," he said, his voice low as he drew me toward the nest in the pergola. "But I need you."

"I need you, too," I murmured, letting him lead me with Bishop staying close behind me.

We reached the edge of the blanket and Knox pulled me closer. His hard cock pressed against my belly, trapped between us, and he brushed his lips against mine. I could feel him fighting to stay in control and not let his wolf take over. And while I didn't care if his wolf took over — I trusted his wolf — I knew he needed to do this. He needed to show me he could be gentle and loving as much as he was wild and commanding.

I sank into his embrace and submitted to his gentleness. He'd been gentle when he'd gone down on me when Sterling had tricked me into hurting myself, so I already knew he was capable of it, but I sensed he needed to prove that to himself.

Behind me, Bishop pressed close and teased his lips over our mating bond, capturing me between them, two men who looked identical but loved me in their own unique ways.

The heat in my core grew hotter, and I moaned at Bishop's attention and kissed Knox back, letting my emotions, my love and desire and burning need for them, flood our bonds.

"Fuck," Knox growled breaking our kiss and jerking away from me.

His breathing was fast, his pupils fully dilated, almost dark enough to suggest his wolf was taking over, but I knew it wasn't. I could feel the beast coloring the emotions rushing between us, could feel its need to possess me and brand himself body, mind, and soul to me, but I could also feel its understanding of Knox's need to be gentle.

Bishop cupped my cheek and turned my head so I could kiss him over my shoulder, his lips taking over where Knox's had stopped. Bishop's desire was just as thick through our mating bond as his brother's, and his kiss hungrier. He plunged his tongue into my mouth, making me gasp, turning the heat within me into an inferno.

"Gorgeous," he praised as he pulled away and undid the ties at the back of my dress.

The garment slid down my body, pooling around my feet and ankles, and Knox's eyes followed the dress's movement, getting darker and darker the lower he looked.

"You have stitches," Knox said.

His voice was so low and filled with darkness, I could barely understand him, but the possessive protectiveness rolling through our mating bond like a thunderstorm about to let loose assured me he wasn't angry at me.

I grabbed his chin and urged him to meet my gaze.

"I earned them," I said, letting both Knox and Bishop feel my pride. "I defended our pack. I am *not* weak."

The words surged like liquid power through my veins and my alpha power unfurled around me.

I might have been shy, uncertain, and afraid, but I wasn't weak. Not anymore.

"You never were." Bishop brushed his lips against the back of my neck. "You're brave and capable. You care so deeply for those who can't protect themselves and I love that about you."

Love and pride surged through my bond with Bishop and joy bubbled inside me.

"You did such a good job protecting those children," Bishop said as his hand inched up my belly toward my breasts. "And you've handled yourself wonderfully with the delegates and their aides."

The joy flared stronger, jolting desire in my core, every word fueling the aching inside me.

Logically I knew I shouldn't need anyone's approval to feel good about myself, but the broken part of my soul craved it. And with Bishop's low sexy voice in my ear and his hands on me while Knox was kissing me as if I were the most precious thing in the world, I'd never felt more loved and accepted and seen.

Knox broke off our kiss with a growl, his desire heavy and thick in our bond, and his nostrils flared, taking in my scent.

Embarrassment flickered through me, an involuntary reaction born from my life before my mates.

"Don't," Knox barked with a snap of power that didn't control me, only made my own power flare stronger. "You smell so good."

He dropped to his knees, buried his nose in my curls, and inhaled deeply.

More wet heat pooled between my thighs, and I cracked my legs open, letting my desire perfume the air.

"Fuck," Knox hissed as he grabbed the back of my thighs and pushed his nose in deeper.

Bishop grabbed my hips and lifted me up, and Knox pushed my legs over his shoulders, fully opening me to him.

His tongue swept through my folds in a long lick that finished with a barely-there flick against my clit, sending more arousal rushing to my core. A responding lust burst through our bonds as Knox lapped at my juices, our alpha powers twirling and sliding against each other in a slow, sensual dance.

Bishop groaned at the double blast of need from me through our mating bond and Knox through their twin bond. His erection, still captured in his pants, pressed against the crack between my cheeks, sending another thrill rushing through me.

What would that be like? Would I enjoy having him push inside me through my puckered hole while Knox was buried deep in my channel?

The thrills turned to molten heat. I wanted both of them inside me, wanted the three of us to be so completely joined for a glorious blissful moment that I didn't know where either of us began or ended.

"Oh, gorgeous," Bishop purred. "What are you thinking?"

The heat of embarrassment rushed across my cheeks, but I quickly shoved it down and pressed back against him as best I could.

"I was thinking—"

Knox teased his tongue inside me and my hips bucked forward.

"You were thinking?" Bishop teased, moving a hand from my waist — letting Knox take more of my weight — and plucking my nipple.

Pleasure shot from that tightened bud to my core, and I rolled my head back as I swallowed a moan.

"What were you thinking?" Bishop asked.

Knox flicked his tongue on my clit and slowly slid a finger inside me, and the moan I was holding back escaped.

"I was thinking of both of you."

"We should be all you're thinking about right now." Bishop plucked my nipple harder, this time adding just a bit of pain to my pleasure, twisting my need higher.

"I was thinking…" I panted as Knox pushed a second finger inside me all while sucking and licking my clit.

My hips bucked faster, my desire tightening, drawing closer to the edge, something both of them could feel through our bonds.

"Of both of you— inside me." Hints of stars flickered behind my lids and I fought to finish my sentence. "At the same time."

AUDREY

Surprise flashed through both of the bonds followed by heavy, consuming lust, along with a flare of alpha power. The sensation sent me crashing over the edge. Knox licked and sucked me through a release that was heightened by the need rolling through my mating bonds.

"You promise?" Knox asked, his gruff voice rumbling through my folds. "You really want that?"

"More than anything," I breathed.

With a growl, he dropped my thighs, grabbed my waist, and rolled back, sliding me onto his thick, hard cock in one smooth stroke.

His pleasure at being buried within me sent a mini orgasm rolling through me, and I gasped, knowing my first full orgasm had just been an appetizer.

Knox might not want to make love to me with his usual ferocity because of injuries that weren't hurting at all at the moment, but that didn't matter. I was already hypersensitive, already halfway to an incredible release, and he could have done the bare minimum at the softest setting and I'd go off, screaming, in no time.

Satisfaction blazed through our bond, and he smirked at me despite him being in the more submission position beneath me.

His grip on my hips tightened, holding me in place, and slowly —
so damned slowly as if he'd taken a lesson out of Bishop's playbook
— he pulled out to just the tip then pushed back in.

My need tightened with just that stroke.

God, he felt so good.

Then Bishop sank to the blanket behind me and ran a heavy
hand down my spine. Shivers followed where he touched me, turning
into a fiery need when he cupped my ass.

A moan escaped my lips, and my head rolled back to rest on his
chest, anticipation of him joining Knox inside me twisting my desire
tighter.

"Wrong direction, beautiful," Bishop murmured in my ear as
Knox pulled out and pushed back in, his girth raking against my
sensitive channel. "This way."

Bishop leaned forward, forcing me to lie against Knox's chest, and
placed my hands on either side of Knox's head.

Knox thrust again and again, his pace still slow and deliberate as
aching, desperate need poured through my bonds.

Bishop ran his hand down my spine again, drawing another
heated shiver, and this time didn't stop to cup my ass. Instead, his
fingers dipped to where Knox was torturing me, playing with my
folds and clit.

My desire spun tighter and my breath picked up. I tried to rock
down to meet Knox's thrusts but his grip was too strong.

Then Bishop slid a finger, slick with my desire, up to my hole. I
jolted at the sensation even though I ached for his touch, and he
teased the tight ring of muscle, quickly melting the jolt into
pleasure.

Knox continued to thrust, his impatience and need seeping
through our bond as he picked up his pace, while Bishop teased more
of my juices to my hole.

I gasped and mewled, my need building, the fire that had barely
cooled from my first orgasm blazing into an inferno. I needed harder,
faster, more more more.

Please. Oh, please.

It wasn't enough, just a torturous tease holding me at aching but never growing into something more.

"You're doing great, gorgeous," Bishop purred, and the pad of his finger pushed against my hole.

Knox thrust again, the stroke more powerful than the last, and Bishop's finger slid inside me with a tingling, heated burn.

A full body shiver rolled through me, raising me from aching to desperate, and my channel started to flutter.

"Stop," Bishop barked.

A blast of his power froze me and Knox stopped mid-thrust, stealing my orgasm.

"Not yet." Bishop pushed his finger all the way in.

My eyes rolled back and I moaned while Knox growled, his body trembling with the effort to keep still.

The tension of not moving, of my aching need roiling with Knox's and Bishop's and our alpha powers whirling around us, twisted me tighter and tighter.

"Bishop, please," I begged. "I need you."

"Not like this," he said, as he slid his finger out and pushed back in. "You're not ready for anyone here. Not yet."

"But—"

He pulled out and pushed two fingers inside with a stronger heated burn that only added to my aching need.

"Soon. We'll work up to it. I'm not going to hurt you."

He leaned over me and brushed his lips over our mating mark while sliding his fingers out then in again.

Lust and determination teased through my bond with him and my channel started to flutter again in anticipation. I couldn't wait to have both of them, to be thoroughly joined with them.

Knox grunted and completed his thrust with a force that jolted through my bond and pushed Bishop's fingers deep inside me. Pleasure roared through my veins and flushed my skin, stealing my breath.

Oh, yes. More.

I wanted more of that. More force, more possession. I liked when my guys claimed me, liked feeling their need for me and only me.

Knox's thrusts grew fast and hard, his control shattering, and Bishop worked my hole, pushing and scissoring, both of them building an ache inside me that twisted tighter and tighter. Every stroke quickly took me higher, up to a grand precipice that I knew meant I'd see stars when I finally came.

Then Knox's control shattered, and with a roar, he buried himself within me. Pleasure erupted through our bond, and with a scream, I flew off the precipice, soaring into a darkness filled with sparkling green flecks, a match to his and Bishop's eyes.

Bliss pounded through me, whirling me around and around, as I could feel Knox's hot jets of cum fill me, connecting with a primal need inside me.

I ground down on him, my core milking him, hungry for every last drop.

The second Knox was spent, Bishop shoved me against his brother's chest and jerked my hips back. Knox's cock slipped out and Bishop replaced him with a vicious stroke that was more Knox's style than his.

Then the dam Bishop had been keeping around his emotions, one I hadn't even realized had been there, shattered, and I could feel his ferocious need. He needed to fill me—

No, his wolf's need. His wolf had been patient, had agreed with Bishop what was best for us in the beginning, but now it was his turn.

He drove into me, giving me the harder and faster I'd ached for earlier. I moaned and gasped, trapped between the two of them, feeling deliciously possessed.

Alpha power crackled around us, stronger and sharper than when I'd been riding Knox. It tormented my sensitive flesh and made Knox's cock, which was trapped between us, harden.

"Fuck," he snarled, his hips bucking up to grind himself into my belly as Bishop drove into me.

Pleasure snapped along my spine and ricocheted to my core. Each powerful thrust raked through my channel, ending at the perfect spot deep inside me that made stars flash across my sight.

"You're so fucking beautiful," Bishop's wolf growled. "You take my cock beautifully, you gasp beautifully, and your scream when you come will be beautiful."

He drove harder, pounding me into Knox who shifted down a bit so when he bucked up, the base of his cock ground against my clit.

Sensation whirled through me, the press of their bodies capturing me, possessing me, protecting me. I didn't want to be without these men, didn't want to think or feel or even live. They were mine. They filled my soul with love and friendship and safety. They were home.

I was home.

Bishop's pace picked up, his thrusts growing uneven, but I didn't care. He and Knox had taken me to the highest precipice and stars already flashed through my vision.

Each powerful thrust and grind against my clit twisted nerves that were already achingly tight closer and closer to the breaking point.

Then Bishop yanked me up, capturing my back against his chest, thrust hard into me, and sank his teeth into my shoulder. I ground down on Knox, and together, all three of us cried out with our release.

The stars in my vision overwhelmed my sight, alpha power erupted around us electrifying my nerves, and I screamed. It was the only way to release all the glorious pressure.

My thoughts whirled, spinning me around and around in a whirlwind of bliss. Flecks of green stars and heady alpha power filled me, and deep satisfaction crashed through my mating bonds.

We collapsed together in a heap, Bishop aware enough to pull the edge of the blanket over top of us.

"I love you," Knox said, his voice a low satisfied grumbled that made my heart swell.

"I love you, too," I whispered, sending love through the bonds to both of them.

Tomorrow we'd still have to deal with the aftermath of the

grimalkin attack and the merchants with their monster killing weapons, who my instincts said I should be wary of, but for right now, I was happy and thoroughly satisfied.

I was with my mates... well almost all my mates — something I wasn't going to think about right now — and needed to stay in this glorious moment. Anything could happen tomorrow, and I needed to hold onto feeling safe and happy and not worry about the future... even if I knew there were things to worry about.

CYRUS

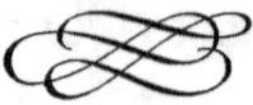

I PACED MY OFFICE, WAITING FOR BISHOP TO ARRIVE. THE SUN HAD barely crept above the horizon, but I'd already been up for hours. Hell, I shouldn't have even bothered trying to go to bed. My mind hadn't settled and I'd barely gotten a few hours of terrible sleep.

Damn it. I felt like everything was spiraling out of control.

Like *I* was spiraling out of control.

I'd caught a glimmer of gold last night and turned to look out the ballroom door and Audrey had been standing there. I hadn't thought she could look more beautiful than when she'd shown up for the city tour yesterday morning wearing a dress that matched the flecks in Bishop's eyes and was designed to show off her mating marks. But last night she'd been breathtaking.

And now I couldn't stop thinking about her, couldn't stop remembering how it felt to bury myself inside her tight, hot sheath, and how my wolf had almost claimed her.

And of course, I hadn't had time to talk with her about anything. I'd had to rush away to deal with the fallout of the attack. And I'd left with a "we need to talk."

Which was the stupidest thing I could have said.

Even I knew you didn't say that to a woman after sex. You told her how beautiful she was, how much you cared about her. Hell, I could have even talked about wanting to protect her — although I had a feeling that would have come out wrong, too.

But no. My alpha mask had slammed into place the second I'd realized I'd lost control of myself and needed to be focusing on the most urgent matter: the aftermath of the grimalkin attacks and those merchants with their dangerous weapons that I felt we had no choice but to buy.

Except that only made me think of everything else going on: helping the injured and those who'd lost loved ones, proper burials, and the deaths of the fighters from the alliance, which I prayed wouldn't turn into a political incident.

Thankfully, Folmar wouldn't demand reparations for Cohnal's injuries even though I could tell she was heartbroken. He was a good man, but their pride wouldn't accept him now as alpha mate — since their primary alphas were always women. No gryphon alpha female would think he, blind in one eye and missing half a leg, would be a worthy mate.

I sighed. Audrey would be so upset when she learned of all that. He'd heroically taken on three grimalkins by himself to protect her along with the women and children in that small square. He'd managed to kill all of them before help had arrived, and Audrey would be pissed that he was going to be punished for it, even if it wasn't an intentional punishment. I'd seen her speak with him during the tour, so I knew she knew him, even if it was just casual. Hell, even if she hadn't known him, she'd still be upset because that was the generous soul that was my mate—

Not my mate.

Not yet.

Someone knocked on my office door and opened it without waiting for my response.

"Good," I said as Bishop walked in.

"What's the plan for today?" he asked, closing the door and pacing to the windows behind my desk.

"Is Knox with her?" I blurted out before I realized what I was saying.

Sisters! I was supposed to be talking about the alliance meetings today because the attacks had changed the agenda.

"They're in bed in her suite," he replied, the corner of his lips twitching.

"There's still an assassin on the loose," I said, and his smile vanished, which wasn't what I'd meant to say, either. Damn it.

I raked my hands over my head, already feeling the braid I wore to keep it out of my eyes loosening.

"That wasn't— I didn't mean—" I blew out a heavy breath.

I wasn't going to be able to keep her off my mind and focus on everything else.

She was my mate. And while she'd proven she was strong and capable when things were desperate, I couldn't stop the instincts screaming inside me saying I needed to protect her... and claim her.

Except there was no way she'd accept me as a mate, not with how I'd treated her. And she shouldn't. She deserved better. It didn't matter if we could both feel something between us. It didn't matter that she'd submitted to my wolf and enjoyed herself in the shower. That didn't mean she accepted me as a mate.

Which meant I needed to court her... one of the things I was an absolute disaster at.

"We need to talk business," I said, my voice gruff. "But you have to tell me how to court Audrey first. I'm losing my mind. There's so much going on, and all my wolf cares about is protecting and claiming."

"And what do *you* want?" Bishop asked.

I stared at the gardens outside my office window, unable to look him in the eyes. He was Audrey's mate, fated to be with her just like Knox was. I'd slept with her a few times now, and her soul hadn't claimed me like it had claimed them. Still—

"She's my mate. *Our* mate," I said.

"No more pushing her away," he replied.

"That's why I need your advice. I open my mouth and I always say the wrong thing."

"You know that's not true."

I stared at him. "My wolf took over and we had sex in the hospital staff shower room. What did I say after when Deacon called me away?"

"You didn't," Bishop groaned already knowing it was going to be something stupid. This wasn't my first time saying the wrong thing to a woman and I doubted it would be my last.

"We need to talk." I raked my fingers through my hair, pulling out most of the braid. "We need to talk. Who says that after sex? Who says that after my wolf almost sank our teeth into her and claimed her?"

"Sisters, Cyrus," Bishop said. "At least you didn't bite her."

"No shit." We wouldn't have bonded, and I'd have just given her another scar, not the mating mark my wolf wanted. She had to accept us first, and that would never happen if I kept doing what I was doing.

"The first thing you need to do is apologize." Bishop leveled a hard look at me. "And do it from the heart. You can't be in control of this."

"I know." My insides squirmed at the thought.

I was the one in charge, the responsible one. *I* took on those burdens so no one else had to, but I knew the tiny voice inside me, begging me to surrender, was right. I just had no idea how to let go.

"Should I get her flowers? Sweets? How do I show her I mean it, that I'm sorry and I'd be a good mate?"

Bishop was so good with women. He always knew the right thing to say and do. Hell, he did it unconsciously and half the females in the pack were in love with him... which was another potential danger for Audrey.

Fuck.

I bit back a growl. Why did I always go there? Why was I constantly thinking of dangers? That couldn't be what I focused on with Audrey. My wolf might think protecting our mate was the only thing that mattered, but even I knew that wasn't the way to win her heart.

She needed mates who believed in her and thought she was strong and competent, even if her strengths weren't physical... because they *weren't* physical. Her strengths were kindness and empathy.

"You need to be honest with her and vulnerable."

My wolf jerked our head toward Bishop and snarled. We did *not* reveal vulnerabilities. We were alpha. The pack needed to know their leader was strong.

"You need to tell her how you feel and why you've been a dick to her," Bishop continued, ignoring my wolf's warning. "And you need to do it without pride and without being defensive. You need to treat her like you're treating me right now."

"I'm not treating her like she's my brother."

"No, you should treat her like an equal and a confidant." Bishop's expression softened. "That's what a mate is. A partner, an equal, someone you trust implicitly, and someone who doesn't judge you for your flaws."

Which was exactly what Bishop and Audrey were to each other. It didn't mean he didn't have to apologize or work to keep their relationship alive and healthy. It meant that they talked it out when something went wrong, and that they had each other's backs when dealing with everyone else.

Me being overprotective undermined Audrey and her relationships. She already had a protector she trusted in Knox and a lover who worshiped her in Bishop. My role was to be her equal, to prove to her I trusted her and valued her opinions, to show her she was and always would be worthy.

And all I needed to do was let go and trust.

I woke to feather-soft kisses along my jaw and disappointment whispering through my mate bond with Knox.

"I have to go," he said as I cracked open one eye and fell into the bottomless depths of his gaze.

"The room—" I started, about to say I understood he had to go outside. Except I couldn't feel the churning unease that Knox always felt when he'd reached his limit for staying indoors.

"Patrol duty," he huffed. "I think I could stay here with you for another couple of hours."

Which was amazing. Sure, the dinner had gone until after sunset and we'd cuddled under the stars after making love before returning to my suite, so we hadn't been here all night. But Knox's time inside should have been up by now.

"It's you," he said, his voice gruff as he nuzzled the sensitive spot behind my ear. "You settle my soul."

Peace and relief washed through the bond. He'd been struggling with his claustrophobia for years and while I hadn't cured it — and doubted I ever would — I'd helped to ease some of the pressure. He had more choice now about how he could live his life, and that made me happy.

"You have to get up, too."

"Right, eavesdropping on alliance stuff," I groaned, wishing I could have another hour— hell, even thirty minutes to stay in bed with my mate, while praying I'd have some free time to talk to Whil.

Because I *had* to talk to Whil about the grimalkins and smoke soon. I didn't want to neglect my problems and have them make everything worse.

Knox looked at me expectantly, waiting for... something.

"You don't have to show me the way. I need to shower first, so I'll just go to the kitchen," I said, dragging myself into an upright position and feeling not nearly as sore as I expected after sex with Bishop and Knox and surviving a fight with three grimalkins. "Eloise or Kira can tell me where to go."

"No," he huffed. "You don't go anywhere alone."

"The grimalkins didn't get anywhere close to the Residence," I protested. "I'll be fine."

But worry poured through our bond and didn't ease up at my words.

"Someone tried to kill you and they're still out there." A growl rumbled in his chest and he hugged me tight. "We're short watchmen and hunters. I have to patrol. But you're not safe without me or Bishop."

A shiver rolled down my spine at the memory of that person attacking and poisoning Bishop. With everything going on, Bishop and Cyrus couldn't spare the time to search for the assailant.

Whoever it was had caught me and Bishop alone, at night, on a dimly lit street. Surely, he wouldn't attack in broad daylight while I was in the Residence.

Except I knew anything was possible and anyone who I didn't know could be the assassin. I could only hope they were going to be more cautious now that Bishop had lived and could identify him by his scent.

And Bishop knowing the assailant's scent didn't rule out everyone in the pack. The Stonehaven pack was large and it would be impossible for the alphas to have memorized everyone's scent.

"Okay," I agreed. "Give me five minutes to shower."

Knox huffed his agreement, and I hurried out of bed, powered through a shower, and changed into a cream-colored dress — one of many that had appeared in my wardrobe between dinner last night and this morning.

This dress was simpler than the previous two I'd worn, without any embroidery, but it still had the higher-than-regular back and thinner-than-regular neck strap to show off my mating marks.

I braided my hair to keep it out of the way and to hopefully look more serious and confident — as if I actually belonged in the alliance's meeting. Then Knox shifted into his wolf and we left my suite through the French doors and walked around the back of the castle to the herb garden and the kitchen door.

All the delegates are taking breakfast in the ballroom, Knox said in my head. *But Bishop said you'd rather eat in the kitchen.*

I gave Knox a grateful smile, knowing he could feel my relief through the bond. I knew I had to spend the next however-many days in the spotlight, having everyone watching me even if I didn't say a word, and I hadn't been looking forward to it.

Just thinking about all those people staring at me, wondering why I was Bishop's and Knox's mate or why I was even in the room made my insides twist.

I'd spent my life trying to be as small and unnoticed as possible and now I had to take up space. An alpha's mate didn't shrink from scrutiny. She faced it head on. Or at least that's what I felt an alpha's mate did. I could be soft and not draw attention to myself, but I couldn't be small anymore.

I didn't *want* to be small.

But I also knew it was going to take time and practice — not to mention be emotionally draining — to go against everything I'd been taught.

I needed to be kind and patient with myself just like I was with the children.

Love and worry crept through my bond with Knox while Bishop's connection held a hint of concern.

I sent my love back to them.

I could do this.

And I wasn't alone.

Knox left me in the kitchen's doorway, bounding out of the garden and heading toward the front of the castle, and I turned to head inside through the open kitchen door.

But Velora stepped through the hall entrance into the kitchen, and I jerked back, pressing my back against the rough, stone wall beside the doorway.

Worry and shame fought for control inside me. I shouldn't have been afraid of Velora. I *wanted* to stand my ground. But I also didn't want to cause a scene and embarrass Cyrus and Bishop in front of the alliance delegates.

And not because it wasn't my place or I was afraid they'd get mad, but because a responsible person didn't air their private business in front of political guests.

I wasn't sure what relationship my guys had with the other leaders, but I refused to be the reason other countries and kingdoms and any other foreign whatever looked down on our pack.

A lot was going on right now, and adding a cat fight between the alpha mate and one of the pack's betas wouldn't help anything.

And that was what it would end up being.

Even if Velora reminded me of where she thought my place was and criticized me, it wasn't to protect the pack. She wanted Bishop, and I'd taken him, and after the look she'd given me when Bishop had pointed out our mating mark, I wasn't sure anyone could make her see reason.

Which was just another problem on top of all the others Bishop and Cyrus had to deal with.

I let my gaze slide over the herb garden as I listened to Velora order breakfast from Kira. She wasn't mean to the cook's assistant but there was still a clear edge of superiority in her tone.

It made the wildness inside me bubble up. How dare she treat Kira as though she was less than her?

Except if I stormed in to protect Kira—

Movement on the far side of the herb garden caught my attention and everything within me froze.

One of the merchants, the short, stocky one strolled past the garden farther from the Residence. That, in and of itself, wasn't an issue. Bishop had mentioned that there was going to be a leaders' only meeting in the morning. No aides or merchants, only translators. It was the tightness and wariness in the merchant's body language that bothered me.

He was trying to look natural, but the *trying* was giving him away with movement that looked rehearsed and repetitive. A glance at a flowering bush, a pause at a tree then another glance and another pause.

Maybe he was just uncomfortable being at the Residence with all the political leaders. I certainly was. Or maybe he was worried about selling the weapons.

But my wildness rejected those explanations. He was up to something and I wanted to know what.

I glanced back in the kitchen to see Velora's back to me while she supervised Kira's cooking, so I crept out of sight of the open kitchen door and after the merchant.

The stocky man in his silky embroidered robe slunk along the hedgerow of another garden then another, going deeper and deeper into the Residence's grounds until he was almost at the towering rock wall at the back.

Three other merchants, dressed in similar clothing waited for him... which was weird. Bishop had said there were only three merchants. That, and I recognized the guy I'd followed and the other two from the town tour, but not the big, muscular man with the dark glare.

"I thought I said ten minutes after their meeting started," the muscular merchant I didn't recognize said.

"The idiot, Jundar, cornered me in the hall," the guy I'd followed replied. "He's interested in making a deal even if the rest of the ridiculous alliance isn't."

"Good," one of the two tall and lanky merchants said. He wore a deep crimson robe with black embroidery, which made his pale skin and short white-blond hair stand out in stark contrast.

"What about the others?" the muscular merchant asked, his voice dropping, making him harder to hear.

I crept closer and knelt beside a large bush, straining to hear their conversation.

"On the fence," the other lean guy said. He wore an olive-green robe with gold embroidery that partially camouflaged him against the rock and trees. "Even Gower. We knew the gryphons, wolves, and Dedearc were going to be a tough sell, but Gower surprised me."

"He's too dependent on the wolves even though the mutts aren't as strong as the gryphons and our grimalkins put the gryphon's heir in the hospital," Muscles said, a vicious, satisfied gleam in his eyes.

My heart stuttered.

Holy shit!

I clamped my hands over my mouth to muffle my gasp. Surely, I'd heard that wrong. *Their* grimalkins? *They* were responsible for the attack?

Were they also responsible for the previous attack? The one that had killed those children?

"I think they need another push," the stocky one said gleefully. "If we prove that these wolves can't even protect their town, Gower will realize he has to buy our weapons."

"They'll get suspicious if another pack attacks so soon," Green Robe said.

"No," Muscles barked. "Emrys is right. They're going to want to talk about all of this for days. Cyrus and Folmar are too cautious and Jundar too eager. They'll butt heads, get all worked up, and *then* we'll release another pack to seal the deal."

"I've already moved our other pack to the pens in Anakar," Red Robe said. "But after that, we'll have to wait four more months for the next litter to be ready."

"That's fine," Muscles replied. "One more push and they'll be falling all over themselves to buy our weapons. Start sowing discord. Let Jundar think Gower and Cyrus don't trust him and whisper around Cyrus's betas that Jundar and Pimryl are thinking of buying in secret, that they want to take over the alliance."

The other three nodded and hurried back toward the Residence while Muscles stood there, his lips twisted in a wicked grin.

I hugged myself tighter, squeezing into the smallest, stillest ball possible, my heart pounding so hard I was sure he, even with his human hearing, could hear it.

Stay calm, I told myself. *Keep your emotions to yourself.* Because the last thing I needed was for Bishop or Knox to come storming back here.

If I could stay hidden, I could tell Bishop and Cyrus what I'd overheard and we'd have the advantage. But that only worked if Muscles didn't know that I'd overheard him.

I just needed to wait until Muscles left.

He chuckled and the wind shifted, carrying the dark reek of the grimalkins along with a whisp of black smoke. I glanced through the bushes as he turned to follow the path around the outside edge of the Residence's grounds, catching a red glimmer in his eyes and another curl of smoke.

Shivers rushed down my spine, my wildness wanting to rise up and defend me, but knowing staying hidden was my best option.

Something was wrong with that man. He was dangerous, more dangerous than just the lightning weapons he and his fellow merchants were selling.

BISHOP

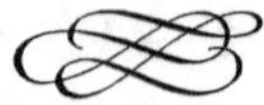

My brother was an idiot. I saw the realization in his expression back in his office, knew he knew what he had to do to win Audrey over, and yet we were still in the scheduled alliance meeting.

He should have postponed everything, even for just fifteen minutes, and checked in on Audrey. He didn't have to grovel and woo her right away, but he needed little acts of consideration, small ways of showing her he was thinking of her to get him going.

Except she hadn't shown up in the dining room for breakfast, most likely wanting to stay away from the public scrutiny for as long as possible, and Cyrus hadn't sought her out.

Of course, she also wasn't in the meeting, and I'd specifically told Eloise and Kira to tell Audrey to join us.

Even more concerning were her muted emotions, making it impossible to tell exactly what she was feeling other than a sense of soft worry — something I often felt from Audrey that didn't necessarily mean there was anything wrong except she usually wasn't trying to block those feelings from me.

I ground my teeth, resisting the urge to glare at Cyrus for being an idiot, and fought to focus on the alliance members.

It was just the six of us, along with a translator for Jundar and

Pimryl. We sat at a round table so no one looked like they were in charge even though Jundar was supposed to be the one who ensured things remained civil and ran smoothly. And while the setting was more casual, everyone was still dressed as if this were a formal meeting.

"The weapons are amazing," Jundar said through his translator, the medals on his crisp military jacket catching the sunlight that poured through the open window.

"Those weapons destroyed buildings in one shot," Folmar growled back, her expression a mix of determination and exhaustion. "They're dangerous."

"With the proper training—" Jundar started but Gower cut him off.

"I don't think we should be debating whether we buy the weapons or not." The muscles in Gower's jaw flexed. "If we don't, we're opening ourselves up for retaliation."

"You honestly think Emrys and his fellow merchants would attack us?" Jundar asked.

I took in a breath to tell him of course Emrys would attack — hadn't the man been paying attention? — when a burst of worry shot through my mating bond before returning to its previous muted level.

What the—?

"Given how he didn't seem upset every time he missed with his weapon, it wouldn't surprise me," Cyrus said, his tone low and cold. "I know that he's personally responsible for the deaths of three of my pack."

Jundar opened his mouth but wisely snapped it shut.

Yeah, arguing with Cyrus about how accidents happen in the kind of fight we'd just faced and how the merchants probably prevented more people from dying wasn't going to help.

"I understand both your concerns," Pimryl said, her soft tone always a surprising contradiction with her size — which was bigger than Cyrus who was one of the biggest men in our pack — along with her fierce lizard-like features.

"Speaker Jundar," she continued. "I can understand how attractive these weapons are for you. Humans are at the greatest disadvantage against grimalkins. But you're right, Alpha Cyrus, these weapons are dangerous. We need to determine if proper training will improve accuracy or find an alternative to help our physically weaker alliance members. They want to be able to protect themselves and not have to rely so strongly on our warriors."

Jundar stiffened at Pimryl's insult — even if it was true — and Gower rolled his eyes.

I shifted in my seat, Audrey's worry still muted but growing stronger as if she were losing her fight to contain her emotions.

"We should ask Emrys for a more structured demonstration," Folmar said. "See if we can determine if accuracy is actually a problem or if—"

Another burst of worry flooded the mating bond— no, *fear*. The emotion stuttering through the bond as if Audrey were trying to hide it from me was fear.

My heart lurched and I jumped to my feet before I realized what I was doing.

Bishop— Cyrus hissed before his eyes widened, realization hitting him — because the only thing that would make me run out of an alliance meeting was Audrey.

"Recess," he barked.

The startled alliance members glanced between us, confusion and surprise on their faces.

"We'll reconvene in an hour," Cyrus said as I raced for the door. "Pack emergency."

Folmar raised an eyebrow at us, a knowing glint in her eyes, but I didn't care if she knew we were rushing off to protect our mate or not. The others would judge us knowing we'd abruptly stopped the discussion for a woman and not a larger problem, but the gryphon alpha knew that we couldn't deny our primal instincts, not with me so newly mated and Cyrus trying to become her mate.

The fear in the bond tugged at me, and I raced down the hall and out the closest door onto the Residence's grounds. My pulse pounded with each step, her emotions getting stronger and stronger.

I had to get to Audrey now now now.

I couldn't let anything happen to her.

The pull around my heart led me deeper onto the Residence's grounds, past my mother's seasonal gardens toward the sheer rock wall at the back.

"What's she doing all the way back here?" Cyrus growled, his gaze scanning the area as the trees and bushes thickened into a more over-grown area.

"I don't—"

Determination and a hint of anger flooded around the fear, and a second later Audrey bolted out from behind a shrub and slammed into me.

I grabbed her before she could stumble back, holding her close to my chest, and she melted into my embrace.

"What's wrong?" Cyrus demanded, his eyes dark with his wolf, his body practically vibrating with his fight to stay in control.

"The merchants have grimalkins."

AUDREY

I TOLD BISHOP AND CYRUS — WHILE IGNORING THE ACHE IN MY CHEST whenever I looked at Cyrus — what I'd overheard, and they hurried me back to the safety of the Residence. Somehow, I convinced Bishop, with Cyrus's agreement, that we couldn't bring what I'd overheard to the other members of the alliance. We needed more than just my say so. We needed proof.

Cyrus quickly dispatched Finn to call Deacon and Knox back to the Residence — since Deacon and Knox were out of even Cyrus's mental reach — and we returned to the leader's only alliance meeting, knowing we needed to buy us enough time to find that proof.

The rest of the day involved hours of discussion where I strained to sit still and look calm while trying to overhear snippets of whispered conversations, particularly among the merchants. But no one said anything that gave away more of the merchants' plans, and I ended the day exhausted and frustrated.

I'd been completely useless, and on top of that, I hadn't found a moment to look for Whil and ask about the smoke that had fluttered out of my mouth when I'd controlled the grimalkins. We hadn't even taken a break when Deacon and Knox returned to the Residence. Cyrus had used his telepathy to tell them what was going on and to search Anakar for proof, and we hadn't had to leave the meeting room.

Thankfully, the dinner ended early. I hadn't felt sick to my stomach or seen any smoke all day so I let Bishop lead me back to my suite where we undressed, cuddled on my bed, and fell asleep.

A few minutes later... or had it been an hour? Two hours? More? My eyes fluttered open.

I took in the familiar towering tree surrounding me, the moist earth and the sweet scent of pine needles. I was in my old pack's sacred grove.

A chill raced down my spine, settling hard and heavy in my gut. The last time I'd dreamed of this sacred grove, Sterling had tormented me, driving a knife into my greatest fears over and over again in an attempt to make me kill myself... because I was forever linked to that monster.

Whil had said she'd magically blocked the connection between us, but she hadn't been able to break it, and that could mean he was invading my dreams again.

My pulse lurched, and I glanced around, searching for a way out of the grove even though I knew it was futile. If Sterling wanted me here, it wouldn't matter if I ran. I'd always end up where I started. I'd always be trapped.

No.

I clenched my jaw, determined to stay calm. It was just a dream. Sterling might be able to control it, but he couldn't affect my body in the waking world. I was still safe from him. We weren't even in the same realm.

The bushes on the far side of the grove rustled, and I scrambled into the underbrush at the edge of the grove, instinct making me hide in the shadows.

A second later, Sterling and Royce appeared, each carrying a slumped figure over their shoulder, one male and one female.

The male wheezed, weakly struggling in Royce's grip as if he were dazed, unable to do anything because his hands and ankles were tied, while the female didn't move at all.

With a grunt, Sterling dumped the woman into the center of the grove. Her long dark hair swept away from her face and my breath stalled in my lungs.

Mila. The only person brave enough to become my friend in my old pack. Sterling and Royce had laughed about tricking her into thinking she and her mate, Porter, had heard the fated mating call because they'd wanted to isolate me. And it had worked. I'd been alone for almost a year.

The guys had said Porter hadn't been involved in their plans, just another unwitting dupe, and Mila had been happy at her mating ceremony, so why was I dreaming of them now?

Or rather, why was Sterling making me dream of them?

Mila groaned and rolled onto her back, her eyes glassy and unfocused as if she were drugged and Royce dumped the man beside her.

"Porter," she moaned, her gaze sliding to the man, her mate, who growled and rolled up to his knees.

"I don't think so," Royce snarled, grabbing Porter's head and slamming his knee into his face.

Mila gasped and Porter dropped to the ground, moaning.

"That's right," Royce said, kicking him in the ribs hard enough to send him sliding across the dirt. "Stay down."

Royce moved to kick him again, but Sterling growled, and a snap of alpha power exploded from him, making Royce freeze.

"I need their beating hearts," he said, his voice filled with menace.

Fear rushed through my body, freezing my breath in my lungs, and Royce dipped his head in submission.

Shadows and wisps of black smoke swirled around Sterling and red flickered in his eyes. Another crushing wave of alpha power roared through the grove, and Mila and Porter moaned while Royce sank to his knees.

I inched farther back into the underbrush despite the wildness inside me rising up and defying Sterling's demand to submit. So far, he hadn't noticed me and I wasn't going to draw attention to myself.

"Good," he laughed, the sound sending more shivers racing down my spine. "Now step back."

Royce scurried to the side of the grove, out of the circle of moonlight, and Sterling pulled a vial containing a red glowing liquid from his pocket.

Just like when he'd tried to sacrifice me to that monster, he dumped the liquid onto the ground and hissed, "Open, Gate of the Realms."

Magic exploded into the grove, crashing against me and stealing my breath. Mila and Porter moaned and Sterling threw his head back and howled with laughter. The power twisted into a whirlwind, picking up dead leaves and small stones while pulling oozing strands of black smoke from the ground. It spun higher and higher, pouring into the night sky and blotting out the stars and moon.

Thunder cracked, sharp and loud, making me jump, and Royce's gaze snapped toward me. I froze, praying he couldn't see me in the gloom. My pulse roared, everything within me screaming to run, get away, stop reliving the moment when I was offered up to a monster. I didn't want to watch Mila and her mate be eaten alive. It had been bad enough hearing it while the monster had been eating Merrick.

Except I knew the second I tried to escape, the dream would change and it wouldn't be Mila and Porter being sacrificed, it would be me.

Lightning sliced through the darkness and Sterling howled with manic joy, drawing Royce's attention. Porter heaved himself back to his knees and strained to break the rope binding his hands behind his back. Mila moaned and writhed, her breathing desperate, sharp gasps, her eyes clearer now as if the drugs were wearing off just in time for her to die.

Save them, Audrey, I screamed at myself. *Save them.*

No. Run!

Another crack of thunder shook me and more lightning sliced through the whirling smoke, tearing open an enormous column of shimmering air, a rip between my old realm and my new one.

Power poured through the rip, bringing with it the putrid reek of the grimalkins, and the smoke thickened. It embraced Sterling, while also rushing around me. It caressed me, resonated with something deep in my soul, and taunted me with how it had leaked from my mouth when I'd make the grimalkins run away.

I could feel the connection between us, the oozing smoke linking us together, the darkness growing inside both of us. Then Mila screamed, dragging my attention to the smoke tearing into her and Porter.

Sterling's laughter deepened and enormous, leathery wings ripped out the back of his shirt. A flush rushed over him, turning all visible skin red, just like the monster he'd summoned, and thick, black ram's horns grew from his temples.

"Yes," he roared, fire blazing from his eyes as he stretched his arms wider and wider, his body growing bigger.

Thick long claws extended from his fingertips, longer and more vicious than a regular shifter's claws, and with a manic grin, he slammed his claws into Porter's chest, tearing into his flesh and ripping out his heart.

Oh, God.

Bile burned the back of my throat and my soul screamed at me.

Do something. Anything. Wake the fuck up.

I squeezed my eyes shut, straining to shut out Mila's panicked screams, Sterling's howls of laughter, and the roaring wind.

It's just a dream. Just a dream.

This wasn't really happening. Sterling wasn't becoming the monster he'd tried to sacrifice me to, and Mila and her mate were safe with his pack. She'd escaped our old pack. She was free.

This was just Sterling torturing me. I needed to wake up and get to Whil. Have her fix the block.

But a part of me, a small, terrified voice inside me, screamed that I was wrong. This was more than a dream.

AUDREY

MY EYES FLEW OPEN, AND I JERKED UPRIGHT, MY SHEETS STUCK TO MY sweat-drenched body as I gasped for air.

"Audrey?" Bishop gasped, jerking upright a second later. "What's wrong?"

"I—" My throat tightened and I struggled to breathe.

It had just been a dream.

Except none of my dreams about Sterling had been *just* anything.

"I have to go to Whil. Now."

I glanced at the window but couldn't tell through the crack in the blinds if it was still the middle of the night or closer to dawn. I didn't want to bother Whil, but I couldn't risk the block in my mind being broken. If Sterling could influence me, I needed to know so I could protect my mates and my pack.

And I needed to know right now.

Bishop grabbed my dress from where it lay on the floor and tossed it to me before pulling on his pants — also on the floor where we'd left them.

"Talk to me, Audrey," he said, worry pouring through our mating bond as we rushed out the French doors in my sitting room.

"I think the block in my mind is breaking."

Please let it just be the block.

But I had a horrible feeling something else was happening. I couldn't shake the ominous feeling inside me or the hint of grimalkin reek caught in my nostrils.

Sterling hadn't tormented me like he had in the other dreams. In fact, the more I thought about it, the more it felt like he hadn't even been aware I'd been there. Without a doubt, he'd have rubbed in how helpless I was while he murdered Mila and Porter and opened a rip in the realms to get to me.

My pulse lurched.

I'd dreamed he reopened the rip. Had the dream been a threat... or reality?

Bishop and I rushed across the Residence's grounds to Whil's cottage, the whimsical glass light hanging above the doorway to the English cottage part of her residence bright in the pre-dawn gray.

With a growl, Bishop banged his fist against the cottage door, making me cringe.

"Whil!" he yelled as he threw open the door and strode inside.

Two wall lamps in the entranceway flared to life, revealing polished wood floors and clean white walls. Straight ahead rose a staircase with a wooden banister carved to look like vines, and a long narrow hall led to the back of the house. To my left stood a wide arch opening into a sitting room.

I peered into the darkness at the end of the hall but couldn't see beyond the warm halo of light. Somewhere, farther back, lay the entrance to the massive greenhouse attached to the cottage.

"Whil," Bishop called again.

"Coming," she yelled back from somewhere above us.

Wood creaked at the top of the stairs, a pale light started to illuminate the walls, and a second later Whil appeared, her perpetual fae glow lighting her way.

"Audrey thinks the block is breaking," he said as Whil hurried down the stairs.

"Sit," she said, jerking her chin toward the archway beside us, "and tell me what happened."

"I had a dream," I told her, crossing the threshold into the sitting room and activating the three magical lamps in the room with my movement.

Three large armchairs and a couch as mismatched as the seating area in the greenhouse, crowded around a squat table covered with books, while more books and knickknacks filled the floor-to-ceiling bookcases taking up all available wall space. The only places where there wasn't a bookcase was the fieldstone fireplace on the interior wall and the two large windows overlooking Whil's perpetually blooming garden.

"And..." I sat on the couch knowing as soon as she checked my magical block, I was going to pass out for most of the day. "And I think there's something else going on."

Bishop sat beside me and pulled me into his lap, holding me tight. Worry tinged with fear whispered through our bond despite the fact that I could feel him trying to block his emotions from me.

"I think I controlled the grimalkins and made them run away. They have an alpha power, and I could feel it, and when those last two came and I was barely hanging on, I screamed at them and, with my own power, willed them to go away," I said, the words pouring out of me.

"What did their power feel like?" Whil asked, and I released the breath I'd been holding even while knowing I hadn't needed to hold it.

Whil and Bishop had always believed me. I'd never had to convince them that what I'd experienced or felt was true.

"It made my skin crawl and upset my stomach and when I used my power on them, black smoke came out of my mouth."

Bishop stiffened, his grip around me tightening, and he buried his nose in my hair.

"It's been over a day," he said, his voice soft even as a torrent of emotions: fear, anger, and frustration roared through the bond. "You should have said something."

"Whil's been at the hospital, Knox is hunting, and you and Cyrus have been dealing with a crisis."

It wasn't as if I'd wanted to keep it a secret. I'd just recognized that there were more important things going on, and I'd wanted to do my part and hadn't wanted to worry anyone.

"The nausea and smoke went away and I thought I could wait until I found a moment to talk to Whil." I leaned back far enough to meet his wolf-darkened eyes. "The second something changed, I told you."

"You should have told me right away," he growled. "You're the priority. You're always the priority."

"You know that isn't true," I said. "The pack—"

"The pack doesn't matter without you." He pressed his forehead to mine and drew in a shuddering breath. "I know you want to protect those who can't protect themselves and you think that sacrificing your needs is how to do that, but it isn't." He huffed. "I already have a brother who always puts himself last. I don't need my mate to do it, too."

More frustration rolled through our bond, and I pushed love back to him. We weren't going to agree on this, and I didn't want to argue. He could teach me how to put me first later, once the crisis with the merchants and grimalkins and whatever Sterling was doing to me was taken care of.

"Whil," I said without turning away from Bishop. "Let's find out what's going on with me."

AUDREY

Whil placed her hands on my temples, and, just like all the other times she'd checked her magic blocking the tether connecting me to Sterling, I took a breath and released it. Her warm, golden power seeped into my head, muddling my thoughts, and I sank back against Bishop.

I drifted on a golden haze, savoring the peace that came with it. For a blissful moment all my worries about what was happening to me and the pack were gone and I felt safe and loved.

Then the haze melted away and I opened my eyes.

I lay on the short, old-fashioned couch in the greenhouse, and Whil sat on the floor a few feet away surrounded by books. Bishop must have carried me out here so Whil could do research while keeping an eye on me.

The sun sat high in the sky, but that didn't surprise me. Whenever Whil checked the block, I lost half a day. Bishop was also gone, which I'd expected. He had pack responsibilities and couldn't sit around all morning waiting for me to wake up.

"So," I groaned as I dragged myself up into a seated position.

Whil glanced up from her book, her expression grim.

That wasn't good.

I focused on my mating bonds. Knox's bond was there but emotionless since he wasn't close enough for me to sense, and Bishop's was muted with only a hint of determination and worry. Which didn't tell me at all if Whil had told Bishop what she'd discovered or not.

"My magic is still blocking the tether," Whil said. "But it's definitely weaker."

"And?" I asked, since still being cut off from Sterling wasn't grounds to be grim.

"The tether has evolved. It's now not just a link between you two, it's also a magical power source," Whil replied. "A dark magic power source."

"Dark magic?" A shiver raced through me despite the humid warmth in the greenhouse.

"Yes, whatever the son of your old pack's alpha did, it's growing in strength."

My stomach churned. I wasn't just tethered to Sterling for the rest of my life, I was caught up in the spell he'd cast to gain more power from that monster.

Oh, God. The last time I'd seen Sterling, he'd had ghostly ram's horns just like the monster. His face had also turned red, but I'd thought that was because he was angry. Now I wasn't so sure.

In my dream, he'd actually become the monster, and that dream had felt too real as if I were witnessing Mila and Porter's murder, not just imagining it. That menacing power had filled the air and caressed my skin, calling out to something inside me, something that rang in recognition.

Was I going to become that monster, too?

The grimalkin's alpha power had felt similar to the power Sterling had used to send those snake shadow monsters after us, a power that had already been hanging in the air around us in Anakar and the surrounding forest.

"Can you get rid of it? Block it?" I asked even as a new horrible thought occurred to me.

I'd run into this realm a weak, pathetic shifter. And now I had power.

Was the power actually mine? Was I actually a female alpha trapped behind a curse that was starting to crumble?

Or was it because of the dark power growing inside me?

If Whil got rid of it, would I go back to being me?

"I tried strengthening the block I already put on the tether," Whil said, "but it isn't strong enough to stop the power from seeping into you." She swept her hands out at the books surrounding her. "I'm researching alternatives."

"We have to tell the guys." As much as I didn't want to add more to their plate, me turning into a monster was important. "I should probably be confined."

"Bishop said you'd say that and has made it clear that's not happening," Whil told me. "And I agree with him. So far, you've only used your power to protect the pack, and the power is growing slowly. I doubt you'll suddenly turn into a power hungry murderous monster, which means we have time to figure this out."

"You don't know that," I insisted.

I didn't want to hurt anyone. In fact, all my instincts were telling me I had to protect the pack. But that only made it more important for me to ensure I wasn't the one the pack needed protection from.

"Audrey," Whil said as she rose and moved to sit on the couch beside me, her expression softening. "Yes, the power is growing inside you, but it's not woven into your soul. It might feel like it, but it's not. Your mate bonds are protecting you. Which means you might have access to that magic, but it's not influencing you."

Except I could hear the "not yet" at the end of her sentence.

KNOX

THE UNEVEN COBBLESTONE ALLEYWAYS OF ANAKAR TWISTED AND turned, thankfully casting deep shadows in the bright midmorning light as Deacon and I in our wolf forms crept toward the heart of Anakar.

As much as it would have been better to sneak around at night, I wasn't dumb enough to risk being caught by the malicious spirits that appeared after sundown.

It was bad enough we could already smell more than a dozen humans, but these humans controlled an unknown number of grimalkins, not to mention had lightning weapons. I didn't want to add evil manifestations of Tzanagoth's power to the mix, so nighttime reconnaissance was out.

Just like every time I crossed onto the land affected by the sleeping malicious god, an ominous power pressed against my senses, making the fur at the back of my neck rise.

Fuck, I hated being in Anakar, and the last time we'd been here snake shadow monsters had exploded from the ground and tried to rip Audrey apart.

All because she'd tried to stand up against the asshole who'd tried to sacrifice her to a monster.

A growl bubbled in my throat. I wanted to tear Sterling apart and piss on his corpse, but the rip between realms wasn't big enough for me to get to Audrey's realm. Of course, that also meant it wasn't big enough for him to get to her, and I was just going to have to be grateful that there was one less threat out there to hurt Audrey.

They've gone down the left passage, Deacon said in my head as he sniffed the ground.

We'd been following the scents from the humans and the foul reek of their grimalkins, keeping to side streets and alleys to avoid detection. I'd hoped the merchants had picked someplace near the outskirts of the complex, but no, every turn drew us closer and closer to Tzanagoth's temple.

I don't like that they're so close to the god's power, I growled back at him.

Some of the myths say that the grimalkins were born from Tzanagoth's magic, Deacon replied. *Maybe they found something here that controls them.*

Sisters, I hoped not. If the merchants could figure out how to turn the grimalkins into weapons, then anyone could. Even if we bought the merchants' lightning weapons our pack would still be in danger. The weapons had a recharging time and wouldn't be able to take out a large pack before the beasts could attack.

We slunk out of the shadows to the wider intersection and hurried after the humans' scent just as the sounds of voices and footsteps came from the road ahead of us.

Shit. We had to get past a long row of buildings before we could slip into a parallel alley.

My gaze leaped from one crumbling structure to the next. Most of the entranceways had collapsed, but enough of the walls still stood that it would be a risk trying to jump over without making a sound — especially since there wasn't a lot of room to move around.

Then I caught sight of a hole where one building had fallen against its neighbor.

In here, I commanded, jerking my nose at the opening.

It was going to be a tight fit, but we only had a few seconds left and no other options.

The voices and steps were coming closer, and the humans were about to walk around the large tree and rubble covering three quarters of the path at the end of the road and see us.

Deacon dove for the hole, shifting to his human form before he reached it, and half slid half squirmed inside. I leaped after him, shifting as well. My wolf was easily twice the size of my human, and if Deacon's human had trouble getting in, it would be impossible for my wolf.

I shoved my head through but my shoulder hit the edge of the still-standing wall.

Shit shit shit.

I needed to get smaller, somehow. If I could get my shoulders through, the rest of me would get through.

Go sideways, Deacon said, grabbing my shoulders, wrenching me onto my side, and hauling me into the cool darkness.

"Did you hear something?" a man asked, his voice pitched a little too high as if he were afraid.

We froze, not risking going farther down the narrow alley we'd crawled into. The slightest move could knock loose the precarious pile of bricks around us. Even just a pebble breaking free could give us away.

"It's just rats," someone else laughed as the footsteps drew closer. "Stop jumping at everything. Raddix said we're protected from Tzanagoth's spirits."

"So *he* says," the first man shot back.

"Jeez," another man said, his voice low and gravelly, and three sets of legs stopped on the road in front of the hole we'd snuck through. "We've been here for over two weeks and nothing's happened."

"Lots has happened. Those spirits scream all night long," Afraid Guy said.

"But they haven't entered our camp," Gravelly Voice shot back. "And it's the middle of the day. There aren't any spirits around. Come on."

"So *you* say," Afraid Guy grumbled as the group walked away.

I glanced at Deacon. Yeah, he'd heard that, too. Raddix, whoever he was, had a way to keep his camp safe from the spirits, which meant someone had found some water or plants or stone or something that could control Tzanagoth's spirits.

Come on, I growled in Deacon's head as I squeezed out from the rubble into the alley and shifted back to my wolf. *Let's find their camp and get the fuck out of here.*

Deacon followed and shifted as well, and we crept in the direction the men had come from.

A few minutes later, we turned onto a short road that ended in brilliant sunlight, and beyond stood Tzanagoth's temple, the only structure in Anakar that hadn't crumbled with age.

My insides churned, an uneasiness settling in my limbs, and I drew close enough to see into the courtyard.

The courtyard was empty with the dry fountain and the monstrous statue of Tzanagoth about to eat his sacrifices standing in the center.

I was about to turn away when something shimmered at the corner of my eye and my pulse stalled.

No. Please no.

I dragged my attention toward the shimmer. It was back and, from the sight of the mangled corpse on the ground in front of it, someone had used a blood sacrifice to open— No, not one sacrifice there were two heads… except there weren't enough body parts for two people.

A growl bubbled in my throat. The man who'd tormented my mate, even tormenting her in her dreams, was back, and if he was powerful enough to open a rip between the realms, I had no doubt he'd actually come to our realm.

I wasn't sure if I could take him out. But I would. I had to.

Because that was the only way to protect Audrey.

AUDREY

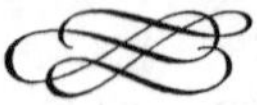

I WOKE WITH A START, SUDDENLY FURIOUS AND COMPLETELY CONFUSED. It must have been another dream, one I didn't remember. Except the second I thought that, I realized the anger was coming from my mating bonds.

Knox was back and he was pissed... except underneath all of that was a churning fear.

"What's wrong?" Bishop asked, his arms around me tightening and his body tense.

When I'd gone to bed, Bishop had still been at the fancy dinner in the ballroom. I'd tried to smile and nod — while also pretending to not understand anyone who used a translator — but it had been hard to focus.

Both Bishop and Whil — and even Cyrus once he'd found out about the dark magic inside me — had assured me I wasn't going to just snap and turn into a murderous maniac, but that didn't ease my fear.

I didn't want to control evil magic. I wanted nothing to do with it. It was still getting stronger inside me and I didn't want to risk it infecting my soul bonds.

And a small part of me was terrified that all the progress I'd made in becoming stronger and recognizing that I did have value was because of the magic. Was the wildness inside me really my wolf awakening or was it the dark magic?

"Audrey," Bishop said, yanking me from my worries. "What's wrong?"

"Knox is back and he's angry."

Bishop frowned then closed his eyes. "Your bond is really strong. I can barely sense him, which means he's still a good five-minute run from Stonehaven." Then he threw back the blankets and sat up. "If he's pissed, he found something in Anakar. Let's go."

I hurried to my wardrobe and pulled out a shirt and pair of pants while Bishop grabbed his clothes draped over the back of the chair in the corner. We quickly got dressed and rushed out of the French doors in my sitting room.

Once again, I was up and it was barely dawn.

"Where are we going?" I asked, surprised that we'd stepped outside instead of staying in the Residence. I'd assumed Bishop would have gone to Cyrus's room to wake him.

"Whil's," Bishop replied, taking my hand.

I glanced up at the two moons still visible in the sky. "She's going to love that."

"If the merchants have a way of controlling the grimalkins, then we're going to want her involved in the planning," he replied, his gaze going unfocused for a second.

"Cyrus is up. He's going to meet us. Now, come on," he said. "We need to keep our pace leisurely so no one knows something is going on."

My heart pounded as we strolled through the gardens toward Whil's greenhouse library cottage. Knox's anger roiled inside me and my wildness started to rise. I needed to move faster, take action, do something even if I knew that there was nothing we could do until Knox and Deacon got back to the Residence.

And even then, I wouldn't be able to do anything because I was wea—

I stopped myself before I could continue that thought. I wouldn't be able to do anything *right now* anyway, even if my mates and Cyrus would let me.

We reached Whil's cottage as Cyrus did and headed around to the side toward the greenhouse entrance while Cyrus banged on the front door.

"How long until Knox gets here?" I asked, struggling to block off some of Knox's anger.

I pushed as much love and support as possible through our bond as I fought to stay calm. Freaking out wouldn't help the situation, and if I was going to help, I needed to look strong and confident.

"He and Deacon are about two minutes out," Bishop replied as he led me through the greenhouse to the mismatched seating area at the back.

Cyrus met us there, and a moment later Whil entered from the cottage part of her house carrying a tray with a teapot and six cups. She set the tray on the table between us, pressed her hands against the pot, and closed her eyes. Golden light flashed around her hands and steam rose from the spout and around the edges of the lid.

Cyrus raised a surprised eyebrow before sitting in the cushioned armchair.

"I figured no one wanted to wait for the kettle to boil," Whil replied as she poured six cups of tea.

"You mean *you* didn't want to wait," Bishop corrected.

"It's not even dawn. Again," she huffed as she sat on the floor in the middle of three piles of books. "If this is what Cyrus thinks it is, I'm going to want tea."

It is, Knox replied in my head, stepping around a leafy plant with Deacon right behind him. *The merchants have set up camp—* "in Anakar and have over four dozen grimalkins," Knox finished, shifting into his human form halfway through.

He lifted me off the couch and took my seat, placing me in his very naked lap.

A shiver of need — that was completely inappropriate — teased down my spine. Knox hummed low in his throat, and the anger in our bond eased as if he'd needed to hold me to get himself back under control even though it hadn't felt as if he were on the verge of going feral.

"Fuck," Cyrus hissed.

"No shit," Deacon added. "We didn't stick around long, but we counted about two dozen swordsmen and all those beasts."

"The rip between the realms is also back," Knox growled, his grip around me tightening. "It's not wide enough for a person to come through, but it might have been at some point. There were the remains of two bodies near it."

My desire turned cold and visions of last night's dream rushed through me. Except it hadn't really felt like a dream, and now I was willing to bet everything that it hadn't been.

Sterling had sacrificed Mila and Porter to open the rip and if their bodies were still there, then the rip had been large enough for them to have passed through. If it hadn't been large enough, there wouldn't be any bodies, they'd have burned to ash before even hitting the ground.

"Sterling is here," I told them.

And he was more powerful than before.

I'd barely escaped his control when he'd tried to get me to walk into the rip and burn up. He'd only had ghostly ram horns then, but if my dream hadn't been a dream but me witnessing what Sterling was doing then he could now turn into that monster.

"We won't let him hurt you," Cyrus said, his alpha power washing over me not in a command but as a protective cocoon. "Ever."

AUDREY

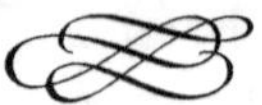

My wildness rose up in response to Cyrus's power, while desire spread low in my core.

Mine. He was mine, and *I* was going to protect *him*, protect all of my mates, and not the other way around.

Cyrus held my gaze, his eyes filled with determination and hunger, and it felt like the air was sucked out of the room. For a moment there was just us, captured in a whirling vortex of desire and need, and my soul ached for him.

We still hadn't had our talk, but if he was going to tell me he couldn't be my mate I was going to scream. He'd sent me heated, possessive glances yesterday when he thought I wasn't looking, and I'd had to grit my teeth to not reciprocate.

We belonged together.

And I refused to let him deny it.

That said, I also knew now wasn't the time to get into it. Cyrus needed to remain focused on saving our pack and so did I. Our relationship could be worked out later.

"We don't know for certain if Sterling is around or if he's even involved with the merchants," Deacon said.

"And the merchants are our first priority," I added. Protecting the pack protected our mates.

"We need to inform the other leaders." Cyrus set his teacup on the table and stood.

"Can we trust them?" Whil asked. "Bishop told me that Speaker Jundar wants to buy the weapons."

"Only because he doesn't know the increased beast attacks are because of the merchants," Bishop replied. "He's honorable. He'll want to put a stop to this, too."

"What we don't want is to tip off the merchants." Cyrus shot me another fierce look with a possessive heat burning in his mossy green eyes then strode out of the greenhouse.

I bit back a groan and sank deeper into Knox's embrace.

"We need a plan to quietly capture the merchants here," Deacon said, his gaze going unfocused for a second. "Finn is on his way."

"Agreed," Bishop replied. "It would be best if the merchants didn't know we were coming."

My thoughts whirled. With that many grimalkins, not to mention the swordmen who also probably had access to those deadly lightning weapons, we were going to need an army.

How many fighters did the pack have left? We were going to be making up the most of it since there wasn't time to call in any cavalry.

From the conversations I'd overheard during dinner last night, the merchants were getting frustrated. I didn't know if they'd figured out Cyrus had been stalling the talks for the previous day and half, but they'd certainly figured out something wasn't right.

The gryphons could get to Stonehaven the fastest even though they were the farthest away, but they still needed a whole day to send a messenger back to their pack then another day for their hunters to show up and that would mean the hunters wouldn't be rested if we then headed straight to Anakar.

Which meant, if we were going to deal with merchants now — and since they could release the grimalkins on us at any time, now was way better than later — it was up to our pack to stop them and we were going to need anyone in Stonehaven capable of fighting.

And that included me. Somehow, I'd killed two grimalkins in the last fight, but more importantly, I could control them... I hoped. In the very least, I was certain I could influence them.

"You're going to need me," I said.

"Absolutely not!" Bishop replied as Knox snarled.

"You've gotten lucky and killed a few grimalkins," Deacon added, "but this is going to be different. There's a chance it won't be one or two of them at a time."

"Which is why you'll need me." I sat up straighter, staying within Knox's grasp because I knew if I stepped away from him, his wolf would lose it. "I can control the grimalkins."

"You controlled two," Whil said as Deacon's eyes widened with surprise.

"What do you mean you controlled them?" Knox demanded.

I turned to meet his wolf-darkened eyes. "Why do you think those grimalkins ran away?"

Knox stared back and his emotions churned through our bond. He was angry and afraid and that mixed with confusion and self-recrimination probably because he hadn't thought to wonder what had really happened.

"Forty-eight is a lot more than two," Bishop said softly.

"It doesn't matter if I can't control all of them. Controlling some will help," I insisted. "Even if I can just get them to hesitate. That might be enough to save someone's life."

"No," Knox snarled, his power crashing over me.

"Yes," I snarled back, meeting his power and forcing it back, proving that I was the more dominant alpha — although it hadn't felt like Knox had used all of his power. "I'm not stupid. I'm not going to run into the middle of them."

"Audrey, please," Bishop whispered, a rush of terror racing through our bond. "We have to protect you."

"And I have to protect *you.*"

I understood how he was feeling. My instincts were freaking out over the thought of my mates facing off against forty-eight grimalkins.

"I don't understand this power, but I have it and I'm going to use it." I was going to save my mates with it before it could turn me into a monster.

The other leaders arrived and we worked out a plan. Today we were going to slowly send wolves, gryphons, and King Gower's men out of Stonehaven so the merchants weren't tipped off. No one wanted to risk the merchants having men around town watching for unusual activity. Jundar's and Pimryl's men would stay since they needed translators, which could be dangerous for everyone involved.

Jundar and Pimryl agreed that they'd lock themselves and their translators into the smaller meeting room for a "leaders only" meeting, and all leaders' aides would distract the merchants saying the alliance was working on a final decision. At noon, Finn would arrest the merchants — since Cyrus and Folmar were certain the merchants would become suspicious by then.

Whil said she could make a sleeping potion with a mix of magic and the sedative we'd gotten from Kelna. She'd then use her magic to swirl it around all the swordsmen while they ate lunch to ensure they were all put to sleep.

Everyone understood why Whil had to join the strike force.

And everyone questioned why I was going along.

"She's killed three grimalkins," Knox growled even though I could feel how much he wanted me to stay safe in the Residence.

Cyrus glanced at me, asking me with a look if I wanted to tell the truth. I was sure he and my guys could tell the others I was going and that was that, but the truth would come out anyway and it was better if everyone was prepared.

"We've discovered Audrey's alpha power is special and she can use it to command the grimalkins," Cyrus said.

Jundar's, Gower's, and Pimryl's eyes widened in surprise while Folmar's narrowed. I could sense her alpha power even though she was a gryphon, but I didn't know if she could sense wolf shifters' powers. And if she could sense mine now, she'd think I was an utter weakling.

"I plan on sticking to the back and helping how I can," I told everyone. They were all bigger than me and trained warriors, and it was clear I didn't have any fight training at all.

"Then it's decided," Folmar said as she stood.

She and Knox left and the rest of us waited a few minutes. Gower left next then Jundar and a few more minutes after that, Bishop and I headed out of Whil's greenhouse.

Outside, the faint light of dawn peeked over the horizon, signaling the start of a new day, and despite my worries, only the soft birdsong and the gentle rustle of leaves disturbed the tranquil morning air. The sun had yet to rise, but there was already a pleasant warmth in the air that spoke of bright summer days ahead.

It was as if nothing had changed.

And yet everything had changed.

And more changes were on the horizon.

I had a growing darkness inside me that terrified me, and yet I knew I had to use it to save my mates and my pack. If I didn't, the merchants with their monsters would destroy them all.

AUDREY

WE HEADED OFF THE RESIDENCE'S GROUNDS WITHOUT STOPPING FOR breakfast or supplies. Knox was going to pack what we needed and meet us at the edge of town with rations, and it was better for us to be seen in Stonehaven early so the merchants would think Bishop was with the other leaders.

For the most part, the streets were quiet, but I could see lights on behind windows and smell bacon and pastries cooking, a sure sign that the town was waking up.

We walked out of Old Town into New Town, the buildings becoming less residential and more commercial, to the large, square hospital with its mismatched architecture. Again, we avoided the courtyard at the front and entered through a modest foyer with the reception desk and comfortable chairs.

A few people napped in the chairs, but there was no one at the desk. It had only been a few days since the grimalkin attack, a lot of people had gotten hurt, and I suspected the staff was still stretched thin. No doubt they'd rationed the healing elixirs for the worst cases and the humans. Nova wouldn't use them all just in case the grimalkins attacked again. Which was smart but meant a lot of people were still suffering.

We took the stairs to the second floor, pausing at the top, and Bishop squeezed my hand.

"Meet me in the garden outside after you've checked on Quinn and Zavier. And remember we still haven't caught that assassin."

A shiver rolled down my spine. That was the last thing we needed on top of everything else.

The memory of his attack shuddered through me. It had been awful feeling so helpless... except, I hadn't been. Bile had burned my throat and my stomach had heaved. Maybe the assailant hadn't run away because Bishop was going to kill him, but because I'd compelled him.

Which was ridiculous. That would mean he was connected to the grimalkins.

"Be careful." Bishop captured my lips in a quick kiss, his love and worry pouring through our mating bond.

"Always," I said, breathless.

He rolled his eyes at me.

Yeah, I hadn't been careful during the grimalkin attack and if I had to do it again, I wouldn't change a thing. We both knew careful went out the window the second someone needed saving.

Bishop headed to the nurses' station at the end of the hall, but I stopped halfway down at Zavier's room.

The door was open a crack and I peeked in. Zavier still lay on the bed in his wolf form and I couldn't tell if he'd moved or not. Shifters could heal some serious injuries, especially if they stayed in whatever form they were in instead of shifting and draining their life force, so if Zavier was still out of it, that wasn't good.

Quinn sat in the chair beside his bed, also asleep clutching Zavier's paw, her face pale and drawn. She'd told me she thought of Zavier like a brother, but there was something more between them, and it was obvious, probably to everyone else but them.

I pushed the door open a little more. Every fiber of my being wanted to reach out and comfort Quinn, to reassure her that everything would be okay. But the truth was, I didn't know.

I had a bad feeling about Anakar and a lot of people could die if we couldn't keep the grimalkins in their pens — and not just those going to fight the merchants. The grimalkins could attack the town again, and Zavier being Zavier would jump into trouble not because it was his job, but because that was the type of man he was.

And if I could keep him from danger— If I could keep *anyone* in the pack safe, I would.

A flicker of wildness whispered through my soul, adding to my determination that I couldn't hide and let everyone else deal with this situation.

I had the power — hopefully. I had to help.

I eased the door shut and forced myself to step away. They needed sleep more than I needed to know how they were doing.

And I needed to get out of the hospital and find some breathing room before I lost it. Every room I passed with the beds filled with injured people was a reminder of the attack.

I couldn't let it happen again.

Funny how just a little while ago, I would have thought I was powerless to do anything, that no one would listen to me or want my help.

And now I didn't care what they thought. My wildness was steadily growing with each step down the hall, each whimper and sob and pained expression I heard and saw.

I didn't think I'd ever felt so angry or so determined. This was my pack and the merchants had hurt them. Mine.

I stormed down the back stairs, shoved open the door at the bottom, and strode into the garden where I was supposed to meet Bishop.

Dozens of people looked up at the sound of the door crashing open, and all eyes locked on me.

Shit.

I didn't want anyone to see me like this, but with the influx of patients, I should have known the hospital garden wouldn't be empty.

I sucked in a sharp breath, determined to will my wildness away. I couldn't do anything about anything right this moment and I needed to look calm.

I also needed to ignore my first instinct to hide from all those eyes along with my fury that hiding was my first instinct.

"Alpha," a tall woman in scrubs said. "I heard you saved the children in the smithy."

My gaze darted around the garden for an escape route while my wildness flared, enraged that I couldn't even control my body.

"Yes," I replied quietly, forcing a tight smile that I hoped conveyed some semblance of strength. "But Jaxon and Finn were there, too."

"I heard you killed a grimalkin," the woman said.

"I heard she killed two," a tired looking man added.

"I heard it was all a lie." Velora's sharp voice cut through the voices of the crowd and everyone fell silent.

The crowd in front of me parted and stepped back, and Velora strolled toward me.

"Everything about you is a lie," she added with a smirk. "I heard you used magic to trick Knox and Bishop into mating with you."

A few people gasped at her words, and a few others hardened their expressions, and everyone else looked upset at Velora. People might have believed her before the grimalkin attack, but even Finn, who'd once agreed with Velora, was supporting me now. No doubt he, along with the children, were talking about how I killed two grimalkins without even shifting.

"Now you're lying about killing grimalkins." She glanced at the crowd. "How could a shifter who's so weak kill a grimalkin?"

My insides twisted, her tone too much like Merrick's when his question was a trap. How could I convince anyone that I'd killed those beasts when everyone could tell I was powerless?

Except I'd killed one, even before my alpha power started to manifest. I'd accidentally killed that grimalkin in Kelna when we're traveling north to break my bond with Knox.

"I challenge you," Velora yelled loud enough that people a block over could probably hear her. "You're a liar and a manipulator. Bishop was supposed to be my mate and you stole him from me. I'm taking him back."

Her claws extended from her fingertips and a soft thump of alpha power hit me. It caught me off guard, forcing me to take a step back, and Velora's sneer deepened.

My pulse thudded. I didn't know this pack's rules for a formal challenge. In my old pack, a challenge was to the death. But if I died, Bishop would die or go crazy.

"Bishop and I have already sealed our mate bond. You can't get rid of me or break us apart."

"Doesn't matter," Velora snarled. "I'm going to tear you up, make you so hideous he'll never be able to look at you again. Then he'll have to take a second mate. He'll make me his alpha mate."

"If you hurt me, Bishop won't love you. He'll hate you."

"He'll finally be able to see the truth!" A manic gleam flashed in her eyes. "Your spell will be broken and Bishop will love me. He'll never look at you again and I'll lock you away to be forgotten. You're weak and pathetic. An alpha shouldn't even bother looking at you let alone one like Bishop."

"Velora—"

"Remember your place and respect me," she screeched. "I'm going to be your alpha. I deserve to be alpha."

My wildness surged, my power thudding hard within my chest.

"Deserve?" I snarled. "You don't deserve anything."

The woman was completely insane. I didn't know how Cyrus or Bishop hadn't seen it. I was sure they'd been aware of Velora's crush, but I had no idea how she'd managed to keep this level of crazy hidden for so long.

And that pissed me off.

She didn't deserve to be alpha and she sure as hell didn't deserve my mate. She wasn't going anywhere near Bishop and I'd be damned if she had any influence over this pack. I'd already lived in a pack with a cruel dictator. I'd never let the people of this pack live with an insane one.

"Being alpha isn't something to be won or deserved," I said, my voice low, dangerous. "It shouldn't be something the strong take because they can or because they want power over others. It's something to be earned. It's an act of full submission to serving the pack."

"An alpha never submits," Velora screamed at me, her power rolling over me in a weak demand to kneel before her.

I squared my shoulders and let her power hit me. She didn't have a strong alpha power and only a few of the bystanders sagged to their knees.

"Why aren't you kneeling?" she demanded, jerking forward a step as if drawing closer to me would make her power stronger.

But she was nothing compared to Cyrus. Hell, half of the people watching this *challenge* were stronger than her.

"Kneel!" she roared, with another weak slap.

"You kneel," I roared back, and my wildness let loose. My power surged from my body, slamming over her and everyone in the garden.

She gasped and dropped to her knees, her eyes wide with shock, along with everyone else.

"I'm not weak and pathetic," I told her, fighting to hold my power back so as not to flatten her like the wildness inside me wanted. "And even if I wasn't an alpha, I wouldn't be weak. My strength comes from my compassion and my determination to protect. I'll never let you take my place. I'll never let a selfish, cruel alpha lead my pack, because it's *my* pack. Mine. Bishop and Knox. They're mine."

A wave of power slipped my grip and slammed into Velora, forcing her to press her forehead against the ground, her power weakly fluttering against mine, unable to even compete.

"This whole pack is mine," I growled. "Mine to serve and protect like an alpha is supposed to. Do you understand me?"

Velora groaned and twisted her head the fraction of an inch necessary to glare up at me with one eye.

"Do. You. Understand?"

BISHOP

I STOOD AT THE HOSPITAL'S BACK DOOR, THE COOL METAL HANDLE pressing into my palm and my eyes fixed on the garden. Power poured from Audrey in great waves, crashing over me and making my knees weak, while everyone else in the garden knelt in submission.

But they were just the bystanders caught up in Audrey's power. Her real target was Velora who lay prostrate on the ground, her head turned just enough so she could glare at Audrey.

"Do. You. Understand?" Audrey snarled, sounding more like Knox than the quiet, shy girl we'd pulled out of the river.

Sisters, she was amazing.

I knew she had a warrior's spirit and now others knew it as well. She wasn't some weakling they could push around and they shouldn't think that because she didn't exude alpha power that they could say and do whatever they wanted with her.

Pride swelled within me and I let it pour through our mating bond. Audrey had come so far from the frightened woman who had been abused by her previous pack alpha.

She'd been forced into silence and invisibility by her previous pack, conditioned to fear speaking up or even being seen, and I had no doubt standing up to Velora made Audrey uncomfortable. I didn't think she'd ever want to draw attention to herself.

And yet, here she was, asserting herself as my mate and claiming her position as alpha.

"Do you?" Audrey pressed, more of her power crashing down on Velora and washing over everyone else.

"Yes," Velora hissed, her words soft but still audible.

Audrey huffed. "I didn't hear you."

"Yes, *alpha*," Velora said, louder this time.

Audrey's power eased, releasing everyone from their submissive position.

I mentally reached out to Harlow. She was an older watchman who should have retired a few years ago and Finn had assigned her to the hospital. With the fear and heightened emotions from the attack, Cyrus and I thought it best if there was someone who could deal with any conflict.

Harlow, I said in her mind. *Meet me in the hospital garden. You need to make an arrest.*

Of course, she replied, and I opened the back door and joined Audrey.

Velora's eyes flashed bright, her hope clear that I'd take her side or that she'd be able to convince me Audrey was dangerous. But I scowled at her. I'd heard everything. She'd threatened to permanently maim my mate and that was unforgivable.

I glanced at everyone else, worried that someone would side with Velora, but most of them looked awed and proud of Audrey. Those who weren't appeared shocked by the display of power they'd just witnessed.

And I couldn't blame them. Audrey didn't radiate any alpha power until it broke through the curse containing it and exploded around her. After, the curse took over again, and she was back to looking like the weakest shifter in existence.

It shouldn't have taken releasing her power to convince everyone she was exactly where she belonged, but it still warmed my heart to see that nobody seemed upset or angry with Audrey for asserting her dominance.

Instead, their eyes held contempt for Velora. Her true, horrible nature had been exposed, and with this revelation, any credibility she had in spreading those nasty rumors about Audrey was now in tatters.

"Velora," I said, struggling to keep my voice even.

My wolf wanted to rip her to pieces for even thinking about doing those things to Audrey, but I couldn't risk looking like I wasn't in control. That would diminish Audrey's strength in standing up for herself, making it look like she needed my protection when she didn't — at least not in this situation.

"Audrey is my fated mate. There won't ever be another woman for me and I knew it the moment I saw her." I glanced at Audrey and offered her a soft smile while sending all my love to her through our bond. "We're destined to be together."

Audrey's love raced back to me in response and the adoration in her expression stole my breath. I'd never tire of seeing that look or feeling her love, and I'd thank the Sisters for the rest of my life that they blessed me with such an incredible mate.

Then Audrey's expression hardened and she turned to Velora.

"I never wanted to be alpha and I still don't. But if it means I can protect this pack, so be it. I don't want to issue commands. That's Cyrus, Bishop, and Knox's job, but in this situation I will," Audrey said. "I strip you of your rank of beta."

"You can't do that!" Velora snapped.

A ripple of Audrey's power swept through the garden. "I think I've proven that I can."

"Bishop—" Velora looked at me with pleading eyes and I placed my hand against the small of Audrey's back.

"I stand by my mate," I said.

"So do I," someone in the crowd mumbled. "Velora is crazy."

Velora jerked around to see who'd spoken, her expression contorted with anger and humiliation. "Who said that? Who dares say that about me."

The back door opened and Harlow strode out. I acknowledged her with a nod, and before I could even tell her what was going on, she assessed the situation and moved to apprehend Velora without hesitation.

When I heard Velora talking trash about your mate, I figured this day would come, she said in my head.

You should have said something, I replied.

The grimalkins attacked and it slipped my mind. I'm sorry, alpha.

Understandable. A lot had happened in the last couple of days, so I couldn't blame her for not coming to me with a worry. All she'd had was a conversation, not any proof that Velora was actually going to do something to Audrey. Even Cyrus, Knox, and I had been worried about Velora but hadn't done anything to prevent this confrontation.

I sighed as Harlow dragged Velora away. Despite my wolf's fury that Velora had threatened our mate, I couldn't help but feel a twinge of sadness for Velora. I'd known she'd been trying to get me to date her and had softly turned her down, but I hadn't known she'd been consumed by ambition and jealousy. If I'd been firmer in my rejection early on, maybe it wouldn't have turned out this way.

But I knew, deep in my soul, that was just wishful thinking. Velora had always been on the path of self-destruction and had done a good job at hiding all the ugly parts of herself.

"Come on," I said, nudging Audrey into movement and leading her out of the garden toward the market.

She leaned close, bumping her shoulder against mine and our fingers brushed. Desire zapped up my arm at the slight contact, and I took her hand in mine, entwining our fingers together. My heart swelled with pride and love for this incredible woman, and I swore I'd do everything in my power to protect her... even if she did want to walk to the heart of Anakar and help us defeat forty-eight grimalkins.

We leisurely strolled down Main Street to the market, even as my insides churned with the urge to hurry, do something, start saving my pack. Audrey's own impatience bled through the bond, fueling mine and making my wolf strain against my control.

I shoved him back down, reminding him we had a part to play.

The merchants could have spies in the city, and if our plan to attack their camp was going to work, we needed the element of surprise.

But damn it. It was hard to concentrate with Audrey's emotions fueling mine.

"Audrey," I murmured to her. "Take a breath. We need to act natural."

"Right." She sucked in a deep breath and released it, some of her tension draining from our mating bond.

After that, I flirted with her, trying to distract her from what was coming. Seeing her blush and smile, so sweet and beautiful, made me fall in love with her all over again.

We reached the market, and Audrey and I strolled along the main paths, taking note of the damage and the progress of the rebuilding efforts while exchanging pleasantries and words of encouragement with those hard at work.

"I can't wait to see this place bustling again," Audrey said brightly to the owner of the bookstore we'd paused at the first time I'd taken Audrey here. I could feel her genuine hopefulness mixed with the urgency to hurry up and protect my pack.

"Thank you, alpha," he replied, and a thread of discomfort slipped down our bond.

"Audrey, please," she murmured.

The bookstore owner hummed and nodded but didn't agree to Audrey's request, and we strolled farther down the street.

"I'm never going to get used to that," she said. "They don't constantly call you alpha."

"They'll stop saying it soon," I chuckled. "They just want to show their respect. You did an amazing thing saving those children. The whole pack is grateful."

Finally, we reached the edge of town and quickly slipped between two still-standing shops and out into the grasslands beyond.

The tall grasses stretched in front of us, the land rolling with rises and dips. The goal was to head north, getting closer to the pack's full-sized sacred grove — not the private one on the Residence's ground

— then head east so it wasn't so obvious that there were wolves running away from Stonehaven.

I led Audrey down a hill and away from town to where Knox waited for us.

He sat in the grass in his naked human form — something he'd been spending more and more time in since mating with Audrey — with a single backpack containing emergency supplies and— was that long black pole in the grass a fence post?

Joy flooded our twin bond. It wasn't nearly as strong as the emotions between me and Audrey, but it was still noticeable, and I was amazed at how Audrey had turned his life around.

Before she'd crashed into our lives, he'd been withdrawn, and I had feared he was slipping beyond my reach and on the verge of permanently going feral.

We'd only recently gotten him back and I hadn't wanted to lose him again. He was my twin. The other half of my soul, just like Audrey was our souls' match.

"Here," he said, picking up the fence post and offering it to Audrey.

Love flooded our bond and she gave him a heart-stopping smile.

"I had one of Jaxon's apprentices sharpen the end into a proper point," he said gruffly, a hint of blush coloring his cheeks. "Just in case."

I didn't want Audrey to be forced to defend herself. Just thinking of her in harm's way made my wolf rage and I knew Knox felt the same.

But neither of us could deny we needed her in Anakar. Hell, even Cyrus had caved, knowing that if she could control the grimalkins even just a little bit, she could save lives.

Which meant Knox was right. If our mate who couldn't shift was going to fight with us, she needed a weapon.

AUDREY

I accepted the spear from Knox while Bishop took off his clothes and put them in the pack. The wildness inside me pulsed stronger, part in desire at the sight of Bishop and Knox's powerful naked bodies, and part in determination, and I wrapped its strength around me while praying it wouldn't fail me when I really needed it.

So far it had always been there when I needed it, but I didn't have any control over it.

"Let's go," Bishop said, taking a step away from the town and shifting into his large black wolf. I'd seen a shifter shift many times before and still the action seemed fluid and beautiful... and heart-breaking.

I shoved back my disappointment as soon as it flickered to life. I didn't want my mates to feel it. I was happy with my life right now — with the exception of the chaos the merchants and their grimalkins had created. I didn't need to be able to shift.

And yet that broken part of me that still hadn't completely healed ached.

I was incomplete.

Sure, I had alpha power now when I really needed it... maybe...

hopefully, but that could be because of the dark magic growing inside me.

My true wolf nature was still imprisoned by my ancestral curse, and there was no way of knowing if my wolf would ever fully awaken.

And I could deal with my insecurities later. I was stronger than I'd ever been before and I had mates who supported me.

My thoughts lurched to Cyrus as I secured the pack over my shoulders and Knox shifted and knelt so I could climb onto his back.

Cyrus was mine and I wasn't going to accept anything less than his bond. My soul and wildness wouldn't let me, and they sure as hell didn't care that he'd hurt me. To them, he'd apologized and treated me with the kindness and respect I deserved. It might have been awkward between us going to the healing pools and coming back, but I couldn't deny that he'd stopped pushing me away.

He also listened to me more and considered my suggestions, even asked for them. I didn't know what was holding him back, especially with the hunger in his gaze every time he looked at me, but I wouldn't accept any more excuses.

I might not have formed a bond with him when we had sex like I had with Bishop, but I knew in the depths of my being that he was the final piece of my destiny.

Bishop took off and Knox followed, the guys slowly increasing their speed to an easy run so I had time to adjust since I only had one hand to hold onto him.

The grasslands stretched before us, a sea of rippling yellow-green rolling hills with the dark splotch of Darkweald in the distance, and the wind whipped at my face and tugged at my hair. The day was turning into the perfect summer's day without a cloud in the sky, but it wasn't enough to distract me from my worries.

It was late afternoon when we reached the campsite, my stomach growling its complaint over skipping breakfast and lunch. It was going to be unimpressed with rations for dinner, but it couldn't be helped. We were trying to amass our warriors in secret. Fires, tents, or even too-loud conversations could give us away even though we were still half a day away from the heart of Anakar.

And we could *not* be discovered. There were a lot of grimalkins — possibly too many for our small force to handle — but the merchants also had their devastating lightning weapons, and I had no doubt some of the weapons were with their swordsmen in Anakar.

It would have been great if we could have attacked them while they slept. We'd have still needed to be sneaky, but darkness and fewer people wandering around lessened the chance we'd be caught. But no one wanted to risk attracting the attention of Tzanagoth's malicious spirits, which were more powerful and active at night.

Which meant Cyrus decided camp was near the river and about twenty feet from the forest with its perpetual mist and ominous power. Knox and Deacon hadn't had time to confirm everywhere the merchant's swordsmen went and we just had to pray they didn't come to this side of the forest.

I slid off Knox's back as Cyrus approached, his gaze capturing mine, reaching into my soul and connecting to the part of me that knew he was mine, before sliding to the fence post-turned-spear in my hands.

"Good idea," he said with a brisk nod. "Grab something to eat. We're just waiting on a few more people."

Our remaining fighters arrived just as the sun was setting. I'd eaten as many tough dried rations as I could and settled on the ground in Bishop's arms with a blanket wrapped around me.

Knox, in his wolf form, lay beside us, his head on his paws, his eyes darting from person to person, on guard. A churning uneasiness rolled through the bond, Knox's fear of being surrounded by too many people, and I pushed loved and confidence back to him because I could also feel his desire to stay with me and Bishop and not hide in the tall grass and deepening twilight.

When I'd first met Knox, he'd wanted nothing to do with me or anyone else except maybe his brothers. He could barely be inside for more than a couple of hours at most and he avoided everyone. He could only stand a small group of people who he was close to, everyone else was too much. And we now had over fifty people standing twenty feet away.

Knox huffed and leaned into me, his unease growing along with his determination to stay, as Cyrus urged everyone to come closer.

"We leave for Anakar at first light," he said, his voice hushed. "Two scout parties will go ahead of us and take out any swordsmen as we go, but I want everyone to keep their eyes open. We can't afford to lose the element of surprise."

Everyone murmured their agreement. Half of them had seen how destructive just a single blast from one of the merchants' lightning weapons could be, and the other half had heard about it. No one wanted to be on the receiving end.

"Our goal is to reach a secure location near the swordsmen's camp and the grimalkins' pens," Gower added. "There we split into three groups. The quick strike group, their immediate backup, and the rest of you, including the medics, in case everything goes sideways."

"We're hoping the everyone-else-group gets bored," Folmar said.

"Better to show up and do nothing than not be there when needed," Deacon said, and the men and women around us nodded in agreement.

And that something was the grimalkins escaping their pens and the merchants being able to use their lightning weapons on us.

The thought sent a shudder of fear rushing through me and Bishop tightened his grip around me.

But with every beat of my heart, my determination grew. I'd protect my mates and my pack at all costs.

As we continued discussing strategies, my thoughts kept drifting to my own role in this battle. I had to hold the grimalkins in place long enough for the others to kill them, but what if I wasn't strong enough?

The fear gnawed at me, but I pushed it down, determined to do my part and protect my friends even as another worry surfaced in my mind: Sterling.

If he truly was in this realm, what would that mean for all of us? He was ruthless and power-hungry, a threat to everyone I held dear.

Except I couldn't let fear control me. I'd faced Velora and put her in her place. I could do the same with Sterling.

I had to.

But first we had to take care of the merchants and protect the pack.

Cyrus woke me just before dawn the next morning with a gentle touch on my shoulder. Slowly, I opened my eyes and was captured in his dark mossy green gaze.

For a second, time stood still between us, and my breath caught in my throat. His power stuttered against mine, as if he couldn't fully control it when he looked at me, but from the yearning in his eyes, I knew it wasn't because he was upset at me.

Heat rose from my core, aching for him to hold me, kiss me, claim me like he had in the shower room in the hospital. But then his alpha-in-charge mask fell into place and he gave me a tight nod.

He wasn't going to address whatever lay between us. Not now. And while I understood his reasons — everyone in the pack was counting on him to lead this mission to success — my wildness wanted to cement her claim on him. He was mine, and I didn't want anything to happen to him before I'd made that perfectly clear to him and everyone else.

"Quick breakfast, then we head out." He jerked his head, indicating I should wake Bishop, who I was half lying on, and went to rouse the few others who were still asleep.

I groaned and stretched. My body was stiff from sleeping on the ground — well, half on the ground — and I pressed my nose against Bishop's neck, breathing in his bright fresh-cut grass sent while savoring the heat radiating from Knox's wolf pressed tight against my back.

Today was the day we stopped future grimalkin attacks or the day I lost my mates because Bishop, Knox, and Cyrus wouldn't give up. They'd give their lives to protect their pack. And I would too.

We ate more rations for breakfast before crossing the threshold into Darkweald and picking our way between the trees and under-brush, risking running into spirits by straying off the trail to avoid detection.

Knox and seven other hunters shifted into their wolves and

prowled around and ahead of us, watching for danger while the rest of us walked as quickly and quietly as we could.

Mist and darkness shrouded the forest, chilling my skin, and the heavy, ominous power I'd felt every time I'd been in Darkweald pressed against my senses.

The evil magic unfurled inside me, a small, insidious darkness that twisted in my stomach. It called to the ominous power pressing down on me, and a mix of fear and relief flickered through me, drawing Bishop's attention.

"I just got confirmation where my—" I glanced at the shifters in front of me. They were close enough to hear me even if I whispered and I didn't want them to think I was a monster — even if I was terrified that I was going to become one.

I pressed a hand over my heart and Bishop nodded his understanding.

Knowing will help Whil figure out how to deal with it, he said in my head. *But you need to focus on right here and now. Don't let this distract you.*

Now it was my turn to nod, and I turned my attention back to the mist and the partially visible trees and underbrush. Cyrus was taking a huge risk in letting me come along, especially if I couldn't get my unwanted magic to control the grimalkins, but I refused to be a burden. I'd promised I'd be helpful, that I'd control the grimalkins, and I would. I had to.

By mid-morning we reached the remains of a stone building with trees, weeds, and tall grass growing around the rubble of the fallen walls and bursting through what was left of the tiled floor.

From there, we moved silently between the decaying buildings, our senses on high alert for any sign of danger even with our scouts searching for trouble ahead of us.

The air was thick with tension and nervous alpha power. No one wanted to face all those grimalkins let alone the swordsmen with lightning weapons, but we were all going to do it if we had to.

Please, God, don't let us have to.

Just before noon, we arrived at our primary defensive position.

The building wasn't very big, probably a thirty by twenty rectangle, and lacked a roof, but all four walls looked solid and sturdy. Collapsed buildings on either side of the structure blocked the windows, leaving only the front and back doors as entry points.

If we had to make our stand here, we wouldn't be able to hold out for long against the lightning weapons, but the confining doorways would force the grimalkins to attack one at a time.

That, however, was only if our plan didn't work.

Please, God, gods, Sisters, anyone. Let it work.

A WEIGHT SQUEEZED MY CHEST AND I FOUGHT TO KEEP MY EXPRESSION strong and stoic. I'd never been so fearful before a fight in my life, and it had everything to do with the woman standing a few feet away, boxed in by my brothers, her mates.

I loved her so much my heart ached, but I couldn't bring myself to tell her she was meant to be my mate, that I'd known the truth the moment she'd woken in the Residence after we'd found her in the river.

Our plan to take down the merchants' swordsmen was a dangerous one, and I couldn't shake the thought of what would happen if something went wrong.

Sure, Knox and Bishop would look out for her, and she had the disturbing dark magic inside her to protect her against the grimalkins — if she could actually control more than two — but knowing that did little to ease my fears.

If push came to shove, she'd risk everything if she thought she could save someone, especially one of her mates.

Which was why I wasn't going to tell her how I felt until this fight was done.

Bishop might be insisting I tell her first, but if something happened to me, I couldn't bear the thought of breaking her heart... because like Audrey, I'd risk everything, even give my life, to protect her and my brothers.

My wolf heaved inside me and I tightened my hold on him. I couldn't afford to lose control. Precision and keeping calm were what I needed right now, not the ferocious fury of my beast.

"Alright, everyone, listen up," I said just loud enough to be heard. "The grimalkins' pens and the swordsmen's camp are close." I pointed in the camp's direction. "They're around the corner then thirty feet to a slightly wider area. The buildings are recessed from the other buildings, which is good for us. It'll give us cover."

"Does everyone remember their assignment?" Gower asked and everyone nodded while Bishop turned to Whil.

"Can you sense them?" he asked.

Whil closed her eyes, her perpetual golden glow brightening for a second. "There's twelve lightning weapons and they're all together, in the direction of the swordsmen's camp."

Perfect. I'd hoped that the merchants wouldn't have armed their swordsmen with deadly weapons and it looked like they hadn't. That didn't mean the swordsmen didn't have access to them, but they weren't carrying them around on patrol and we wouldn't need to keep up with our careful hunting once we'd secured the weapons.

"Alright, let's move," I commanded, and we split into our respective groups.

I led the strike and backup teams, creeping to the corner, our footsteps softly crunching over stone and forest debris.

We reached the corner, and I glanced down the street where the grimalkins' pens and the swordsmen's camp were.

All clear.

Time to do this.

I glanced back at Audrey, my heart aching with the need to protect her.

Please, Sisters. Keep her safe.

Bishop, who stood beside her, caught my gaze, his expression determined. He'd protect her. I knew he would. But the knowledge didn't ease my or my wolf's worries.

I turned back to our target, a pile of rubble thirty feet down the wide road just before the recess in the buildings.

With Knox in his wolf form padding silently beside me and the rest of the strike team following behind us, I carefully slunk down the street, keeping close to the buildings on the same side of the street as the pens.

I reached the rubble and glanced around the edge into the recess. The grimalkins' guard looked bored as he leaned against the open doorway to the building that held the grimalkins' pens.

The large building was just as Deacon had described and as solid as the one I'd chosen for our group's defensive position, which meant if we could take out the swordsmen, the grimalkins would stay contained.

Beside the building containing the grimalkins' pens sat a similarly sized structure. It was in worse condition, with its far corner crumbled almost to the ground, and the archways over the front windows collapsed, leaving only a jagged façade. The front wall, now a mix of fallen windows and uneven edges, ranged between four feet to seven feet high, and through the gaps, I could clearly see and hear the swordsmen sitting around a campfire, eating their lunch and chatting with each other, oblivious to the imminent threat.

Unfortunately, there weren't any nearby alleys, but I trusted Knox to take out the guard before he made a noise and alerted the other swordsmen.

He was the pack's best hunter for a reason, and we were going to need all his skill to pull this off.

Go, I told Knox, and he slipped past the rubble, his enormous black wolf somehow melting into the shadows cast by the ruined building and overgrown brush beside us, the noise from the swordsmen in their camp covering any sound he might have made.

He slunk with ease, getting closer and closer to the guard outside the grimalkins' pens.

My pulse pounded, and my wolf pressed against my control, wanting to let loose and fight.

Someone in the swordsmen's camp laughed louder than the others, drawing the guard's attention. Knox leaped forward and shifted into his human form at the last second. With one clawed hand, he sliced open the guard's throat, and with the other he clamped it over the guard's mouth.

Go, I told Whil, before Knox had even set the dead guard on the ground.

I hurried forward, Whil close on my heels, both of us trying to keep as low to the ground and as quiet as possible. The sound of the swordsmen talking would help if we were careful, but we still had to move fast. Someone could look our way or walk out the door at any second. We couldn't let the swordsmen grab the lightning weapons.

We reached the edge of the crumbling building.

Just a little closer, I told Whil. *We need to get to that lower portion closer to their campfire.*

It was only a few feet away, but even with her magic swirling the potion in the air, it was best to toss the potion as close to the men as possible.

She nodded and pulled the jar of potion from her bag, her hands shaking.

I motioned for Whil to go ahead of me, just as a swordsman stepped out of the entranceway.

His eyes widened in surprise and I leaped forward, extending my claws from my fingertips.

Throw the jar! I commanded.

The swordsman started to draw his sword, but I was faster, slashing my claws through his neck before the weapon was unsheathed.

Whil hurled the jar with all her strength, and it smashed against the ground, releasing a golden mist. Her summer fae glow flared bright and the mist whooshed around those inside.

The men dropped their lunches, scrambling to draw their weapons and attack us, while six of them ran for an open crate on the other side of a row of cots. That had to be where they were keeping the lightning weapons.

The swordsman closest to the doorway jabbed at me with his sword, but I dodged, stepping close to the man, and raked my claws through his stomach and chest.

A growl bubbled in my throat as my wolf surged to the surface, not to take over, but to ensure we had all the power and ferocity needed to protect what was ours.

A few feet away, a man rushed toward Whil, but Deacon was a step behind her. He pulled her out of the way of the man's blade before attacking back.

Folmar and Knox joined him, protecting Whil and keeping the men away from the grimalkins' pens. We just needed to keep them contained until Whil's potion could knock them out.

But as I thought that, two of the swordsmen shoved the cots aside and reached the crate.

Shit.

Folmar, I said. She was the only one who could get past the group of men in front of us to stop the others from using the dangerous weapons.

On it. She leaped into the air, shifting into her majestic gryphon, and used her wings to sail over everyone's heads, landing on the crate and crushing it with her front paws.

The swordsman who'd thankfully hadn't been able to grab a weapon, lurched back with a yelp. He landed on his ass then kept on going, collapsing onto the shattered tiles.

The man beside him collapsed as well, then another and another. Whil's sleeping potion was finally taking effect.

Thank the Sisters.

I blew out a heavy breath, my chest heaving from exertion, and relief washed over me. One slight mishap not counted, everything had gone according to plan. A quick glance told me no one had gotten hurt and we hadn't needed all the extra fighters.

AUDREY

I EASED MY GRIP ON MY SPEAR AND RELEASED THE BREATH I'D BEEN holding when all the swordsmen passed out — Bishop having led our team down the street to the edge of the recess once we'd heard fighting. None of the swordsmen had managed to fire a lightning weapon, and save for being spotted before Whil could throw the potion, everything had gone according to plan.

And yet...

Something didn't feel right.

The air was heavy with the ominous power that felt like it was slowly and steadily growing, and my stomach churned as the dark magic inside me pulsed.

I sucked in a deep breath, determined to ignore my aching belly and the chill settling in my bones.

Cyrus and Knox tied up the unconscious swordsmen, and Whil used her power to magically lock the lightning weapons, preventing anyone from using them, like all of the alliance leaders had agreed on.

Everyone was going to be safe.

Except the wildness inside me screamed that I needed to stay alert.

Something was going to happen. Something—

The ominous power flared, stealing my breath, and the front wall of the building holding the grimalkins' pens exploded.

Debris flew everywhere, and the snarling creatures raced out, half of them rushing into the swordsmen's camp toward Cyrus and the others while the rest stampeded toward my group.

A skin-crawling wave of the grimalkins' alpha power slammed into me along with their heavy foul stench, and the darkness inside me pounded faster. Red light flashed in the eyes of a large grimalkin and my pulse stalled.

The guys had said the grimalkin who'd recently attacked had been more aggressive and possibly smarter than those that had attacked before, and I'd never seen a grimalkin with red eyes.

Maybe I'd imagined it.

But the red flashed again in another grimalkin's eyes, reminding me of the snake monsters Sterling had summoned when he couldn't get me to walk into the rip between realms and kill myself.

And none of that mattered. I needed to harness the darkness inside me and control the monsters before they killed everyone I loved.

I rushed forward, not knowing if I could control the grimalkins in the swordsmen's camp from where I stood. The last time I'd controlled them, they'd been five feet from me, and right now I was at least fifty feet away from Cyrus and the others.

"Audrey." Bishop grabbed my wrist but I jerked free.

"I need to get closer."

"Pretty sure you're close enough," Gower snapped as he swung his sword at a grimalkin's head while two other wolves attacked the beast's haunches.

I jerked my attention away from the grimalkins attacking in the swordsmen's camp to the chaos all around me. Men and women from the backup fighters poured past us, joining the fight, while the medics hung back, waiting for a chance to get to the injured.

Grimalkins kept pouring from the building, and my pulse roared with fear, my breath too sharp and fast. I'd never seen so many of the beasts before, and while I knew Knox had reported that the merchants had over four dozen, it hadn't occurred to me how overwhelming that would look.

Could I even control that many?

Someone screamed and Bishop wrenched me out of the way of a grimalkin's claws.

I had to.

I mentally grasped at the darkness inside me, my stomach seizing with nausea, bile burning the back of my throat, and a ferocious rage bursting to life inside me along with my wildness.

Mine. This pack was mine. Bishop, Knox, and Cyrus were mine.

Mine mine mine.

Black smoke puffed from my mouth and burned across my tongue.

They were going to freeze and they were going to freeze now.

"Submit!" I screamed, releasing a skin-crawling wave of my own alpha power.

All the wolf shifters and gryphons stumbled as if I'd affected them, too, even when the gryphons shouldn't have been able to sense my alpha power, and all of the grimalkins froze.

For a second everyone was staring at me, but instead of cringing away — like I knew I would later — I squared my shoulders and raised my chin, riding the ferocity of my alpha power.

The dark magic heaved against my control and I gritted my teeth.

"Don't just stand there," I snarled. "Kill them."

Cyrus lunged at the grimalkin in front of him and tore his claws through its throat with a shocking spray of brilliant red blood. Next to him, Knox clamped his powerful jaws around another grimalkin's neck, killing it, while Folmar tore into another.

Smoke burned out my nostrils and my stomach heaved.

Hold on and don't puke. Please don't puke.

My grip on the darkness wavered and the ominous power pounded against my senses, straining my control.

The fighters took out ten more grimalkins and I squeezed my eyes shut. I could do this. I *was* doing it. I just... needed... a little more—

My darkness stuttered, suddenly weakening, and the magic slipped through my mental fingertips.

No. Please no.

A grimalkin roared and someone screamed. My eyes flew open to see the remaining grimalkins springing back into action.

Fuck fuck fuck.

I scrambled to regain control of the magic, but it kept stuttering, there and strong one minute, weak and thin the next.

"Alpha," someone yelled.

I wrenched my gaze around, searching for which of my mates was in danger, just in time to see a grimalkin lunge toward me. I was the alpha they were yelling at.

Both Bishop and Gower were busy fending off other grimalkins, there wasn't anywhere to run, and I couldn't count on the dark magic to save me.

With a scream, I wrenched my spear up to stab it, even while desperately trying to seize control of it. But I couldn't grasp the magic, and it heaved its head aside, sending my spear tip scraping against its tough hide.

Shit.

I jerked my spear toward it again as Bishop slammed all of his claws in the beast's haunches and, with a strength I hadn't thought possible even for a shifter, tossed the grimalkin away from me.

"Stay back," he snarled at me, his eyes completely dark, his wolf controlling his body. Then he leaped toward the next closes grimalkin and swiped at it.

Ahead of him, Folmar screamed Whil's name, her voice sliced through the chaos and I wrenched my attention to see her tearing into a grimalkin with her sharp beak and claws, defending Whil from the snarling creature, but there were more surrounding them.

With a roar, Deacon swooped in, grabbed Whil and threw her over his shoulder. He bolted toward me, dodging grimalkin claws and teeth, but one grimalkin was faster than him, raking its sharp claws through his shoulder.

He stumbled and the grimalkin's back legs bunched, ready to pounce.

"No," I screamed, the darkness inside me surging.

I threw out my hand as if that would stop them... and it did. All the grimalkins froze again.

Yes!

But before anyone could kill them, the ground beneath us exploded, and the horrible black flying snake monsters erupted from the earth. Their shark-like teeth snapped hungrily and their red eyes glowed with malevolent intent.

No, oh fuck no.

"Are you fucking kidding me?" Bishop snarled as he killed the frozen grimalkin in front of him then lunged for another.

"Kill the grimalkins first," Cyrus commanded over the yells and screams and hisses filling the air.

The anger inside me blazed hotter, and I tightened my grip on the darkness inside me, determined to keep the grimalkins from fighting.

We were *not* going to lose this fight. We had to kill all of the grimalkins, especially if they weren't as natural as they were supposed to be.

Snakes swarmed around us, tearing bloody chunks out of men, wolves, and gryphons alike. Bishop yanked a snake off his biceps, its many teeth tearing through his flesh, before wrenching away a snake wrapped around Gower's neck, strangling him.

The ominous force pounded stronger and stronger against my senses, making the darkness inside me surge, and half a dozen snakes closest to me dropped to the ground.

Fear, determination, and rage battled inside me. If the dark magic inside me came from Tzanagoth, and Sterling had summoned and controlled the snake monsters. I could too.

But the moment I thought that, the dark magic stuttered, weakening and slipping out of my grasp.

It was just like the last time I'd lost control of the grimalkins, but this time I could feel it being pulled away from me from within me.

Sterling.

It had to be Sterling. We were tethered together and Whil had said that tether was the source of my dark magic.

I didn't know how or why he was involved with the merchants, maybe he'd noticed the battle and was just seizing the opportunity to hurt me, but I knew without a doubt he was responsible for the snake monsters. Even if we killed all of the grimalkins, he'd just keep sending more snakes after us until everyone I cared about was dead.

He had to be stopped, and the wildness roaring inside me along with my burning rage said I was the one who had to do it.

AUDREY

"It's Sterling," I yelled at Bishop as he tore a snake monster in two with his claws. "He's controlling the snakes. We have to stop him."

Without waiting for an answer, I took off, dashing through an opening between two wolves who were each fighting a grimalkin, and past the crumbling building where the swordsmen had made their camp.

With a growl, I concentrated on whatever was pulling on the magic inside me, determined to find its source. It had to be Sterling. How dare he try to fuck with my new life? I was finally happy and content, and that asshole had to keep coming after me.

My footsteps pounded on the uneven ground as I dodge chunks of collapsed buildings, tree roots, and broken flagstones.

Inside me, my dark magic stuttered, strong one minute, weaker the next, and always being dragged from somewhere ahead of me.

Except was I being stupid? What made me think I could possibly stand against Sterling even with my newfound alpha power. He'd become that monster and had to be stronger and—

A new horrible realization hit me. If my alpha power did come from the dark magic and Sterling had control over it, did that mean *he* could control my alpha power?

Fuck. This was the worst idea I'd ever come up with. Sterling was going to murder me.

But my wildness howled, burning with that strange fury that threatened to consume me.

He wouldn't kill me because I wasn't a weakling anymore. *I* would kill him and my fury didn't care that I was eager to commit murder. Sterling had summoned a monster knowing it was going to eat me alive, and if my dream had been true, he'd slaughtered Mila and Porter as well.

He had to be stopped. Permanently.

And I was going to do it.

I rounded a corner and staggered to a stop. Before me lay the grand courtyard in front of Tzanagoth's towering temple. Dead center, beside the fountain with the horrifying statue of Tzanagoth eating people, stood Sterling.

He was a terrifying, living replica of the statue, twice his usual height with bright red skin, large leathery wings, and ram's horns twisting from his forehead. The only reason I recognized him was because he wore the same cruel look in his eyes and the sneer he'd always worn.

Beside him, also smirking, was Royce, except compared to Sterling he looked small and weak. I couldn't believe I'd thought he was powerful. He hadn't tortured me like Sterling had, but Royce's betrayal had been so much worse than anything Sterling had done.

He'd made me believe we were fated mates, that he'd love me for who I was and would rescue me from the nightmare I'd been living in since I was a kid.

He'd crushed the sliver of hope I'd been clinging to, cementing the idea that no one could ever want me.

Behind them, by two of the four pillars marking a large square in the middle of the courtyard, stood the tall shimmering rip between realms.

I hadn't wanted to accept it had actually returned, even though I knew Knox wouldn't lie to me and Sterling and Royce standing in front of me was undeniable proof. It being there meant my nightmare had been real.

And there, on the ground in front of the rip, lay two mangled bodies. From where I stood, it was impossible to tell who Sterling's victims were, but I knew it was Mila and Porter.

Mila had been my only friend in my old pack, the only one willing to risk Sterling's anger, and he'd brutally murdered her.

The wildness and anger within me flared, burning inside me.

"You know who that is, don't you?" Sterling asked with a dark chuckle. "It's the stupid little girl you thought you could be friends with. Turns out with this power—" he flexed his hand and a ball of smoke whirled around his fingers, reveling in his new strength. "I don't need an incomplete mating bond. A complete one will do."

Royce joined his laughter, and my insides churned with disgust, while fear and adrenaline and dark magic pounded through me.

"If you're so powerful, why are you here?" I demanded. "You got your power. You could have stayed in our realm and led all the packs."

He wouldn't have been able to do much more than that though. There were a lot more supernatural beings in my old realm than there were here and some of them were really powerful.

Aaaaand, I'd just answered my question.

I didn't know how he'd guessed that the supers here weren't nearly as powerful as those in my realm, but he must have figured it out or decided it was worth the risk. There, he could only go so far. Here, he could rule the world.

"I'm a god, and this realm is mine." Sterling threw his head back and released a bellowing laugh, the sound cruel and dark, making my skin crawl. "*You're* mine. *My* sacrifice and I'm here to finish the job."

Sterling stretched his arms and wings out and a tidal wave of skin-crawling alpha power, just like the power I felt from the grimalkins, slammed into me.

It stole my breath and wrenched me down to my knees, forcing me to submit to Sterling like I'd always done.

No. Get up. Get up, now.

But I couldn't make myself move. His power crushed me, stronger than anything I'd ever felt before, because I was weak and pathetic and helpless. I wasn't important. No one wanted me. Being with Bishop and Knox was a foolish fantasy because no one wanted to spend the rest of their life tied to a powerless shifter who couldn't shift.

"No!" I screamed, mentally shoving at the thoughts racing through my head, thoughts that weren't mine. They couldn't be mine.

Bishop and Knox loved me.

I. Could. Feel. It.

Our bonds assured me their love was real, and I was *not* going to give in to this asshole and let him destroy everything I'd worked for since I'd gotten here.

I heaved against his alpha power and strained to connect with my wildness and dark magic, but they, too, were crushed under Sterling's power.

"You can't do it," Sterling laughed. "I'm going to slaughter everyone you love, those new alphas of yours, and their whole pack. I'll feed on your despair."

AUDREY

"No!" I yelled back at Sterling. "I won't let you."

I had to protect my mates.

As if thinking of them summoned them, Bishop, Knox, and Cyrus rushed into the Great Square, their expressions fierce.

Knox, in his wolf form, looked practically feral, snarling with his lips curled back showing his teeth. But I couldn't sense his emotions, couldn't tell if he held onto any scrap of humanity.

I couldn't feel Bishop's emotions, either. The power crushing me and raging inside me overwhelmed everything. My stomach ached, but my rage burned through my nausea.

"Get away from her," Bishop commanded, his own alpha power crashing into the courtyard as he raced toward Sterling.

"Don't—" I gasped.

They didn't understand how powerful Sterling was. He was going to murder them.

Before they'd even gotten close to him, he flicked his hand and three men? Beings? Creatures? rose from the ground, black smoke swirling around them. They were identical, each wearing heavy clothes that hid their form and hoods that hid their faces, and they all looked like the man who'd poisoned Bishop.

"Don't let their claws touch you," Bishop yelled as the men screeched an inhuman sound and leaped toward my guys.

"It was you?" I snarled at Sterling.

My guys twisted and leaped out of the way of the smoke men's claws trying to get in a strike while I heaved and snarled. My mates needed me and I was stuck bowing on the ground. I was stronger than this.

Sterling howled with laughter. "That's it, fight me. Squirm against my power. Entertain me."

Like I'd *entertained* him when he and his friends bullied me at school and taunted me about the mother I'd never known and the father who couldn't handle living with the things he'd done in the war?

No.

No more.

My wildness surged. I seized it, wrapped it around the dark magic, and heaved. Power, stronger, wild power, roared through my veins. It tore through Sterling's demand to submit and filled me with strength as I stood.

"I'm not your toy anymore."

Sterling's sneer twisted into a snarl, rage filling his eyes. "You'll always be mine."

He raised his arms, and a flurry of snake monsters burst from the ground around me, snapping and hissing.

One of the snake monsters swooped at my head. I raised my hands to bat it away, but another dove in and wrapped around my neck, squeezing tight. Others sank their fangs into my flesh, but I couldn't feel the pain of their bites.

The dark magic pulsed, stronger and stronger, consuming me.

I had to save my men, had to stop the smoke assassins before they could be poisoned.

With a snarl, I tore the snake from around my neck and the dark magic snapped, a quick, sharp blast.

All the snakes around me burst into smoke and the smoke men screeched, crumbling to ash at my guys' feet.

Surprise and fury flashed across Sterling's expression and it was my turn to look smug.

He was going to pay for everything he'd done to me.

I glanced at my guys, but I couldn't tell if they'd been poisoned or not. But there wasn't anything I could do about it right now. Sterling had to be stopped and then I could pray that I could remove the poison using my own dark magic.

At least, for now, they were free and could help me.

But as soon as I thought that, grimalkins and snake monsters stampeded into the courtyard and they were overwhelmed again. Some of our fighters quickly followed, but not all of them, and I couldn't help worrying that they hadn't arrived because they couldn't, not because they were still fighting monsters elsewhere.

"Kill her," Sterling roared, jerking his chin at Royce. "Get me my magic,"

Royce shifted into his wolf and barreled toward me. I raised my spear, swinging it at him, but he slipped past the weapon and slammed into me, knocking me to the ground.

With a snarl, he dove in to bite me, and I swept my spear up, bashing him in the face with the shaft. He staggered to the side, and I scrambled back, desperate to get on my feet and put space between us.

I don't think so, bitch, he snarled as he lurched forward and snagged my pantleg with his teeth, jerking me closer.

Sterling howled with laughter, and my dark magic heaved within my control, while the grimalkin's alpha power grated against my skin.

I kicked at Royce's head, missed, and kicked again, my heel skimming the side of his face.

"Just fucking die," Sterling roared.

How dare he! How dare he fuck with my life.

"No. Way. In. Hell," I roared back.

I seized my alpha power and slammed it as hard as I could at Royce. I was sure I could resist Royce's command, but I had no idea if I was powerful enough to command him. He was almost as powerful as Sterling, and I had no idea if Sterling had given Royce any special power. There was just too much power and energy snapping through the air to tell.

Royce jerked to a stop and shifted back to a human, his eyes wide with shock.

"You—" he gasped.

"Me," I snarled back, satisfaction pouring through me.

Take that, asshole. I'm not weak anymore.

"Fucking useless," Sterling screamed as he stormed toward me.

Then, between one quick step and another, he shifted into... a monster.

It was more like a grimalkin than a wolf, except it was three times the size and instead of a grimalkin's short, black fur, it had red, leathery skin and a thin tail with a wicked point on the end. Large black wings rose above its body — like the gryphons' wings — and Tzanagoth's trademark ram's horns curled from its forehead.

It— Sterling pounced on Royce, still struggling against my alpha power, and chomped him in half.

My thoughts lurched, unable to fully register what had happened, and bile burned my throat.

Bones crunched, frothy pink drool dripped from Sterling's mouth, and part of Royce's arm dropped to the ground... right beside the rest of him. Legs. Half torso. All slumped on the ground surrounded by a massive pool of blood.

Horror roiled in my stomach and I stumbled back a step, drawing Sterling's attention.

Oh, fuck.

He lunged at me, black smoke and dripping blood pouring from a mouth with too many teeth. In my weak, human form, I didn't stand a chance against him.

I wrenched my spear up to strike him, but he batted it out of my hands, sending it clattering across the flagstones out of reach, then he snapped at me.

With a yelp, I dove out of the way. His teeth tore through the back of my shirt as I scrambled to direct my magic into controlling a grimalkin or snake monster to help me — since I no longer had a weapon and the monsters had overrun even my guys and no one was going to come save me.

Sterling swiped at me with his paw. I tried to leap out of the way, but he still caught me, sending me tumbling across the courtyard just like my spear.

Fuck me.

That strike could have killed me, but he'd pulled his claws. He wanted to torture me first.

I shot my dark magic toward the closest grimalkin but felt Sterling yank it away.

No. Please, no.

The magic was my only chance of surviving.

AUDREY

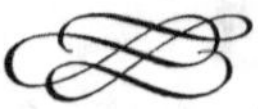

I PUSHED HARDER WITH MY DARK MAGIC, STRAINING TO REACH THE grimalkins, but the power vanished again and Sterling roared with laughter.

Pathetic, he chuckled. *Just give up and die.*

"No," I spat at him.

I'd never just give up. I hadn't through all the years he and his father had tortured me, and I wouldn't do it now. It didn't matter if all my power was from the dark magic, I'd—

My thoughts stuttered. If the dark magic had given me alpha powers, maybe it could awaken my wolf — if only for the fight.

With a new determination roaring through me, I twisted the dark magic inside me, wrapping it up with my wildness. Pain burned through my stomach and across my chest, and smoke poured from my mouth.

Sterling lunged at me, and I scrambled out of the way, my stomach heaving, threatening to expel what little was in it at the sudden movement.

Die, Sterling roared, swiping again. *Just die and give me my power.*

I dove to the side as something snapped inside me. Agonizing pain ripped through every muscle in my body, and I screamed, collapsing to my hands and knees.

Except instead of landing on my hands and knees, I landed on white paws.

Paws.

I had paws.

Wildness coursed through my veins, singing a ferocious song of primal power, as if my soul really was fully connected, my wolf half no longer blocked by a curse cast generations ago.

But I knew it wasn't going to last. I only had my wolf because of the dark magic and as soon as Whil could figure out how to get rid of it, I'd lose my wolf — because she'd either get rid of the magic, or I'd make her lock me away before I turned into a monster like Sterling.

And none of that mattered. Sterling had to be stopped.

I wrenched my attention away from my paws to Sterling, whose eyes were blazing with fury.

Submit! Sterling roared, and a wave of power crashed toward me, aimed at crushing my will and forcing me to obey.

But my wildness flared stronger and my wolf pressed against my senses.

She'd never submit.

Never again.

She released her own wave of alpha power, shattering Sterling's wave before it could even reach me, and Sterling's eyes widened in surprise.

Yeah, my alpha power is stronger than yours, asshole. Barely, and I had no idea if I'd win the next contest of wills. Which meant I needed to end this.

Because I could. I had it in me... and if I couldn't, everyone I loved would die.

I lunged at him, snapping at his throat, but he leaped out of the way just in time. With a growl, he slashed at me with his claws. I twisted to the side, determined to dodge and attack at the same time.

But I wasn't fast enough. Sterling's claws skimmed my side,

leaving behind a burning line of pain even as I managed to sink my teeth into his hind leg.

He roared, wrenching his head to snap at me, but I scrambled back before he could bite me.

We fought, him swiping and biting, his body more powerful than mine, and me dodging and nicking him, with my faster, more agile wolf.

I panted hard, and my pulse pounded as I dodged his claws again.

God damn it. No matter how hard I tried, I couldn't quite reach his throat or underbelly. There was no way I could strike a killing blow, and without a doubt, I was going to get tired before he did.

Sterling's strikes grew harder, more vicious, swatting me this way and that, drawing more stinging lines through my skin. He roared, his movement growing jerky, and I could practically feel frustration radiating from him.

He thought I'd be easy to kill, and I'd proven him wrong.

Well, go me.

With a roar, he shifted back into his monstrous form, towering over me. His claws flew toward me, faster than the swipes he'd been taking in his wolflike form.

Oh, fuck.

I heaved myself to the left, but as I moved, a sharp yank inside my head made me stumble. Inside me, the dark magic twisted tight, no longer within my control.

Icy fear exploded in my veins, and the magic roared stronger, threatening to completely seize my muscles and render me helpless against Sterling's next strike.

He was taking my dark magic and using it against me.

No. I wrenched at my magic, desperate to regain control, while the edge of Sterling's claws tore through my side and sent me flying back.

I hit the ground with a heavy thump that knocked the breath from my lungs, agony screaming through me.

Sharp pain snapped through my head and I fought to stand.

Get up. Just get up.

I had to fight him, but he was in my head. His alpha power hadn't worked on me, so he was using the tether binding us together to manipulate me... just like he'd manipulated me in my dreams to hurt myself.

I gritted my teeth, desperate to keep him out and hold onto my magic, but his power ripped into every cell, and suddenly my paws were hands.

I screamed, my body trembling, getting weaker and weaker, melting back into the nothing I was before I'd met my guys. The rage that had been burning through me flickered, melting into a pinprick of anger, and my soul wept and my wolf howled.

"That's it. Despair. Know that when you're dead, I'm going to tear your alphas limb from limb."

"I won't let you," I gasped back.

"You can't stop me. You're nothing without my power," he sneered, his enormous frame towering over me while I panted, naked on my hands and knees. "You'll always be nothing. You're only good for a sacrifice. Now finish your fate and die."

He lunged at me, his claws already dripping with my blood, and I threw myself back, narrowly escaping his attack.

I crashed onto the flagstones, my arms flung wide but they did little to soften the fall. The impact rattled up my butt and back until my head slammed against the ground. Sparks of black and brilliant light flashed across my vision and my breath burst from my lungs with a whoosh.

I gasped, fighting to breathe as Sterling swiped again.

My pulse roared, my mind screaming at me to move, get up, do something!

I heaved to the side, the world lurching out of focus, and my hand hit my spear.

My ferocious wildness surged, and I thrust my spear up, shoving the tip with all my strength, determination and desperation into Sterling's heart.

The force of his forward movement to reach me pushed the spear deeper into his body, and his eyes widened in shock.

Mine widened in shock as well.

I'd killed him.

A shifter couldn't heal a massive hole in his heart fast enough to save him.

I shoved him to the side so he didn't collapse on top of me and wrenched out the spear. His blood poured onto the flagstones, pooling around my bare feet, but I couldn't stop staring at him.

The monster who'd tormented me from the moment I'd been forced to move into his home with him and his father, who'd tricked me into thinking I'd found my fated mate and had tried to sacrifice me to a monster that was going to eat me alive, was dead.

He couldn't control me anymore, couldn't manipulate me through my dreams, and would never hurt anyone else.

I was finally free.

AUDREY

Relief rushed through me as I sagged back against the flagstones and swept my gaze over the courtyard. With Sterling dead, the snake monsters burst into smoke and vanished and the grimalkins paused mid-fight and shook their heads. Cyrus took advantage of the distraction and killed the grimalkin in front of him, spurring on the others who made short work of the remaining beasts.

Thank, God. It was over.

The medics that had been standing at the edge of the battle, rushed to treat the injured, one heading toward Bishop, who waved him away before taking off his clothes and shifting into his wolf.

Healing his injuries while shifting would drain him, but it meant he wasn't tying up a medic. Knox, who'd fought as a wolf, shifted to his human form to heal and together they walked toward me.

I could feel their love and worry for me rushing through our mating bonds, and my heart swelled with joy. Mine. They were mine.

With that thought, I reached out with the dark magic, searching for signs of the horrible poison. All three of my guys had been poisoned, but before I could freeze in fear, the magic dove into their bodies and, drawing a scream from all three of them, ripped the poison out.

They were safe and it was over.

Finally.

Except the dark magic inside me didn't settle after removing the poison, it grew stronger and stronger, whirling in and around me, stealing my breath.

My stomach cramped and I dropped to my knees. Bile burned up my throat and across my tongue, and I heaved forward, black smoke pouring out of my mouth.

Panic raced through my mating bonds, but I could barely sense it with the dark magic roaring through me.

"Get a medic!" Knox yelled.

He raced to my side, dropped to his knees, and pulled me into his arms. Desperation filled his wolf-darkened gaze, and his alpha power stuttered against my power as he fought to stay in control and not go feral.

Audrey, Bishop said in my head as he pressed his wet nose against my bare thigh.

I could tell he wanted to hold me as well, needed the physical contact to calm his wolf, but knew he couldn't crowd me. The medic needed space to help me and Bishop couldn't take me away from Knox who'd completely lose it if he wasn't holding me.

A second later, Cyrus skidded to a stop beside us, his eyes so dark I wasn't sure who was in control of his body, the human or the wolf. He brushed my hair away from my face as he made space for a medic who thankfully knew enough to not take me from Knox.

I gasped for air, the dark magic growing stronger and stronger and a heavy exhaustion dragging on my limbs. My back heaved, and I vomited up more smoke and bile half onto the ground and half into Cyrus's lap.

"It's going to be okay," he said, not caring about the mess.

"She's bumped her head and has a whole bunch of lacerations that need bandaging," the medic said. "But that doesn't explain the smoke."

"Something has to explain it," Knox snarled.

"It's the darkness inside her," Whil said, nudging the medic out of the way and placing a hand on my forehead, as the medic started binding my wounds. "This close to Tzanagoth's resting place, I can tell the dark magic is his, and it's rushing into her."

"How is it rushing into her?" Cyrus demanded.

"The tether is also gone," Whil replied. "We suspected it was connected to Sterling and now that he's dead all of Tzanagoth's power is pouring into Audrey."

My stomach cramped and I bit back a moan. The guys flickered in and out of focus, and I struggled to keep my eyes open.

If she's getting all of Tzanagoth's power... Bishop said.

"Then the curse on the realm is putting her to sleep," Whil finished.

"You don't know that," Knox snarled.

"She's already on the verge of passing out," Cyrus snapped back then turned to Whil. "Do something. Save her."

"I can't. I'm not strong enough and there isn't anyone in our realm who is," Whil replied.

I raised a trembling hand to caress Knox's cheek but couldn't lift it high enough before the exhaustion dragged it back down. "It'll be okay."

"Nothing will be okay." His voice cracked and my heart broke for him.

He hadn't wanted a mate in the first place and I'd accidentally bound myself to him— No, *fate* had bound us together. It hadn't been an accident at all. Except now I could feel in my soul that living without me, even if I was in a coma, would shatter him.

His grip around me tightened. "I can't lose you."

Bishop whimpered and Cyrus raked his hands through his hair.

"If you can get to Faerie, you can find a sorcerer strong enough to save you," Whil told me. "But that means I have to open a rip."

My gaze slowly dragged up past Cyrus's shoulder to the far side of the courtyard, searching for the rip. Last I'd seen it, it was too thin for us to go through without us touching the sides and turning to ash.

Whil would need to use her magic to widen it, but surely that was easier than creating a new one. But even as I searched for it, I knew the telltale shimmer was gone. It had died with Sterling.

Do you have enough power to open a rip? Bishop asked. *I'm sure you thought about it in the past and you're still trapped in this realm.*

Sadness filled Whil's expression. "I've figured out how Sterling opened the first rip, but—"

But she needed an incomplete mating bond to do it. That was the toll Sterling had made me pay the first time and it had to be the toll now. Except I'd never ask someone to bond with me or anyone else just to create a rip between realms.

"I'll do it," Cyrus said. "I'll bond with Audrey."

My soul soared at his words even as my heart plummeted. He was my mate. We were meant to be together, but I couldn't let him bond with me, no matter how much I wanted it.

And I sure as hell didn't want him mate bonding with me because he felt it was his duty. I wanted him to love me like I loved him.

"No," I said, trying to sound firm and failing, my voice coming out breathy and weak. "If Whil can't make a rip and I fall asleep, you won't be able to seal the bond. You'll go crazy."

"I don't care about that," he said.

"And if she can open a rip and we can't get back?" I asked. "What then?"

"You're not going through the rip without me," he snarled.

"You can't, the pack needs you." Why was he being so insistent? He couldn't just abandon his pack.

"But I need *you*." He cupped my cheeks with his palms, forcing me to look at him. "I've given up a lot of things for my pack, put myself last my entire life, but I won't give up you. I can't."

The heat from his touch seared through my skin, raced down my neck, and swelled around my heart.

Mine. He was mine.

The warmth of our shifter connection was as strong as my connection with Bishop and Knox.

"I love you," he said. "I've loved you from the first moment you woke in the Residence terrified of me, a spark of defiance in your eyes." He squeezed his eyes shut, and a single tear released and trailed down his cheek. "You're my mate, Audrey. You've always been."

My heart sang as my soul wept.

It was too late... but it was better this way.

If he didn't bond with me, he was safe. He wouldn't die from a broken heart or go crazy. There was no guarantee that Whil could make the rip or that we'd be able to find a fae sorcerer who could help us.

Cyrus turned to Whil. "I'm bonding with Audrey and you're making a rip." His attention jumped back to me. "I can't live without you. Please. Let me do this for you. Take me as your mate."

My throat tightened. It was clear in his eyes that he wouldn't take no for an answer and I didn't want to tell him no. I wanted to say yes, wanted to yell it so everyone could hear that my soul was finally fully complete. Cyrus was mine. It was fate and I didn't want to run away from it.

"Yes," I told him, my voice barely a whisper. "I accept your bond."

Joy filled his expression, and he brushed his lips against mine in a soft, quick, heartbreaking kiss.

"It could be a one-way trip," Whil warned. "I've done the research and there's something about the gods' power that's unique to them that the curse gloms onto. The gates to this realm are safe to open, but if the Fae elders refuse to unlock them or you can't find someone who can create another rip, you won't be able to return."

So be it, Bishop said.

"*We* won't return—?" I asked. Whil wasn't including herself. "Whil, this is a chance to go to Faerie. You can finally go home."

Whil's expression softened and she took my hand. "I know. For a long time, I wanted to go back, wanted to talk to and be with other fae, but I can't leave Stonehaven. This pack is my family. There are so many people here I love and care for. In Faerie, I'm barely a sorcerer, but here, my sorcerer ability doesn't matter."

I weakly squeezed her hand, understanding how she felt. I needed to be helpful, too. I hadn't realized how much I wanted a pack until I'd stumbled into this realm. Now that I had one with people who I knew in my soul I needed to protect, I didn't want to leave.

But I also didn't want to fall asleep and never wake up, and I didn't know how me being in a coma would affect Bishop and Knox. Would they be fine or would they slowly start to go crazy as if their mating bonds were dying?

KNOX

I clutched Audrey against my chest, my wolf howling and raging inside me.

I hadn't wanted to be mated to anyone, hadn't thought with my issues that I deserved a mate, and I'd tried so hard to force her away.

I'd told myself we had to break our bond because I couldn't give her the kind of life she deserved. I couldn't stand large crowds or be indoors for more than a handful of hours depending on the size of the space, and it would be cruel to force her to spend the rest of her life with that.

Having a mate meant change and I'd been barely holding onto my humanity as it was.

But in truth, I was afraid. If I opened up to her, she'd know just how afraid I was. She'd see the scared pup who'd been trapped in that cave-in, pinned under all that rock for days. She'd see the beast I'd let myself become to protect that pup.

"Knox," she whispered, her breath warm against my skin.

"I've got you," I said, trying to not let my panic color my tone or bleed through our mating bond. She had to be scared enough by being filled with all that evil magic. I couldn't add the feralness screaming through my soul threatening to completely take over. *I love you.*

Sisters, I loved her so much.

Audrey had become an irreplaceable part of my life. I hadn't told her the truth about my claustrophobia but I had no doubt that she saw the real me. And still, she embraced our accidental mating bond, loving me softly, deeply, and wholeheartedly.

Before her, I'd preferred the wild isolation of my wolf. I'd even let my humanity slip to the background and let my wolf take over. But now, with her by my side, I found myself more comfortable in my human skin, able to spend more time around people and indoors. It was a change I never expected, but one I welcomed for her sake.

Because I *wanted* to do all those things I couldn't do for her. I *wanted* to spend the night, every night, indoors in her bed loving her, wanted to meet with her friends and be social. I wanted to give her the world.

The feralness heaved and my wolf snarled.

I had to protect her, save her. Something. Gods damned something. Now.

"Knox, please," she murmured, her voice barely audible.

"Stay awake, Audrey," my wolf growled, my grip on her tightening. "Stay awake."

Stay with me.

I needed to say more, engage her in conversation to keep her from falling asleep while Bishop, Cyrus, and Whil figured out how to save her. But all I could think of was holding her tight and screaming.

Mine. She was mine. I refused to let her go. If she slept forever, so would I. My wolf and I both agreed.

The feralness could have us. We'd let it consume our consciousness and become the beast everyone thought we were. We were nothing without Audrey.

We didn't want to be anything without her.

Audrey moaned, reminding me that we hadn't lost her yet. She was fighting the gods' curse and we needed to fight for her too.

"I saw your wolf," I blurted out, saying the first thing that came to mind, determined to keep her awake.

Her eyelids drooped, and I gave her a little shake, waking her up.

"Your wolf," I said. "She's beautiful. You have to see her. All white and small. Fast as lightning. We're going to run together through the pack's primary grove once this is over."

My throat tightened as she fought to open her eyes.

"Promise me we'll run together," I insisted, my voice breaking. "Audrey, promise me."

I gave her another soft shake and she groaned, dragging her gaze back to me.

I promise, she said in my head, her telepathy awakening with her wolf.

Love and sadness poured through our mating bond and I pressed my lips to her forehead.

Please, don't leave me.

"Knox." Cyrus's voice jerked me out of my thoughts, reminding me that I was a ferocious beast who'd do anything to protect his mate.

Why the fuck was I sitting there panicking and wallowing?

Because *I* couldn't save her. We were already mate bonded, so I couldn't make an incomplete bond with her, and I wasn't a sorcerer and couldn't just rip the magic out of her.

I couldn't do anything except cling to her like my life depended on it... because it did. Life wouldn't be worth living without her.

"We can't stay in Anakar," Cyrus said, his brow furrowed with concern. "Tzanagoth's spirits could still come out once night falls, and I don't want to risk them screwing everything up."

"Then let's go," I said as I stood.

With Tzanagoth's power rushing into Audrey, I didn't know if his spirits still existed, or if they'd follow us when we left, but it was still smart to leave.

Bishop nodded his agreement, and the four of us marched to where the rest of our party had gathered.

"Deacon," Cyrus said, capturing our betas attention. "You'll need to take charge of the pack while we save Audrey."

The big man nodded, his alpha power stuttered over us like it always did. "You got it."

"We may not return," Cyrus said, his tone thick with emotion. "This could be a one-way trip for the four of us."

Deacon grabbed his shoulder and gave him a fierce grin. "If I found my mate, I'd do whatever it took, too."

"Get our men out of Anakar by nightfall," Cyrus commanded then he called for Folmar to help us return to Stonehaven.

Without question, Folmar called over two other gryphon shifters, and they all shifted and knelt so we could climb onto their backs. With a screech, they took off into the air, racing back to Stonehaven.

It was my first time flying — and from the way my stomach lurched my last — but I couldn't even try to enjoy the trip. My focus remained solely on my mate who was completely limp in my arms, her breathing slow and steady.

The landscape below blurred together, and it felt like an eternity before we finally arrived at the sacred grove on the Residence's property even though it had probably only been a few hours.

Nova and Finn waited for us. Once we'd gotten close enough to town, Cyrus must have told Nova what we needed. They greeted us with fresh clothes and wet towels, so we could clean up after our fight. They'd also packed three packs that included a few healing elixirs, changes of clothes, rations, and a purse with some small gems in case we needed to pay the fae sorcerer to save Audrey.

Carefully holding Audrey, I climbed off Folmar, thanking her gruffly and joining the others. Audrey needed to get cleaned up and changed, she'd be mortified if we took her anywhere unconscious and naked, but I couldn't make myself let her go.

"Here," Nova said gently, handing me a cloth before dribbling two healing elixirs into Audrey's mouth.

"Thanks," I murmured, my attention devoted to Audrey as I wiped away the traces of blood and dirt from her fragile body.

Her eyelids fluttered, making my heart leap, and I gave her a gentle shake, waking her up.

That's it, beautiful, Bishop said. *Stay with us. Just for a little longer. Cyrus needs to profess his love to you for this to work.*

She groaned and, with great effort, opened her eyes wide.

"When you get through the rip, you'll need to find a powerful fae sorcerer capable of extracting the dark magic," Whil instructed. "I can only create a rip to Audrey's realm because our realms are so closely linked, and I can't open a gate directly to Faerie, so you're going to have to find someone who can get you there."

"If you can—" Audrey sucked in a deep breath, struggling to stay awake, while Nova bound her wounds and helped me slide on Audrey's dress — which was easier than trying to dress her in a shirt and pants. "Find a JP agent. They're watchmen for supers in my realm. If they can't get us through a gate to Faerie, they'll know someone who can."

We'll find one, Bishop promised, and I could feel a determination coming through our twin bond that matched mine. *Cyrus, let's do this.*

Cyrus moved to kneel before Audrey, still clutched in my protective embrace. He raised both hands and cradled her face, urging her to meet his gaze. His eyes were filled with sorrow and love and my wolf howled for him.

Cyrus was Audrey's mate as well and even I could tell he'd been an idiot, pushing her away to protect her then putting our pack first, trying to clear up the mess with the merchants before telling her how much he cared.

And now here he was, finally telling her the truth when we could lose her forever.

"I'm so sorry for ever making you doubt yourself and for scaring you," Cyrus said, his voice low. "I swear to spend every day showing you how much you mean to me."

Audrey raised a trembling hand and brushed his cheek, her smile soft and sad.

The vow, Bishop reminded, and Cyrus drew in a steadying breath.

"Blessed be the Great Sisters and her children, and blessed be my sacred vow," Cyrus recited, his eyes turning glassy with tears. "You're my love, my life. My soul recognizes yours as my mate, and I, without reservation, bind my soul with yours for eternity. I love you, Audrey."

"Mine," Audrey said, her words slurred, "Finally."

Whil drew close and gestured for Nova and Finn to give us our packs.

"Get ready." She raised her hands, and her soft, perpetual golden glow exploded in a brilliant light.

A sharp gust of wind swept through the grove and the ground trembled. Whil groaned and dropped to her knees, her eyes squeezed tight and her jaw clenched shut. Her breathing turned short and sharp, and her body shook.

Then, with a sharp *crack*, the air in front of us ripped open revealing a dark field and a forest in the distance. Just like the rip in Anakar, this one was tall, with shimmering edges, but thankfully it was also wide enough to go through.

I tightened my grip on Audrey and stepped up beside Cyrus with Bishop, still in his wolf form, on my other side.

We'll save you, I swore.

Even if I had to let my beast consume me to do it.

BISHOP

Fear tightened my chest. The thought of seeing Audrey unconscious every day and not being able to talk to her or share my life with her making it hard to breathe. She wouldn't be dead. But she wouldn't be alive, either, and I couldn't live with that.

She was too amazing to lose, sweet and shy and funny, with a heart filled with so much love. She was fierce, too. She didn't show it often, but she did when it mattered, and Sisters, she'd shown her ferocious warrior spirit when she'd faced Sterling.

That monster had actually been a monster. He'd looked like the horrible god depicted in the statue outside of Tzanagoth's temple, and she hadn't flinched or hid or even looked afraid. She'd been a goddess of vengeance and justice, and Sterling had deserved everything that had come to him.

And straight ahead lay her salvation.

I stared at the rip between the realms alongside Cyrus and Knox. Whil had used Cyrus's incomplete mating bond with Audrey to create the rip, and while it was the only way to get to a fae sorcerer who might be able to help, I feared for my brother.

We had no idea how long it would take us to get to Faerie and find a sorcerer, and he'd been fighting with his attraction to Audrey before he'd permanently bound his soul to hers. Sure, it was supposed to take a while before the urge from the bond to seal it became overwhelming, but given how much I knew he already loved her, I was certain we didn't have a while.

I chuffed and raised my snout to Knox, who held Audrey, then to Cyrus who stood beside him. Whil had cast the spell, there was no going back, and none of us would go back if we could. All that mattered was saving our mate.

Together we stepped through the rip, careful not to touch the shimmering edges. A shiver rolled through my body, the only indication that we were passing between realms, and then we were in Audrey's realm.

A warm summer night engulfed us, a cool contrast to the mid-day sun that we'd just left. We stood in a field of low grass and right in the middle of a fight... or rather a massacre.

Four men surrounded a man and a woman with strangely mottled skin. Their clothes were ripped and deep gouges — the kind made from small claws — scored their torsos. They lay limp half on the ground and half in the men's arms, all of the men pressed close, one with his lips against the woman's neck in an open-mouthed kiss, another at the man's throat, and the two others lapping at the gashes across their torsos.

What the fuck?

We hadn't been able to see them because of the limited view through the rip even though they were only a few feet away, and every instinct I had screamed that we had to get out of here.

One of the men jerked his head and hissed at us, revealing sharp fangs and blood dribbling down his chin.

My pulse lurched. Audrey had said all manner of supernatural beings — supers as she called them — lived in her realm, and now I was standing face to face with a mythological vampire.

One that looked hungry as hell and, if the stories I'd read were correct, was going to be hard to stop. According to the lore, vampires could move faster than a shifter and could heal at a phenomenal rate.

The other vampires looked up and hissed, their eyes black, their expressions hungry and smug.

"Shit," Knox growled, tensing beside me while a wild rage blasted through our twin bond.

"What do we have here?" a big, bulky vampire asked.

"I think they brought us dessert," another one hissed. This guy was small for a man, but I didn't doubt he was any less dangerous.

"I think both of us should pretend we didn't see anything," Cyrus snarled, his hands flexing and his claws extending from his fingertips. "You don't want this to turn into a fight."

"The puppy thinks he can fight us?" a heavyset vampire laughed and the boringly average looking vampire beside him joined in.

"This puppy knows he can." Cyrus's alpha power rolled off of him revealing just how determined he was.

He knew his power wouldn't affect the vampires, but I doubted he could help himself. Knox was radiating almost as much alpha power as Cyrus, and I could feel mine pouring off me in waves as well.

We'd do anything to protect our mate, and while Cyrus had done a shit job at diffusing the situation, we all knew nothing we said was going to change the vampire's minds.

They can move fast, I said in Cyrus's and Knox's head, the warning only a second before the vampires shot toward us.

Cyrus lunged forward to meet the attack, while Knox jerked out of reach of the heavyset vampire, protecting Audrey with his body and leaving his side open to the vampire's claws.

I bunched down, ready to leap at the heavyset man as his claws dragged through Knox's side, but before I could move, Knox shoved Audrey at me. Darkness filled his eyes and feralness radiated through our bond as he shifted into his wolf form. His wolf had taken over and had already figured out I was the weakest link in this fight.

I'd taken a serious swipe from a grimalkin's claws and had to shift out my injuries, but that had tired me out. I was sure Knox was also tired, but he was a natural born hunter and the feral side of his wolf would keep him going longer than me.

With a huff, I shifted, grabbing Audrey before she fell on the ground. Exhaustion crashed through me, but I forced myself to my feet, determined to put space between me and the fight.

The small vampire rushed toward me, but Cyrus shoved the average looking vampire into the small one making them stumble away from me.

"Get her out of here," Cyrus barked at me, his power snapping into my soul but not forcing me to obey.

Beside him, Knox bit a chunk out of the heavyset vampire's leg, making the vampire howl with pain. The guy staggered but righted himself and dove for Knox.

Again, I turned to run, but the large vampire blocked me.

Fucking hell.

He dove at me, his movements so fast I could barely follow them. Somehow, I manage to jerk out of the way, protecting Audrey from his claws.

But I wasn't fast enough to save myself. Fiery pain sliced through my shoulder and the vampire sneered at me while licking his fingertips.

"You taste good, puppy." His smile grew smug.

And you taste disgusting, Knox mentally yelled at him, making him turn toward Knox just as Knox leaped at him.

Knox's wolf, like mine and Cyrus's, was massive, and he easily tackled the vampire to the ground. With a snarl, he latched his teeth into the vampire's throat and ripped through his flesh.

One of the other vampires screamed, and I glanced up to see Cyrus tearing his claws through the average looking vampire's stomach. The man dropped to his knees, clutching at his insides and Cyrus rammed his knee into the guy's head.

The other two vampires also lay on the ground. The small guy was completely unconscious, his torso shredded by wolf claws, while the heavyset vampire rolled on the ground, moaning, both of his legs gnawed down to the bone and a deep set of claw marks tearing down his side.

Mine, Knox roared as he tipped his head back and howled. Feralness crackled through his alpha power and he stalked toward the heavyset vampire.

"Don't," Cyrus commanded, knowing that Knox was going to finish the man off. "We need to get out of here. We can't get caught with these bodies. We have to find a way to Faerie."

Knox snapped at him and Cyrus's power crushed around us.

"Audrey doesn't need us in prison or spending hours being questioned by the authorities," Cyrus added.

Fine, Knox growled.

I looked up to see where we could go to clean up and for me to put on clothes, as a monster — no, a man? — swooped down from the sky on wide leathery wings.

He was enormous, broader in the chest and easily a foot taller than Cyrus. He also looked a lot like the statue of Tzanagoth back in Anakar with his wings spread out behind him and thin, tall horns protruding from his forehead.

A red mist swirled around him, setting my nerves on edge, and fury radiated off him in almost palpable waves.

Knox growled, the sound low and dangerous, and Cyrus widened his stance, ready for a fight.

Except I knew there was no way we could win a fight against him. That wasn't to say I wouldn't die protecting Audrey, or that my brothers wouldn't die to get me and Audrey a chance to escape, but the conclusion was inevitable. The man radiated power and danger and confidence.

The heavyset vampire groaned and rolled to his hands and knees as if he were going to stand, but the red mist shot out from the winged man's hand and twisted around the vampire's throat.

"If you want to live, stay down," he said, his voice low and commanding. "I don't care that the JP are on their way. I will kill you."

The JP, I mentally said to Cyrus and Knox. *Audrey said to find a JP agent.*

"So, you four," the winged man said, his narrow-eyed gaze sliding over our bodies, taking in our ragged state as well, no doubt assessing how dangerous we were.

"Wrong place, wrong time," I said with a shrug, trying to keep my voice light and praying Cyrus didn't get all possessive, aggressive wolf on him like he had with the vampires. "We'll just be on our—"

A flash of white above and behind the winged man caught my attention and my thoughts stalled.

It was another man, but instead of leathery wings his were softly glowing white feathers and pale light radiated from his eyes.

"An angel," I gasped.

Holy Sisters! I was about to meet an angel.

The angel landed beside the winged man, his gaze on the man and the woman, his expression grim.

"There has to be a way to stop this, Voth," the angel said.

"If I kill the city's new master another idiot will take his place." The winged man, Voth, shot the angel an exasperated look. "And the JP will arrest me."

"Not if that idiot walks onto your property," the angel mumbled under his breath, his words shocking me.

Everything I'd read about angels said they were upholders of law and justice, and this angel was condoning murder.

What else had I read that wasn't true?

The angel turned his attention to us. "You four should come with me."

My stomach churned at his words. I gripped Audrey tighter and took a step back, while Cyrus tensed, and Knox growled, his hackles rising.

The angel frowned. "You're hurt. You need medical attention."

"We're fine. We've got stuff in our packs." I jerked my thumb to where we'd dropped our packs during the vampire fight. "We really should be going."

"You're not going anywhere," Voth said, his red mist billowing around him. "You're going to tell me who the fuck you are. That girl is radiating so much evil power I'm sure anyone with a hint of magical sensitivity can feel it from the next state over."

I didn't know what all that meant, but without a doubt, it was bad.

You run. I'll hold him off, Cyrus said.

No, I snapped back. He and Audrey couldn't afford to get separated.

I'll hold them, Knox snarled.

But with Knox barely clinging to himself, he wouldn't stop fighting until Voth killed him.

Fuck.

Fuck fuck fuck.

The authorities were coming, and if we refused to say something, Voth would tell them we were dangerous. That was what I'd do.

Cyrus opened his mouth to speak but without a doubt that was going to be a disaster so I inched forward.

"It's a long story," I said, trying to keep my voice steady despite my pounding heart.

I had no idea if the man-monster — that looked too much like Tzanagoth — would believe us, but I had a feeling he'd know if we were lying.

Praying that the truth would save us — and save Audrey — I sucked in a steadying breath. "Our mate is possessed by an evil power that's putting her to sleep. We've come from our realm through a rip between realms to this one to find a way into Faerie so we can find a fae sorcerer who can save her."

Voth shot the angel a strange look. It wasn't angry, but it wasn't compassionate understanding, either.

"I'll call him," the angel said as he pulled a thin rectangular box from his pocket.

"Priam," Voth warned before glaring at us. "Fae sorcerers aren't cheap. Can you pay?"

"We can," Cyrus replied as the angel, Priam, rolled his eyes and huffed. "We just need to know where to find him."

"They're mates and they've crossed realms to save her." Priam touched the surface of the rectangular box and it lit up with a bright light. "I'll tell Amiah and she'll make him do it for free."

"He's going to be pissed if you keep doing that," Voth said, but his tone had softened and the red swirling mist thinned.

Cyrus stepped forward, his alpha power still rippling around him, his body still tense. "If you just tell us where he is, we'll talk to him."

"You're not leaving here until I've healed you," Priam said before putting the rectangle to his ear, turning his back on us, and telling someone named Bane to get to the hotel.

"You're also safest here," Voth added as red mist burst around him and his wings and horns vanished, leaving just an enormous man in strangely tailored clothes.

"I'm saying fated mates keep showing up on my doorstep and I've resigned myself to my role in all this."

My wolf whined inside me at his tone. Resigned was the right word. We weren't sure how, but we could tell he wanted more... except I wasn't sure what that meant.

"Come on," Priam said, grabbing our packs. "There's a clinic at the back of the theatre."

I shot Cyrus a wary glance and he shrugged. It didn't matter how understanding Voth seemed, it was clear he wasn't going to let us go. Audrey was too dangerous. Running wasn't an option. We had no choice but to follow the honest-to-goodness angel.

CYRUS

M_Y body burned with need and my hard-as-hell cock ached and wept precum. It hadn't even been an hour since I'd said the vow to create a mating bond with Audrey, and already I was burning up inside to seal it.

Why had I waited so damn long to tell her how I felt?

Sisters, I was so stupid to put the pack first. Bishop had been right, it shouldn't have mattered what was going on even though I hadn't wanted to risk being killed and hurting Audrey because we'd bonded.

Inside me, my wolf paced restlessly, as desperate as I was to get the dark magic out of her and wake her up while my soul screamed at me to save her, wake her, love her.

Please. I'd do anything, risk anything, for her.

With Audrey carried protectively in Bishop's arms and Knox in his wolf form, we followed the angel, Priam, across the field with the strangely short grass toward a large, ten-story building with purple-tinted windows. The structure loomed two hundred feet away on top of a hill and was separated from us by a stretch of hard, black earth that reeked of unfamiliar smells, and held a bizarre collection of large metal and glass boxes on wheels.

I glanced over my shoulder at Voth's massive shadow still

standing behind us. He'd looked more human when his wings and horns had disappeared but without a doubt he wasn't, and I knew if we tried to make a break for it, he'd hunt us down.

Of course, making a break would mean we'd be back to the drawing board looking for someone to get us into Faerie while being dangerously unfamiliar with this realm. And that wasn't good for Audrey.

At least here in Voth's custody — I wasn't going to fool myself and think the situation was anything else — a fae sorcerer was coming to us.

If he wasn't lying.

Which he could be. But all my instincts said the angel wasn't.

I hadn't read any of the books Bishop had about mythical beings from other realms I was never going to meet, so I had no idea what angel personalities were like. Priam had even suggested Voth lure someone onto his territory so Voth could kill him. But even then, the angel's frustration had been because whoever was at war with the man-monster who owned this territory was killing people. No, I believed Priam's words to be true and that he genuinely wanted to help.

And please, Sisters, help.

I turned my attention to Audrey, barely able to look away long enough to avoid walking into the metal boxes on wheels. Even in the moonlight it was clear her skin was too pale, and she hung limp in Bishop's arms, far too still even for someone fast asleep.

My throat tightened and I wanted to howl with frustration. She'd just found herself, her confidence, her power, and her wolf. This couldn't be how it ended. My mate deserved a long, amazing life, filled with Knox's passion and Bishop's laughter.

On top of that, she'd made friends in Stonehaven who I know were going to be upset if she was gone. Nova and Deacon had taken a liking to her, and Finn, much to my surprise had fully submitted to her as a pack alpha and begged her not to banish him from the pack.

And of course, she hadn't. She was grace and love and forgiveness.

She was what a true alpha was supposed to be. She'd risked her life to protect her pack while also gently nurturing them.

I hadn't realized how much our pack and me and my brothers had needed her until she'd crashed into our lives and changed everything.

"This way," Priam said, his voice soft, almost soothing.

He turned away from a grand entrance fully lit by light streaming through the windows of the double doors along with bright lights attached to the brickwork. We walked around down a hill to a tucked-away side of the building, where an enormous door stood beside a smaller, human-sized one, making me even more wary.

My wolf growled low within us, suddenly concerned that he was taking us away from potential help... although really, given our reception when we'd entered this realm, I couldn't count on anyone inside helping us.

Except the angel hadn't lied.

I was sure of that.

But Sisters, it was hard to trust him when the life of my mate was on the line and when all I wanted to do was bury myself inside her and claim her.

Mine.

Always.

Priam opened the human-sized door and walked inside, and I glanced at Knox. Alpha power rolled off him in great waves and his body shook with tension. His ears flattened and he snarled, but followed the angel, and I prayed he'd be able to hold on long enough to help Audrey.

He wasn't going to leave her side until he knew she was safe, but I could tell he was barely holding on to his human consciousness. And I wasn't surprised he hadn't shifted into his human form and taken her from Bishop, even though he needed her to calm himself. His instincts were going wild, just like mine, and if he shifted, he'd exhaust himself. He couldn't protect her if he was unconscious.

Inside, the space opened up into a vast rectangular area filled with a strange, smooth, grayish-white stone. At the back sat a platform that stood at chest height for me and along the righthand wall were a set of stairs, also made from the strange stone.

We followed Priam up the stairs to a metal door, into a plan white hall with stark lights running along the ceiling, where he finally stopped about ten feet down at a small room.

Or rather, a medium-sized room that looked small because a glass wall blocked off the back third. It was crammed with two narrow beds like the bed Nova used in triage, a counter, cupboards, a sink, and a whole array of odd equipment.

"Set her on that bed and let me look at you guys," Priam said as he headed to the sink and washed his hands.

Bishop gently laid Audrey on the bed, his expression a mix of worry and determination while I sat on the other bed, fighting the urge to reach out and touch her, to feel her warmth again, to love her like she deserved.

My precum now dampened the front of my pants, and my cock throbbed as my soul screamed to complete the bond.

But I couldn't, not with her unconscious. She needed to say the vow too, or bond with me like she'd bonded with Bishop and Knox. But I couldn't feel that connection within me, only the burning need threatening to consume me.

Knox snarled, his body tense, ready to attack if Priam blinked in the wrong way.

I was sure the angel noticed — who wouldn't notice a wolf the size of a pony in the middle of their medical clinic? — but he just pulled out gauze and tape and a few other things from the cupboards, set them on a metal tray on wheels, and rolled it over to me.

"Can I touch you?" Priam asked, gesturing toward me. "I'm blessed with the ability to heal. I won't use it if you don't want—" He gestured to the tray. "But it would be faster. I can sense without touching any of you that you're exhausted, and I wouldn't recommend shifting until you've rested. Healing your injuries will help."

I gave him a tight nod and he gently set his hands against my chest. Soft white light radiated around his hands, and a warmth flooded through me that only made my longing for Audrey burn hotter.

The gashes on my arms from the vampires' claws sealed shut as I watched, and I blinked, unable to fully believe that my flesh was mending right before my eyes.

"Oh wow," Bishop breathed. "When the book said angels could heal any wound, I never imagined…"

"If you're not familiar with it, it can look unreal," Priam chuckled. "Like a movie on fast forward or something."

That had been the thing Audrey had tried to explain to Bishop when we'd headed north to break her mating bond with Knox.

My heart ached at the thought. Fuck. I needed her so much. She was mine. She'd always been mine and my wolf was furious at me for being a fucking idiot.

I was about to hop off the table and crawl onto her bed and lie beside her when two men strode into the clinic, making the small room feel even smaller.

Knox hunched, his muscles bunching ready for attack, and he growled, threatening the newcomers. They weren't enormous men like me, but they both had an aura about them that screamed power. It wasn't nearly as much as Voth, but enough that I didn't want to start a fight with them if I didn't have to.

Knox, I said, fighting to keep my mental voice calm. *They could be help.*

They better be help, he snarled back, his attention never leaving the men.

The first guy was strikingly handsome, with blue eyes so pale they were almost clear and spiky white-and-silver hair. His ears were pointed, marking him as the fae sorcerer Priam had called, although his ears were only half the size of Whil's, and his perpetual full-body fae glow — which was a soft white instead of Whil's gold— was only half as strong. A hint of black tattoos poked out from his shirtsleeves and snaked up from the collar of his dress shirt, and everything about him screamed cocky confidence with a dark edge.

The other man was so beautiful he stole my breath even as my need for Audrey erupted into a scorching volcano and made me pant. Little horns poked through his shoulder-length sandy blood hair and his presence screamed sex. Raw, unbridled, mind-blowing sex... something I needed with Audrey. Now now now.

I clench my teeth, biting back a groan, and fought to stay in control of myself. I just needed to wait a little longer. If, of course, these men were actually going to help.

Fuck, I'd make them help if they wouldn't.

It didn't matter that the odds were fifty-fifty of winning a fight against them. I would save my mate and I would claim her.

"So," the fae said, his expression dark, his attention already on Audrey. "Voth said you're from another realm."

"Don't look at her," I snarled.

His sharp gaze snapped to mine, capturing me in endless ice, before the other man bumped him with his elbow and pressed a hand over his heart.

The fae sighed and rolled his eyes. "Fine. I won't poke the wolf shifter whose mate is in trouble."

Knox bristled at that and growled a warning, before Bishop sank his fingers into his fur, trying to calm him.

We already knew Audrey was in danger. That was why we were here.

And now I couldn't stop thinking about what would happen if we couldn't convince these men to help. What if this fae sorcerer thought she was too dangerous or couldn't get the evil power out of her? Would he lock her away, or worse, kill her?

They couldn't. I wouldn't let them.

I opened my mouth to tell them that, but Bishop cut me off.

"We've been told you're a fae sorcerer," he said. "Please save our mate. We have money."

He pulled the small purse with the gems out of one of our packs and opened it up so the other men could see.

The guy with horns whistled and the angel cleared his throat.

"They've traveled between realms to save her," Priam said. "They have to be fated mates, Bane."

The fae pinched the bridge of his nose. "And Amiah just got pregnant again."

The angel's face lit up.

"Titus's," the man with horns said.

"Even more amazing," Priam exclaimed. "But we should save—" He paused and glanced at me.

"Audrey," I replied. "Her name is Audrey."

Bishop introduced us, and the fae turned out to be Sebastian Bane and the guy with horns, Hawk.

"Okay," Sebastian said. "I can already tell from here that I can get that shit out of your mate."

"And he has the juice to open a non-fixed gate and send you home," Hawk added, making Sebastian snort even as he started to roll up his sleeves, revealing that his tattoos traveled up to his elbows.

A shadow crossed Bishop's expression, and I almost leaped from the bed and slapped a hand over his mouth. I could see it in his eyes. He was going to tell them the truth.

But then I remembered these beings might be able to tell if we were lying. We just didn't know anything about them or their abilities.

"The gates to our realm were locked because of a curse. It put the most powerful beings to sleep hundreds of years ago," Bishop confessed. "One of the fae was trapped in our realm and she says she's had time to research the curse and it's safe to reopen the gates. But it might take extra magic to get us there."

"If the gates are locked, how did you get here?" Hawk asked.

"Incomplete mating bond," Bishop replied and Hawk's gaze instantly jumped to me.

Hawk gave a solemn nod. "That's what that is."

Stop talking and fix Audrey, Knox snarled in my head.

"Right." Sebastian strode the three steps to Audrey's bedside and set his hands over her heart, thankfully mindful of where he placed his fingers and palms. Then he closed his eyes and light radiated from his shoulder, turning his white shirt see-through and revealing that his arms and chest were covered in tattoos as well.

A moment later his full-body glow flared blindingly bright, brighter than I'd ever seen Whil's, and my eyes watered because I couldn't look away from Audrey.

Whil had said she wasn't a very powerful sorcerer but I hadn't known until now what that really meant. This man radiated brilliant, blinding power, power that I knew could crush all of us with a single word.

As I watched, the muscles in Sebastian's jaw tightened and Hawk grew tense. Black smoke rose from Audrey, jerking and thrashing against an unseen force, straining to get back inside her.

"Come on, you fucker," Sebastian snarled, and he yanked one of his hands up, drawing out a writhing black core the size of a walnut. "There you are."

With a deep breath, he brought his other hand up and smashed the core between his palms. It exploded into smoke that burst apart and vanished.

"Got it," Sebastian hissed as he sagged forward, clutching the edge of the bed to stay upright.

Hawk stepped close and stared at Audrey's chest, his gaze unfocused. "Looks good."

"It's gone?" Bishop asked and I realized Priam must have used his magic on him while I was distracted since his wounds were healed.

Hawk nodded. "All that's left is a perfect shifter with two and a half mating bonds."

Relief flooded me.

Thank the Sisters. Thank all the sleeping gods. Thank anyone and anything. She was safe.

"Is ah—" Bishop looked at Audrey, his eyes glassy, his relief clear. "Is she still cursed. Her wolf was locked away."

"Cursed?" Hawk frowned.

"There was only the curse woven into the evil power," Sebastian said. "Nothing else."

Which meant my mate had broken her curse when she'd found her wolf while fighting Sterling.

More relief washed through me. I would have loved her whether she had a wolf form or not, but I knew how much not having one had hurt her... that and her white wolf was stunning. I wanted Audrey to meet her.

And even as I thought that, my body burned. My mate was safe and she needed to wake up. I needed to have her, needed her so damned much I couldn't catch my breath.

"Cyrus?" Bishop asked as I felt my wolf take over.

He needed her too and he'd waited too long. He didn't care that she was unconscious, he had to claim her, now now now.

"Fuck," Hawk hissed. "Priam, call Voth. These two need a room, like ten minutes ago. They shouldn't have to seal their bond in here."

"If they used an incomplete mating bond to get here, it shouldn't be affecting him so soon," Priam said as he took his square device from his pocket while also laying a glowing hand over Audrey's heart and healing her. "But you're the incubus. You'd know best."

I had no idea what an incubus was, but he was right. If I didn't get Audrey some place more comfortable, I was going to claim her on this strange, too-narrow bed and she deserved better than that.

AUDREY

I ACHED, NOT A SCREAMING, PAINFUL ACHE, JUST A STEADY, PERSISTENT throb, and my head felt thick, my thoughts muddled. A heaviness dragged at my limbs, making it impossible to open my eyes, so I just lay there, drifting in a dark limbo, lulled by the nothingness in my head.

Whil had said I was absorbing all of Tzanagoth's power and it was putting me to sleep... but I didn't feel asleep. I felt...

I wasn't sure what I felt. Tired? Worn out?

Empty.

I was empty. The pressure that had filled me, that had grown slowly inside me and I hadn't realized was there, was gone. My stomach felt good, no nausea, and nothing burned which meant Tzanagoth's power was gone.

Bishop, Knox, and Cyrus had done it.

But my wildness was gone as well.

A weight squeezed around my heart. I'd feared removing the evil power would also remove my newfound wolf and alpha power, and now I was back to being me.

It stung to think that I'd been so close to having everything I'd wanted, to have a wolf and to be a normal shifter. The loss of the hope that somehow I'd be complete hurt and sliced deep into my soul.

Someone moved beside me, and I realized I was lying on something soft just as the sweet scent of fresh-cut grass enveloped me. Straining, I peeled my eyes open and fell straight into the warm brown depths of Bishop's eyes. They were dark, his wolf close to the surface of his consciousness, and the green flecks sparkled like stars, mesmerizing me like they always did.

Love and devotion flooded through our mating bond, filling the void inside me and warming my heart.

God, I loved this man so much. He was amazing and kind and welcomed me from the moment I'd fallen into their lives, a terrified, barely alive mess.

He'd fallen in love with me the way I was, without alpha power or a wolf, or hell, barely any self-confidence, and I knew in the depths of my soul that he would love me no matter what did or didn't change with me.

Woven through Bishop's love was Knox's, a ferocious passion that made my soul sing. We'd had a rocky start — to say the least — but he'd become a fierce protector. His bond was edged with worry and I could sense he wasn't as close as Bishop, probably outside, unable to control his wolf or his claustrophobia.

I sent a wave of love and thanks through our bond and felt his worry burst into relief and joy.

"Thank the Sisters you're awake," Cyrus rumbled, his voice low and broken.

I dragged my gaze away from Bishop's to look at Cyrus. He knelt beside the bed, looking absolutely terrible, his expression haggard and exhausted and edged with a biting desperation. It appeared as though he hadn't slept in days, and the urge to hold him, claim him, protect him from whatever had caused his suffering, washed over me like a tidal wave.

He'd risked everything just to save me — even his pack if we couldn't get back to his realm.

My throat tightened. We'd have saved so much suffering if he'd accepted what I'd known from the time after we'd returned from the death goddess's land. He wouldn't be suffering now, and him putting it off hadn't helped because he'd ended up saying the mating vows at the worst possible moment.

Of course, I wasn't free of blame, either. I could have been courageous and made him talk to me. I hadn't said anything because I was afraid and I hadn't known if me thinking we were mates was all in my head.

That, and if we had bonded, we'd have had no way of getting to my realm to find a fae sorcerer... which I guess they had.

And now here we were, him staring at me like a starving man, completely strung out on what I knew was a burning need to seal the mating bond.

Except if he looked that bad how long had I been asleep? It usually took weeks, sometimes months, before the compulsion to seal the mating bond drove the bonded mates crazy.

Although in my case, my bonds had been anything but usual.

"How long was I...?" I asked, my voice rough as if I hadn't spoken in a long time.

"Only a few hours," Bishop replied, gently brushing a lock of hair away from my face.

But if it had only been a few hours, why did Cyrus look so utterly broken?

"Audrey." Cyrus's voice cracked and his expression grew more strained, the muscles in his jaw flexing as he fought to control himself.

"You and Cyrus need to talk." Bishop pressed a soft kiss to my cheek and inhaled, drawing in my scent then stood. "Knox and I will be outside."

I watched my mate leave, my heart aching for him, needing to be close to him — to all my mates — even though I knew Cyrus and I needed to embrace our fate... which would involve very little talking.

The door closed behind Bishop, leaving me alone with Cyrus, and I turned my attention back to him.

His gaze locked on mine, the weight of his pain and desire radiating from him, and I could practically feel the lust pouring off him as he stared at me with an intensity that made my heart race.

"I'm sorry," he whispered, his voice laced with anguish. "I'm so sorry for everything."

And I knew he meant it. He'd humbled himself before, just after Bishop had been poisoned, and I hadn't been sure I could trust him, but I understood him better now. He needed to be in control and he needed to protect everyone. It was a primal instinct that drove him, made him do and say whatever was necessary to get the job done even if it hurt someone's feelings.

I didn't agree with his tactics, but knowing changed how I saw a lot of our interactions.

I also knew he loved me. He'd been desperate when Tzanagoth's power was flooding into me, and I recognized his fear. It was the same ferocious fear I'd felt when Bishop had been poisoned.

He was stubborn and too self-sacrificing, always putting his pack above himself, but in some ways, we were a lot alike. Both of us were willing to give up everything to save someone we loved, and we both had a strong drive to protect those around us.

Cyrus gently cupped my cheek, his touch warm and tender as he looked deep into my eyes.

"I meant every word of our mating vow, Audrey," he confessed, his voice gruff. "I didn't say it because I was protecting my brothers. I said it because it's true. Bonded or not, I would have gone crazy if I'd lost you. You're my fated mate and I want to be a part of your life."

Warmth spread across my chest and sank low within me. I could feel the truth in his words, the intensity of his love, and his need for me. It was everything I'd felt from Bishop and Knox.

It felt like our fates had finally aligned.

"I was a fool to have ignored my wolf and the truth. You are an amazing, kind, caring woman, and I'd be the most blessed man in all the realms if you'd accept me as your mate."

Joy and heartache swirled into the mix of emotions inside me. Joy because he was finally saying what I had known in my soul was true, and heartache because we'd suffered so much fighting against the undeniable truth. My chest tightened with emotions I couldn't contain, and I blinked back tears as I reached up to touch his face, feeling his rough stubble against my fingertips.

"You're mine," I whispered, my voice barely audible as my throat thickened with emotion.

"I am," he murmured back, his gaze filled with certainty and love.

I leaned toward him and he met me halfway, our lips connecting in a sweet, tender kiss that sank, slow and sultry, into the depths of my soul.

A hard knot in my soul, that I hadn't even realized was there, unraveled, and my wildness, the power I'd thought I'd lost forever unfurled within my chest. The power was warm, comforting, and something settled inside me.

I was complete.

I didn't know how, but I was.

Then Cyrus's sensual kiss grew insistent, his soft exploration becoming strong and demanding, his grip on his control over the urge from the mating bond slipping. An urgency swelled between us, growing stronger and stronger, and I moaned into his mouth.

"Mate with me," I said against his lips.

"Yes."

AUDREY

With a groan, he crawled onto the bed and pinned me beneath his powerful body. The kiss grew hot and consuming, making me gasp for breath and ache with a soul-deep need for him. Every cell in my body yearned for him to be buried within me and locking our souls together as they were meant to be.

"Cyrus—" I moaned even as I dug my fingers into his hair and drew him closer.

He traced his hands down my neck, leaving a trail of tingling warmth as they skimmed over my bare shoulders, across the front of my dress, and teased my nipples with the barest of touches. My back arched, my body begging for more as pleasure shivered down my spine, pooling like molten lava between my thighs.

His kiss was still strong, edged with desperation, but somehow, he'd held onto enough control to torture me with his touch.

Slowly, so damned slowly, he worked one nipple into an aching, tight bud and then began on the other. My breath turned to ragged gasps, caught between our lips, and I burned for more.

His fingers slid lower, inching down my body with a sensual promise, and I'd never wanted to be naked more in my life. The damned dress was in the way of me savoring the slide of his flesh against mine, and was certainly going to get in the way when he finally reached my aching core.

At the thought, slick heat billowed between my thighs. I moaned, rubbing them together, but it only made the ache inside me worse.

If I'd somehow been blind to everything between us and my soul's voice, I would have known in this instant that I needed him. My body burned for him, for his power and control and protection. He was mine and I was never letting him go.

"Please," I moaned against his lips, writhing beneath his touch, trying to get him to move his hand between my thighs. "I need you, Cyrus."

"Patience," he growled, a wave of alpha power swirling around me, urging me to obey even as his body trembled with the effort to hold himself back. "I refuse to take you like an animal, like I did in the shower room."

The reminder of the shower room shuddered through me, hot and sensual, making me gasp. That had been hot, wild, possessive sex, and I ached for that. But I could also tell Cyrus needed to show me how much he cared and he wasn't going to do that with a quick fuck — no matter how good it had felt.

I groaned in frustration and he chuckled.

"Grab the rungs on the headboard and don't let go." More alpha power crashed over me, this one a sharp snap that had me raising my hands before I fully realized what I was doing. "You touch me. I stop."

His hand froze on my thigh, too far away from where I wanted it. Just being told I couldn't, made me want to tangle my fingers in his hair again, slide my palms over his back, and tear at the shirt covering his gorgeous, powerful body.

"Do you understand?" he growled, his eyes so dark I wasn't sure if he was in control of his body or his wolf... except if his wolf was in control, he'd already be buried deep inside me.

"Do you think you can hold out if you stop?" I asked, my voice breathy with need.

He glared at me and I tightened my grip on the headboard.

Pushing him was a terrible idea. He needed to be in control and right now he was teetering on the edge of disaster. "I understand."

"Good girl," he said, his words shivering pleasure through me. "I'm so proud you accepted me as your mate."

He sat back on his heels, unclipped the dress's catch at the back of my neck, and peeled down the fabric. I squirmed under his gaze as it slid down to my breasts and the hunger in his eyes grew.

"You're so strong in such a beautiful, kind way." With a groan, he dipped forward and flicked his tongue over one nipple then the other, while he reached beneath me and tore through the tie at my back.

My breath hitched and my body thrummed with need.

Touch me. Please, just touch me.

But instead, he inched my dress over my hips and down my legs before tossing it to the floor. Now he knelt at my feet, his breath ragged, his body tense with the effort to hold himself back.

"Come here," I said.

I started to release one of the rungs to urge him closer but saw something flash in his eyes and tightened my grip instead.

"Good girl. So perfect." His gaze dropped to the crux between my thighs, his moss green eyes dark with passion. "Mine."

He pressed his hands against my knees, urging me to open for him, before sliding his palms up the inside of my thighs and burying his nose in my curls. He drew in a deep breath and hummed his pleasure as I ached to reach down and touch him.

Please.

He raked his tongue through my folds, just a brush that swept up my sensitive flesh and flicked against my clit, the sensation jolting the breath from my body.

Oh, yes.

My head fell back and I moaned, liquid fire roaring through my core.

He licked again and again, with harder, longer strokes, making me gasp and moan. I clung to the headboard, my breath heaving with my building need, determined not to let go.

No way in hell was I going to stop this.

My hips started to buck, my core fluttering with the promise of a breathtaking orgasm.

Cyrus growled against me, the rumble vibrating through my flesh and adding fuel to the fire within me.

Oh, yes. More. I needed more but he was keeping me on the edge, teetering on the precipice, his self control mind blowing.

"Cyrus," I begged.

He pushed two fingers inside me and pumped them in and out and sucked on my clit.

Stars flashed behind my lids and my body jerked as glorious bliss exploded inside me, but even as it started to fade, my desire rose again. I needed to seal our bond. He might have started it and I might not have said the vow, but without a doubt a mating bond had formed between us.

Our gazes met and heat rolled between us. With a snarl, he dove up my body, catching himself before he crushed me, and smashed our lips together.

Any control Cyrus might have had was gone. The kiss was hard, ferocious like our kiss in the shower room. I didn't care that his face was covered in my release or that I could taste myself on his lips and tongue. All that mattered was being impaled on the hard-as-steel cock pressing against my thigh just shy of my entrance.

"Fuck me." I grabbed his hair and yanked his head back enough that I could look him in the eyes. "Now."

My wildness surged and my alpha power crashed into his in an intense dance of need and longing.

"Mine," he snarled as his canines extended.

"Then claim me, alpha," I barked back.

He thrust into me with a powerful stroke, our pelvises slamming together, his massive cock bottoming out inside me. Then he jerked back and did it again.

He pounded into me, hard and fast and wild, and I had no idea if I was mating with Cyrus or his wolf. But it didn't matter. Cyrus and his wolf were one, two halves of the same soul. All shifters had a primal, ferocious core, and this was Cyrus's true self. I knew he could be soft and tender and in control — he'd already demonstrated that — but I also knew a beast lived deep within him. Just like one lived within me.

I snarled and raked my fingers across his back, drawing blood, and he responded by fucking me harder.

Just like in the shower room he was branding himself on me, body and soul, and I loved it. I met him stroke for stroke, my wildness and power roaring and my desire burning through my veins.

"Fuck, Audrey—"

He raised his head and our eyes met. Love and ferocious devotion shone in those moss green orbs and my wolf howled inside me.

"Blessed be the moon and her children, and blessed be this sacred vow," I moaned. "I answer the call and join my soul with you, my fated mate."

A powerful bell *gonged* inside me, resounding through my soul and flooding me with certainty. I screamed my release, all of my muscles contracting and brilliant light blazing across my vision. Bliss roared through my body, every nerve firing at once, and my wildness, *my wolf*, howled with victory.

With a guttural roar, Cyrus found his own release, his hot seed spilling deep inside me, and he jerked his head to my shoulder, the one without Bishop and Knox's mating marks, and sank his teeth into my flesh.

Another orgasm tore through me as our bond locked into place and I sank into ecstasy.

Cyrus was my fate, just like Bishop and Knox were and my soul was now complete.

AUDREY

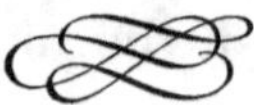

After Cyrus and I sealed our bond, the four of us spent a few days at Voth's luxurious hotel in a room on the main floor with a set of sliding doors leading to the outside for Knox.

We rested and made love while waiting to hear Sebastian's decision on whether it was safe to open a proper gate to our realm and return, not wanting to contemplate what would happen if he said it wasn't.

Sebastian returned on the afternoon of the fourth day, said he'd done his research and that it was safe to open a proper gate and not just a rip between our realms.

That said, he suggested, and the guys agreed, to keep the gate controlled on this side so our realm wouldn't be flooded with demons, humans, and other supernatural beings with dubious intent.

We returned home half an hour later to find that Deacon, Nova, and the rest of the Mountain and Sea Alliance had hunted down and killed the rest of the merchants' grimalkins, but had also agreed to wait ten days before moving on with alliance discussions, hoping we would return.

Our pack had thrown a big party in the center of town — our pack members who hadn't known me and the guys might be stuck in another realm forever thinking the party was because we'd put an end to the grimalkin attacks, something I could fully get behind.

After Cyrus and Bishop concluded the alliance business, they'd turned their attention to Velora who'd been held in a cell in the Residence's basement, no doubt seething with anger and resentment. Knox had voted to kill her, saying she was a serious threat to me, but I begged for forgiveness since with my alpha power I could protect myself.

My forgiveness, however, only went so far, and I said Velora had to be banned from the pack and for everyone in the pack to know that she'd threatened to permanently hurt me so she could have Bishop and be a pack alpha... although I suspected given that we'd had an audience when she'd challenged and threatened me, everyone in the pack already knew.

Now, I stood alone in the Residence's sacred grove, the sun high in the sky, casting dappled light through the ring of trees surrounding me. When I fell into this realm, I'd had nothing — no family, no friends, no safety, and no confidence. I was the girl no one, not even my father wanted, the one Sterling had decided was only good as a human sacrifice so he could gain Tzanagoth's evil power.

But now, I had everything I'd ever wanted. I was safe and loved. I was home.

No one looked down on me and most hadn't cared that I'd had no alpha power and couldn't shift, which still stunned me.

Being around my pack and having them look to me for guidance still made me want to hide — because it was really hard to kick an old habit that had kept me alive most of my life — but I pushed through my discomfort, and most of the pack members were understanding if I was awkward. With that and my mates' love, my confidence grew every day, and I knew someday I'd be able to fully embrace my new life.

A new life that included my wolf.

I was so happy about that. My wolf had finally woken.

Through my own strength of will, and Tzanagoth's power, I'd

broken my curse. I was no longer waiting for the right moment and aching because a part of my soul was forever out of reach.

I was complete, just like I was supposed to be.

With a deep breath, I used my newly enhanced senses to take in the smell of the damp earth and the vibrant greenery, the sound of wind rustling through the leaves, and the feeling of sunlight warming my skin. Everything was richer, deeper, brighter, warmer, crisper, perfect.

I slipped out of my dress, leaving it in a heap on the ground, and, as if I'd been doing it all my life, shifted into my white wolf form.

My first time shifting — when I hadn't been trying to stay alive — had been awkward. I hadn't fully believed I could do it, especially since I still didn't radiate any alpha power until I consciously thought about drawing it out.

But the guys had encouraged me, eager to show me my wolf form, telling me she was beautiful. And she was beautiful. She was easily half the size of the guys' wolves, with delicate paws, ears, and snout, golden eyes, and a stunning, all-white coat.

"Mate," a familiar voice rumbled from behind me as Knox, in his human form, stepped out of the deep shade between the trees.

Mate, I thought back, my gaze meeting his as I marveled over how comfortable he looked in his human form.

When we'd first met, he'd refused to shift into a human. We'd been halfway to the death goddess's temple before I'd even known he and Bishop were identical twins.

And now, he stood with a hint of a grin curling his lips, love radiating through our mating bond, and his hands in his pockets.

With his grin heating, Knox pulled his shirt off over his head and dropped his pants, revealing his stunning, powerful body.

God, I never got tired of looking at him, at all my mates if I was being honest.

He released a slow breath, his grin turning into a smirk, and shifted into his massive black wolf.

My wolf danced from one foot to the other in anticipation, knowing we were going to play from the playfulness radiating through our mating bond, and sure enough, Knot sprang forward and nipped at my haunches.

I hopped out of reach and yipped at him. The game had begun. My wildness rose up, filling me with joyful abandon, and I raced out of the sacred grove with Knox at my heels.

I darted and slipped through the gardens, always avoiding Knox's nips or attempts to pin me. Delight rushed through my veins, feeding off of Knox's happiness, becoming a wonderful, amazing loop of elation.

Knox barked and Bishop in wolf form joined the chase. I raced around the fountain in front of the Residence with the guys hot on my heels. They were bigger than me and could easily beat me in a fight, but I was faster and more nimble.

I careened around the edge of the Residence, barely noticed Cyrus in his wolf form right in front of me, and skidded between his legs before leaping through a narrow slit between a hedgerow.

Well played, Cyrus praised as he leaped over the hedgerow and joined the chase.

I led them on a twisting path through the gardens and around the back of the Residence, evading playful nips and tackles, the joy shifting into something hotter and deeper.

The sensation unfurled through our bonds, heating my soul, and I bounded around the shrubs partially hiding the small patio outside my suite. Between one step and the next, I shifted into my human form and threw open the doors.

Bishop rushed up behind me, also shifting, and scooped me up into his arms, making me laugh with pure joy as the heat within me turned sultry and sank to my core. He bolted through the sitting room into the bedroom and tossed me onto the bed.

With a growl, he dove between my legs, licking and sucking and stealing my laughter, replacing it with pure, burning lust. Knox bounded into the room a second later and captured my lips in a ferocious kiss.

Heat roared in my core, my body instantly aching for my mates as their need flooded me.

"That's it," Cyrus said with a smirk as he sat in a chair near the bed, grabbed his cock, and gave it a slow, hard pump. "I want to hear her scream."

His dark hungry gaze locked on me being ravished by his brothers, and desire shivered from my toes up my body into my scalp.

I moaned as Bishop swiped his tongue over my clit, my pulse pounding, my need screaming for them. I wanted them now, all of them, inside me, filling me, driving me crazy, and making me scream.

Knox tangled his fingers in my hair and raked his tongue against mine, kissing me as if he couldn't get enough — and from our mating bond I knew he couldn't, just like I couldn't.

One of his hands dropped to my breast, roughly kneading the sensitive flesh and turning my nipple into a taut aching bud while Bishop flicked his tongue over my clit sending bolts of pleasure jerking me closer and closer to the edge until I crashed over, shivering and breathless.

"Oh," I breathed making Bishop grin at me.

"That's what I like to hear," he purred as Knox rolled onto his back and pulled me on top of him. The heat and hardness of his cock pressed against my slit and with one powerful thrust, he plunged inside. A rippling aftershock rolled up my body, and I released a throaty moan.

"Fuck," Knox groaned before he gripped my hips, pulled back, and thrust in again and again.

Need burned through my veins, sweeping me right to edge of another orgasm, but then he stopped, his cock buried inside me.

I moaned in frustration even as my pulse picked up in anticipation. Up to this moment, both Knox and Bishop had played with my puckered entrance, getting me ready for one of them, and I knew the moment was now. I was finally going to have both of them inside me and I couldn't wait.

"Ready, mate?" Knox asked, his voice a low seductive growl as he drew me forward so that I lay against his chest.

"Oh, yes," I groaned, my pulse pounding in my ears, my whole body tingling with aching need.

Bishop swiped his fingers through my wetness and rubbed it against my hole, working in one finger, then two, and turning my desire to molten lava.

I yearned for him, for both of them, for all of them, and I knew I always would. These were my mates. Mine. And I hungered for them.

I trembled against Knox, my body trying to writhe against Knox's firm grip, needing more, needing all of Bishop not just his fingers.

"You're doing so beautifully," Cyrus cooed, pulling my attention to him. "But I still haven't heard you scream."

Need filled his expression and precum glistened at the tip of his cock, making my mouth water for a taste of him.

"You're so fucking sexy, Audrey." Cyrus's eyes darkened, his wolf pushing closer to the surface and his lust roaring through our mating bond. "But Bishop, you're moving too fast. We want our mate to enjoy this."

I groaned and Bishop hummed with pleasure. His fingers slowly pulled out of me and he teased my hole before slowly, achingly slowly, pushed his fingers back in.

My breath stalled, and my desire twisted tighter. I'd almost been on the precipice of another amazing orgasm and my whole body thrummed with the need for a release, but Bishop was an expert at edging me... and apparently Knox too because he was practically vibrating beneath me, his breath short and sharp as he fought to stay still and in control.

The thrumming turned into a burning, a desperate need as Bishop tortured me with slow sensual thrusts.

"Please," I whimpered, desperate for release even though I knew Bishop wouldn't let me come until Cyrus said so.

"Patience, love," Cyrus said, his voice deliciously dark.

I trembled and panted, every touch and sensation amplified as I tried to writhe between my two mates and failed because of Knox's grip on me.

Please. Oh please oh please oh please.

I needed faster, harder, pressure, plunging. I needed it all now now now.

"Patience," Cyrus repeated, his voice a low growl that sent shivers down my spine. I could feel the wolf lurking beneath the surface, ready to take control.

Finally, with my body strung so tight I thought I'd burst, hell, I *needed* to burst, Cyrus gave Bishop the nod.

Thank God.

I felt the hard press of his cock against my hole, adding pressure, until he slipped between the tight ring of muscle and carefully, inch by inch giving me time to adjust, pushed inside me.

Oh.

Oh oh oh.

It was all I could think. There was a bit of a burn, and definitely a stretch, and I was full, so damned, wonderfully full, and the rest was glorious sensation.

A small orgasm rippled through me. I moaned, the sound low and throaty, making all my guys groan, and a shudder of pleasure rolled up my body.

"Sisters, Audrey, you're incredible," Cyrus breathed, sending more desire unfurling inside me.

He rose from the chair, his powerful muscles bunching and flexing with the movement as he strode the few steps to the bed. Bishop pulled out to just the tip and Cyrus brushed his fingers down my spine. It was just a tease of a touch, stealing my breath and making me burn with need.

I shuddered and both Knox and Bishop groaned at the sensation.

"Now open up for me, beautiful," Cyrus commanded.

Without hesitation, I opened my mouth, allowing Cyrus to sink his cock inside, hitting the back of my throat. I moaned around him, and he gripped my hair to keep me steady, then he began slow, languid thrusts into my mouth.

Knox and Bishop joined in, pumping into me, and oh God, it was amazing. Incredible. I never wanted it to stop.

With every thrust, I felt their love and desire pouring through our mating bonds which made my own need spiral higher and higher. I teetered on the edge of release, my body burning, lava flowing through my veins.

I needed— I needed—

The guys plunged into me faster and faster, each thrust growing harder giving me exactly what I craved for.

Then a powerful, screaming orgasm tore through me. I screamed like Cyrus wanted and bliss roared through my veins, sending me spinning into ecstasy.

Bishop slammed home inside me and came, grunting with his release. Knox came a second later with a roar, their cocks throbbing as they pumped me full with their seed. Finally, Cyrus groaned between gritted teeth, and his hot, salty cum flooded my mouth.

I swallowed as best I could, but it was like a faucet had been opened all the way and cum dripped down my chin.

Cyrus's deep earthy scent, along with Bishop's bright fresh-cut grass and Knox's rich wood smoke enveloped me. Pride and love flooded my mating bonds, sending another mini orgasm rushing through me, leaving me breathless and floating in a sea of euphoria.

In this moment, I knew I was truly loved and cherished by my mates, and I couldn't imagine a more beautiful feeling.

I WOKE THE NEXT DAY, MY BODY ACHING IN ALL THE RIGHT WAYS, AND peace radiating around my heart. My back was to Cyrus's chest, his arm wrapped protectively around me, and I stared at Bishop's beautiful face, his expression relaxed with sleep.

My lips curled in a smile as I remembered how amazing yesterday afternoon and last night had been. After having all my guys at once, we'd dozed before waking and making love again... before dozing and waking again.

It was no wonder the sunlight streaming through the windows was mid-morning bright.

I stretched, savoring the ache between my legs and connected with Knox's mating bond to see where he was. He'd left just as the sun was rising after being able to control his claustrophobia for longer than he ever had before. But instead of feeling any regret for leaving, all I felt from him was contentment.

That made my smile deepen, and I carefully eased from Cyrus's embrace and wiggled out from the blankets then down to the end of the bed to avoid waking my mates. Cyrus huffed in his sleep and Bishop frowned as if they could tell, even while unconscious, that I was moving away from them.

But I wasn't going far. I could sense Knox just outside my suite and I wanted some cuddles from my gruff mate before everyone else was around.

Free from the bed, I tiptoed to my wardrobe, picked a simple dress, and secured it behind my neck and around my back, not caring that it showed off almost all of my scars.

As much as I hated that I was covered in those permanent marks, something no other shifter had, I also now recognized them for what they were: proof that I was a survivor, that I was strong enough to get through anything, even being sacrificed to a man-eating monster-god.

I hurried out of the bedroom to the French doors in the sitting room, and stepped onto the patio. Knox, in his human form, stood on the edge, his eyes closed, his face tipped up to the sun, basking in it. He wore one of the kilt-like wraps that were popular in Stonehaven and nothing else, and I couldn't help but appreciate his powerful, sculpted back and arms.

A soft sigh escaped me — God my mates were stunning — and he turned to face me, a rare smile tugging at his lips, softening his expression.

"Mate," he growled, and he pulled me into his strong arms and pressed his nose against the top of my head, breathing in my scent.

Rich wood smoke enveloped me and I sank into his embrace. I'd loved his scent from the moment I'd smelled it, even before I'd known it was from the man I'd accidentally mate bonded with.

With one more deep breath, Knox drew away, leaving me aching for his warmth.

"Come," he said. "I have a surprise."

"Really?" I asked.

Knox wasn't a surprise kind of guy. Bishop was. But that only made me more curious.

He nodded and took my hand, leading me away from the front of the Residence and around a corner to a narrow side door.

"Close your eyes," he instructed.

"Close—?"

"Bishop said you had to close your eyes," he huffed, making me giggle and proving that Bishop had a hand in whatever was going on.

I closed my eyes, and with my hand in his, Knox opened the door, guided me inside, and up what felt like an endless flight of stairs that kept going around and around.

When we stopped, another door's hinges squeaked, and we stepped outside. Warm sun heated my face and bare shoulders and a gentle breeze caressed my skin. The scent of the Residence's gardens mingled with something that smelled amazing and familiar but I couldn't quite place, and I could hear voices somewhere, but not tell what they were saying.

"Open your eyes," Knox said, and I obeyed, my breath catching in my throat.

We stood on the Residence's roof, the flat area before me stretching between one of the turrets and a sloped section of the roof.

I turned around, soaking in the breathtaking view of the Residence's grounds and the town beyond the Residence's walls.

Holy smokes, the view was amazing.

Then it hit me. This was a flat area on the roof, more than big enough for a bedroom. Were the guys going to make my dream of a greenhouse bedroom reality?

"Is this...?" I asked.

"It is." Knox grinned back at me. "Your greenhouse bedroom."

"It's going to be amazing," I said, throwing myself at Knox.

He caught me and hoisted me up so I could wrap my legs around his waist. Our lips crashed together and I released all my love and joy into our kiss.

I knew the guys loved me, but that didn't mean my greenhouse bedroom would be a reality. Engineers had to be consulted, weather patterns, and a whole bunch of other things, not to mention taking money from the pack to add a room to the Residence just for me.

"So," Bishop said, startling me and breaking my kiss with Knox. "What do you think?"

He and Cyrus stood in the doorway and I grinned at them.

"I think it'll be amazing." Images of what it could be flitted through my mind. I could already see it, reading nooks hidden by greenery, part of the roof not enclosed for a balcony, and a bed in the center, big enough for the four of us.

"Why don't we get brunch and talk about what needs to be done," Cyrus suggested, his words calm despite the hum of anticipation thrumming through our bond.

I raised my eyebrow at him in question and he raised his eyebrow back at me, refusing to answer.

Something was up, but none of Cyrus's feelings were bad so I was happy to wait... at least until my curiosity got the better of me.

Together, we descended the stairs and stepped outside the Residence, ensuring Knox could stay with us for as long as possible. Bishop laced his fingers with mine, giving me his most brilliant, heart stopping smile and I grinned back at him.

We strolled around the back, toward the herb garden and the kitchen's back door, but I stopped at the sight of a large table. It sat in the only open area in the herb garden and was surrounded by chairs and people. Platters piled high with pastries, fruit, eggs, bacon, and sausages awaited us, and I realized it was the amazing smell I'd detected earlier while standing on the roof.

But what really made me pause were the people. Everyone I cared for was there, Eloise and Kira putting the finishing touches on the table, Quinn and Zavier helping them, while Nova, Deacon, and Lucius chatted.

Quinn noticed us first and rushed toward me.

"Happy birthday!" she said before wrapping me in a tight hug.

I hugged her back, stunned. A while back, I'd mentioned I had a birthday coming up. I didn't remember how it had come up in conversation, but I never expected her to remember or make a fuss, especially with everything that had happened.

"I'm not sure if today is the actual day, but from what you said, I figured today was close enough." She stood back, her expression bright.

"This is amazing," I replied. "Thank you."

Tears welled in my eyes as warmth spread through me. No one had ever celebrated my birthday before — not even my father. Yet here were my new friends, my family, making it seem like the most natural thing in the world even though they'd only known me for a few months.

Bishop spun me around and pressed a deep, sensual kiss on my lips, leaving me heated and breathless.

"We've got an amazing day planned for the four of us," he told me. "Starting with one of Eloise's incredible brunches."

He spun me around, right into Knox's arms who captured my mouth with his usual ferocious passion, adding to the heat building inside me.

If the guys kept this up, I was going to need to skip breakfast.

When I was nearly gasping for air, and melting in Knox's arms, Cyrus pulled me into his embrace, but instead of kissing me, he brushed his lips against my cheek, sending a shiver of anticipation rushing through me.

"And I've got something special saved for you at the end of the night."

Oh, boy. Could we just skip to dessert?

Cyrus's gaze heated and everyone else laughed, making my cheeks flush with embarrassment.

Guess they heard that.

It's okay, beautiful, Bishop said in my mind. *We all know you're still figuring out your telepathy.*

And they did. Everyone had been so kind and understanding as I figured out my new abilities.

I'd never felt so loved before, and while it helped that I could feel my mates' love and devotion through our mating bonds, it was more than that. It was how they treated me with kindness and generosity, and how my new friends did the same.

This was where I belonged.

I'd finally found my place, my pack, my mates, and the people who loved and accepted me for who I was.

I'd finally found home.

OTHER BOOKS BY TESSA COLE

NEPHILIM'S DESTINY

Destined Shadows, prequel story

Destined Darkness, book 1

Destined Blood, book 2

Destined Fire, book 3

Destined Storm, book 4

Destined Radiance, book 5

ANGEL'S FATE

Fated Bonds, book 1

Fated Winter, book 2

Fated Fear, book 3

Fated Despair, book 4

Fated Resolve, book 5

Fated Heart, book 6

ENSNARED BY THE PACK

Wolf Deceived, book 1

Wolf Denied, book 2

Wolf Desired, book 3

Wolf Distressed, book 4

Wolf Decided, book 5

Wolf Devoted, book 6

THE GRECIAN GODDESS TRILOGY

Written with Clara Wils

Kiss of the Goddess, book 1

Power of the Goddess, book 2

Bonds of the Goddess, book 3

SECRETS GODS KEEP

Written with Clara Wils

Craving Demons, book 1

Chaos Demons, book 2

Claiming Demons, book 3

HER BAD BOY WOLVES

Written with Clara Wils

Pack Against the Wall, book 1

Want you Pack, book 2

Pack in Business, book 3

www.ingramcontent.com/pod-product-compliance
Lightning Source LLC
Chambersburg PA
CBHW060421310726
48977CB00001B/1

9 781990 587511